OMNIBUS TWO

elizabeth moon
the serrano connection

This omnibus edition includes
ONCE A HERO
RULES OF ENGAGEMENT

orbit

www.orbitbooks.net

ORBIT

First published in Great Britain in 2007 by Orbit

This omnibus edition copyright © 2007 by Elizabeth Moon

Once a Hero
First published in Great Britain by Orbit 2000
Copyright © 1997 by Elizabeth Moon

Rules of Engagement
First published in Great Britain by Orbit 2000

A CIP catalogue record for this book
is available from the British Library.

ISBN 978-1-84149-485-2

Papers used by Orbit are natural, recyclable products
made from wood grown in sustainable forests
and certified in accordance with the rules
of the Forest Stewardship Council.

Typeset in Caslon by Hewer Text UK Ltd, Edinburgh
Printed and bound in Great Britain by Mackays of Chatham, Chatham, Kent
Paper supplied by Hellefoss AS, Norway

Orbit
An imprint of
Little, Brown Book Group
Brettenham House
Lancaster Place
London WC2E 7EN

A Member of the Hachette Livre Group of Companies

www.orbitbooks.net

CONTENTS

once a hero

DEDICATION

For James, the newest Marine in the family. Semper Fi.

ACKNOWLEDGEMENTS

As usual, many people helped with the details. Tim Bashor, Major U.S. Marine Corps, retired, and presently an exemplary bookstore owner, offered innumerable good suggestions on how to cause trouble aboard a large ship. If you think that part of the book makes sense, it's thanks largely to him. Richard Moon, Malcolm McLean, and Michael Byrd also helped out on specific details. Judy Glaister kept me from making a worse hash of the role of nurses in therapy. Any mistakes are my own (I don't need help to make mistakes . . .). R.S.M. provided the medical texts; the Tuesday Lunch & Ice Skating Club approved the ship design (approved may not be the right word for 'collapsed in helpless giggles'). Consultants for various bits who would prefer not to be named include the ubiquitous M.M. and E.M. and T.B.

1

R.S.S. *Harrier*, Near Xavier

Esmay Suiza had done her best to clean up before reporting as ordered to the admiral aboard her flagship, but the mutiny and the following battle had left her little time. She had showered, and run her uniform through the cycler, but it wasn't her dress uniform – the fight aboard *Despite* had put holes through interior bulkheads and started innumerable small fires, including one in the junior officers' storage compartment. She herself, though clean, had not slept well in . . . however many days it had been. She knew her eyes were bloodshot and sticky with fatigue; her hands trembled. She had the stomach-clenching feeling that her best wasn't good enough.

Admiral Serrano looked like an older edition of Captain Serrano, the same compact trim frame, the same bronze skin. Here the dark hair was streaked silver, and a few lines marked the broad forehead, but she gave an impression of crackling energy held just in check.

'Lieutenant Junior Grade Suiza reporting, sir.' At least her voice didn't shake. Those few days of command had ironed out the uneasy flutter she used to struggle against.

'Have a seat, Lieutenant.' The admiral had no expression Esmay could read. She sat in the appointed chair, glad that her knees held and she made it a controlled descent. When she was down safely, the admiral nodded, and went on. 'I have reviewed your summary of events aboard *Despite*. It seems to have been a very . . . difficult . . . time.'

'Yes, sir.' That was safe. In a world of danger, that was always safe; so she had been taught in the Academy and her first ship postings. But her memory reminded her that it wasn't always true, that a 'Yes, sir,' to Captain Hearne had been treason, and a 'Yes, sir,' to Major Dovir had been mutiny.

'You do understand, Lieutenant, that it is mandatory for all officers participating in a mutiny to stand before a court to justify their actions?' That in a voice almost gentle, as if she were a child. She would never be a child again.

'Yes, sir,' she said, grateful for the gentleness even though she knew it would do her no lasting good. 'We – I – have to take responsibility.'

'That's right. And you, because you are the senior surviving officer, and the one who ended up in command of the ship, will bear the brunt of this investigation and the court.' The admiral paused, looking at her with that quiet, expressionless face; Esmay felt cold inside. They had to have a scapegoat, is that what it meant? She would be to blame for the whole thing, even though she hadn't even known, at first – even though the senior officers – now dead – had tried to keep the youngsters out of it? Panic filled in a quick sketch of her future: dismissed, disgraced, thrown out of Fleet and forced to return home. She wanted to argue that it wasn't fair, but she knew better. Fairness wasn't the issue here. The survival of ships, which depended on the absolute obedience of all to the captain . . . that was the issue.

'I understand,' she said finally. She almost understood.

'I won't tell you that such a court is merely a formality, even in a case like this,' the admiral said. 'A court is never a mere formality. Things always come out in courts to the detriment of everyone concerned – things that might not matter ordinarily. But in this case, I don't want you to panic. It is clear from your report, and that of other personnel—' Which, Esmay hoped, might mean the admiral's niece, '—that you did not instigate the mutiny, and that there is a reasonable probability that the mutiny will be held to be justified.' The knot in Esmay's

8

stomach loosened slightly. 'Obviously, it is necessary to remove you from command of *Despite*.'

Esmay felt her face heating, more relief than embarrassment. She was so tired of having to figure out how to ask the senior NCOs what to do next without violating protocol. 'Of course, sir,' she said, with a little more enthusiasm than she meant to show. The admiral actually smiled now.

'Frankly, I'm surprised that a jig could take over *Despite* and handle her in battle – let alone get off the decisive shot. That was good work, Lieutenant.'

'Thank you, sir.' She felt herself going even redder, and embarrassment overcame reticence. 'Actually, it was the crew – 'specially Master Chief Vesec – they knew what to do.'

'They always do,' the admiral said. 'But you had the sense to let them, and the guts to come back. You're young; you made mistakes of course—' Esmay thought of their first attempt to join the fight, the way she'd insisted on too high an insertion velocity and forced them to blow past. She hadn't known then about the glitch in the nav computer, but that was no excuse. The admiral went on, recapturing her attention. 'But I believe you have the root of the matter in you. Stand your court, take your medicine, whatever it is, and – good luck to you, Lieutenant Suiza.' The admiral stood; Esmay scrambled up to shake the hand extended to her. She was being dismissed; she didn't know where she was going or what would happen next, but – but she felt a warm glow where the cold knot had been.

As the escort outside made clear, where she was going was a quarantine section of officers' country on the flagship. Peli and the few other junior officers were already there, stowing their duffels in the lockers and looking glum.

'Well, she didn't eat you alive,' Peli said. 'I suppose my turn's coming. What's she like?'

'A Serrano,' Esmay said. That should be enough; she wasn't about to discuss an admiral's character on board a ship. 'There's a court coming – but you know that.' They had not so much talked about it, as touched the subject and flinched away.

'At the moment,' Peli said, 'I'm just as glad you had the seniority and not me. Though we're all in trouble.'

She had been glad to lay down command, but just for a moment she wanted it back, so she could tell Peli to be quiet. And so she would have something to do. It took only a minute or two to stow her own meager duffel in the compartment she'd been assigned, and only another to wonder how much the officer evicted from it would resent having to double up with someone else. Then she was faced with blank walls – or an empty passage – or the cluster of fellow mutineers in the tiny wardroom which was all the common space they would have until the admiral decreed otherwise. Esmay lay back on her bunk and wished she could turn off the relentless playback in her head, that kept showing her the same gruesome scenes over and over and over. Why did they seem *worse* each time?

'Of course they're listening,' Peli said. Esmay paused in the wardroom entrance; four of the others were there, listening to Peli. He looked up, his glance including her in the conversation. 'We have to assume they're monitoring everything we say and do.'

'That's standard,' Esmay said. 'Even in normal situations.' One of her own stomach-clenching fears was that the forensic teams sent to *Despite* would find out that she talked in her sleep. She didn't know, but if she had, and if she had talked during those nightmares . . .

'Yes, but now they're paying attention,' Peli said.

'Well, *we* didn't do anything wrong.' That was Arphan, a mere ensign. 'We weren't traitors, and we didn't lead the mutiny either. So I don't see where they can do anything to us.'

'Not to you, no,' Peli said, with an edge of contempt. 'From this, if from nothing else, ensigns are safe. Although you could die of fright facing the court.'

'Why should I face a court?' Arphan, like Esmay, had come to the Academy from a non-Service family. Unlike Esmay, he had come from an influential non-Service Family, with friends who held Seats in Council, and expected family clout to get him out of things.

'Regulations,' Peli said crisply. 'You were a commissioned officer serving aboard a vessel on which a mutiny occurred: you will stand before a court.' Esmay didn't mind Peli's brutal directness so much when it was aimed at someone else, but she knew he'd be at her soon enough. 'But don't worry,' Peli went on. 'You're unlikely to spend very long at hard labor. Esmay and I, on the other hand—' he looked up at her and smiled, a tight unhappy smile. 'Esmay and I are the senior surviving officers. Questions will be asked. If they decide to make an example, we are the ones to be made an example of. Jigs are an eminently expendable class.'

Arphan looked at both of them, and then, without another word, squeezed past two of the others, and Esmay at the door.

'Avoiding contamination,' Liam said cheerfully. He was another jig, junior to Peli but part of Peli's expendable class.'

'Just as well,' Peli said. 'I don't like whiners. D'you know, he wanted me to press the admiral for damage payments to replace a ruined uniform?'

Esmay could not help thinking what the necessary replacements were going to do to her small savings.

'And he's rich,' Liam said. Liam Livadhi, Service to the core and for many generations, on both sides of the family. He could afford to sound cheerful; he probably had a dozen cousins who had just outgrown whatever uniforms he needed.

'Speaking of the court,' Esmay made herself say. 'What *are* the uniform protocols?'

'Uniforms!' Peli glared at her. 'You too?'

'For the court, Peli, not for display!' It came out sharper than she intended, and he blinked in surprise.

'Oh. Right.' She could practically see the little wheels flickering behind his eyes, calculating, remembering. 'I don't really know; the only things I've seen were those cubes back in the Academy, in military law classes. And that was usually just the last day, the verdict. I don't know if they wore dress the whole time.'

'The thing is,' Esmay said, 'if we need new uniforms made, we have to have time for it.' Officers' dress uniforms, unlike regular duty uniforms, were handmade by licensed tailors. She did not want to appear before a court in something non-regulation.

'Good point. There wasn't much left of the stuff in that compartment, so we have to assume that all our dress uniforms were damaged.' He looked up at her. 'You'll have to ask about it, Esmay; you're still the senior.'

11

'Not any more.' Even as she said it, she knew she was, for this purpose. Peli didn't quite sneer, but he didn't offer to help out, either.

'On this, you are the one. Sorry, Es', but you have to.'

Asking about the uniforms brought her to the notice of the paper-pushers again. As captain – even for those few days – she had the responsibility to sign off on all the innumerable forms required.

'Not the death letters,' Lieutenant Commander Hosri said. 'The admiral felt that the families would prefer to have those signed by a more senior officer who could better explain the circumstances.' Esmay had completely forgotten that duty: the captain must write to the family of any crew members who died while assigned to the ship. She felt herself blushing. 'And there are other major reports which the admiral feels should be deferred until Forensics has completed its examination. But you left a lot of routine stuff undone, Suiza.'

'Yes, sir,' Esmay said, her heart sinking again. When could she have done it? How could she have known? The excuses raced through her mind and out again: no excuses were enough.

'Have your officers fill out these forms—' he handed her a sheaf of them. 'Turn them in, completed and countersigned by you, within forty-eight hours, and I'll forward them to the admiral's staff for approval. If approved, that will authorize officers to arrange for replacements of uniforms – and yes, that will include Fleet authorization to forward measurements to registered tailors, so they can get started. Now, we need to deal with the basic reports that *should* have been filed, or ready to file, at the time when you were relieved of command of *Despite*.'

The junior officers were not delighted with the forms; some of them procrastinated, and Esmay found herself having to nag them to finish the paperwork by the deadline. 'None too early,' grunted Hosri's senior clerk, when Esmay brought the reports in. He glanced at the clock. 'What'd you do, wait until the last minute?'

She said nothing; she didn't like this clerk, and she had had to work with him for two straight shifts on the incomplete reports Hosri thought she should do. Just let it be over with, she told herself, even though she knew that the reports were the least of her problems. While she worked on those, the other young officers faced daily sessions with investigators determined to find out exactly how it was that an R.S.S. patrol ship had been captained by a traitor, and then embroiled in mutiny. Her turn would come next.

Forensics had swarmed over the *Despite*, stripping the records from the automatic surveillance equipment, searching every compartment, questioning every survivor, examining all the bodies in the ship's morgue. Esmay could only imagine that search, from the questions they asked each day. First with no visual cues at all, when they asked her to explain, moment by moment, where she had been and what she had seen, heard, and done when Captain Hearne took the ship away from Xavier. Later, with a 3-D display of the ship, they led her through it again. Exactly where had she been? Facing which way? When she said she saw Captain Hearne the last time, where was Hearne, and what had she been doing?

Esmay had never been good at this sort of thing. She found out quickly that she had apparently perjured herself already: she could not, from where she remembered she'd been sitting, have seen Lt. Commander Forrester come out of the cross-corridor the way she'd said. It was, the interrogator pointed out, physically impossible to see around corners without special instruments. Had she had any? No. But her specialty had been scan. Was she sure she had not rigged something up? And again here – lines of her earlier testimony moved down the monitor alongside the image of the ship. Could she explain how she had gotten from her own quarters back *here* all the way forward and down two decks in only fifteen seconds? Because there was a clear picture of her – she recognized herself with familiar distaste – in the access corridor to the forward portside battery at 18:30:15, when she had insisted she was in her own quarters for the 18:30 duty report.

Esmay had no idea, and said so. She had made a habit of being in her quarters for that duty report; it had meant that she didn't have to linger in the junior officers' wardroom and join the day's gossip, or make her report with the others. Surely she would have done so even more readily with the rumors then sweeping the ship. She didn't like rumors; rumors got you in trouble. People fought over rumors and then were in more trouble. She hadn't

13

known that Captain Hearne was a traitor – of course she hadn't – but she had had an uneasy feeling in the pit of her stomach, and she had tried not to think about it.

Not until she'd been dragged through it again did she remember that someone had paged her and told her to come initial the daily scan log of the warhead lockers. Checking the automatic scans had been part of her daily routine. She'd insisted that she had done it, and whoever it was had insisted she hadn't, and finally she'd gone down to see. Who had called her? She didn't remember. And what had she found when she got there?

'I'd made an error entering the scan code,' Esmay said. 'At least – I guess that's what it was.'

'What do you mean?' This interrogator had the most neutral voice Esmay had ever heard; it made her nervous for reasons she could not define.

'Well . . . the number was wrong. Sometimes that happened. But usually it wouldn't enter; it would signal a conflict.'

'Explain, please.'

Esmay struggled on, caught between the social desire not to bore the listener, and the innocent's need to explain fully why she wasn't guilty. She had entered, during her rotation, thousands of scan log codes. Sometimes she made mistakes; everyone did. She did not say, what she had long thought, which was how silly it was to have officers entering codes by hand, when there were perfectly decent, inexpensive code readers which could enter them directly. When she made a mistake, the coder usually locked up, refusing entry. But occasionally, it would accept the error code, only to hang up when the next shift compared its code to hers.

'Then they'd call me, and I'd have to come myself and reset the code, and initial the change. That must be what happened.'

'I see.' A pause during which she could feel the sweat springing out on her neck. 'And from what station did you make the 1830 report, then?'

She had no idea. Going from her quarters – she could see the route clearly in her mind, but she could not remember calling in. Yet if she hadn't, someone would have logged it . . . except that was when, up on the bridge, the mutineers made their move against Captain Hearne. Sometime around then, anyway.

14

'I don't know that I did,' she said. 'I don't remember that I didn't. I got to the weapons bay, reset the codes, initialed them, and came back to my quarters, and then—' By then the mutiny had spread beyond the bridge, and the senior mutineers had sent someone down to keep the juniors out of it if they could. That hadn't worked; there had been more traitors than that.

The investigator nodded shortly, and went on to something else. To a series of somethings else. Finally, over many sessions, they worked their way up to the time when she herself was in charge.

Could she explain her decision to return to Xavier system and try to fight a battle against odds, with no senior officers and substantial casualties?

Only briefly, and obliquely, had she allowed herself to think of her decision as heroic. Reality wouldn't let her dwell on it. She hadn't known what she was doing; her inexperience had caused too many deaths. Even though it came out all right in the end, in one way, it was not all right for those who had died.

If it wasn't heroic, what was it? It looked stupid now, foolhardy. Yet . . . her crew, despite her inexperience, had blown away the enemy flagship.

'I . . . remembered Commander Serrano,' she said. 'I had to come back. After sending a message, so in case—'

'Gallant, but hardly practical,' said this interrogator, whose voice had a twang she associated with central Familias planets. 'You are a protégé of Commander Serrano?'

'No.' She dared not claim that; they had served on the same ship only once, and had not been friends. She explained, to someone who surely knew better than she, how wide the gap between a raw ensign of provincial background, and a major rising on the twin plumes of ability and family.

'Not a . . . er . . . particular friend?' This with a meaningful smirk.

Esmay barely kept herself from snorting. What did he think she was, some prude off a back-country planet that didn't know one sex from the other? That could not call things by their right names? She put out of mind her aunt, who certainly would never use the terms common in the Fleet.

'No. We were not lovers. We were not friends. She was a major, command track; I was an ensign, technical track. It's just that she was polite—'

'Others weren't?' In the same tone.

'Not always,' Esmay said, before she could stop herself. Too late now; she might as well complete the portrait of a provincial idiot. 'I'm not from a Fleet family. I'm from Altiplano – the first person from Altiplano to attend the Academy. Some people thought it was a hoot.' Too late again, she remembered that expression's Fleet meaning. 'A regrettably laughable imposition,' she added, to the raised eyebrows. 'In our slang.' Which was no stranger than Fleet slang, just someone else's. Which was the point: Heris Serrano had never laughed at it. But she wouldn't say that to those eyebrows, which right now made her wonder which great Fleet family she had just insulted.

'Altiplano. Yes.' The eyebrows had come down, but the tone of condescension hadn't. 'That is a planet where the Ageist influence is particularly strong, isn't it?'

'Ageists?' Esmay scrambled through what she knew of politics at home – she had not been home since she was sixteen – and came up with nothing. 'I don't think anyone in Altiplano hates old people.'

'No, no,' the man said. '*Ageists* – surely you know. They oppose rejuvenation.'

Esmay stared at him, now thoroughly confused. 'Oppose rejuvenation? Why?' Not her relatives, who would be only too happy if Papa Stefan lived forever; he was the only one who could keep Sanni and Berthol from each other's throats, and those two were essential.

'How closely do you follow events on Altiplano?' the man asked.

'I don't,' Esmay said. She had left it behind gladly; she had discarded without watching the newscube subscription her family sent her. She had finally decided, in the bleak aftermath of a nightmare in which she was not only stripped of her commission but sentenced to a term of hard labor, that she would never go back to Altiplano, no matter what. They could throw her out of Fleet, but they couldn't make her go home. She had looked it up:

16

no judicial action could force someone to return to their planet of origin for crimes committed somewhere else. 'And I can't believe they really oppose rejuvenation . . . at least, I can't imagine anyone I know thinking that way.'

'Oh?'

Since he seemed interested, the first person in years who had shown any interest at all, Esmay found herself telling him about Papa Stefan, Sanni, Berthol, and the rest, at least insofar as it bore on their likely attitude towards rejuv. When she slowed down, he interrupted.

'And is your family . . . er . . . prominent on Altiplano?'

Surely that was in her file. 'My father's a regional commander in the militia,' she said. 'The ranks aren't equivalent, but there are only four regional commanders on Altiplano.' It would be the height of bad manners to say more; if he couldn't figure out from that where she stood socially on her home planet, then he'd have to suffer in ignorance.

'And you chose to go into Fleet? Why?'

That again. She had dealt with that in her first application, and during the entrance interviews and the military psychology classes as well. She rattled off the explanation that had always seemed to go best, and it sank into the investigator's unresponsive gaze.

'Is that all?'

'Well . . . yes.' The smart young officer did not talk about wish fulfillment, the hours she'd spent in the manor orchard staring up at the stars and promising herself she'd be there someday. Better to be matter-of-fact, practical, sensible. No one wanted wild-eyed dreamers, fanatics. Especially not from worlds that had only a couple of centuries of human colonization.

But his silence dragged another sentence out of her. 'I loved the thought of going into space,' she said. And felt herself flushing, the telltale heat on her face and neck. She hated her fair skin that always showed her emotions.

'Ah,' he said, touching his stylus to his datapad. 'Well, Lieutenant, that will be all.' *For now*, his look said. It could not be the end of questioning; that wasn't how things worked. Esmay said nothing except the polite formula he expected, and went back to her temporary quarters.

17

She had not realized until the second or third shift aboard the flagship that only she, of the young mutineers, had a private compartment. She wasn't sure why, since there were three other women, all crammed into one compartment. She'd have been happy to share – well, not happy, but willing – but the admiral's orders left no room for argument, as Esmay found when she asked the officer assigned as their keeper if she could change the arrangement. He'd looked disgusted, and told her no so firmly that her eardrums rattled.

So she had privacy, if she wanted it. She could lie on her bunk (someone else's bunk, but hers for the duration), and remember. And try to think. She didn't really like either, not alone. She had the kind of mind that worked best alongside others, striking sparks from her own and others' intransigence. Alone, it whirred uselessly, recycling the same thoughts over and over.

But the others did not want to talk about what bothered her. No, that was not quite honest. She did not want to talk to them about those things either. She did not want to talk about how she felt when she saw the first casualties of the mutiny – how the smell of blood and scorched decking affected her, how it brought back memories she had hoped were gone forever.

War isn't clean anywhere, Esmay. Her father had said that, when she'd told him she wanted to go into space, wanted to become a Fleet officer. *Human blood and human guts smell the same; human cries sound the same.*

She had said she knew it; she had thought she knew it. But those hours in the orchard, looking up at the distant stars, clean light on clean darkness . . . she had hoped for something better. Not security, no: she was too much her father's child to wish for that. But something cleanedged, the danger sharpened by vacuum and weapons that vaporized . . .

She had been wrong, and now she knew it in every reluctant cell of her body.

'Esmay?' Someone tapped on her door. Esmay glanced at the timer and sat up hurriedly. She must have dozed off.

'I'm coming,' she said. A quick glance in the mirror; she had the flyaway sort of hair that always needed something done to it. If it had been acceptable, she'd have cut it a centimeter long and let it be. She swiped at it, both hands, and palmed the door control. Peli outside, looking worried.

'Are you all right? You weren't at lunch, and now—'

'Another interview,' Esmay said quickly. 'And I wasn't really hungry anyway. I'm coming.' She wasn't hungry now, either, but skipping meals brought the psychnannies down on you, and she had no desire to be interviewed by yet another set of inquiring minds.

Supper sat uneasily in her stomach; she sat in the crowded little wardroom not really listening to the others talk. It was mostly guesses about where they were, and when they would arrive, and how long it would take to convene the court. Who would sit on it, who would represent them, how much trouble this would cause them in the future.

'Not as much as being under Captain Hearne if she'd gotten away with it,' Esmay heard herself say. She hadn't meant to say anything, but she knew she was the only one really at risk in court. And here they were chattering away as if all that mattered was a possible black mark that might keep them from promotion ahead of their group.

They stared at her. 'What do you mean?' Liam Livadhi asked. 'Hearne couldn't have gotten away with it. Not unless she took the ship straight over to the Benignity—' He stopped, looking suddenly pale.

'Exactly,' Esmay said. 'She could have done that, if Dovir and the other loyalists hadn't stopped her. And we could all be Benignity prisoners.' Dead, or worse than. The others looked at her as if she had suddenly sprouted a full suit of battle armor with weaponry. 'Or she could have told Fleet that Heris Serrano was the traitor, that the accusations were false, and she had fled to save her ship and crew from a maniac. She could have assumed that no one could defeat a Benignity assault group with only two warships.' And even Heris Serrano had not done so; Esmay had recognized the peril even as she ended it. Without her own decisive entry into battle, Serrano would have perished, and all witnesses to Hearne's treachery with her.

Peli and Liam looked at Esmay with more respect than she'd had from them yet, even in battle. 'I never thought of all that,' Peli said. 'It never occurred to me that Hearne could have gotten away with it . . . but you're right. We might not even have known – only those on the bridge actually heard Captain Serrano's challenge. If one more bridge officer had been a Benignity agent—'

'We'd be dead.' Liam rumpled his Livadhi-red hair. 'Ouch. I don't like the thought that I might have disappeared that way.'

Arphan scowled. 'Surely they'd have ransomed us. I know *my* family—'

'Traders!' Liam said, in a tone that made it sound like a cognate of traitors. 'I suppose your Family does business with them, eh?'

Arphan jumped up, eyes blazing. 'I don't have to be insulted by people like *you*—'

'As a matter of fact, you do,' Liam said, leaning back. 'I outrank you, trade-born infant. You're still just an ensign, in case you hadn't noticed.'

'No quarreling,' Esmay said. This she could handle. 'Livadhi, he can't help who his family is. Arphan, Livadhi is your senior; show respect.'

'Whooo,' murmured Peli. 'The ex-captain remembers the feel of command.' But his tone was more admiring than scornful. Esmay was able to grin at him.

'As a matter of fact, I do. And keeping you juniors from messing each other's uniforms is easier than fighting a battle. Shall we keep it that way?'

Expressions ranging from surprise to satisfaction met her gaze; she kept the smile on her face and eventually they all smiled back.

'Sure, Esmay,' Livadhi said. 'I'm sorry, Arphan – I shouldn't have chosen this time, if any, to slang your family. Lieutenant Suiza's right. Friends?' He held out his hand. Arphan, still scowling, finally shook it, muttering something about being sorry. It did not escape Esmay's notice that he had chosen a combination of address which claimed her as a friend, while emphasizing her authority to Arphan. She could do that sort of thing if she thought of it, but she had to think; Liam Livadhi, and the others born into Fleet families, seemed to do it as naturally as breathing.

2

Harborview Industrial Park, Castle Rock

The conference room had been swept and garnished, ensuring that it was empty of the security demons whose probing eyes and ears, and busy tongues, would have had a field day. Outside, two offices away, an efficient receptionist would deal with any calls; the rest of the staff were busy on assigned projects. The three partners who had formed Special Materials Analysis Consulting looked at the moment more like business rivals than old friends. Arhos Asperson, short, compact, dark-haired, leaned forward, elbows on the polished table, as Gori Lansamir reported on the results of clandestine research. Across from him, Losa Aguilar lay back in her chair, consciously opposing him in gesture as in attitudes. The lounging posture did not suit her; with her lean body went an energy usually expressed in action.

'You were right, Arhos. In-house projections at Calmorrie are that demand will rise steeply, especially for repeat procedures where the last procedure used drugs from a questionable source.' Gori scowled, an unusual expression on his normally amiable face. Arhos nodded.

'In other words, last week's blip in the price of a first-time rejuvenation wasn't a blip at all.'

'No.' Gori pointed to details in the chart he'd displayed. 'Ever since the king resigned, there's been talk about adulteration of the components. The shakeup in the Morreline family holdings suggests to me it may be even bigger than what's alleged in the suits already filed.'

'I suppose we should be glad we didn't get ours done last year,' Losa said. Arhos looked at her; had there been a hint of smugness in her tone? Probably. Losa enjoyed rightness as a personal fiefdom. Usually he didn't mind, but when she disagreed with him that buzzsaw certainty hurt.

'Not to our credit, since we couldn't afford them last year – or this, with the price increase. I suppose we could get one of us done—' Arhos glanced at his partners. Gori might go along with that, but Losa never would. Nor would he himself, unless he was the one to get rejuv.

'No,' Losa said quickly, before Gori could say anything. 'For the same reasons we didn't pool funds to do one of us last year.'

'You don't have to make your distrust quite so obvious,' Arhos murmured. 'I wasn't suggesting it – only pointing out that we could afford only one this year, too. It's taken us five years to save up that much – and with the price expected to rise steeply—'

'We need more contracts,' Gori said. 'Surely with all that's happening in the Fleet right now, we can find a niche?'

'We should have an advantage,' Losa said. 'We shouldn't be under any suspicion, like the major suppliers and consulting firms.'

'That might help.' Arhos had his doubts. Somehow even when the witch-hunters were out, the good old firms seemed to find a safe hideout. 'We do good work; we've had Fleet contracts through Misiani . . . if anyone notices the sub-sub-contractors at a time like this.'

'That's what you're worried about? That we're not noticeable enough?'

'In a way. The thing is, they have no way of knowing whether we subs perform well because we're good, or because we're under the thumb of the main contractor. Thus no reason to trust us on our own.'

'We've had a few . . .' Losa began. Then she shrugged, before Arhos could say it. 'But not enough of the juicy ones. Our profit margin's too low.'

'No, and the real problem, I'm convinced, is that we aren't rejuved yet. The big firms all have rejuved executives now.'

'We're not that old.'

'No, but – Gori's not as boyishly cute anymore. None of us look like bright young kids. Look, Losa, we've been over this before . . .'

'And I didn't like it then . . .' She had abandoned the fake slouch for her more normal upright posture; he had never seen anyone but a dancer with such a back and neck. He could remember the feel of it under his hands . . . but that had been years ago. Now they were only partners in work. He pulled his mind away from the thought of Losa rejuved to . . . perhaps . . . eighteen . . .

'Look, it's simple. If we want to survive in this field, we have to convince clients we're successful. Successful consultants are rich – and rich people are rejuved. We're still getting contracts, but not the best contracts. In ten years, the kind of contracts we're getting will go to the new bright young things – or to our present competitors who've managed to afford rejuv.'

'We could cut back—' That was Gori, with no conviction in his voice. They had discussed this before; even Gori didn't really want to live like an impoverished student again.

'No.' Arhos shook his head. 'It's suicide either way. To save out enough for rejuv, even one at a time, we'd have to cut expenses – this office for one – and that would make us look like losers. We need to rejuv – all of us – within the next five years. With the revelations about those contaminated drugs, the price will go up and stay up just when we need it most.'

'Which comes down to more contracts,' Losa said. 'Except that we can't do more without hiring more – and that drives our cost up.'

'Maybe. We need some new ideas, contracts that will give us a higher margin of profit, and not require any more expenditures.'

'From your tone I'd gather you already have some.'

'Well . . . yes. There are specialties which pay a much higher rate . . . for which we are already qualified.'

Losa's lip curled. 'Industrial sabotage? We don't want to try *that* with Fleet . . . not with the current mood.'

'Public opinion's on their side right now because of the Xavier affair – that Serrano woman is a hero – but in the long run what they'll remember is one hero and three traitors.'

'And we're to be traitors too?'

Arhos glared at her. 'No, not traitors. But – none of us got into this work because of any particular love for the Familias bureaucracy. Remember why we left General Control Systems. And then, as subcontractors, we've had the same piles of paperwork—'

'You're talking about working outside Familias space? Won't that just mean a whole new set of paper-pushers to contend with?'

'Not necessarily. Not everyone outside is as tangled in red tape as the Familias. And it isn't necessarily against Familias interests . . . at least I don't see it that way.'

'You want rejuvenation,' Losa said sharply, leaning forward.

'Yes. And so do you, Losa. So does Gori. None of us have been able to increase our profits within the confines of Fleet contracts and subcontracts: too many fish in this pond, many of them with more teeth. So either we give up our ambitions, which I for one am not willing to do, or we find another pond. Ideally a pond that connects with this one, so we don't lose all the goodwill we've built.'

Losa heaved a dramatic sigh. 'All right, Arhos . . . just tell us.'

He let himself smile. 'We have a potential client who would like to have us disable a self-destruct device on a service ship.'

'Whose service ship? Fleet's?'

Arhos nodded.

'Not blow it up – disable its self-destruct?'

'Right.'

'Why?'

Arhos shrugged. 'In this kind of situation it's not my business why . . . though I could speculate, I'd rather not.'

'And who is this potential client?'

'He didn't say whom he worked for, but a little discreet data probe allowed me to estimate a very high probability that he's an agent for Aethar's World.'

Losa and Gori stared at him as if he'd sprouted horns. 'You were talking to the Bloodhorde?' Losa asked, having beat out Gori by a breath.

'Can we trust him?' asked Gori.

'Not really,' Arhos admitted, spreading his hands. 'But the offer was . . . generous. And I suspect we can work up from it – he didn't sound as firm as he thought.'

'What kind of service ship?' asked Gori.

'A deep space repair ship, one of those floating ship-factories crewed like an orbital station. Why anyone would put a self-destruct on it in the first place, I can't understand – it sounds dangerous to me; what if the captain goes crazy? And they want it disabled, is all.'

'I hate the thought of dealing with the Bloodhorde,' Losa said. 'And here we're talking about twenty or thirty thousand people—'

'Military personnel,' Arhos said. 'Not ordinary people. They signed up for the risk. That's what they're paid for. And we need the cash. If we don't get the new rejuv procedure soon—'

'But the *Bloodhorde*, Arhos! All those hairy, beefy types with their Destiny garbage! They belong back on their home planet, whacking each other with clubs and sitting around drunk singing . . .'

'Of course they do.' Arhos grinned at her. 'They're barbarians, and we all know it. That's why I'm not worried . . . Fleet will be able to contain them just as they always have. And this job doesn't require us to damage Fleet—'

'Disabling a ship system—'

'A system that's never been used and never will be. DSRs never get into combat anyway, so I don't know why they even have self-destruct devices. I'd think they'd go the other way, make it impossible to blow them up. But apparently they do have such things, and the person who contacted me wanted it turned off.'

Losa sat up straight. 'It's obvious, Arhos you can see—'

He held up his hand. 'I don't want to see – speculate, rather. It will have no effect on the DSR's function as a repair and maintenance facility; it won't kill anyone; it won't do anything but keep some ham-handed ensign from blowing the ship up by accident. In a way, you could think of our action as damage control . . .' Losa snorted, but he ignored her and went on. 'And the good news is . . . they offered, before I started dickering, a fee that will cover rejuvenation for two of us.' Into the silence around the table, he dropped the last piece of bait. 'I got them up another half mil, and that means we have enough for all three of us. Net, not gross. After the job, of course.'

'The complete—'

'New, with the newest, certified drugs. A margin for inflation while the job's on.'

Losa's thin face glowed. 'Rejuv . . . just like that Lady Cecelia . . .'

'Yes. I thought you'd see it that way.' Arhos cocked his head at Gori. 'And you?'

'Mmm. I don't like the Bloodhorde, what I've heard about them, but . . . probably most of it's propaganda anyway. If they were so quarrelsome and technologically backward, they wouldn't have been able to hold their empire together the past century. I suppose it's in a solid currency?'

'Yes.'

Gori shrugged. 'Then I don't see a problem, as long as it's within our technical expertise. As you said, it's not like we're actually doing any damage to a ship, or to peoples' lives. A self-destruct isn't a weapon; we're not really depriving Fleet of anything.' He thought a moment, then added. 'But how're we going to get aboard the ship? And where is it?'

Arhos grinned, this time more broadly. 'We're going to get a contract. A *legitimate* contract. There's one up for bid, just posted this morning in fact. All the Fleet weapons inventory needs recalibration – the word is, they're afraid more traitors like Hearne could have diddled the guidance systems codes. It's such a big job, they've decided to put it out to all qualified consultants with the right clearances, regardless of size. I put in our bid on the way back.'

'But what if we'd said no to the other—?'

'Then we'd have had a legitimate job. I bid for the contract in Sector 14 only, giving as a reason our small staff. It was listed as a bonus project, because of the distance from major nexi. I think we fit that profile very well – and besides, we can dicker with whoever gets it if we don't.'

'As long as we *do* get paid,' Losa said, with an edge of fierceness.

'Oh, we will. The Bloodhorde representative is coming tomorrow – standard first-visit negotiations, but I want full security backup. He's likely to turn mean, for all that he's wearing a suit. He won't know about the other contract, and I'm going to try to get an additional travel and expense budget out of him.'

26

'Who else are we taking in on this job?' Gori asked.

'The Fleet part of it, the usual team. This part – only the three of us. We don't want to share the fee, after all.'

'There's only one tricky point,' Arhos said. 'That's the civilian/ Fleet interface on Sierra. It's the Sector HQ of a red-zoned sector . . . they do more than just glance at ID there.' He glanced across the broad desk at the blond man in the expensive business suit.

'Your IDs will be in order,' the blond man said. He lounged back in his chair as if it were a throne, a posture which made the suit look as if it had been made for someone else, someone who knew how to sit without sprawling.

'We could avoid the problem entirely by traveling with Fleet from somewhere else – Comus, for instance.'

'No.' Flat, rude, arrogant.

'Explain.'

'It is not my place to explain. It is yours to comply with the contract.' The blond man glared at the others.

'It is not my place to be stupid,' Arhos said. With a flick of his gaze, he ensured the blond man's continued existence for a space of time. How long depended on his mood, which the blond man was not helping. He reminded himself that the consulting fee transferred to the firm's account would pay for three and a half rejuvenations at the rate Gori had calculated would apply when they were through with the job. Fleet's fee for recalibrating all those weapons would give them something to live on. If they killed this messenger, they would have to deal with someone who might be worse. 'If you want this done neatly, as you said, then you should listen to the experts.'

'Expert sneaks.' That with the trademark Bloodhorde sneer. Clearly the blond man had no respect, a condition dangerous in itself, beyond unpleasant. Arhos allowed an eyelid to droop. Before it rose again, the blond man was gasping for breath, the noose around his thick neck grooving the skin. The chair in which he sat had flipped restraints onto his arms, and tightened them. Arhos did not move.

'Insults annoy us,' he said mildly. 'We are experts – that's why you hired us. It is part of our expertise to travel unnoticed, accepted. It is my opinion that waiting until Sierra Station to enter Fleet jurisdiction will bring unwelcome notice. Civilian contractors, special consultants, normally join up with Fleet transport closer to their point of origin.' He smiled. The blond man's face had turned an ugly puce; he made disgusting noises. But the blue eyes showed no fear, not even as they dulled with oxygen deprivation. He nodded, and the noose sprang away from the blond man's neck as if someone had pushed it. Someone had, remotely. . . .

'Mother-devouring scum—!' the blond man croaked. He yanked hard, but the chair restraints held his arms down.

'Experts,' Arhos said. 'You pay us, we do your job – cleanly, thoroughly. But don't insult us.'

'You will regret this,' the blond man said.

'I don't think so.' Arhos smiled. 'It is not my neck which has a mark from a noose. Nor will it.'

'If I were loose—'

Arhos cocked his head to one side. 'I would have to kill you, if you attacked me. It would be most unfortunate.'

'You! You are too little—'

'Bloodhorde barbarian!' That from the other person in the room, the woman who had said nothing before, whose quiet demeanor fit the subordinate role she had seemed to have. 'Do you still think size is everything, after all your defeats?'

'Peace, Losa. It is no part of our contract to instruct this . . . individual . . . in the realities of hand-to-hand fighting. We have no reason to give him gratuitous data.'

'As you wish.' She sounded more sulky than submissive.

'Now,' Arhos said. 'We will expect half the fee on deposit with our bankers by midday tomorrow, the next fourth when we arrive at Sierra Station, and the final fourth when we have completed the task. No—' as the blond man started to speak. 'No, don't argue. You lost your bargaining advantage when you insulted us. You can always hire someone else if you don't like my terms. You won't find anyone as good – you know that already – but it's your choice. Take or leave – which?'

'Take,' the blond man said, still hoarse from the noose. 'Greedy swine . . .'

'Very good.' No need to mention that every insult now – after that warning – would raise the price of the job. One did not have to like one's customers if they produced enough profit, and Arhos – the best in his field – knew to a single credit how much it took to satisfy his feelings.

Though the job itself was intriguing, a challenge he would not have thought of by himself, but one well worth the attempt. Not attempt, he thought . . . the achievement. He had no doubts; they had not failed in an assignment in years. Getting this buffoon out of the office quietly was the only problem that concerned him, once the buffoon had thumb-printed a credit authorization.

'Nasty,' Losa said, after the man had left. 'And dangerous.'

'Yes, but solvent. We don't have to like them . . .'

'You said that before.'

'It's true.'

'He scared me . . . he wasn't afraid, he was just angry. What if they want revenge for the insult?'

Arhos looked at her, and wished she'd make up her mind what kind of person she was. 'Losa . . . this is a dangerous business, and it's never bothered you before. We have good security; we'll be taking precautions. Do you want that rejuvenation, or don't you?'

'Of course I want it.'

'I think you're just annoyed that I found the contract, and not you.'

'Maybe.' She sighed, then grinned, as she rarely did now. 'I must need one, turning into a cautious old lady before my time.'

'You're not an old lady, Losa, and now you never will be.'

R.S.S. *Harrier*

By the time the flagship reached sector headquarters, Esmay had begun thinking of the court as a door to freedom—freedom from the tensions and rivalries of a cluster of scared junior officers with not enough to do. While it made legal sense, she supposed, to keep them all isolated and relatively idle, it felt like punishment.

Even the largest ship has limited resources for recreation; duties normally fill most of its crew's time. Esmay tried to make herself use the teaching cubes – she encouraged the others to use them – but with a knot of uncertainty lodged in the middle of her brain, the rest of it couldn't concentrate on anything as dry as 'Methods for back-flushing filters in a closed system' or 'Communications protocols for Fleet vessels operating in zones classified F and R.' As for the tactical cubes, she already knew where she'd gone wrong coming back to Xavier, and there was nothing she could do about it now. Besides, none of the tactical cubes considered the technical problems she'd faced in starting a battle with a ship which had suffered internal damage in a mutiny.

She could not work hard enough by day to ensure restful sleep at night. Physical exhaustion might have done that, but her share of the gym time wasn't enough to achieve that. So the nightmares came, night after night, and she woke sweat-soaked and gritty-eyed. The ones she understood were bad enough, replays of the mutiny or the battle at Xavier, complete with sound and smell. But others seemed to have drawn from memories of every training film, every military gory story she'd ever heard . . . all jumbled together like the vivid shards of a shattered bowl.

She looked up at a killer's face . . . she looked down to see her own hands slimy with blood and guts . . . she stared into the muzzle of a Pearce-Xochin 382, which seemed to widen until her whole body could slide down inside it . . . she heard herself begging, in a high thin voice, for someone to stop. . . . NO. That time when she woke, tangled in damp bedding, someone was pounding on her door and calling for her. She coughed a few times, then found voice enough to answer.

It was not a door, but a hatch: she was not home, but aboard a ship, which was better than home. She took the deep breaths she told herself to take, and explained to the voice outside that it had been just a bad dream. Grumbles from without: some of us need our sleep too, you know. She apologized, struggling with a rush of sudden, inexplicable anger which urged her to yank open the . . . hatch, not door . . . and strangle the speaker. It was the situation; tempers would naturally flare, and she must set an example. Finally the grumbler left, and she lay back against the bulkhead – the safe gray bulkhead – thinking.

She had not had such dreams in years, not since leaving home for the Fleet prep school. Even at home, they'd been rarer as she got older, although they had been frequent enough to worry her family. Her stepmother and her father had both explained, at tedious length, their origin. She had run away once, after her mother died, a stupid and irresponsible act mitigated by youth and the fact that she was probably already sick with the same fever that killed her mother. She had found trouble, a minor battle in the insurrection now known as the Califer Uprising. Her father's troops had found and rescued her, but she'd nearly died of the fever. Somehow, what she'd seen and heard and smelled had tangled with the fever during the days in coma, and left her with the bad dreams of something which had never really happened. Not as she dreamed it, anyway.

It made sense that being in a real battle would bring back those old memories and the confusion the fever engendered. She really had smelled spilled guts before; smells were particularly evocative . . . that was in the psychology books she had read secretly in Papa Stefan's library, when she had believed she was crazy as well as lazy and cowardly and stupid. And now that she understood where the nightmares had been leading, trying to link her past experiences with her present, she could deal with this consciously. She had had nightmares because she needed to make the connection, and now that she had it, she would not need the nightmares.

She fell asleep abruptly, dreaming no more until the bell signaled the time to wake. That day she congratulated herself on figuring it out, and instructed herself to have no more nightmares. She was tense at bedtime, but talked herself out of it. If she dreamed, she did not remember it, and no one complained of the noise she made. Only once more before they reached Sector HQ did she have a nightmare, and that one was even easier to understand. She dreamt she came into the court-martial and only when the presiding officer spoke discovered that she was stark naked. When she tried to run out, she could not move. They all looked at her, and laughed, and then walked out, leaving her alone.

It was almost a relief to find she could have *normal* nightmares.

At Sector HQ, her replacement uniforms were ready, delivered directly to the quarantine section aboard the ship by guards who clearly felt this beneath their dignity. The new clothes felt stiff and awkward, as if her body had changed in ways that measurements could not reflect. She had used the minimal fitness equipment in the quarantined section daily, so the difference wasn't flab. It was . . . something more mental than physical. Peli and Liam groaned dramatically when they saw their tailors' bills; Esmay said nothing about hers, and only later realized they assumed she had no resources beyond her salary.

For the first time, the young officers were called before the admiral as a group. Esmay wore a new uniform; so did everyone else. An armed escort led them; another closed in behind. Esmay tried to breathe normally, but could not help worrying – had something else gone wrong? What could it be?

Admiral Serrano waited, expressionless, as they all filed into the office, packed in so close that Esmay could smell the new fabric of their uniforms. The admiral had responded to each formal greeting with a little nod, and a flick of her eyes to the next in line.

'It is my duty to inform you that you have all been called before a court to explain, if you can, the events leading up to the mutiny aboard *Despite* and the subsequent involvement of that ship and crew in action at Xavier.'

Esmay heard nothing from behind her, but she felt the reaction of her fellow officers; though they had known it must happen, the formal words delivered by an admiral of the Fleet struck with awesome force. Court-martial. Some officers served from commissioning to retirement without being threatened with an investigation, let alone a hearing before some Board . . . and certainly without standing a court-martial. A court-martial was the ultimate disgrace, if you were convicted; it was a blemish on your career even if you were acquitted.

'Because of the complexity of this case,' the admiral went on, 'the Judge Advocate General has chosen to handle it with utmost circumspection but also utmost gravity. The precise charges have not been determined for each of you, but in general, the junior lieutenants can expect to see charges of both treason and mutiny, which the JAG is not considering mutually exclusive defenses, one for the other. That is, if you were a party to treason, this does not defend against a later charge of mutiny, and vice versa.' The admiral's bright black eyes seemed to bore into Esmay's. Did she mean something *particular* about that? Esmay wanted to blurt out that she was not and had never been a traitor, but discipline kept her jaw locked.

The admiral coughed delicately, clearly a social cough, a punctuation in what she said. 'I am authorized to tell you that the reason for this is the high level of concern about Benignity influence in the officer corps. It would not have been feasible to ignore that possibility in this case; your defense counsels will explain it to you. The ensigns are being charged with mutiny only, except in one case where investigation is still in progress.'

'But we haven't even seen a defense lawyer!' complained Arphan from the back. Esmay could have swatted him; the idiot had no right to speak.

'Ensign . . . Arphan, isn't it? Did anyone give you leave to interrupt, Ensign?' The admiral needed no help from a jig to squash a feckless junior.

'No, sir, but—'

'Then be silent.' The admiral looked back at Esmay, who felt guilty that she had not somehow gagged Arphan, but the admiral's look conveyed no rebuke. 'Junior Lieutenant Suiza, as the senior surviving officer, and former captain of a mutinied ship in combat, your trial will necessarily be severed from that of the officers junior to you, although you will be called to testify in their trials, and they in yours. Additionally, you will face a Captain's Board of Inquiry to investigate your handling of *Despite* in battle.'

Esmay had expected this, in one way, and in another had hoped that one investigation and judicial ordeal might subsume the other.

'Because of the unusual circumstances of the Xavier situation, including the actions taken by Commander Serrano, it has been determined that you should all be transported to Fleet Headquarters for these courts-martial on another vessel.'

Esmay blinked. They didn't trust Admiral Serrano because of her niece? Then she remembered all the rumors – now demonstrably untrue – about Heris Serrano and her departure from Fleet.

'Commander Serrano will of course be facing a Board of Inquiry herself, and three of you will be called to testify to that Board.' Esmay could not imagine who might be thought to have useful information there. 'You will be allowed communications access to notify your families, and if possible speak with them directly, but you are not to communicate with anyone other than your families. Specifically, you are ordered, under penalty, to avoid discussion of this case with anyone in or out of Fleet except your defense counsel and each other. I strongly recommend that you not discuss this among yourselves any more than you already have. You will be closely observed, not always by those who have your interests at heart. You will be met at Fleet Headquarters by your assigned defense counsel, and you will have the usual resources then to prepare yourself for court.' The admiral's gaze raked the lines for a moment; Esmay hoped no one would ask stupid questions, and no one did.

'You're dismissed,' the admiral said. 'Except for Junior Lieutenant Suiza.' Esmay's heart sank through her boot-soles and the deck she stood on. She stood while the others shuffled out, watching the admiral's face for any clue. When they had all gone, the admiral sighed.

'Sit down, Lieutenant Suiza.' Esmay sat. 'This is going to be a difficult time for you, and I want to be sure you understand that. Yet I don't want to panic you. Unfortunately, I really don't know you well enough to know how much warning it takes to scare you too much. Your record, as an officer, doesn't help me along. Can you?'

Esmay kept her jaw from dropping with an effort. She had no idea what to say; for once *Yes, sir* wasn't enough. The admiral continued, more slowly, giving her time to think.

'You did very well at the Academy prep school; you were rated high, not brilliantly, in the Academy itself. I would guess you're not the sort to look up your own fitness reports – is that right?'

'Yes, sir,' Esmay said.

'Mmm. So you may not know that you've been described as "hard worker, willing, not a leader" or "steady, competent, always completes assignments, shows initiative with jobs but not people, leadership potential average."' The admiral paused, but Esmay couldn't think of anything. That's about what she'd thought of herself. 'Some of them say you're shy, and others just say quiet and nondemanding . . . but in a lifetime in the Fleet, Lieutenant Suiza, I've never seen this sort of fitness report – one after another, from the prep school all the way through – coupled with the kind of decisive leadership you showed with *Despite*. I've known some quiet, unassuming officers who were good in combat – but there was always, somewhere in the background, at least one little glint from that undiscovered diamond.'

'It was an accident,' Esmay said, without thinking. 'And besides, it was the crew who did it, really.'

'Accidents,' the admiral said, 'do not just happen. Accidents are caused. What kind of accident do you think would have resulted if Junior Lieutenant Livadhi had been senior?'

Esmay had wondered that; in the aftermath of battle, Liam and Peli both had been sure they would have chosen a different insertion velocity and vector, but she remembered the look on their faces when she'd announced they were going back.

'You don't have to answer,' the admiral said. 'I know from his interviews. He would have sent the same message you did, then hopped back to Sector HQ, hoping to find someone handy. He would not have taken *Despite* back, and although he can justly critique your tactics on system entry, he himself would have been far too late to save the situation.'

'I . . . I'm not sure. He's brave—'

'Courage isn't the whole issue here, and you know it. Prudence and courage make good teammates; cowardice can be as rash as storycube courage.' The admiral smiled, and Esmay felt cold. 'Lieutenant, if you can puzzle me, I assure you that you are puzzling the rest of Fleet even more. It's not that they don't want you to have done what you did – but they don't understand it. If you can hide that level of ability, all these years, under a bland exterior, what *else* are you hiding? Some have even suggested that you are a Benignity deep agent, that you somehow set up Commander Hearne and engineered a mutiny, just to get yourself known as a hero.'

'I didn't!' Esmay said without thinking.

'I don't think so myself. But right now there's a crisis of

confidence all over the Familias Regnant, and it has not spared the Regular Space Service. It was bad enough to discover that Lepescu was making sport of killing Fleet personnel, but to find that three traitorous captains could be dispatched to something like Xavier – *that* has shaken the confidence of Fleet Intelligence, as well it should. By all rights, you should be whisked through the obligatory court as quickly as possible, and then hailed as the hero you are – and don't bother to deny it. You are. Unfortunately for you, circumstances are against you, and I expect you and your defense counsel will have a rugged few weeks. Nor is there anything I can do about it; right now my influence could only harm you.'

'That's all right,' Esmay said. It wasn't all right, not if she understood Admiral Serrano's implications, but she could certainly see why the admiral couldn't change reality. Growing up a senior officer's daughter had taught her that, if nothing else. Power always had limits, and banging your head on them only hurt your head.

The admiral was still looking at her with that intense dark gaze. 'I wish I knew you and your background better. I can't even tell if you're sitting there complacent, reasonably wary, or terrified . . . would you mind enlightening me?'

'Numb,' said Esmay honestly. 'I'm certainly not complacent; I wasn't complacent even before your warning. I know that young officers who get involved with mutinies, for whatever reason, always have a stained record. But whether I'm reasonably wary or terrified – that I don't know myself.'

'Where did you develop that kind of control, then, if you don't mind my asking? Usually our intakes from colonial planets are all too easy to read.'

It sounded like genuine interest; Esmay wondered if it was, and if she dared explain. 'The admiral knows about my father . . .?' she began.

'One of four sector commanders on Altiplano; I presume that means you grew up in some kind of military household. But most planetary militia are less . . . formal . . . than we are.'

'It began with Papa Stefan,' Esmay said. She was not entirely sure it had really begun there, because how had Papa Stefan

36

accumulated the experience he passed on? 'It's not like Fleet, but there's a hereditary military . . . at least, the leading families are.'

'But your file says you were raised on a farm of some sort?'

'Estancia,' Esmay said. 'It's – more than a farm. And fairly big.' Fairly big hardly described it; Esmay didn't even know how many hectares were in the main holding. 'But Papa Stefan insisted that all the children have some military training as they grew.'

'Not all military traditions value the absolute control of facial expression and emotion,' the admiral commented. 'I gather yours does.'

'Mostly,' Esmay said. She couldn't explain her own aversion to unnecessary display of emotion, without going into the whole family mess, Berthol and Sanni and the rest. Certainly Papa Stefan and her own father valued self-control, but not to the degree she practiced it.

'Well . . . I wanted you to know that you have my best wishes in this matter,' the admiral said. She was smiling, a smile that seemed warm and genuine. 'After all, you saved my favorite niece – excuse me, Commander Serrano – and I won't forget that, no matter what. I'll be keeping an eye on your career, Lieutenant; I think you have more potential than even you suspect.'

3

Esmay had time to meditate on those words as the long arm of the Fleet's judicial branch separated her from the other junior officers, put her aboard a courier-escort, and whisked her to Fleet Headquarters a full eight days before the others arrived. She met her defense counsel, a balding middle-aged major who looked more

37

like a bureaucrat than an officer; he had the incipient paunch of someone who avoided the gym except in the last few weeks before the annual physical fitness test.

'It would've made sense for them to link the cases,' Major Chapin grumbled, poring over Esmay's file. 'Starting at the back end, you are the hero of Xavier; you saved the planet, the system, and an admiral's niece's ass. Unfortunately—'

'It was explained to me,' Esmay said.

'Good. At least none of the records are missing. We'll need to prepare separately for the Captain's Board of Inquiry and for each of the main threats of the court martial. I hope you have an organized mind—'

'I think so,' Esmay said.

'Good. For the time being, forget military protocol, if you can; I'm going to call you Esmay, and you're going to call me Fred, because we have too much work to let formalities slow us down. Clear?'

'Yes, sir – Fred.'

'Good. Now – tell me everything you told the investigators, and then everything you didn't tell them. The whole story of your life isn't too long. I won't get bored, and I don't know what's useful until I hear it.'

In the next days, Esmay found that Major Chapin meant what he'd said. She also found herself increasingly comfortable talking to him, which made her nervous. She reminded herself that she was a grownup, not a child who could throw herself at any friendly adult when she needed comfort. She even mentioned the nightmares, the ones connected to Xavier.

'You might want to consider a psych session,' he said. 'If it's bothering you that much.'

'It's not now,' she said. 'It was those first days after . . .'

'Sounds normal to me. If you're sleeping well enough to stay alert . . . there's an advantage in not going for a psych evaluation now, you see, because it might look as if we're going to plead mental incompetence.'

'Oh.'

'But by all means, if you need it—'

'I don't,' Esmay said firmly.

38

'Good . . . now about this petty thievery you said was plaguing the enlisted lockers . . .'

Circumstances conspired to shift the date of the court martial so that the Captain's Board met first. Major Chapin grumbled about this, too.

'You don't take counsel to a Board of Inquiry, so you'll have to remember everything we've talked about by yourself. You can always ask for a short recess and come ask me, but it leaves a bad impression. Damn it – I wanted you to have experience before you went in alone.'

'Can't be helped,' Esmay said. He looked mildly surprised, which almost annoyed her. Had he expected her to complain when it could do no good? To make a useless fuss, and to him?

'I'm glad you're taking it that way. Now – if they don't bring up the matter of the damage to the nav computer, you have two choices—' That session went on for hours, until Esmay felt she understood the point of Chapin's advice, as well as the advice itself.

The morning the Board hearing began, Chapin walked her into the building and all the way to the anteroom where he would wait in case she asked for a recess and his guidance. 'Chin up, Lieutenant,' he said as the door opened. 'Keep in mind that you won the battle and didn't lose your ship.'

The Board of Inquiry made no allowances for the irregular way in which Esmay had arrived in command of *Despite*, or so it seemed from the questions. If a Jig commanded in battle, that jig had better know what she was doing, and every error Esmay made came up.

Even before the next senior officer died of wounds, why had she not prepared for command – surely that mess on the bridge could have been cleaned up faster? Esmay, remembering the near-panic, the need to secure every single compartment, check every single crew member, still thought there were more important things than cleaning blood off the command chair. She didn't say that, but she did list the other emergencies that had seemed more pressing. The Board chair, a hard-faced one-star admiral Esmay had never heard anything about, good or bad, listened to this with compressed lips and no expression she could read.

Well then, when she took command, why had she chosen to creep into one system – the right move, all agreed, given what she found – and then go blazing back into Xavier, where she had every reason to believe an enemy force lay in wait? Didn't she realize that more competent mining of the jump point entry corridor would have made that suicidal? Esmay wasn't about to argue that her decision made sense; she had followed an instinct, not anything rational, and instincts killed more often than they saved.

And why hadn't she thought of using a microjump to kill momentum earlier, when she might have saved two ships and not just one? Esmay explained about the nav computer, the need to patch a replacement chip from one of the missile-control units. And on and on, hour after hour. They seemed far less interested – in fact, not interested at all – in how the *Despite* had blown the enemy flagship, than in her mistakes. The Board replayed surveillance material, pointed out discrepancies, lectured, and when it was over at last Esmay went out feeling as if she'd been boiled until all her bones dissolved in the soup.

Major Chapin, waiting in the anteroom where he'd watched on a video link, handed her a glass of water. 'You probably don't believe this, but you did as well as you could, given the circumstances.'

'I don't think so.' She sipped the water. Major Chapin sat watching her until she had finished that glass.

'Lieutenant, I know you're tired and probably feel that you've been pulled sideways through a wire gauge, but you need to hear this. Boards of Inquiry are supposed to be grueling. That's part of their purpose. You stood up there and told the truth; you didn't get flustered; you didn't waffle; you didn't make excuses. Your handling of the nav computer failure was perfect – you gave them the facts and then dropped it. You let Timmy Warndstadt chew you up one side and down the other, and at the end you were still on your feet answering stupid questions in a civil tone of voice. I've worked with senior commanders who did worse.'

'Really?' She wasn't sure if it was hope she felt, or simply astonishment that someone – anyone – could approve of something she did.

'Really. Not only that, remember what I told you at the beginning: you didn't lose your ship and you made a decisive move in the battle. They can't ignore that, even if they think it was blind accident. And after your testimony, they're much less likely to think it was accidental. I wish they'd asked more about the details; you were right not to volunteer it, since it would've sounded like making excuses, but . . . it annoys me when they ignore briefs. I put it all in; the least they could do is read it and ask the right questions. Of course there will be negative comments; there always are, if something gets as far as a Board. But they know – whether they're willing to admit it or not – that you did well for a junior in combat for the first time.'

The door opened, and Esmay had to go back. She returned to her place, facing the long table with the five officers.

'This is a complicated case,' Admiral Warndstadt said. 'And the Board has arrived at a complicated resolution. Lieutenant Suiza, this Board finds that your handling of the *Despite* from the time you assumed effective command after Dovir's wounds rendered him incapable of taking the bridge, to your . . . precipitous . . . return to Xavier, was within the standards expected of a Fleet captain.' Esmay felt the first quiver of hope that she was not going to be tossed out on her ear, just before being imprisoned as the result of the court-martial.

Admiral Warndstadt went on, this time reading from notes. 'However, your tactical decisions, when you returned to the Xavier system, were markedly substandard. This Board notes that this was your first experience of combat and your first time in command of a ship; the Board makes appropriate allowance for these circumstances. Still, the Board recommends that you not be considered for command of a Regular Space Service vessel until you have shown, in combat situations, the level of tactical and operational competence expected of warship commanders.' Esmay almost nodded; as Chapin had warned her, and she already understood, they could not ignore her mistakes. Such Boards existed to point out to captains that luck, even great good luck, was no substitute for competence.

Warndstadt looked up at her again, this time with one corner of that lean mouth tucked up in what might almost be a smile. 'On the other hand, the Board notes that your unorthodox maneuvers resulted in the defeat of an enemy vessel markedly superior in firepower and mass, and the successful defense of Xavier. You seem well aware of your shortcomings as commander of a ship in combat; the Board feels that your character and your deportment are both suitable for command positions in the future, as long as you get the requisite experience first. Few lieutenants junior grade command anything bigger than a shuttle anyway; the Board's recommendation should have the effect of giving you time to grow into your potential. Now – a complete transcript of the Board's recommendation will be forwarded to you and your counsel at a later date, should you wish to appeal.'

She would be crazy to appeal; this was the best outcome she could have hoped for.

'Yes, sir,' she said. 'Thank you, sir.' She got through the rest of the ritual, the dismissal of the Board and the necessary individual acknowledgement of each member, without being fully aware what she said. She wanted to fall into a bed and sleep for a month . . . but in three days, her court-martial would begin. In the meantime, she had to record her initial statements for the other courtsmartial, including Commander Serrano's.

'Everything's unusual about this,' Chapin said, as one who disapproved on principle of the unusual. 'They had a time finding enough officers to sit on this many different boards and courts at once, and they're short of space, too. So they're shuffling people and spaces, and decided that since you're in such demand they can, after all, accept recorded testimony for some of it. With any luck, you won't actually have to appear in person in all of them . . . they certainly can't yank you out of yours just to answer two questions in some other jig's trial. It rushes you right now, but then your defense is simple anyway.'

'It is?'

'In principle. Were you a conspirator, intending to commit a mutiny? No. Were you a traitor, in the pay of a foreign power? No. Simple. I expect they'll ask all the awkward questions they can think of, just so it looks good, and in case the original investigators forgot to check . . . but it's clear to me, and should be clear to them, that you were an ordinary junior officer who reacted to a developing situation – luckily, in the best interests of both Fleet and the Familias Regnant. The only problem I see . . .' He paused, and gave her a long look.

'Yes?' Esmay finally said, when waiting produced nothing but that steady stare.

'It's going to be difficult to present you as the ordinary junior officer – although your fitness reports support that, putting you right square in the middle of your class – when you became the very unordinary youngest-ever captain to blow away a Benignity heavy cruiser. They're going to want to know why you were hiding that kind of ability . . . *how* you hid that kind of ability. Why were you denying Fleet the benefit of your talent?'

'That's what Admiral Serrano said.' Esmay forced her shoulders back; she wanted to hunch into a little ball.

'And what did you say?'

'I . . . couldn't answer. I don't know. I didn't know I could do it until I did it, and I still find it hard to believe.'

'Such modesty.' Something in the tone chilled her. 'I'm your defense counsel, and more than that I'm an attorney with many years of experience – I was in civil practice and Fleet reserves before I went full-time into Fleet. You may be able to fool yourself, young woman, but you don't fool me. You did what you did because you are unusually capable. Some of that capability showed up on the screening exams you took to get into Fleet in the first place – or had you forgotten your scores?'

She had; she had dismissed them as a fluke when her grades in the Fleet prep school came out only slightly above average.

'I'm now convinced,' Chapin went on, 'that you were not hiding your talents for any obvious reason – such as being a Benignity agent – but you were hiding them. You avoided command track as if it had thorns all over it. I pulled your file from prep school and talked to your instructors in the Academy too. They're all kicking themselves for not noticing, and nurturing, such an obvious talent for command—'

'But I made mistakes,' Esmay said. She could not let this go on. She had been lucky, she had had outstanding senior NCOs who had done most of it . . . she rattled this off as fast as she could, while Chapin sat watching her with the same skeptical expression.

'It won't do,' he said finally. 'For your own good, Lieutenant Suiza—' He had not called her that from the first day; she stiffened. 'For your own good,' he repeated more softly. 'You must face what you are; you must admit how much of what happened was your doing. Your decisions – good ones. Your ability to take charge, to get that performance from those you commanded. It was no accident. Whether the court dwells on this or not, you must. If you truly did not know what you were capable of – if you didn't know you were hiding your abilities – then you must figure out why. Otherwise the rest of your life will be one mess after another.' As if she had spoken, his finger came up and leveled at her. 'And no, you cannot go back to being just another ordinary junior officer, not after this. Whatever the court decides, reality has decided. You are special. People will expect more, and you'd better learn to handle that.'

Esmay struggled to keep calm. One corner of her mind wondered why it was so hard to believe she was talented; most of it concentrated on the need for control.

The Board, technically considered an administrative and not a judicial procedure, had attracted no media attention, but the multiple courts martial of junior officers involved in a mutiny – and then in the successful defense of Xavier – was too juicy to miss. Fleet kept the defendants isolated as long as it could, but Chapin warned Esmay that politics demanded the courts be open to selected media coverage.

'Usually no one much cares about courts-martial,' he said. 'The rare one that has some publicity value is usually kept closed, on the grounds of military necessity. But this case – or rather, all your cases – are unique in Familias history. We've had to court-martial groups of officers before – the Trannvis Revolt, for instance – but we've never had to court-martial a group that had done something *good*. That has the newshounds baying for blood . . . not yours, yet, but any blood that happens to hit the ground. And in a situation this complex, someone's going to bleed.'

Esmay grimaced. 'I wish they wouldn't—'

'Of course. And I don't want you sitting over the screens keeping track of the media; it will only tie you in knots. But you needed to know before you went in that there will be media there, and they'll try to get statements from you between sessions, even though they have been told you are forbidden to give them. Just don't say anything, anything at all, while you're going from the courtroom to the rooms where you'll be sequestered between sessions. I don't have to tell *you* to keep a composed face; you always do.'

Despite the warning, the mass of video and audio pickups, the competing voices of the media interviewers, were like a blow to the face on her first trip between the defendants' suite and the courtroom.

'Lieutenant Suiza, is it true that you killed Captain Hearne yourself—?'

'Lieutenant Suiza, just a word about Commander Serrano, please—?'

'There she is – Lieutenant Suiza, how does it feel to be a hero?'

'Lieutenant Suiza, what will your family think about your being court-martialed—?'

She could feel her face settling into a stony mask, but behind that mask she felt helpless, terrified. A murderer? A hero? No, she was a very junior lieutenant who could happily have stayed in obscurity for decades yet. Her family's opinion of courts-martial . . . she didn't want to think about that. Mindful of the publicity problem, she had sent only the briefest message to them – and asked them not to reply. She didn't trust even Fleet ansibles to keep such messages secure under the pressure of every news service in the Familias.

Inside the courtroom, she faced another bank of media pickups. Even as she followed the ritual of the court, she could not fail to be aware that every word, every fleeting expression, would be broadcast across the worlds for all to see. Chapin, waiting at the defense table, muttered 'Relax, Lieutenant; you look as if you were about to try the court and not the other way around.'

All the cases were linked by the need for officers to testify about each other's behavior – because of the need to determine whether the mutiny resulted from a conspiracy. But Esmay, as the senior surviving officer, had been nominally charged with additional violations of the Code. Chapin had emphasized that the charges were required – that he expected a fairly quick dismissal of most of them, given that no evidence supported them. 'Unfortunately,' he'd said, 'just because Hearne was a traitor doesn't mean that you mutineers are out of danger: if there's any evidence that there was a conspiracy to mutiny before there was clear evidence of Hearne's treachery, then that conspiracy, by itself, is cause for a guilty verdict on that charge.'

But as far as Esmay knew, none of the subordinates not in the pay of the Compassionate Hand had suspected Hearne or the others. She certainly hadn't. Hearne had seemed a bit slapdash in some ways, but she was rumored to be brilliant in combat, and rumor also linked a mild disregard for 'unnecessary' regulations with superior combat ability.

Now she found herself retelling the story of her assignment to *Despite* all over again. Her duties, her usual routine during time off-duty, her responsibilities to officers even more junior, her evaluation of her peers.

'And you had suspected nothing about Captain Hearne, Major Cossordi, Major Stek, or Lieutenant Arvad?'

'No, sir,' Esmay said. She had said this before, about each one separately.

'And to your knowledge, no one else suspected that they were in the pay of the Benignity?'

'No, sir.'

'Did you have a particular relationship with Dovir?' The idea was so ludicrous that Esmay nearly lost control of her expression.

'Dovir, sir? No, sir.' Silence lengthened; she was tempted to explain Dovir's preferences in particular companions, and decided better not.

'And you never heard anything of a plot to mutiny against Captain Hearne?'

'No, sir.'

'No grumbling of any sort, from officer or enlisted?'

That was a different matter. Grumbling filled ships as air did; people had grumbled about everything from the food to the shortage of gym slots; people always did. Esmay picked her words with care. 'Sir, of course I heard people grumble; they do. But not more than on any other ship.'

A huff of annoyance from one of the officers. 'And you have so much experience on so many ships!' he said, dripping sarcasm.

Chapin stood up. 'Objection.'

'Sustained.' The chairman gave the speaker a disapproving look. 'You are aware of the standards, Thedrun.'

'Sir.'

The chair peered at Esmay. 'Please discuss the nature of the grumbling, Lieutenant Suiza. This court is not sure that an inexperienced officer is fully aware of the amount of grumbling that is normal.'

'Yes, sir.' Esmay paused, dragging up from the depths of her memory a few instances. 'When *Despite* was in the yards, before I joined her, the recreation area had been cut by about thirty percent, to allow retrofitting of the enhanced charged beam generator on the portside. That meant losing fifteen of the exercise machines; it would have been nineteen, but Captain Hearne approved a tighter spacing. However, this meant shortening the exercise periods, and some crew could not get their required exercise without getting up on their down shift. Some complained that Hearne should have relaxed the exercise requirements, or installed the other machines elsewhere.'

'What else?'

'Well, there was apparently a sneak thief pilfering from enlisted lockers. That caused a lot of annoyance, because it should have been easy enough to catch, but the scanners never caught anything.'

'They'd been tampered with?'

'Chief Bascome assumed so, but couldn't prove it. It went on for . . . perhaps twenty or thirty days . . . and then it never happened again. The items taken were rarely of great monetary value, but always personal treasures.' Should she mention that they'd been found after the battle, in the cleanup phase, in the locker of someone killed? Yes; she had been taught that withholding information was the same as lying. 'We found the things after the battle,' she said. 'But the person whose locker they were in had died in the original fight.'

'The mutiny, you mean.'

'Yes, sir. Under the circumstances, we just gave the stuff back to the owners – the surviving ones, that is.'

A grunt from the chairman, which she could not interpret.

The trial went on, hour after tedious hour. Most of the time the questions made sense, examining what she had known, what she had witnessed, what she had done. Other times the court seemed determined to follow some useless thread of inquiry – like the kinds of grumbling she'd observed – into a thicket where they would lodge until one of them kicked free and returned to the main issues.

One of the side-issues turned nasty. The hectoring Thedrun had continued to ask his questions as if he was sure she was guilty of something dire. He began asking her about her responsibility in regard to supervising the ensigns. 'Isn't it true, Lieutenant Suiza, that you were charged with ensuring that the ensigns carried out their duties and put in the required hours of study?'

'Sir, that duty rotated among the four senior lieutenants junior grade, under the supervision of Lieutenant Hangard. I was assigned that duty for the first thirty days after *Despite* left Sector HQ, then it devolved onto the next senior, Lieutenant Junior Grade Pelisandre for thirty days, and so on.'

'But as the senior, you were ultimately responsible—?'

'No, sir. Lieutenant Hangard had made it clear that he wished the jig – sorry—'

'Never mind,' the chairman said. 'We do know what the word means.'

'Well, then, Lieutenant Hangard wanted the jig in charge of the ensigns to report directly to him. He said we each needed to feel the responsibility alone for a short time.' Where was this leading?

'Then you are not aware that Ensign Arphan was engaged in illegal diversion of military equipment?'

'What!' Esmay couldn't keep her voice from reacting to that. 'Ensign *Arphan*? But he's—'

'Ensign Arphan,' the chairman said, 'has been convicted of diversion and illegal sale of military goods to unlicensed buyers – in this case, his father's shipping company.'

'I . . . it's hard to believe,' Esmay said. On second thought, she could believe it, but still . . . why hadn't she noticed? How had someone else found out?

'You haven't answered the question: were you or were you not aware that Ensign Arphan had illegally diverted military equipment?'

'No, sir, I was not aware of that.'

'Very well. Now, about the mutiny itself—' Esmay wondered why they bothered to ask questions which the surveillance cubes had already answered. Hearne had attempted to destroy all the records of her conversation with Serrano, but the mutiny erupted before she could. So the court had seen the playbacks, from several angles . . . for Serrano had of course recorded Hearne's transmissions, and the transmissions agreed.

What seemed to worry the court most was the possibility that the junior officers had been plotting even before Hearne defied Serrano. Esmay repeated her earlier statements, and they picked them apart. How was it possible that she had not known Hearne was a traitor before? How was it possible that she had been party to a successful mutiny, if she had not been involved in some plan with the other mutineers ahead of time? Was it really that easy to produce a spontaneous mutiny?

By the end of the second day, Esmay wanted to bang heads. She found it hard to believe that a whole row of senior officers were so incapable of recognizing what lay in front of them – so insistent on finding something other than the plain, obvious truth. Hearne had been a traitor, along with a few others of the officers and some of the enlisted. No one had noticed because, up until the moment she defied Serrano, her actions had not been suspicious.

'You never had any suspicion that she was using illicit pharmaceuticals?' one of them asked for the third time.

'No, sir,' Esmay said. She had said that before. Captain Hearne had never appeared under the influence, not that Esmay would have been able to recognize subtle effects of drugs . . . even if she'd seen that much of Hearne. Esmay had no way to know what she was taking. Nor had she investigated Hearne's cabin after the mutiny to find out. She had had a battle to fight.

More questions followed, on Hearne's motivation; Major

Chapin cut those off repeatedly. Esmay was glad to sit and let him handle it; she felt stale and grumpy as well as tired. Of course she didn't know why Hearne might have turned traitor; of course she didn't know if Hearne had been in debt, had had political connections to a foreign government, had harbored some grievance against Fleet. How could she?

Her own motivations came into question; Esmay answered as calmly as she could. She had harbored no grievance against Captain Hearne, who had spoken to her only a few times. When Hearne's private log came into evidence, she found that Hearne had described Lieutenant Junior Grade Suiza as 'competent but colorless; causes no trouble, but lacks initiative.'

'Do you feel you lack initiative?' asked the board chair.

Esmay considered this. Were they hoping she'd say yes, or no? What hook did they plan to hang her on? 'Sir, I'm sure Captain Hearne had reason to think that. It is my habit to be cautious, to be sure I understand the situation fully before stating an opinion. I was, therefore, not the first to offer solutions or suggestions when the captain posed a problem.'

'You didn't resent her opinion?'

'No,' Esmay said. 'I thought she was right.'

'And you were satisfied with that?'

'Sir, I was not satisfied with myself, but the captain's opinion seemed fair.'

'I notice you use the past tense . . . do you still feel the captain's evaluation of you was accurate?'

'Objection,' Chapin said quickly. 'Lieutenant Suiza's present self-evaluation and its comparison to Captain Hearne's prior evaluation is not an issue.'

At last it wound down . . . all the evidence given, all the questions asked and asked again, all the arguments made by opposing counsel. Esmay waited while the officers conferred; in the reverse of the Board procedures, she stayed in the courtroom while the members withdrew.

'Take a long breath,' Chapin said. 'You're looking pale again . . . but you did very well.'

'It seemed so . . . so complicated.'

'Well, if they let it look as simple as it is, they'd have no good reason for a trial, except that it's the regulations. With all the media coverage, they don't want to make it look easy; they want it to look as if they were thorough and demanding.'

'Can you tell—?'

'How it will come out? If they don't acquit you of all charges, I'll be very surprised . . . they have the Board report; they know you've been chewed on about mistakes. And if they don't acquit, we'll appeal – that'll be easier, actually, out from under the media's many eyes. Besides, they found themselves a bad apple to squash, that young Arphan fellow.'

The officers returned, and Esmay stood, heart beating so that she could scarcely breathe. What would it be?

'Lieutenant Junior Grade Esmay Suiza, it is the decision of this court that you are innocent of all charges made against you; this court has voted unanimously for acquittal. Congratulations, Lieutenant.'

'Thank you, sir.' She managed to stay on her feet during the final ceremonies, which again included greeting each officer on the court, and the prosecuting counsel, who – now that he wasn't badgering her with questions – seemed friendly and harmless.

'I knew we didn't have a chance,' he said, shaking her hand. 'It was obvious from the evidence, really, but we had to go through with it. Unless you'd come in here blind drunk and assaulted an admiral, you were safe enough.'

'I didn't feel safe,' Esmay said.

He laughed. 'Then I did my job, Lieutenant. That's what I'm supposed to do, scare the defendant into admitting every scrap of guilt. You jut didn't happen to have any.' He turned to Chapin. 'Fred, why do you always get the easy ones? The last fellow I had to defend was a mean-minded SOB who'd been blackmailing recruits.'

'I'm rewarded for my virtues,' Chapin said blandly, and they both laughed. Esmay didn't feel like joining in; she felt like finding a quiet place to sleep for a week.

'What'll you do now, Lieutenant?' asked one of the other officers.

'Take some leave,' she said. 'They said it'd be awhile before they had a new assignment for me, and I could have thirty days home leave plus travel. I haven't been home since I left.' She wasn't that anxious to go home, but she knew no other way to escape the media attention.

4

Altiplano

Esmay thought she had outdistanced the last of the newshounds two stops before her homeworld Altiplano. When she came out of the arrival lounge into the main concourse, the bright lights blinded her for a moment. They had figured out where she was going, of course. She set her jaw and kept going. They could have all they liked of her walking from one side of the station to another. They might even get someone on the down shuttle, but once she hit the dirt, they would find themselves blocked. That would be one good to come out of this misconceived home-coming.

'Lieutenant Suiza!' It took a long moment, several strides, for her to realize that one of the yells wasn't a newshound's demand for a comment, but her uncle Berthol. She looked around. He wore his dress uniform, and Esmay groaned inwardly, thinking ahead to the reaction of her Fleet acquaintances when they saw the newsclips of this. When he caught her eye, he quit waving and pulled himself rigid. Sighing, Esmay stopped short, bracing against the expected crunch from behind, and saluted. When her father had sent word that he could not meet her at the station, she'd assumed that meant no one would . . . she hadn't expected Berthol.

'Good to see you, Esmaya,' he said now, opening a path

between them with a glance that sent the newshounds scurrying out of the way.

'And you, sir,' Esmay said, very conscious of the scrutiny of the cameras.

'God's teeth, Esmaya, I'm not a sir to you.' But the twinkle in his eye approved of her formality. The stars on his shoulders glittered as the cameras shifted for better angles, their spotlights crisscrossing. Esmay had told Fleet that her father was one of four regional commanders . . . she had not reminded them what must be in her file, that her uncles Berthol and Gerard were two of the others. 'I guess you didn't starve in Fleet, after all. You know Grandmother is still convinced you can find nothing legal to eat . . .'

Esmay found herself grinning even as she wished he hadn't brought that up. Grandmother was his grandmother, not hers – well over a hundred, and an influence as potent in her way as Papa Stefan in his. 'I'm fine,' she said, and turned, hoping to convince Berthol not to grandstand for the cameras.

'More than fine, Esmaya.' He sobered, and touched her shoulder gently. 'You give us pride. We are more than glad to have you home.' Now he turned; his aides, she noticed now, had been scattered in the crowd and now came together at his back. The glaring lights receded behind them despite raised voices. 'When we get down, we will celebrate.'

Esmay's heart sank. What she really wanted was a quiet drive out to the estancia, and a room with windows open to the rose garden . . . and a full night's sleep, a night that fit her body's rhythms.

'We can't waste this,' he said more quietly, as they walked straight past a departure lounge full of people she didn't know, who were giving her the soft tongue-clicking applause she remembered so well. Berthol ushered her into the waiting shuttle, and into the rear compartment which his aides closed off as they came through.

'What's going on?' Esmay asked. Tension curdled her stomach; she did not really want to know.

'What's going on . . . you'll be fully briefed later,' Berthol said. 'We didn't reserve a full shuttle – we thought it would be too obvious. Natural enough to have a private compartment And there's no way out of the welcoming celebration, though I'm sure you're ready for a vacation at home, eh?'

Esmay nodded. She glanced around at Berthol's aides. The militia ranks were not those of Fleet, exactly; the insignia, except for stars marking flag rank, were completely different. It came back to her in a rush. Infantry, armor, air, navy – what her Fleet called, somewhat disparagingly, 'wet-fleet.' All four branches here, all of them older than she was. The one wearing armor tags had an ear-wire, and now he turned to Berthol.

'General Suiza says it's all ready, sir.'

'Your father,' Berthol said. 'He's in charge down there, for reasons that will become clear later. In the meantime, there'll be a formal ceremony at the shuttleport – blessedly brief, if I know your father – then a parade into town, and a formal presentation at the palace.'

'Presentation?' Esmay squeezed that in when Berthol took a breath.

'Ah—' He seemed embarrassed a moment, then lowered his voice. 'You see, Esmay, when it was your action that saved an entire planet, and then you don't even get a token of recognition from your Fleet . . .'

Dear God. Esmay scrambled through all the possible explanations she could make – that he would not understand – and realized it was no use. They had decided that *her* Fleet had not sufficiently honored her, and it would do no good to point out that her acquittal was itself acknowledgement and reward. Besides, she knew that someone had put in a recommendation for a medal – which made her skin itch to think of it. She wished they'd just forget it. But this—

'And it's not like you're just any shaggy pony out of the back lots,' Berthol went on. 'You're a Suiza. They're treating you—'

'Very well, Uncle Berthol,' she said, hoping to stop him, if she couldn't stop the ceremony.

'No – I don't think so. Nor does the Long Table. They've voted to give you the Starmount—'

'No,' Esmay breathed. She was uneasily aware that something deep inside disagreed, and breathed *yes*.

54

'And a title of your own. To be converted if you marry on Altiplano.'

Dear God, she thought again. She didn't deserve this. It was ridiculous. It would cause . . . immense trouble either way. No matter that Fleet would not realize it had been intended as a rebuke – they would find it awkward, and that made her awkward.

'Not much of a steading with it,' Berthol said. 'In fact, your father said he'd provide that; it's that little valley where you used to hide out . . .'

Despite herself, Esmay felt a stab of pleasure at the memory of that little mountain valley, with its facing slopes of poplar and pine, its grassy meadows and clear stream. She had claimed it years before in her mind, but had never thought it would be hers. If it could be . . . she remembered some R.S.S. regulations she was afraid might interfere.

'Don't worry,' Berthol said, as if he could read her mind. 'It's under the limit – your father ran a new survey, and chopped it short at the upper end. It's under the glacier there. Anyway, if you need to refresh yourself on the protocol of the award ceremony . . .'

She did, of course. The data cube the major with the armor insignia handed her contained not only the ceremony, but a precis on recent political developments, and her family's position on all of them. The Minerals Development Commission was still squabbling with the Marine Biological Commission over control of benthic development. Some things never changed, but in the years she'd been gone the focus of the battle had shifted from the Seline Trench, as the colonies of interest to the biologists died, and were mined for their rich ores, to the Plaanid Trench, where new vents nourished new vent communities. That quarrel would have been unimportant on many worlds, but on Altiplano the Minerals Development Commission represented the Secularists, while Old Believers and the Lifehearts controlled the Marine Biological Commission. Which meant that an argument over exactly when a benthic vent community was dead and could be mined might erupt in religious riots around the entire planet.

'Sanni,' Berthol said, when she had clicked off the cube reader, 'is involved with the Lifehearts again.'

Esmay remembered vividly the moment when her romantic feelings about the night sky became utter certainty that she would have to leave her home forever. Her aunt Sanni – Sanibel Aresha Livon Suiza – and her uncle Berthol, screaming at each other across the big dining room at the estancia. Sanni, a Lifeheart as rigid in her piety as any Old Believer. Esmay found the Lifeheart philosophy attractive, but Sanni in a rage terrified her. Yet it was Berthol who had thrown the priceless chocolate pot, shattering its painted water lilies and swans, scarring the wide polished table. Her own father had walked in on the end of that, with Sanni scrabbling on the floor for shards and Berthol still yelling. And Papa Stefan, two paces behind him, had shamed them both into apologies and hand-shakings.

Esmay hadn't believed it. Whatever was wrong between Sanni and Berthol stayed wrong, and was still wrong, and here she was back in the middle of it.

'It's not my problem now,' she said. 'I'm only here for a short leave—'

'She likes you,' Berthol said. His gaze flicked to his aides, who were studiously ignoring this. 'She says you're the one sane member of your generation, and now you're a hero.'

Esmay felt herself reddening. 'I'm not. All I did—'

'Esmay, this is *family*. You don't have to pretend. All you did, you babykin, was survive a mutiny, come out on top, and then defeat a warship twice your size.'

Bigger than that, Esmay thought. She didn't say it; it would only make things worse. 'It didn't know I was there until too late,' she said.

'So you were smarter than its captain. Hero, Esmay. Get used to it. You're carrying our flag out there, Esmay, and you're doing very well.'

She was not carrying *their* flag, but her own. They would not understand that, even if she dared say it to them. And Berthol sounded too much like Major Chapin, too much like Admiral Serrano. She had been a hero by accident – why wasn't it as obvious to the others as it was to her?

'And Sanni's very proud of you,' Berthol went on. 'She wants to talk to you – ask you all about Fleet, about your life. If you're meeting anyone eligible, if I know Sanni.' He laughed, but it sounded forced.

She had left for a good reason. She should have stayed away. Yet at the thought of the whole family for once approving, for once seeing her as an asset rather than a very chancy proposition, her heart beat faster. The Starmount . . . when she'd been a little girl, she remembered the first soldier she'd seen awarded the Starmount, a lean, red-haired fellow who walked lopsided. She had stared and stared at the medal on its blue and silver ribbon that dangled around his neck until a disapproving grownup made her apologize and then quit following him. No one from Altiplano could be indifferent to the Starmount . . . and she didn't have to tell Fleet how she felt.

At the shuttlefield, the only media wore the green and scarlet uniforms of the Altiplano Central News Agency. No one tried to speak to her; no one tried to crowd close. She knew that her walk from the shuttle through the terminal to the waiting car would be only one clip in the finished story, narrated by a senior 'analyst.' No one would try to interview her; here that was considered rude and disrespectful.

Her father, backed by a wedge of other officers, gave her the same formal salute Berthol had; she returned it, and he gave her the semiformal hug and kisses, not fatherly, but from commander to junior about to be honored. She was introduced to his senior aide, to the next senior; she was led through a corridor where a solid block of militia provided complete privacy – in their terms, which meant from civilian eyes – for her few moments in the ladies' retiring room, where she found two tiring maids ready to apply fresh makeup and attempt to do something about her flyaway hair. That ended in a spritz of scented stuff which would leave her scalp itchy for two days – but this once, she didn't mind. In moments they had whisked off her R.S.S. uniform jacket, pressed it, and after a look at the shirt beneath, insisted on replacing it with a clean one from her luggage.

Refreshed, and to her surprise cheered by these ministrations, Esmay came back out, into the midst of a low-voiced argument between her father and her uncle.

'It's only one cloud,' her uncle was saying. 'And it might not rain—'

'It's only one bullet,' her father said. 'And it might miss. I'm not taking the chance. When her hair gets wet – Oh, there you are, Esmaya. There's a line of storms moving into the city; we're going to go by car—'

'It's not nearly as impressive,' Berthol grumbled. 'And it's not as if you expected her to do any *real* riding.'

She had assumed by car; she'd forgotten that on Altiplano all ceremony involved horses. She thanked some unknown deity for the gift of a possible rainstorm and her father's distaste for the frizzy mess her hair became if it got damp. At least no one from Fleet was here, to make a joke about a backwoods military that still used horses.

Of course the parade still had horses, even though she was in a car. From the protection of the car, she watched the perfectly drilled cavalry swing into position before and behind, the horses moving in unison, their glossy haunches bunching and relaxing. The riders, their backs upright, hands quiet, faces set in a neutral expression that would not vary if a horse stood up on its hind legs . . . not that one of those well-trained animals would. Beyond the horses, a crowd on the sidewalks, faces peering from the windows of the taller buildings. Some of them waved the gold and red Altiplano colors.

She had not been home for just over ten standard years. She had left as a gawky teenager, who in memory seemed the very model of adolescent incapacity. Nothing had fit, not her body nor her mind nor her emotions. From not fitting at home to not fitting in the Fleet prep school had been a tiny, natural transition. By the time she had graduated from the Academy, she had expected to be the odd one out, the one whose reactions were not natural.

She had not realized how much those feelings had been due to age and then the real displacement of leaving her home world before her adult identity had solidified. Now, in the light of Altiplano's sun, with her body held by Altiplano's gravity, she began to relax, feeling at home in a way she had not since she was a little girl. The colors were *right* in a way they had not been for years; her very bones knew that this gravity, not one standard G, was the right gravity.

When she stepped out of the car, and walked up the red stone steps of the palace, her feet found the right intervals without effort. These steps were the right height, the right depth; this stone felt solid enough; this doorway welcomed; this air – she took another long breath – this air smelled right, and felt right all the way down to the bottom of her lungs.

She looked around at the people now crowding into the hall around her. Humans were humans, but the shapes of humans varied with their genome and the worlds they lived on. Here the bone structure looked familiar; these were the faces she had known all her life, prominent cheekbones and brows, long jutting chins, eyes set deeply under thick eyebrows. These long arms and legs, big bony hands and feet, boxy joints – these were her people, her look. Here she fit in, at least physically.

'Ezzmaya! S'oort semzz zalaas!' Esmay turned; her ears had already adapted to the Altiplano dialect, even in her family's less-obvious form, and she had no trouble understanding the welcome she'd just been given. She didn't immediately recognize the wizened old man in front of her, stiffly upright and wearing the brilliant braid of a former senior NCO, but her father's senior aide murmured into her earplug. Retired master sergeant Sebastian Coron . . . of course. He had been part of her life as far back in childhood as she could remember, always crisp and correct, but with a twinkle for his commander's elder daughter.

Her tongue, hearing the familiar speech, curled into the trills without her having to think of it. She thanked him for his congratulations in the formal phrases that brought a broader grin to his face. 'And your family – your bodysons and heartdaughters? And don't I remember that you have grandlings now?'

Before he could answer, her father had extended his own hand to Coron. 'You can come visit later,' her father said. 'We need to get her upstairs—' Coron nodded, gave Esmay a stiff short bow, and stepped back. As her father led her away, he said 'I hope you don't mind – he's so proud of you, you'd think he was your father. He wanted to come—'

'Of course I don't mind.' She glanced up the green-carpeted stairs. She had always loved the stained glass window on the landing, that poured rich gold and blood-colored light onto the carpet. Palace guards in black and gold stood stiff as the banister rails, staring at nothing. As a child, she had wondered whether they would be so stiff if tickled, but she'd never had the chance . . . or the daring . . . to try it. Now she climbed past them, bemused by the mixture of memories and present feelings.

'And he wants to hear about it direct from you – at least some of it . . .'

'That's fine,' said Esmay. She would rather tell old Coron than any of the fresh-faced young militia officers now surrounding them. Coron had taught her more of the basics than her father probably knew; she had pored over the handbooks on small-unit tactics under his watchful eye all one summer down in Varsimla.

'He does get a bit carried away,' her father went on. 'But he saved my skin often enough.' He looked ahead to the upper hall, where a cluster of men in formal dress waited in a semicircle. 'Ah . . . there we are. The Long Table advisors – did you have time in the car—?'

She had not, but that's what the earplugs were for. Most of them were men she had met before, in the way that the children of a household meet distinguished guests. She would not have remembered that Cockerall Mordanz was Advisor on Marine Resources, but she did remember that he'd once fallen off during a polo game and her uncle Berthol's pony had neatly jumped over him. The current Long Table Host, Ardry Castendas Garland, had once slipped coming into their dining room, and knocked over the little table with the hot towels on it; her greatgrandmother had scolded her for staring.

'Esmay – Lieutenant Suiza!' the Host said now, catching himself and returning to the formality appropriate to the ceremony. 'It is an honor . . .' His voice trailed away, and Esmay allowed herself an interior smile. Altiplano lacked the right honorific for someone like her: female, a military officer, a hero. She felt conflicting impulses to help him out, and to let him stew in his problem: they, after all, had wanted to make her a hero. Let them come up with something. 'My dear,' he said finally. 'I'm sorry, but I keep remembering the sweet child you were. It's hard to grasp what you've become.'

Esmay could cheerfully have slapped him. Sweet child! She had been a sulky, awkward teenager, the successor to an awkward child . . . not sweet, but difficult and strange. And what she was now should be simple enough to grasp: a junior officer of the Regular Space Service.

'It's clear enough,' said another man, one she didn't recognize. Opposition Leader, her earplug said. Orias Leandros. He smiled at her, but the smile was intended for the Host. He would make political profit of her . . . he thought.

'Host Garland,' Esmay said quickly. She didn't like either of them, but she knew where her family duty lay. 'You can be no more amazed at my present predicament than I am. My father tells me you plan an award – but, you must realize, you do me too much honor.'

'Not at all,' Garland said, back in balance again. He shot the briefest glare at his rival. 'It's obvious that your family inheritance of military ability continues down the generations. No doubt your sons—' He stopped, trapped again in the assumptions of Altiplano and the usual phrases. What would have been a fine compliment to a man sounded almost indecent applied to a woman.

'It has been so long,' Esmay said, changing the subject before Orias Leandros could say anything damaging. 'Perhaps you would introduce me to the other advisors?'

'Of course.' Garland was sweating a little. How had he ever been elected Host, when he was still as clumsy in word and deed as ever? But he got through the introductions well enough, and Esmay managed to smile with the right intensity at all the right people.

The award ceremony itself felt odd, because Esmay could not feel anything at all. She was too aware of the faint murmur of the earplug, coaching her through the required lines, of the expressions on the faces around her . . . the embarrassment she'd felt when first told of the award could not penetrate the concentration needed to do it right. The Starmount itself, a disk with the blue and black enamel representing a mountain against the sky, the little diamond glittering at the peak, aroused neither pride nor guilt. She bent her head to let the Host put the wide blue-and-gray ribbon around her neck; the medal felt lighter than she'd expected.

Then it was only a matter of standing in the line, saying the ritual greetings and thanks to those who filed past her: pleased, how kind, thank you, how lovely, how kind, thank you so much, very kind, how pleased . . . until the last of the line, a white-haired old lady related to Esmay's grandmother in some complicated way, had passed from her father to her, and from her to the Host. She had a few minutes to sip the tangy fruit juice and taste the pastries, then her father hurried her into the car again for the trip home.

She would like to have stayed longer; she was still hungry, and some of the faces that had blurred past had been friends once. She would have liked a chance to shop in town, to get herself some new clothes. But she had no more to say about it than when she'd been a schoolgirl. The general said it was time to leave, and they left. She tried not to resent it.

'Papa Stefan,' her father said to her. 'He didn't feel well enough to come in, but he had planned a family reception.'

She could not imagine Papa Stefan anything but well; he had been white-haired even in her childhood, but vigorous, riding and working alongside his sons and grandchildren. Things had changed, then. She had known they would, eventually, but – it was hard to feel the same gravity, breathe the same air, recognize the same smells, and think of change. The buildings they drove past, the substantial stone blocks that housed stores and banks and offices, were the same she had always known.

Outside the city, the grasslands surged up to the mountains, as always. Esmay looked out the window, relaxing into that familiar view. The Black Teeth, between which dark spires lay the legendary lair of the Great Wyrm. As a child, she'd believed the dragon stories were about her own world; she had believed the lair was stuffed with dragon's treasure. She'd been bitterly disappointed to find out that the Great Wyrm was the code name of the rebel alliance that had (so legend went) massacred the original owner of Altiplano and all his family. A school field trip to the 'lair' showed it to be a perfectly ordinary bunker built into the cliff on one side of a canyon.

South of the Black Teeth were other peaks of the Romilo Escarpment, lesser only by contrast to the Teeth. Esmay squinted across the kilometers of shimmering light, looking for the gap in the line, the grassy embayment of her family's estanica. There – the trees marked it out, the long lines of formal plantings along the road and the drives.

The car slowed, pulling off the road. Her father leaned closer. 'I don't know if you still observe,' he said. 'But it's customary, when someone returns from a long journey . . . and anyway, I'm going to light a candle.'

Esmay felt the heat rise to her face. Bad enough to forget, but to have her father suspect she'd forgotten was worse. 'I, too,' she said. She clambered out of the car, stiff and feeling even more awkward than stiffness would explain. She hadn't thought of the ceremonies since she left home; she wasn't sure she remembered the words.

The shrine, built into the estancia gate wall, had a row of fresh flower wreaths laid out below the niche. She could smell the faint sweet scent of the wreaths, and the stronger aroma of the great trees that loomed above. Even as an imaginative child, Esmay had never been able to see any meaning in the blurred shape of the statue in the niche. She had once been unwise enough to say it looked like a melted blob. She had never said it again, but she'd thought it often enough. Now, she saw with fresh eyes, and it still looked like a grayish, shiny melted blob, taller than it was wide. Around its base, the candle cups were clean as always, the little white candles in a box to one side.

Her father took one, set it in the green glass cup, and lit it. Esmay took another, lit it from her father's flame, and got it into a cup without burning her fingers. Her father said nothing, and neither did she; they stood side by side, watching the flames writhe in the breeze. Then he plucked a needle from one of the trees, and laid it in the flame. Blue smoke swirled up. Esmay remembered to stoop and find a pebble to lay in the wax of her candle.

Back in the car, with the windows now open to the steady breeze, her father still said nothing. Esmay leaned back, enjoying the many shades of green and gold. The drive, bordered with rows of narrow conifers, ran straight for a kilometer. On the right were the orchards, past blooming now. She could just see knots of green fruit on some limbs . . . on the far side, the first plums should be ripening. On the left, the family polo fields, mown in crisscross patterns . . . someone was out there, stooping, stamping divots back in. Nearer the house, flower gardens burst into riotous color. The car swept around the front, into the wide gravelled space large enough to review a mounted troop. It had been used for that, years back. A broad portico, shaded by tangled vines thick as trees at the root . . . two steps up to the wide double-door . . . home.

Not home now.

Nothing had changed . . . at least on the surface. Her room, with its narrow white bed, its shelves full of old books, its cube racks full of familiar cubes. Her old clothes had been removed, but by the time she came upstairs, someone had unpacked her luggage. She knew, without asking, what would be in each drawer. She undressed, hanging her uniform on the left end of the pole: it would be taken away and cleaned, returned to the right end of the pole. Presently the right end of the pole had two outfits she did not own – someone's suggestion of what to wear to the family dinner. She had to admit they looked more comfortable than anything she had bought off-planet. Down the familiar hall to the big square bathroom, with its two shower stalls and its vast tub . . . after shipboard accommodations, it seemed impossibly large. But just this once . . . she slid the door marker to 'long bath' and grinned to herself. She did like long hot baths.

When she came downstairs, in the long cream-colored tunic over soft loose brown slacks, her father and step-mother were waiting. Her stepmother, born elegant, gave an approving nod, which for some reason made Esmay furious. No doubt she had chosen that tunic, had it put in Esmay's closet . . . for a moment Esmay thought of ripping it off and throwing it . . . but R.S.S. officers did not behave like that. And her half-brothers were watching, and others coming into the hall. She smiled at her step-mother, and shook the offered hand.

'Welcome home, Esmaya,' her stepmother said. 'I hope you will like dinner . . .'

'Of course she will,' her father said.

Dinner was in the informal dining hall, its wide windows

opening on a tiled courtyard with a pool . . . Esmay could hear the gentle splash of the fountain even over the murmur of voices, the scraping of feet on the tiled floor.

She started toward her old place out of habit, but someone sat there already – a cousin no doubt – and her father was leading her up the table, to sit at Papa Stefan's left hand. Great-grandmother was not at the table; she would be waiting to receive Esmay afterwards, in her own parlor.

'Here she is, at last,' her father said.

Papa Stefan had aged; he was thinner, the skin looser over his bones. But his eyes were still sharp; his mouth, even as he smiled at her, still firm.

'Your father tells me you remembered the proper offering for return,' he said. 'Do you also remember the proper blessing of food?'

Esmay blinked. Once away from Altiplano, she had shed all concern about clean and unclean foods, blessings and cursings, as happily as she'd shed the traditional under-garments considered appropriate for a virtuous daughter. She had not expected this honor . . . as much test as honor, as everyone knew. Ordinarily only sons and sons of sons asked blessings on the food at dinner; daughters and daughters of daughters asked the morning grace at the breaking of the night's fast, and at the noon meal everyone held silence.

She looked down the table to see what was on the great platters . . . it made a difference . . . and was even more surprised to see the five platters that meant a whole calf had been butchered in her honor.

She had never heard of a woman speaking at such a time, but she knew the words.

'Back from the waste . . .' she began, and continued through the whole, stumbling only momentarily over the nested clauses where the prayer expected a male speaker and she had either to speak of herself in the masculine or change the words. 'From father to son it came to me, and so I sent it on . . .' She had not thought about her own culture in any detailed way after the first year or so in the Fleet prep schools; she had not noticed how confining the language really was. Fleet had shocked her at first,

65

with its assumption of easy relationships between the sexes, with 'sir' used for both men and women. In Fleet, the important terms for parents distinguished between gene-parents and life-parents, not between mothers and fathers. On Altiplano, they had no word for 'parents,' and while they knew of modern methods of reproduction, very few would ever use them.

She finished the blessing, still thinking of the differences, and Papa Stefan sighed. Esmay glanced at him; his eyes twinkled.

'You didn't forget . . . you always had a good memory, Esmaya.' He nodded. The servants stepped forward; the great platters were shifted to the sideboards for carving, while bowls of soup were offered.

Fleet food had been good enough, but this was the food of her childhood. The thick blue bowl with the creamy corn soup, garnished with green and red . . . Esmay's stomach rumbled at the familiar aroma. The spoon she lifted had her family's crest on it; it fit her fingers as if it had grown there.

The first salad followed the corn soup, and by then the meat had been sliced and layered on blue platters swirled with white. Esmay accepted three slices, a mound of the little yellow potatoes that were a family specialty, a scoopful of carrots. It was worth the long wait to have food like this.

Around her, the family carried on soft-voiced conversations; she didn't listen. Right now all she wanted was the food, the food she had not let herself realize she missed. Puffy rolls that could have floated up into the sky as clouds . . . butter molded into the shapes of heraldic beasts. She remembered those molds, hanging in a row in the kitchen. She remembered the rolls, too – no use letting them get cold, when they were dry and tasteless. They deserved to be soaked in new butter or drenched in honey.

When she came up for air, no one seemed to be paying attention to her anyway. They had finished eating; servants were taking the plates away.

'It's a matter of pride,' Papa Stefan was saying to her cousin Luci. 'Esmaya would not fail in anything that touched the family honor.' Esmay blinked; Papa Stefan's notion of family honor had wildernesses no one had ever explored fully. She hoped he wasn't hatching up one of his plots with her assigned the role of heroine.

Luci, the age Esmay had been when she left, looked much as Esmay remembered herself. Tall, gangling, soft brown hair pulled back severely, with escaping wisps that ruined the intended effect, clothes that were obviously intended for a special occasion, but looked rumpled and dowdy instead. Luci looked up, met Esmay's eyes, and flushed. That made her look sulky as well as unkempt.

'Hi, Luci,' Esmay said. She had already greeted Papa Stefan and the elders; the cousins were far down the list of obligatory greetings. She wanted to say something helpful, but after ten years she had no idea what Luci's enthusiasms were – and a very clear memory of how embarrassing it was when elders assumed you still liked the dolls you'd played with at five or seven.

Papa Stefan grinned at her and patted Luci's arm. 'Esmaya, you will not know that Luci is the best polo player in her class.'

'I'm not that good,' Luci muttered. Her ears looked even redder.

'You probably are,' Esmay said. 'I'm sure you're better than I am.' She had never seen the point of milling about chasing a ball on horseback. A horse was mobility, a way to get off by herself, into places vehicles couldn't go, faster than anyone could follow on foot. 'Are you playing on the school team, or the family team?'

'Both,' Papa Stefan said. 'We're looking for championships this year.'

'If we're lucky,' Luci said. 'And speaking of that, I wanted to ask about that mare Olin showed me.'

'Ask Esmay. Her father bought a string for her to put out on the grant, and that mare was one of them.'

A flash of anger from Luci's eyes; Esmay was startled both by the gift of horses, and her cousin's unexpected reaction.

'I didn't know about that,' Esmay said. 'He hadn't mentioned anything.' She looked at Luci. 'If there's one you wanted in particular, I'm sure—'

'Never mind,' Luci said, standing up. 'I wouldn't want to deprive the returning hero of her loot.' She tried to say it lightly, but the underlying bitterness cut through.

'Luci!' Papa Stefan glared, but Luci was already out the door. She didn't reappear that evening. No one commented, but they were already drifting from the table . . . she remembered from her

67

own adolescence that such a thing would not be spoken of in company. She did not envy Luci the rough side of Sanni's tongue that would not doubt work her over in private very shortly.

5

After dinner, Esmay went to the private apartment where her great-grandmother waited. Ten years ago, the old lady had still lived apart, refusing to inhabit the main house because of some quarrel that no one would explain. Esmay had tried to wheedle it out of her, unsuccessfully. She had not been the kind of great-grandmother who encouraged the sharing of secrets; Esmay had been scared of her, of the sharp glance that could silence even Papa Stefan. Ten years had thinned the silver hair, and dimmed the once-bright eyes.

'Welcome, Esmaya.' The voice was unchanged, the voice of a matriarch who expected reverence from all her kin. 'Are you well?'

'Yes, of course.'

'And they feed you decently?'

'Yes . . . but I was glad to taste our food again.'

'Of course. The stomach cannot be easy when the heart is uncertain.' Great-grandmother belonged to the last generation which adhered almost universally to the old prohibitions and requirements. Immigrants and trade, the usual means of fraying the edges of cultures, had brought changes that seemed great to her, though to Esmay hardly significant compared to Altiplano's difference from the cosmopolitan casualness of Fleet. 'I do not approve of your gallivanting around the galaxy, but you have brought us honor, and for that I am pleased.'

'Thank you,' Esmay said.

'Considering your disadvantages, you have done very well.'

Disadvantages? What disadvantages? Esmay wondered if the old woman's mind was slipping a bit after all.

'I suppose it means your father was right, though I am loathe to agree, even now.'

Esmay had no idea what Great-grandmother was talking about. The old lady changed topics abruptly, as she always had. 'I hope you will choose to remain, Esmay. Your father has chosen for you the reward of bloodstock and land; you would not be as a beggar among us—' That was a dig; she had complained, just before she left, that she had nothing of her own, that she might as well be a poor beggar living here on sufferance. Great-grandmother's memory had not slipped at all.

'I had hoped you might forget those rash words,' she said. 'I was very young.'

'But not untruthful, Esmaya; the young speak the truth they see, however limited it is, and you were always a truthful child.' That had some emphasis she could not interpret. 'You saw no future here; you saw it among the stars. Now that you have seen them, I hope you can find one here.'

'I . . . have been happy there,' Esmay said.

'You could be happy here,' the old lady said, shifting in her robe. 'It is not the same; you are an adult, and a hero.'

Esmay did not want to distress her, but across the impulse to comfort came the same impulse to honesty which had led to that earlier confrontation. 'This is my home,' she said, 'but I don't think I can stay here. Not always . . . not for ever.'

'Your father was an idiot,' her great-grandmother said, on the trail of some other thought. 'Now go away and let me rest. No, I'm not angry. I love you dearly, as I always did, and when you go I will miss you extremely. Come back tomorrow.'

'Yes, Great-grandmother,' said Esmay meekly.

Later that evening, in the great library, she found herself comfortably ensconced in a vast leather chair, with her father, Berthol, and Papa Stefan. They started with the questions she'd expected, about her experiences in Fleet. To her surprise, she found herself enjoying it . . . they asked intelligent questions, applied their own military experience to the answer. She found herself relaxing, talking about things she had never expected to discuss with her male relatives.

'That reminds me,' she said finally, after explaining how Fleet handled the investigation of the mutiny. 'Someone told me that Altiplano has a reputation for being Ageist – opposed to rejuvenation. That's not so, is it?'

Her father and uncle looked at each other, then her father spoke. 'Not exactly against rejuvenation, Esmaya. But . . . many people here see it as bringing more problems to us than it could solve.'

'I suppose you mean population growth . . .'

'Partly. Altiplano's primarily an agricultural economy, as you know. Not only is this world suited to it, but we have all those Lifehearts and Old Believers. We attract immigrants who want to live on the land. Rapid population growth – or slow growth long continued – would start encroaching on the land. But – consider what it means to a military organization, for a start.'

'Your most experienced personnel wouldn't get too old for service,' Esmay said. 'You . . . Uncle Berthol . . .'

'Generals are two a credit . . . but of course, the most experienced you have – the fellow who can always cobble up a repair for your landcruiser or your artillery – will stay useful and perhaps even pick up more expertise. Experience counts, and with rejuvenation you can accumulate more experience to learn from. That's the positive. The negative?'

Esmay felt that she was back in school, being forced to perform in front of the class. 'Longer lives for the seniors mean fewer slots for juniors to be promoted into,' she said. 'It would slow down career advancement.'

'It would stop it in its tracks,' her father said soberly.

'I don't see why.'

'Because it's repeatable now. The rejuvenated general – to start at the top – will be there forever. Oh, there'll still be some slots for promotion – someone will die of an accident, or in a war. But that's not many. Your Fleet will become the weapon of an expansionist Familias Regnant empire—'

'No!'

'It has to, Esmay. If rejuvenation gets going—'

70

'It's already widespread; we know that,' Papa Stefan said. 'They've had the new procedure forty years or more now, and they've tried it on a lot of people. Remember your biology classes, girl: if the population expands, it must find new resources or die. Changes in population are governed by birth rate and death rate: lower the death rate, as rejuvenation does, and you've got an increase in population.'

'But the Familias isn't expansionist.'

'Huh.' Berthol snorted and hitched himself sideways in his chair. 'The Familias didn't announce a grand campaign, no, but if you look at the borders, these last thirty years . . . a nibble here, a nibble there. The terraforming and colonization of planets which had been written off as unsuitable. Peaceful, cooperative annexation of half a dozen little systems.'

'They asked for Fleet protection,' Esmay said.

'So they did.' Her father gave Berthol a glance that said *Be quiet* as clearly as words. 'But our point is, that if the population of Familias worlds continues to increase, because the old are being rejuvenated – and if the population of Fleet continues to increase for the same reason – then this pressure can move them toward expanding.'

'I don't think they will,' Esmay said.

'Why do you think your captain went over to the Black Scratch?'

Esmay squirmed. 'I don't know. Money? Power?'

'Rejuvenation?' her father asked. 'A long life and prosperity? Because, you know, a long life *is* prosperity.'

'I don't see that,' Esmay said, thinking of her great-grand-mother, whose long life was now coming to an end.

'A long *young* life. You see, that's the other thing that bothers me about rejuvenation. Longevity rewards prudence above all . . . if you live long enough, and are prudent, you will prosper. All you have to do is avoid risk.'

Esmay thought she saw where he was going, but preferred not to risk charging ahead. Not with this canny old soldier. 'So?' she asked.

'So . . . prudence is not high on the list of military virtues. It is one, sure enough, but . . . where are you going to get soldiers who

71

will risk their lives, if avoidance of risk can confer immortality? Not the immortality of the Believers, who expect to get it after they die, but immortality in this life.'

'Rejuvenation may work in a civilian society,' Berthol said. 'But we think it can cause nothing but trouble in the military. Even if you could retain all your best experienced men, you would soon be out of the routine of training recruits – and the population you served would be out of the routine of providing them.

'Which means,' he went on, 'that a military organization with anything but mud between the ears is going to see that it must limit the use of rejuvenation . . . or plan on a constant expansion. And at some point it's going to run into a culture of younglings, a culture which doesn't use rejuvenation, and is bolder, more aggressive.' He had never been able to resist belaboring a point.

'It sounds like the old argument between the religious and the nonreligious,' Esmay said. 'If immortality of the soul is real, then what matters most is the prudent life, to make sure the soul qualifies for immortality . . .'

'Yes, but all the religions we know of which offer that prize also define such prudence in more stringent terms. They require active virtues which discipline the believer and curtail his or her self-ishness. Some even demand the opposite of prudence – reckless-ness of life in the service of their deity. This makes good soldiers; it's why religious wars are so much harder to end than others.'

'And here,' Esmay said, to preempt Berthol, 'you see rejuvena-tion rewarding – encouraging – merely practical prudence, pure selfishness?'

'Yes.' Her father frowned. 'There will no doubt be good people rejuvenated . . .' Esmay noted the assumption that good people would not be selfish. It was a curious assumption for a man who was himself rich and powerful . . . but of course he didn't define himself as selfish. He had never had to be selfish, in his own terms, to have his least wish satisfied. 'But even they will, over several rejuvenations, realize how much more good they can do alive, in control of their assets, than dead. It's easy to lie to yourself, to convince yourself that you can do more good with more power.' He was staring blankly at the books; was this self-assessment?

72

'And that's not even considering the dependency created by reliance on rejuvenation,' Berthol said. 'Unless you have control of the process, adulteration—'

'As happened recently—' her father said.

'I can see that,' Esmay said, cutting off the obvious; she was not in the mood for a longer lecture from Berthol.

'Good,' said her father. 'So when they offer you rejuvenation, Esmaya, what will you do?'

For that she had no answer; she had never even considered the question before. Her father shifted the topic to a reprise of the ceremony, and soon she excused herself and went to bed.

The next morning, waking in her own bed in her own room, with sunlight bright on the walls, she was surprised by a sense of peace. She had suffered enough bad dreams in this bed; she had been half-afraid the nightmares would recur. Perhaps coming home had completed some sort of necessary ritual, and they were forever banished.

With that thought, she hurried down to breakfast, where her stepmother offered the morning grace, and then out into the cool gold of a spring morning. Past the kitchen gardens, the chicken runs where every hen seemed to be clucking her readiness to lay eggs, and every rooster crowed defiance at the others. She had heard them faintly through her window on the front side of the house; here they were deafening, so that she was not tempted to slow and look at them.

The great stables smelled as always of horses and oats and hay, pungencies that Esmay found comforting after all these years. There had been a time when she resented them, back when she, like all the children, had been expected to muck out her own pony's stall. Unlike some of the others, she had never enjoyed riding enough to make the work worthwhile. Later, when a horse became her escape route into the mountains, she was old enough that she no longer had the daily chores to do anyway.

Now she walked down the stone-flagged aisle, the great arches opening to her left into one of the exercise yards. On her right, rows of stalls with the dark narrow heads of horses peering out. A groom came out of a tackroom at the sound of her steps.

'Yes, dama?' He looked confused; Esmay identified herself and his face relaxed.

'I was wondering – my cousin Luci mentioned a mare she'd looked at – that Olin showed her—?'

'Ah – the Vasecsi daughter. Down here, dama, if you'll follow me. Excellent bloodlines, that one, and has done very well in training so far. That is why the General chose her for your foundation herd.'

Outside the mare's stall, a twist of blue and silver; Esmay looked down the row and saw more such twists. This was her herd, picked by her father, and although she could exchange them, it would shame him. But to make a gift of one mare, to Luci – that would be acceptable. She hoped.

'Here, dama.' The mare had her rump to the door, but when the groom clucked she swung round. Esmay recognized the qualities for which her father had chosen the horse: the good legs and feet, the depth of heart-girth, the strong back and hindquarters, the long limber neck and well-bred head. Solid dark brown, just lighter than black – 'You would like to see her move?' the groom said, reaching for the halter that hung beside the stall.

'Yes, thank you,' Esmay said. She might as well. The groom led the mare out of the stall, across the aisle, and out into the courtyard. There, in the open ring, the groom put the mare through her paces, which accorded with her conformation. A long, low walk, a sweeping trot and long level canter. This was a horse to cover the ground, mile after mile, and yet she would be handy as well. A good mare. If only Esmay cared particularly—

'I'm sorry I was rude,' Luci said, from the arches. Her face was in shadow; her voice sounded as if she'd been crying. 'She's a lovely mare, and you deserve her.'

Esmay walked nearer; Luci had been crying. 'Not really,' she said quietly. 'I'm sure you heard all about my regrettable attitude towards horses back when I left.'

'I inherited your trail horse,' Luci said without answering the comment. She said it as if Esmay might be angry about it. Esmay had not thought about old – Red, had that been his name? – in years.

'Good,' Esmay said.

'You don't mind?' Luci sounded surprised.

'Why should I mind? I left home; I couldn't expect the horse to go unused.'

'They didn't let anyone ride him for a year,' Luci said.

'So they thought I might flunk out and come back?' Esmay said. It didn't surprise her, but she was glad she hadn't known that.

'Of course not,' Luci said, too quickly. 'It's just—'

'Of course they did,' Esmay said. 'But I didn't fail, and I didn't come back. I'm glad you got that horse . . . you seem to have inherited the family gift.'

'I can't believe you really haven't—'

'I can't believe anyone really wants to stay on one planet,' Esmay said. 'Even when it feels right.'

'But it's not crowded,' Luci said, flinging out one arm. 'There's so much *space* . . . you can ride for hours . . .'

Esmay felt the familiar tension in her shoulders. Yes, she could ride for hours and never come to a border she need worry about . . . but she could not eat a meal without wondering if some old family grievance were about to explode. She turned to Luci, whose eyes kept following the mare.

'Luci, would you do me a favor?'

'I suppose.' No eagerness, but why would there be?

'Take the mare.' Esmay almost laughed at the shock on Luci's face. She repeated it. 'Take the mare. You want her. I don't. I'll square it with Papa Stefan, and with Father.'

'I–I can't.' But naked desire glowed from her face, a wild happiness afraid to admit itself.

'You can. If that's my mare, I can do what I want with her, and what I want to do is give her away, because I'm going back to Fleet . . . and that mare deserves an owner who will train her, ride her, breed her.' An owner who cared about her; every living thing deserved to be cared about.

'But your herd—'

Esmay shook her head. 'I don't need a herd. It's enough to know I have my little valley to come home to . . . what would I do with a herd?'

'You're serious.' Luci was sober again, beginning to believe it would happen, that Esmay was serious, and that different.

'I'm serious. She's yours. Play polo on her, race her, breed her, whatever . . . she's yours. Not mine.'

'I don't understand you . . . but . . . I do want her.' Shy, sounding younger than she was.

'Of course you do,' Esmay said, and felt a century older, at least. Embarrassment hit then – had she seemed this young to Commander Serrano, to everyone who had a decade or more on her? Probably. 'Listen – let's go for a ride. I'll need to get back in shape if I'm going to visit the valley.' She couldn't yet say 'my valley' even to Luci.

'You could ride her – if you wanted,' Luci said. Esmay could hear the struggle in her voice; she was trying hard to be fair, to return generosity for generosity.

'Heavens, no. I need one of the school horses, something solid and dependable . . . I don't get any riding in Fleet.'

Grooms tacked up the horses, and they rode out toward the front fields, between the rows of fruit trees. Esmay watched Luci on the mare . . . Luci rode as if her spine were rooted into the horse's spine, as if they were one being. Esmay, on a stolid gelding with gray around its eyes and muzzle, felt her hip joints creaking as she trotted. But what was her father going to say? Surely he had not expected her to manage a herd from light years away? Had he expected to manage them for her? As Luci cantered the mare in circles around Esmay, she decided to go the whole way.

'Luci – what are you planning to do?'

'Win a championship,' said Luci, grinning. 'With this mare—'

'In the long run,' Esmay said. 'Strategy, cousin.'

'Oh.' Luci halted the mare, and sat silently a moment, obviously wondering how much to tell her older cousin. *Is she safe* was written on her face as if with a marker.

'I have a reason for asking,' Esmay said.

'Well . . . I was going to try for the vet course at the Poly, though Mother wants me to study "something more appropriate" at the University. I know there's no chance of getting on the estate staff here, but if I qualified, I might somewhere else.'

'I suspected as much.' Esmay meant it benignly, but Luci flared up.

'I'm not just dreaming—'

'I know that. Get the hump out of your back. You're serious, just as I was serious . . . and nobody believed me, either. That's why I had the idea—'

'What idea?'

Esmay nudged her horse, and it ambled over to Luci's mare. The mare twitched her ears but otherwise stood still. Esmay lowered her voice. 'As you know, my father gave me a herd. The last thing I need is a herd, but if I try to give it back, he'll be hurt and I'll hear about it forever.'

Luci's face relaxed; she almost grinned. 'So?'

'So I need someone to manage my herd. Someone who will make sure that the mares go to the right stallions . . . that the foals get the right training, and are actually put on the market—' Family horses almost never went to market. '—And so forth,' Esmay said. 'I would expect to compensate the manager, of course. The eye of the master fattens the herd . . . and I will be far away, for a very long time.'

'You're thinking of me?' Luci breathed. 'It's too much – the mare, and—'

'I like the way you handle her,' Esmay said. 'It's how I'd want my horses handled, if I wanted horses at all . . . and since I have them, that's what I'd like. You could save up the money for school – I know from experience that it impresses them if you fund your own escape. And you'd get the experience.'

'I'll do it,' Luci said, grinning. Despite herself, Esmay thought back to the previous night's conversation. Here was someone for whom prudence could never swamp enthusiasm.

'You didn't ask what I'm paying,' Esmay said. 'You should always find that out first . . . what it's going to cost, and what you're going to get.'

'It doesn't matter,' Luci said. 'It's the chance—'

'It matters,' Esmay said, and surprised herself with the harshness of her voice; the horse under her shifted uneasily. 'Chances aren't what they seem.' Then, at the look on Luci's face, she stopped herself. Why was she being negative, when she had just been admiring Luci's impetuosity? 'Sorry. Here's what I want from you – a fair accounting of costs and income. Midsummer – that should give you time to write it up after the foal crop arrives.'

'But how much—' Now Luci looked worried.

'You didn't ask before. I'll decide later. Maybe tomorrow.' Esmay nudged her mount, and started off toward the distant line of trees beyond the canter track; her cousin followed.

She had forgotten about the old man at the reception until a servant announced him after lunch, when she had lingered in the kitchen over a second piece of rednut pie smothered in real cream.

'Retired soldier Sebastian Coron, dama, requests a few moments of your time.'

Seb Coron . . . of course she would see him. She wiped the last of the pie from her mouth, and went out to the hall, where he stood at ease, watching one of the younger cousins practice the piano with Sanni standing by, counting the time.

'Reminds me of you, Esmay,' he said when she came forward to shake his hand.

'It reminds me of hours of misery,' Esmay said, smiling. 'The untalented and unrhythmic should never be forced to go beyond learning a few scales . . . once we've admitted how hard it is, we should be let off.'

'Well, you know, it's in the old law.' It was, though Esmay had never understood why every child, with or without ability or interest, should be forced through ten years of musical training on a minimum of four instruments. They didn't make all children learn soldiering.

'Come on in the sitting room,' Esmay said, leading him to the front room where women of the family usually received guests. Her stepmother had redone it again, but the bright floral-patterned covers on the chairs and long padded benches were in a traditional print. This one had more orange and yellow, and less red and pink, than Esmay remembered. 'Would you like tea? Or something to drink?' Without waiting for an answer, she rang; she knew that with his arrival the kitchen staff would have started preparing the tray with his favorites, whatever they were.

She settled him in one of the wide low chairs, with the tray at his side, and herself chose a seat to his left, the heart-side, to show her awareness of the family bond.

Old Sebastian twinkled at her. 'You have done us proud,' he said. 'And it's all over for you, the bad times, eh?'

Esmay blinked. How could he think that, when she was still in Fleet? She had to expect other combat in the future; surely he realized that. Perhaps he meant the recent trouble.

'I certainly hope I never have to go through a courtmartial again,' she said. 'Or the mutiny that led to it.'

'You did well, though. That's not exactly what I meant, though I'm sure it was unpleasant enough. But no more old nightmares?'

Esmay stiffened. How did he know about her nightmares? Had her father confided to this man? She certainly wasn't about to tell him about them. 'I'm doing all right,' she said.

'Good,' he said. He picked up his glass, and sipped. 'Ah, this is good. You know, even when I was still active, your father never stinted the good stuff when I came here. Of course, we both understood it was special, not something to be talked about.'

'What?' Esmay said, without much curiosity.

'Your father, he didn't want me to talk about it, and I could see his point. You'd had that fever, and nearly died. He wasn't sure what you remembered, and what was the fever dreams.'

Esmay fought her body to stillness. She wanted to shiver; she wanted to gag; she wanted to run away. She had done all those, in past times, without success. 'It was the dreams,' she said. 'Just the fever, they said, something I'd caught when I ran away.' She managed a dry laugh. 'I can't even remember where I thought I was going, let alone where I got to.' She did remember a nightmare train ride, fragments of something else she tried not to think about.

She did not know what tiny movement – a flicker of eyelid, a tension in the muscles along his jaw – but she *knew* at once that he knew something. Knew something that she did not, which he longed to convey and felt he must conceal. Her scalp prickled. Did she want to know, and if she did, could she get him to tell her?

'Well, you went to find your father . . . that was simple. Your mother had died, and you wanted him, and he was right there in the midst of a nasty little territorial dispute. That was when the Borlist branch of the Old Believers had decided to pull out of the regional planning web, and take over the upper rift valley.'

Esmay knew about that miscalled dispute: the Califer Uprising had been a civil war, small but intense.

'No one realized you could read that well, let alone that you could read a map . . . you hopped on your pony, with a week's food, and set off—'

'On a *pony*?' She could hardly imagine that; she had never liked riding that much. She'd have expected her young self to sneak a ride on a truck bound for town.

Seb looked embarrassed – she couldn't imagine why – and scratched at his neck. 'Back then you rode like a tick on a cowdog, and just as happy. You were hardly ever off your pony, until your mother died, and they were happy enough to see you back on it. Until you disappeared.'

She couldn't remember that – couldn't remember a time when she would have chosen to spend all those hours on a horse. What she remembered was how much she hated it, the lessons and the sore muscles and all the work of picking out hoofs and grooming and mucking out a stall. Could this be true, that an illness had wiped out not only her pleasure in horses, but all memory of a time when she had enjoyed them?

'I guess you'd planned pretty well,' he went on, 'because they couldn't pick up your traces anywhere. No one thought of what you'd really done; they thought you'd gotten lost, or gone up in the mountains and had an accident. And no one ever knew the whole story, because you didn't make a lot of sense when we found you.'

'The fever,' said Esmay. She was sweating now; she could feel it, like a sick slime all over.

'That's what your father said.' Sebastian had said it before; now his voice echoed with her memory, and her new adult ability to interpret nuances of expression compared the two versions and found hidden disbelief.

'My father said . . .?' Esmay said, carefully neutral, not looking at his face. Not directly, anyway; she could see the pulse in his throat.

'You'd forgotten it all, with the fever, and all for the better, he said. Don't bring it up, he said. Well, I guess you know by now it wasn't *all* a dream . . . I suppose those Fleet psychnannies dug it out and helped you deal with it, eh?'

She was frozen; she was simmering in her own terror. Cold and hot at once, closer than she wanted to some terrible truth, and yet not able to move away. She could feel his gaze on her head, and knew if she looked up she would not be able to hide her terror and confusion. Instead, she busied her hands among the little dishes of breads and condiments, pouring the tea, handing over a delicate cup and saucer with the spray-pattern touched with silver . . . she could hardly believe her hands were so steady.

'Not that I could have argued with your father, of course. Under the circumstances.'

Under the circumstances Esmay could cheerfully have wrung his neck, but she knew that wouldn't work.

'It was not only my duty to him as my commander, but . . . he was your father. He knew best. Only I did wonder sometimes if you remembered something from *before* the fever. If perhaps that was what changed you . . .'

'Well, my mother had died.' Esmay got that out past her tight throat. Her voice, too, was steady as her hands. How could that be, with terror shaking the roots of her mind? 'And I was sick so long—'

'If you'd been my daughter, I think I'd have told you. It helps the trainees to talk things through after a bad engagement.'

'My father thought differently,' Esmay said. Dust was no dryer than her mouth; she felt drought-cracks opening in her mind, bottomless mouths to trap her . . .

'Yes. Well, anyway, I'm glad you had the chance to deal with it in the end. But it must've been hard when you had that traitor captain to deal with, that second betrayal—' The almost musing tone of his voice sharpened. 'Esmaya! Is something wrong? I'm sorry, I didn't mean—'

'It would be most helpful if you could simply tell me the story from your point of view,' Esmay managed to say; her voice was thickening now, the dust compressing into angular blocks of rock-hard clay. 'Remember, I had only my own somewhat fragmentary memories to go on, and the psychannies found them somewhat inadequate.' The psychannies would have found them inadequate, if they'd found them at all, but they hadn't. They had assumed that anyone with her background would have had any such problems dealt with earlier. And she, convinced by her family's insistence that everything in the nightmares was just fever dreams, had been afraid to let them know she had problems. She'd been afraid of being labeled crazy or unstable, unfit for duty ... rejected, to come home a failure. Was this why her family had assumed she'd fail, even to the point of keeping her trail horse unassigned?

'Perhaps you should ask your father,' Coron said doubtfully.

'I suspect he would be displeased at having his judgment questioned,' Esmay said with all sincerity. 'Even by the Fleet's psychiatric specialists.' Coron nodded. 'It would be a help, if you wouldn't mind.'

'If you're sure,' Coron said. She had to meet his eyes a moment; she had to endure the worry in them, the tightness of the lines around his eyes, the furrowed brow. 'It's not a pleasant matter – but of course you know that already.'

Nausea bucked in her gut, sending sour signals to her mouth. Not yet, she begged it. Not until I know. 'I'm sure,' she said.

It had been a time of riot and civil disorder, when a single small child, if determined and sure of herself, could travel by pony and then by rail some thousand kilometers. 'You'd always been good at explaining yourself,' Coron said. 'You could come up with a story the moment you were caught out. I suppose that's why no one really noticed you – you spun some yarn about being sent to an auntie or grandmother, and since you didn't act scared or confused, and you had enough money, they let you on the trains.'

All this was supposition; they had not been able to trace her path between the time she left the pony – they never found it, but in those days it might well have ended up in someone's stew pot – and the last part of her journey, the train she'd taken right into disaster.

'The last despatches home had given your father's station as Buhollow Barracks, and that's where the train would have gone. But in the meantime the rebels had overrun the eastern end of the county, putting everything they had into an assault aimed at the big arms depot at Bute Bagin. The force at Buhollow Barracks was too small to hold them, so your father had rolled aside to hook around and cut them off from the rear, while the Tenth Cav moved up from Cavender to hit them in the flank.'

'I remember that,' Esmay said. She remembered it from the records, not from real memory. The rebels had counted on her father's reputation which had never included leaving a plum like Buhollow unprotected . . . they had planned to immobilize his forces there with part of their army, while the rest went on to Bute Bagin and the supplies there. Later, his decision to abandon Buhollow and trap the rebel army would be taught as an example of tactical brilliance. He had done what he could for the town. The civilian population of Buhollow fled ahead of the rebels; they had been told which way to go. Most of them survived.

But Esmay, crammed in amongst refugees from earlier fighting, had ridden the train two stops too far. Both sides had mined the railroad; although the official reports said a rebel mine had blown the low bridge over the Sinets Canal just as the locomotive passed, Esmay had never been sure. Would any government admit its own mines had blown up its own train?

She did remember the enormous jolt that slammed the carriage crooked. They had been going slowly; she had been stuffed between a fat woman with a crying baby and a skinny older boy who kept poking her ribs. The jolt rocked the carriage, but didn't knock it over. Others weren't so lucky. She could just recall jumping down from the step – a big jump for her at that age – and following the woman and her baby for no reason other than that the woman was a mother. The skinny boy had poked her once more then turned away to follow someone else. Streams of frightened people scurried away from the train, away from the blowing smoke and screams at the front end of the train.

She had lost track of direction; she had forgotten, for the moment, which way she was supposed to go. She had followed the woman and baby . . . and they had been following others . . . and then her legs were too tired, and she stopped.

'There was a little village the locals called Greer's Crossing,' Coron went on. 'Not even one klick from the train track, where the shipping canal turned. You must've gone there with others from the train wreck.'

'And that's when the rebels came through,' Esmay said.

'That's when the war came through.' Coron paused; she heard the faint slurp as he sipped his tea. She glanced up to meet a gaze that no longer twinkled. 'It wasn't just the rebels, as you know only too well.'

I do? she thought.

'It was right about there the rebels realized that they were being herded into a trap. Say what you like about Chia Valantos, he had a tactical brain between his ears.'

Esmay made a noise intended to indicate agreement.

'And maybe he had good scouts – I don't know. Anyway, the rebels had been on the old road, because they had some heavy vehicles, and so they had to go through the village, to get across on the bridge. They were making a mess of the village, because the people around there had never been supporters. I suppose they thought the people from the train had something to do with the loyalists . . .'

The old memories forced themselves up, lumping under her calm surface; she could feel her face changing and struggled to keep the muscles still. Her legs had begun to hurt, after the hours on the train, the crash, the fall . . . the woman, even with a baby, had longer legs and took longer steps. She had fallen behind, and by the time she got to the village it was gone. Already the roofs had collapsed; what walls remained were broken and cantways. Smoke blew across streets littered with stones and trash and tree limbs and piles of old clothes. It was noisy; she could not classify the noises except that they scared her. They were too loud; they sounded angry, and tangled in her mind with her father's voice scolding her. She wasn't supposed to be so close to whatever made those noises.

Blinded by stinging smoke, she had stumbled over one of the heaps of old clothes, and only then recognized it as a person. A corpse, her adult mind corrected. The child she had been had thought it a silly place for someone to go to sleep, a grown woman, and she had shaken the slack heavy arm, trying to wake an adult to help her find her way. She had not seen death before, not human death – she had not been allowed to see her mother, because of the fever – and it took her a long time to realize that the woman with no face would never pick her up and soothe her and promise that everything would be all right soon.

She had looked around, blinking against the stinging in her eyes that was not all smoke, and saw the other piles of clothes, the other people, the dead . . . and the dying, whose cries she could now recognize. Even across the years, she remembered that the first thought she could recognize was an apology: I'm sorry – I didn't mean to . . . Even now, she knew this was both necessary and futile. It had not been her fault – she had not caused the war – but she was there, and so far untouched, and for that, if nothing else, she must apologize.

That day, she had stumbled along the broken lane, falling again and again, crying without realizing it, until her legs gave out and she huddled into the corner of a wall, where someone's garden had once held bright flowers. The noise rose and fell, shadowy figures moving through the smoke, some wearing one color and some another. Most, she knew later, must have been the terrified passengers on the train; some were rebels. Later – later they all wore the same uniform, the uniform she knew, the one her father and uncles wore.

But she didn't remember. She couldn't remember, not all of it. She had remembered, and they'd said it was dreams.

'It'd have been better, I always thought, if they'd told you,' Sebastian said. 'At least when you got old enough. Bein' as the man was dead, and couldn't hurt anyone again, least of all you.'

She did not want to hear this. She did not want to remember this . . . no, she *could* not. Fever dreams, she thought. Only fever dreams.

'Bad enough for it to happen at all, no matter who did it. The rape of a child – sickening. But to have it one of ours—'

She fixed on the one thing she could stand to know. 'I . . . didn't know he was dead.'

'Well, you father couldn't tell you that without bringing up the rest of it, could he? He hoped you'd forget the whole thing . . . or think it was just a fever dream.'

He'd said it was a fever dream; he'd said it was over now, that she'd always be safe . . . he'd said he wasn't angry at her. Yet his anger had hovered around her, a vast cloud, dangerous, blinding her mind as the smoke had blinded her eyes.

'You're . . . sure?'

'That the bastard died? Oh yes . . . I have no doubt at all.'

The invisible mechanisms whirled, paused, slid into place with a final inaudible crunch. 'You killed him?'

'It was that or your father's career. Officers can't just kill their men, even animals who rape children. And to wait, to charge him – that'd have brought you into it, and none of us wanted that. Better for me to do it, and take my lumps . . . not that there was anything worse than a stiff chewing out, at the end of it. Mitigating circumstances.'

Or extenuating . . . her mind dove eagerly into that momentary tangle, reminding her that extenuation and mitigation were, although similar, applied to different ends of the judicial process, as it were.

'I'm glad to know that,' Esmay said, for something to say.

'I always said you should be told,' he said. Then he looked embarrassed. 'Not that I talked about it, you understand. I said it to myself, I mean. It was no use arguing with your father. And after all, you were his daughter.'

'Don't worry about it,' Esmay said. She was finding it hard to pay attention; she felt the room drifting slowly away, on a slow spiral to the left.

'And you're sure you got it all sorted out, all but him being dead, I mean? They helped you in the R.S.S.?'

Esmay tried to drag her mind back to the topic, from which it wanted to shy away. 'I'm fine,' she said. 'Don't worry about it.'

'No . . . I was real surprised, you know, when you wanted to go off-planet and join them. Figured you'd had enough combat for any one life . . . but I guess it's your blood coming out, eh?'

How was she going to get rid of him, politely and discreetly? She could hardly tell him to go away, she had a headache. Suizas did not treat guests that way. But she needed – how she needed – some hours alone.

'Esmaya?' Esmay looked up. Her half-brother Germond grinned shyly at her. 'Father said would you come to the conservatory, please?' He turned to Coron. 'If you can excuse her, sir?'

'Of course. It's your family's turn now – Esmaya, thank you for your time.' He bowed, very formal again at the end, and withdrew.

6

Esmay turned to Germond, now fifteen, all ears and nose and big feet. 'What – did Father want?'

'He's in the conservatory with Uncle Berthol . . . he said you'd be getting tired of listening to old soldiers' tales, for one thing, and for another he wanted to ask you more about Fleet.'

Her mouth was dry; she could not think. 'Tell him . . . tell him Seb's gone, and I'll be out in a few minutes. I've gone upstairs to . . . to freshen up.' For once, the impenetrable assumptions of Altiplano society worked in her favor. No male would question her need to be alone for a few minutes with an array of plumbing fixtures. Nor would they rush her.

She went up the stairs by instinct; she was not seeing the brass rails holding the carpet snug to the risers, the scuffs on the steps themselves. Her body knew how to get up the stairs, around the corners, where to find the switches that gave her absolute privacy.

She leaned against the wall, turned on the cold-water tap, and put her hands into it. She wasn't sure why. She wasn't sure of anything, including the passage of time. The water cut off automatically, just as it would aboard ship, and she nudged the controls again. Abruptly she threw up; the curdled remains of lunch slopped into the clean swirl of water and disappeared down the drain with it. Her stomach heaved again, then settled uneasily. She cupped her hand under the faucet, and drank a handful of the cold, sweet water. Her stomach lurched, but steadied. She had never been prone to nausea. Not even then, not even when the pain was so bad she'd been sure she was being torn apart. The real pain, not the imagined pain induced by fever dreams.

87

In the mirror, she looked like a stranger – a gaunt old woman with flyaway dark hair, face streaked with tears and vomit. This would never do. Methodically, Esmay took a towel from the rack, wet it, and cleaned her face and hands. She rubbed her face hard with the dry end of the towel, until the blood returned and the greenish tinge of nausea disappeared under a healthy pink. She attacked her hair with damp hands, flattening the loose strands, then dried her hands. The water stopped again, and this time she didn't turn it back on. She folded the damp towel, and hung it on the used rack.

The woman in the mirror now looked more familiar. Esmay forced a smile, and it looked more natural on that face than it felt on her own. She should put on something, she thought, looking to see if she'd spotted her shirt. A few drops showed, dark against the pale fawn. She would change. She would change into someone else . . . her mind stumbled over something in the smoke that was all she could see.

Still navigating by habit, she unlocked the door, and returned to her own room. By the time she'd taken off the shirt, she knew she'd have to change from the skin out. She did that as quickly as she could, taking what lay on top in her drawers, and glancing at herself only long enough to be sure the wide collar lay flat and untwisted around her neck. The pallor had gone; she looked like Esmay Suiza again.

But was she? Was Esmay Suiza a real person? Could you build a real person on a foundation of lies? She fought her way through the choking dark clouds in her mind, trying to cling to what she remembered, what Seb Coron had told her, to any logic that could connect them.

When the smoke-cloud in her mind cleared, the first thing she recognized was smug relief: she had been *right*. She had known the truth; she had made no mistakes. Her adult mind intruded: except for the stupidity of leaving home in the first place, the idiocy of a child trying to travel cross-country in the midst of a civil war. She batted that critical voice down. She had been a child; children were, by definition, ignorant of some things. In the essentials – in recognizing what she had seen, in telling the truth about what happened – she had been right.

Rage followed that moment of delight. She had been right, and they had lied to her. They had told her she was mistaken – that she was confused by the fever . . . or was there even a fever? She had started to call up the household medical records before her critical voice pointed out that of course the records would show such an illness, such a hospitalization. It could have been fabricated, all of it – how would she know? And to whom did she want to prove it?

To everyone, at that moment. She wanted to drag the truth before her father, her uncle, even Papa Stefan. She wanted to grab them by the neck, force them to see what she had seen, feel what she had felt, admit that she had in fact endured what she had endured.

But they already knew. Exhaustion followed exhilaration just as it followed fever; she could feel the familiar languor in her veins, dragging her down to immobility, to acquiescence. They knew, and yet they had lied to her.

She could keep her own secret, and let them think theirs safe, run away again as she had run before. They would be comfortable still, indulged by her complicity.

Or she could confront them.

She looked again in the mirror. That was the person she would become, if she became an admiral like Heris Serrano's aunt. The diffidence, the uncertainty, that had mocked her so often had burned away in the last hour. She did not yet feel what she saw in that face, but she trusted the eyes that blazed out at her.

Would he still be in the conservatory? How long had this taken? The clock surprised her; she had been upstairs only half a local hour. She headed for the conservatory, this time with all senses fully awake. It might have been the first time she came down the stairs . . . she felt the slight give in the sixth from the bottom, noticed a loose tack on the railing side of the carpet, spotted a nick in the railing itself. Every sight, every smell, every sound.

Her father and Berthol were stooped over a tray of bedding plants with one of the gardeners. Her new clarity of vision noticed every detail of the plants, the notched petals of fire-orange and sun-yellow, the lace-cut leaves. The gardener's dirt-blackened fingernails where his hands were splayed out on the potting table. The red flush along the sides of her uncle's neck. White lines in the skin of her father's face, where he had squinted against the sun so long that the creases had not tanned. A loose thread on the button of Berthol's sleeve button.

Her foot scraped on the tile floor because she let it; her father looked up.

'Esmaya . . . come see the new hybrids. I think they'll do very well in the front urns . . . I hope old Sebastian didn't wear you out.'

'He didn't,' Esmay said. 'In fact, I found him quite interesting.' Her voice sounded perfectly calm, perfectly reasonable, to her, but her father started.

'Is something wrong, Esmay?'

'I need to talk to you, Father,' she said, still calm. 'Perhaps in your study?'

'Something serious?' he asked, not moving. Rage surged through her.

'Only if you consider a matter of family honor serious,' she said. The gardener's hands jerked; the plants shivered. The gardener reached for the box of planters, and he murmured something. Her father lifted his chin, and the man grabbed the box and scuttled away, out the back door of the conservatory.

'Do you want me to leave?' her uncle asked, as if he were sure she would say no.

'Please,' she said, this time testing her own power to put a sting in it. He flinched, his eyes shifting to her father, then back to her.

'Esmay, what . . .?'

'You will know soon enough,' Esmay said. 'But I would prefer to speak to Father alone, just now.'

Berthol flushed, but turned away; he did not quite slam the door going out.

'Well, Esmaya? There was no need to be rude.' But her father's voice had no power in it, and she heard an undertone of fear. The little muscles around his eyes and nose were tense; the contrast between his tanned skin and the untanned creases had almost disappeared. If he'd been a horse, his ears would have been flat and his tail switching nervously. He should be able to put the sum together: she wondered if he would.

She came toward him, running her hand through the fronds of one of the sweetheart palms; it still tickled. 'I talked to Seb Coron – or rather, he talked . . . and I found it most interesting.'

'Oh?' He was going to brazen it out.

'You lied to me . . . you said it was all a dream, that it didn't happen . . .'

For a moment, she thought he would try to pretend he didn't understand, but then a quick wash of color rose to his cheeks and drained again.

'We did it for you, Esmaya.' That was what she'd expected to hear.

'No. Not for me. For the family, maybe, but not for me.' Her voice did not waver, which surprised her a little. She had decided to keep going even if her voice broke, even if she cried in front of him, which she had not done in years. Why should he be protected from her tears?

'For more than you, I admit.' He looked at her from under those bushy brows, gray now. 'For the others – it was better that one child suffer that confusion—'

'Confusion? You call that *confusion*?' Her body ached with remembered pain, the specific pains that had specific causes. She had tried to scream; she had tried to fight him off; she had even tried to bite. The strong adult hands, hardened by war, had held her down easily; bruising her.

'No, not the injuries, but not being sure what had happened – you couldn't tell us who, Esmaya; you didn't really see him. And they said you would forget . . .'

She felt her lips pulling back from her teeth; she saw in her father's expression what hers had become. 'I saw him,' she said. 'I don't know his name, but I saw him.'

He shook his head. 'You couldn't give us any details at the time,' he said. 'You were exhausted, terrified – you probably didn't even see his face. You've been in combat now as an adult; you know how confusing it is—'

He doubted. He dared to doubt, even now, her knowledge. A bright ribbon of images from *Despite* rippled through her mind. Confusing? Perhaps, in terms of organizing information to relate in court, but she could see the faces of those she had killed, and those who had tried to kill her. She always would.

'Show me the regimental roster,' she said, her voice choked with rage. 'Show me, and I'll point him out.'

'You can't possibly – after all these years—'

'Sebastian says he killed him – that means you know who it is. If I can point him out, that should prove to you that I do remember.' That you were wrong, and I was right. Why it mattered so much to prove this was not a question Esmay wanted to examine. Proving a general wrong was professional suicide and military stupidity. But . . .

'You can't possibly,' her father said again, but this time with no strength. He led the way to his study without another word; Esmay followed, forcing herself not to strike him down from behind. He moved to the console, and stabbed at the controls. Esmay noticed that his fingers were shaking; she felt a calm satisfaction. Then he stepped back, and she came forward to look.

The faces came up, six to a screen. She stared at them, one part of her mind sure that she would know, and another sure that she wouldn't. Had her father even called up the right year? He wanted her to fail, that was clear enough. He might have cheated – but she could not believe that of him, even now.

Suizas did not lie . . . and he was her father.

He had lied before, *because* he was her father. She tore her mind away from that dilemma and stared at the screen.

She did not recognize most of the faces at all. She had no reason to; she had not been to Buhollow Barracks after her father was posted there. She found a few faces vaguely familiar, but unthreatening. They would have been men who had served with her father before, even among the household guard at the estancia. Among them, a much younger Sebastian Coron, whom she recognized instantly . . . so her memory was clear in some details that far back.

She could hear her father's breathing, as she scrolled through the list. She did not look at him. It was hard enough to focus on the screen, to breathe through the tightness in her throat. Screen after screen . . . she heard her father shift in his chair, but he did not interrupt. Someone came to the door; she heard the rustle of clothing, but did not look up. Her father must have gestured, for without a word she heard the rustle of clothing retreat, and the gentle thud of the door as it shut.

Through the entire enlisted ranks, and she had not found that face her mind refused to show her. Doubts chilled her. The face she remembered had been contorted with whatever emotion makes men rape children . . . she might never find it among these solemn, almost expressionless faces in the catalog. It must be here . . . surely Coron would have told her if it had been someone in another unit, or an officer.

Or would he? She made herself keep going, to the officer ranks. There at the head was her father, no gray in his hair, his mouth one long firm line. Beneath, in descending order, the . . . her breath caught. Yes. Her heart fluttered then raced thunderously in her chest, spurred by the old fear. He stared out of the page, sleek and handsome, the honey-colored hair swept back . . . she remembered it darker, matted with sweat and dirt. But no doubt at all, not one.

She searched his face for clues to his choices . . . for some mark of depravity. Nothing. Regular features, clear gray eyes – coloring not that common on Altiplano, but much prized. The little button of an honor graduate, the braid on his epaulet that declared him an eldest son, of whom more was expected. His mouth was set in a straight line, a conscious copy of her father's . . . it looked no crueler. His name . . . she knew his name. She knew his family. She had danced with his younger brothers, at the Harvest Games, the year before she left Altiplano for the stars.

Her mouth was too dry to speak. She struggled to swallow, to clear her tongue. She had struggled then, too. Finally she got out a word: 'This.' She laid her finger on the image, surprised at the steadiness of her hand; her finger didn't tremble at all.

Her father got up; she could hear him coming up behind her and fought not to flinch away. He grunted first, as if someone had slugged him in the belly. 'Gods! You *did* – how did you—?'

Anger released her tongue. 'I told you. I remember.'

'Esmaya . . .' It was a groan, a plea, and his hand on her hair was another. She slid aside from it, pushing herself away from the console, scrambling out of the chair.

93

'I didn't know his name,' she said. Amazingly, it was easy to keep her tone even, her words crisp. 'I was too young to have been introduced, even if he'd been at our house before. I couldn't tell you his name, or give the kind of description that an adult might have been able to give. But I *knew*. You did not show me the rolls then, did you?'

Her father's face, when she looked, might have been carven in bleached wood; it looked dry and stiff, unnatural. Was that her vision, or his reality? Her gaze wandered away, around the room, just noticing the familiar things before moving on to something else. In her mind, more and more of the certainties shifted, as if stone walls had been only scenery painted on movable screens. What did she really know about herself, about her past? What could she rely on?

Against this chaos the past years in Fleet stood firm: she knew what had happened there. From her first day in the prep school to the last day of the court-martial, she knew exactly what she had done, and who had done what to her. She had created that world for herself; she could trust it. Admiral Vida Serrano, an easy match for her father, had never lied to her . . . had never screened anyone else, at her expense.

Whatever she had had to suppress, to limit, in herself in order to make this haven was expendable. She didn't need to find the part of herself that had loved to ride, or paint, or play antique instruments . . . she needed to keep herself safe, and she had managed that quite well. She could give up Altiplano; she had already done it.

'Esmaya . . . I'm sorry.' He probably was, she let herself think, but it didn't matter. He was sorry too late and too little. 'If – *since* you remember, you probably need therapy.'

'Therapy *here*?' That got out before she could control the emotion in it, the scorn and anger. 'Here, where the therapists told me it was all my imagination, all fever dreams?'

'I'm sorry,' he said, but this time with an edge of irritation. She knew that tone; he could apologize, but that was supposed to be the end of it. She was supposed to accept that apology and let it go. Not this time. Not again. 'I – we – made a mistake, Esmaya. We can't change that now; it's past. I can't possibly convince you

94

how badly I feel about it – that it was a mistake – but there were reasons. I asked advice . . .'

'Don't,' she said harshly. 'Don't make excuses. I'm not stupid; I can see what you would like to call the realities. He—' she could not bring herself to dirty her mouth with the name. 'He was an officer, the son of a friend; there was a civil war in progress; you could not risk a feud—' Memory reminded her that the young man's father had commanded a sizable force himself. Not merely a feud, but potentially a lost war. Her military training argued that a child's pain – even her pain – weighed less than an entire campaign. But the child she had been, the child whose pain still shaped her reactions, the child whose witness had been denied, refused that easy answer. She had not been the only victim – and for the victims, no victories sufficed . . . the victories were not for them, did not help them. Yet defeat promised only more of the same. She squeezed her eyes shut, trying to force back all the feelings that wanted to escape, shut them back into the darkness. 'It did not take rejuvenation to make you *prudent*,' she said, throwing at him the only new weapon she had.

A short silence, during which her father's breathing was almost as harsh as hers had been that bitter day.

'You need help, Esmaya,' her father said, finally. His voice was almost back to normal, warm and steady; the general in command of himself, a lifetime's habit. She wanted to relax into the promise of fatherly love and protection.

She dared not. 'Probably I do,' she said. 'But not here. Not now.' Not with the father who had betrayed her.

'You won't come back,' he said. He had never been stupid, only selfish. That wasn't entirely fair, but neither was he. Now he looked at her, as straight a look as he might have given a commander he respected. 'You won't come back again, will you?'

She couldn't imagine coming back, but she wasn't quite ready for that negative commitment. 'I don't know. Probably not, but – you might as well know . . . I've worked out a deal with Luci for the herd.'

He nodded. 'Good. I shouldn't have done that, but . . . I suppose I was still hoping you'd come home for good, especially when they treated you like that.'

And you treated me better? hovered on her lips but did not quite emerge. Her father seemed to hear it anyway.

'I understand,' he said. He didn't, but she wasn't going to argue, not now. Now she wanted to get away, far away, and have some time alone. She suspected she would have to spend some time with Fleet psychnannies in the end, but for now . . . 'Please, Esmaya,' he said. 'Get help in your Fleet, if you won't accept it here.'

'I'm going to ride out to the valley,' she said, ignoring that. He had no right to tell her what to do about the wound he'd inflicted. 'Just for a day. Tomorrow. I don't want company.'

'I understand,' he said again.

'No surveillance,' she said, meeting his gaze squarely. He blinked first.

'No surveillance,' he agreed. 'But if you stay overnight, please let us know.'

'Of course,' she said, her voice relaxing even as his had. They were alike in ways she had never noticed; even in her anger she suddenly felt the urge to tell him about the mutiny, knowing that he would not find her actions surprising, inexplicable, as the Familias officers had.

She walked out into the afternoon, feeling nothing but a great light emptiness, as if she were a seed pod at summer's end, ready to blow away on the first autumn stormwind. Across the gravel drive, crunching under her feet. Between the beds of flowers whose color hurt her eyes. Across the sunlit fields beyond, where shadows shifted and moved and called her name, but she did not answer.

She came back when the sun fell behind the distant mountains, tired in ways that had nothing to do with walking however far she'd walked, and went into the dim entrance hall, where the smell of food and clatter of dishes stopped her short.

'Dama?' Esmay whirled, but it was one of the servants, offering a tray with a cup and a folded note. She shook her head to the cup of tea, took the note, and went upstairs. No one followed, no one intruded. She lay the note on her bed, and went down the hall to the bathroom.

The note, as she'd half expected, was from her great-grandmother. *Your father told me I am now free to talk to you. Come see me.* She put it on the shelf above the clothes pole and thought about it. She had always assumed that her father obeyed his grandmother, as she obeyed her grandfather; though men and women had different roles, elders always ruled. She had thought so, anyway, imagining the chain of authority coming down, link by link, from eldest to youngest through all the generations.

Had her great-grandmother really known the truth and *not* told her? How had her father gained so much power?

She lay back on the bed, and as the hours passed she could not find the strength to move, to get up and bathe or change her clothes or even turn away from the square of sky she could see darkening from blue to gray to the star-spangled midnight. It was all she could do to blink her eyes when they burned from staring at the window; it was all she could do to breathe.

In the first light of dawn, she struggled up, stiff and miserable. How many mornings she had wakened stiff and miserable, hoping to see no one on the way to the baths, on the way out . . . and here she was again, supposedly a hero – she would have laughed at the thought if she could – once more alone at the top of her father's house, once more awake and miserable after a sleepless night.

She told herself, firmly, in the tone she thought Admiral Serrano would use, to get a grip on herself. A deep breath of the morning air, sweet-scented with the nightblooming flowers on the house wall. She made it to the bathroom, showered, brushed her teeth. In her room she dressed in riding clothes; when she came down the stairs she heard the familiar clatter in the kitchen where the cooks were already at work. If she put her head in, hoping for a taste of the first baking, they'd want to talk to her. She went on, past the kitchen, to the storeroom. Inside on the right, if the custom hadn't changed, was a stone jar of trail bread. Anyone could grab a handful, if headed out to do early chores.

The stable, busy as always by daylight . . . the grooms and their helpers scurrying from stall to stall, buckets clattering. She went to the stable office, where she found her name at the top of the list of the day's riders. Her father had done that, probably the night before, and she felt no gratitude. In another hand, someone had written in a horse's name, Sam.

'Dama?' One of the grooms. 'When you're ready, dama.'

'I'm ready,' Esmay said through a dry throat. She ought to have taken a water bottle too, but she didn't want to go back for it. The groom went ahead of her, down the aisle of that barn and into another and out again into the small training ring, where a bored brown horse leaned its chin on the rail where it was tied. A trail saddle, slicker tied neatly behind the cantle, saddlebags, water bottle . . . her father must have specified that, too. She hadn't needed to take the trail bread. A trail bridle, easy to unclip the bit so the horse could graze, a long lead-line now clipped into the hitching rail's permanent loops.

The groom offered his linked hands, and she mounted; he unclipped the lead and handed her the end to tuck into the saddle ring. 'He is good, but not too fast,' the groom said, and opened the gate into the upper pastures.

She turned the horse's head into the trail that would, hours later, lead to her valley. Eventually her stiff body relaxed into the rhythm of its walk, and she made herself look around. Morning light lit the recesses of the mountains on her right, and the vast rolling pastures that spread from their foot as far east as she could see.

She could remember riding out here from childhood. She had always taken a deep breath, going out the gate, because it meant freedom. Thousands of hectares, dozens of trails, hidden wooded hollows even in this open grazing land, and all the intricate topography of the mountains . . . no one could find her, once she was out of sight of the house. Or so she'd thought.

She took the deep breath, and it caught in her throat. Anger sat on one shoulder, and grief on the other; the stink of old lies filled her nose and she could not think of anything else. She had lived through the assault itself – she had, thanks to Seb Coron, outlived the assailant. But she had not outlived the effects . . . worst of all effects, the lies.

The horse ambled on, carrying her along as time did, mere passage without change . . . without the right change . . . without healing. She could ride forever – the horse slowed, and she looked up to find they'd come to a fork in the trail; she legged it to the right – and it would not help. Nothing would help. Nothing *could* help. Nothing on Altiplano, at least.

At the second fork, she turned right again. It was stupid, going to the valley when she felt like this, and yet it had helped before. At other bad times in her life, she had gone there and found peace, at least for awhile. She rode on, seeing little, hearing little. It hurt so much. It hurt beyond hurting, to the point where pain became a white fog, as the physical pain had been then.

She argued with herself, part of her defending her family even now. It wasn't true they had done nothing: the man was dead. *But that was Seb Coron, doing it for her father, not her father doing it for her.* And what if Coron had lied about that? It wasn't true that her father hadn't cared: he'd done what he thought would help. *But it hadn't helped, and he hadn't changed his mind. He, whose rule had been 'If one thing doesn't work, try another.'*

She rode beside the creek now, but its spring-full rushing made only a white noise she found annoying. It was too loud. In the shade of the trees, she felt cold; in the sun she felt scorched. The horse sighed, and pulled a little toward the water. She halted it, clambered off feeling every stiff muscle, and led it down to drink. It laid its lips on the water and sucked; she could see the gulps rising up its gullet. She waited until it was finished, until it lifted its head and gave her a look and then tried to stray off toward some buttonweed twigs. She didn't want to climb back on, but she had to.

She walked instead, leading the horse, until her legs felt better. By the sun, it was late morning. She didn't really want to go on to the valley but where else could she go? Someone would ask, knowing where she always went . . . she pulled herself back into the saddle, and rode on.

The valley was smaller than she remembered, and she could feel nothing for it. The pines, the poplars, the creek, the meadow. She looked around it, trying to feel something . . . it was hers, it would always be hers . . . but all she felt was pain and emptiness. She slid off the horse and took the bit out of its mouth. She could walk around and let it graze for an hour before heading back. She remembered to loosen the girth, then took down a water bottle and drank. Her body wanted food, but her mind did not; she made it halfway through the lunch the cooks had packed for her before her mind won the battle, and she threw up what she'd eaten.

She felt faint, then, and sat on the cold ground with her head down on her knees; the horse snatched at the grass nearby, the ripping and chewing of grass punctuating her thoughts. What could she do? Emptiness behind her, emptiness before her.

In the middle of that emptiness, those few vivid moments when she had done something right, and saved someone else. Heris Serrano. Vida Serrano. What would they say now, if they knew all this? Would it explain what the admiral had wanted explained? Would it change anything? Or would it be worse, far worse, to let them know what had happened to her? She already had black marks against her; she had known from childhood that nothing in a military career is ever completely forgotten or forgiven. If she became not only the colorless, ordinary young officer from a backwoods planet, who just happened to do the right thing once and save a Serrano neck . . . if she admitted that she was damaged, fractured, prone to nightmares . . . that had to put her in more jeopardy. That had to risk being thrown out, sent home . . . except she had no home. Not this valley, not anywhere.

When her head cleared a little, she made herself drink again, and eat the other half of lunch. This time it stayed down. It tasted like dust and wood, but it stayed down.

She was home well before dark, handing over the dry, cool horse to the groom with thanks. Her stepmother hovered in the hall; Esmay nodded politely.

'I rode too far,' she said. 'I need a long bath, and bed.'

'Could I send up a tray?' her stepmother asked. It was not her stepmother's fault. It had never been her stepmother's fault; she wasn't sure her stepmother even knew. If her father had kept it such a secret, perhaps she didn't know even now.

'Thank you,' Esmay said. 'Soup and bread would be fine – I'm just too tired.'

She was able to get herself in and out of the bath, and she ate the food on the tray when it came. She put the tray back out in the hall, and lay on the bed. She could just see the corner of her great-grandmother's note on its shelf. She didn't want to see it; she didn't want to see anything.

The next morning was marginally better. Luci, who clearly knew nothing, wanted her to come watch a schooling session with the brown mare. Esmay could think of no polite way out of it, and partway through the session came out of herself far enough to notice that the problem with the canter depart was Luci's failure to keep her outside hip in place. Luci accepted this with good grace, and offered a tube of liniment for Esmay's obvious stiffness. They went in to lunch together.

In the afternoon, her conscience would not let her avoid her great-grandmother any longer.

'You are very angry with me,' her great-grandmother said, not looking up from her embroidery. She had to use a thick lens and a special light, but she worked on it every day, Luci had said.

'I am angry,' Esmay said. 'Mostly with him, I think.' Meaning her father, which surely her great-grandmother knew.

'I am still angry with him,' her great-grandmother said. 'But I'm too old to put much energy into the anger. It's very tiring, anger, so I ration it. A sharp word a day, perhaps.'

Esmay suspected humor at her expense, but the old woman's face had a soft vulnerability that she'd never noticed before.

'I will say I was wrong, Esmaya. It was how I was brought up, but it was still wrong of me. Wrong not to tell you, and wrong to leave you as I did.'

'I forgive you,' Esmay said quickly. The old woman looked at her.

'Don't do that. Don't lie to me, of all people. Lies added to lies never make truth. You don't forgive me – you can't forgive me that fast.'

'I don't . . . hate you.'

'Don't hate your father, either. Be angry with him, yes: he has hurt you and lied to you, and anger is appropriate. You need not forgive him too soon, any more than you forgive me. But don't hate, because it is not natural to you, and it will destroy you.'

'I'm going away, as soon as I can,' Esmay said. 'And I'm not coming back.'

'I know.' Again, a sense of vulnerability, but not intended to

101

sway her decision. Her chin firmed. 'Luci told me about the herd. You are right, and I will argue for Luci when the time comes.'

'Thank you,' Esmay said. It was all she could say; she kissed the old woman and went away.

The days crept by, then the weeks. She counted them off; she would not cause a scandal by moving to the city for the rest of her leave, but she could not help watching the calendar. her resolve had hardened: she would go, and never return. She would find someone – not Luci, who had no feel for it, but someone else – to become the valley's guardian. Nothing here meant anything to her now but pain and sorrow; the very food tasted bad in her mouth. She and her father had spoken each day of other things; she had been amazed at both of them, the way they could evade any mention of or reference to that disastrous afternoon. Her stepmother took her shopping in the city; she allowed herself to be draped in suitable clothes; she packed them into her duffel to take along.

Then it was the last week . . . the last five days . . . the last four. She woke one morning stabbed by the sorrow that she had been *in* her valley, but she had not *seen* it. She had to go one more time; she had to try to salvage something, some real memory that was also a good memory, from her childhood. She had been riding almost every day, just to keep Luci company, so if there was a horse free, she could go now, today.

For the dama, there was always a horse free. A trail horse? Of course, dama, and the saddle, and the bridle. And might the groom suggest that this horse accepted hobbles well? Very good. She went back into the kitchen, and collected a lunch. She felt, if not happy, at least positive . . . the pull of Fleet, she thought, the knowledge that in just a few days she would be back in her new home, forever.

The valley opened before her, magical again, as it had been in her childhood . . . as she would remember it in the moment of her death. It hardly deserved the name of 'valley,' although when Esmay had first seen it, she'd been so young it seemed large. Now she could see that what she remembered was merely a saucer in the side of the mountain, a grassy glade in which a small pool trickled away in a murmuring stream that would become a rushing noisy stream only further down. On one side were the dark pines, secretive, rising from rocky ledges, and facing them were the white-boled poplars with their dancing leaves. In this brief mountain spring, the new grass was spangled with pink and yellow and white, the wind-flowers and snowflowers . . . a few weeks later, the tall scarlet and blue lupines would bloom, but now all the flowers lay close to the ground.

Esmay leaned back in the saddle and took in a deep breath. She wanted to breathe in and in, filling herself with the resinous scent of pine, the crisp scent of mint and grass, the sweetness of the flowers, the tang of poplar and even the sour rank smell of the lush weeds near the water. She could feel tears rising, and she clamped down on her emotions. Instead of crying, she dismounted, and led her horse forward to drink from the pool. Then she removed the saddlebags, and slung them over her shoulder. She led the horse to the fallen pine – still there after all these years – and unsaddled it; she put the saddle over the leaning trunk, then hobbled the horse before removing the bridle.

The horse worked its way back out into the sunshine, in the meadow grass, where it set to grazing. Esmay settled herself on the convenient rock she had placed years before, and leaned back against the saddle. She unbuckled the left saddlebag and took out the meat-filled pasties Veronica had packed. She would have five hours of peace here, before she had to start back.

She could hardly believe it was hers now. She belonged to it, to this chill rock with its multicolored lichens, to the trees and the grass, to the mountain itself . . . but by law and custom, as their saying went, it was now hers. By custom and law she could bar anyone from trespassing here . . . she could fence it, shield it, build a house here that no one ever entered but herself.

It had been her dearest dream, once. A little cabin, one or two rooms, all to herself, with no memories in it, here in this golden place. She had been a child then; in her daydream, food had appeared on the table without any effort of hers. Breakfast had been . . . had been cereal with cream and honey. Someone else, some invisible magical person, had washed the sticky bowl. She had always been out for lunch, usually perched on a rock high above, watching the sky. Dinner, in those dreams, had been fish from the stream, sweet-fleshed mountain trout, lightly fried.

Not this stream; it was too small, but downstream a few kilometers. She had fished there, the time she camped here for a week: reality, not dreams, by then, the summer she was eleven. The fish were as tasty as she'd imagined, but the hike back and forth had convinced her that she would have to find another food source.

Papa Stefan had been furious; so had her father, when he came back from the situation in Kharfra (there was always a Situation in Kharfra). Her stepmother had panicked, convinced that Esmay had killed herself . . . remembering that unsavory row, Esmay felt herself knotting up, the cold of the stone striking deep. She pushed herself off the rock and walked out into the sun, stretching out her arms to it.

Even at eleven she had known she would never kill herself, no matter what. Had Arris ever told her father? Probably not. She would have been afraid to introduce any more tension, any more difficulty, between father and daughter. Poor Arris, Esmay thought, closing her eyes against the sun as she lifted her face to it. She had been six years too late with her sympathy, six years too late with her shock and horror. Now she could understand how futile Arris must have felt, with a stepdaughter so awkward, so independent.

Esmay walked down the slope to the open grass. She crouched, putting a hand to the ground. It was cool – only on the hottest midsummer day would the ground feel warm up here – but not as cold as the rock. She let herself down onto the grass, and leaned back with her hands clasped behind her head. Above, the morning sky burned blue, the exact blue that felt right, that made her happiest. She had never found that blue on another planet. Under her shoulders and back, the land upheld her with just enough pressure.

'You're not making it easy,' she said to the glade. Here and now, she could not imagine leaving Altiplano forever, giving this up forever. The horse, a few rods away, waggled an ear at her but went on munching.

She stretched out on her side, and looked at the flowers, reminding herself of their names. Some were original terraforming rootstock, and others had been developed here, for this particular world, from Terran gene lines. Pink, yellow, white, a few of the tiny blue-violet starry ones she had privately named wish-stars. She had had private names for all of them really, taken from the plant names in the old stories, whether or not they were really related. Campion and rosemary and primrose sounded pretty, so she used them; harebell sounded silly to her, so she didn't. She touched them now with a fingertip, renaming them: pink rosemary, yellow campion, crisp white primroses. It was her valley, these were her flowers, and she could give them her names. Forever.

She looked over at the horse. It was grazing steadily, not so much as an earflick to indicate any danger. She leaned her head back on her arm again. She could feel the warmth of the sun where it touched her, and the coolness of the shadows. She felt herself relaxing, as she had not relaxed since she arrived – or for how long before? – and let her eyelids sag shut. She rolled her face into the fragrant grass to get the annoying sun off her eyelids . . .

And woke with a jerk and a cry as a shadow stooped over her. Even as she lunged up, she recognized the horse. It snorted and plunged away, fighting the hobbles, frightened because she was.

It had only wanted a treat, she told herself. Her heart was racing; she felt sick to her stomach. The horse had settled uneasily a short distance away, watching her with pricked ears.

'You scared me,' Esmay said to the horse. It blew a long rattling sigh at her, meaning Me, too. 'It was your shadow,' Esmay said. 'Sorry.' She looked around. She had slept at least an hour, more likely two, and she could feel the heat of sunburn on her ear. She had worn a hat . . . but not when she lay down. Idiot.

When her heart slowed, she felt better, rested. Lunch, her stomach reminded her. She walked back to the rock, shaking the kinks out of legs and arms, and then took her hat and the lunch sack back into the sun. Now she was ready for that meat pasty, and the horse would enjoy the apple.

After lunch, she walked down by the stream, and let her mind loose again. She had come home, and found the truth, and it had

105

not killed her. She didn't like it – it hurt, and she knew it would continue to hurt – but she had survived the first terrifying hours as she had survived the initial assault in childhood. She felt shaky, but not in danger of dissolution.

Was she ready to give this up, this lovely valley that had helped her cling to sanity so often? The stream chuckled and splashed at her feet; she knelt and put her hand into its icy flow. She loved this sound, the smell of the pungent herbs on its bank, the feel of icy water on her hands and face when she knelt to drink. She loved the heavy *tonk* of stone on stone when she stood on the uneven one that rocked back and forth.

She did not have to decide now. She had years . . . if she stayed in Fleet, if she qualified for rejuvenation, she had many, many years. Long after her father died, long after everyone who had betrayed her died, she could come home to this valley, still young enough to enjoy it. She could build her cabin and live here in peace. It would not have to hurt to return; she could avoid that pain just by persisting.

Against this vision rose the vivid, eager face of her cousin Luci, Luci willing to risk struggle, conflict, pain . . . the opposite of prudence. But Luci had not suffered what she had suffered. Tears burned in her eyes again. If she gained her peaceful valley at the end by simply outlasting those who had betrayed her . . . Luci would be old, perhaps dead . . . because how many normal lifetimes would she live, before she had earned retirement and the peace of her valley?

She would like to have Luci for a friend as well as a business partner, Luci who now looked up to her, as she could not recall anyone in the family looking up to her before.

'It's not fair,' she said to the trees and the slopes and the gurgling water. An icy breeze slid down the creek bed and chilled her. Stupid complaint; life was not about fairness. 'He *lied* to me!' she screamed suddenly. The horse threw up its head, ears pointed at her; somewhere upstream jays squalled and battered their way through thickset twigs.

Then it was quiet again. The horse still watched her with the suspicion of the edible for the eater, but the jays had flown away, their scolding voices diminishing. The water gurgled as before;

106

the breeze failed and came again like the breath of some vast being larger than mountains. Esmay felt her rage draining away with it, not really gone but its immediate pressure eased.

She spent another hour wandering around the glade, drifting in and out of moods like the clouds drifting in and out of sight above the slopes. Sweet memories of her childhood trips – of learning to climb on the boulders at the foot of the cliff, of the time she found a rare fire-tailed salamander under the ledge of the creek's largest pool – swept over and under the other memories, the bad ones. She thought about climbing the cliff again, but she had not brought any climbing gear, and her legs were already stiff and sore from riding.

Finally, as the afternoon shadows began to climb the boulders, she caught and saddled the horse again. She found herself wondering if her father had told Papa Stefan ... or only Great-grandmother. She wanted to be furious with Great-grandmother for not overruling her father, but she had used up her store of anger on her father. And besides – when she'd come back from the hospital, her great-grandmother had not been in the house at all. Was that *why* she had moved away – or been sent away?

'I am still an idiot child,' she said to the horse, as she unlooped the hobbles and prepared to mount. The horse eyed her and flicked an ear. 'Yes, and I scared you out of your wits, didn't I? You're not used to that kind of behavior from Suizas.'

She rode down the shadowy trail beside the stream deep in thought. How many of the family knew the truth, or had known it? Whom, besides Luci, could she trust?

The upper pastures, when she came to them, were still in sunlight, out of the shadow of the mountains. Far away to the south, she saw a drift of cattle moving slowly. In the distance, the buildings of the estancia were nested in green trees like little toys, bright-painted. For some reason she felt a rush of joy; it passed through her to the horse, which broke into a trot. She didn't feel her stiffness; without realizing she was going to, she legged the horse into a canter, and then let it extend into a gallop. Wind burned in her face; her hair streamed back; she could feel each separate tug on her scalp and the power of the galloping animal beneath her lifted her beyond fear or anger.

*   *   *

107

She walked the last mile in, as she had been trained to do, and grinned at Luci who was just coming in from polo practice when they met in the lane.

'A good ride?' asked Luci. 'Was that you we saw galloping in the upper fields?'

'Yes,' Esmay said. 'I think I've remembered how to ride.'

Luci looked worried, and Esmay laughed.

'The deal is good, Luci – I'm going back to Fleet. But I'd forgotten how much fun it can be.'

'You . . . haven't seemed very happy.'

'No. I haven't been, but I will be. My place is out there, as yours is here.'

They rode in together; Esmay did not have to say more, because Luci was ready to talk for hours about the brown mare's talents and her own ambitions.

7

The team from Special Materials Analysis came off the commercial line at Comus along with all the other passengers, some hundred and thirty. Here, in the interior of the Familias, the customs checks were perfunctory. A glance at the ID, a glance at the luggage . . . their matching briefcases, matching duffels, all with the company logo.

'Consultants, eh?' said the customs inspector, clearly proud of his guess.

'That's right.' Gori smiled at the man, that friendly open smile which was just a bit too memorable sometimes. Arhos wondered if he should have let Gori come – but Gori was the best with such devices, faster by thirty seconds than anyone else. He would edge their profit up on the Fleet contract, too – thirty seconds a hundred times a day was fifty minutes off the top.

'What a life,' the customs man said. 'Wish I could be a consultant—' He passed them through.

'They always think it's glamorous,' Losa grumbled, audibly enough. 'If they had to be on the road all the time, hear the complaints at home—'

'You didn't have to marry that loser,' Pratt said. This was an old script, one they could improvise around for an hour.

'He's not a loser, he's just . . . sensitive.'

'Artists,' Gori said. 'I don't know why intelligent women always fall for losers who claim they're creative—'

Losa huffed, something she did well. 'He's not a loser! He's sold three works—'

'In how long?' asked Gori.

'Stop it,' Arhos said, as any manager would. 'It's not important – Gori, let her alone. She's right; people think our job is glamorous, and if they knew what it's really like, on the road all the time, working long hours for people who are already angry they had to hire us, they'd know better. But no more personal problems on this trip, all right? We're going to be stuck out here long enough without making it seem longer.'

'All right,' Gori said, with a sidelong look at Losa.

'I need to stop in here,' Losa said, ducking into a ladies' without looking at Gori at all. Arhos glared at Gori, who shrugged. Pratt shook his head. The two junior women, technicians newly hired from a large firm which hadn't offered them enough challenge, glanced at each other, and made a tentative move toward the ladies'.

'Go on,' Arhos said. 'We've got enough time.'

'She's the sensitive one,' Pratt said, continuing the argument even without Losa.

'Stop it. It doesn't help, and we can't run her life.' The rest of the team caught up with them, and formed a clot in the passage until Losa and the other women reappeared. Then, not speaking, they moved on to the gate that divided Fleet space from civilian space. Here, instead of a bored civilian customs inspector, they faced a cluster of alert, edgy, military guards.

'Arhos Asperson, Special Materials Analysis Consulting,' Arhos said, handing over his ID case. 'And this is the contract—' A data cube, embossed with Fleet's own insignia on one side, and an elaborate marbled etching on the others. It had taken them two years to develop a duplicate of Fleet's equipment, so that they could fabricate their own cubes rather than having to steal and reprogram them. Then they'd gotten this perfectly legitimate contract, and hadn't needed to use their fake.

'Yes, sir,' the first guard said. 'And how many in your group?'

'Seven,' Arhos said. He stood aside, while the second guard collected everyone's ID cases. He would have worried, on Sierra Station, even with a real Fleet cube. . . . though they had used the faked Fleet cubes before, and faked ID before, Fleet was unusually alert, thanks to the repercussions from Xavier. Here, he expected no trouble – and in fact the cube reader had already accepted, then spat out, the fake cube.

'All clear, sir,' the guard said. 'We'll have to check all the luggage, of course.'

'Of course.' He handed over his own duffel and briefcase. Standard civilian electronics: datapads, cube reader, cubes, portable computers in all sizes from pocket to briefing, communications access sets, data probe wands . . .

'You can't use this shipboard, sir,' the guard said, holding up the comm access set and the data wand.

'No, I understand. Last time out, your people provided a shielded locker.'

'We can do that, sir,' the guard said, with obvious relief. Inexperienced consultants sometimes insisted that they would not give up any of their equipment . . . they got no more contracts. The other guard, Arhos noticed, was calling someone in Fleet territory, and soon a lowly pivot appeared with a luggage truck and a lockable container for the restricted electronics.

'You don't have to lock it up now,' the guard said. 'If you want to place calls from the Fleet areas, that's permissible from any blue-coded booth. But before boarding—'

'We understand,' Arhos said. He knew there would be another search before they boarded.

The Fleet area of Comus Station had its own eating places, its own bars, its own entertainment and shopping outlets and even public-rental sleeping. They had plenty of time before their ship left.

'What exactly is your area of expertise, Dr. Asperson?'

Arhos allowed his mouth to quirk up at one corner, restrained amusement at the naivete of the question. 'My degrees are in logical systems and substrate analysis.'

The young officer blinked. '. . . Substrate?'

'Classified, I'm afraid,' Arhos said, with a little dip of the head to take the edge off.

'Lieutenant, I believe you have duties forward,' said the lieutenant commander at the head of the table.

'Oh . . . of course, sir.' He scurried out.

'I'm sorry,' the lieutenant commander said. He wore no name tag; none of the officers aboard such a small ship wore them. 'Please forgive us – we're not usually carrying civilians—'

'Of course,' Arhos said. 'But you understand our situation—?'

'Certainly. Only – I didn't recognize your firm's name.'

'Subcontractors,' Gori said, grinning. 'You know how it is – we used to work for the big firms, one and another of us, and then we struck out on our own. Got our first jobs as sub-subs, and now we're all the way up to sub-contractors.'

'It must be hard, going out on your own after working for a big company,' the officer said. Arhos thought he was buying the whole story.

'It has been,' Arhos said. 'But we're past wondering how we're going to pay the rent.'

'I imagine you are,' the officer said, with a knowing smile for the quality of the clothes they wore, the expensive cases they carried.

'Not that it's easy profit,' Arhos said, putting in the earnest emphasis that impressed the military so well. 'We're working harder than we used to – but it's for ourselves. And you, of course.'

'Of course.'

At Sierra Station, they had no customs to pass, nothing but a long walk down one arm of the station and out another. An escort, ostensibly to ensure that they didn't get lost; civilians did not

111

wander the Fleet sections of stations – especially stations this near the borders – without an escort. In the comfortable ease of someone who had not intended mischief anyway, the team ambled along, chatting aimlessly about the food they'd had, and the food they hoped to have.

Koskiusko's docking bay was actually a shuttle bay. Here, Arhos handed the contract cube to the ranking guard, who fed it into a cube reader.

'I'll call over, sir, but it'll be at least two hours before a shuttle comes in. The little pod's halfway over with an arriving officer, and the shuttle's already loaded with cargo – no room for you, and it's down at Orange 17 anyway.'

'No problem. Is there someplace to get a drink, meanwhile?'

'Not really – there's a food machine just down the corridor there, between the toilets, but nothing really good.'

'Nothing edible,' grumbled another guard. 'Station food service's supposed to replace those snacks before they turn green but—'

'We could call in for something,' the first guard said. 'They deliver from civ-side, but there's a fee—'

'That would be great,' Arhos said. 'The ship we came in on was skewed five hours off Station time by the last jump, and I for one would enjoy something. And if it's near a break for you—'

'No, thank you, sir. Here's the order list . . .'

'Ever been aboard a DSR before?' asked the bright-eyed young man who escorted them from the docking bay.

'No . . . main station yards, a couple of cruisers, but no DSR.'

'Let me get you a shipchip,' the youngster said. He touched a control panel, entering a sequence so fast that Arhos couldn't figure out the placement of sensors on the unmarked surface. Something bleeped, and tiny disks rattled into a bin below the panel.

Arhos looked at his and wondered how to activate it.

'Voice,' the young man said promptly. 'It'll project a route from your position to the location you name – for the low-security areas, that is. If you need access to the high-security areas, you'll have to get it reset. That'll be in ship admin, which it'll guide you to. I mean, I will, that's where you're going first, but any other time—'

'Thank you,' Arhos said. Behind him, the rest of the team murmured appropriate thanks as well.

They were passed from desk to desk in the admin bay, collecting ship's ID tags, access cards for a variety of spaces, and a new set of shipchips. Then someone came to fetch them to the admin offices of the 14th Heavy Maintenance Yard.

'We don't have slideways, but we do have lift tubes,' they were told. 'Don't try to hitch a ride on the robo-carts – they're programmed to stop if they sense extra mass.'

They spent the first several days looking over the inventory, and discussing their plan with the senior technician, a balding master chief named Furlow.

'I think Headquarters has its nose up its tail again,' Furlow said at the first meeting. 'Rekeying *all* the weapons guidance codes? That assumes the people doing the job are competent and loyal.' He gave Arhos a sideways look. 'Not that I'm saying you aren't, but it's too big a job to go without hitches.'

'You're probably right,' Arhos said. 'But I'm not going to pass up a contract . . . it's how we make a living.'

'Yes, well . . .' A heavy sigh. 'I know you've got clearances from transcendent deities or something, but on my watch, these weapons are my responsibility and I'll have one of my people with you.'

'Of course,' Arhos said. 'We don't want any misunderstandings either. This is the protocol we were sent – I'm assuming you have the other part—'

'Yes, sir, I do.' The chief took Arhos's version and peered at it. 'Scuzzing waste of time, but it'll work. How long did *you* tell 'em it'd take?'

'Five minutes per weapon, an hour to retool between types. That's what it took on the racks they mocked up for us to bid on.' Arhos allowed himself to smile. 'We were one minute faster than the next fastest on each, and a solid ten minutes faster in retooling. Then when they had us work on a patrol craft, we were able to work that fast even in tight situations. We weren't told what your inventory was, of course. We're just supposed to do it until it's done. Then when the other ships return from deployment, we'll do theirs as well.'

'I imagine,' the chief said, 'that there weren't many people that wanted to spend a standard year or more out here in Sector 14.'

'Not that many,' Arhos admitted. 'Fleet had a lot of contracts to hand out for this work, and most of 'em were either bigger, smaller, or in more popular places. We happened to fit the profile for this one – and we performed well in the test series.'

'Umph.' The chief didn't look any happier, but at least seemed slightly less hostile. 'Well, you have your work cut out. We store the weaponry for all of Sector 14. There's no rear supply depot out here, because of security concerns – Sierra Station gets a fair bit of civilian traffic, and we know some of it's Bloodhorde agents.'

'We'd better get started, then, hadn't we?'

The chief still didn't move. 'It's not going to be that easy. This thing is big, but not big enough to hold inventory like that in convenient arrays. Weapons and guidance systems are stored separately, and since the guidance systems are compact, we've squirreled them away wherever they'd fit. It's not anything like the way you worked on that patrol ship. At least we have an automated system. Let me show you some video.' He ran his hand over the control panel on his desk, and a display came up on the wall. 'That's one of the inventory bays in which guidance systems are stored.' Racks rose from the deck to the overhead, the familiar pattern of automated inventory systems controls along the vertical rails. 'Because the guidance systems are small, and most of the time we're not restocking the warships, we fit them in by size, not by type.'

'So we're going to have to go through there and pull them out one at a time?'

'Not quite that bad. One rack at a time, though. This bay, right now, has . . .' The chief flicked another control that brought up a display on his desk. 'Eight thousand two hundred sixty-four ASAC-32 modules. But they're on at least eight different stacks, and I'd bet that someone has moved at least a few of them when restocking other goods, and hasn't bothered to update the file.'

'Won't your automated system do that?'

'So-so.' The chief wobbled his hand in the age-old gesture. 'High-security items have a tracer that sounds off if they're removed from that hold, but not if they're moved a few meters.

We'd have spent all our time rekeying the tracers – we're always having to move things in and out.'

'So you know they're in there, and you probably know where most of them are, but . . .'

'But not all. Which is why it's a stupid idea, thought up by someone who's never seen a big repair inventory.' The chief grinned. 'I hope they're paying you a daily allowance, and not by piece, or you'll be here forever and earn nothing.'

Arhos wasn't sure that prospect would bother the chief, but it certainly bothered him. He had worried that the job wouldn't take long enough – that he'd have to stretch it out – that they wouldn't need to wander over enough of the ship to find the self-destruct. Instead . . . they would be here far too long, and although they'd have wide access they might be too busy to use it.

'I wonder if someone leaked this problem to Burrahn, Hing & Co., and that's why they didn't bid on this job,' he said, and watched the chief's face. No flicker, but . . . but someone had to have leaked it. Damn the Bloodhorde! 'At least we are getting a per diem . . . but it's going to be a bitch.'

Arhos eyed his partners and gave a meaningful glance at the gray cylinder on the table between them. Fleet would expect them to disable the simpler scans of their compartment; Arhos had not concealed the device. Now he turned it on. Telltales blinked hotly: it had detected signals it could not fog. He'd expected that. Right now, it was important for Fleet to think its more delicate scans worked here. What lay concealed within the familiar cylinder, under the Morin Co. seal, was for later use, and more private conversations. His partners would know that, and would interpret what he said in the light of the caution now necessary.

'We have a problem,' Arhos began, when the team had assembled. Quickly he repeated the chief's explanation of the way weapons guidance systems were stored on *Koskiusko*. 'It's going to take a lot longer than we thought. It might be better to start with the weapons on the warships, since they're in the arrays we know—'

'But our contract states that we should begin with the DSR,' Losa said, playing up beautifully.

'Yes, but they didn't tell us the whole story. With this arrangement, there'll be a lot of dead time – we'll be waiting around while they figure out where some of the weapons are. I'm considering whether to discuss a restructuring of the whole job.' It would be difficult, with a signed contract; he would have to prove that Fleet had not provided necessary information. He wasn't sure he could trust that Chief Furlow to give evidence, if it came to that.

'A suggestion . . .' Gori said.

'Go ahead.'

'Why not split the team, and send some of 'em over to the larger warships? That way, the manhours lost in dead time won't be as great.'

'Possibly . . . in fact, that's a good idea. We won't have to worry about them . . .' Noticing anything, he didn't say, but Gori's upward twitch of eyebrow meant he'd understood exactly what Arhos didn't say.

'We don't look like whiners, we get the job done faster . . . and we're here to show that our top people cope with the unexpected.' Losa sounded enthusiastic; her eyes sparkled. Arhos thought it over, liking the idea better every moment. The one thing they'd worried about was having one of their own people notice something. Yet the Fleet contract had required a larger team. This way – this way he got rid of those bright, inquisitive minds, in a way that could cast no suspicion on the partners.

'Good, then. I'll speak to the admiral's office. If we're sending people off, we need to do that before we leave Sierra.'

From Altiplano to Comus Station, Esmay traveled by civilian carrier, a regularly scheduled passenger ship. In the thirty days of her leave, other news had come to dominate the screens. No one seemed to recognize her in her civilian clothes, for which she was grateful. She divided her time between her own quarters and the ship's palatial fitness equipment. It felt odd to be aboard a ship and have no duties, but she was not about to call attention to herself by hanging around the crew looking wistful. Better to sweat on the exercise machines, and then cool off in the pool. She was vaguely aware that some of the other passengers who regularly used the fitness equipment might have wanted to chat, but

116

swimming steady laps made that difficult. In her quarters, she worked her way through one teaching cube after another, everything in the ship's library that seemed relevant.

At Comus, she chose to walk the distance from the liner's docking bay to Fleetgate rather than taking a slideway. She needed to do a bit of shopping; she wanted to replace every bit of clothing she'd brought from Altiplano. It was wasteful, she admitted, to throw away perfectly good garments . . . but she wanted nothing to connect her to her past. When she found a Space Relief outlet store, she emptied her cases, and then handed over the cases, all but her Fleet duffel.

She needed little, really. A few comfortable things for lounging, one good dress outfit. She found all that in the first store she entered, picking the things hastily. It didn't really matter what she wore when she was off-duty. She was eager to get back to Fleet territory. When she arrived at the Fleetgate, the sentry's cheerful 'Welcome home, Lieutenant!' sent her mood up three notches.

Esmay found her new assignment posted to her private mail when she checked in. She had expected a tour on Comus itself – else why send her out here in the first place? – but her orders directed her to Sierra Station, there to take up her duties with the Fourteenth Heavy Maintenance Yard aboard the *Koskiusko*. She'd never heard of that ship; when she looked it up in the Table of Ships, she discovered that it was a DSR, a deepspace repair ship, part of the second-wave deployment out of Sierra Station.

Someone must be seriously annoyed with her. Repair ships were huge, ungainly, complicated, and totally unglamorous. Worse, DSR ships were a logistics nightmare, the natural and lawful prey of every inspector general: it was impossible to keep them in perfect order, up to nominal inventory, because they were always losing parts to some other vessel. Legitimately, but inevitably, the paperwork lagged reality.

For this, among other reasons, very few people – except the specialists who actually did the repairs on other vessels – wanted assignment to a DSR. Young officers considered such an assignment proof that someone was down on them; Esmay followed the herd in this, if nothing else, and took it as evidence that exoneration by the official court hadn't convinced someone of

117

her innocence. She looked up the next available transfer to Sierra Station. Because she had arrived on Comus almost 24 hours before her leave was up, she could just catch a Fleet supply run to Sierra . . . and she had no good excuse not to catch it, since her duty status went active the moment she logged on to pick up her orders.

Esmay checked – the supply ship had space available, and she had two hours to report aboard. A bored clerk stamped and validated her original and amended orders, updated her hardcopy ID and her files. She dashed in and out of the tiny PX to pick up her new insignia – the clerk told her that her promotion to lieutenant had come through while she was on leave – and get a *Koskiusko* shiptag for her duffel. That wasn't required, since she hadn't signed aboard, but her duffel was more likely to arrive there if it had a shiptag than a name-and-number. When she got to the docking bay for the supply ship, she found herself in a queue with half a dozen other Fleet personnel making a transfer. No one stared at her; no one seemed to know who she was or care. Most of the talk was about a parpaun match played recently between the crews of two ships in dock – apparently someone had kicked all three of the possible goals in one play – but Esmay had never really understood parpaun. Why two balls? Why three differently colored goals? Why – she often thought to herself, but would not say – bother? Now she was glad to hear the others full of enthusiasm for something that banal, and she hoped that her moment of fame had already vanished.

The supply ship was hauling parts that would resupply *Koskiusko*; its exec had noticed her orders, and put her to work checking the inventory. Sixteen days of counting impellers, gaskets, lengths of tubing, fasteners of all kinds, tubes of adhesive, updates to repair manuals (both hardcopy and cubes) . . . Esmay decided that someone at Headquarters *really* hated her.

She was good at this kind of thing; she didn't find it difficult to keep her concentration. On the fourth day, she noticed that of the 562 boxes supposed to contain 85mm star-slot fasteners with threads of pitch 1/10 and interval 3mm, one was labeled for 85mm star-slot fasteners with threads of pitch 1/12 and interval 4mm instead. Two days later she found three leaky tubes of adhesive, which had glued themselves to neighbouring tubes in a container; it was clear from the discoloration of the labels that they had been flawed from the beginning; she noted that. She could see why this was necessary – someone would find the errors and better now than in the midst of an emergency repair – but it wasn't the glamorous sort of job she'd thought of when she had dreamed of leaving Altiplano. Either time she'd left Altiplano.

She wondered if she'd spend her entire time aboard *Koskiusko* doing the same thing. That would make a very long two years. She didn't want notoriety, exactly, but she would like something more interesting than bean-counting.

In her off-shift, she listened to the sports fans, hoping for a change in topic, but they seemed to have no other interests. Apparently, they had all played on a parpaun team at one time or another, and after they'd rehashed the recent match they were happy to tell each other in detail about every match they'd played. Esmay listened long enough to understand at last what the rules were, and why two balls (each team had its own ball, and scores could be made with the opponent's ball only on the third, 'neutral' goal. It still seemed an unreasonably complex game, and as boring as any other for nonplayers to listen to.

She finally gave up and started reading the supply ship's tech support cubes. Inventory control, principles and practice. The design of automated inventory systems. Even an article on 'static munitions recognition systems' – which she couldn't imagine needing – was better than the eighty-eighth rehash of a game she hadn't seen and didn't care about anyway. She was sure she'd never come face to face with a Barasci V-845 mine or its nastier cousin, the Smettig Series G, but she stared at the display until she was sure she would know them again if she were unlucky enough to see one.

Sierra Station served both Fleet and civilian interests, but Fleet predominated. Two long arms docked only military vessels; Esmay watched the names scroll past on the wardroom screen. *Pachyderm*, the oldest active cruiser, and Fleet's largest. *Plenitude, Savage*, and *Vengeance*, cruisers much like Heris Serrano's *Vigilance*. *Plentitude* had a star by its name – it was the flagship of

119

some combat group. A gaggle of patrol craft: *Consummate*, *Pterophil*, *Singularity*, *Autarch*, *Rascal*, *Runagate*, *Vixen*, *Despite* . . . *Despite*? What was *Despite* doing here?

Esmay felt cold all over. She had left that very lucky (in one way) and unlucky (in another) ship almost the full length of Families space away . . . she had not expected to see *Despite* again unless she was transferred to its sector. Why had they moved it at all? And why, of all places, *here*?

She didn't want to know. She didn't want to see that ship again; the memory of victory could not erase the memory of what had gone before, that bloody mutiny, and the mistakes she had made later.

She shook that off. She couldn't afford to be upset by it, and it was unlikely she'd have anything to do with *Despite* and her new captain.

Koskiusko, the screen read, blinking now because she had put a tracer on the name. She noted the concourse and docking number in her personal compad. One corner of the screen turned yellow, then flashed their arrival dock number in blue. Esmay referred to the station map . . . *Koskiusko* was out at the far end of the longest arm, but she could get there without going past *Despite*.

When she made it to the gate area, a pair of Fleet security personnel checked her orders again. To her surprise, they made no move to open the access hatch. 'It'll be a few minutes, Lieutenant,' one of them said. He had sergeant's stripes on his uniform, and his unit patch read Sierra Station, not *Koskiusko*. Esmay noticed that nowhere on the deck of the gate area were the traditional stripes defining ship space from station space. 'They've sent a pod but it's not here yet.'

'A pod?'

'DSRs don't actually dock at stations.' The tone was carefully respectful, though Esmay had the feeling she had just asked a stupid question. 'They're too big – the relative masses would play hob with each other's artificial gravity.' A pause, then a neutral, 'Would you like to see *Koskiusko*, Lieutenant?'

'Yes,' Esmay said. She'd already shown she was ignorant; she might as well learn what she could.

'Here, then.' Up on the gate display came a blurry view of

120

something large; the view sharpened, leaped nearer, and finally stabilized as the biggest and most unlikely excuse for a ship Esmay had ever seen. It looked like the unfortunate mating of an office building with a bulk-cargo tank and some sort of clamshell array. 'Those funny-looking things are on the main repair bays,' the sergeant said helpfully. 'They've got 'em open now, testing. As you can see, an escort can fit all the way in, and even most patrols . . . then the ports swing down . . .'

That opening was the size of an escort? Esmay revised her assumptions about size upward steeply. Not just an office building, but – she realized that the array of lights beyond a rounded bulge was another 'office building.' It looked nothing like the DSR stats she'd seen at the Academy six years before. The two DSRs they'd been shown designs of had been built like clusters of grapes, with a single cylindrical repair bay running through the cluster. When she said that, the sergeant grinned.

'*Koskiusko* wasn't commissioned then,' the sergeant said. 'She's new – and she's not the same as she was, either. Here – I'll show you a design plot.'

This came up in the three standard views, plus an angled one similar to that Esmay had seen. In design, the DSR still looked like several disparate (but large) components had been squashed together. Five blunt arms ran out from a central core: that was the 'office building' part. Two adjacent arms had the clamshell arrangements on them. Behind those trailed great oblong shapes labeled 'drive test cradle.' The arm adjacent to neither 'main repair bay' had the tanklike object – larger, Esmay realized, than any tank she'd seen – stuck on its end like a bulbous nose. Without the tank, it would have looked like an orbital station specialized for some industrial process.

'What is that tank?' she asked, fascinated by this impossible oddity.

'Dunno, sir. That was added about three years ago, maybe two years after she was commissioned. Ah – here's your pod.' The display blinked out, then reappeared as a status line; Esmay heard the clunk as the pod docked, then the whistling of an airlock cycling. Finally the status light turned green, and the sergeant opened the hatch. 'Good luck, sir. Hope you enjoy your tour.'

Esmay found the pod unsettling. It had no artificial gravity; she had to strap into the passenger racks and hang there facing a ring of ports. The pilot wore an EVA suit; his helmet hung on a drop-ring just above him, suggesting that the EVA suit was more sense than worry. Through the pod's wide ports she could see entirely too much of Sierra Station and its docked vessels, barnacles on a floating wheel. Station navigation beacons and standing lights played over them, glittering from the faceted hulls of pressurized bulk cargo tanks, gleaming from brightly colored commercial liners, and scarcely revealing the matte-dark hulls of Fleet vessels, except for pricks of light reflected from shield and weapons fittings. Beyond, a starfield with no planets distinguishable. Sierra System had them, but not out here, where the station served primarily outsystem transport. Sudden acceleration bumped Esmay against the rack, and then ceased; her stomach lagged behind, then lurched forward.

'Bag's on the overhead, if you need it,' the pilot said. Esmay gulped and kept her last meal firmly in place. 'We're over there—' The pod pilot nodded to the forward port. A tangle of lights that diverged as they came nearer. Suddenly a glare as a searchlight from one arm flared across another, revealing the hull surface to be lumpy and dark . . . and big. Esmay could not get used to the scale.

'Passenger pod docking access is near the hub,' the pilot said. 'That gives passengers the easiest access to personnel lifts and most admin offices. Cargo shuttles and special cargo pods dock near the inventory bays for the specific cargo. Minimizes interior traffic.' He leaned forward and prodded the control panel; deceleration shoved Esmay against the straps. Closer . . . closer . . . she glanced up to the overhead port, and saw the vast bulk of the DSR blocking out most of the starfield – then all of it.

Exiting the pod into the passenger bay, Esmay stepped across the red stripes that signaled where the ship formally began (something that had no relation to its architecture) and saluted the colors painted on the opposite bulkhead.

'Ah . . . Lieutenant Suiza.' The sergeant at the dock entry looked back and forth from her ID to her face several times. 'Uh

. . . welcome home, sir. The captain left word he wanted to see you when you came aboard . . . shall I call ahead?'

Esmay had thought she'd have time to put her duffel away first, but captains had their perks. 'Thank you,' she said. 'Can you tell me my bunk assignment?'

'Yes, sir. You've got number 14 in the junior officers section of T-2, 'cross ship from where we are now. This is the base of T-4. Do you want someone to take your duffel down?'

She didn't want anyone messing with her things. 'No, thanks. I'll just stick it in a temp locker for now.'

'It's no trouble, Lieutenant. The temp lockers are out of your way to the captain's office anyway . . .'

She also didn't want to start with a reputation for being difficult. 'Thanks, then.' She handed over the duffel, and accepted the sergeant's directions to the captain's office . . . turn left out that hatch, take the second lift up five levels to Deck Nine, then left out of the lift and follow the signs.

The wide curving corridor matched the size of the ship; it belonged on an orbital station, not a warship. Esmay passed the first bank of lift tubes; the signs made it clear she was on Deck Four, which on an ordinary ship would be Main, not that any ordinary ship would have signs. At the second bank of tubes, she stepped in and watched the numbers flash by. Eighteen decks . . . what could they find to put on eighteen decks?

She stepped out of the lift tube on Deck Nine. Here the wide curving corridor that went around the core had the gray tile she associated with Main Deck in ordinary ships. Across from the lift tube openings a corridor led away, she supposed down one of the arms . . . T-5, said the sign on the overhead. A clerk sat at a desk in an open bay to one side. Esmay introduced herself.

'Ah. Lieutenant Suiza. Yes, sir, the captain wanted to see you right away. Captain Vladis Julian Hakin, sir. Just let me buzz the captain . . .' Esmay could not hear any signal, but the clerk nodded. 'Go along in, sir. Third on your left.'

This captain had had a wooden door substituted for the standard steel hatch; this was not unusual. It was somewhat unusual for it to be closed when a visitor had been announced. Esmay knocked.

'Come in,' came a growl from the other side. She opened the door and entered, to find herself facing the top of a gray head. The captain's office had been carpeted in deep green, and paneled in wood veneer. The Familias seal hung on the bulkhead behind the captain's desk on one side, and a framed copy of some document – probably his commission, though she couldn't see it – on the other.

'Ah . . . Lieutenant Suiza.' That seemed to be the greeting of the day. In Captain Hakin's tone of voice, it sounded more like a curse than a greeting. 'I hear they consider you quite the hero on Altiplano.' Definitely a curse. The distinction between *on Altiplano* and *here in the real world* might have been printed in red with less emphasis.

'Local interest, sir,' Esmay said. 'That's all.'

'I'm glad you realize that,' Captain Hakin said. He looked up suddenly, as if hoping to catch her in some incriminating expression. Esmay met his gaze calmly; she had expected repercussions from the awards ceremony, that was only natural. His glance flicked down to her uniform, where the silver and gold ribbon was *not* on the row allotted to non-Fleet decorations. By law, she was entitled to wear major awards from any political system within the Familias Regnant; by custom, no one did unless on a diplomatic assignment where failure to wear a locally awarded decoration might insult the giver. Junior officers, in particular, wore no personal awards except when in full dress uniform. So Esmay had the S&S, the ships-and-service ribbons appropriate to her past service, including the two decorations awarded *Despite*'s crew for the recent engagement – and, incongruously, the Ship Efficiency Award won under the late Captain Hearne. Traitor Hearne might have been, but her ship had topped the sector in the IG's inspection.

'Yes, sir,' Esmay said, when his gaze flicked back to hers.

'Some captains would be concerned about a junior officer who had been involved in a mutiny, no matter how . . . er . . . warranted the action was later shown to be.'

'I'm sure that's true, sir,' Esmay said, unruffled. She had dealt with this sort of thing all her life. 'There must be some officers who remain concerned even after a court has considered the matter in detail. I can assure the captain that I will not overreact to such concern, if anyone expresses it.'

Hakin stared. What had he thought, that she'd turn red and bluster, trying to justify herself? She had stood before a court; she had been exonerated of all charges; she need do nothing but live out her innocence.

'You seem very sure of yourself, Lieutenant,' Hakin said finally. 'How do you know that I am not one of those so concerned?'

Idiot, thought Esmay. His determination to prick her had overcome his good sense. No answer she could give would entirely ease the tension he had created. She chose bluntness. 'Is the captain concerned?'

A long sigh, through pursed lips. 'About many things, Lieutenant, of which your potential for mutiny is only one minute particle. I have been assured, by those who are supposed to know, that the public reports of your courtmartial were in fact accurate . . . that there is no suspicion of your having conspired to mutiny ahead of your captain's treacherous act.' He waited; Esmay could think of nothing helpful to say, and kept quiet. 'I shall expect your loyalty, Lieutenant.'

'Yes, sir,' Esmay said. That she could do.

'And have you no corresponding concern that your next captain might also be a traitor? That I might be in the pay of some enemy?'

She had not let herself think about that; the effort pushed her response into exclamation. 'No, sir! Captain Hearne must have been an aberration—'

'And the others as well? You're happier than I, if you can believe that, Lieutenant.'

Now what was he getting at?

'We've had investigators all over every ship in the Fleet – and that's reassuring only to those who think the investigators can't be bent. A mess of trouble that Serrano woman caused.'

Esmay opened her mouth to defend Heris Serrano, and realized it would do no good. If Hakin seriously believed that Serrano had 'caused trouble' by unmasking traitors and saving the Familias from invasion, she couldn't change his mind. She could only ruin her own reputation.

'Not that she isn't a brilliant commander,' Hakin went on, as if she had said something. 'I suppose Fleet must count itself lucky to have her back on active status . . . if we do get into a war.' He looked at Esmay again. 'I'm told Admiral Vida Serrano is pleased with you . . . I suppose she would be, since you saved her niece's neck.'

That, too, was unanswerable. Esmay wished he would get to the point, if his point was not merely to needle her, trying to get some sort of reaction.

'I hope you don't have a swelled head from all the attention, Lieutenant. Or some kind of psychological trauma from the strain of the court-martial, which I've been warned is sometimes the case, even with a favorable verdict.' From his expression, he would want some kind of answer this time.

'No, sir.' Esmay said.

'Good. I'm sure you're aware that this is a time of crisis for both the Fleet and the Familias. No one knows quite what to expect . . . except that on this ship, I expect everyone to attend to duty. Is that clear?'

'Yes, sir.'

'Very good, Lieutenant; I'll see you from time to time as the mess rotations come around.' He dismissed her with a nod, and Esmay went out trying to suppress a resentment that she knew would do her no good. No one lasted long in any service with a 'why me?' attitude; she wasn't to blame for the things held against her, but what was new about that? In the history of the universe, Papa Stefan had taught them all, life was unfair more often than not . . . life wasn't about *fair*. What it was about had filled more than one evening with explosive argument . . . Esmay tried not to think about it more than necessary.

She handed her order chip to the clerk in the front office. 'What's my duty assignment, do you know?' He glanced at it and shook his head. 'That's the 14th Heavy Maintenance Yard, Lieutenant: Admiral Dossignal's command. You'll need to report to his Admin section . . . here—' He sketched out a route on her compad. 'Just keep going clockwise around the core, and you'll come to it at the base of T-3.'

'Is the bridge on this deck?' asked Esmay, gesturing to the color-coded deck tiles.

'No, sir. The bridge is up on 17; this ship's too big for the usual color-codes. There is a system, but it's not standard. We call this command deck because all the commands have their headquarters units here. That's just for convenience, really; it cuts down the transit time.' Esmay could imagine that in a ship this size any hand-carried message could take awhile to arrive. She had never been on a ship where the captain's office and the bridge were not near each other.

On her way around the core, she passed another obvious headquarters, this one with a neat sign informing her that it was the Sector 14 Training Command, Admiral Livadhi commanding. Underneath were smaller signs: SENIOR TECHNICAL SCHOOLS ADMIN OFFICE, SENIOR TECHNICAL SCHOOLS ASSESSMENT, SUPPORT SYSTEMS. She walked on, past the base of another wing, this one labeled T-2. That was where she would be living, but she didn't have time to explore it now. On and on . . . and there ahead she saw a large banner proclaiming *Fourteenth Heavy Maintenance Yard: The Scrap Will Rise Again*. Below that, smaller signs directed the ignorant to the administrative offices. There, a bright-eyed pivot-major sent her directly to the admiral's chief of staff, Commander Atarin. He greeted Esmay's appearance in a matter-of-fact way she found reassuring. He had already read her report on the inventory aboard the supply ship, and seemed far more interested in that than her past.

'We've been trying to nail our supplier on these leaky adhesive tubes for a couple of years,' he said. 'But we couldn't prove that the supplies were damaged before we got here. I'm glad old Scorry – the XO on that supply ship – thought of having you go over the stock on your way here. We may finally get some leverage on them.'

'Yes, sir.'

'How much experience do you have with inventory control?'

'None, sir,' Esmay said. Her record cube, she knew, was on the XO's desk, but he might not have had time to look at it.

'I'm impressed, then, especially that you caught those fasteners. Most people give up after fifty or sixty items. Or assume the computer will catch it. It's supposed to, of course – there's supposed to be automatic labeling, right from the manufacturing machinery. Zero-error, they keep claiming. Never have *seen* zero errors, though.' He grinned at her. 'Of course, it could be someone from the I.G.'s office, putting little tests in our path, to see if we're alert.'

That possibility hadn't occurred to Esmay, though sabotage had. But he hadn't been on *Despite*.

'Of course, it could also be enemy action,' he said. She hoped he hadn't seen that on her face. 'But I'd rather believe in stupidity than malice.' He looked down at his desk display. 'Now let's see . . . your last duty was on a patrol craft – your emphasis on your last few cruises was scan technology. Frankly, we have plenty of scan tech experts aboard now, all more experienced than you in the field. It would do you good to branch out, get some expertise in other ship systems—' He looked up as if expecting her to disagree.

'Fine, sir,' Esmay said. She hoped it was fine. She knew she needed to learn about other systems, but was he just determined to keep her away from scan, because scan was political?

'Good.' He smiled again, and nodded. 'I expect most of you juniors think DSR is a bad assignment, but you'll discover that there's no better way to learn what really keeps ships operational. No ordinary ship deals with as many problems as we do, from hull to electronics. If you take advantage of it, this tour can teach you a lot.'

Esmay relaxed. She recognized someone happily astride his favorite hobby horse. 'Yes, sir,' she said, and wondered if he would go on.

'Personally, I think every officer should have a tour on a DSR. Then we wouldn't have people coming up with bright ideas – even installing bright ideas – that they should know wouldn't work.' He reined himself in with a visible effort. 'Well. I'm going to assign you to H&A first – Hull and Architecture, that is. You'll find it a lot more complicated than your basic course at the academy.'

'I expect so, sir,' Esmay said.

'You'll be working with Major Pitak; she's on Deck Eight, portside main, aft third of T-4 . . . you can ask someone from there. Had time to stow your gear yet?'

'No, sir.'

'Mmm. Well, technically you're not on duty until tomorrow, but—'

'I'll go see Major Pitak, sir.'

'Good. Now, the admiral will want to meet you, but he's tied up right now in a meeting, and I don't expect he'll be free until tomorrow or the next day. Check back with me, and I'll set it up. You might want to take a look at the command structure here – it's more complex than you'd find in most assignments.'

'Yes, sir.'

Not only the command structure was complex, Esmay discovered. She headed clockwise from T-3, where the 14th Heavy Maintenance had its administrative offices, to T-4, sure that she had now caught on to the *Koskiusko's* peculiar structure. At the hub end of T-4, she found an array of personnel and cargo transport tubes, and took the personnel lift down to the eighth deck. There she faced an axial passage wide enough for three horsemen abreast, and plunged into it, looking for the third crosswise passage. She passed one administrative office after another, each occupied by busy clerks: Communications Systems, Weapons Systems, Remote Imaging Systems . . . but nothing labeled Hull and Architecture. Finally she stopped and asked.

'Hull and Architecture? That's on the portside main passage, sir. You'll have to go back to hub and clockwise to it—'

Esmay suspected a joke at her expense. 'Surely there are cross-passages?'

A quickly-suppressed laugh. 'No, sir . . . T-4 has one of the main repair bays . . . nothing goes straight across at this level, from Deck Three up to Deck Fifteen.'

She had forgotten the repair bays. She felt annoyed with herself and the clerk both. 'Oh yes. Sorry.'

'No problem, sir. It takes awhile for anyone to get used to this place. Just take this passage back, turn left—' The civilian term seemed right for something this size, Esmay realized. 'Then look for the P-designations on the bulk-heads. That's portside main – if you keep going, you'll get to portside secondary, which you don't want. Hull and Architecture is about as far down portside main as we are down starboard, so . . .'

So she had given herself a lot more walk than she wanted. 'Thank you,' she said, with what courtesy she could muster past her annoyance. This ship shouldn't need any fitness equipment, if everyone got lost occasionally.

Although she felt the length of the hike in her legs, she had no more trouble finding Pitak's office. The portside main passage was easy enough, and at the third passage aft she found a pivot who directed her the rest of the way.

Major Pitak wasn't in that office. The pivot had said something about 'the major's on a bit about something' but Esmay didn't know what that meant. She glanced up and down the passage. Crewmen moving along as if they knew what they were doing, and no major. She thought of going to look, and decided not to play that game. She would simply park here until Pitak came back.

She glanced around. On the bulkhead facing the entrance was a display of metal pieces. Esmay wondered what it was, and moved closer to read the label below. COMMON WELDING ERRORS it said. Esmay could see the big lopsided blob at the one joint, and the failure of another blob to cover the joint . . . but what was wrong with the rest of them?

'So you're my new assistant,' someone said behind her. Esmay turned around. Major Pitak looked like her name sounded: a short, angular woman with a narrow face that reminded Esmay uneasily of a mule.

'Sir,' Esmay said. Pitak scowled at her.

'And no background at all in naval architecture or heavy engineering, I notice.'

'No, sir.'

'Do you at least have *some* background in construction of anything? Even a chicken house?' It was clear that Pitak was furious about something; Esmay hoped it wasn't her own presence.

'Not unless helping put a roof back on a stable after a windstorm counts,' Esmay said.

Pitak glared a moment longer, then softened. 'No . . . it doesn't. Someone must be mad at both of us, Lieutenant. Sector HQ stole three of my best H&A specialists, promoted my assistant off this ship, and left me short . . . and now they've sent you, whatever your background is.'

'Scan, mostly,' Esmay said.

'If I were religious, I would consign their sorry tails to some strenuous afterlife,' Major Pitak said. The corner of her mouth twitched. 'Blast it. I never can stay mad long enough to singe them properly, and they know it. All right, Lieutenant, let's see what you do know. Whatever it is, it's not enough, but at least you haven't done anything stupid yet.'

'I've hardly had time, sir,' Esmay said. She was beginning to like the major, against all expectation.

'There's a naive statement,' Pitak said. She had moved to her desk, where she yanked at a drawer without effect. 'I've been sent idiots who managed to screw up before I'd met them.' Another yank, this one hard enough to shift the desk itself. 'For instance, this drawer . . . it never has worked right since your predecessor times two thought it would be clever to rekey the lock. We still don't know what he did, but none of the command wands work on it, nor does anything else but brute force and profanity.' Without changing expression, Pitak launched a blistering stream of the latter at the drawer, which finally yielded with a squawk.

Esmay wanted to ask why anyone would use such a pesky drawer – why not clean it out and leave it empty? – but this was not the time. She watched Pitak rummage through the contents, coming up with a couple of data cubes.

'You probably wonder why I put anything in here,' Pitak said. 'Frankly so do I, but there's little enough secured storage down here – not with all the specialists we have aboard, people who know all the tricks of every security device since the latch. They sent some background on you, but I haven't looked at it yet, which I hope you won't hold against me.'

'No, sir.'

'For pity's sake, Lieutenant, loosen up. Find a seat somewhere. Let's see here . . .' She inserted the cube in a cube reader as Esmay looked around for something to sit on. Every horizontal surface was crusted in clutter; the two chairs had piles of hardcopy that looked like inventory lits. Pitak glanced up. 'Just shove some of that onto the floor. Danton was supposed to clean it up yesterday,

131

but he's in sickbay with some crud he caught . . . I think we'd do better to let them brew their nasty chemicals on board; they always get sick ashore.'

Esmay set a pile of paper carefully on the floor, and sat down. Pitak was scowling at the cube reader's display.

'Well. For a mutineer and a hero, you're awfully quiet, Lieutenant Suiza. Trying to cover your tracks?'

Esmay couldn't think of anything to say.

'Hmm. The strong, silent type. Not mine, as you've already discovered. Planetary militia family . . . ye gods, one of *those* Suizas!' Esmay hadn't had that reaction from anyone in Fleet before; she could feel her eyebrows going up. Pitak stared at her. 'Do they *know*?'

'I'm not sure what you mean, sir.'

A disgusted look, which Esmay felt she deserved. 'Don't play your games with me, Lieutenant Suiza. I mean, does Fleet understand that 'planetary militia' is an understatement when applied to the Suiza family of Altiplano?'

'I had assumed they did,' Esmay said cautiously. 'At least, when I applied, there was a background check, and surely they found out.'

'You're a careful pup,' Pitak said. 'I noticed that "had" – what do you think now?'

'Uh . . . most don't realize it, but I presume someone must.' Esmay wanted to know how Pitak knew – surely she wasn't from Altiplano herself. Esmay had thought she was the first.

'I see.' Pitak scrolled through the cube contents; Esmay presumed it was a precis of her record. 'Interesting place, Altiplano, but I wouldn't want to live there. Ah – at least you were on the science branch at the Academy . . . interesting. You didn't take the usual courses for someone going command track. What did you think, technical?'

'Yes, sir.'

'And then you end up the most junior officer ever to command a patrol vessel in combat – and win. I'll bet someone's looking into your background again. Well, I'll tell you what, Lieutenant – the most important thing you can do right now is learn your way around this ship, because when I have something for you to do, I don't want you to spend an hour finding out where it is. So – next three days, while we're docked, go everywhere and see everything and be ready for an orientation exam when you come back. That's 0800 on the 27th – clear?'

'Yes, sir,' Esmay said. Curiosity burned away the last shreds of her caution. 'If the major doesn't mind – how did you know about Altiplano?'

'Good for you,' Pitak said, grinning now. She had a strange grin, in that narrow face, all teeth somewhat bigger than seemed possible to fit in it. 'I was wondering if you'd get up the nerve to ask. Met a fellow one time I thought of hitching up with, back when I was a jig and things weren't going too well. Spent a leave on Altiplano, with his family. Heard all about the Suizas and their relations, and the local politics, but the whole time he was extolling the beauties of those big rolling plains and snow-capped mountains. I was wishing for a nice tight spaceship. Especially after a gallop over the plains in a rainstorm – I was sure I'd be fried by lightning, and I was so sore I couldn't walk for days. I suppose you ride?'

'When I have to,' Esmay said. This was not the time to mention her own herd, which she hadn't wanted anyway. 'It's – expected, riding. But I chose space.'

'My kind of woman. Now – get out of here and start learning where things are. I warn you, my exams are no joke. Here – this is what you need.' She tossed over a data cube. 'That and good legs.'

'Thank you, sir,' Esmay said.

'0800 on the 27th.'

'Yes, sir.' Esmay paused, but the major didn't look up. She retraced her way back to the hub corridors, then looked up her assigned quarters and figured out a route to that compartment. T-2 should be back the way she'd come, counterclockwise . . . then up the personnel lift, and . . . she paid close attention to the axial passage designation, even though T-2 wasn't split by a repair bay . . . somewhere around here. . . .

8

Her compartment was small, but her own – lieutenants had that bit of privacy. Her duffel was waiting on the bunk, its seals unbroken. She stowed her gear in the locker, activated the status board, and confirmed her identity to the computer's flat-voiced inquiry. On a bulkhead a colored plan explained the officer housing arrangement. T-2 was configured for personnel housing: decks of enlisted bunking, broken into large bays for most, with two- or four-person compartments for the most senior. An entire deck for junior officers, with ensigns in ten-man bays, jigs in two-person compartments, and lieutenants in separate compartments, ranging outward by seniority. Above her was a deck of billeting for field grade officers, and above that a deck for the flag officers; she blinked at the number of admirals aboard.

Messing was in the same wing: two levels of food storage, kitchens, and dining halls. Exercise rooms, gyms, pools, even team sports space – she groaned at the thought of more parpaun enthusiasts – and on the top decks, open gardens. Gardens? Some space stations had gardens, but no Fleet vessel she'd ever been on. She thanked whatever beneficent deities had not assigned her to Environmental; it must be unbelievably difficult on a ship like this.

She looked around her compartment again. She hadn't minded ensign bunking, when she'd been that junior. Some automatic device in her brain kept the worst dreams away when she was sleeping in a public space. Lack of privacy when awake had rarely bothered her either; she had not had much free time to miss it. Now . . . now she would have to hope that the nightmares didn't

134

wake her neighbors on either side. Her conscience pointed out that she could always go to Medical and request help from the psychs; she ignored it.

She had no messages waiting; she was not expected anywhere in particular. Which meant she could take a look at Pitak's assignment on the cube, if she could find a cube reader free. The console informed her that she had her own cube reader . . . it took her a moment to find it; she had never seen one in the fully-stowed position. Most people left them half-open at least, for the next user.

The cube contained what looked like ordinary ship schematics. Not ordinary, exactly – this ship wasn't ordinary – but nothing she couldn't have pulled off the general user base and displayed on her own console. Esmay called up the schematics on the console to check that.

Not quite the same. Passages that went through on one schematic dead-ended in the other . . . lifts were in slightly different places. Esmay scowled at the display. Was the major trying to play her for a fool, or was the ship's own database wrong? If so, why?

She looked for the nearest non-match, which was back on T-3, where a cross-corridor on Deck Three that the ship's database said ran through 'Forming Workshop 2-B' ended on Pitak's data cube before reaching the workshop; according to her data, 'forming workshop 2-B' couldn't be reached except by a detour around 'Die Storage.'

Only one way to find out. She glanced at the time . . . she could get up there and back to her assigned mess in T-2 before the next meal.

Back to the hub end of T-2, then clockwise to the base of T-3 . . . she was getting the hang of this. She located the personnel lift tube beside a cluster of four labeled CARGO ONLY.

The personnel lift light changed to green, and Esmay punched in. When the second light came on, she stepped in and felt a quick double lurch of her innards before she came to rest at the hatch eight decks down. Waiting there was another lieutenant, male, with a couple of ensigns in tow.

'I don't know you,' the lieutenant said, as she stepped out. 'Are you assigned here?'

135

'Just aboard, sir,' Esmay said, hoping she didn't have the bug-eyed look that usually followed a short hop on the lift tube. 'Esmay Suiza, assigned to Hull and Architecture . . .'

'Oh, yes.' He extended a hand; he had a good hand-shake. 'Tai Golonifer. Short for something horrible and familial, don't ask. I heard you were coming; I'm with 14th Maintenance staff. Are you busy at the moment?'

What was this? 'I'm assigned to Major Pitak,' Esmay said, intentionally oblique.

'You're busy,' Golonifer said, as if there were no doubt. 'I'm not surprised she's already got you running all over the ship. But meet these two – also newbies – Ensigns Anson and Partrade.' The two ensigns returned Esmay's handshakes – Anson had a chilly, damp palm, and Partrade's felt as if he'd lined it with saddle leather. 'See you at mess,' Golonifer said. 'Come on, guys, down the tube we go.'

Esmay turned away and looked around her. She needed the starboard main axial passage for T-3. On this deck, the corridor was wide enough to drive a small truck through, and the inlaid guidelines for transport carts, along with marked pedestrian lanes on either side, suggested that small trucks did in fact drive it, at speed.

A soft rushing . . . she glanced back and saw a flatbed carrier loaded with canisters rolling smoothly along the guideline, its red sensor blinking like a mad red eye. Five meters from her, its automatic warning bleated three times . . . then it was past. Ahead, Esmay saw it slow and swing into a large hatch on the outboard side. When she got to the hatch and looked in, she saw a long robotic arm plucking canisters off the carrier and placing them on racks. Someone in the compartment yelled – she couldn't hear clearly – and the arm stopped in mid-move, with one canister in its pincers.

She couldn't stand there all day – she would have the rest of her tour to figure out what was going on in there. She set off again. The first cross-passage was double the width of the one she was using, with warning lights as well as mirrors at the corners. Esmay glanced at the mirrors, even though the lights were green. Far down the inboard side something large and lumpy with flashing yellow lights sat motionless, with little dark figures swarming over it . . . she blinked, startled again at the distances inside this ship.

Esmay almost missed the second cross-corridor; a dark slit opened on either side, barely one pedestrian wide, and lit only by wide-spaced lights. Again she stopped and peered at it. On a cramped escort, this might be a normal width – but it didn't fit with the others she'd seen. The third aft was the most normal so far, if anything about this ship was normal. Three could have walked abreast, if they didn't mind banging hands now and then. Evenly spaced hatches opened off it on either side. The fourth aft was much like it . . . a passage that might have been on any ship, save for its length. The fifth, the one she'd come to see . . . she turned inboard.

Forming Workshop A was right where both Pitak's cube and the ship's own schematics said it should be. Esmay wasn't sure what a forming workshop was, but she could tell that it was important. Guide lines for robotic carts streaked the floor, curving into one hatch after another. Through the open hatches she could see long arrays of equipment that meant nothing to her: cylinders and inverted cones, racks of nozzles mounted overhead on tracks, great blank-faced cubes with warning logos on them.

Ahead of her, the passage ended in a sealed hatch. Esmay glanced again at her notes. The ship's computer evidently thought this passage continued . . . and perhaps it did, past the obstruction. NO ADMITTANCE WITHOUT AUTHORIZATION in yellow on red . . . and Esmay suspected that some of the little gleaming knobs on the hatch seal were actually video sensors.

She retraced her way to the longitudinal passage, and followed the indirect path suggested by Pitak's cube. It took longer than she'd expected . . . she kept being surprised at the size, and annoyed with herself for still being surprised. But she found Forming Workshop B where Pitak's cube said it would be, and on this side the obstruction looked like an ordinary hatch with the label DIE STORAGE.

A soft tone rang through the ship, and she glanced at her handcomp. Almost late – she would have to hurry, and she was on the other side of the ship from territory she was already thinking of as home. She didn't bother to compare Pitak's data with the ship's own this time; she jogged forward on the portside main passage, back around the hub passage, popped into the first passenger tube, and fetched up at her assigned mess only just ahead of the gong.

Here she found that lieutenants were expected to head a table of jigs and ensigns. She had met none of them yet. They introduced themselves politely and she tried to sort out names and faces. She said little, listening to them and hoping to find out something to make them memorable. The light-haired ensign on the left had a scrape on his left hand; surely by the time it healed she'd have another reason to know him. The jigs seemed a bit stiff, as if they were afraid of her. They must have heard about the court-martial, but was that all?

'Lieutenant Suiza, did you really meet Admiral Serrano?' That was an ensign, not the blond one but a thin dark young man with green eyes. Custis, his nametag said.

'Yes, I did,' Esmay said. Ensign Custis opened his mouth to say more, but the blond ensign elbowed him visibly and he shut it again. A brief silence followed, during which Esmay ate steadily. Out of the corner of her eye, she could see Custis glancing at her from time to time. Finally he got his courage up again.

'You know her grandson's aboard . . . Barin Serrano . . .'

'Toby!' That was the blond, disapproving. Esmay didn't rise to that bait, but she did wonder if coincidence or Serrano influence had anything to do with a young Serrano's assignment.

'If you'd eat without talking, you wouldn't get your foot in your mouth,' said one of the jigs further down the table. Esmay looked up in time to see a Look pass from that jig to another one. Great. Something mysterious which would, no doubt, end up on her shoulders.

She put her fork down; her appetite had disappeared. 'Admiral Serrano's a very interesting person,' she said. That was always safe . . . she hoped. From the startled looks of the two jigs, perhaps it wasn't. 'Not that it wasn't an alarming situation.' Now everyone was looking at her. A year ago, she might have felt her face flushing, but the publicity around the court-martial had taken care of that. She smiled around the table. 'Any of you ever serve with Admiral Serrano?'

'No, sir,' said the senior jig. 'But she's a Serrano, and they're all pretty much alike.' His tone tried for superior, that of the one with secret knowledge, but its very smugness defeated its intent. Esmay knew exactly what he didn't know. For the first time she realized she could enjoy this.

'I don't think I'd put it that way,' she said, leaning forward a little. 'Frankly, having served under both of them—' She had served under Admiral Serrano only remotely, and briefly, but this was no time for precision on that point. 'Admiral *Vida* Serrano, that is, and Commander *Heris* Serrano . . .' Thus reminding everyone that a lineup of all the admirals and commanders Serrano would take up a fair length of deck. 'I thought them quite individual. Nor is the difference all seniority.' Let them make what they could of that.

'But isn't Commander Serrano – Heris Serrano that is – the admiral's niece?'

Esmay let her eyebrows go up at this appalling lack of manners. 'What, precisely, are you suggesting?'

'Well . . . you know, they all stick together. Being related so close, I mean.'

Esmay had not imagined that kind of prejudice aimed at anyone but Fleet outsiders like herself, those who had enlisted from some planet. The Serranos were Fleet royalty, one of the fourteen private military forces that had combined into the Regular Space Service of the Familias Regnant. Through the white rage she felt, her mind reacted as if pricked, correlating remarks made months ago, even years ago, as early as her second term in the Fleet prep school. She had always ignored them, labeled them pique or envy or momentary annoyance. If those people had been serious . . . if there were serious resentment of the Serranos – and possibly some of the other First Fourteen – someone should know. She should know, and she should not lose her temper and shove this brash youngster's face in the stew.

Her temper bucked, like one of the green colts in training, and she rode it down, hoping her eyes showed none of the strain.

'I think with a little more experience you won't either think or say things like that, Jig Callison,' Esmay said in the mildest tone she could manage. Callison turned red, and looked down. Someone snickered; she didn't spot who.

Conversation, naturally, died, and she pretended to eat the rest of her dinner. When the senior lieutenant tapped on his glass for attention, Esmay felt more relief than curiosity. She found it hard to keep her attention on the announcements of who had the duty, and almost missed her introduction. She stood, off-balance mentally if not physically, and nodded to the faces that seemed only pale and dark blurs.

After the meal, she left for her quarters as soon as she could. She was annoyed with herself for her immediate prickly response to the mention of the Serrano name. And why was she so blurry? Usually she could focus on new people without much trouble.

When she thought about it, she realized that she had actually run about thirty standard hours without sleep. Her transport ship had come in on its own schedule, skewed a full shift and a half from the *Koskiusko*. Shiplag . . . luckily she never had much trouble with it. One night's sleep seemed to rearrange her internal timer . . . but right now she wanted that sleep badly. She wasn't on the watch schedule yet, so she set her personal timer to allow ten hours.

Her compartment filtered out most of the noises . . . she could just hear the bass thump of someone's music cube, DUM-da-DUM-DUM, over and over. She didn't like it, but it wouldn't keep her awake. She logged off the status board, and stretched out on her bunk. She had just time to wonder if she would have nightmares when she fell asleep.

Beside her, Peli leaned out to toss a gasser into the passage. A blue line traced the air just above his head and he jerked back. Esmay pressed the filters snugly into her nostrils and peered through the helmet visor. When the smoke obscured normal vision, her helmet sensors gave her a wiggly false-color view of the corridor. She snaked out into it, hoping that whoever'd been shooting at them didn't have a similar helmet. They thought they'd gotten to the locker before the traitors, but none of the juniors knew how many helmets were supposed to be in that locker.

Ahead, someone braced into an angle of a hatch, weapon at ready.

Esmay couldn't see the features, but she could hear, with the clarity provided by the helmet external pickups, the words 'Get this bunch of little fuckers, and we'll have only Dovir to worry about—'

She braced her own weapon and fired. The wiggly pink-and-green image blew apart; something wet and warm splashed her arm. She ignored it. Through the dense stinging fog, she slithered on, attention focussed on the helmet's input . . . aware that behind her Peli and the others followed, that somewhere Major Dovir still led the few other loyalist officers. . . .

The fog lifted in ragged wisps . . . ahead she could see the scorched lines on the bulkheads . . . she did not look at the deck except when she had to, when she would have fallen over the obstructions . . . but even so she saw them. Heaps of old clothes, dirty and stained, scattered here and there . . . she would not think of it now, she would not, later was soon enough. . . .

She woke in a sweat, heart pounding. Later. Later was now, when she was safe. She turned on her bed light, and lay staring at the overhead. They had not been heaps of clothes; she had known it even then. Her father had been all too right – warfare was ugly, no matter where. Guts and blood and flesh stank the same in a spaceship as in the aftermath of a street riot. And she herself had added to that stench, that ugliness. She and the other juniors had fought their way up the ship, onto the bridge, where Dovir, mortally wounded, held the command chair after Hearne was dead. Dovir, his guts slipping out of his hands, had given her that one glazed look . . . his voice, struggling for control, as he gave his last orders. . . .

She blinked, trying not to cry. She had cried; it didn't do any good. She felt slimy all over, the sweat cold and slick now, the bedclothes damp and tangled around her. It reminded her of her aunt's description of menopause, waking up sweaty and then having cold chills. Or something like that. She forced her mind back to this place and time. Thinking about home wouldn't help her at all.

According to the chronometer, she had slept a solid seven hours. She could try for another short nap . . . but experience suggested that she wouldn't really sleep. Better would be a shower – it was late third shift on this ship – and an early start on the working day.

No one was in the big shower room; she let the hot water warm her and wash away the fear-stink. As she came back down the passage, she heard someone's alarm go off. Not hers – she had carefully shut hers off. Then, from down the passage, another alarm. She made it into her compartment before those alarms stopped, and when she emerged, it was to find two bleary-eyed ensigns on their way to the showers, and a jig leaning on the bulkhead folding down the top flap of his uniform boot.

'Sir!' they all said, coming to more or less upright posture. Esmay nodded, feeling the momentary glow of virtue that accompanies an early rising, clean teeth, and the evidence that one's associates are still half-asleep.

She did not let herself dwell on that. She had work to do – not only learning the ship, as Major Pitak had said, but figuring out why the major's data cube and the ship's records were so different. All that day, except for hurried meals, Esmay mapped the real ship against two dissimilar records. Major Pitak's data cube was right except once, far in the bow end of T-1, Deck Thirteen, when neither fit the reality. A hatch had disappeared completely, replaced by a bulkhead painted in garish stripes. As Esmay stood there, wondering what the pattern meant, a bald senior chief bustled out of the nearest cross-passage, and hurried toward her.

'What are you – oh, excuse me, sir. Can I help you find something?'

Esmay had not missed the tension . . . something was clearly going on. But it was not yet her job to find it. She smiled instead. 'I'm Lieutenant Suiza,' she said. 'Major Pitak told me to familiarize myself with the entire ship by 0800 on the 27th, and I thought there was a hatch up here to the electronics warehouse facility.'

'Oh . . . Major Pitak,' the man said. Evidently Major Pitak was well known outside her own bailiwick. 'Well, sir, the ship's database hasn't caught up to renovations. The electronics warehouse access is up that way.' He pointed. 'I'll be glad to show you.'

'Thanks,' Esmay said. As they turned away, she said 'This bulkhead pattern – is it something they didn't teach us, or—?'

A red flush went up the back of his neck. 'It's – probably unique to DSR ships, Lieutenant. They're so big, you see . . . the

142

captain's permitted some nonreg markings to keep newbies oriented.'

'I see,' Esmay said. 'Very sensible – I've gotten lost several times already.'

The red flush receded; she could hear relaxation in his voice. 'Most people do, Lieutenant. That pattern just lets people know that what the ship's schematics show isn't there any more – they haven't gone the wrong way, exactly, but the way's changed.'

Something about the intonation of that almost put a capital letter on 'way.' Esmay stowed that slight emphasis for later consideration, and followed the chief outboard, then forward again, to a hatch clearly labeled ELECTRONICS WAREHOUSE FACILITY. Under that official label was another.

CHECK OUT WITH DUTY CHIEF
BEFORE YOU REMOVE ANY PARTS:
THIS MEANS YOU!

Esmay thanked her guide, and went in. It looked like any storage facility she'd seen, as large as most on major bases. Racks of containers labeled with part numbers; bins with the most commonly needed parts piled loosely. A jig she had not yet met came out from a warren of racks.

'Sher, is that you – oh, sorry, sir.' Esmay went through her explanation again, introducing herself to Jig Forrest. He seemed eager enough to show her the whole warehouse.

'I just wondered – my ship schematic showed a different entrance.'

'Before my time,' he said. 'I know – I got lost trying to find this place when they sent me up from the 14th. We share this warehouse with Training – those technical schools people are always needing more parts in the lab. That's why they moved this warehouse. I don't think they update the ship's schematics often enough, especially since this is a DSR – it's important for us to know where we are. But you know how it is, Lieutenant: no one asks jigs for their opinion.'

Esmay grinned. 'I do indeed. And I suspect, new as my extra bar is, that no one asks lieutenants their opinion either.' At least not until the middle of a mutiny, when everyone else was dead. But

143

this fresh-faced young man with the coppery hair hadn't been through that.

'You must be with Major Pitak,' he said now, and at her expression laughed again. 'She always sends her new juniors out to find impossible corners of the ship. I've never been in H&A, for which I thank whatever gods govern the assignments.'

'At least I know where this is now,' Esmay said. 'And I'd better get back to my list.'

She was glad for the years of open-country navigation on the estancia . . . she had no problem retracing her route down and aft, and arrived in the junior officers' section in plenty of time to freshen up before taking her assigned table at mess. Now that she was wide awake, she found it easier to engage them in conversation.

Callison, the senior jig, had a graduate degree in environmental engineering. Partrade, the junior jig, worked in administration – a specialty still called paper-pushing, though relatively little of it was on paper. The five ensigns at her table included one in Hull and Architecture, two in Weapons Systems, and one each in Medical Support and Data Systems.

Esmay wondered if any of them had served aboard a ship in combat, but didn't like to ask. She had spooked them enough the previous night. Partrade brought the topic up without her having to ask.

'Was the Xavier action your only experience in combat, Lieutenant Suiza?'

Esmay managed not to choke on her peas. 'Yes, it was.' End of sentence.

'I've never even served on a warship,' Partrade went on, with a glance around. 'I don't think anyone at this table has. They put me in Maintenance Administration right away, and I've been on the *Kos* for five solid years.'

'I was on *Checkmate*,' one of the ensigns said. 'But we never did anything but patrol.'

'Be grateful,' said Esmay, before she could stop herself. Now they all stared at her. She hated this. She felt too young and too old at the same time.

'If the lieutenant doesn't want to talk about it, don't push her.'

That from the lieutenant at the next table, whom Esmay now remembered was the one she'd met outside the lift tube. 'Dinner's not the time for gory stories anyway.' He winked at Esmay. She grinned in spite of herself.

'He's right,' she said to her table. 'It's not a fit topic at the table.' Or among strangers, she realized. Now she understood why the veterans tended to cluster apart to tell their tales, why they had fallen silent when she and other juniors had tried to overhear them. 'Any of the rest of you have any experience?' She was surprised to hear in her own voice the same slight emphasis to the word which she had heard from more senior, and experienced officers. Their heads shook. 'Well,' she said. 'Then we won't be tempted to bring up things like that at dinner.' Her smile would, she hoped, take the sting out of that. 'Now . . . Zintner, you're in H&A. Was that your intent at the Academy?'

'Yes, sir.' Zintner, who must have stood on tiptoe to make the minimum height requirement, almost sparkled in her seat. 'My family's been in shipbuilding forever – a long time anyway. I wanted to work on military hulls . . . that's where the good new stuff is.'

'And this is your first assignment?'

'Yes, sir. It's great. You've met Major Pitak – she knows so much – and we get to work on everything, once we're out with the wave.'

'Mmm. My background's scan technology, so I don't know much about H&A. I expect you'll be teaching me a lot.'

'Me, sir? I doubt it – the major's got me working on a technical manual right now. She'll probably tell Master Chief Sivars to take you on.'

Direct contradiction was rude, but the ensign looked too bouncy to have intended any rudeness. She was simply full of what she was doing. Esmay understood that. She turned to the jigs. Callison was pleasantly willing to discuss the less disgusting processes that kept the ship's crew alive, and had amusing anecdotes of the sorts of things that went wrong. It had not occurred to Esmay that a few insect egg cases caught in the mud in someone's hiking boots could hatch and cause serious problems, but apparently they had, on another ship. That story led Partrade

145

to regale them with a story about the time an unnamed junior lieutenant transposed a few numbers and caused a massive overdraft of his ship's account . . . everyone had been bumped up ten grades, so the whole ship was crewed – according to the computer – by officers, and the captain outranked the sector commander.

One of the many differences from home that Esmay savored was this . . . that they could talk about their assignments at dinner. On Altiplano, nothing related to one's work could be discussed at dinner, even if all at the table were working together. She found that unnatural . . . here, a flurry of shop talk would unwind naturally into other topics.

'Are you ready for my exam?' Major Pitak asked when she reported.

'Yes, sir,' Esmay said. 'But I do have a question.'

'Go ahead.'

'Why doesn't the ship's schematics agree with reality – or with the schematics on your cube?'

'Excellent. How many discrepancies did you find?'

Esmay blinked. She hadn't expected that reaction. She began to describe the discrepancies, starting at the bow and working aft. Pitak listened without comment. When she had finished. Pitak made a note on her pad.

'I believe you found them all. Good work. You asked why we have discrepancies, and that's not a question I can answer. I suspect it's the new AI subroutines, which actively protect data considered especially important. A software glitch, in other words, though we can't seem to convince the Fleet systems designers that it's a problem. They take the view that architecture, once launched, shouldn't change . . . which is probably true for most hulls.'

Esmay thought that over. 'So you create new data cubes individually when you change architecture.'

'Right. We can actually change the main system for a time – usually an hour or so before it "heals" itself and repairs what it thinks is a data injury.'

'But there were two places where your data cube didn't match the reality.'

146

Pitak grinned at her. 'I gave you an old data cube, Lieutenant – to see if you'd really check things out. The stupid ones come back all confused, complaining that they can't find their way by ship schematics. The clever ones check out one or two locations, then come back with a list of discrepancies between my cube and the ship schematics. Good, honest officers who aren't afraid of work do what you did – they check *everything*. That's what I want in my section . . . people who skip the details in H&A kill ships, and we're here to save them.'

'Yes . . . sir.' Esmay thought about that. It was an efficient way of separating lazy and careless from diligent and careful, but she wondered what other tricks Major Pitak had waiting. It would, she thought, be some exam. 'Thank you, sir, for explaining.'

Pitak looked at her oddly. 'Thank you for passing the test, Lieutenant – or hadn't you figured that out yet?'

She hadn't, and now she felt stupid. 'No, sir.' Stupid, gauche . . . she felt her ears burning and hoped the glow didn't come through her hair.

'A one-track mind, I wonder, or . . . of course you are a dropsquirt.' That in a thoughtful voice with no edge to it.

'Dropsquirt?' Esmay hadn't heard that before, though it sounded pejorative.

'Sorry. DSR vessels develop their own local slang . . . almost a local dialect, though we try not to be too impenetrable. It means Personnel of Planetary Origin, the official term . . . someone squirted into deepspace work from a drop – a gravity well. And someone junior, which is when you can really tell the difference. One doesn't expect dropsquirts to get all the nuances of Fleet social structure right away . . . when did you join, Suiza?'

'Prep school, sir.' Esmay thought of the years she'd been in a Fleet environment. Two in prep school, four in the Academy, a tour as ensign, and two assignments as jig. If she hadn't caught on by now, would she ever? She'd thought she had – her fitness reports always commented on her quiet, mannerly demeanor. What was she doing wrong, besides getting involved in mutinies?

'Hmm. Technical track, most of the way.' Pitak gave her a long look. 'You know, Suiza, we technical types have a reputation for being a little dense in some things. Wouldn't surprise me if you are too. That doesn't bother me, and won't cause you as much trouble here as it would on a warship. But since you are not from a Fleet family, you might want to think about opening your sensors to a little wider band. Just a suggestion – not an order.'

'Yes, sir,' Esmay said. She felt a little dizzy. What was she doing wrong? What was so obvious? She knew she didn't have an accent any more; she had tried so hard . . . but Major Pitak had moved to her process chart.

'To get you up to speed in H&A, you're going to have to take a couple of quick courses. Right now all we have is a minor little plate repair job for an escort – it'll be done before you're through with the tapes, and you'll be more use to us then. How are you with tools? Ever done metal fabrication? Ceramics or plastics molding?'

'No, sir.'

'Mmm. All right, then. Take these tapes down to Training, and run through them as many times as it takes. Then come back here, and I'll set you up with some instructors. You've got to know how a process is supposed to be done before you can supervise it.'

That made perfect sense, and Esmay had never minded learning new things. 'Yes, sir,' she said, accepting a thick stack of tapes for the machines.

'We'll probably be out on deployment before you're through with the tapes,' Pitak said. 'Take what time you need.' Then she shook her head. 'Sorry – you're naturally thorough – I don't have to warn *you* against rushing through them.'

'Sir.' Esmay backed out, with very mixed feelings. One side of her mind felt ruffled and itchy; another part felt soothed and confident.

Scheduling sessions in Training took longer than she had expected. The techs in charge of the banks of machines explained. 'A DSR needs more specialties than any other kind of ship. And we have to know everything – all the old stuff, and all the new stuff, and anything someone's come up with to make repair easier. Our people are always retraining. The rest of Fleet just thinks it retrains, with its predictable little drills every so many days. But we'll get you in, Lieutenant, don't worry. And

Major Pitak knows what the situation is – she's not going to blame you.'

Nonetheless, it would be three standard days before Esmay could get a machine, and then only on third shift.

'Do you have anything similar that I could go over on my cube reader?' she asked. The tech ran the tape titles through his scanner.

'Yes, but this is really technical stuff, Lieutenant – what I have on cube is much more basic. The intermediate stuff's all been checked out – in fact, it's overdue.'

'I'll take the basic,' Esmay said. 'A good review for me.' She took the cubes, and gave the tech her tapes, to be held for her session. Back in her quarters, she inserted the first cube. An hour later, she was very glad she hadn't been able to get time on the machines right away. The basic level cube was already past her. She sat back, blinking, and realized she'd have to take it in short doses.

Almost lunchtime. She wasn't really hungry, but she did feel stiff and stale. What she wanted was exercise. She changed to shorts and padded shoes, and followed the directions (in this case identical) given by the ship's schematics and Major Pitak's cube to the junior officers' workout area.

Aside from being bigger, it was much like the exercise compartments she'd seen on other ships. Rows of machines for exercising this or that group of muscles, enclosed spaces for pair games played on a small court, a large open space with mats for tumbling and unarmed combat practice. Half a dozen or so junior officers occupied various machines, and two were sparring on the mats. She checked the charts. At this time of the cycle, only a few machines were reserved; she could use almost anything. Esmay avoided the riding simulators, and climbed onto something said to simulate cross-country walking on snow. She had no desire to walk on real snow – she had done that – but it was better than pretending to ride horses by sitting on an arrangement of pistons and levers.

She had just begun to work up her heart rate when someone called her name. She looked around. It was one of the ensigns from her table . . . Custis? No, Dettin, the blond with the scrape, now healed.

'I just wondered if you'd talk to our tactics study group about the Xavier affair,' he asked. 'Not necessarily your own role, though of course we'd like to hear it, but just how you saw the battle as a whole.'

'I didn't see the battle as a whole,' Esmay said. 'We got there late, as you may have heard.'

'Late?' His brow furrowed. Could he really be this ignorant.

'The ship I was on was captained by a—' it was extraordinarily hard to say 'traitor' right out loud to a youngster like this. 'Captain Hearne left the Xavier system before the battle,' she said. She didn't know why she said it that way; she had not cared that much for Captain Hearne. 'It was only after the—' *mutiny* was another hard word to say, but this time she got it out. 'Only after the mutiny, when all the senior officers had died, that I took the ship back.'

She did not expect the look on his face, the expression of someone who has just seen impossible dreams fulfilled. 'You – that's like something out of *Silver Stars*.'

'Silver stars?'

'You know – the adventure game series.'

Shock knocked out her control. 'It was *nothing* like an adventure game!'

He was oblivious. 'No, but in the eighth series, when that young lord had to overcome the wicked prince and then lead the ships in battle . . .'

'It's not a game,' Esmay said firmly, but with less heat. 'People get killed for real.'

'I know that,' he said, looking annoyed. 'But in the game—'

'I'm sorry,' Esmay said, 'I don't play adventure games.' *I only fight wars*, she wanted to say, but didn't.

'But will you talk to our tactics group?'

She thought it over. Perhaps she could make clear the difference between game and reality. 'Yes,' she said. 'But I'll have to check my schedule. When do you meet?'

'Every ten days, but we could move the meeting time if you wanted.'

'I'll check,' Esmay said. 'Now – I've got to finish my set.' He went away, and she worked until she felt she'd worked off not only the stiffness of study, but the unreasonable anger she'd felt at being compared to a gaming hero. By the time she'd cooled down again, she began to think whether she should have been quite so quick to agree . . . even if she hadn't agreed to a specific time. Should she talk to a pack of ensigns about the Xavier affair? If she kept her own part to a minimum, and discussed the way Heris Serrano had held off a superior force, surely that could do no harm.

9

She was trying to think whom to consult, when she remembered that she needed to make an appointment to meet Admiral Dossignal. Now, while she was working her way through the basic level training cubes, would be an ideal time. She contacted Commander Atarin's clerk, and an hour or so later the message came back that the admiral would see her at 1330. So at 1315, she presented herself at the admiral's office suite, where Commander Atarin happened to be delivering a pile of cubes.

'How's Hull and Architecture, Lieutenant?'

'Very interesting, sir. Major Pitak has me taking some courses, since I had no background.'

'Good; she's very thorough. Has she given you the ship test yet?'

'That came first, sir.'

'Ah.' His eyebrows rose and fell. 'Well, you must have passed, or I'd have heard about it. Good for you. How are you getting along in the junior mess? Settling in all right?'

'Fine, sir,' Esmay said.

'This ship's so big, none of us can get to know everyone. Sometimes people coming in from smaller craft find that very unsettling. If you have any special interests, you might take a look at the recreational group roster. We encourage people to have acquaintances outside their own work sections – even commands.'

'Well, sir, the juniors' tactics discussion group did ask me to speak on the Xavier action.'

'Oh? Well, that's not exactly what I had in mind, but it's a start. And they showed some initiative in asking . . . who was it?'

'Ensign Dettin, sir.'

'Mmm . . . I don't know Dettin. But I'm sure they've all heard something about Xavier, and are curious to know more. I might drop in . . .' Was that a threat, or a warning, or mere interest? 'Ah – the admiral's ready.'

Admiral Dossignal was a tall man with craggy features and big-knuckled hands that fiddled with things on his desk. Despite this, he seemed more relaxed than Captain Hakin, and considerably more welcoming.

'I've read the notations your Board made in your file, Lieutenant Suiza . . . and though I can understand their concern about your decisions, I do not share them. I have complete confidence in your loyalty to the Familias Regnant.'

'Thank you, sir.'

'No thanks necessary, Lieutenant. Although we need to smoke out the other traitors we surely have – Garrivay and his cohorts cannot be all of them – we must have trust, or we have no cohesion.' He paused, but Esmay found nothing to say. When he resumed, it was in a different tone, less somber. 'I understand you and Major Pitak are getting on well . . . and Commander Seveche?'

'I've only met him, sir,' Esmay said. The head of Hull and Architecture had spoken to her only briefly; he had seemed even busier than Major Pitak when she saw him.

'I'm sure you've heard this before, but I must say it's unusual to have a lieutenant assigned here without having gone through one of the advanced technical schools first. You may find it necessary to take some courses . . .'

'I'm already signed up for one, sir.'

'Good. By your record, you're a quick learner, but heavy maintenance is a lifetime's study.' He glanced back at his desk display. 'I see you've had recent home planet leave. How did your family react to all the publicity?'

Esmay tried to think of a tactful way to phrase it. 'They . . . went overboard, sir.'

'Ah? Oh, I suppose you mean the medal?'

Of course it was already in her file; she knew that. 'Yes, sir.'

'But that was the government, not your family . . . You have . . . a father, stepmother, half-brothers?'

'Yes, sir. Also aunts, uncles, cousins . . . it's a large clan, sir.'

'Did they approve of your joining us?' The warm brown eyes sharpened.

'Not . . . entirely, sir. Not at first. Now they do.'

'We have no other officers from your planet, you see. The last was some thirty years ago.'

'Meluch Zalosi, yes, sir.' A Zalosi of the Coarchy, which no longer existed, but had been, at one time, a political force. The Zalosi, though, were servants of the Coarchs. Meluch, the gossip went, had been the illegitimate child of the Tributine Coarch and a Zalosi guard, farmed out to a distant Zalosi relative. He had proven to carry the distinctive feathery brows of the Coarch's line – a dominant trait – and when he qualified for the Fleet entrance exams it had seemed the best solution to everyone. Meluch himself had not been asked; he was a Zalosi, to go where the Coarchy directed.

'I wondered,' Admiral Dossignal went on, breaking into her musings, 'why so few? Altiplano is, I understand, an agricultural world. We usually get quite a few recruits from ag worlds.'

'It's not the usual sort of ag world, sir.' Esmay paused, wondering how much to explain. The admiral would have ample data available if he really wanted it.

'And why is that?' he asked. Perhaps he simply wanted her analysis, rather than the raw data.

'No free-birthers,' Esmay said succinctly. All the other reasons came back to that: with population growth under control, there were no idle hands to ship offplanet. Immigrants had to agree before they were accepted; if they already had reproduced, they had to agree to pre-emptive sterilization.

'But your family – how many sibs do you have?'

153

'Two, sir. But they're my father's second wife's, on her permits.' She did not mention what he could probably guess, that the birth limits were enforced more strictly on other families. Her father could have sired more children, but he had transferred his remaining permits to Sanni, who wanted them.

'I . . . see. And their attitude towards rejuvenation?'

She hesitated. 'I . . . know only my father's view, and my uncle's. They expressed concern about the effect on population stability, although the competitive value of ever-increasing experience would have a positive effect.'

'Mmm. So the senior military personnel on Altiplano have not been rejuved?'

'No, sir.'

'Did you sense any resentment of the Familias on that basis?'

Esmay felt uncomfortable, but answered with the truth as she saw it. 'No, sir, none. Altiplano's an independent; the admiral is no doubt aware that we have no sponsor with a Seat in Council, and Council policy affects us only inasmuch as it affects commercial law.'

'There's been some unrest, especially since the revelation about that mess on Patchcock,' the admiral said. 'There's now a strong political faction opposed to rejuvenation on the grounds that the rich old will exploit the poor unable to afford rejuvenation.'

'I don't think anyone on Altiplano feels exploited by the Familias,' Esmay said. 'Occasionally by each other . . .' More than occasionally, but she didn't see how her limited knowledge of Altiplanan local politics would make the situation clear. She didn't say the first thought that popped into her head, which was that any force trying to exploit Altiplano would have its work cut out for it.

'I'm glad to hear it,' the admiral said. 'I'll be seeing you from time to time – officers of the 14th get together regularly . . . Commander Atarin will let you know the next event.'

'Yes, sir; thank you.'

The first thing Esmay did after coming back from her interview with the admiral was pull a diagram of the various commands aboard the DSR. She had thought she understood how the chains of command ran, and who reported to whom about what . . . but several things the admiral had said left her confused.

A few hours later, she was only slightly less confused, but considerably entertained. With very few exceptions – and DSRs were the primary exception – Fleet vessels had a simple command structure, with the captain at the top, and authority descending rank by rank through the officers to the enlisted personnel. An admiral aboard a flagship had no direct authority over the ship's crew: all orders had to flow through the regular captain.

But the size of the newer DSRs had tempted Fleet to treat them as mobile bases. Rather than maintain separate technical schools and laboratory facilities at Sector HQ, staff had decided to put them abroad the *Koskiusko*, which needed most of the equipment anyway. Thus the *Koskiusko* had multiple commands, each headed by an admiral, which were expected to use the same facilities – and even the same experts – for different purposes. If Fleet had wanted to create a venue for massive turf battles, it could have invented no better arrangement.

Esmay found the debris of such battles in the files. The Special Materials Fabrication Facility, for instance: it was supposed to serve the 14th Heavy Maintenance Yard by making all the materials needed to maintain an inventory of structural members. But it also served the Senior Technical Schools, where students learned to make such materials, and the Special Materials Research Lab, where the most inventive materials scientists struggled to develop new materials with exotic properties.

On the first deployment a massive fight developed between the 14th Heavy Maintenance, which wanted a larger inventory of the crystal-bonded structural members for repair, and the other two commands, which insisted that they needed a guaranteed minimum access to the facility to fulfill their missions.

That argument had risen through the various chains of command until the admirals involved were, as Pitak put it, 'locked in a room to fight it out until only one emerged victorious.' The solution – a compromise reached with all admirals still alive and kicking vigorously – satisfied no one, but its inconvenience suggested that complaint would only make things worse.

Even the traditional division between the ship's crew and its

155

passengers had eroded. Though in theory Captain Hakin had the ultimate authority for the ship's security and functioning, his crew was outnumbered many times by the personnel of the 14th Heavy Maintenance Yard. When a previous Yard commander wanted to run an 'outrigger tube' between T-3 and T-4, between the lateral docking bays, he'd done so. Esmay found the furious correspondence launched by the then captain to the admiral then commanding the 14th Heavy Maintenance, and the directive from Sector HQ that the offending tube would be allowed to remain. The captain had been reassigned.

No wonder the ship's architecture didn't match the computer specs, and everyone needed update cubes to keep track of the changes!

Above the ship level, the chain of command looked more like a tree diagram. Captain Hakin's superior was Admiral Gourache, commander of this wave, whose superior was the Sector 14 commandant, Admiral Foxworth. Admiral Dossignal, however, reported directly to the sector commandant; he was responsible for all maintenance functions in the sector. Admiral Livadhi was Training Command's representative in this sector, and not under the sector commander at all: Fleet Headquarters had taken over all training functions sixty years before. Similarly, the medical command had its own separate chain, this time running back to Admiral Surgeon General Boussy, back at Rockhouse.

Her father would never have put up with this mess. On Altiplano, the military medical service was firmly and formally subordinate to the operational command. *Yes, and that's how he was able to conceal your trauma,* her memory prompted. *No one was going to argue with the hero of the war . . .*

That wasn't fair. She wasn't even sure it had been a military hospital. She wasn't going to think about it anyway. She put the displays away; she understood the command structure well enough now. She could start preparing for her presentation to the discussion group in two days.

The *Koskiusko* had a personnel complement the size of a small city or large orbital station, and the officer list alone was as large as the crew of any normal ship. Esmay knew that, in the intellectual sense, but when she saw the mass of ensigns jamming the lecture hall and crowding the passage outside, numbers became experience.

'You're not all in the tactics discussion group, surely,' she said to Ensign Dettin, who had offered to introduce her.

'No, sir. But a lot of others wanted to come – I'll have to shift some of them out, because they're overloading the compartment . . .' She could see that. All the seats had been taken long ago; ensigns were crowded knee to knee in front, and were sitting squashed together in the aisles and in back. They were jamming the passage outside, too.

She watched Dettin trying to shoo them back out, to no avail. She should, she realized, have told someone more senior about this . . . if she'd thought it would be more than a dozen or so ensigns, she would have. Dettin wasn't getting anywhere, and it was her responsibility. She reached for the microphone. 'Excuse me,' she said. Silence fell, chopping off words in mid-utterance. 'How many of you are regular members of the tactics discussion group?'

A few hands went up, about what she'd expected originally.

'This meeting was scheduled for that group,' Esmay said. 'We can't have a mob scene like this; it's not safe. Those of you who are not members of the discussion group will have to leave, until we're sure we have seating for that group, and then we'll see how many others we can accommodate.'

Low mutters of protest, but these were ensigns and she was a full lieutenant now. Squirming awkwardly, those crammed into the aisles began to stand up; those in front waited, perhaps hoping for a reprieve, but Esmay gave them a stern look. Slowly, more awkwardly than necessary, they heaved themselves up and shuffled out. She could hear raised voices from the passage, but first things first. Some of those in seats were now standing; some sat as if glued in place. She hoped those were all discussion group members.

'Ensign Dettin.' He looked mildly embarrassed. 'Make sure all the discussion group have seats – you know them all, don't you?'

'Yes, sir.'

'When they're seated, and if it's agreeable to the others, I don't mind having any spare seats filled. But that's all.'

'Sir.' He glanced around, his lips moving as he ran down some internal list. 'All here but two – they may be outside.'

'Go check on them. By name.'

He made his way up the crowded aisle and called out into the passage. A knot of ensigns congealed in the opening, and finally two more elbowed their way in. That left seats for another two dozen, Esmay figured. She wished she knew a fair way to allocate those seats, but it was too late for that. More quickly than they'd left, more ensigns came in until all seats were filled.

Dettin introduced her, excitement edging his voice. The lights dimmed, except where she stood. The eager young faces faded into a blur with highlights of eyes and teeth. She had not expected that, but after standing in the glare of flag officers' disapproval, she was not about to crumple in a merely visual spotlight.

She had prepared a display cube with the same information given in court: the geometry of the Xavier system, the disposition of Fleet vessels, available Xavieran and civilian vessels, the number and armament of the invaders. She had been over this so many times, for her counsel and for Board of Inquiry and for the court-martial, that she could have explained in her sleep just how outnumbered Serrano had been even before Hearne defected.

When she put up the first display, a faint sigh came from her audience. Breathless silence while she spoke, reciting the familiar sequence. Some of it she knew only by report, and she said that. But the events themselves were so compelling that no one seemed to mind: the Benignity intrusion, the lagging pair of Benignity ships . . . possibly a new tactic, possibly malfunction. No one knew for sure. The successful attack on those ships, the damage to one assault carrier, the effective ambush of the killer-scout sent to form its own ambush. The long and dangerous harrying of the invaders in their course to Xavier, the loss of the space station, the damage to the Xavieran cities.

'Only a scorch, after all,' she heard someone mutter. She stopped short; silence returned, thick and tense. She could not see, against the glare of light focussed on her, who had spoken.

'*Only* a scorch . . . someone thinks a scorch is a minor problem? Let me show you video . . .' She switched to that, the former capital of Xavier on one side of the screen, as it had been, a small city of wide streets and low stone buildings, gardens and tree-shaded parks. That was file footage from Fleet databanks; Xavier's own records had all been destroyed.

On the half screen, an uneven field of rubble, the shattered remains of trees, the languid columns of smoke twisting in their own heat, a damage assessment team from Fleet in their protective gear. The video pickup had zoomed in on dead bodies, human and animal. Esmay recognized a dead horse, if no one else did. 'All population centers,' Esmay said, 'were reduced like this. Fire destroyed outlying settlements, as well as millions of hectares of pasture and farm crops. A "scorch" is intended to leave the planet barely habitable for the Benignity's own troops, with return to agricultural production in three to five years. That doesn't leave much for the people who live there.'

'But weren't they all killed?' someone asked.

'No, thanks to the foresight of Commander Serrano and their own government. Most of the population survived in remote regions – they have caves, I heard – but their economic base is gone. It will take a generation or two just to recover what they lost.' She could imagine the sequence; Altiplano had suffered similar damage during the Succession Wars when their Founder had died. The years of hunger, while they reestablished their agricultural base. The years after that when just enough to eat was no longer enough. As distant as they were, they could not expect much help from the rest of the Familias, once some new crisis caught public attention.

Silence again, this time with a different flavor.

'Let's begin with the situation as it first appeared to Commander Serrano.' Esmay changed displays, to show the Xavier system again. 'Xavier had been troubled by periodic incursions over the past few years, that appeared to be independent raiders of some sort. These had threatened the orbital station, and in fact had damaged it on more than one occasion. Xavier's defense consisted of outmoded, undersupported Demoiselle-class ships, of which only one was really space-worthy by the present. The others had been cannibalized for parts to keep that one working. Xavier is off regular passenger service, and ships out its agricultural products – mostly large-animal semen, ova, and frozen embryos − aboard locally-owned private vessels. Nearly all its mining production is used locally, for building up the infrastructure.'

Esmay had not known any of this until she read Heris Serrano's brief − concise, but hardly brief in the usual terms − to the admiral. She had found it easy to follow, because Altiplano and Xavier had many similarities.

'The government enlisted Commander Serrano, then acting as a civilian captain of a private yacht − but a very well-armed one − in defense against just such a raider. As you might expect—' she allowed herself a brief smile '—the unsuspecting raider didn't have a chance.'

'How big was it?' came from the back of the room.

'According to scan reports at the time, it was an Aethar's World raider—' Esmay flashed the hull specifications on the display. 'Commander Serrano anticipated its attack course, and was able to surprise it.'

'But that wasn't the whole battle, was it? One lousy little raider?'

'No, of course not.' Esmay changed displays again, to show the location of Xavier relative to Benignity and Familias territory. 'Commander Serrano's scan techs noticed another ship in system, which appeared to be an observer . . . she suspected that the raider's attack was merely a probe for a larger invasion force. She transmitted that concern to the nearest Fleet headquarters.'

'And got a bunch of traitors,' came a mutter from midway back.

'Not a "bunch,"' Esmay said. 'Most of the officers and crew of all three ships were loyal, or things would have turned out very differently. Fleet dispatched a small force, under the command of Dekan Garrivay. Two patrol ships, one cruiser. The captains of all three ships were prepared to cooperate with the Benignity, but that is not true of others.'

'Exactly how many traitors were there, and how do we know they were all discovered?'

'I don't know the answer to either question,' Esmay said. 'Some died fairly quickly − it's impossible to determine their alliance. And it's possible − though unlikely − that some traitors did not reveal themselves during the fighting on each ship. The last estimate I saw was that five to ten percent of each crew was actually traitorous – that includes both officers and enlisted.'

She watched the sideways looks, as the young officers estimated how many of the people in the room that would be.

'Naturally, most of them were in fairly senior, critical posts. Five traitorous ensigns wouldn't do the enemy as much good as one captain and the senior scan tech. The problem for the Benignity, as I understand it, is that the sort of thing they planned at Xavier required their longstanding agents to identify themselves to each other – a very risky affair. This need to confer was their undoing.'

Esmay skipped rapidly past the still-classified methods by which Koutsoudas had overheard the conspirators in the midst of their plotting.

'Commander Serrano had to prevent Garrivay from destroying Xavier's orbital station, and she needed those ships to defend from the expected invasion. That meant she had to relieve Garrivay and the other traitorous captain of their commands, identify any other traitors, and rally the loyal crews.'

'Well, but she's Admiral Serrano's niece,' someone said. 'She could just say so—'

Esmay almost grinned. Had she ever been that naive, even before she went into Fleet?

'Commander Serrano, remember, was operating as a civilian, whose resignation from Fleet had been highly publicized. There is some evidence that Commander Garrivay worried about what she might do, especially the influence she might have on the Xavieran government. He was trying to discredit her there. But consider: you are a civilian – at least apparently civilian – and you are on a space station where two Fleet vessels are docked. Another one is on picket at a distance. How are you going to gain access to the docked ships? We don't let civilians just wander in. And once in, how are you going to convince an ignorant crew that their captain is a traitor, and you should be allowed to take over? Would you, for instance, readily believe that your captain was a traitor, just because someone told you so?'

She saw comprehension of the difficulties on most faces.

'I didn't,' she said, fighting down the tension of that confession.

'All I knew of the situation – as a jig on *Despite*, under Kiansa Hearne – was that we were on patrol, while the rest of the group was docked. I knew nothing about an invasion; we thought we had come to Xavier to babysit some paranoid colonists who had panicked over a perfectly ordinary random raid. A lot of us were annoyed that we'd missed the chance to compete in the annual Sector war games . . . we felt our gunnery was outstanding.'

'But surely you suspected—'

Esmay snorted. 'Suspected? Listen – my real concern was stuff disappearing out of personnel lockers. Minor theft. I didn't worry about the captain . . . the captain was the captain, doing her job of commanding the ship. I was a mere jig, doing my assigned job, which was servicing the automatic internal scanners and trying to find out who was getting into the lockers, and how. When the . . . mutiny started on *Despite*, I was so surprised I nearly got shot before I caught on.' She waited for the nervous giggles to die down.

'Yeah – like that. It was ridiculous . . . I couldn't believe it. Nor could most of us. That's why conspirators are always a step ahead of the people who get real work done . . . they can count on that surprise.'

'But how *did* Serrano get command?' someone asked.

'I can only tell you what I heard,' Esmay said. 'Apparently, she and some of her former crew got aboard by some ruse, asked to talk to Garrivay in his office. By good fortune – or perhaps she had some way of knowing – some of the other conspirators were there. She and her crew . . . killed them.'

'Right away? You mean they didn't try to talk them out of it?'

Esmay let that lie in a stillness that was as scornful as her own. When the stirring began, she ended it by speaking. 'When someone has determined on treason – is commanding a ship, and planning to deliver helpless civilians to the enemy – I doubt any moral homilies would change his mind. Commander Serrano made a command decision; she eliminated the most senior conspirators as quickly as possible. Even then it wasn't easy.'

Esmay put up new displays. 'Now – Captain Hearne took *Despite* – with me, and the rest of the crew – quickly out of Xavier system. Our exec was also involved, but the next junior officer was both loyal, and on the bridge to hear Commander Serrano's transmission to Captain Hearne, requesting her return to station and her assistance in defending Xavier. He actually began the mutiny, appealing to the bridge crew . . .' She stopped, flooded in memories of the next few hours. The contradictory orders on the ship's internal communications, the total confusion, the time it took – which now seemed inexplicable – for the loyalists to realize that a mutiny was necessary, and that they'd have to use deadly force on their crewmates.

'From the tactical point of view,' she said, forcing all that back down, 'Commander Serrano faced a very difficult task. The Benignity force arrived almost simultaneously with her assumption of command. Had she waited even a few more hours, it would have been impossible. The Benignity force—' Esmay outlined its specifications, reminding her audience of the usual tactics used by Benignity strike forces. Now, describing decisions and actions she had not personally witnessed, she found it easier to be calm and logical. This ship here, these over there, expected and unexpected choices of maneuver . . . results, neatly tabulated without reference to the people whose lives had just been changed forever.

All too soon, she had to come back to her own experience. She skipped over the internal battle for control of *Despite*. She had relived that too many times for the court to do it again, for these callow youngsters. But they needed to know how the battle ended, including the mistakes she had made.

'We came in too fast,' she said, displaying yet another visual. 'My concern was that we might arrive too late, and I assumed that any insertion barrage would be sufficiently dispersed. As you know, calculation of real elapsed time in multiple FTL hops is difficult at best – but the error is usually negative, not positive. As it happened, we made it through insertion safely, and skip-jumped to here—' she pointed. 'Without dumping enough residual vee. We were short-crewed, with some damage to the nav computers, so I couldn't get a quick solution to a microjump that would have allowed the right angular motion. So . . . we blew past Xavier, and in that interim *Paradox* took fatal damage.' More than eighteen hundred dead. Her fault. War left no margin for mistakes. She remembered the desperate scramble on the bridge of her ship, the bridge crew fighting to get control, to get a jump solution that would let them get back in time to do some good.

'We got a jump solution,' she said, leaving out the rest of it, that instant when she had to accept it, with the risk, or not. The risk had been substantial – the confidence interval on that very unorthodox jump was broad enough that they could have gone right into Xavier itself. 'And we came out of jump with a clear shot up the rear of the Benignity command cruiser.' And a vector that gave them only one chance for that shot. The crew that had resented losing a chance to become the Sector gunnery champions had made their shot in the narrow window . . . and then had managed to reposition *Despite* in a stable orbit.

'The Board of Inquiry,' Esmay said, 'did not approve of the means, though they liked the results.' She didn't want to discuss that; she hurried on to show how the Xavieran defenses had contributed: the suicidal use of phase cannon on a shuttle, the improvised mines, little *Grogon*'s few telling shots, the yacht's astonishing defeat of the killer-ship.

'Only because they weren't expected,' Esmay pointed out. 'The Benignity ship intended ambush – post-battle analysis picked up enough transmissions to know that – and simply didn't know the yacht was there. When it shut down active systems to lie low for several hours, it was an easy target.'

'What difference would it have made if *Despite* had also been in the Xavier system the whole time?'

An intelligent question, but difficult. 'By the ship stats, it would have improved the odds ratio only about fifteen percent. To my own knowledge, *Despite* had the best weapons performance in the Sector: whatever Hearne's failings, she demanded and got quick and accurate fire from her crew. But if it had stayed, it would have been a known quantity, and Commander Serrano's force would still have been outnumbered and outgunned. I haven't seen any of the senior analysts' reports, but my own guess is that its contribution throughout the long battle would have been less than its effectiveness as an unexpected opponent at the end. That is, however, only my guess – it does not change the fact that the lack of another hull severely limited Commander Serrano's choices of action – and that its absence was the result of treason.'

Silence, attentive and almost breathless. Esmay waited. Finally someone shifted, a very audible rasp of clothing against the seat cushions, and that broke their immobility. Ensign Dettin clambered up to take the podium, and thank her for her talk. Hands rose for more questions, but Esmay caught sight of senior rank in the rear. When had they come in? She hadn't noticed . . . but certainly no ensign guarding the door from other ensigns would refuse entry to the handful of majors and lieutenant commanders gathered there.

Dettin saw them, finally, and stopped short in his closing remarks. 'Uh . . . sir . . .?'

Commander Atarin, Esmay finally recognized as he moved out of the dimness back there and into the light. 'I presume you'd be willing to give the same briefing to senior officers?'

A shiver of apprehension ran down her backbone. She couldn't tell if he was angry, or amused; she didn't know whether to apologize or explain. Both were bad ideas, her family heritage reminded her. 'Of course, sir.' She choked back the automatic qualifiers: if she wasn't really qualified, why was she showing off to the ensigns?

'If I could have a word . . .' he murmured, his glance raking the ensigns, who immediately began scrambling from their seats to leave by the other entrance.

'Of course, sir.' Esmay retrieved her display cube from the projector, and came down from the dais. Major Pitak was not one of the officers there, and she didn't recognize any of the others besides Atarin. They gazed at the departing ensigns with the kind of neutral expression which she interpreted as trouble on the half-shell and bubbling from the broiler. Atarin said nothing more until the ensigns had gone.

'Very clearly explained, I thought,' he said then. Esmay did not relax; from his tone he might have been discussing a textbook, and she wasn't sure whether she was being considered the textbook's author or its topic. 'I was impressed with your analysis of your own errors.'

Textbook case of junior officer putting feet clumsily in mouth, then.

'Just how badly was that nav computer damaged?'

A factual question she could answer. 'It had taken direct fire – we'd replaced components from storage, but we couldn't get the microjump functions within 80 percent of normal function.'

One of the other officers spoke up. 'Couldn't you have used components from the weapons board? There's duplication in some of that, if I recall.'

'Yes, sir, there is. But we didn't want to risk having any delay in target acquisition or getting a firing solution.'

'Umm. So you were skip-jumping with a faulty system . . . a bit risky, wasn't it?'

Esmay could think of no real answer but a shrug; one did not offer shrugs. 'Somewhat risky, yes sir.' It had been terrifying at the time, as the confidence intervals broadened and she had had to feel her way from one jump to the next. Instinct, she had been well taught, made a lousy guide to navigation in space.

'When I read the Board of Inquiry report,' Atarin said, 'I didn't notice that they acknowledged the difficulty with the nav computer. I presume you mentioned it.'

'It was in the record, sir,' Esmay said. She had not dwelt on the difficulties it presented; it would have been whining, making excuses.

'Yes. Well, Lieutenant Suiza, I think you'd better expect an invitation to the senior tactics discussion group. I quite realize that you aren't a senior analyst – but I doubt we can resist having a firsthand account of so . . . striking . . . an engagement.'

'Yes, sir.'

'And you might want to check the orientation of your illustration eight . . . I think you've got the axes rotated ninety degrees . . . unless there was a reason for that.'

'Yes, sir.'

With a nod, Atarin led the other officers out. Esmay felt like falling into one of the seats and shaking for a half hour, but Dettin was peeking in at her, obviously hoping to chat.

'So you don't think she's rousing the ensigns to any sort of . . . undesirable activity?'

'No, sir. You know how ensigns are: they'll go after anyone with real experience to talk about. They love gory stories, and that's what they were hoping for. Instead, she gave them a perfectly straightforward account, as unexciting as possible, of an innately thrilling engagement. Absolutely no self-puffery at all, and no attempt to romanticize Commander Serrano, either. I've invited her to address the senior tactics discussion group – she'll get more intelligent questions there, but I suspect she'll answer them as well.'

'I don't want to make her into some sort of hero,' Admiral Dossignal said. 'It will rile our touchy captain. Too much attention—'

'Sir, with all due respect, she *is* a hero. She has not sought attention; from her record she never did. But she saved Serrano's ship – and Xavier – and we can't pretend it didn't happen. Letting her discuss it in professional terms is the best way to ensure that it doesn't become an unprofessional topic.'

'I suppose. When is she speaking? I'd like to be there.'

'The meeting after next. We have that continuing education required lecture next time.'

When Esmay reported to duty the next day, Major Pitak said, 'I hear you had an interesting evening. How does it feel to have an overflow audience? Ever thought of being an entertainer?'

The nightmares that had kept her awake most of the night put an edge in Esmay's voice. 'I wish they hadn't asked me!' Pitak's eyebrows rose. 'Sorry,' Esmay said. 'I just . . . would rather put it behind me.'

Pitak grinned sourly. 'Oh, it's behind you, all right – just as a thruster's behind a pod, pushing it ever onward. Face it, Suiza, you're not going to be an anonymous member of the pack ever again.'

Just like my father, Esmay thought. She couldn't think of anything to say.

'Listen to me,' Pitak said. 'You don't have to convince me that you're not a glory-hound. I doubt anyone who's ever served with you or commanded you thinks you're a glory-hound. But it's like anything else – if you stand in the rain, you get wet, and if you do something spectacular, you get noticed. Face it. Deal with it. And by the way, did you finish with that cube on hull specs of minesweepers?'

'Yes, sir,' Esmay said, handing it over, and hoping the topic had turned for good.

'I hear you're on the schedule for the senior tactics discussion group,' Pitak said. Esmay managed not to sigh or groan. 'If you've got any data on the hull damage to Serrano's ship, I'd like to hear about it. Also the Benignity assault carrier that blew in orbit . . . mines, I think it was . . . it would be helpful to know a little more about that. The mines and the hull both. I realize you weren't in the system for long afterwards, but perhaps . . .'

'Yes, sir.'

'Not that it's tactics proper, but data inform tactics, or should. I expect Commander Serrano made use of everything she knew about H&A.'

Forewarned by this exchange, Esmay was not surprised to be buttonholed by other senior officers in the days that followed. Each suggested particular areas she might want to cover in her talk, pertaining to that officer's specialty. She delved into the ship's databanks in every spare moment, trying to find answers, and anticipate other questions. Amazing how connected everything was . . . she had known the obvious for years, how the relative mass of Benignity and Fleet ships governed their chosen modes of action, but she'd never noticed how every detail, every subsystem, served the same aims.

Even recruitment policy, which she had not really thought of as related to tactics at all. If you threw massive ships in large numbers into an offensive war, seeking conquest, you expected heavy losses . . . and needed large numbers of troops, both space and surface. Widespread conscription, especially from the long-conquered worlds, met that need for loyal soldiers. Recent conquests supplied a conscripted civilian work force for low-level, labor-intensive industries. A force primarily defensive, like the Familias Regular Space Service, manning smaller ships with more bells and whistles, preserved its civilian economic base by not removing too many young workers into the military. Hence hereditary military families who did not directly enter the political hierarchy.

Fascinating, once she thought about it this way. She couldn't help thinking what widespread rejuvenation would do to this structure, stable over the past hundred or more years. Then she surprised herself when she anticipated the next set of hull specs on Benignity killer-escorts . . . on their choice of hull thickness for assault carriers. How had she known? Her father's brusque *You're a Suiza!* overrode the automatic thought that she must have seen it before somewhere, she couldn't possibly be smart enough to guess right.

By the time of her second presentation, she felt stuffed with new knowledge barely digested. She'd checked her illustrative displays (yes, number eight had been rotated ninety degrees from the standard references) and assembled what she hoped were enough background references.

10

'Looks like you came prepared,' Major Pitak said, as Esmay lugged her carryall of cubes and printouts into the assigned conference room. This was a large hall in the Technical Schools wing, T-1, its raked seating curved around a small stage.

'I hope so, sir,' Esmay said. She could think of two dozen more cubes she might need, if someone asked one of the less likely questions. She had come early, hoping for a few minutes alone to set up, but Pitak, Commander Seveche, and Commander Atarin were already there. Her chain of command, she realized.

'Would you like any help with your displays?' Atarin asked. 'The remote changer in this room hangs up sometimes.'

'That would be helpful, yes, sir. The first are all set up on this cube—' she held it out. 'But I've got additional visuals if the group asks particular questions.'

'Fine, then. I've asked Ensign Serrano to make himself available – I'll call him in.'

Serrano. She hadn't met him yet, and after what she'd said at dinner, no one had gossiped more about him in her presence. She hadn't wanted to seek him out. What could she have said? *I saved your aunt's life; your grandmother talked to me; let's be friends*? No. But she had been curious.

Her first thought when he walked in was that he had the look of a Serrano: dark, compact, springy in motion, someone whose entire ancestry was spangled with stars, someone whose family expected their offspring to become admirals, or at least in contention. Her second was that he seemed impossibly young to bear the weight of such ambition. If he had not worn ensign's insignia, she'd have guessed him to be about sixteen, and in the prep school.

She had known there were young Serranos, of course, even before she got to the *Koskiusko*. They could not be hatched out full-grown as officers of some intermediate grade. They had to be born, and grow, like anyone else. But she had never seen it happen, and the discovery of a young Serrano – younger than she was – disturbed her.

'Lieutenant Suiza, this is Ensign Serrano.' The glint in his dark eyes looked very familiar.

'Sir,' he said formally, and twitched as if he would have bowed in other circumstances. 'I'm supposed to keep your displays straightened out.' Generations of command had seeped into his voice, but it was still expressive.

'Very well,' Esmay said. She handed over the cube with her main displays, and rummaged in the carryall. 'That one's got the displays that I know I'll need – and here, this is the outline. They're in order, but in case someone wants to see a previous display, these are the numbers I'll be calling for. Now these—' she gave him another three cubes, '—these have illustrations I might need if someone brings up particular points. I'm afraid you'll have to use the cube index . . . I didn't know I'd have any assistance, so there's no hardcopy listing. I'll tell you which cube, and then the index code.'

'Fine, sir. I can handle that.' She had no doubt he could.

Other officers were arriving, greeting each other. Ensign Serrano took her cubes and went off somewhere – Esmay hoped to a projection booth – while she organized the rest of her

170

references. The room filled, but arriving officers left a little group of seats in front as if they'd had stars painted on them. In a way, they did . . . the admirals and the captain came in together, chatting amiably. Admiral Dossignal nodded at her; he seemed even taller next to Captain Hakin. On the captain's other side, Admiral Livadhi fiddled with his chair controls, and Admiral Uppanos, commander of the branch hospital, leaned toward his own aide with some comment. Atarin stood to introduce Esmay; with the admirals' arrival, the meeting started.

Esmay began with the same background material. No one made comments, at least not that she could hear. All her displays projected right-side-up and correctly oriented . . . she had checked them repeatedly, but she'd had a nagging fear. This time, her recent research in mind, she added what she had learned about the Benignity's methods, about the implications of Fleet protocols. Heads nodded; she recognized an alert interest far beyond the ensigns' hunger for exciting stories.

When the questions began, she found herself exhilarated by the quality of thought they implied. These were people who saw the connections she had only just found, who had been looking for them, who were hungry for more data, more insights. She answered as best she could, referencing everything she said. They nodded, and asked more questions. She called for visuals, trusting that the Serrano ensign would get the right ones in the right order. He did, as if he were reading her mind.

'So the yacht didn't actually get involved in the battle? Aside from that one killer-escort?'

'No, sir. I have only secondhand knowledge of this, but it's my understanding that the yacht had only minimal shields. It had been used primarily to suggest the presence of other armed vessels, and would not have fired if the Benignity vessel hadn't put itself in such a perfect situation.'

'It can only have confused them briefly,' a lieutenant commander mused from near the back. 'If they had accurate scans, the mass data would show—'

'But I wanted to ask about that ore-carrier,' someone else

171

interrupted. 'Why did Serrano have it leave the . . . what was it? Zalbod?'

'It's my understanding that she didn't, sir. The miners themselves decided to join in—'

'And it shouldn't have got that far, not with the specs you've shown. How did they get it moving so fast?'

Esmay had no answer for that, but someone else in Drive & Maneuver did. A brisk debate began between members of the D&M unit . . . Esmay had never been attracted to the theory and practice of space-drive design, but she could follow much of what they said. If this equipment could be reconfigured it would give a 32 percent increase in effective acceleration. . . .

'They'd still arrive too late to do any good, but that's within the performance you're reporting. I wonder which of them thought it up . . .'

'*If* that's what they did,' another D&M officer said. 'For all we know, they cooked up something unique.'

Esmay snorted, surprising herself and startling them all into staring at her. 'Sorry, sir,' she said. 'Fact is, they cooked up a considerable brew, and I heard about the aftermath.' Scuttlebutt said that Lord Thornbuckle's daughter had been dumped naked in a two-man rock-hopper pod . . . supposedly undamaged . . . and the pod jettisoned by mistake into the weapons-crowded space between the ore-carrier and Xavier. Esmay doubted it was an accident . . . but the girl had survived.

Brows raised, the officer said, 'I wonder . . . if they added a chemical rocket component . . . that might have given them a bit of extra push.'

The talk went on. They wanted to know every detail of the damage to *Despite* from the mutiny: what weapons had been used, and what bulkheads had been damaged? What about fires? What about controls, the environmental system failsafes, the computers? The admirals, who had sat quietly listening to the questions of their subordinates, started asking questions of their own.

Esmay found herself saying 'I'm sorry, sir, I don't know that,' more often than she liked. She had not had time to examine the spalling caused by projectile hand weapons . . . to assess the effect of sonics on plumbing connections . . .

'Forensics . . .' she started to say once, and stopped short at their expressions.

'Forensics cares about evidence of wrongdoing,' Major Pitak said, as if that were a moral flaw. 'They don't know diddly about materials . . . they come asking *us* what it means if something's lost a millimeter of its surface.'

'That's not entirely fair,' another officer said. 'There's that little fellow in the lab back on Sturry . . . I've gone to him a few times asking about wiring problems.'

'But in general—'

'In general yes. Now, Lieutenant, did you happen to notice whether the bulkhead damage you mentioned in the crew compartments caused any longitudinal variation in artificial gravity readings?'

She had not. She hadn't noticed a lot of things, in the middle of the battle, but no one was scolding her. They were galloping on, like headstrong horses, from one person's curiosity to another's. Arguments erupted, subsided, and began again with new questions.

Esmay wondered how long it would go on. She was exhausted; she was sure they had run over the scheduled meeting time – not that anyone was going to tell the captain and senior officers to vacate the place. Finally Atarin stood, and the conversation died.

'We're running late; we need to wrap this up. Lieutenant, I think I speak for all of us when I say that this was a fascinating presentation – a very competent briefing. You must have done a lot of background work.'

'Thank you, sir.'

'It's rare to find a young officer so aware of the way things fit together.'

'Sir, several other officers asked questions ahead of time, which sent me in the right directions.'

'Even so. A good job, and we thank you.' The others nodded; Esmay was sure the expressions held genuine respect. She wondered why it surprised her – why her surprise made her feel faintly guilty. The admirals and the captain left first, then the others trailed away, still talking among themselves. Finally they were all gone, the last of them trailing out the door. Esmay sagged.

'That was impressive, Lieutenant,' Ensign Serrano said as he handed her the stack of cubes. 'And you kept track of which display went with which question.'

'And you handled them perfectly,' Esmay said. 'It can't have been easy, when I had to skip from one cube to another.'

'Not that difficult – you managed to slide in those volume numbers every time. You certainly surprised them.'

'Them?'

'Your audience. Shouldn't have – they had recordings of the talk you gave the juniors. This was just fleshed out, the grown-up version.'

Was this impertinence? Or genuine admiration? Esmay wasn't sure. 'Thanks,' she said, and turned away. She would worry about it tomorrow, when Major Pitak would no doubt keep her busy enough that she wouldn't really have time. The young Serrano gave her a cheerful nod before taking himself off somewhere.

The next morning, Major Pitak said, 'You know, there are still people who think that mutiny must've been planned ahead.'

Esmay managed not to gulp. 'Even now?'

'Yes. They argue that if Hearne knew she was going to turn traitor, she'd have her supporters in key positions, and it would have been impossible to take the ship without doing critical damage.'

'Oh.' Esmay could think of nothing further to say. If after all the investigation and the courts-martial, they wanted to believe that, she didn't think she could talk them out of it.

'Fleet's in a difficult situation right now . . . what with the government in transition, and all these scandals . . . I don't suppose you'd heard much about Lepescu.' Pitak was looking at her desk display, a lack of eye contact that Esmay realized must be intentional.

'A few rumors.'

'Well. It was more than rumors – that is, I know someone who knew . . . more than she wanted. Admiral Lepescu liked war and hunting . . . for the same reasons.'

'Oh?'

'He got to kill people.' Pitak's voice was cold. 'He hunted

people, that is, and your Commander Serrano caught him at it, and shot him. A result that suits me, but not everyone.'

'Was he a Benignity agent?'

Pitak looked surprised. 'Not that anyone noticed. I've never heard *that* rumor. Why?'

'Well . . . I heard that Commander Garrivay – who had the command of—'

'Yes, yes, the force sent to Xavier. I don't forget that quickly, Suiza!'

'Sorry, sir. Anyway, I heard he had served under Lepescu. And Garrivay *was* a Benignity agent . . . or at least a traitor in their pay.'

'Mmm. Keep in mind that there are officers on this ship who served under Lepescu some time back. Far enough back not to be caught by Serrano, but . . . that might not be a healthy thing to speculate about, whether he was an agent or not.'

'No, sir. Anyway, he's dead, so it doesn't matter.' The moment it was out of her mouth she wished she hadn't said it; the look on Pitak's face was eloquent. It mattered, if only to the dead, and given Pitak's expression it mattered to some of the living too. It probably mattered to Heris Serrano. 'Sorry,' she said, feeling the hot flush on her face. 'That was stupid . . .'

'Um. Just watch yourself, Lieutenant.'

'Sir.'

Since she didn't have another public appearance to get ready for, she headed for the gym when she came offshift. She'd missed out on her regular exercise.

The gym was crowded at this hour, but almost at once one of the machines came vacant, and the jig who'd been leaning against the bulkhead waiting waved her on. 'Go on, Lieutenant. I'd really rather have one of the horsebots.'

Esmay climbed onto the machine and set it for her usual workout. She had been aware of quiet competition to have the machine next to hers in the exercise room, the eagerness to invite her onto wallball teams despite her indifferent play, the little favors offered casually. She supposed it would go away in time, when people forgot about her so-called fame. She had never had really close friends in Fleet, and she didn't expect to acquire any now. Her mind hung on that thought. Why shouldn't she have friends? If people liked her, and they seemed to . . .

It was only her transient fame. It had nothing to do with her real self.

Could she be sure?

She worked harder, until she was breathless and sweating and all thought of friends had vanished in the struggle for breath and strength.

At dinner, she listened to the chatter at her table with a mind uncluttered by worry about a coming presentation. Ensign Zintner's enthusiasm for Hull & Architecture reminded her of Luci's uncomplicated enthusiasm for stock breeding. She could like Zintner. She glanced around the mess hall, and found another female lieutenant watching her. It made her feel itchy, and she looked back at her plate. The hard workout had damped her appetite; she would be hungry in three hours, but not now.

On her way out, two other lieutenants stopped her. 'If you don't have duty tonight, would you like to come watch a show with us?' They had asked before, but she had been preparing for the discussion group presentation. Now she had no excuse ready. She agreed to come, expecting to slip away after a few minutes.

Instead, she found herself locked into a row of others, with someone leaning over the back of her seat to speak to her. When the show started, she had that much peace, but as soon as it was over, she found herself the center of attraction.

It was ludicrous. It could not be real liking, real interest. It was only her notoriety. She hated herself for enjoying it, even the small amount that she did enjoy. She shouldn't like it; the only legitimate way for an Altiplano woman to be the center of attention was as matriarch of a family. Her great-grandmother would scold . . . her great-grandmother was light years away, if she was still alive.

Esmay shivered, and someone said 'Are you all right . . . Esmay?' She looked over. A lieutenant . . . Kartin Doublos . . . so the use of her first name was not familiarity, but the normal usage between those of the same rank off duty.

'I'm fine,' she said. 'I just thought of my great-grandmother.' He looked puzzled, but shrugged it off.

Over the next weeks, she noticed that the interest in her, the competition for her attention, did not slack off. It puzzled her. What could they hope to gain? What were they trying to prove?

Tickling at the edge of her mind were all the things Admiral Serrano had said . . . that legal counsel had said . . . and her father . . . and Major Pitak. She pushed them aside. She could not cope with a demand to break out of the comfortable safe niche she had created for herself. She would crawl back into it, pull it around her, an inviolable shield.

The nightmares came oftener, further proof that she was not, could not be, the person these others seemed determined to see. Not every night, but especially after those times when someone had talked her into a game, a show, some recreation which had – as far as she could tell – no connection with the content of either set of dreams. She started running a noise generator in her compartment, hoping it would cover any sound she made. No one had complained, but when she woke, heart pounding, at 0300, she was always afraid she had cried out in real life the way she had in the dream.

The dreams tangled, the helpless child caught in a war she did not understand merging abruptly into the terrified young officer belly-down on a bloody deck, firing into the haze.

She considered going to Medical. She would have to, if it affected her performance. So far it had not, that she could tell. Pitak seemed pleased with her progress; she got along fine with Master Chief Sivars, whose massive frame was so unlike Seb Coron's that she was startled only occasionally by the same kind of attitude.

'And how is Lieutenant Suiza shaping, Major?' Commander Seveche asked, at the quarterly review.

'Very well, of course.' Pitak looked down at the record cube she held. 'She's worked hard to get herself up to speed, though she has no background in heavy engineering and she'll never be the technical help that Bascock was.'

'She shouldn't be technical track at all,' Seveche said. 'That presentation to the senior tactical came out of a command-track mind.'

'She asked for technical,' Admiral Dossignal said, but with the quirk in the corner of his mouth that his subordinates knew meant he was playing devil's advocate.

'I think it was the colonial background,' Seveche said. 'I looked up Altiplano's cultural index. Even though she's a general's daughter, they have no tradition of women commanders.'

'Of women in the military, period,' Dossignal said. 'I saw the same report.'

'Well, then. And the juniors are around her like bees around honey.'

'Which she isn't comfortable with,' Pitak said. 'She's muttered to me about it, claims not to understand it. If that's honest, and I think it is, she's got no insight into her abilities . . .'

'Which you say aren't technical.'

'Well . . .' Pitak considered. 'I don't want to overstate it. She's got the brains, and she's applying herself. I can't speak for her qualifications in scan, but she's merely a studious amateur where H&A's concerned. And there's her habit of seeing everything in operational terms.'

'Example?'

'Well . . . she's completed the second course in hull design, and I assigned her a report on the modifications necessary to support the new stealth hardware. I was looking for the usual, what I'd have gotten from Ensign Zintner: where to install it based on its need for power, its effect on the center of gravity, and so on. All technical. What she came up with was an analysis of the performance changes in terms of operational capability. I pointed this out, and she blinked twice and said "Oh – but isn't that what really matters?"'

Seveche and Dossignal laughed. 'Yes,' said the admiral, 'I see what you mean. To her, everything matters because of its use in battle—'

'Which is what's supposed to matter to us,' Pitak said. 'I know that . . . but I also know that I personally get sidetracked into neat engineering problems, technical bits for the sake of technical bits. She doesn't appear to, and I wonder if she ever did, even in scan.'

'I doubt it,' Dossignal said. 'Because of her record on Xavier, they sent along the entire personnel file. Along with all those ordinary fitness reports, in which she came up bland and colorless and mediocre, there are her Academy ratings. Guess which courses she topped out in?'

'Not tactics and maneuver?'

'No . . . though she was in the top 5 percent there. Try military history. She wrote a paper analyzing the Braemar Campaign, and was invited to consider an appointment to postgraduate work as a scholar. She turned it down, and applied for technical track instead, where she'd never excelled.'

'That's odd,' Pitak said, frowning.

'It's more than odd,' Dossignal said. 'It makes no sense. I can't find anything in the file to show that she was counseled against command track, though I do find the usual comments about non-Fleet family backgrounds down in her prep school files. Yet they assigned her to technical track, purely on the basis of her request and her fairly mediocre scores.'

'What were her personal evaluations?'

'What you'd expect for an outsider who wasn't pushing for command track . . . I don't know why we still use those things. If Personnel would ever go back and check officer performance against the predictions of the personal evaluations, they'd have to admit they're useless. She came out midrange in everything except initiative, where she was low-average.'

'On which I'd rate her quite high,' Pitak said. 'She doesn't wait to be told, if she knows what she's doing.'

'The question is, what do we do about her?' Dossignal asked. 'We've got her for a couple of years, and we can teach her a lot about maintenance . . . but is that the best use of her talents?'

Seveche looked at Atarin and Pitak. 'I'd have to say no, sir, it's not. She's a good speaker, a good tactical analyst – she might make a good instructor. Or . . .' His voice trailed away.

'Or the kind of ship commander she was in the Xavier action,' Dossignal said. Silence held the group for a moment.

'That's a risky prediction,' Atarin muttered.

'True. But – compare her even to officers several ranks ahead of her, in their first combat command. I think we'd agree that she has abilities she has shown only rarely – abilities Fleet needs, if she's really got them and can unlock them. I see that as our task: getting this potentially outstanding young officer to show her stuff.'

'But how, sir?' asked Pitak. 'I like the girl, truly. But – she's so reserved, even with me, even after this much time. How do we get the lid off?'

'I don't know,' Dossignal admitted. 'Engineering is my strength, not combat. I know we can't ask Captain Hakin, because he's half-convinced she's a mutineer. But if we all agree that the best use of Lieutenant Suiza is elsewhere, then at least we'll be looking for opportunities to nudge her that way.'

Atarin chuckled suddenly. 'When I think of all the youngsters who fantasize being heroic ship captains . . . all the untalented children of famous families . . . and here's a shy, inhibited genius who just needs a good kick in the pants—'

'I just hope we can administer that kick in the pants before life does,' Pitak said. 'However hard we kick her, reality can do worse.'

'Amen to that,' Dossignal said. He picked up another file. 'Now – let's get to the ensigns. Zintner, for instance—'

Esmay had not run into the Serrano ensign for some time; she had seen him occasionally playing wallball or working out with someone on the mats, but he had never approached her. Now, the rotation in table assignments put him at hers. She nodded at him as the others introduced themselves.

'You're in remote sensing, aren't you, Ensign?'

'Yes, sir.'

'Your first choice?'

'Actually no.' He made a face. 'But I had a short-term assignment right out of the Academy, and then I was off-schedule for normal ship rotations.'

'It's a wonder,' a jig to his right said. 'I thought Serranos got whatever they wanted.'

The Serrano ensign stiffened for an instant, but then shrugged. 'It's a reputation perhaps not quite deserved,' he said, in a colorless voice.

'And what's your specialty?' Esmay asked the jig. What was his name? Plecht, or something like that.

'I'm taking an advanced course,' the jig said, as if that should impress her. 'I'm doing research in low-temperature material fabrication,' he said. 'But probably nobody would understand it unless they were working in the field.'

Esmay considered her options, and decided on blandness. He was making enough of an idiot of himself already. 'I'm sure you're very good at what you do,' she said, with as little expression as she could manage. It was still too much; two of the ensigns, but not Barin Serrano, snorted and choked on their soup.

On the way out, she got two invitations to come watch the junior officers' parpaun semifinals match.

'No, thank you,' she said to each. 'I really should spend some time in the gym myself.' It was not an excuse; she was still having trouble with nightmares anytime she did not work out to exhaustion. She was sure she would outlast them in time, but for now she was spending a couple of hours a day in the gym.

The parpaun matches had thinned out the gym; Esmay saw only three others, each engrossed in his or her own program. She turned on her favorite machine. Someone had left the display wall on its mirrored setting; she faced her reflection and automatically looked away from the face. Her legs, she saw, looked hard and fit. She should probably do more with her upper body. But what? She didn't feel like swimming, or using the machines designed for upper-body-building. What she wanted was a scramble up some rocks, nothing really hard but movements less regular than a machine would demand.

'Excuse me, Lieutenant . . .'

Esmay jumped, then was furious with herself for reacting that way. She looked; it was Ensign Serrano, with what she privately considered *that look* on his face.

'Yes?' she said.

'I just wondered . . . if the lieutenant . . . would like a sparring partner.'

She stared at him in sheer surprise. It was the last invitation she'd expected from a Serrano . . . from him. 'Not you!' got out before she could censor it; he flushed but looked stubborn.

'Not me? Why?'

'I thought you were different,' she said.

This time he understood; the flush deepened, and then he went

181

as pale as a bronze-skinned Serrano could and pulled himself up angrily. 'I don't have to suck up to you. I have more influence in my family—' He stopped, but Esmay knew what he would have said – could have said. With the Serrano Admiralty behind him, he didn't need her. 'I liked you,' he said, still angry. 'Yes, my cousin mentioned you, and yes, of course I saw the media coverage. But that's not why—'

Esmay felt guilty for misjudging him, and perversely annoyed with him for being the occasion of her misjudgment. 'I'm sorry,' she said, wishing she felt more gracious about it. 'It was very rude of me.'

He stared at her. 'You're *apologizing?*'

'Of course.' That got out before Esmay could filter it, the tone as surprised as his and making it clear that in her world all decent people apologized. 'I misinterpreted your actions—'

'But you're—' He stopped short again, clearly rethinking what he had started to say. 'It's just – I don't think it needed an apology. Not from a lieutenant to an ensign, even if you did misunderstand my motives.'

'But it was an insult,' Esmay said, her own temper subsiding. 'You had a right to be angry.'

'Yes . . . but you making a mistake and me being angry isn't enough for an apology like that.'

'Why not?'

'Because—' He looked around; Esmay became aware of un-natural silence, and when she looked saw the other exercisers turning quickly away. 'Not here, sir. If you really want to know—'

'I do.' While she had a captive informer willing to explain, she wanted to know why, because it had bothered her for years that Fleet officers routinely shrugged off their discourtesies without apology.

'Then – no offense intended – we should go somewhere else.'

'For once I wish this was home,' Esmay said. 'You'd think on a ship this size there'd be someplace quiet to talk that didn't imply things . . .'

'If the lieutenant would consider a suggestion?'

'Go ahead.'

'There's always the Wall,' he said. 'Up in the gardens.'

'Gardens don't imply things?' Esmay said, brows rising. They certainly did on Altiplano, where *They're in the garden* meant knowing smirks and raised brows.

'No – the Wall. The climbing wall. Even if you haven't ever climbed a real rock . . .'

'I have,' Esmay said. 'You mean they have a fake rock wall?'

'Yes, sir. And the parpaun match is on the way.'

Esmay grinned, surprising herself. 'I always heard Serranos were devious. All right. I'd like to try this fake cliff.'

The cliff, when they arrived, was festooned with would be climbers wearing all the accouterments of their sport. Esmay stared up at the safety lines swinging from the overhead. 'Sorry,' Barin said. 'I thought they'd be gone by now – it's past the time the climbing club usually finishes, and no one else ever seems to use it.'

'Never mind,' Esmay said. 'They're not paying any attention to us.' She examined the cliff closely. The indentations the climbers were using for their feet and hands were molded fiber-ceram, attached to the cliff face with metal clamps. 'It looks like fun.'

'It is, though I'm not very good at it.' Barin peered upward. 'But one of my bunkies is an enthusiast, and he's dragged me along a few times. That's how I know when they're *usually* done.'

'Come on up . . .' someone yelled from far above.

Esmay fitted her hand into one of the holds. 'I don't think so – I don't have any gear, and besides . . . we had a conversation going.'

'A conversation or an argument?' Barin asked, then flushed again. 'Sorry, sir.'

'No offense taken,' Esmay said. Around the base of the fake cliff, decorative rocklike forms had been placed to mark off the climbing area from the garden beds. She found a comfortable niche and sat down. 'I'm not letting you off, though. If you can explain the protocols of apologies in Fleet, I'll be forever grateful.'

'Well, as I said, what you called an insult is not that important . . . I mean, unless you really wanted my friendship, and that's personal. Is it on your world?'

On her world, duels would have been fought, and honor would have been satisfied, for the apologies Fleet never bothered with. Would he think her people barbaric, because they cared? 'It's different,' Esmay said, thinking how to say it without implying what she really felt about their manners. 'We do tend to apologize easily for things . . .'

He nodded. 'So that's why Com – some people think of you as tentative.'

Esmay ignored the slip, though she wondered which commander. 'They do?'

'Yes . . . at least that's what I've heard some people say. You apologize for things we – sorry, most of the Fleet families – wouldn't, things we just take for granted. So it seems as if you're not sure of what you're doing.'

Esmay blinked, thinking back down her years in Fleet, from the prep school on. She had made a lot of mistakes; she had expected to. She had been guided by the family rules: tell the truth, admit your mistakes, don't make the same mistakes twice, apologize promptly and fully for your errors. How could they think that was weakness and uncertainty? It was willingness to learn, willingness to be guided.

'I see,' she said slowly, though she still didn't understand. 'So . . . when you make a mistake you don't apologize?'

'Not unless it's pretty massive – oh, you say you're sorry, if you step on someone's foot, but you don't make a procedure out of it. Most mistakes – you own up, of course, and take the responsibility, but the apology is understood.'

It was not understood, Esmay was sure, nearly as well as an apology properly delivered in plain speech. However, if they chose to be rude about it, she couldn't change that. 'Is it offensive?' she asked, intent on mapping the edges of Fleet courtesy.

'Oh no, not offensive. A little bothersome, if someone's always doing it – it makes seniors a bit nervous, because they don't know how sincere it is.'

Esmay felt her brows rising. 'You have insincere apologies?'

'Of course,' he said. Then he took another look at her face. 'You don't,' he said. Not a question.

'No.' Esmay took a long breath. She felt as if she'd ridden out into a dry riverbed and sunk hock-deep in quicksand. She went on, quickly, keeping her voice as unemotional as possible. 'In our – on our world, an apology is always part of taking responsibility for errors. It accompanies action taken to redress the wrong and ensure that the error is not repeated.' That was almost a quote from the Conventions. 'An insincere apology is like any other lie.' Serious, she meant, and her mouth tingled at the memory of the hot peppers that had impressed her with the importance of telling the truth, no matter how unpleasant. She had not suspected her father of an insincere apology . . . just one far too late and insufficient.

'Fascinating,' he said; by his tone he meant it the right way, real interest and not idle curiosity about the barbarians. 'It must be very different, if you didn't know – I mean—'

'I understand what you mean,' said Esmay. 'It's – a new idea for me, that apologies could get me into trouble.'

'Not trouble exactly, but the wrong idea about you.'

'Yes. I take your point. Thank you for the information.'

'You don't have to thank—' Again that bright-eyed look. 'But you do, don't you? Thanking goes with apologizing . . . your world must be terribly formal.'

'Not to me,' Esmay said. It wasn't formality, it was caring about how others felt, caring how your actions affected them. Formality was Founders' Day dinners, or the awards ceremonies, not one of the twins coming in to apologize for having broken her old blue mug.

'Do we – I mean, do the others born into Fleet – seem rude to you?'

Should she answer that? She couldn't lie, and he had been unexpectedly honest with her. 'Sometimes,' Esmay said. She forced herself to smile. 'I expect that I sometimes seem rude to you – or them.'

'Not rude,' he said. 'Very polite – extremely polite, even formal. Everyone says how nice you are – so nice they couldn't figure out how you could do what you did.'

Esmay shivered. Did they really think rudeness went with strength, with the killing way, that someone who said please and thank you and I'm sorry couldn't fight or command in battle? A grim satisfaction flowered briefly: if the Altiplano militia ever came offplanet, Fleet wouldn't know what hit them. *Pride is a blossom of ashes*. The old saying rang in her ears. *Bitter in the mouth*,

185

sharp to the nose, stinging to the eyes, and blown away on the first wind from the mountains. Plant no pride, lest you harvest shame. She almost shook her head to free it from that old voice.

'I'm not sure myself how I did what I did – besides making a great number of unnecessary mistakes.'

'Mistakes! You stopped a Benignity invasion—'

'Not by myself.'

'Well, no, you weren't out there on your white horse galloping across the stars alone.' He sounded as sarcastic as he looked.

This time Esmay took the offensive. 'Why do you people use that image so much? The white horse thing, I mean. Yes, we use horses on Altiplano, but where did you get the idea that they're all white?'

'Oh, that's not about *you*,' he said. 'Nor Altiplano. It's from the Tale of the White Knights, who all rode white horses and spent their time doing great deeds. Didn't you have that in your libraries?'

'Not that I know of,' Esmay said. 'Our folk tales ran to Brother Ass and the Cactus Patch. Or the Starfolk and the Swimmers of Dawn. The only heroes on horses we know about were the Shining Horde.'

He blinked. 'You really do come from another culture. I thought everybody had grown up with the White Knights, and I never heard of the Swimmers of Dawn, or Brother Ass. The Shining Horde – that wasn't an ancestor of the Bloodhorde, was it?'

'No.' That thought sickened her. 'They're just legends; supposedly they were people with strange powers, who could glow in the dark.' She glared at the twinkle in his eye. 'Without getting too close to atomics,' she said firmly.

The climbers, now near the base of the wall, ended that conversation. Esmay went over to see what equipment they used – much like that she'd used at home – and was offered more help than she wanted if only she'd join the climbing club. They would teach her; she could start on the easy end.

'I've scrambled around some boulders,' she said.

'Well, you should come join us,' one of the climbers said. 'We can always use new members and soon you'll be right up there—'

he pointed. 'It's like nothing else, and this is the only ship I know with a real Wall.' He was so clearly entwined in his hobby that Esmay felt no embarrassment; he would have welcomed anyone willing to climb off the flat deck. 'Come on – just go up a little, and let me see how you move. Pleeease?'

Esmay laughed, and started up the wall. She had never done as much climbing as her male cousins, but she had learned how to reach and shift her center of gravity without swinging away from the slope. She made it up a meter or so before losing her grip and slithering back down.

'Good start,' the tall climber said. 'You'll have to come again ... I'm Trey Sannin, by the way. If you need climbing gear, there's some in our club lockers.'

'Thanks,' Esmay said. 'I might do that. When's your meeting time?' Sannin told her, then led the other climbers away. 'And thank you,' she said to Barin. 'I'm sorry I misjudged you, and you'll just have to put up with my apology – at least this time.'

'Gladly,' he said. He had an engaging grin, she noticed, and she felt an impulse to trust him even more than she had already.

That night she slept free of nightmares, and dreamed of climbing the cliffs of home with a dark-haired boy who was not quite Barin Serrano.

11

Over the next few decads, Esmay found herself chatting with Barin Serrano even away from the mess hall. They had gone climbing once, with the club, and after a couple of hours of sweating on the Wall, she could not be shy with any of the climbers, let alone Barin. Then they had found themselves in the same corner during one of the officer socials, simply because Ensign Zintner had cornered a tray of the best cookies and they'd spotted her doing it.

Esmay did not let herself notice that the nightmares were not as intense on the evenings she spent with Barin and his friends. Instead, she concentrated on what he could show her about the unofficial customs of Fleet. Gradually, she thought of him less and less as 'that nice Serrano boy' and more and more as the kind of friend she had not known she wanted.

In his company, she found herself making other friends. Zintner, whose lifelong background in heavy engineering made her the ideal person to ask for references when Pitak had handed Esmay a problem she couldn't solve. Lieutenant Forrester, who came to the climbing club meetings about half the time, and whose sunny attitude brightened any gathering. She began to realize that not all the people who approached her were interested only in her notoriety.

Once she began to enjoy herself more, she started worrying that she was being too social, neglecting her studies. 'I still don't know what I should do to help Major Pitak,' she said to Barin one shipnight. She felt guilty about going to the gym to play wallball when she could have been studying. Pitak seemed pleased with her progress, but if a ship needed repair right now, what could she actually *do*?

'You're too hard on yourself,' Barin said. 'And I know what I'm talking about. Serranos have a reputation for being hard on themselves and each other . . . you're off the scale.'

'It's necessary,' she said. When had she first discovered that if she had high enough standards, no one else's criticism mattered?

'Not that far,' he said. 'You're locking down a lot of what you could be, could do, with that kind of control.'

She shied away from that. 'What I could do, is study.'

He punched her arm lightly. 'We need you; Alana's not feeling up to a game, and that leaves us short.'

'All right.' She wanted to cooperate, and it bothered her. Why was she reacting like this, when she was immune to the tall, handsome Forrester, who had already asked her what Barin probably never would? She didn't want complications; she wanted simple friendship. That was pleasure enough.

The wallball game turned into a wild melee because most of the players agreed to play a variable-G game. Esmay argued, but was outvoted. 'It's more fun,' Zintner said, setting the AI control of the variable-G court for random changes. 'You'll see.'

'Out of black eyes,' said Alana, who was refereeing this match. 'I won't play VG games, and neither should you, Esmay.'

'Be a sport,' someone on the other team called. Esmay shrugged, and put on the required helmet and eyeguard.

An hour later, bruised and sweaty, she and the others staggered out to find that they had plenty of spectators.

'Chickens,' Zintner said to those watching through the high windows of the court.

'It's easier on you shorties,' said the tallest player on the other team. 'If all the blood rushes to your head, it doesn't have time to go as fast.'

Esmay said nothing; her stomach was still arguing about which way was up, and she was glad she had eaten little for lunch. She refused an invitation to take a cooling swim with the team, and instead showered and changed. By then she was hungry. Outside the showers, she found Barin nursing a swollen elbow.

'You're going to have that checked, aren't you, Ensign?' she said. They had discovered a mutual distaste for medical interventions, and now teased each other about it.

'It's not broken, Lieutenant,' he said. 'I believe surgery won't be necessary.'

'Good – then perhaps you'll join me for a snack?'

'I think I could just about manage to get my hand to my mouth,' he said, grinning. 'It was Lieutenant Forrester's fault, anyway. He went for my shot, and got his knee in the way of my elbow.'

Esmay tried to work that out – in a variable-G game, a lunge could turn into an unplanned dive and end in a floating rebound – and gave up.

As they ate, she brought up her past experience with his family for the first time. 'I served on the same ship as Heris Serrano, back when I was an ensign. She was a good officer – I was in awe of her. When she got in that trouble, I was so angry . . . and I didn't know what I could do to help, if anything. Nothing, as it turned out.'

189

'I met her just one time,' he said. 'My grandmother had told me about her – not everything, of course, only what was legal. She sent me with a message; she wanted to use only family as couriers. We weren't sure which of us would find her, and I was the lucky one.' From the tone, Esmay wasn't sure he thought it was lucky.

'Didn't you like her?'

'Like her!' That, too, had a tone she couldn't read. Then, less explosively, 'It's not a matter of *liking*. It's – I'm used to Serranos; I'm one myself. We tend to have this effect on people. We're always being accused of being arrogant, even when we aren't. But she was . . . more like Grandmother than any of the others.' He smiled, then. 'She bought me dinner. She was in a white rage when I first showed up, and then she bought me dinner, a really expensive one, and – well, everyone knows what she did at Xavier.'

'But you ended up friends with her?'

'I doubt it.' Now he looked down at his plate. 'I doubt she's friends with any Serrano now, though I hear she's speaking to her parents again.'

'She wasn't?'

'No. It's all kind of tangled . . . according to Grandmother she thought they would help her when Lepescu threatened her – and they didn't – and then she resigned. That's when Grandmother told everyone to leave her alone.'

'But I thought she was just on covert ops then.'

'That too, but I don't know when – or what was going on. Grandmother says it's none of my business and to keep my nose out of it and my mouth shut.'

Esmay could imagine that, and wondered that he broke the prohibition even this much. She had prohibitions of her own that she had no intention of breaking, just because she'd found a new friend.

'I met her, of course, after Xavier, but only briefly,' Esmay said. In the dark times before the trial, when she had been sure she'd be thrown out of Fleet, the memory of the respect in those dark eyes had steadied her. She would like to have deserved that look more often. 'There were legal reasons for keeping us apart, they said.' Then she turned the topic to something less dangerous.

A few days later, Barin asked her about Altiplano, and she

found herself describing the rolling grassy plains, the mountain scarps, her family's estancia, the old stone-built city, even the stained glass she had liked so much as a child.

'Who's your Seat in Council?' Barin asked.

'Nobody. We have no direct representation.'

'Why?'

'The Founder died. The Family we served. Supposedly, half the militia died along with the Family. There are those who say otherwise, that the reason no one from Altiplano has a Seat in Council is that it was a mutiny.'

'What does your grandmother say?'

'My *grandmother*?' Why should he think her grandmother's words had any weight . . . oh, of course, because *his* grandmother was Admiral Serrano. 'Papa Stefan says it's a ridiculous lie, and Altiplano should have a Seat or maybe four.' At his look, she found herself explaining. 'On Altiplano, we're not like Fleet . . . even if we're military. Men and women don't usually do the same things . . . not as life work, that is. Most of the military, and all the senior commanders, are men. Women run the estancias, and most of the government agencies that aren't directly concerned with the military.'

'That's odd,' Barin said. 'Why?'

She hated to think about it, let alone talk about it. 'It's all old stuff,' she said dismissively. 'And anyway, that's just Altiplano.'

'Is that why you left? Your father was a — a sector commander, you said? — and you couldn't be in the military?'

Now she was sweating; she could feel the prickle on the back of her neck. 'Not exactly. Look — I don't want to talk about it.'

He spread his hands. 'Fine — I never asked, you never got upset, we can just talk about my relatives again if that's all right.'

She nodded, stabbing her fork into food she barely saw, and he began a story about his cousin Esser, who had been consistently nasty during long vacations. She didn't know if it was true; she knew it didn't matter. He was being polite; she was the occasion for more politeness, and that in itself was humiliating.

That night the nightmares recurred, as bad as the worst she'd had. She woke gasping from the battle for *Despite* only to find herself in the body of that terrified child, helpless to beat off her

191

assailant . . . and from that relived the worst of the time in hospital. Dream after dream, all fire and smoke and pain, and voices telling her nothing was wrong even as she burned and writhed in pain. Finally she quit trying to sleep, and turned the light on in her compartment. This had to stop. She had to stop it. She had to get sane, somehow.

The obvious move presented itself, and she batted it away. She had enough bad marks on her record, with the Board of Inquiry and the court-martial and then that ridiculous award from Altiplano . . . let her get a psych note in her record and she'd never get what she wanted.

And what was that? The question had never presented itself so clearly before, and in that bleak night she looked at it straight on. She wanted . . . she would have said safety, awhile ago. The safety Fleet could give her from her past. But the man was dead, the lie exposed . . . she was safe, in that way. What did she really want?

Fragments popped into her mind, as brief and bright as the fragments of traumatic memory. The moment on the bridge of *Despite* when she had given the order to go back to Xavier system . . . the moment when she'd given the order to fire, and the great enemy cruiser had gone up. The respect she'd seen on the faces of those at her briefing, when even the admirals – even the captain, in spite of himself – had admired the way she presented the material. Even the admiration of the juniors, which she half-hated herself for enjoying. The friendships she was beginning to have, fragile as young plants in spring.

She wanted that: those moments, and more of them. Herself in charge, doing the right things. Using the talents she had shown herself were hers. Recognition of her peers; friendships. Life itself.

The critical side of her mind pointed out tartly that she was unlikely to have many such moments as a technical specialist, unless she made a habit of serving on ships with traitorous or incompetent captains. She wasn't as good at the technical bits as others; she studied hard, she achieved competence . . . but not brilliance.

You're too hard on yourself. She was not hard enough on herself. Life could always be harder; it was necessary to be hard first. *You're locking down what you could be.* What did he think she could be, that Serrano ensign? He was only a boy – *a Serrano boy*, her critical self reminded her. So . . . he thought she wasn't using all her talents. If he knew anything. If, if, if . . .

She could hardly apply for command track now, this many years into technical. She didn't even want command track. Did she? She had hated combat, from the first moment of the mutiny through to that last lucky shot that burst the enemy cruiser like a ripe seedpod. She pushed down the memory of the feeling that had accompanied the fear, the sick disgust with the waste of it . . . that feeling entirely too seductive to be reliable.

Who knew what they felt at such times anyway? Perhaps she could go into teaching – she knew she was good at presenting complex material. That history instructor had even suggested it. Why had she fled from that offer into the most unsuitable specialty? Her mind thrashed around like a fish on a hook, unable to escape the painful reality that she had trapped herself stupidly, blindly. Like a fish indeed . . . she, who was meant to swim free. But where?

The next morning, she was tired enough that Major Pitak noticed.

'Late night, Suiza?'

'Just some bad dreams, Major.' She made it as dismissive as she could without rudeness. Pitak held her gaze a long moment.

'Lots of people have post-combat dreams, you know. No one will think less of you if you talk them over with someone in Medical.'

'I'll be all right,' she said quickly. 'Sir.' Pitak kept looking, and Esmay felt herself flushing. 'If it gets worse, sir, I'll keep your advice in mind.'

'Good,' Pitak said. Then, just as Esmay relaxed, she spoke again. 'If you don't mind telling me, what made you choose technical instead of command track?'

Esmay's breath shortened. She hadn't expected to face that question here. 'I – didn't think I would be good at command.'

'In what way?'

She scrambled to think of something. 'Well, I – I'm not from a Fleet family. There's a natural feel.'

'You honestly never wanted to take command of a unit until you ended up with *Despite*?'

'No, I . . . when I was a child, of course I daydreamed. My family's military; we have hero tales enough. But what I really wanted was space itself. When I got to the prep school, there were others so much better suited . . .'

'Your initial leadership scores were quite high.'

'I think they gave me some slack for being planet-born,' Esmay said. She had explained it to herself that way for years, as the leadership scores dropped bit by bit. Until Xavier System, until the mutiny.

'You're not really a technical-track mind, Suiza. You work hard, you're smart enough, but that's not where your real talent is. Those briefings you gave the tactical discussion groups, that paper you wrote for me . . . that's not the way a tech specialist thinks.'

'I'm trying to learn . . .'

'I never said you weren't trying.' From the tone, Pitak could have intended the other meaning; she sounded almost annoyed. 'But think of it this way: would your family try to make a draft horse out of a polo pony?'

For some reason the attempt to put the problem in her culture's terms made her stubborn; she could almost sense her body changing, long dark legs and hard hooves sinking into mud, leaning backwards, resisting. 'If they needed a load hauled, and the pony was there . . .' Then, before Pitak exploded, she went on. 'I see your point, sir, but I never thought of myself as . . . as a pony mismatched to a load.'

'I wonder what you *did* expect,' Pitak said, half to herself. 'A place to work,' Esmay said. 'Away from Altiplano.' It was the most honest thing she could say, at that point, without getting into things she never intended to discuss with anyone, ever.

Pitak almost glared. 'Young woman, this Fleet is not "a place to work away from home."'

'I didn't mean just a job—'

'I should hope not. Dammit, Suiza, you come so close . . . and then you say something like that.'

'Sorry, sir.'

'And then you apologize. Suiza, I don't know how you did what

194

you did at Xavier, but you had better figure it out, because *that* is where your talent lies. And either you use your abilities or they rot. Is that clear?'

'Yes, sir.' Clear as mud in a cattle-trampled stock tank. She had the uneasy feeling that Barin wouldn't be able to explain this one, in part because she would be too embarrassed to ask.

'I put the bug in her ear,' Pitak said to Commander Seveche.

'And?'

'And then I nearly lost my temper and pounded her. I do not understand that young woman. She's like two different people, or maybe three. Gives you the impression of immense capacity, real character, and then suddenly flows away like water down a drain. It's not like anything I've seen before, and I thought I'd seen every variety of strangeness that got past the psychnannies. She's all there . . . and then she isn't. I tried to get her to go talk to Med about her combat experience, and she shied off as if I'd threatened her with hard vacuum.'

'We aren't the first commanders she's puzzled,' Seveche reminded her. 'That's why it was such a surprise . . .'

'One good thing is she's coming out of her shell with some of the other juniors,' Pitak said. 'She and that Serrano ensign and some others.'

'The young Serrano? I'm not sure that's a good idea. There were two Serranos at Xavier.'

Pitak shrugged. 'I don't see a problem. This one is too young; those were much her seniors. Besides, they're not plotting; they're climbing the Wall and playing team games together occasionally. My thought was that maybe the Serrano arrogance would get through her shell, whatever it is, and release that natural command ability.'

'Maybe. She's not seeing just him, you say?'

'No. I hear about it mostly from young Zintner, who plays wallball with them. She says Suiza hates variable-G games but is a good sport. I haven't asked, but she's told me that two or three young men are pursuing Suiza, without much success. "Not really a cold fish when you get to know her, but reserved," is what Zintner said.'

Seveche sighed. 'She must be hiding something; they always are, the juniors, even when they think they're not.'

'And we aren't?' Pitak said.

'We are, but we know we are. The advantages of maturity: we know where our bodies are buried, and we know that anything buried can be exhumed. Usually at the wrong moment.'

'But Suiza?'

'Let her be for a bit; see if she gets somewhere on her own, now that you've planted the idea. We've agreed she's not stupid. She'll be here a couple of years, anyway, and if she hasn't unstuck herself by the end of the next review period we'll try again. If, as we said before, life doesn't give her the necessary kick in the pants.'

Esmay stared at her work, feeling resentful. She knew that was an unsuitable feeling for any junior officer . . . unproductive, not useful, even if justified. In this case it wasn't even justified. She liked Major Pitak and trusted in her honesty; if Pitak said she didn't have a technical mind, then she didn't have a technical mind. She tried to ignore the self-pitying self that wanted to whine about all the hours of study, the diligence, the self-sacrifice . . .

'Stupid!' she said aloud, startling herself and Master Chief Sivars, who had come in to bring something to Major Pitak. 'Sorry,' Esmay said, and felt her face heat. 'I was thinking about something else.'

'That's all right, Lieutenant,' he said, in the indulgent voice of the very senior NCO to the very junior officer he tolerates out of misguided affection. Or so it seemed to Esmay, making her even more resentful.

'Chief, how can you tell which junior personnel are going to have a knack for technical stuff?'

He gave her a look that clearly said this wasn't her business, or his, but then leaned back against the bulkhead and answered. 'Some of 'em come in with such a genius for it you don't have the slightest doubt. I remember a pivot, six or seven years ago, straight out of basic, who had blown the top off the placement exams. Well, we'd had high-scorers before . . . but this kid couldn't touch something without making it work better. In two days, we knew what we had; in a decad, we were just holding our breath hoping he wouldn't get crosswise of anyone important, because he did have a way of speaking his mind.' He grinned at the memory. 'That was before we were on *Kos*, you understand; she was under construction, and we were working out of Sierra Station. Major Pitak was a lieutenant then, same as you are now, except she was herself, if you know what I mean. Well, this kid snapped back at her one day, and she went the color of bad polyglue. Then she blinked, and looked at me, and said the kid was right, and walked out. Told me something about both of 'em, though of course I had to give the kid what-for, for sassing an officer. It wasn't really sass; he just knew what he knew, and didn't bother to hide it.'

'And the ones that aren't quite that good?'

'Well . . . I can tell the ones that'll work hard, of course. That always helps. Anyone with enough smarts to pass the placement exams can learn enough to be useful if they work at it steadily, the way you've done. But nothing replaces the knack, the feel . . . I can't explain it, Lieutenant. Either they have a feel for the material, or they don't. Some of 'em have it real narrow . . . they may be technical geniuses in scan, say, and useless for anything else. Others have a knack for a lot of things in the technical area – they can work almost any system.'

'Are you ever wrong?' Esmay asked.

He chewed his lip. 'Sometimes . . . but usually it's not to do with their talent. I've missed other things about them, things that interfered. I remember a sergeant minor, transferred in from Sector 11, with scores off the chart. That was odd in itself – why would another sector let him go, if he was so good? But we were short-handed, like we always seem to be, and he was awfully good.'

'So what was wrong with him?'

'Pure meanness. Turned out he got his kicks making trouble: on his own crew, in barracks, everywhere. Set people against each other, skinned the truth to the bone but always in ways that he could explain as not really lies. Nothing he did was against regulations . . . he was careful about that . . . but by halfway through his tour we'd have done anything to get rid of him. I would, anyway. I'd just been promoted to master chief; I wanted my section to run smoothly and here he was stirring things up. We finally got rid of him, but it wasn't easy.' By the tone, he did not want to explain how, and Esmay didn't ask. 'Then there was a kid who was smart enough when he could keep his mind on the job, but he was always in emotional hot water over something. Or rather, somebody. We finally got him to Medical and they had some treatment, but then he wanted to transfer. I heard later he was doing fine over in Sector 8.' He gave Esmay a smile as he pushed himself up and started out. 'Just keep plugging away, Lieutenant; you're doing fine.'

So even he knew she wasn't that good at this. Esmay resisted the childish urge to throw something at that broad back.

At dinner that evening, she said less than usual, listening to the chat at her table. The self-proclaimed genius of special materials research wasn't talking either; he had the abstracted expression of someone trying to solve problems in his head. Barin Serrano was describing his attempt to recalibrate a gravscan in which, as he put it, 'someone had been tap dancing on the connections.' He sounded happy enough, and the jig at the far end, talking about her current love affair, sounded even happier.

Perhaps it was only lack of sleep that made her want to crawl under the table. She had had nightmares all night, and a confusing and disappointing talk with her commander; of course she felt down. She didn't eat dessert, and decided to go to bed early.

'Found it,' Arhos said. 'It's a good tricky one, too.'

'Not too different from what we were told, I hope,' said Losa.

'No . . . but apparently the captain's a bit paranoid, moves it around from time to time. And checks out the circuitry periodically, to make sure it works.'

'So we have to fix it with a built-in test circuit to fake the test?'

'Yes. I've got the details . . . amazing how some of these people will talk if they think you sympathize with their problems. There's a petty-light who's convinced the captain is down on him because of a practical joke actually concocted by someone else . . . he was so anxious to convince me how unfair and unreasonable Hakin is, that he practically handed me the whole mechanism on a chip.'

'So when can we do it?'

'The captain tested it two days ago. He's using some schedule of his own devising, but he's never yet tested it within five days of a previous test. So if we do the main part tomorrow, that should give us a few days to test the test, as it were.'

'I hope this is all right,' Losa said, frowning. 'I mean – we're stuck on this ship now, and we can't pretend we don't know what it's for . . .'

'I can,' Arhos said. 'In anticipation of immortality, I can pretend any number of impossible things.'

'But if the Bloodhorde shows up . . .'

'Here? Where our very efficient escorts will chase them into the arms of the neighboring cruisers? I refuse to worry; there's nothing we can do. As far as I'm concerned, there's a dangerously paranoid captain on this ship, who might at any time see a dust spot on a vidscan and decide it's an enemy fleet – and then decide it's his duty to blow us all away. While I'm on this ship I *particularly* want that device out of his control, lest I lose my chance at a long happy life because of some knotheaded captain's mental quirk.'

'You're not happy about it either,' Losa said with satisfaction.

'Yes, I am.'

'No . . . every time you get flowery like that it means you have doubts. Serious doubts. I think we ought to put the controls in our own hands.'

Arhos considered. 'Not a bad idea, that. If nothing else, it will keep you satisfied. Gori?'

'I like it. What time tomorrow?'

'Well – the easiest access will be through the inventory bay on Deck Ten, the one across from T-4. And there are weapons components in that bay.'

'How fortunate,' Losa said.

'Especially since the computer indicates they're located in exactly the right place . . .'

'You fiddled, Arhos.'

He grinned. 'What use to have the ability, if no use is made of it? It's true that I . . . transposed some numbers in the database, but . . . it was in a good cause.'

'I hope so,' Losa said soberly. 'I do hope so.'

With their most advanced equipment, they were able to locate and fox the scan which supposedly kept anyone from tampering with the device. It took a day or so to create the blind loops they'd insert while they worked. Another day or so to create a convincing errand in that bay again.

Then they were in, and the device in its casing looked just as they'd expected.

'The tricky bit,' Arhos said, but he didn't sound worried. Rapidly the case came open, the controls yielded to their intrusion, the codes changed . . . and the telltales stayed a friendly green.

'Might as well run the test,' Gori said.

'Might as well – we've got ten minutes.' Arhos nodded to Losa, who pricked her intercept into the captain's control line and then inserted a two-layer code. The telltales changed, in sequence, from green to yellow. She inserted another code, and they went back to green.

'Lovely,' Gori said. 'I really do like it when we're right the first time.'

'If we *were* right,' Losa murmured.

Arhos grinned. 'Three rejuvs, Lo. Three, first-class, guaranteed with the best drugs. We were right.' He finished cleaning up, putting everything back as they'd found it, even to the tiny piece of metal filing that just happened to have lain a half a centimeter in from the right front corner of the case. 'We're going to live forever,' he said, backing out, wiping the deck behind him. 'Forever, and be very, very rich.'

That night they brought out one of their treats from home, and toasted each other. For the benefit of the ship's scan, they congratulated themselves on their progress so far in getting the weapons rekeyed. It made a delicious joke. Arhos sank into sleep and dreamed of the future, when he would be so rich, and so well known, that he'd never have to take a Bloodhorde contract again.

12

Esmay was asleep, having a different dream for once, when the alarm bleeped, bringing her upright even before she woke. All down the passage she could hear voices; her heart stammered and she felt cold sweat break out. But even as she dressed, the nature of the emergency became clear: ships coming in for repair. Not a mutiny. Not combat. Not – she told herself firmly – as bad. For her.

Even as she dressed and scampered along the passage and up ladders to her section, she felt the gut-twisting lurch of a ship overpowering its way through a jump point. Fear crawled back up her spine, vertebra by vertebra. DSRs were not built for racing and jumping; DSRs moved at the leisurely pace appropriate to their mass and internal architecture. She understood now, after the time in Hull & Architecture, why it wasn't a matter of adding more power – what the trade-offs were, in making *Koskiusko* so big and so massive. What had happened? Where were they going? And more important, were they fleeing with trouble on their tail, or running toward it?

Hull & Architecture, like every other section, swarmed like a kicked anthill. In the departmental briefing room, Commander Seveche was putting a cube in the display. 'Ah . . . Suiza. Hook up your compad, this is going to be interesting.' Esmay plugged in her compad, and made sure it was set to record the display directly. Most of H&A was in the room when Seveche started his briefing; the rest straggled in within a few minutes.

'This is what we know – and we all know that it will be worse. *Wraith* is a patrol ship, commissioned ten years ago, out of the

Dalverie Yards – one of the SLP Series 30 hulls—' A couple of low groans, which Esmay now understood. The SLP Series 30 had well earned the nickname 'slippery,' meaning its architecture lent itself to unauthorized and possibly damaging revisions. 'She's been in combat against the Bloodhorde, and despite their technological inferiority, they managed to wipe most of her scan systems and then bludgeon her with heavy explosive. There was shield failure of the starboard arc, forward of frame 19—' Esmay now knew exactly where frame 19 was on that class and series. '– with resulting damage to the forward weapons pods, and a hull breach here—' Seveche's pointer circled the intersection of frame 19 with truss 7.

'And she's coming *in*?' Someone less inhibited than Esmay had voiced her surprise exactly.

'She was lucky,' Seveche said. 'They knocked out her scans, but not the scans of her hunting partners. *Sting* and *Justice* were in the system, and they blindsided the Bloodhorde ships, drove them off. *Wraith* had heavy casualties of course, but they were able to patch things up enough to make it through one jump point. They couldn't manage two: the hull patch was leaking again, and they had nothing more to use on it. So – as you all no doubt felt – we're jumping out to meet them.'

No one said it this time, but the tense faces around Esmay revealed their thoughts. DSRs stayed well behind any line of war for a very good reason . . . they couldn't fight, maneuver, or get away. If they were attacked . . .'

'I did remind our captain that old *Kos* isn't an escort,' Seveche said wryly. 'But we should be fine. Half our protection jumped ahead of us, and the rest with us. We'll have *Sting* and *Justice* as well. And it looks like all the experimental stuff on *Justice* worked.'

'How long do we have?' asked Pitak.

'We expect to come into the same system in—' Seveche looked at the chronometer. 'Seventy-eight hours and eighteen minutes. We'll be making a series of fast-insertion jumps, coming out of the last at a slow relative vee; they'll tow *Wraith* out to us.'

Seveche went on with the briefing. 'We won't know more about the hull damage until we come out of the last jump: we're pushing this ship to its max, and not hanging around anywhere to pick up messages. For all we know, *Wraith* won't make it until we arrive.'

By the time *Koskiusko* came out of its last jump, Esmay had been all over the ship on errands for Major Pitak. 'Don't be insulted, but you still don't know enough to be really useful – and I need someone to keep up with all the other departments. Ship's comm is overloaded, or will be.'

Esmay didn't feel insulted at all. She was quite willing to check with Inventory Control on the stock of fasteners, star-slot, 85mm, pitch 1/10, interval 3mm (she patted the boxes with a proprietary hand – those were *her* fasteners), to ask the chief in Weapons Systems for an estimate of the damage that *Wraith* might have suffered from its own weaponry exploding when the hull breached, to crawl around the depths of the storage hold full of structural members checking each one with instruments that should detect any dangerous deformities. Everything had been checked before, and would be checked again, but she understood the need. Mistakes happen. The wrong color uniform gets on the person with the . . . no, she didn't have time to think of that.

She had avoided Medical, in the superstitious belief that any wandering psychnanny would see in her face that she had terrible secrets, and she'd be out on a psych discharge before she could argue. But in the last hours before they closed with *Wraith*, Pitak sent her there, to coordinate the search and rescue with what was known about the hull and its problems.

Medical occupied a large chunk of T-5, with onboard operating suites, decontamination suites, regen tanks, neural-assisted-growth tanks, isolation chambers for exotic infectious diseases, diagnostic labs . . . the equivalent of a sector hospital. Esmay found it in the same state of bustle as her own department, and was passed from one desk to another until she located Trauma Response.

Esmay handed Pitak's cube of data – updated since the down-jump by direct transmission from *Wraith* – to the lieutenant in charge of the extrication and trauma transport teams.

'Hang around until I'm sure we understand all this,' he said, stuffing the cube into a reader. The display came up on the wall;

the others milling around settled to look at it. 'Forward hull breach — that'll mean decompression injuries in the nearest compartments beyond the breach—' In the breach itself, it meant deaths, the responsibility of Personnel Salvage, not Extrication and Transport.

'Looks like truss failure here—' he pointed. 'We'll have to cut our way around that. Lieutenant, what'll happen if we cut here and here?' He pointed. Esmay, briefed by Major Pitak, pointed to alternative cuts, already on the cube display in green. He scowled. 'That'll just barely give clearance for our suits — we don't want to snag on anything — and we'll have casualties coming out . . . we need more room than this. We've told H&A before — we need a solid two-meter clearance . . . why can't we make this cut?' He pointed again at his first choice.

Esmay thought she knew, but this was a job for someone with seniority. 'I'll get Major Pitak for you,' she said.

'Do that.'

Esmay found Pitak deep in one of the holds stocked with H&A gear, and patched her through to the E&T commander . . . then backed off as the air heated up around her. She'd never actually heard Pitak swear before, but on this occasion the major left curlicue trails of smoke down the bulkheads. After the first explosion, she settled into explanation.

'—And if you want several dozen *more* casualties and a lot of sharp-edged ejecta floating around, then you go on and cut to your heart's content—'

'Dammit, Major—'

As abruptly as a mule's kick, the major calmed. 'Now — what do you need for your suits? I'll get you space, just tell me—'

'Two meters.'

'Mmph. All right. I'll send Suiza back with a new plan that'll give you two meters — round section or square?'

'Uh . . . square would be nice, but round will do. If it were only one it wouldn't matter, but—'

'Yes, well, if the Bloodhorde were recruits on a first mission, *Wraith* wouldn't be full of holes. I'll get back to you.' Pitak turned on Esmay. 'And why are you looking so surprised? Didn't know I could turn the air blue, or didn't think I could calm down? Either way, it looks bad . . . don't just stare at me, Lieutenant, you're making me nervous.'

'Sorry, sir,' Esmay said.

'Two stinking meters they want. Greedy pigs. I suppose they can't be sure what they'll find in there, and they need space – but they certainly can't cut that one. If I lend them a structural tech to do the cutting, that shorts me on the main job – but it might save some lives and shouldn't cost any. All right – here's what you tell them.' She rattled off a series of contingent plans, and sent Esmay back to the medical deck. Esmay wanted to ask why she didn't just call them on the com, but this was no time to ask Pitak anything.

Eight hours before the last jump point, Esmay and all but essential crew went down for a forced rest period, augmented by soporifics in the compartments. Esmay understood the reason for this – exhausted, twitchy people would make unnecessary mistakes – but she hated knowing that her calm repose had been created chemically. What if something happened and those awake forgot – or had no time – to turn on the antidote sprays?

She was still worrying at that when she woke, feeling rested and alert, to the soft chime of the downshift alarm. It had worked, as usual . . . but she didn't have to like it.

The *Koskiusko* had emerged at near-zero relative vee to the system it entered, the safest way to dump something of its mass out of jumpspace. Before Esmay could get back to Pitak's office in H&A, word had come down that *Wraith*'s tow was within twenty thousand kilometers. That made not only a bull's-eye, but a potential disaster. 'An error of considerably less than a tenth of a percent in exit vee, and we'd have romped right into her and her damnfool fool escorts,' Pitak growled. 'But it does mean we can get to work quickly. Might save a few survivors in the forward compartments.'

Tightbeam comlinks were already up; realtime data poured into *Koskiusko*'s communications shack, to be decoded and routed to the relevant departments. Esmay spent the first hour or so watching the H&A data, and sending it on to the subspecialists. Then Pitak found another job for her. 'Troll the stuff they're sending Drives and Maneuver, and Special Materials. You're good at picking up connections – someone upstairs may have misrouted something we need.'

Pitak herself had a model of the SLP Series 30 hull set up in both virtual and wireframe floor versions in the briefing room. Around it clustered the senior H&A engineers, making changes to reflect the peculiarities of *Wraith* as the data streamed in. Esmay looked up often to peek at the progress. She had seen plenty of computer 3-D displays of ship hulls, but never the scaled-down wireframe that now occupied a five-meter length of the floor. It looked like fun – though the empty space along one forward flank had nothing to do with fun.

She wondered if it was safe to set up for repair so close to the jump point exit lane. What if someone else came through? That wasn't her problem; she shook her head to clear that worry away and went back to scanning the topics routed to SpecMat. There – *that* was her concern, a request to schedule the fabrication of four twenty-meter crystal fibers. She checked the origin . . . if it wasn't someone in H&A, Pitak wanted to know. And it wasn't – it was a damage assessment specialist aboard *Wraith*, who wanted them to replace some communications lines. She called Pitak.

'Aha! Good for you. No, dears, you don't get to pick your own priorities,' Pitak said. She flagged the item, then sent it on to Commander Seveche's stack. 'They always want to, though,' she said, grinning at Esmay. 'They think they're helping us, figuring out what they need, when they don't realize the sequencing problem. We can't start anything in the SpecMat until we know everything we need at the structural level. If we get the sausage busy working on things we don't need yet, so it can't do what we need immediately, then either we lose that job or sit around like ducks on a pond until it's done.'

'What will come first?' Esmay asked, since Pitak didn't seem in a hurry to get back to the floor model.

'After assessment and evacuation, we have to clear away the old damage – there's always something you can't see until you get the skin off and expose at least ten meters you think is undamaged. I don't care what they say about diagnostic equipment, nothing beats cutting into a carcass to find out what the bones look like. Anything this badly damaged requires rebuilding from the main structure on out, just as if it were new. It's harder, because we do try to save some of the old . . . we save time and material, but it's not as efficient as building it whole. My guess is that the first things we'll want out of SpecMat are much longer crystals, grown in clusters and resin-bonded in the zero-G compartment. These will be stabilizing scaffolds for the real repair later. Then we'll want the big framing members . . . and it can take weeks to do those. No one's yet figured out how to grow the long ones and the ring ones in the same batch. Meanwhile, the die-and-mold sections can be working on little stuff like hatch frames and hatches. But the communications linear crystals come much later.'

'I . . . see.' Esmay felt she understood much better why Pitak had her doing this apparently unimportant job. She knew a lot more about hulls than she had, but this matter of sequencing repairs had never occurred to her. It made sense, now she thought of it.

'How'd you like a little adventure?' Pitak asked.

'Adventure?'

'I need someone to do a visual survey of the hull breach, and everyone I've got is busy. You'd need EVA gear – go over with the first teams, carry a vidcam and transmitter, and record everything for me.'

'Yes, sir.' Esmay wasn't sure if she was more excited or scared.

'It'll be about six hours, they think, when they're in position.'

Esmay had never done EVA since the Academy – and that was from a training shuttle hanging just a kilometer from a large station, in sight of a habitable planet. Out here, even the local star was far away, hardly a disk at all and giving minimal light. *Koskiusko*'s brilliant lights flooded the near flank of the *Wraith*, casting sharp black shadows. Esmay tried not to think of the nothing around her, and the way her stomach wanted to crawl out her ears, and looked instead at the damaged ship. She hadn't seen the outside of a ship with her own eyes, rather than vidscan . . . and it was instructive.

Like most Familias warships, *Wraith* had a long rounded profile that could have been confused with airstreaming – but was instead the result of a compromise of engineering constraints. Shield technology dictated the smooth curves: the most efficient hull shape for maximum shield efficiency was spherical. But spherical ships had not proven themselves in battle; it had been impossible to mount drives – either insystem or FTL – to provide the kind of reliable maneuverability needed. The only spherical ships now in service were large commercial freight haulers, where the gain in interior volume and ease of shielding from normal space debris was worth the decreased maneuverability.

So a patrol craft like *Wraith* had a more ovoid shape, giving it a distinct longitudinal axis. Forward, its bow should have been a blunt rounded end, only slightly pointier than the stern. What Esmay saw instead was a crumpled mess, the shiny glint of fused and melted skin where it should have been (as the undamaged hull was) matte black. Aft, the smooth curves of the drive pods appeared to have suffered no damage, though she'd heard that Drives and Maneuver were worried about the effect of jumping with an unbalanced hull.

She dared a look over her shoulder, even though that twist made her swivel around the safety line like a child's toy. *Koskiusko*'s vast bulk blocked out the stars well beyond the banks of search-lights that held the patrol craft in their gaze. She wasn't even sure where the working lights on its exterior became stars against the dark.

Someone punched her shoulder. Right. Get on with the job. She pulled herself along, taking no more sight-seeing looks. *Wraith*'s damaged hull inched closer. Now she could see the pale tracks of fragments – of the weapons or the hull itself she didn't know – against the dark normal hull coating beyond. The entry gaped, jagged and unwelcoming. Something whispered against her suit helmet, and she jerked to a halt. A firm tap on her shoulder sent her on. In a moment her brain caught up and she realized it must be minute ejecta from the breached hull: probably ice crystals from the continuing air leak the crew had not been able to seal completely.

She hit the red section of line: only ten meters from the attachment. Ahead of her, someone had already clipped on the first of the branch lines that would frame the working web. But this was Esmay's station for now. She locked the slide on her safety line, clipped on the secondary stabilizing line that would confine her rotation to one plane, and waved the others past.

With the vidscan recorder aimed at the hole and the work going on, she could avoid thinking about where she was. Major Pitak wanted details – more details – even more details. 'Don't rush,' she'd said. 'Take your time – stay at the ten-meter line until you're sure you've shown me everything you can from there. You won't be in the way of the scaffolding crews, but you will be able to see a lot. Every detail can help us. Everything.'

So Esmay hung in her harness and worked the recorder's eye along the edge of the hull breach. Everything? Fine, she would spend a few minutes on those pale tracks, on the way the hull peeled back *there* to expose a twisted truss, on the odd bulge forward of the breach. By the time she'd filled half a cube from that location, the scaffolding crew had placed the major grid lines that would define the location of specific damage sites. Esmay signaled her intention to the chief, received permission, and clipped on to one of the cross-lines.

Really, she thought, it wasn't that bad out here. Once the stomach adapted to zero gravity, it was kind of fun, scooting along the line with only an occasional tug . . . a red tie bumped her hand, and she grabbed. Her arm yanked at her shoulder, and she spun dizzily, cursing herself for forgetting that she was supposed to move *slowly*. When she got herself straightened out again, someone's helmet visor was turned her way; she could imagine what they thought. Another dumbass lieutenant learns about inertia. She would have apologized, except that they weren't supposed to use the suit radios unless it was a real emergency.

She was now on the opposite side of the hull breach, nearer the bow. From this angle, she could see into the hole better – or the searchlights had found a better angle. She forced herself to look in . . . but she didn't recognize any bodies. The mess inside all looked mechanical, like a child's toy that had been stepped on. Twisted, broken, shattered . . . all the words she knew for destruction. Slowly, recording, she made sense of it. The forward bulge came from a separation of the forward framing members – they had sprung, like an old-fashioned barrel-ring, under concussive force, and the shattered truss had gone with them.

Pitak would want to know how far forward the bulge extended. It could be mapped from *Koskiusko*, if no one was using the near-scan . . . but someone would be. Esmay looked at the bulge and wished she could ask the major. If she could get on the other side of it with the recorder . . . but there was no scaffolding line there. She thought of asking the scaffolding chief to string one for her, and thought again. They were far too busy to do favors for one curious lieutenant. No, she would either string one herself, or not. Not didn't sound like a good option. She had four additional lines slung to her own suit, just as all the scaffolding crew had . . . so it was only a matter of setting the hooks.

She left the big vidscan behind, without admitting to herself the reason. She didn't intend to come loose and drift away; it was just good sense to leave the vidscan where it would be easily found. The one built into her helmet would do well enough for this short excursion. She clipped the end of one of her long lines into the ten-meter safety ring, then edged along the scaffolding line to the hull itself. Her short safety line slid along the scaffolding line on its ring. The scaffolding line was anchored with a double pin-and-patch. She ran her long line through the ring that attached there, which took longer than simply clipping in, but was more secure.

She put a boot on the hull and tested. Nothing. She had halfway hoped that *Wraith*'s internal artificial gravity would give some adhesion, but it might not even be functioning. She could put short-stick patches on her boots, or she could just go on . . . it would be easier to go on, and she could always put the patches on if she couldn't make progress.

She fished a stickpatch out of her toolband with her right hand, positioned it on the end of her gloved middle finger and gave the slightest push with her left hand. She slid to the end of her safety line, slowly. Reaching out cautiously, she touched the stickpatch to the hull; it adhered just as it was supposed to. Now she could stick a pin to the patch . . . she hoped. She left her right hand on the stickpatch, and fumbled for a pin. There it was. When she reached over slowly, her safety line tugged at her waist. She had definitely gone as far as she could go with that on. She got the pin stuck to the stickpatch with its own quick-setting backing, then opened a connecting ring, locked her long line into it, and clipped the ring into the pin's opening.

The next move had a certain finality – when she unhooked her safety line from the scaffolding cable, she was depending on her own ability to set patches and pins. Caution reminded her that she was not a specialist in EVA work . . . that she would not have the right reactions if something went wrong. Esmay grinned at caution, alone inside her helmet. She had listened to caution and what good had it done her? First they thought she was dull, and then they thought she was a wild radical.

It wasn't that different from climbing the rocks at the head of her valley, or the exercise wall in the *Kos*. Reach, place a stickpatch, a pin, clip into the pin, move past that protection to the next. Twenty pins along, and she was beyond the bulge of damage . . . though the bow shield outlet access points, which should have been smooth glossy nubs protruding a few centimeters from the hull surface, were instead jagged-edged holes. Esmay turned up the light on her helmet vidscan to examine them more closely. Something glinted, ahead of her. More debris – and surely Major Pitak would want a picture of it. She placed another pin, clipped in carefully and finger-walked herself nearer.

Then tried to push herself back, and made a move violent enough to fling her off the hull, to hit the end of her line. She tried to swim herself into a position where she could see, where she wouldn't be flung back into the hull . . . what if there were *two* of them?

Was she even sure of what it was? And even if it was, it could be the *Wraith*'s own weapons, by chance stuck to its own hull by . . . by some reaction Esmay couldn't begin to understand. She forced herself to breathe slowly. Mine. It was a mine, exactly like the ones in the handbooks of enemy weaponry she'd been looking at in the supply ship on the way to Sierra Station.

Meanwhile, she reeled herself in, hand over hand, coming in too fast to her last clip; she bumped the hull with bruising force, and would have bounced free except that she grabbed the pin and outward line in one hand and the inward line with the other and let her arms take the strain. Now she wished she had stickpatches on her boots – it seemed she hung there a very long time, bouncing back and forth. Finally the oscillations died down. With great care, she reached inward for the next clip, then unclipped from the pin. Twenty . . . twenty-two . . . twenty-seven pins in all, each requiring slow, careful movement to pass. She thought several times of using her suit comunit – but was that mine an emergency now? If no one else approached it before she warned them – and the scaffolding crew was still setting up their workspaces in the hull breach.

When she made it back to the scaffolding cable and clipped on her safety line, she felt it must have taken a half-shift at least. But her chronometer didn't agree. Barely an hour had passed. She retrieved the big vidscan, and looked around for the scaffolding chief. She couldn't go back to the *Koskiusko* without warning someone here. She spotted him at last, and edged from line to line until she could tap his shoulder, and then the message board he carried. His helmet nodded. Quickly, Esmay drew a clumsy sketch of the bow – the bulge, then the location of the mine. MINE she printed in careful letters.

He shook his head. Esmay nodded. He pointed to the big vidscan and drew a question mark. She had to shake her head, and point to the scan lens in her helmet. FOLLOW he signed, and led her along the scaffolding to a com nexus. While she was gone, they'd strung a direct line from ship to ship, and passed a wire into *Wraith*, so that the ships could talk without unshielded transmission. Esmay and the scaffolding chief both hooked their suits to the nexus.

'What do you mean, mine?' the chief asked. 'And what were you doing that far up the bow, anyway? Your safety line isn't that long.'

'You saw the bulge of damaged frame,' Esmay said. 'I went to scan it for Major Pitak. I put out stickpatch pins and clipped in. And when I got beyond the bulge, I was scanning damaged shield nodes . . . turned up my suit scan lights . . . and there it was.'

'A mine, you say.' He sounded unconvinced.

'It looks like the illustrations in the handbooks. Not one of ours, either. A Smettig Series G, is what it looked like to me.'

'What kind of fuse, did you see that?'

'No.' She didn't want to say it, but she couldn't leave it at that. 'I tried to jump back and . . . lost contact with the hull.'

'So . . . you don't have full documentation?'

212

'No.' She didn't even know how much of the mine her scan had picked up. How long had she looked at it before panicking?

'If it is a mine . . .' He sighed, the exasperated sigh of someone who does not want one more complication in a day already stuffed with complications. 'Well . . . hell. I see you have to report it, and if it *is* a mine we'll have to do something . . .' His voice trailed off, someone who didn't know what to do next. He looked at her, and her intention to say anything vanished. She was an officer; it was her job to make decisions. This is what came of ignoring caution, she thought bitterly, as she tried to think who to report this to, aboard *Koskiusko*. The simple answer was Major Pitak, but an enemy mine stuck aboard a ship under repair wasn't simple.

Pitak's reaction, when Esmay finally got her on the other end of the connection, was hardly reassuring. 'You think you saw a mine . . . an enemy mine.' Flat, almost monotone. 'And you may or may not have gotten it on the vid . . . ?'

'Yes, sir. I . . . pushed off too hard. I was afraid . . .'

'I should hope so.' That with more energy. 'You know, Suiza, you do have an instinct for drama. An enemy mine. Not everyone would think of that.'

'Think?' She wasn't sure if she heard scorn or genuine amusement in the major's voice. Or something else.

'Thinking is good, Suiza. Now the first thing you do, is tell the chief to get his crew the hell away from *Wraith*. Then you get your sorry tail back out there and get some decent vidscan of this putative mine. I hope you have enough air . . .'

'Uh . . . yes, sir,' Esmay said, after a quick glance at her gauges.

'That's reassuring.' A long pause, during which Esmay wondered if she was supposed to cut the connection and go. But Pitak wasn't quite through. 'Now I'll go tell our captain to tell *Wraith*'s captain that a totally inexperienced junior officer on her first real EVA thinks she saw an enemy mine stuck to his ship and while she didn't get any good pictures the first time, she is now taking pictures which, if the mine doesn't blow her up, may show us whether she's right. And give us a clue how to do something about it.'

'Yes, sir.'

'That did not require an acknowledgement, Suiza. Can you think of any mistake you haven't made yet?'

'I didn't set it off,' Esmay said, before she could stop herself. A harsh bark of laughter came over the com.

'All right, Suiza . . . send the crew home and go bring me some decent pictures. I'll see what I can do to scare up a bomb squad.'

The scaffolding chief was quite willing to take the orders of a junior officer; he scarcely bothered to utter a ritual grumble. Esmay didn't wait for the crew to leave. She fished out stick-patches for her boots, checking twice to be sure she had the kind that would not adhere permanently. She didn't want to be stuck there like an ornament. Then she used one of her safety lines and extra clips to sling the big vidscan on her back.

This time the trip was easier, with the pins already in place, and the grip of her boots on *Wraith*'s hull. She could walk part of the way between the pins, paying out line to herself from the clip before . . . it was easy to see, from this position, that she had not laid a straight course in the first place. She had angled across the bulge, rather than taking the shorter route straight forward. She didn't look at anything but the pins, the clips, the line itself, until she was almost at the twentieth pin. Then light flooded over her from behind, washing out the fainter light from her helmet, and she missed the pin. When she turned to look, her helmet visor darkened automatically; she could see that one of *Koskiusko*'s big lights had turned away from the hull breach to search along the bows. Evidently Major Pitak had reached the captain. . . .

She reached again for the pin, and clipped into it safely. In the brighter light, the edges of the shattered shield nodes cast jagged shadows that striped the hull's dull black. Things looked different now . . . she couldn't see the mine, but it had to be close. Another pin, and another, and another . . .

EEEEERRRRP! Esmay jerked to a halt, and slammed her feet into the hull. The whiny, irritable, noise demanded her attention. A light flashed red in front of her . . . emergency . . . oh. She leaned her chin on the comunit switch.

'Don't move,' a voice said in her ear. 'Look down, knee level, 10 o'clock . . . but don't move.' Esmay looked down, half her gaze cut off by the helmet. Something . . . something *moved*. Something small, perhaps the size of her ungloved fist, dark and glossy, rising on a thin wire stalk that gleamed in the searchlight . . . she

214

wanted to tip her head and see where it was coming from, though she knew without seeing. 'Just don't move,' the voice said again. 'With any luck it will think you're part of the ship.'

Just as she opened her mouth to ask, the voice added, 'And don't talk. We don't know what its sensor characteristics are.'

The little black ovoid on its wire – the programmable sensor pod of a smart mine – rose higher . . . she could see it clearly now, and presumably it could see her. Sweat sprang out on her whole body at once; it tickled abominably as it rolled down her ribs, down her belly . . . she wanted to scratch. Not as bad as she wanted to run.

She was part of the ship. She was a . . . an automatic repair mechanism. Turned off at the moment, non-functional . . . she tried not to breathe as the sensor swayed nearer, sweeping in a conical pattern dictated by the stiffness of its wire stalk and the vibrations induced at its source. She had been in scan herself; she knew what such a small package might contain. It could already have matched her thermal profile to that of 'human in EVA suit' if that was part of its programming. It could have recorded her skeletal density, her respiratory rate, even her eye color.

And if it had done all that, she was already dead, she just hadn't been killed yet.

The little pod on its stalk continued to revolve . . . but it was lower again. She didn't know what that meant. Would a smart mine bother to retract its sensor array before blowing up? She could barely see it now, above the sight rim of her helmet. Then it was below her vision . . . she was not tempted to bend over and look more closely.

'Sorry, Lieutenant,' came the voice in her ear again. 'Our searchlight brought your shadow up past its threshold. But you were dead right – it's definitely a mine, and definitely an enemy weapon.'

Dead right . . . she didn't like that at all.

'We've got a hazardous equipment assessment team on the way,' the voice went on. 'Just don't move.'

She had no intention of moving; she wasn't sure she would ever be able to move again. A few moments later, the tremors began, behind her knees; she struggled to control them. How sensitive was the sensor pod? Which little twitch might set it off? Reason suggested that she'd been moving more before, and it hadn't reacted . . . but reason had no control over her hindbrain, where panic danced its jig on her spine.

She was very bored with being that scared by the time the voice spoke again.

'You put down a good line, Lieutenant. Don't move . . . we're at the next pin, we can see you clearly.'

She wanted to turn and see them, see something friendly, even if that was the last thing she saw . . . but she did not move.

'We're afraid if we douse the spotlight, that'll trigger another search sequence, and we don't know how it's programmed.'

The voice didn't have to say more; she remembered that some mines were set to go after a specific number of searches had been triggered, even if they didn't find anything. She might have triggered an earlier search, when she first flung herself away from the thing.

'If we're lucky, it's looking for a match to something specific, which we don't resemble, but . . .'

She wished the voice would shut up now . . . what if the mine reacted to minute vibrations carried through someone's suit? Even hers. Surely they had someone watching it . . . surely they had a plan. . . .

'*Wraith*'s given us an update on what's beyond the hull breach – they're evacuating personnel now.' A pause; she tried not to think. Then, 'How's your suit air? Give me a one-letter answer: A for ample, S for short, C for critical, then a number for minutes remaining.'

Esmay looked, and was startled to see how far down the gauge had gone. 'S,' she said. 'Sixteen.'

'I'd call that critical, myself,' the voice said. 'Here's what we'll do. Someone's going to come up behind you, trying to match your profile and cast the same shadow, and pop on an external reserve. Don't move. He'll do all the hooking up from his end.'

'Yes, sir,' Esmay said. Her eyes had locked onto the air gauge; the number flicked down to fifteen, and it was definitely in the red zone.

216

'Breathe slowly,' the voice said. 'You're not doing any work; you may have longer than that.'

Fear burns oxygen. She remembered that, along with other pithy sayings. It was amazingly hard to breathe slowly because you needed to save oxygen . . . she tried thinking of other things. Would she feel the vibration of the person coming up behind her? Would the mine's sensor pod notice it? That kind of thought didn't help her take slow breaths. She tried to send her mind back to her valley, that favorite and reliable relaxation exercise, but when the gauge flicked to fourteen, she gasped anyway. Don't gasp. Don't look at the gauge. It will either go down to zero, or it won't.

She did not feel the vibration; what she felt first was a tiny push that made her sway forward. She stiffened against it. Then something tapped the back of her helmet, and a new voice spoke in her ear.

'Doin' good, Suiza. Just don't wiggle . . . while I . . . get this tank attached . . .' Random bumps and prods, which she tried to resist so that she wouldn't move enough to trigger the pod's notice. She eyed her oxygen gauge. Nine. Had she really been standing there waiting more than six minutes? Apparently so. The gauge flicked down again, to eight. She could hear clicks and squeaks from her suit as her unseen rescuer tried to hook up the auxiliary tank with the least possible movement.

'Gauge?' asked the voice.

She looked. Now it read seven. 'Seven,' she said.

'Damn,' said the voice. 'It's supposed to – oh.' She didn't know what that 'oh' meant, and it infuriated her. How dare they mean whatever 'oh' meant? An irritating scritch, repeated over and over, as she tried not to watch the gauge. It seemed a long time, but it hadn't flicked down to six when the indicator whipped over to the green section.

'Gauge?' asked the voice again.

'Green,' Esmay said.

'Number,' the voice said, with a bite of disapproval.

Esmay swallowed the 'uh' she wanted to make and blinked to focus on the number. 'One four seven.'

'Good. Now I'm going to hook into your telemetry – you've been out more than your suit's rated for—'

Another set of scritches; Esmay didn't care. She was breathing; she would not run out of oxygen.

'Your internal temp's low,' the voice said. 'Turn up your suit heater.'

She complied, and warmth rose from her bootsoles. The tremor she'd been fighting to control eased – had it been only cold, and not panic after all? She wanted to believe that, but the sour smell of her sweat denied it.

13

'We have a problem, Suiza,' said the voice in her ear. Esmay thought they could have said something more helpful. She knew they had a problem – *she* had a problem. 'If that's the only mine, if it blows it will probably damage only those forward compartments, which as far as anyone knows are empty anyway. And you, of course.'

No comment seemed necessary.

'We haven't spotted any other mines – but we can't figure out why there's only one. If there is only one.'

Did they expect her to figure it out?

'It's not like the Bloodhorde, but there's no doubt that the ships that attacked *were* Bloodhorde ships. Came right in for the kill – *Wraith* got unequivocal scan data – and then broke off when *Sting* and *Justice* closed and started raking them.'

Esmay wondered about that. By rumor, if a Bloodhorde group closed with prospect of a kill, it would not break off just to avoid contact with another ship. Unless its ships were having trouble . . . she wished she could see the scan data herself. Not likely, if the mine blew. But . . . she dared a transmission. 'Were they close enough to plant the mine by hand?' she asked.

'Don't transmit,' the voice said. 'If it hears you—'

'You wanted to know why,' she said. 'Is *Wraith*'s scan tech available?'

'Wait.'

She could imagine the scene in *Koskiusko*'s communications shack – perhaps Major Pitak was there; certainly the captain was. A different voice came with a tiny physical tap on her EVA suit. 'You're going to upset 'em, Lieutenant.' That voice sounded amused; she wasn't sure what it meant. She shrugged enough to move the shoulders of the suit; a chuckle came through the link. 'You got an idea, huh? Good for you. I can't figure out why that thing hasn't blown us both – but I'm willing to live with that.' Another chuckle. Esmay felt her own stiff face relaxing into a grin.

'Suiza, just in case you've got an idea, we've patched you through to the *Wraith* senior scan tech. Just try to keep your transmissions short, do you understand?'

'Yes, sir. Did the Bloodhorde ships come close enough for an EVA team to plant the mine by hand, or by pod?'

A pause. Then yet another voice. 'Uh . . . yes . . . I suppose. We were trying to rotate, because of the damage to the starboard shields and hull. They got pretty close . . .'

Esmay wanted to yell 'NUMBERS, dammit!' but she could hear a roar in the background that might be the scan tech's supervisor saying the same thing, for the next transmission gave her the figures she wanted. Close enough indeed; her mind raced through the equations for both EVA and pod movement . . . yes. 'How soon after that did the Bloodhorde ships pull away?'

'As soon as *Sting* and *Justice* came back,' the tech said. Esmay waited, confident in that background bellow. Sure enough, the tech came back on with the precise interval. Esmay felt as if someone had run a current down her spine. Maybe they'd spotted the Fleet ships before they were fired on, or maybe they hadn't. They'd planted a smart mine, programmed for a specific task, and then they'd gone away, leaving *Wraith* damaged but not killed. And why?

What did the Bloodhorde expect to happen next? A damaged Familias military vessel would not be abandoned, so they couldn't

219

have hoped to capture it – in fact, if they had, why mine it? Damaged Familias vessels . . . went to repair facilities. Either dockyards, in this case too far away for a cripple like *Wraith* to reach, or the mobile dockyards called DSRs . . . *Koskiusko*. What would the Bloodhorde know about DSRs? Whatever was in the public domain, certainly – and Esmay knew that the public knew DSRs were capable of taking the smaller Fleet ships into the DSR's vast central repair bay.

That made sense. She thought it all through, then transmitted it. 'The Bloodhorde chose a small ship to disable, planted a smart mine, then withdrew, so that *Wraith* would lead the way to a DSR. The mine's programmed to go off when *Wraith* enters the repair dock – disabling the DSR. It's not strong enough to destroy it, but it would probably be unable to make jump—'

'Certainly unable to make jump,' came Pitak's voice in her ear.

'And thus would be immobilized for attack.' Esmay paused, but no one said anything. 'Either they followed *Wraith* and her escort to this system, or the mine will also have a homing module to lead them here. They want the DSR, almost certainly for capture, since they could have covered *Wraith* with enough mines to blow the whole DSR if they'd wanted.'

Another long pause, during which the contact hissed gently in her ear. Then: 'It makes sense. Never thought the Bloodhorde were that sneaky . . . and what they want a DSR for, unless they've got significant battle damage somewhere . . .'

Esmay rode the wave of her confident intuition. 'They lack technical skills they need; they don't have a military-grade shipyard. They want a DSR to upgrade their entire space effort. In one blow they get manufacturing facilities, parts, and expert technicians. Given a DSR, they could upgrade any of their ships to Fleet equivalency – or quickly learn to manufacture their own cruisers.'

The long hiss that followed conveyed both horror and respect. 'Of course,' someone said softly.

'Which means,' Esmay said, 'that this thing won't go off until the parameters match whatever they think the inside of a repair bay looks like, or until someone tries to remove it. It doesn't know it's been detected until we try to do something about it.' Relief weakened her knees; she leaned back against the unseen person behind her. 'Which means we can walk away and it won't blow – as long as we don't put *Wraith* in the repair bay.'

'Not so fast,' said Pitak, over a gabble of other voices. 'You still need to get good scan on it.'

'Not active,' Esmay said. 'But yes, I can do vidscan.' Without waiting for orders or permission, she moved, leaning over to aim at it. There it was, the blunt-ended cylindrical shape, the little sensor pod on its wire now retracted to form a knob on the cylinder. She could pick out a serial number, and one of the swirling shapes that meant something in the language of Aethar's World. Probably something rude; the outside of Bloodhorde ships were usually decorated with slogans intended to shock and frighten their neighbors.

She patched the vidscan signal to her headset, and waited for Pitak to say they had enough data. Finally she heard, 'That's enough – now the guy behind you is going to withdraw—' A final tap on her shoulder, and then she saw the shadow cast by *Koskiusko*'s light waver as he left. The smart mine's sensor pod didn't move. Curious, but welcome. She waited a little longer, watching her oxygen display count the seconds and minutes, then lifted one stickpatched boot from the hull. The sensor pod stirred, rotating on its wire stalk.

'The sensor pod's moving a bit,' Esmay said. 'How about dousing the light while I get loose.'

'We were afraid the change might trigger something,' the voice said.

'If it's programmed for repair bays,' Esmay said, 'then light will activate the matching program, but dark will turn it off.'

The light behind her vanished, and with it the crisp shadow she'd cast. She turned up the sensitivity of her helmet scan, and just made out the mine . . . the sensor pod did not move. Slowly, she folded herself up as much as the EVA suit allowed, so that she could grip her safety line close to the pin and kick the other boot free. No movement from the sensor pod. Slowly, she worked herself hand by hand backwards, around the curve of the hull, until she was out of sight of the mine. Then she stuck her boots onto the hull and walked back to the line connecting *Wraith* to *Koskiusko*. There the specialists of the bomb squad waited for her, in the strange bulky suits she had seen only in training cubes.

'Suiza, come back to *Koskiusko*,' she heard.

'Yes, sir.' She wanted to know what the bomb squad was going to do about the mine; now that she was here, she might as well stay. But the voice in her ear had left her no options. And she'd need another auxiliary tank to stay out longer.

'Good job, Lieutenant,' said one of the bomb squad. 'Glad you figured out it was safe for me to come back.'

'Me, too,' Esmay said, then hooked herself to the transfer line and pushed away.

By the time she had clambered out of her EVA suit, she felt like collapsing in a heap on the deck. The undersuit clung to her nastily; she hated having to stand around in it while the chief in charge of suits examined and checked off the condition of the one she turned in. After one glance, she ignored the big mirror at the end of the bay; her hair looked like dirty felt glued to her head.

Showered and properly dressed once more, she headed to the compartment number waiting in her message bin. T-1, Deck 9, number 30 . . . that was in the administrative area of the Senior Technical Schools, down the passage from Admiral Livadhi's office.

The conference, when she got there, consisted of Captain Hakin, Admiral Dossignal, Admiral Livadhi, Commander Seveche and Major Pitak from Hull and Architecture, and two lieutenant commanders she did not know. One wore the insignia of the 14th Heavy Maintenance, with the collar flashes of weapons systems; the other, also with weapons collar marks, wore the armband of ship's crew. The captain spoke first.

'Well, Lieutenant . . . glad your guess about the mine's programming turned out to be right. At least as far as you were concerned.'

'Me, too, sir.' Esmay hoped the edge in the captain's voice had as much to do with the situation as with her.

'I don't suppose you've had time to figure out how we're going to evacuate *Wraith* and repair her without triggering the mine's recognition program?'

'No, sir.' He was definitely displeased with her; that frosty glare could mean nothing else.

'What I'd like to know is how much time delay is built into that program,' said Commander Seveche, after a quick glance at Dossignal. 'Would they have sent it open-ended, or would they have built in a hard delay, for just this situation?'

Eyes shifted to Esmay but she had nothing to say. Shrugging was inadvisable in the midst of that much brass, so she simply didn't say anything.

'Do we have any Bloodhorde analysts aboard?' asked Dossignal, looking at Admiral Livadhi.

'Not really, Sy. They pulled the best for some sort of policy/ strategic planning thing back at Rockhouse, and the next best is on the flagship with Admiral Gourache. I've got an instructor for the tactics course, but his specialty is Benignity history. He's hitting the databanks . . .'

'Abandoning *Wraith* is not an option,' the captain said. 'The admiral's made it clear that we're not to give the Bloodhorde any chance at advanced technology, and even stripped, that hull has too many goodies to let fall into the hands of the Bloodhorde, or even a random pirate. If she can't be repaired well enough to get her back to safety—'

'She can be,' Admiral Dossignal said. 'This is exactly the kind of damage we're equipped to repair. The only question is how to do it safely, without risking the integrity of *this* ship.' He glanced at Commander Seveche, who took over.

'We have to repair that hull breach, and reset the engines, or she won't make jump again . . . and that means working all around that mine, even if we don't stick her into the repair bay. I'd like to hear from the weapons experts.'

The captain nodded, and the crew weapons officer spoke. 'Given the kind of mine, there are several approaches we can use, depending on the amount of damage tolerable on *Wraith* . . .'

'*Wraith*'s already got enough damage—' Pitak sounded outraged. Dossignal held up his hand and she subsided.

'We realize you want to minimize any further damage, but there's a trade-off between speed and safety here. We can get the remnants of *Wraith* in to repair faster if some additional damage is acceptable; if not, we're looking at a long period of preparation in an already damaged ship – dangerous time, for both the workers and both ships – to attempt something which may not be possible.'

'Explain what procedures you might use,' the captain said.

'Ideally, we'd detach the mine, enfold it in a foam-mold casing, and set it off at a safe distance. However, we – Lt. Commander Wyche and I – believe that there's considerable risk of detonating the mine if we try to detach it. So the next best thing is a foam bed both interior – behind the hull where it's attached – and on the exterior. Here the problem is how much of the interior needs to be foamed. And that homing signal we suspect, though that depends on which kind it is.'

'How long before you can set it off?'

'That depends on what H&A tells us.' He turned to Commander Seveche. 'Will we need to foambed the interior as well? How much additional damage would such a mine cause?' With a gesture, Seveche passed the question to Pitak.

Pitak scowled; Esmay recognized thought in progress. 'There's already so much damage forward – we're going to have to replace most of the structure anyway. On the other hand, it's stretching our resources, especially if we expect an attack. Do you think it's an aimed charge, or just a straightforward blow-em-up?'

He shook his head. 'If they went to the trouble of hand-placing this thing, I'd bet on a directed charge, probably with substantial penetrating power. It's definitely a hull-cracker.'

Someone down the table stirred. 'But if they wanted to disable the DSR, wouldn't the charge be directed outwards?'

'Not necessarily,' Pitak said. 'An explosion of that magnitude, in the repair bay, could be expected to damage sensitive equipment – certainly enough to keep us from withdrawing *Wraith* and closing the bay.' She paused, and no one interrupted. 'Sorry, but I think you'd better foambed the interior, at least these compartments—' She called up a display, and highlighted some of the forward compartments. 'If we can possibly save these: seventeen A, eighteen A and B, and twenty-three A, it'll save us considerable time on the repairs.'

'Then – with the precautions we need to protect personnel –

we're talking 96 hours to foambed those compartments and the exterior—'

'Why the exterior?' asked someone else.

'Because we don't want pieces flying around hitting us,' Pitak said. 'Or the rest of *Wraith*.'

'And I'll need additional squads,' he said. 'The more people, the faster it'll go. As long as they're not working in close, it should be safe enough.'

'Unless it has a fixed delay of some kind—'

'Unless stars sprout horns . . . sure, that'd kill us all, but there's no way to know but go.'

'Very well, commander,' the captain said. 'I presume damage control would have personnel trained to spray a foam bed?'

'Yes, sir.'

Captain Hakin turned to his exec. 'Make sure he gets what he needs. Major Pitak, can H&A do anything to expedite this?'

Pitak nodded. 'Yes, sir. With the captain's permission, I have construction crews standing by to widen access to the compartments that must be foamed; they've been clearing debris already—'

'I thought we pulled everyone out,' the captain said.

'We did, sir, but when tactical analysis concluded that the mine had its programming set for our internal bay, I sent them back over.'

'Very well. Keep me informed.' With that, the captain rose; everyone stood as he left. Pitak beckoned to Esmay.

'Lieutenant, you're not ready to direct a crew in this kind of situation; I want you to hold down the office – be my communications link. I'm going over myself.'

'Yes, sir.'

Pitak started down the passage; Esmay followed.

'You'll be in charge of expediting the transfer of materials and tools as we need them. I've set up a model in my office, but it'll need modification – they always do. Keep in mind the limited staging area on *Wraith*. We don't want things backing up there.'

The model lasted only about an hour, then Pitak was calling in changes, and Esmay thought of nothing but her assignment. She relayed requests for tools, for materials, for personnel. Several glitches required intervention from above; she sicced Commander Seveche's office on the stubborn senior chief in the Technical Schools who didn't see why an instructor in weapons systems should dismiss a class and go help deal with the mine. He'd argued that the 14th was supposed to have its own bomb disposal squad . . . but polite requests through appropriate channels soon produced a cheerful woman with one prosthetic hand and her custom EVA suit slung on her back. Esmay directed her to the right EVA hatch, and went back to work.

She would like to have watched the work on *Wraith*; she knew only vaguely what a 'foam bed' was, and what it was supposed to accomplish. But Pitak's construction teams had found more casualties in the forward compartments, most dead and the rest unconscious.

'The artificial gravity failed up here, along with the communications lines – some shrapnel, probably, sliced them like a hot knife. It's a wonder any of 'em are alive, and I don't know how many will survive – they look pretty bad. But they're all out now, so you can send over the next load of stuff as soon as they're logged clear of the lanes.'

Esmay looked at the cluttered screen that now represented everything between *Koskiusko* and *Wraith*. A query to the scan supervisor tagged the medical evac pod on her screen; when it was out of the way, she put a priority tag on the shipment Pitak had asked for, and talked to the sergeant minor in T-3 responsible for sending it off.

She was concentrating so hard on keeping up with Pitak's requests that she jumped when the sergeant at the other console said 'Wow!' and then 'Good thing they foamed it . . .'

'The mine?' she asked, when she got her breath back.

'Yeah. Want a replay?'

She couldn't resist; he transferred the replay to her console. *Wraith*'s hull breach no longer faced *Koskiusko*; she could just see the edge of it. That meant the mine was out of line of sight; the viewpoint shifted. Now, where she remembered the mine should be, there was an irregular grayish blob strongly side-lit by *Koskiusko*'s floods.

'They took this from a pod,' the sergeant said. 'Relayed on tightbeam . . . they had several out there watching.'

This view closed in, until she could see that the blob looked like whipped cream or icing piped into a slumpy cylinder. As she watched, another blob of foam appeared, rising then slipping sideways to seal off the end of the cylinder.

'They foamed all the compartments inboard,' the sergeant said. 'And foamed a cylinder around it, aiming it away from us . . . then finally put a lobe over the top. That's when . . .'

It blew; the blob of the foam bed burst apart, and something shot out the top, away from *Wraith*.

'All the ejecta went the right way,' the sergeant said. 'Good design. Reports are that very little blew in the interior. All they have to do now is get all that foam back out, and we can do that in the big bay.'

'I don't understand how it works,' Esmay said. 'I thought if you confined an explosion, that only made it worse.'

The sergeant shrugged. 'I don't really understand it either, but I had a buddy back in Sector 10 who was in their bomb squad. He said you had a choice – you could try to aim it somewhere, and let all that energy escape in a direction that didn't bother you, or you could put enough padding around it to absorb the force.'

'But the foam bed blew apart—'

'Well, maybe it needed to be thicker . . . but it was thick enough to aim the ejecta in a direction that doesn't bother us. Notice where it's going?'

'Away from *Kos* is all I know or care,' Esmay said.

'Toward the jump point exit,' the sergeant said, grinning. 'We can always hope some fool Bloodhorde ship comes roaring in here and gets a mouthful of its own bullet.'

'Suiza!' That was Pitak, wanting to know if she could find someone to go into inventory and get the lights and limbs of the idiot who insisted they didn't have any more temporary hull curtains in stock and would have to wait until more were fabricated. 'I know what I've used,' Pitak said. 'And I know what I put into stock, and what was on the inventory when we left Sierra Station. There ought to be sixteen more of 'em, and I want 'em two hours ago.'

*   *   *

'Lots of blood,' said the nanny at the forward triage station.

'At least they're breathing.' The extrication team rolled the slack shape in blood-soaked uniform off the board and onto a gurney with practiced skill, then reached for the next. 'They're all unconscious; we did a quick-scan of the first two and found blood levels of slow-oxy . . . probably someone popped the emergency supply when the hull blew.'

'So you don't have a survey?'

'No – if they aren't missing limbs, we're just bringing them out with all due precautions.' All due precautions to preserve whatever spinal cord integrity was left.

'Number?'

'Thirty or so, I think. I'm not sure yet. We're just now getting access to the most forward compartments.'

The extrication team turned away, heading back for another load.

Esmay watched as *Wraith*'s damaged bow edged into the repair bay. It was easy to forget how large that bay was, empty, but the ship gave a reference for the eye.

'Suiza!' That bellow had to be Pitak. 'Quit looking at the view, and give me a readout.'

'Yes, sir.' Esmay glanced at her board. Pitak's concern was the change in center of gravity as *Wraith* entered *Koskiusko*'s artificial gravity field. Rapid changes could stress the internal structure of *Koskiusko* beyond safe limits. 'Is *Wraith*'s artificial gravity on in any part of the ship?'

'No, it's not.'

'There's a torque force developing in the contralateral midsections . . . only 5.4 dynes right now, but it's increasing in a linear relationship to the mass of *Wraith* within *Kos*'s field.'

'That's expected . . . not desirable, but expected. Transfer a plot of that to my screen and to Power.'

'Yes, sir.' Esmay locked in the curve, keyed for the transfers, and continued to watch her board. Her gaze kept twitching upward to the view of *Wraith*'s approach, but she yanked it back each time. The strain she'd noticed dipped below the curve; she called Pitak. 'It's dropped below line—'

'Good. That means Power is compensating. But watch for that bulge ahead of the damage – that's something we can't really model for the field generator.'

Centimeter by centimeter, *Wraith* edged in. When the mooring lines were secured, warning bells rang throughout the DSR. 'Cradles shifting in T-minus 15 minutes. Cradles shifting—'

Esmay transferred her final readouts to Major Pitak and Power, then withdrew to a monitoring station behind the double red lines. Only a few essential personnel would ride the cradles during shift.

'I hate to think what that mine would have done to the cradle mechanisms,' someone said behind her. She glanced back. Barin Serrano, his dark brows lowered.

'It's taken care of,' she said. She wondered what he was doing there; his assignment, in scan, wasn't needed at the moment.

'Lieutenant Bondal sent me down here to see if Major Pitak had decided where to put the new RSV units,' he said, anticipating her question.

'She hasn't told me – but I'll check for you. Have you heard anything about Bloodhorde ships coming in?'

'No . . . and I'm sure I would have, because . . . well, anyway, I would have. But I do know that *Sting* and *Justice* have jumped out.'

'Why?'

'They delivered *Wraith* . . . and they're supposed to be patrolling out wherever they were. Maybe they thought they'd spot anyone following *Wraith*'s trail in.'

Gar-sig (Packleader) Vokrais woke to the bustle of a medical ward; when he turned his head, he saw his pack-second Hoch staring back at him.

'What happened?' he asked, in his best Familias Standard.

'Effing sleepy gas,' Hoch said. 'We got hauled in as casualties . . . I don't think this is the same ship.'

They lay, listening to the chatter around them.

'We're on the DSR,' Hoch said finally, with a wolfish grin. 'Right inside.'

'All two of us,' Vokrais said. He lifted his head cautiously since no one seemed to be paying any attention to him. He was wearing a clean pale blue shift of some crinkled fabric, and all up and down the rows of beds were the rest of his assault team dressed the same way. Most of them, anyway. He counted only twenty-five of the original thirty, and Tharjold wasn't there – their technical expert, the one who knew most about Familias technology. Nor Kerai, nor Sij . . . his mind ticked off the missing, and consigned them to either of the two possible eternal destinations. The rest were there, all butt-naked in hospital gowns . . . but all awake now, staring at him in wild surmise.

Before he had time to worry about how he was going to get his team clothed and out of medical, a heavyset man with a scowl worthy of a Bloodhorde senior sergeant bustled down the aisle between the beds.

'All right, sleepyheads,' he said. 'You're awake, and none of you got worse than a dose of trank. Come with me – I'll get you clean clothes and put you to work . . . we'll need your help to get *Wraith* repaired.'

'Our IDs?' Hoch asked. He sounded half-strangled, but it was probably just his attempt to control his accent.

'I've got 'em – already passed on the stats to Supply, so you'll have something close to fitting.'

Vokrais rolled out of bed, surprised to find that he wasn't at all dizzy. The others followed; he saw arms twitch as the automatic habit of saluting conflicted with awareness of their position. Their guide didn't notice; he was scowling at a list in his hand.

'Santini?'

Vokrais scrabbled through his memory of the alien vocabulary, and finally remembered that the nametag on the uniform he'd stolen had been something like that, in their misbegotten tongue. 'Uh . . . yes, sir?' Someone sniggered, three beds down, to hear him say 'sir' to a Familias enemy. Someone would feel the lash for that later.

'Wake UP, Santini. Listen – says here you were a specialist in ventilation?'

'Sir,' Vokrais said, wondering which of several meanings he knew for that word mattered here. Ventilation? As in, artificial breathing? As in, perforating?

'That's good – I'll send you over to Support Systems as soon as

230

you've got your gear. Oh, and Camajo?' Silence again. Vokrais prayed to the Heart-Render that someone would have the sense to say something.

After too many heartbeats, Hoch coughed – an obviously fake cough, to Vokrais's ear – and said, 'Yes, sir?'

'I guess you're all still a bit dazed – they told me to give you another hour, but we need help now. Camajo, you'll report to Major Pitak, in H&A. Now, let's see . . . Bradinton?'

This time, the others caught on quicker, and someone said 'Yes, sir,' almost brightly. Vokrais wondered if the others remembered the names on the uniforms they'd stripped from dead men, or if they were just answering blind. It probably didn't matter. Supposedly the Familias ships had a fancy way of figuring out who was really one of their own, but so far he hadn't seen any sign of it.

Eventually all of them had answered to their new names – names which felt uncomfortable even held so lightly, names with no family chant behind them. For a moment Vokrais wondered if the strangers had families . . . if those families had chants of their own . . . but this was not the right kind of thought for the belly of an enemy ship. He pushed it away, and it fell off his mind like a landsman off the deck of a dragonship in rough seas. Instead he thought of the battle to come, the hot blood of enemies that would soak his clothes, not cold and clammy this time but properly steaming. He had not minded stripping the dead and putting on their blood-soaked uniforms . . . not after the rituals of the Blooding . . . but it had been distasteful to feel it already cold.

His pack followed him through the enemy ship; he could feel their amusement even as his own bubbled just beneath the surface. The enemy . . . more like prey than enemy, like sheep leading a wolf into the fold in the mistaken notion that it was a sheepdog. Even as he accepted a folded pile of clothes, he was sure that his pack could have taken this ship bare naked, with only their blood-hunger. Instead . . . he dressed quickly, carefully not meeting anyone's eyes. He had worn Familias clothing before, in his years as a spy . . . the soft cloth, the angled fastenings, felt almost as familiar as his own.

The lack of weapons didn't. He missed the familiar pressure of needler and stunner, knocknab and gutstab. Familias troops carried weapons only into battle . . . and DSRs didn't fight.

The helpful enemy had leapfrogged them over the first two phases of the plan, handing them the chance to disperse throughout the ship. With any luck at all – and the gods definitely seemed to be loading luck upon them – no one from *Wraith* would notice that the men wearing the uniforms of shipmates were not shipmates at all.

Vokrais followed the route displayed on the palm-sized mapcom, sure that he could deal with whatever he found when he arrived.

'No, I'm not going to send anyone from *Wraith* back over there – not after they've been knocked out for a week or so with sleepygas. Their cogs won't be meshing for another two shifts, and we don't want accidents.' Vokrais heard the end of that and wondered whether feigning mental illness would do anything useful. Probably not. They might send him back to the medical area, where he could end up in bed with no pants on. Better to seem dutiful but slightly confused – the confusion at least was honest enough.

Familias technology impressed him as it had before – so much of it, and it worked so well. No familiar stench of sweat and gutbreath. Clean air emerged from one grille, and vanished into another; the lights never flickered; the artificial gravity felt as solid as a planet. The little communications device and the data wand he'd been given were smaller and worked better than their analogs on the Bloodhorde ships.

This was what they had come for, after all. The technology they had not been able to buy or steal or (last and least efficient ploy) invent. Bigger ships, better ships, ships that could take on Familias and Compassionate Hand cruisers and win. The technicians to keep the technology working . . . Vokrais eyed the others around him. They didn't look like much, but he had somewhat overcome the prejudice of his upbringing; he knew that smart minds could hide in bodies of all shapes. But hardly one in fifty looked like any kind of warrior.

Meanwhile . . . meanwhile his pack was dispersed throughout the DSR, very handily. Probably several supervisors would decide, as his had, to assign them simple duties. Eventually a meal would come, and they'd have access to eating utensils, so easily converted to effective hand weapons.

An hour . . . two. Vokrais worked on, willing enough to sort parts, package them in trays, stack them on automatic carriers. There was no hurry; they had gained time by being put to sleep and admitted as casualties, an irony he hoped to be able to share at the victory feast with his commander. Once he caught a glimpse of another pack member, carrying something he didn't recognize; for an instant their gazes crossed, then the other man looked away. Yes. Huge as this ship might be, they would locate one another, and their plan would work. And the longer they had to explore it, to learn its capabilities, the easier to slit its guts open when the time came.

Esmay glanced up as a shadow crossed her screen. CAMAJO, the nametag said, clipped to a uniform that fit its wearer like a new saddle . . . technically fitting, but uneasy in some way. The insignia of a petty-light had been applied recently, and not quite straight, to his sleeve.

'I was told to report here,' the man said. 'To Major . . . Major Pitak.' His eyes roved the compartment as if scanning it for hidden weapons; his glance at Esmay had been dismissive. Her skin prickled. He reminded her of something – someone – her mind, suddenly alert, scrabbled frantically in memory to figure out what. She looked back at the screen before she answered.

'She's in with Commander Seveche. Are you from *Wraith*?' She couldn't imagine anyone from *Koskiusko* giving her quite that look. It wasn't the 'you're not really Fleet are you?' look, or the 'you're that kid who commanded *Despite*, aren't you?' look, or any of the others she'd have recognized.

'Yes . . . sir.' The pause snagged her attention away from the screen graphics again. 'We were . . . in the forward compartment . . . the sleepygas . . .'

'You're lucky to be alive,' Esmay said, instantly forgiving the man's odd behavior. If he'd been through all that, he could still be affected by the drug. 'We've got *Wraith* in now; work's already started. You can wait here for Major Pitak, or at Commander Seveche's office.'

'Where's Commander Seveche's office?' the man asked. The shipchip in his pocket bleeped, and he peered cross-eyed at a space between him and Esmay. She knew what that meant – the shipchip was projecting a route.

'Just follow your shipchip,' she said. He turned, without the proper acknowledgement; Esmay started to say something, but . . . he had been gassed, and might be still a bit hazy. Something wasn't quite right . . .

'Petty-light . . .' she said. He stopped in mid-stride, then turned jerkily. Something not right at all. His eyes were not the eyes of someone dazed by drugs . . . his eyes had a bright gleam half-hidden behind lowered lids.

'Yes . . . Lieutenant?'

She could not define what was wrong . . . it was not anything so positive as disrespect, which she had experienced often enough. Respect and disrespect occurred in a relationship, a connection. Here she felt no connection at all, as if Petty-light Camajo were not Fleet at all, but a civilian.

'When you do see Major Pitak, tell her that the simulations for fabrication have arrived from SpecMat.'

'The simulations have arrived . . . yes . . . m . . . sir.' Camajo turned, moving more decisively than someone fogged on sleepy-gas, and was gone before Esmay could say more. She scowled at the screen. *Yes . . . m . . . sir?* What had he been about to say?

She felt uneasy. Had *Wraith* had traitors on its crew? Was that why it had suffered such damage? Why was Camajo alive, uninjured, after such a hull breach between him and the rest of the ship?

This was ridiculous. She had not noticed anything amiss in *Despite*, had not recognized that any of the traitors were traitors. She had not been uneasy this way then. Perhaps that experience had made her paranoid, willing to interpret every discrepancy as ominous. Camajo had been lucky, that was all, and now he was disoriented, on a strange ship with none of his familiar companions.

That didn't work out. The casualties on *Despite*, traitor or loyal, none of them had stumbled over the familiar Fleet greetings and honorifics. With blood in his mouth, as he died, Chief Major

Barscott had answered 'Yes, sir . . .' to Esmay. How many of the survivors in those forward compartments had been lucky? How lucky? And was it luck?

Camajo's eyes . . . his gaze . . . reminded her of her father's soldiers. Groundpounders' eyes . . . commandos' eyes . . . roving, assessing, looking for the weaknesses in a position, thinking how to take over . . . Take over what?

Scolding herself, Esmay flicked to the next screen, but her mind wandered anyway. In the civil wars – she called it that now, though to her family it was still the Califer Uprising – both sides had tried infiltrating the others' defensive positions with troops wearing stolen uniforms, using stolen ID. It had worked a few times, even though both knew it was possible. She'd never heard of such a thing happening in Fleet. Ships weren't infiltrated by individuals . . . they were attacked by ships. Very rarely in Fleet history were attempts at hostile boarding mentioned; battle zones were too dangerous for EVA maneuvers. Pirates sometimes boarded individual commercial vessels . . . but that wasn't the military. It would take . . . it would take a single badly damaged Fleet ship, one that could not detect the movement of individuals in EVA gear . . . a hull breach that let them in . . . a way to get the right uniforms . . . no. She was being silly.

Major Pitak came in while she was still arguing with herself. 'That Camajo fellow from *Wraith* must be still half-tranked,' she said, dropping a half-dozen cubes onto her desk. 'I couldn't get out of him *which* simulations were in . . . sent him on down to E-12; they can use him for a runner if nothing else. Can't cause much trouble that way.'

Esmay lost her argument with prudence. 'Major, I was wondering about a security breach . . .'

'Security breach! What are you talking about?'

'Camajo. I'm not sure, but . . . something wasn't right.'

'He'd been out for a week; that scrambles anyone's brain. How could he be a security breach?'

'He just didn't react the way he should,' Esmay said. 'The way he looked at me – it wasn't a tranked-out sort of expression.'

Pitak looked at her, alert. 'You've been through one mutiny; if it hasn't made you paranoid, maybe you would notice something wrong. So you think he might be a traitor, like Hearne and Garrivay?'

'No, sir. I was thinking . . . what if someone infiltrated *Wraith*. Through the hull breach maybe. Couldn't Bloodhorde troops have gotten in there, before *Wraith* jumped out?'

'You mean like boarding a watership in a pirate story? Nobody does that, Suiza, not in real life in deep space. Even pirates send people over in pods. Besides, how would they survive through jump?'

'Well . . . there were survivors in the forward compartments.'

'But those were *Wraith* crew, in *Wraith* uniforms, with their names on the crew list. I was there myself, Suiza. I didn't see anything that looked like Bloodhorde commandos, just wounded who'd been knocked out by sleepygas to conserve oxygen.'

'You're sure?'

Pitak looked at her with a combination of exhaustion and irritation. 'Unless you're suggesting that the Bloodhorde cleverly dressed their soldiers in our uniforms – uniforms that just happened to have the right ID patterns in the cloth, and the right nametags on the pockets – and wounded them, drenched them in their own blood, then left them there to jump in a damaged ship—?'

'I suppose they really were wounded?'

Pitak snorted. 'I'm no medic – how would I know? They were unconscious and covered with blood, wearing our uniform. What more do you want?'

It was a silly question, but Esmay didn't bother to point that out. The itchy feeling between her shoulders wouldn't go away. 'Camajo wasn't wounded . . . I think I'll check with sickbay, if you don't mind.'

'Snarks in a bucket, Suiza, why don't you keep your mind on your work – or am I not giving you enough? Let Medical worry about the wounded, unless you want to transfer over there—'

'No, sir.' Esmay heard in her own voice the stubborn conviction that she was right.

Pitak glared at her. 'You're worried about something.'

'Yes, sir.'

'Spit it out then.'

'Sir, I . . . I have a bad feeling—' Pitak snorted and rolled her eyes like a skittish mare; Esmay persisted. 'The thing is, sir, if they could get close enough to hand-plant a mine, they could have put some troops aboard.'

'Without anyone noticing? That's—'

'Sir, *Wraith* was isolated at the time of the attack; individuals in EVA gear – or even in small pods – wouldn't have shown up on scans by *Justice* and *Sting*; *Wraith*'s own scan was badly damaged. The tactical analysis suggested that the Bloodhorde might want to capture a DSR, not just destroy one. I know we don't usually consider the Bloodhorde as having this sort of planning ability, but consider: if they can get a commando team aboard the DSR, they could cause enough disruption to make it easier for a follow-up ship or wave of ships to board and capture it.'

'I can see where that might be a plan, Suiza, but I repeat: those wounded wore our uniform. *Our* uniform, with the Fleet recognition code in the weave . . . you think they stole a bale of our cloth and made up uniforms, then stole *Wraith*'s personnel list—'

'No, sir.' Esmay's mind raced, trying to catch up to her intuition. 'Suppose . . . suppose they boarded, forward of the breach, counting on the confusion. Communications to the forward compartments failed, with the damage . . . so whatever they did up there wouldn't be known aft. They could have overpowered any uninjured crew, killed them, put on their uniforms, spaced their own uniforms and the dead—'

'It still sounds like something out of an adventure cube, Suiza, not like real life.' Pitak chewed her lip. 'Then, on the other hand, the Bloodhorde go for the dramatic. You would argue then that the blood belonged to the real RSS personnel, now dead – and that inside those bloody uniforms, the enemy were unwounded?'

'Yes, sir, unless jump transit did them some harm. Those compartments weren't any too sound, you said.'

'No . . .' Pitak glowered at her. 'I must say, Suiza, your passion for completeness can be a real pain sometimes. We had enough to do already.' She reached for the comm switch. 'But I'll check.'

For the time it took for Pitak to work her way through the obstacles the medical section put in the way of the merely curious, Esmay tried to settle to her own assignment. The lines and figures blurred on the page . . . she kept seeing in her mind what she had not seen with her own eyes, the dark compartments of *Wraith*'s bow section, cluttered with debris and unconscious men and women. Men and women with Camajo's − or whatever his name really was − eyes, the alert eyes of those on a mission. She ran her stylus along a column of figures, trying to force her mind to some useful task.

A change in the tone of Pitak's voice brought her upright, fully alert.

'Oh?' Elaborately casual, that. 'Interesting − I helped evacuate some of them, you know, and they were covered with blood − yes. I see. Just the effect of the sleepygas? Are they still in sickbay then?' Her voice sharpened. 'When?' Her eyes met Esmay's. 'I see.'

Esmay waited, as Pitak closed the circuit.

'If you retain this habit of being right, Suiza, you're going to be hated.' Esmay said nothing. 'They weren't wounded, any of them. Twenty-five males . . . seemed a little dazed and confused when they woke up, and three hours ago they were sent off to various workstations around the ship. Camajo, as we both know, was sent here, to H&A. If they were Bloodhorde . . . that many Bloodhorde loose in our ship could do us real damage . . .'

'Yes, sir.'

'And I don't even know where they are. A petty-chief named Barrahide, from Personnel, came and got them. Not somebody from *Wraith*, because all *Wraith* personnel who aren't in sickbay are busy helping our people with damage assessment.' As she talked, Pitak was scrolling through the communications tree. 'Ah. Here we are. Extension . . . 7762.' Another call, but this time Pitak talked as she waited for someone to pick up on the other end. 'That's *if* they're Bloodhorde. They might not be. We need someone from *Wraith* . . . or rather, the captain does. But I'll see what Barrahide can tell me.'

'Someone might take a look at the communications lines from the forward compartments to the rear in *Wraith* . . . was it explosive damage or were they cut?'

'Good idea, Suiza. You call my chief and tell him to check − Oh, Chief Barrahide? Listen, about those *Wraith* crew you took out of sickbay . . .'

14

Barin tried not to think about Esmay Suiza; he had enough to do, if only he could concentrate on it. Besides, she was two ranks above him; he was a mere boy to her. He told himself that, but he didn't believe it. She respected him; after that first disastrous argument, she had treated him as an equal. He felt himself scowling. This wasn't about respect, exactly. It was about . . . he squirmed, trying to push the thought aside. Planet-born, and higher-ranked . . . he had *no* good reason to be thinking of her that way, and he was. Her soft brown hair made Serrano black look harsh . . . her height made Serrano compactness look stubby. The back of her neck . . . even her elbows . . . he didn't want to feel this, and he did.

Serranos, his mother had said, fall hard when they fall. He had taken that as he took most of the things he was told about his inheritance, with far more than one grain of salt. His mother was not a Serrano; her occasional sarcasms might be envy. His adolescent crushes had been obvious even to him as temporary flares of hormonal activity. He had expected to find someone, if he ever did, in the respectable ranks of Fleet's traditional families. A Livadhi, perhaps. A Damarin – there was one of his year, a sleek green-eyed beauty with the supple Damarin back. If they had been assigned to the same ship . . . but they hadn't been.

This was unsuitable. He knew that. Grandmother would raise those eyebrows. Mother would sigh that sigh. His distant cousin Heris would . . . he didn't want to think about her, either. By rumor she had chosen an unsuitable partner, but he didn't think that would make her sympathetic.

The part of his mind that had not wandered off down this seductive lane prodded him back to alertness. Commander Vorhes would have his head on a platter if he didn't get those scan components out of inventory and down to the repair bay in a hurry. He shook his head at his own folly, and caught an amused glance from another ensign he knew.

'Heads up, Serrano – you hear about the mysterious intruders?'

'Intruders? What intruders?'

'Some casualties off *Wraith* who weren't that badly hurt, so we put 'em to work, and then they disappeared. About that time someone in Hull and Architecture went spacey and started claiming they were Bloodhorde agents or something . . . anyway, nobody can track 'em down, and there's a sort of alert—'

'Nothing official yet?'

'No—' A loud blat-blat-blat interrupted them. 'Unless this is it.'

It was. 'All personnel report to nearest lift tube bay on Decks Seven and Eight for identification confirmation . . . All personnel . . .'

Barin and the others in sight drifted toward the nearest lift tube bay. 'This is silly, you know,' the other ensign said. 'They'll never find anyone in this maze . . . five arms, the core, eighteen decks, all the dead space here and there, let alone the inventory bays . . . it's impossible.'

'If it's really a Bloodhorde assault group, they'd better find 'em,' Barin said. 'Anyway, we've got internal scan in every compartment.' He remembered what Esmay had told him about the internal scan evidence used in her trials. 'They'd have to know how to disable it to escape detection. Shouldn't be that hard to track 'em, even in a ship this size.'

'What could they do, anyway? If we don't find them, they'll just rattle around. It can't be but a few—' The other ensign slowed as the crowd ahead came in sight.

Barin thought of what Esmay had told him about the mutiny and what he'd heard of Heris Serrano's capture of Garrivay's cruiser. 'It doesn't take many to create havoc,' he said. 'If they get command of the bridge . . .' All at once the ship which had seemed too large to be a ship, too safe to be interesting, felt fragile in the immensity of space. He tried to tell himself again that internal scan would find the intruders . . . but there were compartments without full pickup. And the volume of data alone would make it easy to miss significant details. That new AI system which had already glitched on keeping up with changes in the layout . . . could it really handle a job like this?

He joined the line forming in front of a *Koskiusko* crewman wearing Security patches. Ahead of him, others asked the questions he wanted answered, but the answers weren't coming. 'Just look in here,' they were all told. 'Handprints there. You'll feel a prick . . . now move along . . .'

Full ID checks? Barin hadn't been through a full ID check since he entered the Academy. Did they really think someone could fake a retinal scan or handprint pattern? *Could* someone fake all that? He shifted from foot to foot. Behind him the line thickened. It was taking at least a minute to process each person and hand out a new ID tag. He occupied his mind with the obvious calculation . . . a max of sixty people an hour through each checkpoint, and they had only ten checkpoints? It would be hours and hours before they'd confirmed and issued new tags to the whole crew . . .

'Look in here, sir . . . and your hands . . . you'll feel a prick.' He blinked from the flash as the machine checked his retinal pattern; he felt a sharp prick as it drew his blood to check against his record. The machine bleeped, and Barin took the bright pink tag they offered. Unlike his old one, it didn't have his picture, just the shiny strip that would allow scan to recognize him as legitimate. Even as he walked off, on his way to inventory for the parts Vorhes had wanted, he saw more security personnel arriving with more screening equipment.

He took the tube up to Deck 13, and gave his request to the master chief who was supervising the automated retrieval system. She did not have one of the new pink ID tags, but nodded toward his.

'I expect the captain'll shut down the automated system soon, and then I can go get my new tags. You're lucky you got here now.'

Inside, the noise of the shifting racks was only half as loud as usual. Soon enough, one of the little robocarts slid up to the door with his order; the chief checked it off.

'Do you need transport, sir?'

Barin eyed the load and decided he could manage. 'No, thank you.'

'Fine, then.'

He picked up the packaged components and decided not to take the tube back down . . . he could walk around the core, clockwise with the traffic, then take the ladder up to Deck Twelve and be in the Tech Schools inventory for the other things Vorhes wanted. And he might see something . . . his pulse quickened. If they were intruders, and if they were Bloodhorde, what would they look like? All he knew about the Bloodhorde was that they favored tall blonds.

As he passed the base of T-5, he could see into the ship security bay, which looked like a kicked anthill. Why couldn't he have been in the ship's own crew? He could imagine himself easily as that lieutenant of security, the one scowling at him now as if to wonder what an ensign from the 14th's remote sensing section was doing here. It would be a lot more interesting than his job . . . he wouldn't see any intruders, or any enemy on the outside either. He strode on, wishing hives on the person who'd assigned him to scan on a DSR, instead of something suitable to a Serrano.

The schools inventory, when he got there, was empty. He leaned on the counter, tempted to stick his wand in the console and find out where the parts were that he wanted. It wasn't safe, really . . . if everyone was lined up getting new ID tags, who was making sure the intruders didn't get into someplace like this? Although why they'd want to . . .

He heard footsteps coming, and felt his pulse quicken again. What if it was intruders? He glanced around and saw nothing useful as a weapon . . . but the plump sergeant who puffed into view wore a new pink ID tag.

'Sorry, sir,' he said, his cheeks scarlet with exertion. 'I had to run up all the ladders . . . they've turned off the lift tubes, just in case, which is ridiculous . . . it only makes more work for the rest of us.'

Barin handed over his list. 'Perhaps they're concerned that the intruders might cut the power to the lift tubes.'

'You don't think they would!' The sergeant paused in the act of entering the access codes.

242

'I don't know what they'd do,' Barin said. 'But if someone wanted to cause trouble, that's one way to do it.'

'Stupid,' the man said, and completed the entry. 'Let's see . . . aisle 8, level 2, tray 13. Just a moment, then.' The schools inventory had never been automated, and Barin waited while the sergeant found his items and handed them over. Barin signed the terminal and headed back. Should he use the ladders here . . . T-1 was probably less crowded . . . or go on around and straight down in T-3?

He split the decision, dropping to Deck Six, then going around core to T-3 for the final descent to Deck Four.

Vokrais had found the place, one of the maintenance shafts for the lift tube clusters, this one at the inboard junction of T-3 and T-2 on Deck Six, on his way to the meal at which he'd picked up the disgustingly dull knife and fork now hidden under his jumpsuit. He'd found Metris again, and passed the word. Metris would pass it on, as he would. How long did they have? His blood sang with excitement, clearing away the dregs of the sleepygas. This was nothing like the usual ship boarding, when they blasted their way in, weapons in hand, to take swift control of some fat, lazy trader. This was a real challenge.

He wondered if anyone had noticed their weapons and equipment, back on *Wraith*. They'd found the mine – that was common gossip, which they were glad to tell a presumed *Wraith* crewman. 'Would have blown you to hell and back,' someone had said to him. 'If our people hadn't found it and foamed it down.'

But had they foamed the inner compartments too? If so, his favorite knives and tools might be safely embedded in the foam, and he could retrieve them later. It had been his grandfather's battle knife too . . . he wanted it back.

They needed weapons. He knew he could take any two or three of these effete technicians barehanded, but there were thousands of them. His whole team together could kill dozens, but it would not be enough. Somewhere on this monster ship were weapons of all sorts, hand weapons and ship weapons, ammunition, powerpacks . . . everything. He just had to find it.

His supposed supervisor wasn't watching him closely; he walked off casually in the direction of the dumps . . . no, they called them 'heads' for reasons he'd never figured out. He was willing to call any of these fools shithead, but it still seemed an odd name for the receptacle. He felt eyes on him, and glanced back to see his supervisor, looking annoyed. The man shrugged as Vokrais went on through the door.

Inside were three others, a man and two women. Vokrais eyed the women. The Bloodhorde hired some female mercenaries, but they fought in all-female units. That was the natural way, otherwise men would think of nothing but rut, day in and day out. He was thinking of it now, as the tall redhaired one was washing her hands. She looked into the mirror, met his gaze, and scowled at him. Scowl all you wish, Vokrais thought. You will be tossed on my spear before morning. Or another one would; it didn't really matter.

When they left, he explored the echoing space with its seamless hard floor, its shiny walls. He found two other doors; one opened into a storage closet, and one into a different corridor. He tested the top of the closet – he could get out that way, if he had to – but chose to walk out the other door as if he had come in that way. Here he would have no pesky supervisor watching his every move. He tried to remember where his pack-second had been sent, and thought of using the data wand.

He pushed it into one of the dataports, and flicked through the controls coding queries.

'Need some help?' someone asked at his elbow. Vokrais managed not to strike, but his move was sudden enough that the man – older, gray-haired – stepped back, startled.

'Sorry,' he muttered. 'Timing still off . . .' and he gestured to his ID tag, which had the *Wraith* shipcode on it.

'Oh – I thought perhaps you were lost or something. That's a slow-stream dataport; if you want a quick answer to anything, there's a fast-stream down there.'

'I would like to find the other survivors,' Vokrais said. He struggled to remember the names on the uniform tags. 'Camajo, Bremerton . . .'

'Ah . . . you know their numbers?'

No, he didn't know their mythical numbers that went with their mythical names. He shook his head, not trusting his voice.

'A search on *Wraith* should get 'em,' the man said, and put his own wand into a port a few meters away. Vokrais noticed that this one had a double ring around it, blue and green. The one he had been using had a double band of yellow and green. 'Here you are,' the man said then. 'I'll transfer it to yours . . .' He reached for Vokrais's data wand, then snugged it next to his for a moment, and handed the wand back.

'Thanks,' Vokrais remembered to say; the man nodded and strode off. He looked at the display options, and walked down the corridor as if thinking, looking at the names and duty assignments coming up. Would that man remember him? Report him? Would anyone be expected to know about the color codings on the dataports? He'd felt smug that he'd recognized a dataport at all.

Hoch was indeed in Hull and Architecture, in wing T-3 and on Deck Four. Vokrais considered the distance and cursed to himself. What misbegotten brain-dead fool of an engineer had designed this ship . . . it made no sense. A space station with an oversized drive, that's what it was, not a ship at all. He was wasting too much time hunting people, but he could hardly get on the shipspeaker (surely they had a shipspeaker) and call.

He spotted another of his people lounging along looking the picture of a lazy incompetent, and signaled him. Sramet wandered over, and Vokrais told him where to meet, and that he would find Hoch. 'And don't slouch like that,' he said, as he finished. 'At least look like you're on business.' Sramet nodded, and put on the character of earnest, hardworking dullness as if he had pulled a mask over his head.

And that was another thing lost in *Wraith* . . . not only their technical expert and their weapons, but their tools, and their special gear that included disguises and camouflage.

Hoch, when he found him, was being chewed out by one of the Familias NCOs, who finished a scathing description of his abilities with a couple of ethnic slurs aimed at his presumed planet of origin. 'And you can take your sorry tail back to Commander Atarin's clerk, and explain that Petty-major Dorian won't have you on the crew, is that clear?'

Hoch caught Vokrais's eye, but his expression of sullen incompetence did not change. 'Yes, sir,' he said, in a strangled voice.

'Get on with it, then.' The NCO, suppressed fury in every line of his body, stalked off down the passage. Hoch looked straight at Vokrais, this time with the expression of his mind: he would kill that one, when he found him again.

'We have a place,' Vokrais said, as they walked back the other way. He gave the location, then said, 'I need to find more – only two others so far . . . this thing is too big.'

'I'll go too . . . do you know where they are?'

Vokrais was able to repeat the trick, as he thought it, of mating his data wand with Hoch's to transfer the list of personnel locations. 'We're going to be discovered soon,' he said. 'I can feel it. We don't fit in with these . . . people.'

'Slaves,' Hoch said, in their tongue, and Vokrais looked at him sharply.

'Careful. We still have to do it.'

'In my sleep, packleader.' That in a lower voice still, but still in their tongue.

'Soon, then,' said Vokrais, in the Familias. 'Make one sweep clockwise – they all seem to go clockwise on the big passage around the core – and then meet. I want to make one trip as far unship as I can get before they realize we're aboard.'

'Why should they? They're half-asleep, sheep ready for shearing.'

'Go, packbrother,' Vokrais said. Hoch's eyes gleamed, and his arm twitched; he moved off to the left. Vokrais went across to the nearest cluster of lift/drop tubes and shot upward. He had enjoyed the swift ride many times on his visits to Familias space stations; the Bloodhorde had sufficient trouble with the technology of gravity control that they used lift tubes rarely, never for such distances. He didn't suppose it would take him all the way to the top, but there it was: Deck Seventeen.

He stepped out into the same wide curving corridor, here less busy than down on Deck Four. He walked along briskly, as if he knew where he was going. A bored guard stood at an opening that might lead to the bridge, on the core side; Vokrais didn't try to look in. His shoulders itched; he knew he was being watched. He walked on, most of the way around the core, surprised to find no other lift tube clusters, as there had been on the lower decks. Did only one set come this far? He didn't want to go back past the first guard, like someone who had lost his way.

He came to another guarded opening. Here the guard looked more alert, eyes shifting back and forth. Vokrais could see the bulge of lift tubes ahead, but before that was a wide opening into T-2 . . . it had the label above . . . and he remembered that the dining hall had also been in T-2. He looked in and almost stumbled in amazement. The place was full of plants, green plants.

He turned in through the door as if this was what he'd intended all along, and felt the guard's attention drop from him like a heavy load. Beneath his feet, something that almost felt like soil cushioned his steps; on either side were the plants, from ankle to waist-high, some with colorful flowers on them. He ambled along a path, seeing no one. Paths met the one he was on, diverged, wound around taller plants that made screens so that he could not tell how large this place was.

Water pricked his face; when he looked up, he could see a foggy halo around the lights far overhead. The path ended abruptly in a waist-high wall of fake stone − he felt it, and was sure it was molded. A path ran beside the wall to rustic fake-stone steps to his left. Below . . . below was more garden, and one enormous tree rising up past him to end fifteen meters over his head. Behind it, a rough-looking gray wall with patches of blurred white, on which someone was splayed out as if for sacrifice: arms wide, legs stretched apart. As he watched, someone laughed, far below, and the figure heaved upward, lost its grip, and fell.

Vokrais watched the fall, waiting for the satisfying thunk, but instead the climber jerked to a halt in midair, and hung swinging. Now he could see the thin line, looped far above and coming back to the hand of someone standing beside the wall.

He started down the steps. Were the Fleet planners finally schooling their troops in hostile boarding techniques? But if so, why not have them in the gear they'd need? Why practice in thin short pants and little raglike shirts?

From the garden on Deck 16, he ran down one of the sets of stairs − stairs in stairwells, as in a building, not ladders as in a real ship – to Deck 14, then went out on the main curved passage again to catch the drop tube down to Deck 6. He could have used the access shaft itself, checking it out as he came, but he was eager to see how many people Hoch had collected.

When he came through the hatch, he saw nothing at first, which was what he expected to see. Above and below, the shaft seemed empty, a smudged gray tube with a spiral ladder curling around bundled cables and pipes in the middle. Vokrais grinned, noting where lights had burnt out in helpful places, and whistled a few notes.

His pack reappeared, one after another moving out of the shadows, out of hatches that opened into other access tunnels, out of whatever cover they'd found. One by one they came up or down the ladder to cluster near him. One, three, four, six, ten . . . plus himself and Hoch. Twelve only, and not enough. He scowled at Hoch.

'Is this all?'

'No . . . but all who could come safely right now. Three more coming, when they can slip away. Sramet saw Pilan and Vrodik, but couldn't speak to them long enough. Geller is the only one nobody's seen or reported on.'

'Who has weapons?' he asked, pulling out the knife and fork he'd taken.

'They don't carry weapons,' Sramet said, sounding disgusted. 'Not even the ones with Weapons Systems patches.'

Two others had stolen dinner knives; Brolt had already started to sharpen his to a stabbing point.

'The contractors?'

'They're here,' Hoch said. 'But we haven't contacted them yet.'

'So we don't know about the mechanism.' Vokrais thought a moment. 'It would be better to find out for ourselves, without asking them. I don't trust them.' His distrust had brought them all here; he had argued, successfully, that even if the scum were honest, they might panic and undo the job once they realized their own necks were in danger. Later his plan had expanded; if they were quick enough, his warband would have the entire glory to themselves, the richest capture in the history of the Bloodhorde.

'We could take them . . . we could make *sure* they did it right.'

Vokrais grinned. 'We do need a few hostages.'

'They won't care—' Hoch said. The Bloodhorde didn't. Anyone careless enough to get caught was worthless; even if he escaped later, he wouldn't be trusted again for a long time.

'Familias is different. Besides, we need some of their technical tricks. We're supposed to know how to do things we don't understand.' They nodded; they'd all found that out in only the few hours. Astounding that a warship crew, even down to the fewest of stripes, would be expected to understand all the gadgetry . . . but so it had proved. Only the fact that they'd been gassed, and assumed to have residual problems from that, had kept them from being discovered simply by their ignorance. 'If we get one of the right family, it'll slow 'em down. They'll stop to think about it; they'll try a rescue. Then we get more.'

'So you want us to pick certain needles out of a stack of thousands?'

'If they come handy. Here – shove that wand into the 'port and let's get a crew list.' It was a blue-and-green ringed port, he noticed. Hoch put his wand in, and information appeared in little glowing letters, projected on the air itself.

At first, the long list of names meant nothing. Then Vokrais remembered the Familias habit of putting organizational charts on the system, and figured out the right code to ask for. 'We want someone in scan, so they can tell us how to disable their miserable systems without blowing them away,' Hoch said.

'The question is, do we want someone on the ship's crew, someone from the schools division, or the heavy maintenance division?'

'Heavy maintenance,' Vokrais decided. 'From what I heard, they've made all sorts of modifications to the original ship's architecture . . . the crew may not know about it, but those in maintenance will.'

In a few minutes, they had a list of personnel assigned to Remote Sensing, 14th Heavy Maintenance Yard. 'Commander Vorhes,' Vokrais muttered. 'That won't work – he'll be surrounded by people all the time. Lieutenant Bondal . . . Ensign Serrano . . .' He looked up, grinning. 'Serrano. Wasn't that the bitch who caused us trouble at Xavier?'

'And an important Fleet family. Even though he's only an ensign, that'll make them take notice.'

'If he knows enough,' Hoch said. 'He's only an ensign. The lieutenant I found in Hull and Architecture isn't an expert . . . the junior officers can be sent here for short runs.'

'If he doesn't know enough, we can snatch another from scan – the family connection alone will be useful.'

'Hostage or vengeance?'

'Well . . . we tell *them* it's a hostage.' Another low chuckle; they understood that. This Serrano cub would go back to his family – if he did – toothless and tamed, a warning not to interfere with Bloodhorde nobles. 'Now – have you all used the mapping function on these things?'

Heads shook, and Vokrais glared at them. They'd come for the technology; they should be learning to use it. The data wands weren't difficult. He put his own in the port this time, telling them about the fast and slow ports as if he'd known all along. Then he switched to the open display, and the ship graphics glowed before them.

'We need a higher access probe to find everything we want,' he said. 'So we need to kill someone in ship security – with lots of stripes – and use theirs. But here you can see . . .' He pointed out the bridge, the secondary command center tucked in between the two FTL drives, the medical decks and the ship security offices on T-5. 'They'll have weapons in security – even these sheep must run amok sometimes – and if we knock out their security personnel, we've eliminated resistance.' All that counted, all that knew how to fight in any organized way. 'In medical, they'll have more of that sleepygas, and the antidotes—'

'Eye for eye,' murmured Hoch, grinning. Bloodhorde tradition, to return insults as exactly as possible, before the final blood-letting.

The loud blat-blat-blat of some alarm made them all look around. Then the muffled voice that must be a transmitted announcement. Hoch stuck his data wand back in the 'port, this time choosing the faster display, which only the user could see.

'They caught on,' he said after a moment. 'They're pulling everyone in for identification checks, full-scale . . . whatever that

250

means.' Vokrais was impressed. After that sloppy beginning, he'd expected to have days to wander around unnoticed before being found out. But this was better. He grinned at his pack.

'They know something's wrong, but they don't know where we are. It'll take them awhile to do the checks and issue new ID tags. Hours, probably. In the meantime, they won't even know how many of us there are. Vanter, Pormuk—' These were not their Fleet names, but their own. 'You'll get us new tags. Try to dispose of the bodies where it'll take awhile to find them. Get the data wands, too. If you see any more of our people, sweep them up. Hoch, take two – three if you must – and get those contractors; we need to know where the self-destruct is, and be sure the captain can't use it. The rest of you, come with me. We need weapons, especially as we're short-handed right now.'

'We come back here . . . ?'

'No. They have gardens on this ship, if you can believe it. Maybe more than one, but at the top of T-2, Decks 16 and 17. Lots of places to hide, and many ways in and out. There's a big tree – you can't mistake it – and an assault wall.'

'If we're seen . . . ?'

'Capture or kill, and don't capture more than you can handle on the move. They know they've got trouble; we'll show them how much.' Low growls answered him; they liked this much better than pretending to be softbellied Fleet techs. 'Go.'

Captain Hakin, wearing his own new ID tag, looked as grim as expected when he met with the other senior officers aboard. He had called them to the officers' lounge nearest the bridge, where officers just going off or coming on duty met informally. Now the room was guarded by security personnel, their wary eyes watching everyone in sight.

'The *Wraith* crew members who came aboard as casualties from the forward compartments have not appeared for ID checks,' he said. 'We have forwarded what little videoscan we have to Captain Seska aboard *Wraith*, and he is sure that at least eight of those were never his personnel. He is showing every image to his remaining crew, to check on the ones he said he wasn't sure of. But we must assume that all twenty-five *Wraith* casualties who were not injured, and who were sent to work assignments by Chief Barrahide, are actually impostors. We do not know where they came from; I understand that Lieutenant Suiza had a notion that they might be Bloodhorde intruders. If so, this ship is in even more peril than we thought.'

'Any sign of a Bloodhorde ship?' asked Admiral Dossignal.

'No, Admiral. However, the situation with regard to our escort is . . . tenuous.'

'Tenuous?' asked Admiral Livadhi.

'Yes . . . *Sting* and *Justice*, as the admiral recalls, were assigned to patrol the same area as *Wraith*. Their captains insisted on returning to that patrol area, arguing that they could then guard the exit jump point there if the Bloodhorde tried to use it. That made sense, before we knew about the mine on *Wraith*; they'd been long gone by the time we suspected that intruders had come aboard.'

'And our present escort?'

'Is useless if the intruders gain control of this ship – they could destroy *Koskiusko*, of course, if they were ordered to do so, but who is to give the order? I have made it clear to both captains that they should do precisely this, if they think the ship has been captured, but they have not yet agreed. Captain Plethys said he did not feel certain he could know that the ship had been irrevocably lost, even if he could not make positive identification of an officer on the crew list on a comlink. He argued that communications capacity might be interdicted by the intruders without their actually gaining control—'

'Which is quite possible,' Admiral Livadhi put in.

'Quite so. In fact, any type of signal which I tried to imagine could, in theory, be interdicted by the intruders before they gained control. Captain Martin agreed with Captain Plethys, and added that he did not wish to be responsible for the considerable destruction of life and materiel, even if the intruders did appear to control this ship. He argued that the rest of the wave will no doubt return to guard us, and offered his ship to go and explain the situation. I insisted that he stay, but I'm not sure he will.'

'You think he'll desert us in the face of enemy attack? That's treason!'

'There are no enemy ships on scan,' Livadhi pointed out, hands steepled. 'And he knows he can do nothing about the intruders already aboard. He probably thinks that will clear him with a Board.'

'Not if I'm around to argue it,' Dossignal growled.

'I agree . . . but if I remember Captain Martin, and I believe this is the same Arlen Martin I once attempted to teach Military Justice to, he's got a mind like an eel. Twisting and slithering away is his nature. I never did understand why he was given a ship.'

'So you think he'll go,' Captain Hakin said.

'Probably. Certainly, if his scan techs can locate an enemy ship at a distance where he thinks we can't . . . and then he'll claim he didn't know it was there. He doesn't make mistakes, you see.'

Hakin looked even grimmer. 'Then, sirs, I'm faced with a dilemma which you have probably already anticipated . . . when do I throw the switch?'

'The switch?'

Hakin sighed. 'The admiral will recall that this ship, unlike vessels intended for combat, carries a self-destruct device and my orders are unequivocal. If I believe that the *Koskiusko* is in imminent danger of capture by a hostile force, I am to prevent such capture and appropriation by the enemy . . . by destroying the ship and – if necessary – her entire complement of personnel.'

'But . . . are you *serious*?'

'Quite.' Hakin looked ten years older at the word. 'We've talked about how useful this ship would be to the Bloodhorde – their own private shipyard capable of manufacturing two or three fully-armed cruisers just with the materiel in inventory, and with resupply of the most basic type, capable of building a battle group. Right now it's full of the very people who know how to use it – some of whom, faced with torture or death, would cooperate with the Bloodhorde, at least long enough to train replacements.'

'Nobody would—!' began Livadhi.

'Begging the admiral's pardon, but no military organization in the history of man has had zero failure rate in any system, including the human system. The recent action at Xavier – and for that matter Captain Martin – shows that Fleet is no exception. Besides, even if every person now aboard this vessel chose death, the Bloodhorde can hire civilians from all over the galaxy to operate what they can't figure out.'

'But surely – we're not at that point yet. There are only a few Bloodhorde aboard; security will no doubt pick them up in a few hours—'

'The point at which I *should* push the button is before the Bloodhorde have a chance to prevent it working. Do you think they haven't assumed such a device exists? Do you think they're not looking for it right now, disarming it if they've found it? They don't want to lose this ship any more than we do – but the only way I can ensure that we don't lose it is to destroy it.'

Dossignal looked at him compassionately. 'You're right, Captain, that's a tough decision. Are you asking for advice?'

Hakin grimaced. 'It's my decision . . . my responsibility . . . but I'll be glad to hear your ideas on choosing the right time. Only realize that I know the right time must be too soon rather than too late.'

'How do you test the device integrity?' asked Livadhi. 'And what's your normal test cycle?'

'It's tested weekly, by partially arming the device – it has its own control board, with the usual sensor array and so on. I have a vidscan of it, so I can see the attached status lights, and I also have scan that reports whether the circuits are functioning correctly.'

'So . . . have you tested it since the intruders came aboard?'

'Not yet. My concern, though, is that even if it tests out now, they could find and disable it at any time.'

'You've put a guard on it?'

'Yes . . . but as you know we need security personnel in other areas, including searching for the intruders. They might overpower the guard.'

'Still, that should give you some warning. If the guard doesn't report . . . if the vidscan changes. You *can* test the system while the guard is there, can't you?'

'Yeees . . .'

'Would you like a witness to the test?'

'Yes, I would.'

'Then my suggestion is that you test it now – immediately. And my second suggestion is that you jump back out of this system, which would make it harder for the Bloodhorde group we expect to find us.'

'And for our ships as well,' Captain Hakin said.

'Yes, that's true. But avoiding a Bloodhorde assault group seems more important at this juncture . . . I'm convinced that with over 25,000 loyal personnel on board, we can deal with the intruders – be they Bloodhorde commandos or any other hostile group – as long they aren't reinforced by outside forces.'

'Very well.' Hakin spoke to the guard at the door, and led them across to the bridge.

15

'The Captain asketh, and the Admiral respondeth,' said Lieutenant Bondal, staring at his status board.

'Sir?' Barin pulled himself away from another daydream, this one of himself rescuing Esmay Suiza from faceless Bloodhorde goons.

'All that vidscan that's supposed to be watching every square centimeter of this ship . . . which in theory could find the intruders?'

'Mmm?'

'Isn't there, or isn't working, and the captain has quite reasonably asked the 14th to come to his aid. So we – you and I, for example – replace, install . . . and somehow I suspect the intruders, whoever they are, will manage to undo what we did, right after us.'

'I hope not,' Barin said. 'Why doesn't the captain seal off the different wings? He could do that, couldn't he?'

'He could blow us all to glory if he wanted to, or turn off the artificial gravity, or . . . I don't know why he's done what he's done, or why he'll do what he's doing, and it's not my problem. Scan is my problem.' He sighed, heavily, and began to make notes. 'I know you went to inventory only an hour or so ago, Ensign, but you'll have to go back.'

'It's what ensigns are for,' Barin said cheerfully. 'That's what you said yesterday: scutwork, gofering . . .'

'And making smart remarks. Yes, well, you're on your way to a successful career as an ensign, laddy-o.'

Barin winced dramatically. Lieutenant Bondal had a freakish sense of humor, but was easy to work with if he thought it was appreciated. And he knew his business, which made the teasing worthwhile.

Traffic in the corridors was down except for the line still backed up at the ID station. Barin flashed his pink pass at the guard before entering the lift tube. It was like being back at school, where you'd had to have a hall slip to use the toilet. He decided not to make that remark to the grim-faced guard watching him. In the aftermath of the shipwide identification verifications, Barin understood why the automatic inventory racks had been disabled. With hostiles aboard, the captain didn't want anyone confused by the sudden shift of a rack . . . if it shifted now, they'd know it was enemy action. Still, that made retrieving a component stored on the second-to-top rack, at the rear, a time-consuming procedure. He looked up, checking the rack numbers. Yes, 58GD4 was up there, and what he needed should be on it. He looked at the maintenance ladder with its warning signs and tangle of safety harness . . . DANGER: VIBRATION FROM MOVING RACKS. CLIP IN BEFORE USING. But the racks wouldn't be moving, and putting on the harness would slow him down. On the other hand, he'd look pretty stupid if he slipped for some reason and broke an arm. Lieutenant Bondal would be furious; they were shorthanded already, what with the intruder scare.

Sighing, he got himself into the harness. It felt awkward; he was three-quarters sure he didn't need it. The safety clip fit around a rod beside the ladder steps, but had to be unclipped and reclipped every five or six rungs. He glanced around; he hoped no one was watching his clumsy caution. Up the first level, then the second. It was annoying to stop and unclip and clip every single time, even though he was getting faster at it. Somewhere across the compartment, he heard a clang and a muffled curse. His heart raced a moment, then quieted. It had to be a crewmate; the last reported sighting of the hostiles had been two decks down and over on the starboard side . . . a kilometer away, and only five minutes before. Should he call out and identify himself? Probably.

'Yo,' he said. A distant voice replied with an indistinct bellow that seemed to be a familiar grade and name, with a questioning intonation on the end. He heard the rhythmic sound of footsteps coming nearer.

'—You all right?'

'Fine,' Barin said, from his perch now eight racks off the deck. He could see a brown head moving along an aisle, a familiar uniform, though the angle was wrong to see insignia. 'Up here,' he said.

The person looked up, and grinned. 'See you. You hear me trip over the vent hatch someone left undogged?'

'Vent hatch undogged?' Barin didn't like the sound of that. 'Where?'

'Back there.' Closer now, the man pointed back toward the compartment entrance. Barin saw by his stripes that he was a sergeant minor. 'Inboard ventilation access hatch . . . probably some idiot guardsman went through looking for the bad guys and forgot to close it behind him.'

'We can hope,' muttered Barin. He felt cold, and he wasn't sure why. He glanced around. The inventory racks ran up to the overhead, fifteen meters from the deck, divided by aisles and cross-aisles usually humming with robotic carriers. He couldn't see far in any direction but along that one aisle. The racks he climbed beside were a half-meter high, but the ones across from him were a full meter . . . some full, and some partly empty. Plenty of room for someone to hide, even in the half-meter racks.

'What were you looking for?' he asked the other man.

'57GD11, code number 3362F–3B,' the other said promptly. 'Scrubber port covers. Should be around here somewhere.'

'I'm on 58GD4,' Barin said. 'If that's any help.' He watched as the other man peered at one rack after another.

'Ah – here it is.' The other man started up the ladder of a stack two down from Barin without putting on the harness. Barin started to say something to him, but shrugged. He hadn't needed his own harness so far. He turned back to his own ladder; he had a long way to go.

By the time he was up ten more levels, he was breathing hard. A vertical fifteen meters wasn't like the short 3-meter ladders he was used to. The climbing wall was only ten meters. Still . . . he was over halfway. He looked up; the remaining racks seemed to loom over him. He glanced around for the other climber.

No sign of him. Had he found his items and gone away? Barin leaned out against the safety belt, trying to see . . . nothing. When he looked down, nothing but deck showing in the aisle. Odd. He'd have expected the other man to say something when he left. Barin shrugged, finally, and climbed up another rack level, reaching up over his head to clip in the safety line.

As his eyes came level with the rack edge, he had just time to think 'How odd' before the cold round muzzle of a riot gun prodded him under the chin. It looked exactly like the ones that ship security carried.

'Don't move.' The voice had no expression. Barin stiffened for a moment he would later realize was critical, and then someone grabbed his ankles. He arched back, trying to kick loose; the barrel of the gun slammed into the side of his head hard enough to stun. He struggled, but now something had caught his safety harness and pulled him hard against the ladder – his feet – then his arms – and finally another blow to the head that dropped him into a dark hole where he was only vaguely aware of being dragged off the ladder and onto the chill metal mesh of the inventory rack.

He felt too many things to sort out easily. His feet, bumping over some surface with regular obstructions. His shoulders, painfully cramped from the traction on his arms. His head throbbed, with occasional flashes of brighter pain that left ghostly spikes across his vision. Other things hurt too – his ribs, his left hip, his wrists – but *where was he*?

He tried to ask this, but chocked on the gag in his mouth. Something soft – cloth or another soft material, that he could not

258

spit out, though he tried. The part of his brain that could think suggested caution . . . waiting to see what happened . . . but between the choking and the dark his body's instincts opted for action. He flared his nostrils, trying to suck in more air, and twisted as hard as he could. Someone laughed. Blows crashed into him, from all sides; he tried to curl up defensively, but someone yanked his legs out full-length, and the beating didn't stop until he had passed out again.

'You're a Serrano,' the voice said.

Barin concentrated on breathing. His nose felt like a pillow-sized mass of pain, and no air went that way; his captors had loosened the gag so he could breathe through his mouth. It had been made clear that this was a privilege they could revoke at any moment. He could barely see through his eyelashes, which seemed to be glued together. When he tried to blink, his eyelids hurt, and his vision didn't clear.

'We don't like Serranos,' the voice went on. 'But we do recognize your value as a hostage . . . for now.'

He wanted to say something scathing, but the noise in his head didn't allow for creative endeavors. He wanted to know where he was, who his captors were, what was happening.

'You might even be valuable enough to let live past the capture of this vessel,' the voice said. 'It's possible that you'd even make it to Aethar's World . . . a Serrano in the arena would be a profitable attraction.'

His remaining intelligence smugly pointed out that these must be Bloodhorde soldiers . . . the hostiles that everyone was searching for . . . and wasn't there something about the arena combats on Aethar's World? Slowly, grudgingly, his memory struggled through the haze of pain and confusion to find the right category and index . . . and offered a precis of what Fleet Intelligence knew about the arena.

Barin threw up, noisily.

'Well, that's one reaction,' his captor said, running something cold and metallic up and down his spine. Barin couldn't tell if it was a firearm or the hilt of a knife. 'I always look forward to Fight Week. But then I've never been on the sand myself.'

'It could be that knock on the head,' said another.

'No. He's a Serrano, and I have it on good authority that they are solid granite all the way through.'

It was not a good sign that his captors were talking so much. Barin struggled to think what it meant, in all permutations. It meant they felt safe. They must be somewhere they did not expect to be found . . . or overheard, which meant they'd done something to the ship's sensors. The stench of vomit made him gag again; it didn't seem to bother his captors, who kept on chatting, now in a language he didn't understand.

They left the gag loose, which argued that they didn't want him to choke on his vomit if he heaved again. He blinked, and one eye cleared suddenly, giving him a view of uniforms that looked exactly like his own, only cleaner. A *Wraith* ship patch on the arm nearest him, with the stripes of a corporal. He couldn't see the nametag. Another beyond . . . he blinked again, and his other eye came unstuck.

Now he could see that one was watching him closely, cool gray eyes in a broad face. The nametag read Santini; the stripes indicated a pivot-major. The expression said killer, and proud of it.

Barin struggled to regain the moral high ground. He knew what was expected of a Serrano in a tight fix: triumph, despite all odds. Escape, certainly. Capture the bad guys, ideally. All it took was brains, which he had, and courage, and physical fitness – both of which he was supposed to have. His grandmother could do it in her sleep. Any of the great Serranos could.

He didn't feel like a great Serrano. He felt like a boy with no experience, whose nose was at least as big as a parpaun ball, who hurt all over, who was surrounded by big dangerous men who intended to kill him: helpless, that is. He hated feeling helpless, but even that resentment couldn't wake the surge of defiant anger he needed.

Do it anyway, he told himself. If he couldn't feel brave, he could still use his brain. He let his eyelids sag almost shut again. That man was not a pivot-major named Santini, but he had a name . . . and perhaps his companions would use it. He might learn what it was even though he didn't know their language. At least he should be able to figure out the command structure of this group, just by observation.

The man he was watching said something, and Barin felt a sharp tug at his hair. He stifled a groan, and opened his eyes again. 'You don't need to sleep, boy,' said the man. His accent was no stronger than others Barin had heard within the Familias, but it had a hard contemptuous edge that even his first Academy instructors had not used. They had not cared if he passed or failed; this man did not care if he lived or died. 'You need to learn what you are.' A few words in that other tongue – Barin didn't even know what to call the language the Bloodhorde used – and someone behind him laid something cold and hard along the side of his neck.

From behind, another gabble of the strange tongue; the man across from him grinned. Pain exploded in his neck, down his arm; he felt as if it were bursting, as if his fingers had disintegrated into shards of pain flung meters away from him and still hurting. Before he could scream, the filthy gag was back in his mouth. Tears streamed from his eyes; his whole body shuddered. Then it was over.

'That's what you are,' the man said. 'Entertainment. Keep it in mind.' He said something else, and they all stood. Barin was yanked to his unsteady feet, and dragged along with them as they moved off down a passageway he had never seen before. And not a single vidscan pickup in sight.

'Bad news,' Major Pitak said as she came in from a briefing. Esmay looked up. 'Security's found a body stuffed in a utility closet on Deck 8, T-2, and it was someone who'd had a pink tag. Neck broken, neatly and professionally. Also, they've got a hostage – maybe. Ensign Serrano.'

'Barin!' That got out past her guard; she told herself it was no time for silly embarrassments.

'He was sent to get something out of inventory – none of the automated systems are running – and never came back. When his unit went looking for him, they found a harness tucked into the rack he'd have been on, and a smear of blood – as if there'd been more and someone had been careless wiping it up.'

'They'd have had to knock him out to take him,' Esmay said.

'So you'd think. Commander Jarles and Commander Vorhes are both furious, and nearly got into a flaming row right there at the briefing. Why was he sent alone, and why didn't someone raise the alarm sooner, and so on. The admiral was not happy with them, to put it mildly. The captain . . . I don't even want to discuss. Scuttlebutt has it that he got crosswise of a Serrano twenty-odd years ago. If that kid gets killed aboard his ship, he's going to have the whole family down on him.'

'But Bar − Ensign Serrano is surely more important than any feud.' Even as she said that, she knew it was wrong. Family was family, but a family would not jeopardize its standing for a single individual. Hers hadn't.

Pitak shrugged. 'He's one ensign, on a ship with over 25,000 personnel. The captain can't let concerns about Serrano affect his primary concern: the safety of his ship.' Her gaze sharpened. 'You've spent some time with him recently, haven't you?'

'Yes, sir.'

'Mmm. Something going on there?'

Esmay felt her face heating up. 'Not really . . . we're just friends.' It sounded as lame and false as it felt. What *had* she been feeling, around Barin? She hadn't done any of the things that regulations prohibited between senior and junior officers in a chain of command, even though they weren't in the same chain of command. But she had . . . if she was honest . . . wanted to do some of those things. If he did. He had never indicated that he did. She forced herself to look Pitak in the eye. 'After he helped me at that briefing for the senior tactical discussion group, we talked a few times. I liked him, and he knew a lot of things about Fleet which they never taught us in school.'

'I'd noticed some changes,' Pitak said, without specifying their nature. 'Coaching you, was he?'

'Yes,' Esmay said. 'Admiral Serrano and others had mentioned that I . . . confused, I think was their term . . . people because of mannerisms which are normal on Altiplano. Barin was able to define what I was doing wrong—'

'I wouldn't say exactly wrong,' Pitak murmured.

'And show me what the Fleet customs were.'

'I see.' Pitak rocked back and forth in her chair for a long moment, staring past Esmay's elbow. 'Suiza, everything in your record says you're level-headed and not a troublemaker. But you've never had a partner, that anyone knows about. Have you?'

'No.' Direct challenge had gotten the answer out of her before she realized she was giving it. The blush came afterwards. 'No, I . . . I just didn't.'

'Umm. And you're not on any medication that would explain it. Are you?'

'No, sir.'

Pitak sighed heavily. 'Suiza, you're ten years too old for this advice, but in some ways, if I didn't know better, I'd think you were ten years younger. So try to take it as well-meant. You're ripe for a fall, and Barin's the only male you've spent more than a work-shift with. Whether you know it or not, you're on the slide now . . .'

'No.' That came out in a low whisper. 'I won't . . .'

'There's nothing *wrong* with it, Suiza,' Pitak said sharply. 'You're only a lieutenant; he's an ensign – that's a fairly common level of difference. You're not his commander. The only problem is . . . he's now in enemy hands, and we've got an emergency. I need your brain clear, your emotions steady. No racing off to do useless heroics and try to rescue your lover.'

Lover? Her heart pounded; her stomach was doing freefall into her boots. 'He's not . . .'

Pitak snorted, so like a lead mare that Esmay was startled into a grin. 'Young woman, whether you have actually been skin to skin or not, he is the first man you've cared about since you were grown. That's clear enough. Admit it, and you'll deal with it better.'

Could she admit it? Was it true? She had had those vague wishes, those inchoate fantasies . . . Barin's hands would not be like those other hands. The uniform was different. She dragged herself away from all that, and fought down the flutter in her diaphragm. 'I . . . do care . . . a lot . . . what happens to him. I – we hadn't talked about – anything else.' She almost said 'yet' and saw that Major Pitak had added it without hearing it.

'All right. Now you've faced it, and now you have to face this:

you and I have nothing to do with the search for Barin, for the intruders, for anything else. It's our job to get *Wraith* back in service before a Bloodhorde battle group pops out here and blows us all away – or worse, captures us. Whatever happens to Barin Serrano cannot be as bad as the capture of this ship by the enemy. Is that clear?'

'Yes, sir.' It was clear, in the part of her mind that was free to think clearly. The word 'capture' rang in her mind with the finality of steel on stone. If they did not do their work, they might all be captives . . . and she knew she could not handle that. The vision sparkled in her mind – the quiet, competent, ordinary Lieutenant Suiza going completely and irrevocably crazy, the moment she became a captive again. However much she cared for Barin . . . she could not let that happen.

'Good. I didn't think you'd do anything foolish, but the little I know about Altiplano suggests that you might have triggers set which would push you into some stupid rescue attempt.'

'They are going to try one, though, aren't they?' Esmay asked.

'I don't know.' Pitak looked away. 'The most critical thing is to find the intruders before they do any significant damage. Rescuing one ensign has to be a lower priority. What's really twisting the captain's tail is the fear that they'll disable the self-destruct.'

'The self-destruct?'

'Yes. The captain is not about to let us be captured by the Bloodhorde – they could build cruisers with this facility and the expertise of our people. He's told the admirals that he'll blow us up first.'

'Good,' Esmay said, before she thought. Pitak looked at her oddly.

'Most of us aren't happy about that,' Pitak said. 'We admit the necessity but . . . you like it?'

'Better than captivity,' Esmay said. The tremors were gone; the fear receded.

'Well. You never cease to amaze, Suiza. Since your brain seems to be working well enough, I'll answer some questions you'll no doubt ask in five minutes if I don't. We aren't jumping out of this system, because we can't. I don't know why. It might be that the intruders sabotaged the FTL drive . . . it might be that the fast-sequence jumps we did coming in shook something loose. Drives and Maneuver is on it. I need you to do a search, since you're good at that: if we assume that the fast-sequence jumps caused some structural damage or shift, what would it be?'

'Yes, sir.'

'If you come up with anything, buzz me. We've got those *Wraith* structural supports coming over the line, and I need to be there for the installation.' She started out the door, and then turned back. 'Oh yes: the new procedures are that no one goes anywhere alone, and that includes the head. We know that at least one of the intruders now has a current ID badge – no doubt they'd like more. The captain may decide to firewall the ship, but right now there's not enough security personnel to man the access points. We're supposed to be alert for any strangers, anyone we're not used to seeing around, though on a ship this size that's not much use. I certainly wouldn't know half the instructors over in T-1 by sight, let alone the students.' She sighed. 'This is going to be a real bitch to implement. Rekeying thousands of IDs every day, and rechecking all personnel they're given to. All of us wearing tagtales, all of us going around in bunches.'

'Are we all going to move into open bays for sleeping?'

'I hope not.' Pitak scrubbed at her head. 'I can't sleep like that anymore; I'm old enough to be wakened by snorers. But it may come to that, though it means leaving a lot of compartments vacant – which can only help the intruders. Anyway, the captain's asked the flags for more personnel for security – and I understand there were words exchanged about that between our admiral and Livadhi. But we've got to get *Wraith* back in action. If, as we suspect, there's a Bloodhorde battle group coming here to pick us off, we'll need every bit of help we can get.'

'Is that possible – I mean, you said it would take—'

'Longer than we have. I know. Hull repairs alone should run sixty to seventy days . . . then there's refitting the internal systems, installing the weapons, testing. But there's nothing else to do. Maybe they'll be late – maybe they'll get lost. Maybe our fleet will come back. Or maybe they'll get the self-destruct fixed and we won't have to worry about anything . . . at least those of us who

265

don't believe in an afterlife. Do you? Is that why you think it's a good idea?'

'Not . . . exactly.' She didn't believe in the afterlife her great-grandmother had taught her about, where the dead were placed on the level they'd earned like pots of flowers on a stand. But she found it hard to imagine nothingness, an absolute end.

'Mmm.' Pitak looked as if she'd like to say something more, but someone called her from the passage and she left without another word. Esmay looked at her screen a moment, and then at the bulkhead. Barin a hostage . . . Barin dead? She could not imagine either of those . . . not Barin, so brimful of energy, so much a Serrano. It was not her assignment. Pitak had warned her. But . . . of all the people on this ship, she was the one who had actually fought on shipboard.

There must be others. Security personnel had experience; that's what they trained for. She wasn't trained. She had no weapons.

She was thinking the wrong things. She wasn't thinking at all. Memory splashed her mind with the images of battle in *Despite* . . . she could imagine that behind the partition between her cubicle and the rest of the offices, someone lurked with a weapon.

Ridiculous. Yet she could not just sit there; she itched to be . . . somewhere, doing . . . something. She scolded herself for letting a brief experience of command turn her head. With a shipful of admirals on down, they weren't going to let a lieutenant in Hull and Architecture do anything but look up statistics in computer files.

Barin had dozed off, but woke when he heard an approaching noise. Help, maybe? Instead it was another of the intruders, with two men and a woman in civilian clothes. Barin knew, in a general way, who they were: civilian technical advisors, experts, contractors hired to do something in weapons systems. He'd never actually met any of them, though he'd seen them in the corridors and lift tubes occasionally. Ordinary middle-aged civilians, he'd thought. Of no interest to him, since they weren't working in his area. Now they stared at him as if he were a monster too. He supposed he looked pretty bad, with his swollen nose and bruised face, but they didn't have to look as if they thought it was all his fault.

'You lied to us,' one of the Bloodhorde said. 'You were paid to fix this, and you didn't. When we looked, the lights were green.'

'But we *did* fix it,' said the taller man earnestly. 'We fixed it so that it wouldn't work, but the captain would think it did work. That's why all the telltales are green. He could run his system test, and it would come up—'

'They're not green now,' his captor said.

'What happened?' The man leaned past his captor to look, and turned an interesting shade of pale green. 'You – did you tear those wires out?'

'To make sure it wouldn't work, yes. Because you lied to us.'

'But I didn't lie. Now he knows it doesn't work – and he could have a backup—'

'You were supposed to disable all self-destruct devices.' That with a series of shoves that ended when the man bumped into the bulkhead. 'You were *paid* to do that!' Another, harder shove; the man staggered. 'So if you left one, then you have broken your word to us, and . . . we take that very seriously.'

'But – we don't know – we did what you said—' The man looked as if he couldn't quite believe the situation; he kept glancing at Barin and away again.

'Fix it again so that it looks to the captain as if it's working,' the Bloodhorde leader said.

'But the captain will know it's been tampered with – fixing it now won't convince him. Someone would have to tell him . . . I could go tell him I could fix it, they know we're experts in weapons systems, and then I could—' The man didn't have time to flinch away before he was dying, the blade deep in his throat and a hard hand squeezing his mouth, stifling his last bubbling scream. Blood spurted, then flowed, then stopped, filling the compartment with the smell of blood so strong it almost covered the stench of death itself.

The woman screamed, a short cry cut off in terror as one of the others slapped her. The killer let the dead man fall, and then wiped his bloody hand across his own mouth, then the woman's. 'They don't call us the Bloodhorde for nothing,' he said, grinning. With the same knife – and it seemed even worse to Barin that he didn't wipe it clean between the killing and the mutilation – he sliced off the dead man's left ear, bit it hard once, and then tucked it away in his uniform. 'Now,' he said to the second civilian. 'You will fix this so it looks as if it's working.'

The second man, shorter and darker-haired than the other, hurried to comply. When he had done, the telltales showed green again.

'That's got it,' he said.

'Is this right?' the killer asked the woman.

'Yes . . . yes it is right,' she said.

'If you know that, we don't need him,' the killer said, and caught the smaller man by the collar, half-choking him. 'We'd rather . . . work . . . with you.'

'No!' The woman lunged, but one of the others caught her. She tried to fight free, but she had no skill, and no strength to make up its lack. 'No, let him – please—'

The killer laughed. 'We heard what you said about the Blood-horde . . . how you taunted our agent.'

She turned even whiter.

'You dared to bind him . . .' He twisted the man's collar until the man's face purpled. 'You threatened. You had a noose around his neck . . . and now you have a noose around *your* neck. Even barbarians, as you call us, understand poetic justice.'

Barin could not look away; there was a fascination in this that disgusted him with himself. The killer twisted . . . twisted . . . and horribly, slowly, the dapper little man about whom Barin knew nothing died, his struggles weaker and weaker until they ceased.

'We pay our debts,' the killer said to the woman. 'All of them, the ones you know about and the ones you don't. Do we think size is everything? I believe that was your complaint, was it not? Then I believe you should have a chance to experience size in a way suitable to you in particular.'

The woman gave Barin a frantic glance, and the killer laughed. 'You think he could help you? This boy with a broken nose, that we captured as easily as we took you?'

He had to do something. He couldn't just lie here doing nothing . . . but no matter how he struggled, he couldn't loosen the very efficient bindings they'd taken from ship security.

Through all that followed, he struggled, rasping his wrists raw, earning a random cuff now and then from men more amused than concerned with his efforts. The woman struggled too, but it did her no good; one after another they took her, in ways that Barin's inexperience had not imagined. Finally her struggles, her gasps and moans, died away, and she lay still. He couldn't tell if she was dead, or just unconscious. She had been some kind of traitor apparently . . . he had gotten that much from what they'd all said . . . but no one deserved what had happened to her.

One of the men spoke to the other in their language, something Barin could tell was meant as a joke. The one on her pushed himself up, laughing, and then turned to Barin. He grinned even wider.

'The boy's upset,' he said. 'Maybe she was his girl?'

'Too old,' said one of the others. 'A nice boy like him wouldn't have a woman like that.'

'I'm sure he has a girl somewhere on this ship,' the first one said. 'We'll have to be sure we find her.'

He would have heaved again if he'd had anything left.

'What I don't understand is how they found the self-destruct so fast,' Captain Hakin said. 'Not that many people know where it is . . .'

'They grabbed those civilian contractors,' Admiral Dossignal said.

'But how would they know? They're weapons specialists; they've been busy recalibrating the guidance systems . . . oh.'

'If someone suborned the civilians, then they could have disabled the self-destruct – they could have found it while appearing to be working on weapons in inventory. I see . . .'

'What I don't understand is why they were snatched, if they'd already done their job.'

'They hadn't,' the captain said. 'Remember – until an hour ago, all the signals were secure.'

'Considering the quality of work they did on the weapons, *if* they'd done it, I'd expect it to be undetectable,' said Commander Wyche. 'I'd bet they were snatched simply for their weapons expertise . . . with the data wands the intruders got from the three we know they killed, they'd have high enough access to find that out.'

'So now the self-destruct is out of my control.' Hakin glared at the admirals. 'I should have used it.'

'No,' Dossignal said. 'It was the handiest way, the easiest and least obvious way, for you to have the power of destruction, but it wasn't the only. On this ship, with what we've got in inventory, and the expertise in the 14th alone, we can prevent capture. We will.'

'I hope so,' the captain said. 'I sincerely hope so, because if you don't we are not the only ones who will suffer for it.'

'*Wraith* gives us another possibility,' Commander Wyche said. '*Wraith?*'

'She still has a third of her weapons, all in portside mountings. And she still has ample firepower to blow *Kos*. Not from the repair bay – the way she's locked into the cradles, even if she blew herself, there's a 72 percent chance that most of *Kos* would survive. We'd have to reposition her mounts, which would take days. But if we can get her into a position to fire on the core area—'

'She can't maneuver!' said Commander Takkis, head of Drives and Maneuver. 'We dismounted the drives when she first came in, and it would take days to remount them. Besides, I have everyone working on the FTL drive for *this* ship.'

'I was thinking of the drives test cradle. She doesn't have to maneuver to be slung on there and then towed into position . . . even, if you wish, at the extremity of the lines. The test cradle's own drive would be sufficient, if necessary, to move her into the best firing position for *Kos* . . . or she could get some shots off at the Bloodhorde.'

A moment of silence, as they thought it over. Dossignal and Livadhi both nodded. 'It could work – certainly, as far as destroying *Kos* is concerned, and quite probably she could do a fair bit of damage to the Bloodhorde ships.'

Captain Hakin was nodding too. 'If those weapons have not been taken off *Wraith*, and we're absolutely sure they haven't been tampered with, then we've got our fail-safe back . . . as long as they're not depleted taking potshots at the enemy.'

'No . . . I can see that there'd have to be strict limits of use, but that should leave enough to do some damage. Especially if we had something else. One of the shuttles, maybe. In the Xavier action, the planetary defense used a couple of shuttles to good effect.'

'They used them for mine-laying . . . I don't think that would work here.'

'If only we could Trojan-horse them, the way they did to us.' Livadhi smiled briefly. 'It would be *so* satisfying.'

'Get aboard a Bloodhorde ship? I don't see how. Since they do it, they know it can be done – they'd be watching. And our people would be trying a hostile boarding, against resistance.'

'I was thinking . . . if we had any native speakers of their language, if we could locate one of these intruders and sweat some recognition codes out of him, then our people could pretend to be their own team coming back.'

'Won't work.' Admiral Livadhi scowled in surprise at the lieutenant commander two seats down. 'Sorry, sir, but – we shouldn't waste time with schemes bound to fail. The Bloodhorde special operations teams – which is what we have aboard – are all members of one lineage. Each team is, I mean. They train together for years, and develop their own distinctive argot. Commander Coston, who went back to Rockhouse recently, had been doing a special study on Bloodhorde special ops. Our people can't imitate a Bloodhorde pack – not without a lot of training we don't have time to give. As well, we have only thirteen people aboard who speak the language with anything like suffi-cient fluency, and their accents indicate different origins.'

'We don't need negativism now, Commander Nors,' Livadhi said. 'We're at the stage of thinking up possibilities.'

'Sorry, sir. Well . . . suppose one of the Bloodhorde ships were close in . . . and empty or nearly empty of its crew. We've developed a fairly good model of a Bloodhorde ship's control systems, working from the commercial models they're built on, and information from scavenge. It wouldn't take long to train our experienced warship crews to use it – or for that matter, import our own scan equipment.'

'Just where do you plan to find a close-in Bloodhorde ship with its crew off it?' asked Hakin with some sarcasm. The question hung a moment, as they all considered, then the same idea flickered across several faces. Hakin's turned grim. 'No. Absolutely not. I am not going to allow *more* Bloodhorde troops aboard my ship, just for the chance of capturing one of theirs.'

'They'd probably like to use one of the repair bays,' Dossignal said slowly. '*Wraith's* in one – they know that. The other's empty . . . the best place for a smallish ship to dock, anyway. Full of stuff they want.'

'No!' Hakin said, more loudly.

'Do you have any information on Bloodhorde boarding procedures, Commander?' Dossignal asked, ignoring Hakin for the moment.

Nors thought a moment. 'All we have is reports from the few civilians who survived a Bloodhorde raid on a large civilian ship. They come in wearing protective gear that functions as both EVA and battle armor . . . they were in that case quite willing to damage the ship they'd captured to gain control of it. None of the civs we talked to could tell one level of weapon from another, but one of them did describe something capable of holing interior bulkheads with one shot. Here, though, we're assuming they want a DSR entire. I expect they'll do as little damage as possible in capturing it . . . but they do have to board.'

'Another possibility,' said Commander Wyche, 'is the weaponry aboard a Bloodhorde ship in a repair bay. Suppose it could be immobilized there. Then its weapons would give us yet another self-destruct capability. They have forward-mounted weapons in every class.'

'*If* we were able to get aboard and take control.'

'I think we can take that as given, sir. If they just sit there, they aren't accomplishing anything . . . they can't shoot at us without doing the damage they don't want, and besides, they have no reputation for being patient. I think we can count on them coming out, with an intent to take control of key systems.'

'Which is why we can't let them do it,' Captain Hakin said. 'It would take your people some time to get aboard, get control of their ship, and *maybe* be able to use it to defeat their other ships or destroy us . . . and in the meantime, I'd have a shipful of enemy . . . NO.'

'So the real problem is getting them off their ship without

letting them onto ours,' Admiral Livadhi said. He put his fingertips together. 'You know . . . there might be a way. If we could shut off the repair bay – that whole wing—'

'We could just take it apart,' Admiral Dossignal said.

'Take it apart?' Captain Hakin asked.

'Yes . . . Commander Seveche, review the original construction data and all later modifications . . . there may be a way to cut one of the repair bays loose – unobtrusively, of course – and isolate it from the rest of *Koskiusko*.'

In less than an hour, Seveche returned with the data ready to display; he set up the large screen and lit it.

'Here, you see: when they assembled *Kos*, they planned for possible changes by using temporary attachments—'

Hakin turned red. 'You mean we've been working in a ship that's not really held together—?'

'No, sir. It is held together, and quite well . . . but it would take only hours, not days, to detach it again. These pressure clamps . . . these connectors here . . .' Seveche pointed to them on the display. 'All this can be undone fairly easily. Relatively, I mean. The seal between T-4 and the core cylinder is a large expansion joint of sorts.' He switched to another display. 'As *Kos* was assembled, before an arm was locked on, the near end of these things were fastened to the core . . . and then the outer end to the arm. As the arms moved in to mate with the core, the corrugations compressed, giving additional safety margin to the join.'

'Yes, but – I presume you plan to stretch them out again. Do you really expect them to be sound after all this time?'

'I don't see why not,' Seveche said. 'We've used the same material over the same span of time, with multiple compressions and extensions, with no failure. Besides, we can have the locks on each side shut. The way the arms are made, there are airlocks on the inner end of each deck.'

'I know that, Commander,' Hakin said. He sounded annoyed. 'But I'm sure they'll notice that the inner hatches are locked, and then they'll blast them—'

'They won't. We can rig temporary cross-dock access . . . they don't know what it's supposed to look like.'

'Then when it detaches, it'll depressurize—'

'Not if someone is there to lock the hatches.' Seveche looked to Dossignal for help.

'We're going to take casualties, whatever we do,' Dossignal said. 'To protect us from capture, you're prepared to destroy the ship and crew. I understand that, and it may be necessary. But I believe we have a chance to save both the ship and much of its crew if we can hold out until Admiral Gourache returns. Denying the enemy the use of a ship – using it ourselves – and using what firepower *Wraith* has left – is the only way I see to do that. I'm sure we'll have volunteers enough for the most hazardous of these hazardous missions.'

'We'll have to have someone commanding each section that's freed – with the authority to do what they must, whatever that is. Divided command would be disastrous, and we can't be sure that communications will hold.'

'Which means we've got to get those people involved in planning right away—'

'I don't like it,' Captain Hakin said. 'It's scrabble law: the whole ship is my command, and you're proposing to break off pieces and give them an independent command. Separated, they'll be even easier meat to the invaders—'

'Captain, we're offering a suggestion that gets us both off the hook. *Koskiusko* was assembled from previously independent sections in deep space. You know that. T-4 and T-3 even had names – *Piece* and *Meal* may've been stupid names, but names. They might have been commissioned as ships in their own right, if Fleet had not decided to try for a unified DSR. It's reasonable to maintain that they're both directly under the 14th—'

'You'll have to crew them,' Hakin said. 'You're not taking any of the crew I need to secure *Kos*.'

Was it capitulation? Admiral Dossignal looked at Hakin a long time.

'You know, Vladis, if it's really going to stick in your craw, you can write a report.'

'I intend to,' Hakin looked even grimmer. 'Partly to question your authority to nominate a captain for any vessel in this sector: that's Foxworth's job, or, at the lowest level, Gourache's.'

'I see your point. But I'm going to do it anyway, and we can all hash it out with a Board, if not a court, later.'

Hakin shook his head. 'It won't improve the odds, and it just makes my job harder . . .'

'I don't see how, since we're almost certainly ridding you of most of your intruders, and one of the ships trying to attack you. Now as for crew, we have the uninjured survivors of *Wraith*—'

'Which will be needed to serve *Wraith*'s weapons,' Livadhi said.

'Their weapons crews certainly. Since *Wraith* won't be maneuvering, I don't know about their bridge crew. I hate to waste a captain with combat experience aboard a crippled ship. We're not overburdened with such officers.'

Commander Atarin spoke up. 'Admiral, I have prepared a list of all officers and enlisted aboard with combat experience in the past three years. They're rank-ordered by specialty and performance – not just experience – in combat.'

'Good. Let's see . . . oh, my.'

'What?' Hakin craned his neck, trying to see.

'We have ample combat-experienced weapons specialists, because the senior weapons technical course is running. Scan . . . not much problem there. We're short environmental systems specialists, but this should be over fast enough that it won't be critical . . . we can have our people in self-contained gear. Communications is also short, but most scan techs are cross-trained in communications and we have plenty of scan techs. What we don't have is ship commanders. Or rather, we have just enough: *Wraith*'s captain for *Wraith*, and Lieutenant Commander Bowry, who's here for a special course, to command the Bloodhorde ship.'

'I don't suppose we'd be lucky enough to get more than one of them . . .'

'I doubt it. Why would they bring in more than one ship at a time? If they gifted us with such riches, we'd just have to find someone to take it . . . but that gets us down to fairly junior officers with very little experience of ship command in combat.' Dossignal considered telling them who, precisely, but he knew Hakin would have particular objections to Esmay Suiza.

16

Esmay found what might be a possible cause of the failure of the FTL drives, and took that to Major Pitak, who was overseeing the transport of the long crystal bundles from the Special Materials Fabrication Unit to T-3 and *Wraith*. Even bundled, they were more flexible than Esmay had expected, as she watched the special transport teams eased them along the transport track. She had known, intellectually, that all ships had such framing members . . . she had known that they had a lateral flexibility which was essential to the design. But these shivering, wriggling lengths seemed far too frail to trust lives to in deep space.

Pitak gave her a brief glance and turned back to watch. 'Ah, Suiza . . . find something?'

'It's only a possibility.'

'Good enough. Have you seen these before?' She went on before Esmay could answer. 'Wiggly, aren't they?' She sounded pleased.

'More than I thought,' Esmay said honestly. Vidscan screens showed the entire route, from the exit port at the end of the SpecMatFab, up over T-1, the core, and down again between T-3 and T-4. 'Why didn't they put the repair bays on the same side of the ship as SpecMat? Wouldn't it have been easier to transfer things like that?'

'Yes, but that turned out to be the least important design consideration. If it really interests you, when this crisis is over, you can look it up in the design archives . . . the whole argument is in there.' She punched up the view in one screen, and pointed to the bundles. 'Now that's a good set. After awhile, you'll be recognizing good strands from bad by the oscillations alone. If we didn't have this other crisis, I'd send you over to SpecMat to watch them during breakoff.'

Esmay was just as glad to miss that. She had heard from others about the more spectacular breakoffs, when the test sequences induced more oscillation than a faulty crystal could withstand, and shards flew with a noise that was said to shake reason.

'Let me see what you've got,' Pitak said. She looked at the data Esmay had found and frowned. 'I don't think this is it. The shearing force isn't enough to unseat the AG generators, and you're suggesting that it was AG instability which caused the drive failure, right?'

'Yes, sir.'

'How does it model?'

'They've bumped everyone below department heads off the big computer . . . the little one said it was possible. That's why I brought it.'

'Oh. Well, I don't like the modeling program on the little one for anything but pure structural layups. For this sort of thing we need the Mishnazi series . . . but I imagine they're trying to maximize their data analysis. I don't think this is likely enough to ask for the time ourselves.' She looked at Esmay. 'You should log off and get some sleep while you can – at least a good meal. Have you kept track of who's been to dinner?'

'No, sir, but I can do that as soon as I get back.'

'Do that, then, and thanks for this . . . I think it's sabotage, myself, but D&M asked us to consider it.'

Esmay nodded and withdrew with her escort, a corporal she'd yanked out of the H&A clerical section when she needed to find Pitak. She hated feeling useless. Of course she should eat; of course she should be making sure that everyone in the section did. But . . . she wanted to do more.

She had just reached Pitak's office and started checking on the whereabouts of all the personnel under her command when the comm beeped at her. It was Pitak.

'Right in the middle of a crisis and they have to short me. Suiza, what have you been doing to get the admirals interested in you?'

'Nothing that I know of,' said Esmay.

277

'Well, you're to report to Admiral Dossignal's office immediately, and the note to me says not to expect you back any time soon. It never fails. I get someone trained to the point where they can do me some good, and the brass taketh away.'

'Sorry, Major,' Esmay said, before remembering that she wasn't supposed to apologize. She thought of Barin with a pang. Was he still alive? Was he . . . all right?

'Better get going,' Pitak said. 'And if you have a chance, let me know what's going on. There's an odd feeling in the ship.'

'Yes, sir.'

In the admiral's outer office, Commander Atarin was watching for her. 'Ah – Lieutenant Suiza. Good. We're going directly to a secure meeting room in T-1; our escort will meet us at the lift tube.'

'Sir, may I ask—'

'Not until we're there. And don't look alarmed; you aren't in trouble and we don't want to scare anyone.'

'Yes, sir.'

Two armed pivot-majors, with Security patches, waited by the lift tubes. 'Commander, the captain says it would be better to avoid the tubes,' one of them said. Esmay saw the sheen of perspiration on his face.

'Something happened?'

'I can't say, sir,' the man said. He was breathing a bit too fast.

'Let's go, then.' Esmay and Commander Atarin followed as he led them around the core to the base of T-1. The wide passageway was busier than usual, as if others were avoiding the lift tubes and slideways. They had five decks of ladders to climb; when they emerged from the last, Esmay saw another pair of security guards, these with their weapons in hand, outside a secured hatch. A portable ID booth had been set up nearby, and Esmay noticed the heavy gray boxes and cables of a full-strength blanket system positioned along the bulkhead. Whatever this was about, it was being kept as secure as possible from intrusion.

She and Atarin both went through a complete ID check, retinal scans, palmprints, and blood test. Then the guards at the door checked them in.

Inside, the medium-sized conference room was edged with

more scan-blanketing equipment; in the center, a cluster of officers leaned over a large table with a 3-D model of *Koskiusko* on it. Esmay already knew Admirals Dossignal and Livadhi by sight, as well as Captain Hakin, but she had not met the lean gray-haired full commander who was introduced as *Wraith*'s captain, or his Exec, Lieutenant Commander Frees. Another lieutenant commander named Bowry, who wore no ship patch, but had a collar-pin indicating he was in the Senior Technical Schools for some course. What *was* this?

'Gentlemen.' That was Admiral Dossignal, now seating himself at one end of the table. Esmay saw that places had been prepared, with nametags . . . hers near the far end of the table. She sat just as the others did.

'As you know,' Dossignal said, even before the last chair slid back into place, 'we are in a difficult situation here. In a few minutes, you'll have a chance to review the details of that situation, but the first thing you need to know is that you are all immediately relieved of your former assignments. You are assigned, under my direct command, to a difficult and dangerous mission; this is the first of the meetings you will hold to plan the execution of this mission.' He paused, as if for comment, but no one was unwise enough to make any. 'You also need to know that Captain Hakin is not in agreement with the aim of this mission, and plans to file a letter of protest. I respect his moral courage in so expressing his disagreement, and his loyalty, which has allowed him to cooperate even under protest.'

Esmay glanced at the captain, who went from beet-red to pale in the course of this.

'I take full responsibility,' Admiral Dossignal went on, 'for what is done here, and its outcome. I have so informed Captain Hakin, and have so stipulated in the official log. Is that clear?'

He waited until everyone had nodded.

'Good. Now: our mission is to capture a Bloodhorde ship, and using that and *Wraith*, successfully defend this ship from capture. You are the officers who will command elements involved in this mission, so you are here to plan it.'

'But *Wraith*'s crippled,' said someone – a lieutenant commander whose name Esmay had already forgotten.

'Correct. *Wraith*'s drives are dismounted and she cannot man-euver. But she can be trolled out to the drive test cradle, where her weapons can come to bear on either the Bloodhorde ships or *Koskiusko*, as need requires.'

'*Koskiusko* . . .' someone murmured too audibly.

'If capture appears inevitable, *Koskiusko* must be destroyed. Its capability must not fall into Bloodhorde hands – nor must its thousands of skilled technicians.'

Esmay felt the heavy silence in the room. She supposed the others had worked through this equation before: the Bloodhorde had never been known to free or exchange prisoners, though a few had been rescued from appalling conditions. Thus a quick death – or relatively quick – would be a mercy compared to slavery on one of the Aethar's World planets. But to contemplate the annihila-tion of so many of their own . . .

'We believe – *I* believe – that there is a chance to defend this ship and prevent those deaths,' Dossignal said. 'It's not a good chance, but it is a chance. You are the ones best suited to carry it out. We do not know how much time we have; let's not waste any.'

With that the planning session began in earnest. Esmay had never been involved in mission planning before; she said nothing and listened, wondering how she fit into this. Admiral Dossignal outlined his ideas, then assigned officers to specific tasks. 'Lieu-tenant Suiza,' he said finally. 'Except for the crew of *Wraith*, you have the most recent, and in some ways the most valuable, combat experience.'

Esmay could feel them all staring at her; her breath caught. 'Sir, the admiral knows I was only—'

He cut her off. 'This is no time for humility, Lieutenant. You are the only officer we've got who has actually fought *inside* a ship. And you commanded *Despite*, with remarkable results. I'm not assigning you to command the ship we hope to capture – there's a more senior and more experienced officer – but I am calling on your knowledge of intraship combat.'

'Yes, sir.'

'At the same time, I think Captain Hakin's security squads would benefit from your expertise . . .' He glanced at the captain, whose face reddened. 'We have hostile forces aboard, and we've already taken casualties. Security hasn't located them or prevented the trouble they've caused so far.'

'If the admiral wishes,' Hakin said, through gritted teeth. 'My reservations are on file.' He gave Esmay a look of cold distaste.

'Commander Seveche, you will be responsible for the actual detachment of T-4 from the hub. I leave it to you how you're going to keep the necessary preparations from being recognized by the intruders, whom I'm sure are observing what they can.'

'Yes, sir. I think some judicious tinkering with the artificial gravity controls could provide an excuse . . .'

'Whatever. If events overtake us before detachment is possible, we need a fallback plan. Along with your other duties, Lieutenant Suiza, I'd like you and Commander Atarin to liaise with *Koskiusko*'s security about that. Commander Jimson, you're to make sure that people get what they need out of inventory, without letting any more personnel be captured.'

'We need more security personnel,' Captain Hakin said.

'True, Captain. If it would help you, I'm sure that Admiral Livadhi can suggest individuals now enrolled in one of the tech courses who have sufficient background to be useful and have been aboard long enough to know their way around.'

'I've had Commander Firin make a list already,' Admiral Livadhi said. 'We have twenty-eight enlisted personnel with a secondary speciality in ship security, and another thirty-four who have done security work at some time or other within the past ten years. All are currently qualified with shipboard small arms. In addition, we have more personnel in the remote sensing course than Admiral Dossignal thinks will be needed for the rest of this mission. They can improve surveillance . . .'

'I'll be glad of them,' the captain said, this time with no resentment in his voice.

'I must emphasize the urgency of the situation.' Dossignal said. 'We don't know how long before a Bloodhorde battle group arrives – or how many ships it might contain – or how the intruders will affect our efforts. We—' He stopped as someone knocked on the door. The guard there lifted his eyebrows; Dossignal nodded and the guard pulled the door open.

A disheveled security guard looked straight at the captain. 'Captain, you're needed on the bridge, urgently. We have a situation.'

'Excuse me.' Hakin pushed back his chair.

'What kind of situation?' Dossignal asked. The guard looked at the captain who shrugged irritably.

'Tell him, Corporal.'

'The emergency oxygen conservation system went off on half a dozen decks of T-5, and knocked out everyone in sickbay and the ship's administrative offices. Two people got out and gave the alarm.'

'I'm on my way. You'll excuse me . . .' It was not a question.

'I hadn't thought of that,' Dossignal said. 'I should have – we haven't had any experience of this sort of thing. Lieutenant Suiza . . . can you tell us . . . what sort of mischief might we expect?'

Esmay gathered her scattered wits. 'Sir, they'll try to get weapons, if they don't already have them. With stolen data wands, they can find out where the ship security weapons lockers are, and if they get a data wand keyed for security, it might even give them the access codes. Then they'll try to isolate and immobilize large numbers of the crew, probably by locking them into various compartments. That's what Captain Hearne's allies tried to do to us on *Despite*. Here I suppose they'd try to cut off the wings from the core. They'll damage systems that give them effective control of ship operations . . . environmental systems, including ventilation as they did here, hatch controls, communications, scan. I'd expect them to take hostages from critical positions . . . if they've been loose in sickbay, they'll have medical personnel and supplies, including gas exchange equipment, so that we can't use the equivalent trick on them.'

'And your response would be—'

Through her mind flashed what she knew about the DSR. 'The same tactics would work against them if the captain initiated them. Manually reset the ship's support systems so that each wing is independent for life support, as it was designed, then isolate the wings. They'll be trapped, and outnumbered wherever they are. If they're not in the core section, they won't be able to get to the bridge. If they are in the core section, they won't be able to use the

282

wings for refuge, and ship security can go through the core first, then one wing at a time, until they're located. Ship security will need a different, secure communications system, because we have to assume the present one is already compromised.'

'But if we do that, we won't be able to set up for detaching T-4,' someone said. 'And if the other ships come . . .'

'If we've all been knocked out with sleepygas,' Esmay said, 'we won't be able to detach T-4 either.'

A moment's silence, as the others digested that, and she realized that she had just implied – no, said – that a commander was being stupid.

'Lieutenant Suiza,' Dossignal said. 'I'm putting you in charge of security for the 14th – specifically, T-3 and T-4. Liaise with regular ship security, but don't wait – do what you think needs doing. Atarin, who've you got for her?'

The door opened again; Captain Hakin interrupted without apology. 'They got into Security; they've got the weapons, and gas masks. Riot gas, probably. Maybe more.'

Almost as one, heads turned to stare at Esmay, who was still on her feet.

'As I said,' Dossignal stood also, and the others scrambled up. 'Lieutenant Suiza has been through this before; she correctly anticipated their moves.'

'I'm closing off the wings,' the captain said, as if Dossignal had not spoken.' We'll have to get the support systems isolated, but at least I've ordered the hatches closed, to everything but T-1. I'll give you the new codes, but—'

Outside a confused clatter, followed by soft pops as of something wet being dropped into a deep fryer.

'Captain—!' yelled someone outside. The guard at the door opened it and turned to look out.

Esmay moved before she thought; as the captain started to turn, she tackled him solidly and yelled, 'Shut it!' The captain, cursing, writhed and tried to kick her in the head; she released him, rolled to her feet and yanked the guard away from the door, slamming it . . . without taking a breath.

'What—!' began Dossignal, but stopped when the guard sagged to the floor, his face already bluish gray.

The captain sat up, red-faced and furious. 'You—' he started to say, then gasped and began wheezing.

'Get him up,' Esmay said. 'It's heavier than air . . .' If they didn't think to turn off the artificial gravity. If they didn't come right on through the locked door – she took the guard's weapon and used it to smash the internal doorlock control. *Wraith's* captain and exec scrambled to help the captain up and get him to the table.

'Gas, I presume,' said Admiral Livadhi in a tone of mild intellectual curiosity.

'The bridge . . .' the captain gasped, struggling for breath.

'After we get out of here,' Esmay said. Preferably before the intruders figured out where this compartment's air supply was, and simply poured the gas in that way.

'If we can get out of this compartment, I can suggest a safe – or possibly safe – route away from here,' Lieutenant Commander Bowry said. 'I've been all over T-1 for the past quarter year.'

'The overhead,' Esmay said. 'Or the deck, but I don't know how to get into it.'

'You could just blow a hole in it,' said Captain Hakin sourly.

'Waste of ammunition,' said *Wraith's* captain, Seska. 'We'll go up.' He climbed onto the conference table, and pushed aside one of the overhead tiles. 'Yep. Just like every other space station, though the one we want is over there—'

It took longer than Esmay wanted to get the entire group up through the hole in the overhead; the captain was still groggy and uncoordinated, and made an awkward bundle to lift. Esmay went last, guarding their rear with her single weapon, though she knew it would be useless if the intruders broke in.

But they wouldn't. She knew that, as if she could read minds. They had isolated the captain and the highest ranking officers, and would let them stew in there as long as they wanted. In the seconds ticking away now, they were wreaking as much havoc as they could. They'd be back at the core, trying to take the bridge, if they hadn't already.

In the dim, unhandy space between the tiles of the overhead and the base of the deck above, she followed the others – Lieutenant Commander Frees, in this instance – and wished she knew more about Lieutenant Commander Bowry. Did he really know a way out of this section? And just how had the wings been sealed off from the core? She supposed it was like the fire drills, but she didn't know for sure.

No time to worry about it. Ahead of her, the others had stopped moving. Esmay squirmed around so that she could look back the way she'd come. There was nothing to see but the smudged track of their passage, where they'd disturbed the dust.

Someone patted her leg, and she turned back; they were moving on again, more slowly. After a minute or two, she realized the leaders were slithering out of the overhead, down into a passage.

When she got close enough, she could hear voices.

'Damn near got us all. And you?' That was Admiral Livadhi, sounding more annoyed than alarmed.

A low murmur she couldn't follow. Frees, in front of her, slid out the gap into helpful arms. Esmay gave a last look back and saw nothing . . . but anyone could follow that track. She turned and dropped through feet first. A couple of enlisted men with Tecj Schools patches replaced the overhead panel as she looked up and down the passage.

Some meters in both directions, armed security guards kept watch. One of them had an armor vest and helmet; the other had none. Esmay saw openings into several compartments, but no one moved that way.

'Captain Hakin's still having trouble breathing,' Dossignal said. 'Does anyone know which gas that was?'

'Probably SR-58,' Bowry said. 'They'd have the antidote in the hospital, but—' Esmay didn't know anything about the different kinds of volatiles, but from the tone, the captain's life might still be in danger.

'We can't get there.'

A shout from the outboard end of the corridor startled them. Quickly, but without panic, they moved into the nearest opening. Esmay flattened against the inner bulkhead, and hoped the security guards had the sense to get out of sight themselves. The footsteps came nearer – more than one person, she thought. They paused outside the opening.

285

'Admiral Livadhi likes green pea and leek soup,' the newcomer announced in a conversational tone.

'Carlton,' Livadhi said, grinning. 'In here, Major.'

The major who came through the opening was festooned with equipment; his brows went up when he caught sight of Esmay and her weapon.

'The admiral might want to put this on,' he said, handing over a face filter. 'They've been using sleepy-gas . . .'

'They used worse than that,' Livadhi said. 'Captain Hakin got a faceful; it killed one guard.'

'Yes, sir. I have ten filters with me, and Corporal Jasperson is handing them out to your security detail. Commander Bowry had suggested securing the aid stations and the weapons lockers before he went up to the meeting; we've got enough gear for about fifty. Vests, helmets, comunits, weapons. And the medical supplies.'

'Good work. Where'd you stow it?'

'This way, sir.' Major Carlton led them down one passage, turned into another; two men helped the captain along. Esmay saw more guards, all with gas masks and some with armor. She wondered where they were going, and why waste time going there instead of breaking out of T-1 now, before they were trapped. But she had a weapon, and she stayed back with the rear guard.

Where they were going, it turned out, was a secure briefing room snugged in among the laboratories of Special Materials Research. 'Separate ventilation system, good thick armor all around – it'll take them awhile to get us, long enough to make plans.' Admiral Livadhi turned to Carlton. 'Any medical person-nel in T-1?'

'I've got someone coming who worked in the wing clinic; the only supplies we have are from emergency lockers, because the intruders wrecked the clinic.'

Captain Hakin had collapsed two turns back, and now he barely roused when Livadhi spoke to him. 'Captain . . .'

'Uhhh . . .'

'Captain, we have a legal problem: you are the only *Koskiusko* officer here; we cannot contact the others, and we need to make plans for resistance.'

'We're not going to *resist*,' Dossignal said. 'We're going to get this ship back.'

'Do . . . it,' Hakin said.

'Thank you, Captain; I accept your permission.'

In the next few minutes, the admirals agreed on the new command structure required by the emergency, and on goals. Then they settled to considering how to regain control of the ship.

'We need to get our combat-experienced people over into T-3 and T-4,' Dossignal said. 'That's where we've got part of a ship, and might with luck capture a Bloodhorde ship. The sooner we get those people off on that mission, the better.'

'Through the blast and fire doors . . . ?'

'How else?'

'If they're smart – if they have enough men – they'll be watching all the access points.'

'They don't,' Esmay said confidently. 'There were only twenty-five of them in sickbay.'

'Not a complete team: they usually send a threefold pack, three tens.'

'You mean we missed some?'

'No . . . some may have died aboard *Wraith*. We haven't had time to get into the foamed compartments and look. That'll be where their weapons and gear are, too.'

'But the thing is, they're not going to be able to watch every place we can get through. So where *will* they be?'

'Where they're still in contact with each other, for backup,' Bowry said. 'If they were after the bridge – and I would be, if I were trying this trick – that means they'll be watching on Deck 11, where we might be trying to get to weapons stored in the security weapons lockers, and Deck 17.'

'So . . . let's try Deck 8,' Dossignal said. 'Commander Takkis can get into the core, to the secondary command center, and make sure that the FTL drive isn't working under their command. The rest of us—'

'What d'you mean "us" – you aren't going out there.'

'I certainly am. I belong over there in the 14th, with my people.'

On the way down to Deck 8, they saw no sign of the intruders. Most of the people here were staff or students of the Training

Command, Senior Technical Schools Division. Scattered among them were elements of the ship's crew, mostly security, and researchers from the SpecMat Research Facility. They watched, wide-eyed, as the group passed, masked and armed.

Deck 8 seemed especially quiet when they came out of the stairwell. Esmay, in the lead, stopped short when she saw the first body lying sprawled in the corridor.

'Trouble,' murmured Seveche, behind her.

'And we don't know if it's gas or something else,' Esmay said. There was no other way from here to the firewall doors; she took a breath and edged forward, as quietly as she could.

'Dead some hours,' Seska said as they came up to the body. The man had ship security patches on his shoulder, loose on one corner where someone had hacked at them but given up.

'Maybe that was one of the first,' Dossignal said. 'And the attacker then went on to meet the others . . .'

Esmay wished they would all shut up. She could hear nothing, see nothing. At the first compartment, she looked in. Five corpses lay sprawled on the floor, sagging from chairs onto work surfaces . . . her stomach turned; she swallowed with an effort. Whoever had come here was quick to kill.

Nearer to the core, they could see the solid wall that cut them off from the rest of the ship. Esmay knew now that this was no simple bulkhead, but instead a section of the hull itself, capable of sustaining pressure if the wing detached. It lay against a similar section of the core: two thicknesses of hull. Once these barriers came down, the only way across was by means of the override codes, which could open small airlock hatches.

Admiral Dossignal entered the code, while the others guarded. The hatch did not move. He tried again; again it would not open. 'Commander Seveche,' he said. 'Did you hear the captain give the code?'

'Yes, sir.'

'Then you try it; perhaps I misremembered.'

Seveche also entered the number, but again the hatch did not open.

'Either the captain didn't remember the right sequence, or they've found a way to change it,' Dossignal said.

'Or someone in the crew changed it, perhaps thinking the intruders had it,' Seveche said.

'Amounts to the same thing,' Dossignal said. 'Now . . . There's got to be another way to get through this.'

Seveche grunted. 'Not without the equipment that's over in our section, sir. Two thicknesses of hull – we might manage one, with the tools in SpecMat Research, but not two.'

'What's our communications situation?'

'We can reach Admiral Livadhi on the headsets; so far I've picked up nothing from the rest of the ship. That's what I'd expect with the wings closed off; we'd need higher power.'

'If we can't go inside, how about outside?' asked Captain Seska.

'Same problem, getting through the hull.'

'Over on T-3 and T-4, there are airlocks on every deck,' Seveche said. He had projected a map of T-1 on the bulkhead and was going through it deck by deck. 'This one certainly isn't over-provided with airlocks. There's one out at the end of the Special Materials Fabrication Unit, of course, but—'

'T-1 was designed to be secure from casual interference,' said Dossignal.

'So we have to go all the way through SpecMatFab and hope no one flips the switch. Right. When I design a DSR, it's going to have some add-ons.'

'This one has add-ons; that's part of the problem.' Dossignal looked around at his group. 'We'd better get out there, then. I think we can assume that all the intruders are somewhere else, probably in the core section. Come on—' He strode off, startling them with his haste. Esmay caught a look between Captain Seska and his exec which suggested they weren't any happier than she was with the admiral's assumption that they needn't worry about the intruders. 'Luckily it's on this deck,' Dossignal said. Esmay wished he'd slow down and let some of his escort get ahead of him.

'Admiral—' Seveche said after a few meters. 'Sir – let us catch up—'

Dossignal slowed and turned. 'Mari, there's—' He gasped, and staggered. Esmay realized she'd gone for the deck just as her body smacked into it. So had Seska, Frees, and Bowry; the others stood where they'd stopped, looking around.

289

'DOWN!' yelled Seska, and the rest of them went down. 'Admiral?'

'Alive,' grunted Dossignal. 'And lucky.'

Esmay looked past Dossignal, up the passage, trying to guess where the shot had come from, and what kind of weapon it was. She'd heard nothing until the impact.

'Very lucky,' Seveche agreed, crawling forward.

'Not for long,' said a quiet voice; the figure that stepped out was a lot closer than Esmay had anticipated, and loaded with weapons. 'Drop—'

She had fired almost before she knew it; the intruder's shot ricocheted off the bulkhead as her burst took him apart from neck to hip. Someone – not that intruder – screamed.

She ignored that, made herself get up and move forward, past Admiral Dossignal, through the mess of splattered blood and tissue, to check the opening from which the intruder had come. It was a small compartment lined with shelves of office supplies, and empty now.

'—Two casualties,' Seveche was saying into his headset. 'Deck 8, main passage—'

'You're the one who was in the mutiny,' Captain Seska said to Esmay.

'Yes, sir.'

'Good reaction time. My guess is this one was cut off when the doors went down; if he'd had a partner, we'd already know it.'

Esmay thought about it. 'Makes sense, sir.' She could see nothing, and hear nothing, but the sounds their own party made. 'We could get the admiral into cover in this closet. Just in case.'

By the time help arrived, they had both casualties in the closet, with Esmay and the *Wraith* exec, Commander Frees, watching for more trouble. Dossignal kept insisting that he was all right, that they should go on without him, and once others had arrived, he put it as a direct order.

'I'm not fool enough to think I should go – I'd only slow you down – but you can do nothing useful here, and over there you might save the ship. I've dictated orders for the 14th – Lieutenant Suiza, take this to whatever officer is senior when you arrive. Now go.'

17

Nothing hindered their movement until they reached the access area for the Special Materials Fabrication Unit.

'You can't do that! It's in use . . . there's ninety meters of whisker in the drum now . . .' The shift supervisor for the Special Materials Fabrication Facility was a solid, graying petty-chief, who was not intimidated by a mere four officers. 'You'd have to have permission from Commander Dorse, and he wouldn't—'

'Stand aside, or there'll be ninety meters of whisker and . . . I estimate 1.7 meters of you.' Seska, intent on getting back to his ship, furious with more than the Bloodhorde, was past making polite requests, although he'd started with one.

'Admiral Dossignal will kill me if you get in there and destroy an entire batch—'

'No . . . the Bloodhorde will kill you. The admiral will only break you to pivot and then give you twenty years hard time if you don't get – out – of – the – way.'

'Bloodhorde? What does the Bloodhorde have to do with it?'

'Haven't you heard anything?' Esmay stepped forward, trying to project harmlessness and a pure heart.

'No, I haven't. I've been monitoring a startup whisker for the past five hours and my relief hasn't shown up and—'

Esmay lowered her voice. 'Bloodhorde commandos are loose on the ship, and your relief is probably dead. The only way we can fight them is to get out of T-1 and the only way out of T-1 is through here. I suggest you let us pass, and when we're safely out, let the Bloodhorde in, if they show up. Then do a breakoff early.'

'But that'd be ninety meters wasted . . .'

'Excuse me,' said Frees, to one side. The man's head turned, and Esmay hit him as hard as she could with her weapon. She might have killed him; at that moment she didn't care.

They barricaded the hatch to the passage as well as they could, and climbed quickly into the EVA suits in the nearby locker. They checked each others' suits before opening the first of the lockout hatches that isolated the Special Materials Fabrication Unit from the ship's artificial gravity. Inside was a metal-grid walkway ten meters long, ending in another lockout hatch. Rails ran along either bulkhead, with rings set every half-meter. They went in, closed the hatch behind them, and punched for Airless Entry. The light ahead of them turned green, and they started down the walkway.

Esmay felt herself lifting with each step, as if she were walking in deepening water. In the last meter, her steps pushed her off the walkway completely, and her feet trailed back, lured by the weak attraction of *Koskiusko*'s real mass. She grabbed for a rail, and hoped her stomach would crawl back into her midsection.

'I hate zero-G,' Bowry said.

'I hate the Bloodhorde,' Seska said. 'Zero-G is just a nuisance.'

They cycled through the second lockout hatch into a long dark tube lit by the eerie purple and green glow of the growth tank. It seemed to go on and on, narrowing to a dark point far away. Here Esmay could feel no slightest hint of attraction to any mass. Her stomach slid greasily up into her throat when she moved one way, and back down her spine when she turned the other way. She tried to concentrate on her surroundings. Along one side was a narrow catwalk with a rail above it.

'Remind me again what happens if we disturb the growing whiskers,' Seska said.

'They shatter and impale us with the shards,' Bowry said. 'So we don't disturb them,' Seska said. 'Minimal vibration, minimal temperature variance – we slide on the rail. Not thrashing around, not trying to look. Just relaxed . . . like this.' Esmay watched as he made a circle of his suit glove loosely around the rail, and pushed off from the lockout hatch. He slid away . . . and away . . . and vanished into the darkness. Esmay noticed that he'd pushed off precisely in the axis of motion he wanted; his legs simply trailed behind him.

'I hope there's a bracket on the end of this thing,' Frees said, and did the same thing.

'Lieutenant, it's my turn to be rear guard,' Bowry said. Esmay wrapped her glove around the rail, loosened it in what she hoped was the right amount, then kicked off. It was a strange feeling. She was drawn along effortlessly, as if the rail itself were moving, and she could see nothing but the faint reflection of the greenish purple glow on the bulkhead, a long vague blur of not-quite-color.

When she slowed, she didn't at first realize it. Then the blur steadied . . . she thought it was motionless. Now what? If she moved around too vigorously she could bang into the bulkhead and disturb the whiskers. She moved very slowly, bringing up her other hand to steady herself, then turning to look back the way she'd come. Far away now she could see the little cluster of lights at the lockout hatch. Nearer – something was coming, sliding along . . . too fast. If Bowry hit her, they'd both hit the bulkhead, if not worse. She gripped the rail and pulled herself along hand over hand, trying to let her body trail without twisting.

She couldn't watch and move at the same time, not without twisting. And she didn't want to go too fast; she didn't know how much farther she had to go. She glanced up from time to time, matching speed with Bowry . . . and as he slowed in his turn, she also slowed. Somewhere ahead of her were the others; she didn't want to slam into them, either.

'Slow now,' she heard. She hoped Bowry heard it too; but she didn't look, just put out her arm to brake against her movement. Her legs slewed sideways, but she was able to stiffen her torso and keep them off the bulkhead.

When she turned to look forward, she saw the narrowing rounded end of the fabrication unit, and the big round lock that allowed completed jobs to be taken out. To one side was a smaller personnel lock. Why did they even have locks at this end, when the point of SpecMatFab was its hard vacuum and zero-G? She thought of the answer almost as soon as the question. Of course they didn't want all the debris in space getting into the unit.

The personnel lock was manual, a simple hatch control that required only strength to turn. Then they were outside, clinging to the grabons and loops that Esmay thought were misnamed as 'safety' features. Beside it were a row of communications and oxygen jacks.

'Top up your tanks,' Seska said. Esmay had almost forgotten that standard procedure. She glanced at her readouts; it hardly seemed reasonable to spend the time now for just a few percents. But the others were all plugged in; she shrugged mentally as she pushed her own auxiliary tube into place. Her suit pinged a signal when tank pressure reached its maximum, and she pulled the connection free.

Seska clipped his safety line to the first loop and started pulling himself along, up the rounded end of the fabrication unit alongside the arching supports for the whisker transport system. Esmay followed Frees again, with Bowry behind her, stopping to unclip and reclip her line every time it ran out. When they got to the upper surface – upper as defined by the whisker track – Seska paused.

From here, the size of *Koskiusko* surprised Esmay all over again. The fabrication unit alone was larger than most warships, coated like them with matte black, and studded with the shiny knobs of the shield generators. Beyond it rose the angular outer face of T-1, black against the starfield, with the faint gleam of the transport track rising over its edge.

'Check,' Seska said.

'Two.'

'Three.'

'Four.'

Esmay shivered. Only four of them, out here alone on a ship so big she couldn't see most of it . . .

'We'll take the transport line,' Seska said. 'It'll save us time.' Nobody mentioned how much air was left; no one had to.

Esmay could see on her own suit gauges that they had spent twenty minutes cycling through locks, traversing the long tunnel of the fabrication unit, climbing up this far. And now they had to go back the same distance they'd come, cross the entire ship, find a way down to one of the locks opening into T-3's repair bay. Inside, walking along the decks, even running up and down ladders, they could have done it within the limits of a suit tank. Out here? It didn't matter – they had to. Seska clipped his line onto one of the rails of the transport line and pushed off. They followed.

Esmay had wondered how far beyond the ship's surface artificial gravity projected. As they came over the edge of T-1, with the dome of the bridge ahead of them, she could feel nothing . . . but when she looked, her legs had drifted toward its surface.

The transport track led directly over the domed core of *Koskiusko*, and Esmay thought that if she had not been both rushed and frightened, she would have enjoyed the view. The five blunt-ended wings splayed out around them, the dome itself studded with shield generator points and an array of retractable masts for communications and remote sensing. She looked for, but could not see, any other ship shapes against the stars. The escorts were out there somewhere . . . but too far to occlude a noticeable patch of the starfield.

It was easy to lose track of time in that long traverse of darkness. The glowing numerals inside her helmet flicked through the tenths of seconds, then seconds, then minutes. She did not look at her oxygen gauge; if it went too low, too fast, there would be no helpful bomb disposal team to hook up a new one for her.

'Trouble.' That was Seska; Esmay looked his way. Beyond him, the starfield shifted suddenly. Her mind froze up, but even as Seska said, 'They're maneuvering,' she had figured it out. Someone had decided to rotate the ship . . . and that someone could not be the captain.

But it could very well be the Bloodhorde commandos, in control of the bridge.

She told herself not to panic. She told herself that despite the seeming solidity and immobility of *Koskiusko*, the ship had never been really immobile: all ships moved, all the time, and she was no more likely to lose her grip and fall off when it was under drive than when it was moved only by the old laws of physics. *Kos* wasn't a warship; it couldn't develop the acceleration of the most anemic civilian cargo vessel on insystem drive.

Bowry's voice, elaborately casual, broke into her thoughts. 'Lieutenant – I don't suppose you know whether the FTL drive is irretrievably broken?'

The FTL drive. At once she knew what the Bloodhorde was going to do, and kicked herself mentally for not seeing it before. Of course they were going to take their prize away from possible rescue before trying to open it, like a jay with a sweetnut. 'No, sir,' she said to Bowry. 'Drives and Maneuver seemed to think it was most likely sabotage, but the sequenced jumps out could have knocked something loose.'

'Those escorts ought to be doing something useful,' Seska said. 'Like blowing us away, when they see us moving under power.'

Esmay had forgotten about the escorts, too. Her mouth went dry. Here she was, clinging to the outside of a spaceship under power, which was likely to come under fire . . . her EVA suit felt about as protective as facial tissue.

'Unless our crew's doing it, and they're talking to them.' Bowry didn't sound really hopeful. 'I suppose they could be moving away from the jump point and closer to the escorts.'

'No . . .' That was Frees. 'Looks to me like we're heading for it, but on a different vector . . . without the nav computer, I can't be sure, but – didn't this jump point have four outbound vectors?'

'Yes,' Seska said. 'I can't judge the approach, but you're probably right, Lin. We're less than a half hour from jump, I'd guess, and a lot more than a half hour from any place we can get into the ship. This should be interesting . . . pity we have no way to record the experience of the first people to die going through unprotected jump.'

'The commandos survived,' Esmay said, not knowing she was going to say it. Silence followed; she assumed the others were watching the wheeling starfield that proved *Kos* was moving under power.

'They were in *Wraith*,' Seska said.

'But there was a hull breach and forward shield failure. There's nothing wrong with *Kos*'s FTL shields.' She didn't know anything about shield technology, except that all FTL-capable ships had FTL shields. 'If we get off this thing and down onto the hull . . .'

'Good idea, Suiza.'

It took almost the entire half hour to clamber down, carefully clipping and unclipping and reclipping safety lines, from the high smooth arch of the materials transport track to the hull. Here, for the first time, Esmay could feel through her bootsoles a faint lateral tug, another proof that *Kos* was moving on her own, arguing with the inertia of her former path.

They were perhaps two-thirds of the way across the bridge dome from the Special Materials Fabrication Unit, its bulge hiding from them T-1 and all but the tip of SpecMat. Suddenly, light behind them, a flare that spread into a glow overhead. Esmay ducked instinctively, and looked up. The materials transport track flared into blinding vapor at its highest point, and shed flaming pieces that streamed along a track revealing their progress.

'Let's see,' Seska said. 'Now we're on the outside of a ship headed for jump *and* someone's shooting at us. I wonder where the adventure cube camera crew is?'

'On the other escort, of course,' Frees said. 'That's why they're not shooting at us yet.'

'I would wonder what else could go wrong, but I don't want to give the universe ideas,' Bowry said.

Esmay grinned. She suddenly realized one other thing she'd been missing . . . humor that felt right to her.

'If they're at standard distance, they can't get mass weapons to us before we go through jump,' Seska said. 'And that's only an escort, isn't it? Two more LOS shots ought to wipe them out for recharge, and then we'll be gone.'

'Assuming the other one doesn't fry us,' Bowry said. Light flared again, and this time the haze thickened. The rest of the transport track peeled away. 'Good tracking, but they'll burn out their power supply if they don't let it go.' Abrupt darkness; Esmay blinked, and the stars showed again.

'If the other one wanted to, they'd have done it already. What I heard in the first conference was that one of the escorts was waffling and probably would jump out pretending to go for help.'

'Desertion . . .' mused Frees.

'Butt-covering,' Bowry said. 'How I hate the prudent ones.'

'Doing all right, Lieutenant?' Seska asked, not as if he were worried, just checking.

'Fine, sir,' Esmay said. 'Just trying to remember if there's an airlock access around here somewhere.' Because even if they could survive jump on the outside of the ship, they'd run out of air before they finished . . . even a short jump lasted days longer than the air supply in an EVA suit.

'That's an idea,' Seska said. 'Get back in and go for 'em?'

'No, sir . . . not just the four of us, with only four light weapons. I was thinking, just stay in the airlock, with the outer hatch cracked so no one can get into it from inside, until we drop out of jump. Then go on.'

'Might work,' Seska said. 'We can use suit—'

Koskiusko bulled its way into the jump transition with an uncanny slithering lurch and a vibration that ground its way through Esmay's boots into her sinuses. The stars were gone. She could see nothing beyond the readouts in her helmet and they looked very strange indeed. Her com was silent, as dark a silence as the visible dark around her. Under her, the vibration went on and on, unhealthy for the ship, for the connection of wing to core, for the stability of the drives themselves. If the drives failed, if they dropped out of FTL at some unmapped point . . .

She clung to her handholds, and tried to talk herself out of the panic she felt. Of course it was dark; they'd outrun the light. If her readouts looked strange, she could still see them. Oxygen, for instance, gave her two hours more . . . but as she watched none of the values clicked over. The time-in-suit display was frozen in place, unmoving.

She had never been that good in theory, and she knew little about FTL flight, except that there was no way to define where and when ships were when they vanished from one jump point and reappeared (later, if there had been such a thing as absolute time, which there wasn't.) FTL flight wasn't instantaneous, like ansible transmission; the onboard reckoning might be anywhere from hours to days to – for the longest flight ever recorded – a quarter-standard year. Onboard, inside the hull and the FTL shielding, the clocks worked. Here . . . she forced a breath, which was not reassuring. She was breathing; she could feel the warm movement of her expiration on her cheeks. But the suit time-keeper wasn't keeping time, which meant it wasn't logging the oxygen she breathed, which meant she could run out without even knowing it.

And was it better to know when your oxygen was out? She

shied away from that to a consideration of the suit comm failure. Lights and comm worked fine inside ships in FTL flight . . . why not here, if they were inside the shields?

If they weren't inside the shields . . .

A low moan came through the suit earphones, dragging on and on like a lost cow on a spring night. Esmay couldn't figure out what it was, until it ended in a long hiss. Her mind put the sounds together like pieces of a puzzle: it could have been a word, slowed down. She struggled, trying to imagine what word it could have been, but a piercing jitter followed. She nudged the suit controls, damping the sound – at least that worked. But if the suit coms didn't work, they could all get lost . . .

Something bumped the back of her helmet; she turned cautiously. It had to be one of the others. It bumped again. Now she could hear someone's voice – Seska's – as well as a faint gritty noise where their helmets rubbed together.

'Radios don't work. Have to touch heads. Hook in.' He tapped her arm, and she remembered her safety line. Of course.

Esmay switched on her helmet light, and watched in amazement as the light reached slowly – *slowly* – down like the extrusion of a semisolid adhesive from its tube. When it reached the hull, the edges of the shape it made rippled uneasily, the edges a moire pattern of odd colors. Unfortunately, it illuminated no helpful markers, nothing to suggest which way an airlock might be.

'—Suiza?'

If the light moved slowly, so might comm, the radio waves distorted by whatever the FTL drive did to space and time. Esmay had a sense of waking up from some kindred slowness, as if part of her body were keyed to the velocity of light itself, and lagged far behind them.

'Here,' she said to Seska. She dipped her head; the bar of light from her helmet bent slowly, undulating with the movement. She handed the end of her line to the gloved hand that appeared in the light.

'—know someone who would take one look at that and spend the month in a trance of math, trying to explain it.' That was another voice, fainter, and she worked out that it must be transmitted helmet to helmet, from the other side of Seska. 'Frees linked. Bowry linked.'

'—airlock? Clock's not working.' Of course they had figured out the implications of that for themselves. Where was the nearest airlock? She stared into the darkness, trying to picture this part of the ship, to build up the model from her first days aboard when she studied *Kos*. There was an airlock for the emergency evacuation of bridge crew at the base of the dome, across from T-1, which meant on their present path and perhaps a quarter hour's careful traverse. In the dark she was not sure what their former path had been, but the leakage of the gravity unit helped her find downslope.

'Follow me,' she said, and pointed her helmet downslope. The light beam bent, kinked like water from a moving hose, and rippled off in the approximate direction. Esmay started after it, uneasily aware that she could catch up with her own light source. Just like the idiot captains they taught about in the Academy, who had microjumped their ships out in front of their own beam weapons, and fried themselves. She glanced sideways without moving her head, and saw other streams of light like her own but slightly different in color . . . felt a touch on her back.

'—Follow you,' Seska said. 'Stay in direct contact.'

She felt her way cautiously from one grabbable protuberance to another. It was like climbing boulders in the dark, which she'd done only that one time because it was such a stupid way to get hurt, hanging out over a dark place feeling for nubs and not knowing how far down . . .

Here *down* was a meaningless concept, and she had no idea what would happen if she lost contact with the hull. There was no sensation of external pressure, as there would be from speed in an atmosphere, with wind battering. No, but from deep inside came another pressure, as one body cavity after another insisted that things were wrong, were bad, and shouldn't be moving this way. The worst of the vibration had evened out, it should have been better. Instead, she felt growing pressure in her skull; she could feel the roots of her teeth tickling her sinuses; her eyes wanted to pop out to escape the swelling.

She paused as she felt a tug on the line connecting her to the others. A helmet tapped hers, then steadied.

'—think maybe we're not inside the FTL shielding,' Frees said. 'Just the collision shields.'

Of course. Her memory unreeled the correct reference this time, showing the FTL shield generators affecting a network of spacers set just under the hull covering. Of course the outer hull could not be shielded from FTL influences – it had to travel there.

It was hard not to overrun her light, but she finally figured out just how to position her head and move, so that she could see possible handholds and clip points coming up just out of reach. She passed a communications array, and remembered that it was only a few meters from the airlock entrance. But which way? And exactly how many? She paused there, wrapped her line around the base of the array (and why hadn't it snapped off when they went through the jump point?)

'It's nearby,' she told the others when they'd caught up and touched helmets, for all the world like cows touching noses. 'Wait – I'm going to look.'

A pause. '—Shine in different directions. Might help.' It would. She watched as the two beams she could see looped out on either side of hers. She gave herself five or six meters of line, and scooted out to the end of it, then began circling.

The airlock, when she found it, had a viewport beside the control panel. She clipped in to the bar meant for that purpose, peeked through, and saw only more dark. She didn't want to try turning on the interior lights – why announce to the Bloodhorde commandos where they were?

She tugged a signal on her line, and wrestled with the control panel as she waited for them to catch up. She had trouble making her light stay on the controls while she tried to operate them. The safety panel slid at last, and she looked at the directions. It had been designed for emergency exit, not entrance, so the entrance instructions were full of cautions and sequences intended to keep some idiot from blowing the pressure in neighboring compartments.

She punched the sequence that should work. Nothing happened. She looked at the instructions again. First lock the inner hatch, the button marked INNER HATCH, then the CLOSE switch. Then check the pressurization, TEST PRESSURE. She went that far then read and completed the rest of the sequence. But the lights did not turn green, and the airlock did not open.

'—Have a manual override?' Seska asked. She had not even noticed his approach, or the touch of the helmet.

She looked, and saw nothing she recognized. 'Didn't find one – I tried the auto sequence twice.' She moved aside.

Frees found the override, beneath a separate cover panel, with its own instructions. It was mechanical, requiring a hard shove clockwise, which freed a set of dials that had to be rotated into the number sequence printed on the inside of the cover. Seska and Frees struggled with the lever. She could imagine what they were saying. Fighting with the lever would use oxygen fast.

Esmay stared at the instructions for the automatic sequence, wondering why it wasn't working. Lock inner hatch, test pressurization, enter number of personnel coming in, key in opening sequence for outer lock. She'd done that. She went on reading, past the warnings against unauthorized use, down to the fine print, hoping to find something she'd missed that would get it open.

In that fine print, down at the bottom, the final word was *no*: NOTE: EXTERNAL AIRLOCKS CANNOT BE USED DURING FTL FLIGHT. In even finer print: *This constraint poses no risk to personnel as personnel are not engaged in EVA activities during FTL flight.*

She leaned over and put her helmet against Seska's. 'Some fool must have painted this thing shut,' he was saying.

'No,' Esmay said. 'It won't work in FTL flight. It says that at the bottom.' The others stopped struggling.

'So it does,' Frees said, leaning into her helmet. 'On this panel too. Says we don't need it because of course we aren't out here in FTL. Silly us, being impossible.'

'Wish they were right,' Bowry said. 'All right, Suiza – now what?'

Esmay opened her mouth to protest that – they outranked her; they were supposed to make the decisions – and shut it again, thinking. The oxygen running out, at a rate they could not determine. Time passing . . . somewhere, at least inside the ship, time was passing. Could they make it to their original goal before the oxygen ran out? Could they get in if they did? If all the airlocks were inoperable in FTL flight, they could at least use the air outlets in the repair bays . . . if those worked.

Then it occurred to her that maybe this airlock had an external oxygen feed too . . . some airlocks did, for the use of personnel stacked up waiting to use the lock. She turned back to the control panel and looked. There: traditional green nipple fitting, though only one at this lock. Would it work or was it too automatically shut off because no one would use it during FTL flight?

'Oxygen outlet,' she said, and tapped Bowry, next to her, on the shoulder. He looked, nodded, and turned. She found the recharge hose on the back of his suit, and unclipped it for him.

The oxygen flowlight came on when he plugged in, so at least the ship's system thought it was supplying oxygen.

'Gauge still stuck,' Bowry said. Which was going to make it hard, if not impossible to figure out when the suit tanks were recharged. 'Counting pulse,' he said then. 'Don't interrupt.'

Esmay had no faith that her own pulse was anything like normal, nor did she know how long it would take to replace an unknown consumption, even if she could use her pulse to determine duration. They crouched what seemed like a long time in silence, until Bowry said, 'There. Should do it.' He unplugged from the access, and said, 'Your turn. If you know your heart rate, give it three minutes. Otherwise I can count for you.'

'Others first,' Esmay said. 'They were wrestling with that lever.'

'Don't be too noble, Lieutenant; we might think you were bucking for promotion.' Seska moved over and plugged in, then Frees, and finally Esmay.

'Why three minutes?' Frees asked, while Esmay was still hooked up.

'Because – if I can just get it out – I've got a test that doesn't depend on the suit's internal clock. We'll need more, but I figured three minutes would give us a margin of fifteen, at least. My suit stopped registering at 1 hour, 58.3 minutes. Is that in the range for the rest of you?' It was, and just as Esmay had counted not her pulse but seconds, Bowry said 'Aha!' in a pleased voice.

'It works?'

'I think so. It would help if we could rig some way of getting us all hooked up at once, though, because calculating the differentials for the waiting periods is a bit tricky.'

'Give us an estimate; it'd take too long and we don't have tools—'

'All right. Suiza, you're still hooked up – you'll need the longest time on, then it goes down. I'll count it off for you.'

Esmay wondered what kind of gauge Bowry thought he'd worked out, and how long it was going to be, but she didn't want to interrupt his count. She felt vaguely silly, hanging there in the dark and silence, waiting to be told it was time to unhook herself from the oxygen supply, but tried to tell herself it was better than being dead. Finally – she could not guess how long it had been – Bowry said, 'Time's up. Next?'

When they had all tanked up by Bowry's count, which Esmay could only hope bore some relation to reality, they still had to decide what to do next.

Seska took the lead. 'Suiza – do you know where all the airlocks are?'

'I studied it for Major Pitak's exam when I first came aboard, but I don't really know . . . there are some I do remember. On each deck, between T-3 and T-4, for instance. Once we're on T-3, there are airlocks both inside the repair bay, and opening on the outer face toward T-4.'

'We could just stay here,' Frees said. 'We know where *this* oxygen is.'

'If we knew how long the jump transit was . . . if it's anything more than a day or so, we've got other suit limitations.'

'I don't suppose you know a handy external source of snacks, water, and powerpacks?'

'And toilets?'

Esmay surprised herself with a snort of laughter. 'Sorry,' she said. 'I believe all those substances are restricted to the interior of the ship during FTL flight.'

'Then we'd better head toward the next oxygen access, and hope that we find a way inside before . . . we have to.'

Navigation was going to be their worst problem. Although *Kos*'s hull was studded with more protuberances than Esmay had expected, it was still mostly matte black and unmarked. Creeping, feeling her way, across that great black expanse, she felt like a deep-sea creature, one of those her aunt had shown her pictures of. Some of those, she recalled, clustered around deep-ocean vents that provided warmth and nutrients. How did they find their way? Chemotaxis . . . however that worked. She couldn't figure out an equivalent for it on the hull of a ship in hyperspace, so just kept moving.

An abrupt change in the topography she could see signaled the dropoff, as it were, into the gulf between T-3 and T-4. Esmay struggled to think which direction to move next. Down toward the lower decks in the crease between T-3 and the core? Along the top of T-3? She didn't even know if the great clamshell gantry supports were closed around *Wraith*, or if they'd gone into jump with the repair bay open to the dark.

As if in answer to her question, light reappeared in the outer dark. At least, she supposed it was light, because her eyes reacted to it, and her brain, trying to make what she saw into the shapes she expected. It looked strange, and more like pale smoke blowing than light, thick streams fraying to looser strands as she watched, but it gave an impression of some angular bulk just off to her left, with towering plumes above. Far away, a tumbled trail of light, a badly ploughed furrow, receded redly into the distance.

They had all paused, and moved into the helmet-touching huddle. 'If I were a physicist,' Seska said, 'I just might go crazy. Most of what we've seen since jump hasn't fit most of what I learned about FTL flight. But since I'm a mere ship's captain, I say it's beautiful.'

'The gantries are up,' Esmay said. 'Repair bay's unsealed. If it doesn't have some kind of barrier I don't know about, we should be able to get in that way.'

'Why'd they turn the lights on *now*?' asked Frees.

'Just got the separate power supply hooked up,' Esmay said. 'The Bloodhorde's got the bridge – they probably cut power to the wings, maybe even life support, but each wing actually has its own ship support capability.'

'So we just walk over and hop down one of those openings?'

'Only if we want to hit sixteen or seventeen decks down after a

1-G acceleration. We might be able to climb down the gantry legs . . .' She'd never actually been on the gantries, but she'd seen others up there. The problem was . . . would their friends shoot them first, or give them time to explain who they were?

'Our suitcoms should work in there,' Seska said. 'And maybe they won't see us right away.'

The walk along the topside of T-3 to the first of the openings was easier than the final traverse of the dome, but fraught with its own difficulties. The unhappy light streaming away from the openings illuminated nothing in their path, and a lot was in their path. The sheared roots of the materials transport track supports . . . cables set to brace the clamshells, counterweights for the mechanisms that raised and lowered them . . . at least something was always near at hand to clip the lines to.

Personnel access in normal operations was on the center of curved openings, now clearly downlight of the arching supports themselves. They edged along the opening, and the light changed color as they moved beside it. Even those few tens of meters of uplight . . . were too blue, and a turn of the head made it red.

The personnel lift shaft was where Esmay had remembered it should be. Far, far below, its controls locked down. She could see a section of *Wraith* with her skin off and a crowd of workers in EVA gear clustered around a bundle of crystals that ran out of sight fore and aft.

There was, at least, the comfort of a niche below the hull line, a platform large enough for twenty or more workers to stand waiting for the personnel lift. Esmay started down the ten mesh steps that led down to it. On the second step, ship's gravity caught her feet; she felt glued to the step. By the time she got to the platform, she felt the drag of gravity through every bone, but her head felt clearer. Inside, the light looked normal, if less bright than usual. She glanced around. Only some of the lights were on, spotlighting the workers. Of course – on internal power, they'd conserve where they could.

The others came down, one by one, carefully; none spoke until they reached the platform. Esmay glanced around. Oxy supply lines in the bulkhead . . . a real bulkhead, with the green triangle for oxygen access painted on it. A water tap. Even a suit relief valve . . . suit maintenance really hated people who turned in soiled suits. A movement in her helmet caught her attention – her suit's internal clock was working again, and the oxygen gauge squirted up, then dropped, then rose again slowly to indicate that she had 35 percent of her supply left, one hour and eighteen minutes at current usage.

She started to speak, then realized that if the suitcoms were working properly they could be overheard. And why wasn't she hearing the others. Different circuits?

She found the controls in her suit and switched around the dial. '—Gimme *one* – just *one* – now half . . .'

Back to the other channel, the one they'd used into the jump into FTL. 'They're on a different setting, at least some of 'em are.'

'Makes sense.' Seska was peering over the rail at his ship. 'How do we get down?'

'Carefully,' said Frees, eyeing the emergency ladder which led down to the first horizontal gangway on this side of the repair bay, five decks below. 'If we try to get the lift up, they'll know we're here.'

'Better report now,' Esmay said. 'If we hail them on their own frequency, it might be someone I know. They can get Major Pitak to identify me, anyway.'

'You're right, but – in the grand tradition, it seems a bit tame to let them know. Adventures who've survived unprotected FTL flight ought to do something more dramatic . . . why weren't we provided with those little invisible wire things that spies and thieves are always using to lower themselves from heights?'

'Blame the props department,' Esmay said, surprising herself. They all chuckled.

'Suiza, if you ever get tired of maintenance, I'd be glad to have you on my ship,' Seska said. 'I wondered at first, but now I can see why the admiral wanted you on the operational end of this.'

Esmay's ears burned. 'Thank you, sir. Now – I'll just let them know we're here.' She switched channels, and found herself listening to the end of the previous set of directions.

'. . . Now back a tenth . . . just right . . . *there*.'

'Lieutenant Suiza here,' she said, hoping she wasn't cutting across another transmission.

'What! Who? Where are you?'

'I'm up at the top of the bay, on the personnel platform by lift one. With three other officers: Captain Seska and Lt. Commander Frees of *Wraith*, and Commander Bowry from the Schools. I have an urgent message from Admiral Dossignal for the senior officer in T-3.'

18

'What did you think you were doing hiding out up in the rafters all this time? I was told you were going over to T-1 to some kind of conference with the admiral and Commander Seveche and other important brass.' Commander Jarles, head of Inventory Control, was the senior commander aboard T-3. Esmay had met him briefly, at one of the officers' socials, but she did not know him well. Now he was angry, his stocky body thrust forward in his chair, his cheeks flushed.

'I did, sir.'

'And with everything else going on, you just lazed your way the long way round? You can't tell me you got past the blast doors, or that you didn't hear the allcall telling everyone in this wing to get their tails to assembly points!'

Esmay interpreted the emphasis on 'important brass' to mean that Commander Jarles of Inventory Control had had his nose put out of joint because he wasn't invited to that conference. Now he was feeling very much on his dignity.

'Sir, if I may ask – how is communication with the rest of the ship, especially T-1?'

'We've got a link to T-4, thanks to the access tunnel, but no one else. Why?'

'Then you might not be aware that the captain was gassed and in critical condition; Admiral Dossignal was injured in a firefight, and that's why the admiral didn't come along. I have his orders here.' Esmay fished them out of her pocket and handed them over. Jarles pursed his lips, and gave her a nod that clearly meant *Tell the rest.*

'We couldn't get past the blast doors out of T-1,' she said. 'The captain gave us the override codes, but they didn't work. The admirals felt it was imperative to get Captain Seska and his exec back to *Wraith* – the reasoning's in that order cube, sir. So we got out the SpecMatFab far end, and followed the transport track partway over the ship.'

His eyes widened. 'You crossed the whole ship?'

'Yes, sir. I don't know if the scans here picked it up, but the ship took hostile fire from beam weapons – the shields held, but the transport track was destroyed.' She waited a moment for any questions, then sprang the big one. 'Then it went into jump. That's why it took us so long to get back.'

'You're telling me . . . you were on the outside of this ship . . . during jump insertion?'

'Yes, sir.'

A long pause. 'Lieutenant, you're either crazy or lucky or blessed by some combination of deities I never heard of. The officers with you confirm this story?'

'Yes, sir.'

'All right. I presume you need a little time to . . . eat . . . or something. We've got a scratch mess set up; my clerk'll direct you. Give me a time to read these orders, then I'll want a complete report, down to each breath you took, and from the others as well. You can have an hour.'

Pitak was waiting for her outside. '*Where* have you been?'

Esmay was too tired to smooth it out for her. 'Crossing the outside of the ship during the fighting, the jump, and FTL flight. Thanks, by the way, to whoever turned on the repair bay lights. We were having problems up until then.'

Pitak's brows went up. 'Well. Somehow I suspect I'm losing you permanently for Hull and Architecture. I'll take you down for what passes for food. Where's the admiral?'

'In T-1, as far as I know – he was hurt, but alive. The captain was gassed, and maybe dying, when we left.'

'And here we are, hijacked like any fatbellied trader, going someplace we don't know and into trouble we can only imagine. Much good our escorts did us!'

Esmay found a toilet, then food . . . basic mush, but it was hot and the temporary cook had spiced it with something that gave it an actual flavor. She had expected to feel better after eating, but the warmth in her belly made her sleepy instead; she felt she could sleep standing up, and maybe even walking. It made no sense . . . she woke with her cheek on the table. Major Pitak was a few feet away, talking on the com. Esmay struggled to get her head up as Pitak came back.

'You need sleep,' she said. 'I talked to Commander Jarles, and he said what with the jump and all he'll need longer to assess the admiral's orders. You're going down for a half-shift at least.'

Esmay would have argued, but when she pushed herself up, her head swam. Pitak found her an empty space in a nearby corridor, in a row of other sleeping forms, and before she knew it Esmay was asleep on the hard deck. No dreams troubled that sleep, and she woke clearheaded.

She made her way around the other sleepers, found a working toilet and shower – it was hard to believe that with all the emergencies they still had enough extra water to use for showering, but she needed it. Then she went back to Commander Jarles's office, where she found Commander Bowry dictating his own report of their experiences.

He grinned at her, but kept talking. '—Then the lights came on, which made it easier to find our way to T-3 and the overhead access . . . whatever those openings are really called . . . Anyway, once back inside the ship, we found normal gravity, and our suit instruments began working again.' He turned off the recorder. 'Did you fall in a heap, too? I did, and I've just talked to Seska and Frees aboard *Wraith* – they said they'd barely gotten aboard when they couldn't stay awake. Scared hell out of their crew.'

'Maybe it was being outside the FTL shields,' Esmay said.

'Maybe. Maybe it was having had a long and interesting day.

You know, you're really good at this kind of stuff – how'd you get stuck in a DSR, if you don't mind my asking?'

'That mutiny, probably. I'd guess they didn't want any of those involved where they'd get into similar trouble, and since I ended up commanding, they sent me as far away as possible.'

'Where you promptly found a use for your newly acquired expertise. Yah. They might as well put you back in command track; you're a lightning rod.'

'I was technical track before. Scan.'

'You?' He shook his head. 'Your advisor messed up; you're a natural, and I don't say that lightly. Put in for transfer.'

'That's what my boss here said once. Major Pitak, in Hull and Architecture.'

'Believe it.'

She almost did. From someone like this, a seasoned veteran who had observed her . . . maybe it was true, and maybe she was not just lucky, but good at it.

Commander Jarles came out of his inner office. 'Lieutenant Suiza – glad you're here.' He sounded much more cordial than the day – was it day? – before. 'Hope you're rested, both of you. Captain Seska says he's staying aboard *Wraith*, but Lt. Commander Frees is coming to liaise with us on a plan to retake the *Koskiusko* and fight off any attempted boarding. Lieutenant Suiza, Admiral Dossignal seems to have a lot of faith in you.'

Esmay couldn't think what to say – *Yes, sir* seemed a bit too pushy – but Bowry spoke up.

'Considering that she saved the captain's life, and later the admiral's, I'd say he had reason.'

'I suppose.' He looked down at the files in his hand. 'He wanted you to take over all security for T-3 and T-4, and said you had helped develop a plan to trap a Bloodhorde ship. Frankly, with the admiral out of communication, I'm not comfortable putting that much responsibility on a junior officer I don't know very well. I've consulted with Major Pitak, who gives you a favorable review, but I'm not sure.'

'Got a plan yet?' came a voice from the door. That was Frees, whom rest and food had restored to an almost bouncy quality. 'Captain Seska sends his regards, and says he's got a guess how long we'll be in FTL flight.' He waited a moment for that to sink in, then waved a data cube. 'Nothing wrong with *Wraith*'s nav computers, though she couldn't give us any scan data. But from where we were, there are four primary mapped routes that we know – and know the Bloodhorde knows. They're on all the standard references. Two we can pretty much dismiss; they won't go back where they attacked us, because they can figure that our ships will be out there looking for them. In the same way, they won't back-jump where you came from, because they don't know if there were more Fleet ships there. But there's Caskadian, which has a direct route into Bloodhorde space at Hawkhead. And Vollander, which is offset to most routes, and a long jump to Bloodhorde space . . . but direct, and a long way from any Fleet pickets.'

'Put it up on the screen,' Jarles said. Frees complied, and they stared at the tangle of lines, thicker or thinner with flux values, edged with colors that told which political entities were known to use those routes.

'*Wraith*'s onboard systems say we went through the first jump point some 43 hours ago. We need someone from Drives and Maneuver to give us the figures on this ship's FTL drive, and then we might know which route we're on, and when we might drop out.'

'How long are they for regular travel?'

'Caskadian should be about 122 hours, maybe longer given the slow insertion and assuming the same exit. Vollander would be about 236 hours.'

'Long jumps – longer than we made coming in. I'd expect them to go for the short one, with so few of them aboard.'

'Now on the connecting lines – how does this ship handle series jumps?'

'It doesn't. Or rather, in theory it can, and we did coming out after you, but usually there's a pause of several hours for recalibration between jumps.'

'Besides,' Esmay said. 'They'll want to get more of their people aboard. The intruders have been working as hard as we have – without relief, and shorthanded.'

'So we've got roughly sixty hours before you think we'll come

312

out of jump, and until then all we have to cope with are the ones aboard.'

'Yes, sir.'

'Captain Seska wants to know how far the repairs on *Wraith* can get by then,' Frees said.

Commander Jarles shrugged. 'We have no access to the main inventory stores – and we can't move anything from SpecMat while we're in FTL. I suppose Major Pitak will know about the structural repairs—' Esmay decided this was no time to tell him that nothing was going to come from SpecMat by the exterior transport system until it was rebuilt.

'Sixty hours,' Bowry said. 'Nobody can come in from outside while we're in FTL flight – and surely those Bloodhorde are getting tired by now. There aren't that many – if we can get back in contact with the rest of the ship, we might be able to take control back.'

'And get ready for whatever's waiting when we come out of jump,' Esmay said. 'If they're jumping to a place where they have a battle group waiting . . . how many ships would that be?'

'With the Bloodhorde – five or six, probably.'

'A two-part plan,' Bowry said. 'Get control of this ship, and defeat whatever's waiting for us.'

'For which we need warships,' Jarles said. 'We can't mount weapons on *Koskiusko*.'

'Who's here for Weapons?' Esmay asked. 'I know Commander Wyche is in T-1.'

'It can't be done,' Jarles said firmly.

Esmay looked at him, then glanced at Bowry. Bowry spoke up. 'I think, Commander, to make best use of the resources of the 14th, the senior person in each department should assist in our planning.'

For a moment he puffed around the neck, exactly like the frogs Esmay remembered from home. Then he relented. 'All right, all right.'

When the fourth person started to remind the group that they couldn't do what they usually did, Esmay lost patience.

'Now that we know what we *can't* do, it's time to start thinking

313

what we *can* do. Fifty-eight hours, at this point: what can we do in fifty-eight hours? Thousands of intelligent, inventive, resourceful people, with the inventory we have available, can come up with something.'

'Lieutenant—' began Jarles, but Commander Palas held up his hand.

'I agree. We don't have time for the negatives. Do any of you know what the senior officers were planning in case of a Blood-horde assault?'

Bowry outlined it quickly. 'So,' he finished, 'I'd think that getting a Bloodhorde ship into T-4 would still work. Is there some way to get it . . . sort of stuck, so they can't move it? I think they'd come boiling out, and if they were somehow diverted away from it, some of our people could get in – if it could be unstuck . . .'

'There's that new adhesive . . .' said someone in back. 'Really strong, but depolymerizes in the presence of specific frequencies of sound. We could coat the barriers—'

'That's what we need to hear. Now we know we don't have that many troops capable of close-contact fighting – someone think of a way to immobilize Bloodhorde troops, who will be wearing EVA battlesuits.'

'So gas won't work,' someone muttered. 'If we knew the signal characteristics of the suits . . .'

'What about gluing *them* down?'

'Then our people couldn't get to the ship – the stuff stays tacky too long.'

'You'll think of something,' Esmay said. 'Now – about getting to the rest of the ship—'

'Once we're out of FTL, we could rig a communications cable back around to T-1 . . .'

'Once we're out of FTL, the airlocks will work. And we have lots of EVA suits; our people work in vacuum a lot.'

Commander Bowry nodded. 'Then to head the team that's going to get *Wraith* as ready as possible to be put out on the drive test cradle: Major Pitak, because she's Hull and Architecture.'

'I'll need to pull people from—'

'Go ahead. If there's a conflict, get back to me. Commander

Palas, could you head the team that will plan the capture of a Bloodhorde ship, assuming we can get one into T-4.'

'Certainly. May I ask where you'll get your crew?'

'That was my first assignment from Admiral Dossignal; I'll choose a crew from those who've served aboard warships fairly recently. Lieutenant Suiza, I'd like you for my exec, when the time comes, but in the meantime, I'd like you to work on the assignment Admiral Dossignal gave you: prepare Security here to defend these wings against the intruders. I suspect they'll try to get into T-4 to prepare it for their own ships.'

'Yes, sir.' Esmay wondered how she could possibly get ready for both, but having argued against negative thinking, she knew better than to say anything.

Vokrais grinned happily at his pack. Bloodied, bitten, but not defeated, and they had the bridge, its surviving crew demoralized and – at least temporarily – cooperative. The ship had made its jump into FTL without falling apart. The wings were locked off, helpless. Three of them had been reduced, at least largely, to unconscious dreamers and corpses. T-3 and T-4 so far held out; he'd expected more resistance there, but it didn't matter. When they came out of jump in a few hours, the ship pack would be waiting, with enough warriors to manage them. After all, they had no real weapons over there, and they were only mechanics and technicians anyway.

His people had even gotten some rest; it didn't take the whole pack to subdue these weaklings. Three of them were sleeping now. By making the bridge crew work longer shifts, they'd kept them tired enough that there'd been no sign of rebellion. He stretched, easing his shoulders. They had done everything they'd set out to do, done it better than predictions; their commander had not believed they'd be able to get the ship through jump. He was waiting for a message; he'd be delighted to get the whole prize.

Still, he hated leaving any part of the job undone. He had missed out on four years of raiding; the pack had fewer shipscars than any other of their seniority. They'd paid – paid dearly, in honor and opportunity – for the preparation necessary for this operation. He didn't want to share the glory with anyone. If he could offer his bloodbond the ship entire, he could raise his banner any time he chose, independent command.

He glanced around. Hoch looked bored; he had tormented the Serrano cub until all the fun was out of it. Three of his remaining pack would be enough to hold the bridge against the unarmed, spineless sheep that now sat the controls.

Excitement roiled in his gut again. 'Let's do it,' he said in his own tongue. His pack looked up, eager. Who should stay behind? As he described what they were going to do, he looked at their faces, looking for the slightest hint of weakness, exhaustion, or even worse, contentment.

First they would unlock the barriers to T-4 . . . with the crippled *Wraith* in T-3, most of the personnel would be in T-3. Could they repair *Wraith* in time? He doubted it, but even if they did it could not outfight a whole ship pack. Vokrais considered which deck they should use. According to the ship maps, Deck 17 contained hydroponics and even a few small gardens tucked among the gantry supports. Unlikely anyone would be watching for them up there, and they'd have a good view of the entire repair bay. They could work their way down, using their weapons and gas grenades to subdue anyone in their way, and drive them to a holding area at the base . . . and they had no way out. Not if he opened only the Deck 17 hatch . . . they'd be sure to close it behind them.

Corporal Jakara Ginese kept her eyes on her screens, obedient and to all appearances as scared as all the rest. She had not indulged in the sidelong glances that got Sergeant Blanders a beating; she had not struggled when one of the Bloodhorde fondled her and told his friends what he planned to do with her later. Above all, she had not revealed, by the slightest change of expression, that she understood everything they said in their own language. While she could do nothing, she did nothing.

But now . . . she thought it over, while appearing to cower away from the leader's rough bloodstained hands. 'You will be good, won't you?' he asked. 'You wouldn't think of giving any of us trouble . . .' She gave a little moan, and trembled, and told herself that it would be over soon, one way or the other.

She was sitting the wrong board, though the Bloodhorde hadn't figured that out. They'd come in screaming and shooting, and by the time they'd done, what with bodies all over the floor and the noise everyone was making . . . they hadn't noticed her changing nametags with a dead woman. At that point, she wasn't sure why she'd done it. Some instinct had urged her, and when they left the communications board empty, and she moved to environmental, where Corporal Ascoff usually sat, she began to think what she could do. None of her shipmates had commented, though she'd gotten some looks . . . but after what happened to Sergeant Blanders they didn't look anywhere but at their own work.

The environmental systems board cross-linked to ship security, another board the Bloodhorde had left empty after they changed the override codes. Possibly they didn't know that; she wouldn't have known it, sitting comm as she usually did, but she and Alis Ascoff had been working the same bridge shift long enough to share details of their work. Either Security or Environmental might have reason to close off the wings from the core, or take control of life support.

If they were watching too closely – as they had with ten of them always alert, always stalking around behind people – she could do nothing. But if they left only three . . . at some point, she would not be observed for a moment, and . . . what would be the best thing to do? If she opened all the wings, would the sleepygas simply spread to the core and put everyone there to sleep?

The captain had gone to T-1 to confer with the admirals. She knew that; she'd seen the captain on the bridge shortly before the Bloodhorde commandos burst in and took over. So if the captain was still alive, he was in T-1, and maybe the admirals too. If he wasn't gassed. If he wasn't dead.

If you can't make up your mind, her mother always said, do something anyway. Luckily, the core environmental system needed frequent adjustment when it was cut off from the wings. She had explained this, earnestly, when she first needed to touch the board. The Bloodhorde had leaned over, far too close for comfort, and stared at the display a long time before giving her permission to touch it. After the tenth or eleventh change, they'd

317

paid less attention, only asking now and then when the display showed a yellow band instead of green just how long she proposed to let it go?

The three left behind would be nervous. She listened as the others left, and did not turn around. Someone else did; she heard the blow and the angry command to get back to work. They would be watching . . . but would they understand? A yellow flicker on her board, just as before. The core, unlike the wings, did not have a large hydroponic/garden area for oxygen production and carbon dioxide uptake; oxygen was supplied from electrolysis of the water in the Deck 1 pool, and she had to keep the hydrogen collectors from overfilling. As well, she needed to put new CO_2 scrubbers online. She started to enter these commands, and as she expected one of the three came up behind her.

'What now?'

'The hydrogen, sir.' She pointed. 'It needs a new collector unit. And I need to put another ten CO_2 packs online.'

'No tricks, understand?' The muzzle of his weapon stroked her cheek. She shuddered, nodded, and her fingers trembled as she entered the values. She heard him walk away.

The question now was, how long did she have, and how could she do the most the quickest? She would open the T-1 access, she'd decided, but not T-5, because she knew T-5 had been gassed. If she had time, she'd reset the override codes for all the wings, so that the captain or any of ship's security who were still alive and awake could use them.

'Sir!'

Admiral Livadhi looked up; one of the security guards stood panting in the doorway. 'Yes?'

'Sir, the hatches are open . . . we're not cut off from the core . . .'

'All the hatches? All decks?'

'Yes, sir – at least, that's what the system says.'

Livadhi looked over at Dossignal, who was hunched awkwardly in his chair. 'I don't think this is *their* doing.'

'No – I'd say go for the bridge, with everything we have.' They had planned an assault on the bridge, but had not been able to breach the barrier.

'You can handle this end?'

'I can hardly run yours,' Dossignal said, grimacing. 'Having been stupid enough to get shot.' Then he grinned. 'Confusion to our enemies,' he said.

'I intend a good deal worse than confusion,' Livadhi said, and spoke into his headset. 'Bridge team: go ahead.'

'You stupid—!' The snarl came just before the blow that knocked her to the deck. Corporal Ginese would have been furious with herself for not remembering that the barrier status lights showed clearly on the board, if she'd been able to think. A savage kick in the ribs curled her around the pain. She said nothing. She thought, with all the intensity of her being, *Please, please, please . . . let it work. Let someone be alive there, awake . . .*

Now two of them were on her; she heard bones snap as one of them kicked savagely at her arms, her ribs. It hurt more than she'd expected . . . and more noise . . . she couldn't think why it should be so noisy, all that clatter and roar and shouting. If they were going to make that much noise, why not just shoot her?

She hardly noticed the blows had ceased . . . then it was quiet again. Someone wept in the distance. Nearer, footsteps . . . she wanted to flinch away, but couldn't move.

'I think . . . she's alive,' someone said.

Not one of them. Not someone from the bridge. She opened the eye that would open, and saw what she had hoped to see: shipmates, armed, and just beyond them, a Bloodhorde corpse. She smiled.

'They're trying to get through the barrier up on Deck 17,' the sergeant minor said. 'They've got the core-side barrier open, but the interlock we put on the wingside barrier's holding.'

'Are they really committed?'

'It sounds like it.'

'Then I think it's time for Brother Ass and the Cactus Patch,' Esmay said.

'What?'

'Folk tale from my home planet, slightly revised. As long as we

319

provide enough resistance, they'll be sure we didn't want them there. Only we *do* want them there, because it's our trap.'

'How long do we make 'em wait?'

'Long enough to—' A shout from down the passage.

'Suiza!'

'Yes?'

'Our people have the bridge! The barriers are operable on the old override codes!'

Esmay swung back to her comunit. 'Now – let them in now.' If they knew they'd lost the bridge, they might not come into the trap. 'Be sure to lock the gate behind them, once they're onto another deck.' By all combat logic, they should be hoping to clear T-4 from the top down . . . if they found the top deck empty, they should go looking for resistance.

The scan techs had installed additional surveillance near the hatch and in the passages beyond. Esmay watched as the hatch slid aside . . . the Bloodhorde commandos still wore their Fleet uniforms, now bloodstained and filthy, under light armor they'd stolen from the ship security. Helmets and respirators . . . they couldn't be gassed, but the respirators were noisy enough to affect their hearing. The helmets were supposed to compensate with boosted sensitivity . . . but that had its shortcomings. They each carried several weapons, the light arms intended to suppress shipboard violence.

'They're outnumbered, but we're still outgunned,' said the petty-chief looking over her shoulder.

'Guns aren't the ultimate weapon,' Esmay said. Would they choose the well-lit passage ahead, or the dim one to the left, among the garden rows? They'd had only a few concussion shells, taken from *Wraith*'s damaged starboard battery, and she hadn't been able to seed every possible route.

As she'd hoped, they headed down the dimmer passage. They moved as she remembered her father's troops moving, cautious but swift. It was on the basis of that trained advance that she'd planted the shells where she had . . . and when they passed the marked point, the shells burst around them. Esmay had the sound turned down . . . but they hadn't. They were flat on the deck, firing at nothing, and unable to hear anything but the racket they made and their own ringing ears . . . she was sure of that.

The top level of T-4 was too big for them to check thoroughly; she had counted on that, and on their reaction to resistance. From one position to another, they followed what seemed to be a retreating force of slightly lesser strength. They would be trying to pick up its communications through their helmets . . . surely they would change channels until they found it. And what they heard would sound authentic . . . Esmay had discovered that the 14th had its own Drama Club, its members eager to create and record a script full of dramatic conflict. It had multiple branches, just in case the enemy didn't follow the main plotline, and one of the communications techs cued the different segments while watching the vidscan to see what the intruders were really doing.

She keyed to listen herself for a moment.

'Hold 'em at Deck 15 – we can hold 'em if they don't come down that inboard ladder—'

'Corporal Grandall, cut off that ladder—'

'—Here's the ammo, sir, but we're running—'

Sure enough, on the vidscan, the Bloodhorde had turned back, looking for, and finding, the inboard ladder. Poppers wired into sensors blew off as they started down. Smoke swirled . . . Fleet uniforms wrapped around bundles of insulation moved, fell, were dragged backwards.

'Whiteout! Whiteout! They're on the ladder—'

'HOLD them—'

'We're TRYING – NO! They got Pete!'

'—More gas masks! They're using more . . .'

It would have been fun to watch, like being behind the scenes when an adventure cube was being taped, except that more than half the sites needed someone live, on the scene, to produce a realistic effect. The enemy didn't know which targets were live, but Esmay did. She had argued at first for a less risky approach – dousing the intruders with that adhesive, if nothing else – but the capture of an enemy warship would be easier if it thought it was coming into a ship controlled by its own people.

Ideally, they'd get to the base of the repair bay just as the ship came out of FTL flight. They'd find the lockers of EVA suits; they'd open the repair bay – it was all set up for automatic use, with new – and newly aged and scuffed – control panels and instructional labels.

Esmay switched to the secure link to the bridge: they had opened a T-3 access hatch and fed an optical link through it. She knew the captain was alive, but in critical condition, now in a regen tank in Medical, which had been purged of the sleepygas. The casualty count was rising, as search teams found more and more bodies . . . most were bodies, but a few had been wounded. Barin hadn't been found yet.

A jolt like stepping off a ledge in the dark bumped her spine on the chair. She glanced at the clock. An hour early?

'Jump point exit,' said someone unnecessarily. Moments later: 'Caskadian System, low-vee exit.'

So they were where they'd expected to be, and in one piece. A low-vee exit meant scan would clear soon, and they'd know how much trouble they were in. Esmay wondered what jump exit would have looked like from outside and shuddered. They could not have survived the whole trip outside, she was sure.

'Prelim scan: six, repeat six Bloodhorde ships. Weapons analysis follows . . .'

Now where were the Bloodhorde intruders? She looked back at the vidscan . . . at Deck 10. Too far up; she wanted them able to contact their own ships, and for that they had to be at Deck 4.

'Release, release!' she said. The communications tech nodded, and switched to the final segment: anguish, terror, harsh breathing . . . resistance melting away in panic. Predictably, the Bloodhorde team followed, and although they came out into the repair bay control compartment with some remnant caution, they didn't hesitate long.

They had made good use of their data wands . . . one pair went straight to the control centers, and the others to the EVA lockers. The communications tech put on the post-battle tape – if they kept listening, they'd hear individuals trying to find each other, trying to decide what to do, where to take the wounded.

The two who could speak – or at least understand – the Bloodhorde dialect tuned in the output of the communications desk in the repair bay. What would they say to their ships?

*   *   *

The Bloodhorde ship looked nothing like the sleek blackovoids of the Fleet.

'Damn converted tramp hauler,' someone muttered through the comlink. Esmay wished they'd shut up, but she agreed. Slightly larger than a Fleet escort, and perhaps a third shorter than a patrol craft, its hull had a more angular outline suggesting its origin as a civilian freight carrier.

'Part of that's bare metal,' someone else said. Esmay spotted the oblong patch, glinting dully in the repair bay's spotlights. The rest was probably the same organoceramic material that most ships used, its scarred uneven coloring suggesting patches of different ages and origins. Along the flank, bright-painted symbols that must mean something to the Bloodhorde. Near the nose, rows of stylized eyes and jagged teeth. She shivered.

The ship edged in, still untethered but now in easy reach of the grapples. Someone nudged her; she followed the gesture to see tiny figures in EVA gear moving on the plates of Deck One. That would be the Bloodhorde intruders, come out to welcome their friends and let them aboard. One of them moved to the control board for the grapples on her side; another stood at the controls for the other set of grapples.

She could not see their hands on the controls, but she could see the result, the shift of the grapple heads as they moved into position, and the sharp pings in her helmet as the grapples released from the heads and then impacted the ship. The sling buffer at the inboard end of the repair bay deployed, as if released by the grapples . . . they hoped the Bloodhorde would think that. She watched the intruder at the grapple controls spin around, and imagined his surprise. But nothing more happened. He made some hand signal to another of his team, out of her sight, then turned back to the controls.

The Bloodhorde ship barely moved, drawn by the retracting grapples. Esmay boosted the magnification on her helmet scan, and watched as the intruder pushed the grapple controls to maximum. She grinned through her tension. She'd thought they would do that . . . the plan would work anyway, but this was a bonus.

The ship moved faster, as all the grapples exerted full power. They must think the sling buffer would halt it if it moved too fast . . . and it would . . . after jolting the passengers a bit.

She watched in fascination as the ship moved slowly, inexorably, past the marked safety point . . . stretching out the grapples again, swinging like a ball on an elastic line. As if in automatic response, another buffer sling deployed – and another. The enemy ship rammed into them, nose first, stretching the first to its limit – one . . . two . . . bands ruptured and flung back across the bay with an indescribable noise. The impact shook the entire bay. *Now* . . . would they notice anything? The second held, and the third, barely deformed. The enemy ship shuddered, held by the buffer slings' adhesive coating and the taut grapples behind.

'We did it,' she said aloud. 'We got ourselves a warship!'

19

'And two problems,' said the woman on scan in the bridge. 'Take a look—'

The second and third Bloodhorde ships kept coming, now obviously aiming for the drives test cradles.

They should have thought of that. They'd assumed the Bloodhorde would be cautious, would test with one ship until they were sure it was safe. Not their style . . . of course they'd get in close with as many as possible, and with those small ships it was not hard to maneuver in close.

'Now what, genius?' murmured Major Pitak. Esmay stared, her mind watching possibilities that flickered past more rapidly than the turning dials of a biabek game.

'We won't be able to get *Wraith* out now,' someone else said. 'We should have done that first—'

Wraith, trapped in the repair bay, immobile, capable of blowing itself, but probably not the rest . . . unless its self-immolation ignited the others' weaponry. Would it? Was that good enough, the best she could hope for?

No. She wasn't playing for any outcome but victory. Her terms.

'We take them both,' she said. 'The ones on the test cradles. Then we get *Wraith* out . . . and the other Bloodhorde ship, if we can. It's actually better – evens the odds—'

'But we don't have crews for that many – and they're not even our ships.'

After the first panic had come a surge of exhilaration; she felt as if her mind was working at double speed. 'Oh, yes, we do. We have thousands of the top experts on every ship system right here – right now.'

'Who?'

Esmay waved her hand, indicating both wings. 'Think about it. D'you really think our people can't figure out the controls on Bloodhorde ships? They're simple. D'you think our people can't offer effective resistance to Bloodhorde troops, if we turn them loose? I think they CAN. I think they WILL.'

They had to. And it was better. Even if they just got two, the odds were almost even . . .

Bowry had seen it too. 'We'll have to scramble, though, to get two – no, three – crews ready to board. They'll be down in less than an hour.' He grinned at her. 'Well, Lieutenant, I think I'll have to find another exec – you're going to have to take one of those ships yourself.'

'Me?' But of course, her mind insisted. Who else? The most terrifying thing about it was that she didn't feel as scared as she should be. 'Right,' she said, before he could say anything else. 'Which one?'

'The T-3 cradle – because I've already got a crew assembled here. Maybe Captain Seska can free some of his crew for you.'

'Yes, sir.' She was already thinking who she wanted.

'Whoever gets control of a ship first takes group command,' Bowry went on. Esmay hadn't thought of that, but they would need to coordinate. 'My advice, if you're first, is to get that thing off the cradle – don't wait for me – and fire on the first ship you can locate.'

Vokrais was furious. After all they had accomplished, that pighead of a ship pack commander was going to let two more shiploads board. He knew what that would mean – they'd be claiming credit for kills he and his men had made; they'd be marking loot.

'There is no need,' Vokrais said. 'We have this ship at our mercy. Only the troops aboard *Deathblade* are needed. What if the Familias ships are following? If you take two more ships out of formation, how will you beat them off?'

'You assured me they could not follow, having no idea where you are.' The ship pack commander sounded entirely too complacent. When Vokrais had started this mission, the ship pack command had been promised to his own warclan. Now it had gone to the Antberd Comity, on whose graves he would spit if he got the chance. Ambitious, rich with loot they never bled for, he didn't know why the Overband let them get away with it. And here was another one, not even an Antberd, but a hireling . . . he had met Cajor Bjerling at the arena once, and hadn't liked him then.

He wanted to slug someone, and unfortunately they'd dumped the Serrano cub for safekeeping before they came to T-4.

'I claim this ship,' he said. He wouldn't get it, but at least the claim would be registered. 'I claim the blood shed, and the riches won, the deaths and the treasures, for the men who won them.'

'It's big enough to share the glory,' Bjerling said. 'And soon enough to divide the loot when the deed is done.'

'The deed is done,' Vokrais argued.

'You need not fear my justice,' Bjerling said. 'Unless you want to challenge my honor.'

Of course. In the middle of the operation he was supposed to challenge the commander? Even if he won, the Overband would not be pleased with him.

'I do not challenge your honor,' he said. 'Only remember who opened this ship like an oyster.'

'You are not likely to let me forget,' Bjerling said. 'The troops in *Deathblade* will await the arrival of those from *Antberd's Axe* and *Antberd's Helm* before they maneuver.'

In other words, Vokrais thought sourly, he would have no chance to show the *Deathblade* troops, whose commander he knew well, how he had conquered. The others would overwhelm everything.

'May his wife grow spines in her fur,' said Hoch quietly.

'If only it were possible,' Vokrais said, enjoying the idea. 'So we have to wait around for them all to land – assuming those incompetents can actually land on the test cradles – and get inside? Just stand here like targets?'

'He would not be ill-pleased if any of these people did kill us – greedy swine. We shall be extremely careful, packsecond. There is no reason, with so many eager to find loot, for us to take risks.'

Hoch chuckled. 'Perhaps we might even disappear?'

'Not that, I think. After all, our people are in charge on the bridge. Perhaps we should go back and be sure they know who's being so helpful.' Assassination on a mission was unusual, but not unheard of, and Vokrais felt in the mood to kill someone. 'Let these people find their own way in; it will be good practice for them. Not all boardings are unopposed.'

Esmay had just made it back to T-3 when she was called to one of the communications nodes.

'I hear we're about to be trapped in here,' Seska said, sounding angry.

'Not for long,' Esmay said. 'We're going to take the ship behind you, and the one coming in to the T-4 test cradle. As soon as we're clear, they'll warp *Wraith* out.'

'Better odds,' Seska said, sounding slightly less angry. 'Save me one, why don't you? I presume you'll be taking one of them yourself?'

'Yes – the one behind you; Commander Bowry's already got his crew over in T-4.'

'Who's going to take the one that's docked? Or were you going to leave that one where it is?'

'Leave it – we don't have the crew.'

327

'And I presume you have a plan to get to the test cradle and board? What if they dump their troops and take off again?'

'In that case, you're not blocked, and Bowry can take the ship of theirs that's in T-4. But what we hear through their transmissions is that they're planning to stay awhile – it's made the commando leader mad – he thinks they're stealing his glory.'

'Good. And good luck, Lieutenant.'

Esmay went back to the command center set up in the 14th's headquarters area.

'I've got a list of volunteers for your crew, Lieutenant,' said Commander Jarles. 'You seem to be quite popular.' She wasn't sure if this was sarcasm or honest surprise. 'They're sorted by specialty, then rank-ordered by those with experience in ships similar to the enemy's. I told them to wait for you in R-17.'

'That's wonderful, sir.' It was indeed; the only problem was knowing how many she should take.

'We've got a link now to the other wings. One of the instructors over in Admiral Livadhi's command has done a tactical analysis – he suggests—'

An alarm went off.

'They're going through somewhere!' Esmay said.

'They're not even off that ship yet,' said Commander Palas. 'We've been watching.'

'Then it's the others – the original intruders. But why? And where?'

'Warn the bridge,' Jarles said. 'That'll be where they're going – they may not know we've taken it back. Lieutenant Suiza, pick your crew and get in position – I think we can ignore that tactical analysis.'

Esmay took the list and looked at it on her way down to R-17. Petty-major Simkins, Drives and Maneuver, had operated the commercial equivalent of the Bloodhorde hulls during the three years he'd tried making it in the civilian world. Two others had less, but some, experience with those ships. Scan – she hoped they'd be able to take some of their own aboard, or tight-link to *Koskiusko*'s bridge. No one had a lot of relevant experience, but there was a pivot-major, Lucien Patel, that the entire Remote Sensing unit thought was another Koutsoudas. Worth a try, anyway. For backup in scan, she picked the one person with recent combat experience, and another because he had both commercial and military background. Communications, that was critical . . . that one, and that one, and a backup. Environmental she wouldn't worry about – they'd fight in their suits, and either win this in a hurry or die in a hurry. Weapons – she really needed good weapons people. There were five that seemed to stand out from the rest of the list.

When she got to the meeting place, she was startled by their response – the swift approving murmur, the eagerness on their faces. They looked at her as if she could make this mad enterprise easy. She felt her own heart lift, and gave them back the grin they seemed to be waiting for.

'Told you,' she heard someone say. 'She's got a plan.'

Not yet, she didn't, but she did have a crew list. She read it out, and those named came forward; others looked disappointed.

'Can't you use a few more?' asked a burly sergeant who looked vaguely familiar. 'If there's someone aboard, if there's a fight. I've won my share of barroom brawls.'

Extras with that attitude couldn't hurt. Esmay nodded, and another half-dozen clustered around. Others lingered, but didn't come forward.

'The rest of you – if you haven't heard, some of the original intruders have gone back into the rest of the ship. And there are plenty of troops coming in. I'm sure you can think of something appropriate to do. The plans we had for dealing with the troops aboard one Bloodhorde ship now need to work for three times that number.'

The really worrisome problem was how to get to the drives test cradles unobserved. Both repair bays were now open and flood-lit, so that any movement across the gap might be seen . . . would be seen if the Bloodhorde were looking for it. Even though she and Bowry both had guides – specialists who were test cradle supervisors – so that they could approach the keel of the test cradle rather than its upper deck where ships rested – they would be in sight of anyone watching from the repair bays for part of the distance. Esmay did not want to trust that no one would glance over and notice a string of EVA suits going the wrong direction.

'We need something else to get their attention,' Esmay said. 'More smoke-and-mirrors, like we used to get the intruders well into T-4, but big enough to enthrall however many of them come out.'

'If we turned the lights out, they couldn't see you as well.'

'Not at first, but they probably have lights of their own. They'll be expecting something . . .'

'We're supposed to have been partially disabled . . . what if our lights go off, then flicker back on? If they've got those fancy faceplates on their helmets, that'll give 'em fits.'

'I'll bet we can look really inept,' someone else said. 'Fluctuations in the artificial gravity, flickering lights – it could seem like the power's out of control.'

'But not until we're on our way,' Esmay said. 'And that means after most of them are off the test cradles – the timing's going to be tight.'

'Trust us, Lieutenant,' said one of the people she had not picked for her crew. 'We're trusting *you*.'

Good point. Esmay nodded at her. 'Fine – I'll leave it to you, then. Come on, folks – let's get suited up and see about wiping out a Bloodhorde battle group, or whatever they call themselves.'

The Bloodhorde ships disgorged EVA-suited figures in clumps that reminded Esmay of strings of frog spawn in the lily ponds back home. Little shiny blobs, two and three together, silvery in the light from the repair bay. They kept coming and kept coming, more than Esmay would have thought would fit in such a small ship.

'Do they know how visible they are?'

'Probably. It helps them find each other, after all . . . though I don't know if other ships they attack have so much light outside. Why would they? It's depressing to think how visible *we're* going to be.' EVA suits were intended to be seen; it was a safety feature.

'Too bad we didn't think to spray ourselves matte black or something.'

Her gaze fell on the rolls of sheathing for *Wraith*'s denuded flanks. 'The skin.'

'What?'

'The sheathing . . . those rolls . . . they wouldn't shine . . . If only we'd thought of that earlier. But now they'd see us if we tried to use them.'

'It's easy enough to peel off the hull,' said one of the techs. 'Just takes a sonic generator set at the right frequency, depolymerize the adhesive. What were you thinking, wrap it around you? It's not that flexible.'

'How flexible is it?'

'It'd make a roll about this big—' The man held out his arms.

'In other words, several of us would fit into it, in our suits?'

'Oh, sure.'

'Would it be any good against scans?'

'Most of 'em, certainly, small as you'd be.'

But they had no time; it could take an hour to cut and roll enough tubes, and they didn't have an hour. Esmay put that out of her mind and said, 'What else might give us some cover?'

'Well – we can't use the high-speed sprayers in the repair bays, 'cause they'd see it, and besides that's part of the plan—' Esmay wondered what plan, but didn't interrupt to ask. 'But there's the little hand sprayers in the Small Parts Coating workbay.'

One of the EVA suit techs shot down that idea – paint might eat through the fabric, and they had no time to experiment – so they'd prepared to go as they were, silvery suits and all, when one of the cooks' assistants came running up with an armload of dark green waste sacks.

'We'll look like a row of green peas,' muttered Arramanche.

'Better than silver beads,' Esmay said. 'At least they're dark, and not shiny.'

Ahead of her, the base of the test cradle loomed, clearly visible in light from the repair bay. Visible too was their shadow, enlarging as they neared. In its center was the little red blinking dot of the rangefinder on her helmet, giving her the distance and rate of approach.

'Now,' said Esmay. The lights went out; she had only her helmet readout to go on, and a single chance to make any adjustments that had to be made. But presumably the Bloodhorde attackers would be startled by the change in light – they'd be looking for people in the repair bays, where they were. Seb Coron had told her about night fighting, that no one could resist looking to see where a light had just come on, or gone out.

Nearer – five meters . . . four . . . she pushed the makeshift control and a little jet of gas spewed out; she felt the shove as if the ones behind her were leaning on her back. Three meters . . . a very slow progression to two, then one, then she tucked her head, rolled, and felt her boots thud on the hull; her knees took up the impact easily.

The base of the drives test cradle was a maze of cables and attachments, but the test cradle supervisor they'd found knew where the nearest hatch was. Once inside, they rose through the shaft with only short tugs on the line. Then they were at the upper hatch, and Esmay peered through . . . there was the Bloodhorde ship, an angular dark bulk against the starfield. She couldn't tell if it was occupied, not until she had the instruments in the test cradle up and running. That was a job for the supervisor, who grunted and fumbled around for a moment. Then—

'It's got active scan leaking all over it,' he said. 'Can't do much without them noticing. Good thing is, with them putting out that much, they're not likely to notice anything we put on the cable. Want me to signal *Kos*?'

'Yes.'

In moments the signal came back: their arrival had been logged, and they were waiting for Bowry's report from the other test cradle. Esmay reminded herself that his team had had longer to travel, that they had crossed below the line of the Bloodhorde troops coming in. Then, when she thought she couldn't wait another moment, the signal came.

'Ready?'

'Go.' This was only one tricky bit in the many tricky bits of the plan. Keeping it simple had not been an option. They needed to focus Bloodhorde attention on the repair bays, away from the assault teams who were after Bloodhorde ships. What they had to work with was more in the nature of handwaving and colored smokes than real weaponry or the skill to use it – but to the repair crews of a DSR, handwaving and colored smokes were second nature. Esmay didn't know what they were going to do, only that it would occur in sixty-second bursts of maximum distraction. They hoped.

The first of the Bloodhorde reinforcements had made it to the cradles when the lights went out. They cursed the stupid Familias sods who had not the sense to surrender without playing childish tricks, and turned on their own searchlights. The beams made harsh moving shadows of the construction machinery, the cradle supports, grapple housings, gantries and the robotics that sprouted on them like barnacles on a dock. In the vacuum of the open repair bays, the laser rangefinders left no trace; the first victims didn't even see the little colored dots on their suits for squinting into that mass of bright lights and shifting shadows. More curses in the headphones, but they knew how to deal with this kind of resistance. It was tricky, with their own ship now moored in T-4, but they lobbed in some of the little mines called bouncers, and waited until three or four of them had blown up. They had proximity fuses, but would recognize patches on Bloodhorde EVA suits, which made them only very dangerous to play with.

They came on, alert for any more direct resistance. A hundred more had made it alongside their own ship, alongside *Wraith*, when the lights came back on, flickered on and off several times, and then went out again. Helmet filters darkened, oscillated in response to the rapid changes, and finally cleared as the darkness came back. Again their own lights probed the darkness, and they remembered the confusion they'd seen. They were not novices, to be put off by such basic ploys. They didn't bunch up; they moved along in a disciplined skirmish line, until their forward elements reached the airlock at the hub end of the repair bay.

Then the big robotic sprayers, which had slid down the gantries centimeter by centimeter in the light, dropping meters whenever the lights weren't on them, rotated, aimed . . . and fired thick yellow liquid at them. It dispersed to a fine spray in the vacuum, a spray that adhered with equal rapidity to their suits, including the helmet viewplates.

Not all of them got a full dose. Some, near the nozzles, were physically thrown off their feet by the force of the spray, and of those a few managed to curl protectively into balls, so their helmet faceplates weren't entirely obscured. But it took a critical few moments to realize what had happened, and its effect. In those few moments, their formation disintegrated. A few battered and blundered their way to airlocks. But the rest were blind, their external sensors clogged with spray, in some cases stuck fast to the deck by having unfortunately stepped on a coat of spray before it set completely.

The suits were powered; they could pull free. But they couldn't see; they couldn't get the paint off with gloved hands . . . in fact, though they didn't know it, they'd have needed an unusual solvent to remove the paint without eating through the faceplate.

'They're wrathy,' said one of those who could understand the language coming out of those suit radios. 'They're cursing the name and the war clan of someone named Vokrais.' Down on the deck of the repair bay, the brilliant yellow suits seemed almost to glow in the shadowy areas. Evidently those mixing the paint had added reflectants and fluorescents to it.

'Good. How many of them did the trap miss?'

The external vidscans, hastily rigged a few hours before to cover areas not usually monitored, showed several clusters of Bloodhorde invaders around the outer edges of the repair bays.

'Perhaps fifty – a hundred—'

'Let's keep them occupied.' The sprayers lifted much faster than they'd come down, the beaked nozzles rotating inward. Other machinery shifted up and down, back and forth, in an elaborate dance intended to look vaguely menacing. Would that keep the attention of the Bloodhorde from what was happening behind them? One enterprising operator detached one of the sprayers from its usual mounting, and sent it toward the repair bay opening, as if in search of more troops to spray. He ran it out on a boom, its nozzle swinging threateningly from side to side, and watched on the vidscan as the Bloodhorde troops shifted uneasily on their lines. One of them raised a weapon . . . and let off a triumphant screech of Bloodhorde when his shot holed the paint reservoir.

He hadn't thought what would happen if he succeeded: the bursting reservoir meant a cloud of dispersing paint, still tacky enough to cloud several more faceplates. More screamed curses came over the radio; the other troops lost the last remnants of discipline, and rushed into the repair bay.

Esmay pulled herself into the ship. Both outer and inner hatches were open, which argued that anyone aboard would be in an EVA suit. She edged across to the inner hatch, noting the slightly greasy feel of a substandard artificial gravity generator, and peered around. She was looking into a large open compartment with rows of upright stanchions, each fitted with a top crossbar and several loops. It looked nothing like anything she'd seen in a Fleet vessel. Then she realized how handy that apparatus would be for someone getting into an EVA suit without help. This was where the Bloodhorde troops prepared for boarding.

Where was their bridge? Was anyone there? She waved two of her people forward, and two aft. She herself went forward, behind the other two. She saw the leader's arm lift, and held her breath . . . they and Bowry's team had the only five needlers available, weapons that were safe to use in the confines of a warship's bridge.

His hand jerked twice, and then he moved forward. Esmay followed, alert for movement from any direction. There was none. On the bridge, the Bloodhorde had left two – she had no idea what their duties had been – and both were dead.

'Let's get this ship going,' she said. Someone dragged the bodies back to the big compartment near the locks; the specialists moved to their areas.

The controls looked familiar enough, despite the odd lettering on the labels.

'This'll do, Captain,' said Petty-Major Simkins. Esmay started to say she wasn't the captain, when she remembered that she was . . . at least for the moment. A captain, if not the captain. Simkins was her engineering section, ordinarily in Drives and Maneuver. 'It's just a basic small freighter perked up with some weaponry . . . shields aren't more than civ level. If the others' shields are no better, it'll only take a few hits.' That it would take only a few enemy hits to destroy them was understood.

'Weapons?' she asked. That was Chief Arramanche, who held up a finger for a moment's more grace.

'We've got . . . almost a full arsenal of missiles, Captain,' she said then. 'Ample for the mission. But this thing has no beam weapons.' Which meant they'd have to come close to be sure of a kill.

'Scan?' Esmay asked.

'Power . . . on . . . Captain, we're operational.' Lucien Patel had a light, almost breathy voice, but it sounded confident enough. 'And we have . . . there's *Kos*'s signal . . . the three other Bloodhorde ships. One's probably a pirated superfreighter, and the other's about this size.'

Vokrais eyed the empty curved passage uneasily. Something was different, and he couldn't be sure what.

'Which deck is this?' he asked.

'Four.'

'I'm going to check the air,' he said. He pulled down the mask, and lifted the helmet. The lights . . . had they or hadn't they told that bitch to cut the lights below Deck 8? He couldn't remember. The smell . . . it seemed fresher than he remembered, but that might be breathing through that mask for hours. He couldn't see or hear or smell anything definite, but he could not relax. Every since he'd found that Bjerling was commanding, he'd had the feeling that things were going wrong.

'Trouble, packleader?'

'Nothing I can taste,' he said. 'But—' His team was short-handed now – they were so few, and Bjerling hated him, he was sure. If Bjerling's people killed them all, it could be blamed on the Familias troops. Who would ever know?

'We need a hostage,' he said finally. 'Someone Bjerling would want . . . maybe those admirals if any of them are still alive.'

'The Serrano cub?' Hoch asked.

'No – if he's still alive, he's still just a cub. Bjerling will have to talk to us if we have important prisoners, and enough of his people will hear to bear witness. Otherwise . . .'

'The bridge?' Hoch asked.

'I suppose.' He was in the trough of the waves now, the sky far

336

away and the sea cold and near . . . the space between waves of battle joy, where he could feel exhaustion and hunger and realize that it wasn't over yet. 'Yes. The bridge.'

Running up the stairs ahead of the rest, his rage came back and the energy with it. Bjerling's sons should all have shriveled balls; his daughters should all whore for prisoners in the arena. The Antberd Comity should fall to quarrels and jealousy, its last survivor dying poor and crippled—

He saw the little pile of trash an instant too late to stop and had just long enough to recognize what it might be instead, and extend his curses to the entire Familias Regnant when the stairwell erupted in flame and smoke and he died, unrepentant.

The question they couldn't answer ahead of time was what the other Bloodhorde ships would do. Now, as they powered up *Antberd's Axe*, Esmay kept mental fingers crossed.

'Think we ought to trust their life support?' asked one of her techs.

'No,' Esmay said. 'Lift off when ready, maximum acceleration – ours, not theirs.'

Antberd's Axe bounded off the drive test cradle like a bucking horse; its gravity generator compensated only a little, and Esmay's knees buckled.

'Wow!' said Simkins, sitting helm. 'I guess they moved the red line over . . .'

Eighteen decks of T-3 flashed past, and a howl of Bloodhorde that Esmay assumed was invective crackled from the speakers around the bridge.

'They're annoyed,' said the pivot-major sitting the communications board. She was supposed to know some Bloodhorde. 'They think their captain got bored and went off to play. But I now know our name: *Antberd's Axe*.'

'Where's the other one?' Esmay asked. She couldn't interpret the blurry scan she saw. 'Scan—?'

Bowry's voice came over her headset, scratchy but recognizable. 'We're off. I'm taking the big one,' he said.

'Scan—'

'There!' The scan image steadied, still grainy but now she could

337

interpret what she saw. Bowry's Bloodhorde ship, that must be, veering from hers toward the biggest blip on the screen. The Bloodhorde flagship, if they had flagships. Esmay looked for her own target, which had been parked, as it were, some thousand kilometers on the far side of *Koskiusko*, where it had a clear shot down the throat of anyone coming through the jump point.

Had it mined the jump point? She suspected not. Setting minefields wasn't a Bloodhorde sort of thing to do, even if they had put that mine on *Wraith*. It didn't matter . . . she was going there anyway. The third Bloodhorde ship, positioned insystem of the DSR from the jump point, would require a separate attack run. From where it was, missile attack would risk blowing *Koskiusko*; she hoped it was like this one in having no beam weapons.

Arramanche said, 'Got it. Ready on your order, Captain.'

'That ship wants to know what you think you're doing,' communications said. 'They're saying this is no time for dancing with the bear, whatever that means.'

Wait, or shoot now? Her mind grappled with the geometry of it, their motion relative to *Koskiusko*, to the Bloodhorde ship, to the other Bloodhorde ship, the distance, the velocity of the weapons, the probable quality of the other ship's shields, its maneuvering ability. 'Hold it,' she said. 'We're going closer.'

Going closer was like riding a polo pony; *Antberd's Axe*, whatever its shortcomings by Fleet standards, bounced happily from heading to heading with no resistance. She had been right to close; the other ship could dodge as well . . . instead, it held its position, as if certain she was no threat.

'The big one's moving,' Lucien said. 'Putting out quite a plume, but Bowry should have it . . .'

'Range in, Captain,' Arramanche said.

'Go ahead,' she said. Arramanche hit the controls; the whole ship shuddered, with every departing missile.

'It's no wonder they don't mount beams on this thing – it'd fall apart,' said Simkins.

'On track!' yelled the scan tech on *Kos*. 'You've got—'

The screen flared, and their target disappeared.

'Good shot,' Esmay said. 'Now – let's go after that third one.'

'Two down,' said the *Koskiusko* contact. That must have been Bowry, in the other Bloodhorde ship. Surely they hadn't gotten *Wraith* out that fast.

'Lovely shot,' Lucien said. Esmay glanced at his screen, and saw that it was now much crisper than before. Maybe he was a genius.

Their ship's artificial gravity wobbled as Simkins tried to maneuver sharply enough to get a good angle on the third Bloodhorde ship. It had boosted toward *Koskiusko*, then veered as both Esmay and Bowry went after it.

'It's launched missiles,' Lucien said, just as *Koskiusko*'s scan tech told them the same thing. 'Tracking . . . one flight at *Kos* and one each at us and Bowry. Lousy aim . . . you'd think with a target the size of *Kos*—'

Esmay ignored that, and told Simkins to get the last bit of acceleration out of the ship.

'We're not going to make it,' Arramanche said. 'It—'

Wraith's position lighted up on Lucien's scan.

'All hot,' Lucien said. 'I didn't know they had that much left—'

'Got him,' said Seska calmly in Esmay's headset. And the entire portside array of beam weapons focussed on the fleeing Blood-horde ship, overwhelming its shields . . . the screen flared again, a final time.

'Captain to Captain,' Bowry said. 'I'd say there'll be no rank-pulling on this raid, eh? One each, that's pretty fair shooting. Even if two of them were sitting ducks.'

'Not our fault,' Seska said. 'Besides, you two had to get 'em with their own guns – that brings the challenge up to an acceptable level.'

'Thank you,' Bowry said.

Esmay grinned at her crew. 'All right, let's get this thing back to *Kos* before someone else takes a potshot at us.'

'There's nobody in this system who'd dare,' Arramanche said.

Esmay brought *Antberd's Axe* back to the test cradle with no flourishes; a *Koskiusko* crew waited to talk them into the docking pad and tie the little ship down with 'appropriate care.' She supervised the powerdown, the locking of weapons; she made sure the two Bloodhorde corpses were bagged and turned over to the deck crew. Simkins handed her the little red key – an actual key, she was startled to note, completely unlike the command wands that Fleet used to unlock controls – and she tucked it into the holdall of her suit. Then she followed the others out of the ship, and closed the hatches herself.

When they got back to *Koskiusko*, back into aired space and out of suits that had acquired a stench all their own, Esmay thought she wanted only three things: a shower, a bunk, and word about Barin Serrano. Instead, she found herself the center of a shouting, laughing, crying, dancing mass of people. Her crew, *Wraith*'s crew, Bowry's crew, coming at a dead run through the tunnel, and at least half the people who'd been left in T-3. She was hugged, pummeled, cheered. She and the other two captains were lifted shoulder high, carried through the passages toward the core . . .

Where she saw Admiral Dossignal, standing a little lopsided, near the lift tube cluster. Seveche and Major Pitak were beside him, watching her.

The crowd slowed, still exuberant but aware of stars and their implication. Esmay managed to wriggle down, and then make her way out of the crush.

'Sir—'

'Good work, Lieutenant! Congratulations to all of you.'

'Is there any word . . . ?'

'Of Ensign Serrano?' That was Major Pitak, sober-faced; Esmay braced herself for the worst. 'Yes . . . he was found; he's alive, but badly hurt.'

But alive. He had not died because she'd done nothing. With the knowledge that he was still alive – and surely if he was alive, he would be fine when he got out of the regen tanks – her heart lifted to impossible heights. She turned back to the crowd, hunting for those she knew.

'You did it!' she yelled at Arramanche. 'You did it!' to Lucien. 'We DID it!' with all the others, to all the others.

Admiral Dossignal leaned over to speak to Pitak through the din. 'I think we can quit worrying, Major. I do believe life has given her that kick in the pants.'

340

20

By the time Esmay finally got some sleep, while others headed *Koskiusko* back toward Familias space, her initial euphoria had worn away. She woke several times, her heart pounding from dreams she couldn't quite recall. She felt angry, but couldn't find a target for her anger. The Bloodhorde intruders were dead; no use to be angry with them. Nothing seemed right . . . but of course schedules and ship's services were still upset. Those who had been aboard *Antberd's Axe* with her came around for more congratulations; it was hard to give them the responses they deserved. She wanted to, but she felt empty of anything but unfocused irritation. When Lieutenant Bowry sought her out and told her he'd be glad to give her a strong recommendation for a switch to command track, she felt a prickle of fear.

Another sleep cycle helped, but in the next, one of the nightmares caught her again, this time vivid enough that she woke hearing herself cry out. She turned on the light, and lay staring at the overhead, trying to slow her breathing. Why couldn't she get over this? She was not that child any more; she had proven it. She had commanded a ship – *Despite* didn't count, but she allowed herself credit for *Antberd's Axe* – and destroyed an enemy vessel.

Only because it had suspected nothing; only because its captain had been stupid. Her mind led her through the many ways every decision she'd made could have gone wrong. She had been hasty, impulsive, just like that child who had run away. She could have gotten everyone killed.

Others thought she had done well . . . but she knew things about herself they didn't. If they knew everything, they'd under-

341

stand that she could not really be qualified. Like a novice rider who might stay on over a few fences, she had been lucky. And she'd been supported by skilled crew.

It would be safer for everyone if she went back into obscurity, where she belonged. She could have a decent life if she just kept out of trouble.

Admiral Serrano's face seemed to form before her. *You cannot go back to what you were.* Esmay's throat tightened. She saw the faces of her crew; for a moment she could feel the surge of confidence that had freed her to make those critical decisions. That was the person she wanted to be, the person who felt at home, undivided, the person who had earned the respect the others gave her.

They would not respect her if they knew about the nightmares. She grimaced, picturing herself as a cruiser captain who followed each battle with a round of nightmares . . . she could see the crew tiptoeing around listening to the thrashing and moaning. For a moment it seemed almost funny, then her eyes filled. No. She had to find a way to change this. She pushed herself up, and headed for the showers.

The next shift, word came down that Barin was out of regen and could have visitors. Esmay didn't really want to know what horrors he'd endured, but she had to visit him.

Barin's eyes had no light in them; he looked less like a Serrano than Esmay had ever seen him. She told herself he was probably sedated.

'Want some company?'

He flinched, then stiffened, looking past her ear. 'Lieutenant Suiza . . . I hear you did good things.'

Esmay shrugged, embarrassed again. 'I did what I could.'

'More than I did.' That with neither humor nor bitterness, in a flat tone that sent prickles down her spine. She could just remember that flatness in her own voice, in that time she didn't want to think about.

She opened her mouth to say what he had, no doubt, already been told, and shut it again. She knew what others would have said – it had been said to her – and it didn't help. What would help? She had no idea.

342

'I don't belong,' Barin said, in that same flat voice. 'A Serrano . . . a *real* Serrano, like my grandmother or Heris . . . they'd have done something.'

In the split second before she spoke, awareness of what she was going to say almost clamped her jaw shut. Against the ache of that, Esmay got out the first phrase. 'When I was caught . . .'

'You were captured? They didn't tell me that. I'll bet you gave 'em a rought time.'

Anger and fear together roughened her own voice until she hardly recognized it. 'I was a child. I didn't give anyone a hard time . . .' She could not look at him; she could not look at anything but the moving shadows in her mind as they came clear out of the fog. 'I was . . . looking for my father. My mother had died – a fever we have on Altiplano – and my father was off with his army, fighting a civil war.' A quick glance at his face; now his eyes had life in them again. She had accomplished that much. She told the story as quickly, as baldly, as she could, trying not to think as she told it. The runaway . . . the fat woman on the train . . . the explosions . . . the village with dead bodies she had first thought were sleeping. Then the uniformed men, the hard hands, the pain, the helplessness that was worse than pain.

Another quick glance. Barin's face had paled almost to the color of her own. 'Esmay . . . Lieutenant . . . I didn't know . . .'

'No. It's not something I talk about. My family . . . had insisted it was a dream, a fever dream. I was sick a long time, the same fever my mother had had. They said I'd run away, gotten near the front, been hurt . . . but the rest of it was just a dream, they said.'

'The rest of it?'

It felt like knives in her throat; it felt worse. 'The man . . . he was . . . someone I knew. Had known. In my father's command. That uniform . . .'

'And they *lied* to you?' Now Serrano anger flashed in his eyes. 'They lied to you about that?'

Esmay waved her hand, a gesture her family would have understood. 'They thought it was best – they thought they were protecting me.'

'It wasn't . . . it wasn't someone in your own family—?'

'No.' She said it firmly, though she still wasn't sure. Had there

343

been only that one assailant? She had been so young – she had had uncles and older cousins in that army, and some of them had died. In the family book of remembrance, the notations said 'died in combat' but she was well aware now that notations and reality were not the same thing.

'But you . . . went on.' Barin looked at her directly now. 'You were strong; you didn't . . .'

'I cried.' She got that out with difficulty. 'I cried, night after night. The dreams . . . they put me in a room at the top of the house, at the end of the hall, because I woke them up, thrashing around so. I was afraid of everything, and afraid of being afraid. If they knew how scared I was, they would despise me . . . they were all heroes, you see. My father, my uncles, my cousins, even my Aunt Sanni. Papa Stefan had no use for crybabies – I couldn't cry in front of him. Put it behind you, they said. What's past is past, they said.'

'But surely they knew – even I know, from my foster family – that children don't just forget things like that.'

'On Altiplano you forget. Or you leave.' Esmay took a deep breath, trying to steady her voice. 'I left. Which relieved them, because I was always trouble for them.'

'I can't believe you were trouble—'

'Oh yes. A Suiza woman who did not ride? Who would not involve herself with stock breeding? Who did not flirt and attract the right sort of young men? My poor stepmother spent years on me, trying to make me normal. And none of it worked.'

'But . . . you got into the Fleet prep school program. You must have recovered very well. What did the psychnannies say? Did they give you any additional therapy?'

Esmay dodged the question. 'I had read psych texts on Altiplano – there wasn't any therapy available there – and after all I passed the exams.'

'I can't believe—'

'I just did it,' she said sharply. He flinched, and she realized how he might take that. 'It's not the same for you.'

'No . . . I'm a grown man, or supposed to be.' The bitterness was back in his voice.

'You are. And you did what you could – it's not your fault.'

344

'But a Serrano is supposed to—'

'You were a captive. You had no choices, except to survive or die. Do you think I never tortured myself with 'A Suiza is supposed to—'? Of course I did. But it doesn't help. And it doesn't matter what you did – if you spewed your guts—'

'I did,' Barin said in a small voice.

'So? That's your body . . . if it wants to vomit, it will. If it wants to leak, it will. You can't stop it.' She was aware that she was talking to herself as much as Barin, telling the self that had grieved so long what it had needed to be told.

'If I'd been braver . . .' in a smaller voice still.

'Would bravery have kept your bones from breaking? Your blood from flowing?'

'That's different – that's physical—'

'Vomiting isn't?' She could move again, and now she stepped closer to the bed. 'You know you can make anyone vomit with the right chemicals. Your body produces the chemicals, and you spew. A leads to B, that's it.'

He moved restlessly, looking away from her. 'Somehow I can't see my grandmother admiral puking all over a musclebound Bloodhorde commando just because someone mentioned the arena combat.'

'You had been hit in the head, hadn't you?'

He twitched, as if he'd been poked in his sore ribs. 'Not that hard.'

Esmay fought down a flash of anger. She had tried; she had told him things she had not told anyone else, and he was apparently determined to wallow in his own pangs of guilt. If someone could wallow in pangs . . .

'I just don't know if I can face it,' Barin said, almost too quietly to hear over the soft buzz of the ventilator.

'Face what?' Esmay asked, her voice edged.

'They'll . . . want me to talk about it.'

'Who?'

'The psychnannies, of course. Just as they did with you. I . . . don't want to talk about it.'

'Of course not,' Esmay said. Her mind skidded away from his assumption that she had had therapy.

345

'How bad is it, really? What do they say?' A pause, a gulp. 'What do they put in your record?'

'It's . . . not too bad.' Esmay fumbled through her memory of those texts, but couldn't come up with anything concrete. She looked away, aware that Barin was now staring at her. 'You'll do fine,' she said quickly, and moved toward the door. Barin raised a hand still streaked with the pink stain of nuskin glue.

'Lieutenant – please.'

Esmay forced herself to take a deep breath before she turned back to him. 'Yes?'

His eyes widened at whatever he saw on her face. 'You . . . you *haven't* talked to the psychs, have you? Ever?'

The breath she'd taken had vanished somewhere; she could not breathe. 'I . . . I . . .' She wanted to lie, but she couldn't. Not to him; not now.

'You just . . . hid it. Didn't you? By yourself?'

She gasped in a lungful of air, fought it into her chest, and then forced it out through a throat that felt stiff as iron. 'Yes. I had to. It was the only way—' Another breath, another struggle. 'And it's better . . . I'm fine now.'

Barin eyed her. 'Just like me.'

'No.' Another breath. 'I'm older. It's been longer. I do know what you're feeling, but it gets better.'

'This is what confused people,' Barin said, as if to himself. That non sequitur snagged her attention.

'What do you mean, confused?'

'It wasn't just the difference in Altiplano social customs and Fleet's . . . it was this secret you had. That's why your talents were all locked up, hidden . . . why it took combat to unlock them, let you show what you could do.'

'I don't know what you're talking about,' Esmay said. She felt a tremor in her mind like that of stepping onto the quaking surface of a bog.

'No . . . but . . . you need help as much as I do.'

Panic; she could feel her face stiffening into a mask of calm. 'No, I don't. I'm fine now. It's under control; as you say, I can function.'

'Not at your best. I heard about your best; Grandmother said the combat analysis was unbelievable . . .'

For a moment it seemed funny. 'Your grandmother wasn't on the Board of Inquiry.'

His hand flipped a rude gesture. 'Boards of Inquiry exist to scare captains into heart attacks and ulcers. What I heard, through the family, was how the real commanders, who have combat experience, saw it.'

Esmay shrugged. This was only slightly more comfortable than the other topic.

'And no one, Grandmother included, could understand how you did it . . . there was nothing in your background, she said.'

'My father is not a bad tactician,' Esmay said stiffly, aware that the reflexive annoyance was not entirely honest.

'I imagine not. But not all children inherit the talent – and those that do usually show it earlier. You didn't even choose command track.'

'I took advice,' Esmay said. 'It was pointed out to me how difficult outsiders found it to succeed in higher command in Fleet.'

'Argue all you want,' Barin said, hitching himself up in the bed. This time he didn't wince. 'I still say, as Grandmother said, that you were hiding something, something that kept you from showing what you could do.'

'Well, it's not hidden now,' Esmay said. 'I did command that ship . . . actually now, two of them.'

'Not that,' he said.

'I told you,' she said then. 'It's not hidden.'

'I'm not a psychnanny. D'you think my telling *you* about my experience would be sufficient?' Despite his attempt at persuasion, she heard the covert plea: he hoped she'd agree that he need not talk to anyone else about it.

'No.' She took a quick breath and hurried on. 'They know already; you have to talk to them. And they'll help you, I'm sure of it.'

'Ummhmm. So sure that you will talk to them too?'

'Me?'

'Don't.' He lay back against the pillows. 'Don't play with me . . . you know you're not healed. You know you still need help.'

347

'I . . . they'll throw me out . . . a mutineer who hid craziness in her past . . . they'll send me back . . .' She noticed after she'd said it that Altiplano had become 'back' and not 'home.'

'They won't. Grandmother won't let them.'

The sheer Serrano arrogance of this took her breath away; she laughed before she thought. 'Your grandmother doesn't run everything in Fleet!'

'No . . . I suppose not. But it doesn't hurt to have her on your side, which you do. She's not about to lose an officer she considers brilliant.' He sobered. 'And . . . if you talked to them about your problem . . . you see, I don't know anyone else who's been . . . who ever . . .'

'You want a partner, is that what you're saying?'

He nodded without speaking. Clear in his expression was the effort it cost him to pull himself out of his own pain long enough to reach out to her.

Her heart pounded; her breath came short. Could she?

'You already told me,' he said then. 'It's not like it'll be the first time for you.'

When you hit the ground, Papa Stefan had always said, it was too late to be scared of being bucked off. You had already survived the worst . . . now all you had to do was catch the horse and get back on.

'I caught the horse,' Esmay said; she almost laughed at Barin's confusion. 'All right,' she said, knowing the panic would come again, but able at this moment to face the pawing, snorting shadow, to walk toward it. 'I will talk to them – but you have to cooperate too. I want a Serrano ally closer to my own age than your estimable grandmother or your ferocious cousin. Is that a deal?'

'Deal. Although I'm not sure you've got the right adjective with the right relative.'

Major Pitak looked up when Esmay came back from sick bay. 'How's the boy?'

'Shaken up, but healing. He's got to see the psychs, he says.'

'Standard,' Pitak said. 'Is it bothering him?'

'As much as it would bother anyone,' Esmay said, and gathered her courage again. The shadow condensed from a cloud of smoke to a dire shape, snorting fire. 'Major . . . back before all this happened, you said perhaps I should see the psychs . . . about what happened on *Despite*.'

'Is that still bothering you?'

'Not . . . just that. I know we're shorthanded, but – I'd like to do that.'

Pitak gave her a long, steady look. 'Good. Go find out how long it will take, and let me know. You're in enough good graces right now that nobody's going to grudge you some help. Would you like me to call over there and find out when they can take you?'

'I . . . thank you, Major, but I think I should do it myself.'

'You don't have to do everything the hard way, Suiza,' Pitak said, but it had no sting.

Setting up an appointment was absurdly easy. The appointments clerk didn't ask for details when she said she wanted a psych appointment, just asked if it was urgent. Was it urgent? She could put it off by saying it wasn't . . . but putting it off hadn't solved it before.

'Not an emergency,' she finally said. 'But . . . it's . . . interfering with things.'

'Just a moment.' Of course they were busy, Esmay told herself. Barin wasn't the only one with urgent needs relating to the recent action. All those who'd been captives, she expected, and some who'd simply seen too much death, too much pain.

Another voice came over her headset. 'Lieutenant Suiza . . . this is Annie Merinha. I need just a few bits of information, in order to place you with the individual most likely to help you.'

Esmay's throat closed; she could say nothing, and waited for the questions as if they were blows.

'Is this related only to the recent events, or is it something else?'

'Something else,' Esmay said. She could barely speak.

'I see that you were in a difficult situation aboard *Despite*, and received no psych support services subsequently – is this related to that?'

She could say yes, and be telling the truth . . . but not the whole truth. She could tell them the rest later, surely . . . but lies had started this, and she wanted it over. 'Partly,' she said. 'There's . . . it's all mixed up with . . . with other things.'

'Predating your entrance to the Regular Space Service?'

'Yes.'

'There's nothing on your record . . .'

'No, I . . . please, I can't explain it . . . like this.'

'Certainly.' A pause, during which Esmay imagined damning check marks on a laundry list of mental illness that would bar her forever from anything she wanted to do. 'I can see you at fourteen hundred today. T-5, Deck Seven, follow the signs to Psych, and ask the front-desk clerk. You're on the schedule. All right?'

It was not all right; she needed more time to get herself ready for this . . . but she could hardly complain that they were helping her too quickly.

'That's fine,' she said. 'Thank you.'

'You'll need about two hours. We'll arrange the rest of your sessions once we've met.'

'Thank you,' Esmay said again.

She glanced at the time. 1030. She had that long to live as she had lived, however that was. It felt like doom coming down on her. She went to tell Major Pitak she would be gone for several hours.

'That's fine. In the meantime, I want you to have lunch with me.'

Her stomach roiled. 'Major . . . I'm really not hungry.'

'True, but you're also tied up in knots. I'm not asking what it's about, now that you're getting help, but I'm also not letting you mope around by yourself. Soup and salad – you need something before you go over there and spill your guts. It's going to be exhausting.'

Through the meal, Pitak kept up a series of anecdotes that didn't really require a response from her. Esmay ate little, but appreciated the thoughtfulness.

'Lieutenant Suiza.' The clerk smiled at her. 'I know you don't know me, but – we all want to thank you for what you did. *I* spent most of the time flat out, having dreams I can't even remember, no good to anyone. If it hadn't been for you—'

'And a lot of others,' Esmay said, accepting the file the clerk handed her.

'Oh, sure, but everyone knows you took that Bloodhorde ship and fought them off. They ought to make you a cruiser captain, that's what *I* think.' The clerk looked at a screen at his desk and said, 'There – the room'll be ready in just a couple of minutes. We like to freshen it up between . . . d'you want something to drink?'

Her mouth was dry again, but she didn't think she could drink; her stomach had knotted shut.

'No, thank you.'

'Your first time with psych support?' Esmay nodded; she hated to be that transparent.

'Everyone's scared beforehand,' the clerk said. 'But we haven't killed anyone yet.' Esmay tried to smile, but she didn't really think it was funny.

Nubbly toast-brown carpet ran halfway up the bulkheads, here painted cream; a fat-cushioned couch with an afghan draped over one end and a couple of soft chairs made the little compartment look more like a particularly cozy sitting room. It was quiet, and smelled faintly of mint. Esmay, aware that she had stopped in the doorway like a wary colt halfway through a gate, forced herself to go on.

'I'm Annie Merinha,' the woman inside said. She was tall, with a thick braid of light hair going silver at the temples. She wore soft brown pants and a blue shirt with her ID tag clipped to the left sleeve. 'We don't use ranks here . . . so I'll call you Esmay, unless you have a favorite nickname.'

'Esmay's fine,' said Esmay through a dry throat.

'Good. You may not know that a request for psych support authorizes whoever works with you to have complete access to your records, including all personal evaluations. If this is a problem, you'll need to tell me now.'

'It's not,' Esmay said.

'Good. I called up your medical record earlier, of course, but that was all. There are some other things you need to know about the process before we get started, if you feel you can understand them at this time.'

Esmay dragged her wits back from their hiding places. She had expected to have to tell everything at once . . . this was much duller, if less painful.

'The slang for most of us is psychnannies, as I'm sure you know. That's reasonably accurate, because most of us are nannies, not medtechs or psychiatric physicians. You're from Altiplano, where I believe they still call nannies nurses, is that right?'

'Yes,' Esmay said.

'Do you have any cultural problems with being in the care of a psychnanny rather than a physician?'

'No.'

Annie checked off something. 'Now: you need to know that although our sessions are confidential, there are limits to this confidentiality. If I have reason to believe that you are a danger to yourself or others, I will report that. This includes participation in certain forms of religious or political activity which could be a danger to your shipmates, and the use of proscribed substances. Although you may choose to attempt concealment of any such activity, I must in conscience warn you that I'm very good at spotting lies, and in any event dishonesty will markedly affect the value of your treatment. Do you want to go on?'

'Yes,' Esmay said. 'I don't do anything like that . . .'

'All right. Now we get to the heart of it. You said you had problems connected both with your experiences on *Despite*, and with other experiences from before you joined the Service. I would have expected problems existing when you joined to have been dealt with at that time.' She stopped there. It took Esmay a long moment to realize that this was an implied question.

'I . . . didn't tell anyone.'

'You concealed something you knew was—?'

'I didn't know . . . at that time . . . what it was.' *Only dreams, only dreams, only dreams* pounded her pulse.

'Mmm. Can you tell me more about it?'

'I thought – it was only nightmares,' Esmay said.

'There is a question on the intake physical about excessive nightmares,' Annie said, with no particular emphasis.

'Yes . . . and I should have said something, but – I didn't know

352

for sure they were excessive, and I wanted to get away – to get into the prep school . . .'

'How old were you then?'

'Fourteen. The first year I could apply. They said the application was good, but to wait a year or so, because they'd already filled up, and besides they wanted me to take extra courses. So I did. And then—'

'You did get into the prep school. The dreams?'

'Weren't as bad, then. I thought I was outgrowing whatever it was.'

'You didn't know?'

'No . . . they said it was only dreams.'

'And now you know differently?'

'I do.' That sounded as grim as she felt. She met Annie's eyes. 'I found out when I went home. After the court-martial. That it was true, it was all real, and they lied to me!'

Annie sat quietly, waiting for her breath to steady again. Then she said, 'What I understand you to say is that something happened when you were a child, before you joined Fleet, and your family lied, told you it had never happened and you only dreamed it. Is that true?'

'Yes!'

Annie sighed. 'Mark down another one for the misguided abusive families of the world.'

Esmay looked up. 'They're not abusive, they just—'

'Esmay. Listen. How painful was it to think you were going crazy because you had unreasonable, disgusting, terrifying bad dreams?'

She shivered. 'Very.'

'And did you have that pain every day?'

'Yes . . . except when I was too busy to think about it.'

Annie nodded. 'If you tormented someone every day, made them miserable every day, scared them every day, made them think they were bad and crazy every day, would you call that abusive?'

'Of course—' She saw the trap, and turned aside like a wild cow swerving to avoid a gate. 'But my family wasn't – they didn't know—'

'We'll talk about it. So the first problem you have is these dreams, that turned out not to be dreams, of something bad that happened when you were a child. How old were you when it happened?'

'Almost six,' Esmay said. She braced herself for the next questions, the ones she wasn't sure she could answer without coming apart.

'Do you still have the same dreams, now that you know what it is?'

'Yes, sometimes . . . and I keep thinking about it. Worrying about it.'

'And your second problem has to do with your experiences aboard *Despite*?'

'Yes. The . . . the mutiny . . . I've had dreams about that, too. Sometimes they're mixed up, as if both things were happening at once. . . .'

'I'm not surprised. Although you haven't told me yet what kind of childhood trauma it was, there are parallels: in both instances you were under someone's protection, that protection failed, and someone you trusted turned out to be against you.'

Esmay felt particularly stupid that she hadn't figured this out for herself; it seemed obvious once Annie had said it.

'I presume the mutiny on *Despite* involved a lot of close-contact fighting aboard?'

'Yes . . .'

'So of course the Bloodhorde intrusion here would rekindle the same feelings – and tie into the earlier trauma as well.'

'I wasn't quite as scared this time,' Esmay said. 'Not at the time, anyway.'

'Luckily for the rest of us. Now – have you ever told anyone about the events in your childhood?'

Esmay felt her shoulders hunching. 'My . . . my family already knows.'

'That's not what I asked. Have you ever told anyone since you grew up?'

'One person . . . Barin Serrano . . . because he was feeling so bad. About having to consult you, and . . . and what happened.'

'Barin Serrano . . . ? Oh. The ensign in sickbay – he's assigned to someone else. Interesting. You're friends?'

'Yes.'

'It must have been hard for you to tell him . . . how did he react?'

Esmay shrugged. 'I don't know what a normal reaction is. He was mad at my father.'

'Good for him,' Annie said. 'That's what I'd call a normal reaction. Now . . . since you've told it once, do you think you could tell me?'

Esmay took a breath and plunged into the story again. It was no easier . . . but no harder, even though Annie was a stranger. When she faltered, Annie asked just enough to get her started again. Finally – she was sure it had taken hours – she got to the end. 'I thought . . . thought maybe I'd gone crazy. From the fever, or something.'

Annie shook her head. 'That's one thing you don't have to worry about, Esmay. By any definition of sanity, you're well onto the sane side . . . you always were. You survived enormous trauma, physical and emotional, and although it damaged your development, it didn't stop it. Your defenses were normal ones; it was your family's response which, if it manifested in an individual, would be called insane – or at least unsound.'

'But they weren't crazy . . . they weren't the ones waking up everyone in the house at night screaming. . . .' It was absurd to think of her family as crazy, those normal people walking around in everyday clothes, carrying out normal lives.

'Esmay, nightmares are not a symptom of insanity. Something awful happened to you; you had nightmares about it: a normal reaction. But your family tried to pretend it hadn't happened, and that your normal nightmares were the real problem. That's a failure to face reality – and being out of touch with reality *is* a symptom of mental illness. It's just as serious when a family or other group does it, as when one person does it.'

'But . . .'

'It's hard to connect your normal family – living their everyday lives – with your mental image of insanity? I'm not surprised. We'll talk more about this, and your other problems, but let me reassure you: you are sane, and the symptoms you've had are treatable. We'll need to spend some time at it here, and you'll have

355

some assignments to complete on your own. They should take about two hours, between our sessions, which I'm setting up twice a decad for now, every five days. Now: do you have any questions about the process?'

Esmay was sure she had questions, but she couldn't think of them. She had an overwhelming desire to lie down and sleep; she felt as tired as if she'd been working out for two hours.

'You will probably have some somatic symptoms for the first several sessions,' Annie went on. 'You'll be tired, perhaps achy. You may be tempted to skip meals or binge on desserts . . . try to eat regularly and moderately. Allow extra time for sleep, if you can.'

21

All very well to say that, but what good was time for sleep if she couldn't sleep? Esmay acquired an intimate knowledge of every flaw in the surface of bulkhead and overhead, every object in her quarters. When she shut her eyes, she felt wider awake than before, heart racing. At meals, she dutifully forced down one mouthful after another, mimicking whoever sat fourth down on the left, taking a bite when he or she did. No one seemed to notice. She felt suspended in a hollow sphere; nothing seemed quite within reach.

To her surprise and relief, no one seemed to expect her to do more than routine work, even though the ship was shorthanded. Pitak handed her endless lists of inventory to check, progress notes on *Wraith's* repair to enter into the database. She was vaguely aware that this was routine clerical work, more suited to a pivot or corporal, but she felt no rancor. The simple tasks engaged her fully, kept her busy. Whatever burst of energy had sent her across the ship, into the enemy's craft, into battle, had vanished. Someone else could figure out how to get *Koskiusko* back to Familias space, back to the rest of the Fleet deployment. Someone else could worry about *Wraith's* repairs, about internal damage, even about casualties. She couldn't quite manage to care.

In the next session, Esmay found herself defending her family again. 'They didn't understand,' she said.

'You had the nightmares. You screamed so much, you said, that they banished you to a distant part of the house—'

'It wasn't banishment—'

'For a child to sleep alone that far from anyone else? I call that banishment. And you had changed in ways that most adults would recognize as a response to stress. Hadn't you?'

Seb Coron had said she loved to ride, until after that. She had been outgoing, ebullient, eager, adventurous . . . but all children grew out of the easy joy of early childhood. She tried to say that to Annie, who insisted on reflecting it back to her in other interpretations. 'Whenever a child's behavior changes suddenly, there's a reason. Gradual change is not so diagnostic – exposure to new experiences can mean new enthusiasms replace the old. But sudden change means something, and a child's family is supposed to notice, and look for the cause. In your case, of course, they already had a cause they knew about.'

'But it wasn't connected . . . they said I'd just gotten lazy. . . .'

'Children don't "just get lazy." That's an adult's quick label for some behavior they don't like. You had liked riding before . . . then you quit, and forgot you'd ever enjoyed it. And you think that's not related to a sexual assault?'

'I . . . suppose it could be.' Her whole body twitched, like a horse's skin trying to flick off a biting fly.

'Do you remember whether the assault was in a building or outside?'

'All the buildings were destroyed . . . at least partly. I'd found a corner . . . taller than I was, but only a little . . . there was . . . was straw, and I'd crawled into it . . .'

'What did it smell like?'

Her breath caught again . . . a whiff of that smell, not the

357

smoke but the other smell, blew across her mind. 'Barn,' she said, so softly she could barely hear herself. 'It was a barn. It smelled like home. . . .'

'That's probably why you were in it, your nose leading you to something that didn't scare you silly. So there, in a place you had thought safe – remember, smells go straight in to the emotional center of the brain – you were assaulted in the most terrifying way by someone whose uniform you had previously associated with safety. Is it any wonder you hated cleaning stalls later?'

Astonishment all over again. 'I wasn't just lazy,' she said, half-believing it. 'Or being a sissy about the horses moving around. . . .'

'No – your accurate memory told you that barns weren't really safe, that bad things could happen if you were trapped in a corner. Your brain was working fine, Esmay, trying to keep you safe.'

Even as her ears heard, her mind denied. 'But I should have been able to—'

'Whoa.' Annie held up her hand. 'In the first place, you could no more change the new insight your experience gave you than a low-level computer can change the program you feed into it. The part of your brain that's concerned with survival is a very low-level computer; it doesn't care about anything but connecting sensory input to danger and food. If you'd had proper treatment early on, with neuroactive drugs, the worst of the damage could have been prevented . . . but there would always have been a trace of it. That's what life is, after all: that's why mindwipes are illegal.'

'You mean I'm stuck with it forever?' If she was going to be stuck with it, why go through therapy?

'Not exactly. The kind of work you're doing now, thinking through it bit by bit, will lessen the effect. There are still drugs we can give, to stabilize your insights and put a sort of shield between your present awareness and the ingrained connections while the new connections become stronger.'

'What about the nightmares?'

'Those should diminish, possibly disappear forever, though you might get a recurrence in another period of extraordinary stress. Other patterns of thought which have impeded your development

– as a person and as an officer – will change with continued practice.'

'I don't like the idea of drugs,' Esmay said.

'Good. People who like the idea of drugs have usually medicated themselves with things that don't work and leave neurons flapping in the breeze. You don't have to like your medicine, you just have to trust me to know when you need it.'

'Can't I do it without?'

'Possibly. Slower, and with more difficulty, and not as certainly. What do you think the drugs will do, turn you into one of those people in horror cubes, who drags around in an asylum in ratty slippers?'

As that was the image that had come to mind, Esmay could think of nothing to say. Her head dipped in a weak nod.

'When you're ready for drugs, Esmay, I'll tell you exactly what to expect. Right now, let's get back to the other connections between what happened and the things you quit doing, quit enjoying.'

She had quit enjoying horses; that still shocked her more than the nightmares. She had not even remembered enjoying them; the image Seb Coron gave her, of a child hardly ever off her pony, felt alien. How could she have been that child, and become this woman? Yet if she believed him about the rape, she had to believe him about the pony. It would mean nothing to Fleet, she was sure, but in her own family that by itself had made her different, inferior.

Could it really be just a matter of smells, of her olfactory system going its own stubborn way, associating the smell of barns and horses with all the terror and pain of that day? It seemed too simple. Why couldn't her nose have associated all the pleasure she'd had, if that pleasure had been real?

Her nose chose that moment to comment on the smell of dinner, which she had been forking into her mouth without thinking about it. She hadn't noticed anything for days, but now a smell got through, and she realized that her mouth was full of ganash stew. She hated ganash stew, but she couldn't spit it out. She gulped, managed that mouthful, and took a long swallow of water. 'Come play ball, Lieutenant?' someone asked. Who was that? Her mind thrashed around, not finding a name for the pleasant-faced young woman. Barin would have known. Barin . . . had not been around for awhile. Therapy, she reminded herself. He probably felt like she did, in no mood for games.

She needed an excuse. 'No thanks,' she said, putting the words together like parts of an intricate model, keeping careful control of tone and volume and pitch changes. 'I need to work out – maybe another day.'

From there to the gym, uncrowded in the aftermath of the battles. Everyone's schedule was upset, not just hers; she scolded herself for being absentminded and climbed on one of the tread-mills. When she glanced aside, her gaze caught on the mechanism of the virtual horse. She had not been on one in her entire Fleet career; she had never considered using one. If she didn't enjoy riding real horses, why bother with a simulator?

It wouldn't smell like a real one. The thought insinuated itself, and her mind threw up a picture of Luci on the brown mare, two graceful young animals enjoying movement. Pain stabbed her – had she been, *could* she have been, like Luci? Could she have had that grace?

Never, never . . . she lunged forward on the treadmill, driving with her legs, and almost fell. The safety rail felt cold against her palms. She forced herself to slow down, to move steadily. The past was past; it would not change because she learned more, or wanted it to.

'Evening, Lieutenant.' A jig, moving past her to the horse. He mounted clumsily, and Esmay could tell by the machine's move-ment that he had set it for basic mode, a slow trot in a straight line. Even so, he was off-rhythm, posting just behind the beat.

She could do better. Even now, she could do better, and she knew it.

She had no reason to do better. This life had no need for expertise in riding. She reminded herself of the smell, the dirt, the misery . . . her mind threw up images of speed and beauty and grace. Of Luci . . . and almost, tickling at the edge of awareness, of herself.

*   *   *

360

On the wall of Annie's room – she thought of it that way, though she had no reason to think it was really Annie's room – a flatscreen displayed a vague, misty landscape in soft greens and golds. Nothing like Altiplano, where the mountains stood out crisply against the sky, but it was a planet; she felt grounded by even that little.

'In your culture,' Annie began, 'part of the global definition of woman or girl is someone to be protected. You were a girl, and you were not protected.'

I wasn't worthy of protection ran through her mind. She curled into the afghan, not quite shivering, and focussed on its texture, its warmth. Someone had crocheted it by hand; she spotted a flaw in the pattern.

'A child's reasoning is different,' Annie said. 'You were not protected, so your child's mind – protecting your father, as children do and the more strongly because your mother had just died – your child's mind decided that either you were not *really* a girl, or you were not a *good* girl, and in either case you did not deserve protection. My guess would be that your mind, for reasons of its own, chose the "not really a girl" branch.'

'Why do you say that?' asked Esmay, who had been remembering the many times someone had told her she was a bad girl.

'Because of your behavior as an adolescent and adult. The ones who think they're bad girls act like bad girls – whatever that means for their culture of origin. For you, I suppose it would have been having affairs with anything that had a Y chromosome. You've been conspicuously good – at least, that's what your fitness reports say – but you haven't formed any lasting relationships with either sex. Also, you've chosen a career at odds with your culture's definition of women, as if you were a son rather than a daughter.'

'But that's just Altiplano . . .'

'Yes, but that's where you were raised; that's what formed your deepest attitudes towards the basics of human behavior. Do you fit in, as a woman, in your society?'

'Well . . . no.'

'Are you far enough from their norm to make them uneasy?'

'Yes . . .'

'At least you haven't taken the whole-bore approach: some

people in your situation chose to reverse both parts of the definition and define themselves as "bad, not-girls."'

'Does that mean I'm . . . not really a woman now?'

'Heavens, no. By the standards of Fleet, and most of the rest of Familias, your interests and behaviors are well within the definition. Celibacy's unusual, but not rare. Besides, you haven't considered it a problem until now, have you?'

Esmay shook her head.

'Then I don't see why we should worry about it. The rest of it – the nightmares, the flashbacks from combat, the inability to concentrate and so on – are matters for treatment. If, when the things that bother you are resolved, you find something else to worry about, we can deal with it then.'

That made sense.

'My guess – and it's only a guess, not an expert opinion – is that when you've got the rest of this straightened out, you'll find it easy to decide whether you want a partner, and if you do, you'll find one.'

Session after session, in that quiet cozy room with its soft textures, its warm colors . . . she had quit dreading them, though she wished they weren't necessary. It still seemed slightly indecent to spend so much time talking about herself and her family, especially when Annie refused to excuse her family for their mistakes.

'That's not my job,' Annie said. 'It may, in the end, be your job to forgive them – for your own healing – but it's not your job or mine to excuse them, to pretend they didn't do what they did do. We're dealing in reality here, and the reality is that they made what happened to you worse. Their response left you feeling less competent and more helpless.'

'But I was helpless,' Esmay said. She had the afghan over her knees, but not her shoulders; she had begun to recognize, by its position, how much stress she was feeling.

'Yes, and no,' Annie said. 'In one way, any child that age is helpless against an adult – they lack the physical strength to defend themselves without help. But physical helplessness and the sensation of helplessness are not quite the same thing.'

'I'm confused,' Esmay said; she had finally learned to say so. 'If you're helpless, you feel helpless.'

362

Annie looked at the wall display, this time a still life of fruit in a bowl. 'Let me try again. The sensation of helplessness implies that something could have been done – that you should be doing something. You don't feel helpless if you don't feel some responsibility.'

'I never thought of that,' Esmay said. She felt around inside herself, prodding the idea . . . was it true?

'Well . . . did you feel helpless in a rainstorm?'

'No . . .'

'You might be frightened, in some situations – perhaps severe weather – but not helpless. The opposed feelings of helplessness and confidence/competence develop through childhood as children begin to attempt interventions. Until you have the idea that something is doable, you don't worry about not doing it.' A long pause. 'When adults impose responsibility on a child for events the child could not control, the child is helpless to refuse it . . . or the guilt that follows.'

'And . . . that's what they did,' Esmay said.

'Yes.'

'So when I got angry, when I found out—'

'A reasonable reaction.' She had said this before; this time Esmay could hear it.

'I'm still angry with them,' Esmay said, challenging.

'Of course,' Annie said.

'But you said I'd get over it.'

'In years, not days. Give yourself time . . . you have a lot to be angry about.'

With that permission, it began to seem a limited anger. 'I suppose there are worse things . . .'

'We're not talking about other peoples' problems here: we're talking about yours. You were not protected, and when you were hurt they lied to you. As a result, you had a lot of bad years, and missed a lot of normal growing experiences.'

'I could have—'

Annie laughed. 'Esmay, I can guarantee one thing about your child self before this happened.'

'What?'

'You had iron will. The universe is lucky that your family did

363

get a sense of responsibility into you, because if you'd chosen the "bad" branch, you'd have been a criminal beyond compare.'

She had to laugh at that. She even agreed to take the neuro-actives Annie said she was ready for.

'So, how's it going with the psych stuff?' Barin asked. It was the first time since his release from sickbay that they'd had a chance to talk. They had come to the Wall, but no one was climbing. Just as well; Esmay didn't feel like climbing anyway. When she looked at the Wall, she saw the outside of the ship, the vast surfaces that always seemed to be just over vertical.

'I hate it,' Esmay said. She hadn't told Barin about the trek across the *Koskiusko*'s surface in FTL flight; even this topic was better. The weird effects of unshielded FTL travel did not bear thinking about. 'It wasn't too bad when I started, just talking to Annie. It actually helped, I think. But then she insisted I go to that group thing.'

'I hate that too.' Barin wrinkled his nose. 'It wastes time . . . some of them just ramble on and on, never getting anywhere.'

Esmay nodded. 'I thought it would be scary and painful, but half the time I'm just bored . . . .'

'Sam says that's why therapy happens in special times and places . . . because listening to someone talk about themselves for hours *is* boring, unless you're trained to do something in response.'

'Sam's your psychnanny?'

'Yes. I wish you were in my group. I'm still having trouble talking about it to them; they want to make a big thing about the physical damage, the broken bones and all. That's not what was worst. . . .' His voice faded away, but she felt he wanted to talk to her.

'What was worst, then?'

'Not being who I'm supposed to be,' he said softly, looking away. 'Not being able to do *anything* . . . I didn't manage to put a scratch on them, slow them down, anything . . . .'

Esmay nodded. 'I have trouble forgiving myself, too. Even though I know, in my mind, that it wasn't possible, it still feels as if it was my weakness – mental weakness – that didn't stop them.'

'My group keeps telling me there was nothing I could do, but it

364

feels different to me. Sam says I haven't heard it from the right person yet.'

'From your family?' Esmay asked, greatly daring.

'He means me. He thinks I think too much about the family, in quotes. I'm supposed to make my own standards, he says, and judge myself that way. *He* never had a grandmother like mine.'

'Or a grandfather like mine,' Esmay said. 'But I see his point. Would it help if your grandmother told you you'd done as much as you could?'

Barin sighed. 'Not really. I thought about that, and I know what I'd think if she did. *Poor Barin, have to cheer him up, give him a boost.* I don't want to be "Poor Barin." I want to be who I was. Before.'

'That won't work,' Esmay said, out of long experience. 'That's the one thing that won't work. You can't be who you were; you can only become someone else, that you can live with.'

'Is that all we can hope for, Es? Just . . . acceptable?' He glowered at the deck a moment, then looked up, with more of the Serrano showing than Esmay had seen for awhile. 'I'm not happy with that. If I have to change, fine: I'll change. But I want to be someone I can respect, and like – not just someone I can live with.'

'You Serranos have high standards,' Esmay said.

'Well . . . there's this Suiza around who keeps setting me an example.'

Examples. She didn't want to be the one setting examples; she hadn't been able to live up to any. New insight pounced on that, turned it inside out, put it in the imaginary sun to air. As a child, she had copied the people she loved and admired; she had tried to be what they wanted, as much as she understood it. Where she had failed was not only not her fault – it wasn't, in the larger context of the Fleet and Familias Regnant, even failure.

Fleet seemed to think she had set an acceptable example. Now that the *Koskiusko* was back with its companions, she heard rumors of the reactions in high places. Her head cleared, little by little, from the initial murk of therapy . . . she saw that Pitak and Seveche were not just tolerating her weak need for therapy; they

365

wanted her to take the time she needed. The ensigns and jigs at her table at mess treated her with the exact flavor of respectful attention which a lifetime's experience of the military told her meant genuine affection.

They liked her. They liked *her*, they respected *her*, and not her fame or her background, which they didn't know anyway. She was the only Suiza – the only Altiplanan – any of them had ever met, and they liked her. With reason, Annie said when she confessed her embarrassment, her confusion. Slowly she came to believe it, each day's experience layering a thin glaze of belief over the self-doubts.

From time to time she looked at the virtual horse in the gym, wondering. She had not told Annie that it had begun to haunt her. This was something she had to work out for herself. Automatically now her mind picked that thought up and played with it. Denial? No – but this was something she *wanted* to work out for herself. A choice she would make, when she was free to make it.

'I could get attached to the old girl,' Esmay said, peering out the observation ports to the patterns of lights on T-1 and T-5. 'She's an amazing ship.' She and Barin had found a quiet corner of the crafts activity compartment; the climbing club was busy on the Wall, and Barin had confessed he felt no more eagerness for climbing than she did. She thought he looked a lot better; she knew she felt better . . . she had had no nightmares for the past twenty days and was beginning to hope they were gone forever.

'You're going to transfer to Maintenance Command?' Barin looked up from the model he was putting together, the skeleton of some exotic beast. She could not read his expression, but she saw tension in the muscles of his face.

'It's tempting . . . there's a lot more to learn here . . .'

'Fine for a sponge,' Barin said, in a tone that suggested what he thought of sponges.

'Fretting, are we?' Esmay asked, wrinkling her nose at him. 'Eager to get back to the *real* Fleet?'

He flushed, then smiled. 'Therapy's going well, even the group part. It may even – in the very long run – turn out to be something worthwhile.'

'Look out all admirals . . . someone's after your job?'

'Not quite. By the time I get to that age, there may be no slots for new admirals anyway. That's another reason to get back into my own track as soon as possible.' He cleared his throat. 'How's your stuff going?'

'Stuff? I'm not shy about it, Barin. The sessions have helped. I still wish I knew how much of the change was me, and how much was in those medications, but . . . they say it doesn't matter.'

'So what are you going to do? Back into technical track, into scan?'

'I'm transferring,' Esmay said. 'If they approve, which I hope they will. So far they're being encouraging.' She still found it hard to believe how encouraging. Gruff Pitak had practically leaped over the desk, and she had undeniably grinned.

'Transfer to *what*, you annoying woman?'

Esmay ducked her head, then faced him squarely. 'Command track. I think it's time a few dirtborn outsiders held command.'

'Yes!' His grin lit the compartment. 'Please . . . when you get your first *legal* command . . . wangle me a place in your crew.'

'Wangle?' She pretended to glare at him, but her face wouldn't stay straight. 'You Serranos can wangle all you want, but Suizas expect to *earn* command.' He made a face and sighed dramatically. 'Gods help us all – we let the Suizas off Altiplano.'

'Let?' Esmay reached out and tickled him. Startled, he dropped the model onto the desk.

'You touched me!'

'I'm an idiot,' Esmay said, feeling herself blush.

'No . . . you're human. Overwhelmed by my charm.'

Esmay laughed. 'You wish!'

'Yes, I do,' he said with a sudden change of expression. Slowly, he reached out and touched her cheek. 'I do wish an alliance with this Suiza of Altiplano. Not just because Suiza has pulled Serrano out of trouble twice now, but because . . . I do like you. Admire you. And most desperately wish you'd like me enough to welcome me into your life.' A pause she knew was calculated. 'And into your bed.'

Her pulse raced. She wasn't ready for this, she hadn't let herself think about it since Pitak's lecture during the crisis. Her body informed her that she was lying, that she had thought of very little else whenever she had the chance. 'Uh . . .'

'Though not if the prospect disgusts you, of course. Only if . . . I never thought you'd touch me, aside from whacking me firmly with your elbow or knee in a wallball game.' He was joking now, flushing a little himself, and Esmay felt moved to perform a rescue.

'I'm shy,' she said. 'Inexperienced to the point of total ignorance, barring what I saw on the farm as a girl, which I hope is a long way from anything you were thinking of, as it involved biting and kicking and hobbles.'

Barin choked back a laugh. 'Esmay!'

'Inexperienced, I said. Not, you will notice, unwilling.'

In the long silence that followed, watching the shifting expressions play over his face, feeling the first feather-touch of his fingers on her face, on her hair, Esmay laid the last fiery ghost to rest.

Awards ceremonies all had the same structure; she wondered if all recipients felt a little silly, so far removed from the mood in which they'd done whatever it was that got them honored. Why the discrepancy? Why had the Starmount stricken her to silent awe when she saw it on someone else's uniform, while she had felt first nothing much, and then a sort of shamed confusion, when she wore it herself? As Admiral Foxworth spoke briefly to each recipient, she found she could believe that the others deserved their medals – that those awards were real. It was hers that felt . . . wrong.

The sessions of therapy rose up like a mirror in her mind. From a vague shape against darkness her own face came clear, as real as any other. She was real . . . she had done what she had done, and its worth lay not in anything *they* said about it. What bothered her . . . she struggled with it, fought to bring it out where she could see. Why was it right for others, but wrong for her? *You don't deserve it*, said part of her mind. She knew the answer to that now, knew the roots of that belief and could pull up those roots no matter how often the wrinkled seed sprouted. But what else? If . . . if she became that person who could be honored, who could be recognized in public as honorable, then . . . then what? Then someone might . . . look up to her as she had looked up to that young man. Might expect her to be what the award made her seem, what they judged she was ready for.

She almost grinned, making that connection.

She could remember, down the years, from before the trouble, an instructor telling some hapless student: 'Don't tell me I over-mounted you: shut up and *ride.*' And then he'd looked at her, the little Esmay knee-high to the tall horses, watching from the ringside, and said, 'This one'll show you.' He had tossed her up to another horse – the first time she'd been on a horse and not a pony. She'd been more excited than scared, too young to know she couldn't do what she was told to do – and not knowing, she'd stayed aboard. It had felt like flying, so high above the ground, so fast. She could almost feel that grin stretching her face. 'Like that,' the instructor had said, lifting her down. And then he'd leaned close to her. 'Keep that up, little one.'

She wasn't riding ponies any more. She was out in the world, on the big horses, taking the big fences – and she would just have to live up to her reputation as the horses and fences grew bigger . . . .

'Lieutenant Esmay Suiza.' She stood, came forward as directed, and listened as Admiral Foxworth read the citation. She waited for him to pick up the ribbon his aide held on a tray, but instead he raised one bushy gray eyebrow. 'You know, Lieutenant, I've seen the summary of the Board of Inquiry.' Esmay waited, and when the silence lengthened wondered if she was supposed to answer that. Finally he went on. 'The final paragraph specifically notes that you are not to be in command of any combat vessel until such time as you have demonstrated competence in relevant training exercises. Yet I find that your citation says you took command of the vessel *Antberd's Axe* which subsequently engaged enemy vessels in a hostile encounter. Your commander praises your initiative, when I would think he should condemn your blatant disregard of the findings of that Board of Inquiry.' He looked at her, his face now blank of all expression. 'Do you have anything to say, Lieutenant?'

All the things she wanted to say, and must not, tangled in her mouth. What was right? What was safe? What was . . . true?

Finally she said, 'Well, sir, my recollection is that the Board said I should not command any *R.S.S.* combat vessels until further training . . . it didn't say anything about Bloodhorde ships.'

A long moment of utter silence, during which Esmay had ample time to regret her boldness and consider the power of angry admirals. Maybe she had overmounted herself, maybe the fence was too high. Then a slow grin creased his face and he looked past her to the rest of the assembly. '*And* she can think on her feet,' he said. The crowd roared; Esmay felt the blood rushing to her cheeks. The admiral picked up the decoration and pinned it on. 'Congratulations, Lieutenant Suiza.'

On the far side of the fence, the ground was still there; she would survive this time, and she would keep riding forward. Coming back to her seat, she caught Barin's eye; he was sparkling all over with delight in her, and she indulged herself with a moment's fantasy . . . Suiza and Serrano. Yes. Oh, my, *yes*.

rules of engagement

DEDICATION

In memory of the victims of the Jarrell, Texas, tornado, May 27, 1997, and especially Brandi Nicole Smith and Stacy Renee Smith, and their mother, Cynthia L. Smith.

ACKNOWLEDGEMENTS

The usual suspects (you know who you are . . .), with special thanks to Ellen McLean and Mary Morell for helping with the psychology behind the pathology. Mary managed to read the first draft and make intelligent comments even as the rain poured down, the roof leaked, and a dead mouse turned up in the guest room. This is heroic manuscript help. Diann Thornley let me pick her brain about what kinds of things are taught in junior officers' leadership courses. Ruta Duhon helped me think through one of the final bits of excitement over lunch one day, probably because she was tired of hearing me complain that I was stuck. Anna Larsen and Toni Weisskopf each contributed a specific nudge to the emotional side of the plot. Kathleen Jones and David Watson took on the task of 'cold reading' the final draft aloud, and did it in just a few days. Their comments markedly improved the *new* final draft. Debbie Kirk, as always, found more typos than anyone else and gently nudged my erratic spelling back toward consistency. Certain anecdotes contributed by persons who asked not to be named added grit to the fictional reality.

Special mention must be made of the bits of Texana which decorate this story. Some are real (other Texans know which), some are fictional, some are Texas mythology of the future. The misappropriation and distortion of Texas history and traditions by characters in the book does not in any way represent my attitude towards that history or those traditions. Readers with a knowledge of history and a sense of irony may be amused by the juxtaposition of certain characters' surnames; the intended references all predate the 20th century. (It was tempting, but not *that* tempting, to play in contemporary Texas politics.) Any coincidence of name is purely accidental. The movements mentioned as ancient history in the text are, however unfortunately, alive and sick in the 20th century; it would be not only useless but dishonest to pretend that the New Texas Godfearing Militia did not derive its nature from elements all too close to home, in Waco, Fort Davis, and even Oklahoma City.

1

Regular Space Service Training Command,
Copper Mountain Base

Halfway up the cliff, Brun realized that someone was trying to kill her. She had already shifted weight from her left foot to her right foot when the thought penetrated, and she completed the movement, ending with her left foot on the tiny ledge almost at her crotch, before she gave her brain a 'message received' signal.

Instantly, her hands slicked with sweat, and she lost the grip of her weaker left hand on the little knob. She dipped it into her chalk, and reached for the knob again, then chalked her right hand and refound that hold. That much was mechanical, after these days in training . . . so someone was trying to kill you, you didn't have to help them by doing something stupid.

She argued with herself, while pushing up, releasing her right leg for the next move. Of course, in a general way, someone was trying to kill her, or any other trainee. She had known that coming in. Better to lose trainees here than half-trained personnel in the field, where their failure would endanger others. Her breath eased, as she talked herself into a sensible frame of mind. Right foot *there*, and then the arms moving, finding the next holds, and then the left leg . . . she had enjoyed climbing almost from the first day of training.

A roar in her ears and the sudden sting on her hand: she was falling before she had time to recognize the noise and the pain. A shot. Someone had shot at her . . . hit her? Not enough pain – must've been rock splinters – then she hit the end of her rope, and swung into the cliff face with a force that knocked the breath out of her. Reflexively, her hands and feet caught at the rock, sought grips, found them, took her weight off the climbing harness. Her head rang, still; she shook it and the halves of her climbing helmet slid down to hang from the straps like the wing cases of a crushed beetle.

Damn . . . she thought. Reason be damned, someone was trying to kill her – her in particular – and plastered to a cliff in plain sight was not her idea of a good place to be when someone was shooting at her. She glanced around quickly. Up – too far, too slow, too exposed. Down – 150 feet of falling in a predictable vertical line, whether free or on the rope. To the right, nothing but open rock. To the left, a narrow vertical crack. They had been told not to use it this time, but she'd climbed in it before, learning about cracks and chimneys. If she could get there . . .

She pushed off, and the next shot hit the cliff where her head had been, between head and right hand. Splinters of rock sprayed her hand, the right side of her face. She did not fall. She lunged for the next hold, not in a panic but with the controlled speed of someone who knew just where each hold would be. Whoever it was had some reason not to fire on automatic, at full speed. But now they knew which way she was going. They could adjust their aim . . . she took a chance, and her foot slipped on one hold. For an instant, she hung from her arms, feet scrabbling . . . then she found the hold, and the next. The sheltering crevice was just ahead – this time it was her left hand that slipped, when she reached too far, and even as she cursed, the next shot shattered the hold for which she'd reached, loosing a shower of rock.

She didn't hesitate. The breakage offered new holds; in a second she was into the crevice, yanking hard on the rope for more, for enough to move into deeper cover. What she hoped the shooter didn't know was alignment of the crevice. Here, she was as vulnerable as on the cliff face, apparently held in a vertical groove. But the forces which had made the crevice had produced an almost spiral fracture. Not ten feet above she could be safely hidden from the shooter.

The rope from below dragged at her. No more slack. They hadn't understood . . . or were they part of the plot? She yanked again, unsuccessfully.

Our Texas, Formerly Kurzawa-Yahr Joint Investment Colony

Mitchell Langston Pardue, Ranger Bowie of the New Texas Godfearing Militia on Our Texas, sat in his heavy carved chair and waited for the Captain to finish reading his report. He stroked the carving on the right arm – supposed to resemble the Old Texas animal called a dilla, whatever that had been – and thought how he could imply that the Captain was an idiot without actually saying so.

'Mitch, you payin' attention?' Pete Robertson, Ranger Travis and Captain of Rangers, had a querulous waver in his voice that made Mitch want to slap him upside the head with something heavy. He was getting old, with a wattled neck like a turkey gobbler.

'You bet, Captain,' he said. 'You say we need about thirty more of them nukes from Familias Regnant's space fleet, in order to top up the first depot. Your timetable for hittin' the Guernesi is runnin' behind a little . . .'

'It's stopped in its tracks like a mule in a swamp,' the Captain said. 'An' if we wait too long, they won't make the connection we want.' The Guernesi had reacted with vigor to the theft of a shipload of tourists, and had gotten them back, though with casualties. Then they'd imposed a trade embargo, and blown up a couple of ships to make their point that they held a grudge about the ones who had died. 'We've gotta get more weapons. And there's somethin' wrong with our main agent at their space fleet headquarters – the last signal we got from him makes no sense.'

'He's gettin' old, though,' Sam Dubois, Ranger Austin said. 'He's had one of them proscribed procedures . . .'

'He was rejuvenated,' Mitch said, using the correct term. 'They started rejuvenating their most senior NCOs about ten, fifteen years ago, and he's one of 'em. If they hadn't, likely we wouldn't have got anythin' from him.'

'But it's an abomination,' Sam said. Stubborn as rock, Sam was, and tighter than a tick to Parson Wells.

'Yes, it's an abomination,' Mitch said. 'I'm not sayin' it's right. But the devil takes care of his own, sometimes, and them rejuvenations have been working awhile now. The man's only eighty; his mind should be fine even if he hadn't had the drugs.'

'But it's not,' the Captain said, with a triumphant look at Mitch. 'Look at this here.' He passed down a sheet of paper.

Mitch looked at it. 'Gobbledegook,' he said after a glance. 'Did he change ciphers or something?'

'No. I think he's taken to some heathen practice – or that rejuvenation is eating his brain. I've heard about that.' His next glance at Mitch was calculating.

'Could be,' Mitch said. Everyone knew he had read more widely in the dangerous literature of biomodification than was strictly approved by the parsons. The Captain was trying to trap him into a discussion that would prove his contamination, but Mitch was smarter than that. Instead, he had his own plan.

'Well?' Sam said.

'Captain,' Mitch said formally. 'I'd like to make a proposal.'

'Sure,' the Captain said. His gaze didn't waver. Mitch could have laughed; the idiot still thought Mitch would incriminate himself.

'You know you gave me permission 'way last year to do some work in the Familias myself—'

'Yeah—'

'Well, sir, I cast bread on the waters and let me tell you, there are hungry souls out there all athirst for the true word of God.' Now the others all nodded, leaning forward. 'I found us some agents here and there – in big trading firms, and one in a regional weapons depot, an assistant station master – and we've been getting a nice little flow of illicits in here for about six months.'

Mitch pulled out his own report and passed it around. 'More'n that, gentlemen, any time we want an entire cargo hold loaded with nukes or anything else, I've got just the person to do it. What I thought was, I'd go on and tell 'em to load up, and then go get us

380

a transport as well as the weapons. There's this ship that takes a shortcut through a deserted system – a fine place for an ambush.'

'Ah – and you want our help, Ranger Bowie?'

'No sir, I don't. With all respect, sir, there's too much goin' on to pull resources from the rest of our people. What I thought was, I'd take all of the Bowies, and take care of this little chore – and that should put us back on track for knocking the Guernesi flat on their tails.'

Silence, during which the others digested this, and looked for ways to profit from it. Mitch made himself sit still, and observed.

'What about the crew?' the Captain asked finally.

Mitch shrugged. 'Our usual rules. We still need more females, if we can find some that aren't too badly contaminated.'

'You know, we've had to mute damn near every foreign female we've brought in,' Sam said. 'And I worry about their effect on our women.'

Mitch smiled. 'We're real men; we can control our women.' The others quickly nodded; nobody wanted to admit to having a problem in that area. 'Besides, we know God approves, because the imported women have strong, healthy babies, fewer of 'em born with defects.' That, too, was unarguable. A child's defects reflected parental sin; if healthy children came from women brought up in sin, then it must be because God celebrated their release from the abominations of the ungodly.

'If Parson Wells will bless your mission, Ranger Bowie, you have my approval,' the Captain said formally.

Just wait until he, Ranger Bowie, was Captain of Rangers, and then see if he rolled over like that for anyone. Mitch nodded, and when the parson came in he explained the proposed mission again. Parson Wells pursed his lips, but finally nodded. 'Just be sure to avoid contamination, Ranger Bowie.'

Mitch smiled. 'Yes, sir, Parson. I got no intention of going heathen.' He had every intention of coming back with weapons, women, wealth – and every intention of making it to the captaincy before he was many years older.

R.S.S. Training Command, Copper Mountain

Lieutenant Esmay Suiza arrived at Training Command's Copper Mountain Base with high hopes only to find herself waiting her turn for security clearance in a big echoing reception hall with two of the ugliest murals she'd ever seen. On the right, over the com booths, a scene of ships in combat in space. They looked nothing like ships as Esmay had seen them from the outside. Realism would have been dull at best, but she couldn't help an internal smirk at the astronomical decorations . . . stars, comets, spiral galaxies. On the left, over the luggage dumps, a scene depicting ground combat, which looked even less realistic than the space one . . . for one thing, nobody's uniform ever stayed that clean. For another, the artist had only a shaky grasp of anatomy and perspective; all the figures looked squashed sideways.

Esmay tried to get her mind back to her own high hopes. A change in track, from technical to command, and she was finally pursuing her destiny, using her best talents. Certainly her commanders thought so. She had made friends, including Barin Serrano who was – if she was honest with herself – much more than a friend. In his admiration, she felt herself more capable; in his concern, she felt herself loved. That still made her uncomfortable: she had never really thought about love, about being loved, and she could hardly believe it had happened, or that it might last. But she still felt the touch of his hands on her face – she pulled herself back from that memory and made herself consider what came next.

She glanced at the space combat scene again and could not help shaking her head.

'Gruesome, aren't they, sir?' asked the sergeant at the first security station. 'Supposed to be very old and valuable, but really – it looks like something done by a half-gifted amateur.'

'That's probably what they got,' Esmay said, grinning. She presented her orders and identification.

'New rules, Lieutenant, require a full med-ID scan before you receive station tags. If you'll follow the yellow line to the next station, they'll get started.'

Security had been tighter all the way across Familias Space, a

382

natural result of all that had happened in the past quarter year. Still, she hadn't expected the level of confirmation required here, at a training base whose only access was through a Fleet-controlled orbital station. Where were intruders supposed to be coming from?

An hour later she was waiting outside yet another security checkpoint. It was ridiculous. How long did it take to do a retinal check, even a full neuroscan? Her stomach growled, reminding her that she'd broken one of the great rules of military life – eat whenever you get a chance. She could have grabbed a snack before leaving the transport, but (her memory mocked her) it was only supposed to be a couple of hours down to Copper Mountain.

In for the retinal check at last. 'Just follow the yellow line, Lieutenant . . .' said the voice behind the screen.

'But can't you just—'

'Follow the yellow line.'

Which ended in another bench to wait on until her name was called. Ahead of her was a whole squad of neuro-enhanced combat troops . . . she'd heard of these but never seen any up close. They looked like anyone else who happened to be carrying about twice the muscle and half the fat of anyone else. They had been chatting, but fell silent as she came up to the bench. She felt fragile beside them.

'Excuse me, Lieutenant—' She looked up to see that they had reshuffled themselves to put one of the women next to her.

'Yes?'

'Are you the Lieutenant Suiza who was on *Despite* and then *Koskiusko?*'

Esmay nodded.

'Lieutenant, I'm really glad to meet you. I – we've always wondered what it's like outside during FTL flight. Would you mind telling us about it? They tell us the debriefing sims won't be out for another six months.'

'It's . . . really odd,' Esmay said. 'First, the starfield disappears—' She was about to go on when the clerk called her name.

'If we don't take you now, you'll be here for hours,' the clerk said. 'These neuro-enhanced jobs take forever.'

Esmay felt a wave of cold dislike rise from the seated squad, and hoped they were aiming it at the clerk, and not her. 'Excuse me,' she said to them all.

'Of course, Lieutenant,' said the woman who had asked her the question. She had green eyes, startling in her dark face. Then she looked beyond Esmay to the clerk, and Esmay was not surprised to hear the clerk's breath catch.

She hadn't had a full neuroscan since she entered the Academy, and it was still as boring as ever, being stuck in the dark maw of the machine following orders to think of this, or that, or imagine moving her left little finger . . .

Finally it was done, and the last yellow line led her back to the desk where her duffel lay waiting for her, along with a handful of ID tags she would need for the facilities she was authorized to enter.

'Junior officers' quarters and mess that way, sir,' the sergeant said, and gave a crisp salute as he passed her through. Esmay returned it and stepped onto the indicated walkway. She had missed out on command training, once she'd chosen technical track, so now she would be taking back-to-back courses – more school! Her own fault, she reminded herself, and yet not a fault to spend much time on. Her Altiplano conscience worried about the quickness with which her retrained neurons pushed away that momentary pang of guilt, and she grinned mentally at it. Her Altiplano conscience, like her Altiplano family, could stay where it belonged . . . on Altiplano.

She signed into the officers' quarters and the officers' mess, showing her clearance tags each time, picked up a duty roster, then a class schedule. She slung her gear into 235-H, one anonymous cubicle in a row of anonymous cubicles, and then headed for the mess. Even if it was between mealtimes for the school, they should have something for officers arriving from different time zones.

The dining room was almost empty; when she walked in, a mess steward peered out from the galleys and then came toward her.

'Lieutenant?'

'I just came in,' Esmay said. 'Our ship was on . . .'

'Fleet Standard. I understand Lieutenant . . . you're overdue for . . . midday, right? Do you want a full meal or a snack?'

'Just a snack.' She would get herself on the planet's schedule faster this way, but she felt hollow as a new-built hull at the moment.

He seated her at a table a discreet distance from the two that were occupied, and left to bring the food. Esmay glanced casually at the others, wondering if they would be in her class. A young woman in fatigues without insignia, her curly blonde hair cropped short, sat hunched over what looked like a bowl of soup. Beside her, an older man in a lieutenant commander's uniform who, from his posture, was laying down the law about something.

Esmay looked away. Unusual to chew someone out while they were eating, but it would be rude to observe. Could this be father and daughter? At the other table, three young men wearing exercise clothes who were, she realized, watching *her*. She met their gaze coolly, and they looked away, not as if they were embarrassed, but as if they had seen all they wanted. Their gaze wandered the room steadily; they ignored the litter of plates and cups before them.

The steward brought out a platter of sandwiches, pastries, and raw vegetable slices arranged in a fan-shaped pattern. Esmay ate a sandwich of thinly sliced cattleope spread with horseradish sauce, several carrot sticks, and was considering one of the curly pastry things which smelled so deliciously of cinnamon and hot apples when the blonde woman erupted.

'I'm *not* quitting!' she said, loudly enough that Esmay could not fail to hear. She was sitting upright now, her face flushed slightly. With that flush Esmay could spot the irregular patches of fresh healing . . . she had been in a regen tank to repair some kind of injury to her face and – Esmay could not help looking – hands and arms.

The older man, with a cautionary glance at Esmay, rumbled something she could not hear.

'No!' the blonde said. 'It's something else – something important. I know—' Then she too looked around, met Esmay's eyes, and fell silent for a moment.

Some instinct prompted Esmay to look not merely down, but – under lowered lids – across at the other table. The three men there now made sense . . . their dismissive assessment of her, their constant surveillance of the room. These were the bodyguards of someone who hired the best – or to whom the best were, by custom, assigned.

Whom were they guarding? Surely not the young woman . . . if they had been, they had failed in some way or she would not have been hurt. A lieutenant commander? Hardly . . . unless he were not a lieutenant commander at all.

She glanced back at the young woman, and was surprised by an expression on both faces so alike that it had to imply a relationship. Her eye, trained on a planet where families mattered, and where she had been expected to recognize even the most distant Suiza cousin, picked out now the similarities of bone and proportion, as well as behavioral quirks like the sudden lift of eyebrow that both older man and younger woman showed at that moment.

'Brun . . .' That carried, in part because the tone was so like the pleading tone her own father had used. Her mind caught on the unusual word. Brun. Wasn't that – ? She clamped her mouth shut on the apple tart. If that was the blonde girl who had been involved in the Xavier affair, then her father was the present Speaker of the Grand Council . . . the most powerful man in the Familias Regnant. What could they be doing here?

Speculation having outrun data, she munched steadily through the tart, studiously ignoring the argument which continued, in lower voices, at the other table. She struggled to remember all the snippets of rumor she'd heard about Thornbuckle's wild youngest daughter . . . a spoiled beauty, a hotheaded fool who had plunged into the thick of intrigue with no training, an idiot who'd ended up dead drunk and naked in a rockhopper's pod in the aftermath of a battle. But also something about being, in some obscure way, Admiral Vida Serrano's protégé, because of her services to the Familias and – most particularly – to Admiral Serrano's niece Heris.

'Excuse me,' someone said. Esmay swallowed the last bite of tart, and looked up. She had been concentrating so hard on not noticing what she shouldn't notice that she hadn't noticed anyone approaching her table.

It was one of the bodyguards. He had no rank insignia on his exercise clothes, but from his face he was older than she.

386

'Yes?'

'You're Lieutenant Suiza, aren't you?'

Despite the therapy, her gut tightened. 'Yes, that's right.'

'Lieutenant Commander . . . Smith . . . would like to meet you.'

'Lieutenant Commander Smith?'

He nodded his head toward the other table. 'Smith,' he said firmly. 'And his daughter.'

For a moment Esmay wished that she had just lived with her hunger until the next scheduled main meal. She had no desire to get involved in whatever was going on, whether it was a matter of father-daughter dissension or some plot against the Familias.

'Of course,' she said, and rose from the table.

The older man and the young woman watched her approach with, Esmay thought, the wrong sort of interest. The older man had the sort of face which might have been pleasant, but presently had locked into a tight mask of concern. The young woman looked both annoyed and afraid.

'Commander Smith,' Esmay said, 'I'm Lieutenant Suiza.'

'Have a seat,' the man said. Although his uniform fitted his tall, lanky body perfectly, she was sure it did not fit his spirit . . . it would have needed stars on the shoulders, and plenty of them.

'This is an unexpected honor,' the man went on. 'I had heard about you, of course, from Admiral Serrano, after Xavier – and now this recent business—'

This, for instance, was not the way a real lieutenant commander would have brought it up. Esmay wondered whether to relieve him of the need for faking a military identity, and had her mouth open when the young woman spoke.

'Dad! Stop it!'

'Brun, I'm merely—'

Now almost whispering, but still angrily, the young woman continued. 'You're *not* really a lieutenant commander and it's not fair.' She turned to Esmay. 'I'm Brun Meager, Lord Thornbuckle's daughter, and this is my father.'

'I'm pleased to meet Commander Smith,' Esmay said, 'under the circumstances.'

His face relaxed a bit, and his mouth quirked. 'Well, one of you young ladies has a bit of discretion.'

'I'm not being indiscreet,' Brun said. 'She could see you weren't really a Fleet officer, and I could see the wheels going around in her head as she tried to figure out how to handle it.'

'One allows prominent people to introduce themselves as they choose,' Esmay said. 'One's private curiosity never intrudes.'

Brun blinked. 'Where are you from?'

'Altiplano,' Esmay said. 'Where, on occasion, senior officials may choose to appear in borrowed identities.'

'And where good manners seem to have penetrated more than in some other places,' Lord Thornbuckle said pointedly. Brun flushed again.

'I don't like deception.'

'Oh, really? That's why you so carefully avoided using your own name when you were coming back to Rockhouse—'

'That was different,' Brun said. 'There was a good reason—'

'There's a good reason *now*, Brun, and if you can't see that I'll go back to calling you Bubbles with reason.' For all his low, even voice and quiet face, Lord Thornbuckle was seriously angry. Esmay wished she were on the other side of the planet. Father-daughter conflict raised ghosts she wanted laid to rest. Brun subsided, but Esmay had the feeling she was not really subdued.

'Perhaps we could continue this in another location,' Lord Thornbuckle said. Esmay could think of no polite way to refuse, and she wasn't sure where her duty lay, as an R.S.S. officer. But she would have to report to class at 0800 local time the next morning, and she had a lot to do in the meantime. Still . . . he was who he was, and even who he wasn't outranked her.

'Of course, sir,' Esmay said.

Thornbuckle nodded to the men at the other table, who stood up. 'I'm afraid we will have an escort.'

That didn't bother Esmay; what bothered her was landing in the middle of whatever mess this was. She noticed that the escort split up, two going ahead and one trailing behind. Were they Fleet? She couldn't tell. She felt she should be able to tell; the civilians aboard *Kos* had been obvious enough. These didn't look like civilians, but they didn't quite fit Fleet, either. Private guards?

388

The conference room they finally entered was small, centered with a table large enough for only eight or so to surround. It had a display console at one end, but Lord Thornbuckle ignored that. He waited until his escort nodded, then sat at one end of the table. Habit, Esmay supposed.

'Sit down, and I'll make this as brief as possible. You haven't been here long, have you?'

'Just got off the shuttle, sir,' Esmay said. 'I'm here for the command courses I missed earlier, and then the standard junior officers' course.' The one that would qualify her to command a ship in combat, according to the Board of Inquiry which had recommended it. Of course, not being qualified hadn't stopped her yet – but she put that out of mind and prepared to focus on whatever Lord Thornbuckle had to say.

'My daughter wanted to take some training with Fleet experts,' Thornbuckle said. 'I agreed, in part because she'd gotten herself in so much trouble without training . . . it seemed the risk-taking genes had all come together in her.'

'And the lucky genes,' Brun said. 'I know they're not enough, but they're also not negligible. That's what Captain – Commander – Serrano said. And her aunt admiral.'

The thought of anyone calling Vida Serrano 'aunt admiral' – even a niece – shocked Esmay. For this girl – for Brun was clearly younger than she was – to do so would have been unthinkable except that Brun had just done it.

'But there've been incidents,' Thornbuckle went on, ignoring what Brun had just said. 'I thought she'd be safer here, on a Fleet training facility—'

'I *am* safer,' Brun said.

'Brun, face the facts: someone shot at you. Tried to kill you.'

Esmay managed not to say what she was thinking, that a Fleet training facility was not, in the nature of things, the safest place in the universe. Live fire exercises, for instance. Was this what the girl had gotten into?

'It wasn't anywhere near a live fire exercise,' Thornbuckle went on. 'That was my first thought, of course. Military training is dangerous; it has to be. But we – and by "we" I mean not only myself, but others who've seen Brun in action – thought it would be less dangerous than turning her loose on the universe untrained.' He spread his hands. 'No – this has been different. I suppose we were just careless. We knew there were traitors in Fleet; that mess with Xavier proved it. But it didn't dawn on me that there might be traitors here, in a training base, until Admiral Serrano pointed it out. We knew that Brun might be at special risk, but we didn't react fast enough.'

'I'm alive,' Brun said.

'You survived with your usual flair,' her father said. 'But you also had to spend a day in the regen tank, which is not what I call coming out unscathed. Too close for comfort is my analysis. You have to have more protection, or you have to leave.'

Brun's shoulders twitched. 'I'll be careful,' she said.

'Not good enough. You have to sleep sometime.'

'Have you identified the nature of the threat?' Esmay asked, to forestall another round of useless argument.

'No. Not . . . precisely. And the worst of it is that I can see a variety of threats. The Benignity's not happy with their loss at Xavier, and we are sure they have other agents in Fleet. Some have been identified, others haven't. They consider assassination a political tool. The Bloodhorde . . . well, you can imagine how they would like to have my daughter in their control. Then there are my personal enemies among the Familias. A few years ago, I would not have believed any of the Families would make war on personal relations, but now – things have changed.'

'And you – or your advisors – think your daughter should leave this facility?'

'It would be easier to protect her at home, or even on Castle Rock.'

'I would go crazy,' Brun muttered. 'I'm not a child, and I can't just sit around doing nothing.'

'Do you want to join Fleet?' Esmay asked. She couldn't really imagine this obvious rebel wanting to join anything with discipline, but if she hadn't understood . . .

'I did at one time,' Brun said, eyeing her father. 'Now – I'm not sure.'

'She doesn't want to get stuck doing boring things,' Thornbuckle said. Brun flushed.

'It's not that—!'

'Isn't it? When Captain Serrano pointed out how much of her time was spent on boring routine, you said you didn't much like that prospect.'

'I don't, but that's part of any life. I do understand that, just as I understand that the exciting bits are dangerous. You seem to think—'

Esmay jumped in again, as much for her own comfort as for the hope of getting useful information. 'Perhaps you could tell me what you think I might do to help?'

'She needs a' – Thornbuckle paused, and Esmay was sure he was thinking of the word *keeper* – 'Mentor,' he said instead. 'If she's going to stay here, I need to know that someone of her—' Another pause, during which Esmay could almost hear the unspoken, discarded choices: *social standing, rank, type, ability* . . . 'Someone she might respect and listen to, anyway, will be near her. She's been chattering about you and your exploits—'

'I do not chatter,' Brun said, through her teeth.

'So I thought maybe you—'

'She has her own responsibilities,' Brun said. 'And there are the . . . guards.' In that gap was some epithet Esmay was glad the guards had not heard.

'Are you telling me now that you *will* accept the security procedures we talked about?'

'Rather than bother Lieutenant Suiza, yes.' Brun gave Esmay a challenging look. 'She will be busy with her own courses here; they don't exactly give officers time off to play nursemaid to rich girls.'

Esmay interpreted this as having more to do with Brun's determination not to have a nursemaid than any consideration of her own convenience.

Thornbuckle looked from one to the other of them. 'I have seen more cooperative senior ministers of state,' he said. 'Whatever gene sculpting we did on you, Brun, is not going to be repeated again.'

'I didn't ask for it,' Brun said. Again Esmay sensed old arguments lurking below the surface.

'No – but life gives you a lot you didn't ask for. Now – if you promise me that you will cooperate with the new security procedures—'

'All right,' Brun said, not quite sulkily. 'I'll cooperate.'

'Then, Lieutenant Suiza, I'm very sorry to have wasted your time. And I must thank you for your recent actions; you well deserve your recent award.' He nodded at the new ribbon on her uniform.

'Thank you,' Esmay said, wondering if she was just supposed to leave and forget the conversation had ever happened. She turned to Brun and surprised an almost wistful expression on her face. 'If we end up in the same class, I'll be glad to share notes with you. I'm glad to have met you.'

Brun nodded; Esmay got up when Thornbuckle did, and he walked her to the door. 'I'm officially still Smith,' he said quietly.

'I understand, sir.' She understood more than she wanted to, or than he expected. She was glad to get back to her own quarters, where she could deal with her memories of her father in privacy. There, she found a stack of study cubes in the delivery bin, and racked them into the cube reader's storage. Some looked much more promising than others; *Leadership for Junior Officers* made sense, but why did she have to study *Administrative Procedures for Junior Staff*? She didn't want anything to do with administration.

Brun curled up on her bunk under her very non-regulation afghan and pretended to nap until her security detail had finished whatever it was doing and gone to stand outside. As if she were a prisoner. As if she were a naughty child. As if being shot at were her fault.

Her father had done it again. She would have been fine, if he had only been somewhere else, if only she had had time to get well before he showed up. But no. He had to come here, still unsure she should be doing things like this, and embarrass her in front of a roomful of professionals . . .

In front of Esmay Suiza.

She rolled over, and picked up her remote, then flicked on her cube reader, cycling through the selections until she found the one she wanted.

Back on Xavier, while she herself was drunk and incapable (as her father had mentioned more than once), Esmay Suiza had survived the treachery of her captain, the mutiny that followed, and then saved everyone – including Brun – by blowing up the enemy flagship. Brun had followed the court-martial of *Despite*'s crew in the news; she had wondered over and over how that calm young woman with the flyaway hair managed to do it. She didn't look that special – but something in the expression, in the eyes that never wavered, caught at her.

And then the same young woman had been a hero again, in an adventure that seemed like something out of a storycube series . . . she had been outside a ship during FTL flight and survived; she had defeated another enemy. Once more her image filled the news viewers, and once more Brun had imagined meeting her . . . talking to her . . . becoming – she was sure they could become – friends.

When she'd learned that Esmay Suiza was coming here, to Copper Mountain – that she might even be in the same classes – she had been so certain that her luck was running true. Here at last was the woman who could help her be like that, help her combine her uncooperative past experiences into the self she wanted to be.

And now her father had ruined it. He had treated Suiza as a professional, worthy of respect; he had made it clear he thought Brun was a headstrong child. What would Esmay Suiza think now – what *could* she think, when the Speaker of the Grand Council, her own father, had presented her that way? It was impossible that Suiza could see her as a competent adult.

She would not let it be impossible. She would not let this chance go by. There had to be some way to convince Suiza that she was more than a silly fluffhead. Fluffhead made her think of Suiza's hair, which could certainly use some attention . . . maybe Suiza would be approachable on a girl-to-girl level first, and then she could prove what else she could do . . .

At the next main meal, a few hours later, Esmay returned to the mess, and sat with a tableful of jigs and lieutenants who had arrived the day before. She remembered a few of them from the Academy, but had not served with any of them. They knew of her recent exploits and were eager to discuss them.

'What's it like to fly a Bloodhorde raider?' asked Vericour, another lieutenant. In the six years since their graduation, he had gained several kilos and now sported a crisp red mustache.

'Fun,' said Esmay, knowing the expected response. 'Goes like a bat, even if you don't redline it.'

'Shielding?'

'None to speak of. And the weapons systems are amazing for its size. The interior's mostly weapons, very little crew space.'

'They must have lousy shooting, if they missed you—'

'They didn't shoot at us first,' Esmay said. 'After all, I was in *their* ship. They let us get close, and – poof.'

'Yeah . . . that's the way. What're you here for?'

'A whole string of things,' Esmay said. 'I'm changing to command track—'

'You mean you *weren't?*'

'No.' How to explain this one?

Vericour shrugged. 'That's Fleet Personnel for you. Take someone with a flair like yours and shove her into technical, just because they need more techs. They ought to recruit techs, if they want more.'

Esmay opened her mouth to explain it hadn't been Fleet's fault, considered the difficulty of the subsequent explanations, and nodded instead. 'Yup. So now they've let me into command track, and I have to play catch-up. All the stuff I missed—'

'They're not going to drag *you* through command psychology, and all that dorf?'

Esmay nodded.

'When you've actually commanded ships in battle? That's ridiculous.'

In sardonic chorus, everyone else at the table said 'No, that's regulations!' Vericour laughed, and Esmay along with him. She was enjoying herself, she realized, with people who were almost strangers, even without Barin. The discovery that she could enjoy herself like this was new enough that it still surprised her when it happened.

'You know, I heard the Speaker's daughter's here,' Anton Livadhi said, in a lower tone.

'Well, she's run through the whole of the Royal Space Service,' Vericour said. 'I suppose she's looking for new blood.'

Esmay said nothing; she could not say anything without revealing knowledge she wasn't supposed to have.

'Is it true she was floating around in a rockhopper's pod stark naked at Xavier?' Livadhi asked.

'Alone?' asked someone else Esmay didn't know.

'That's the story,' Livadhi said. 'My cousin – you know Liam, Esmay; he was on *Despite* – he said he heard from a buddy on the flagship that she got stewed and somehow ended up out there all alone. But Liam's a bit inventive; I figured Esmay would know if it really happened.'

'Why?' asked Esmay, buying time.

'Because they'd have put a young female officer with her, afterwards,' Livadhi said. 'I figured that would be you.'

'Not me,' Esmay said. 'I was busy doing scutwork on *Despite*. Never even saw her.' Until now, but that was another thing she couldn't tell them.

When she left the table, she glanced around but did not see Brun. Did the girl have meals alone somewhere? She pushed aside the thought that the girl might be lonesome. Brun Meager was not her problem . . . this course was.

2

At 0500 local time the next morning, Esmay shivered in the chill predawn breeze, much cooler than ship standard. The air smelled of growing things, and distance – sharply different from ship air. Some of the others sneezed, but Esmay sniffed appreciatively – it wasn't home, but some of the smells were the same.

Her shivering didn't last long once the exercise started. Esmay grinned to herself – she had always worked out faithfully, but some of these people had not, judging by the sounds they made. She was sweaty, but not exhausted, after an hour and a half; she had surprised herself by coming in fourth in the final run around the drillfield. In the distance, she had seen the irregular cliffs for which Copper Mountain was named emerge from predawn dimness to show the oranges and reds and ochres, when the sun hit them. Vericour was complaining loudly, but good-naturedly; she suspected it was mostly for effect. He didn't seem to be breathing any harder than she was, and it took breath to complain.

'When's your first class?' he asked, as they jogged back to quarters.

'Not class – testing,' Esmay said. 'They think I can test out of some things, to make room for others.' She hoped so; otherwise her schedule would be impossible.

They parted with a wave, and Esmay went in to shower thinking how different he was from Barin. He was older; he was her peer; he was pleasant and handsome . . . and about as exciting as a bowl of porridge.

That first day passed in a blur of activity. She tested out of some sections – she'd been told she probably would – Scan, as she expected, and Hull and Architecture, which she had not. She must've picked up more of that on *Koskiusko* than she'd thought. The military law segment concentrated on treason, mutiny, and conduct unbecoming . . . giving her an unfair advantage, she thought, but she wasn't going to complain. Administrative Procedures, though, was her downfall, along with tables of organization and command chains in areas where she'd never served.

'Your schedule's going to be all over the place,' the testing officer said, frowning. 'If you actually took both courses, back to back, you'd be here five standard months. You've placed out of about half the lower course, and a tenth of the upper . . . let's see now.' He finally produced a schedule that looked impossible for the first two weeks – though he claimed that two of the classes were no-brainers – and merely difficult for the next seven.

She had a few choices, and picked Search and Rescue Basic, and Escape and Evasion; they sounded more active than the optional staff support and administrative methods courses. Besides, she knew they were practical. She didn't want to end up in Barin's situation.

By the end of the first five days, Esmay felt settled in the academic routine. She was carrying about half again as many hours as her classmates, but the pace of instruction was much slower than it had been at the Academy. Early morning PT woke her up for the day's classes, and she didn't have to stay up too late to get all the work completed. Already some of the others had established a habit of going into Q-town when classes let out, eating there instead of in the mess hall. She was almost glad that her extra classes made that impossible for her; she had never socialized off-ship with other officers, and felt shy about it now. Many did not go into town every evening, and whenever she emerged from her room for a break, she would find someone ready to chat or play a quick game in one of the rec rooms.

Administrative Procedures was as dull as she'd feared, though she understood the importance of the course. She tackled it as she had tackled technical data in Scan or Hull Architecture, and found she could remember all the niggling little details even if she was bored by them.

Professional Ethics for Military Officers was another matter. She had started in eagerly, expecting – she wasn't quite sure what, but not what she got. Three lectures on personal relationships left her feeling unsure and guilty about her . . . friendship . . . with Barin Serrano. Example after example where a senior officer's pursuit had damaged, if not ruined, a junior's career. Examples of apparently innocent liaisons, which ended in grief for all concerned. She wondered if he was talking about one of her Academy classmates, a stunning blonde from the Crescent Worlds. She hadn't seen Casea since graduation, but she had heard that she had moved on from classmates to more senior officers.

And yet – the instructor had insisted – Fleet had neither the desire nor the power to prohibit close friendships and even marriage between officers. The standards governing such relationships were, according to the instructor, perfectly clear and reasonable. Esmay could recite them forwards and backwards, without knowing for sure if she and Barin had done anything wrong, or if going where they had talked about going was forbidden. She wished she had someone to ask about it.

To her relief, her Tactical Analysis class did not consider either the action at Xavier or the *Koskiusko* defense; along with her classmates, she plunged instead into a comparison of Familias and Benignity small-ship capabilities and battle performance.

'Lies, damn lies, and statistics,' muttered Vericour, her assigned partner. 'I hate statistical analyses of battles. It's more than just so many tons throw-weight—'

'Mmm . . .' said Esmay, extracting another set of figures from the archives. 'Did you know that the Benignity had better battle performance out of *Pierrot* than we did, after they captured her?'

'No! That's got to be wrong – none of their tacticians use maneuver the way we do—'

'Yup. Renamed *Valutis*, confirmed from salvage . . . their commander got five hits on *Tarngeld*, at extreme range.'

'Says who?' Vericour leaned over to look. 'Uh . . . you trust that scan data from *Tarngeld*?'

'Well . . . it's embarrassing to have to admit you were clobbered by a ship a third your mass, which used to be on your side, so I'd bet on its being accurate. Besides, according to the post-battle plot, nothing else was in that direction. My question is, what did they do to *Pierrot-Valutis* to make her that effective, and are they doing that to their other ships?'

'Wouldn't think so. They didn't at Xavier, did they?'

'Not that I know of, but . . . they had *Pierrot* for three years before she showed up in their lines.'

'Well, someone must've noticed that . . .'

'Yes, but did they apply it?' Esmay handed over the relevant bits. 'If the Benignity does whatever it did to that ship to others of the same size, we've got a new element to worry about.'

'Maybe. But if they could, they'd have used it at Xavier, wouldn't they?'

'I wish I knew what it was . . . it matters if it was some one-time thing that depended on some of our architecture—'

'One really good scan tech? Weapons tech?'

'Maybe,' Esmay said again. 'But if they've got one that good

398

they might have more. I think we ought to make this one of the main points of our presentation.'

'I'm not going to argue with the hero of Xavier and the *Kos*,' Vericour said, with a grin that took the sting out of it. 'It's not something I would have thought of. Maybe you are that smart.'

'I do my best,' Esmay said, grinning back. He wasn't Barin, but he was comfortable.

She was still thinking that when Vericour reached out and touched her hair. Esmay managed not to flinch, but she moved smoothly away.

'Sorry,' he said. 'I just . . . thought you might like it.'

So Barin wasn't the only man who could find her attractive . . . she didn't know whether she found that reassuring or just bothersome. At least she knew for sure that another lieutenant was within the limits allowed by regulations and the ethics class.

'I'm . . . not in the mood,' she said. She couldn't explain about Barin, or claim a preexisting relationship, not yet.

'If you ever are in the mood, just let me know,' Vericour said. 'I'll even swear on whatever you like that it's not just hero worship.'

She chuckled, surprising herself. 'I didn't think it was,' she said.

He grinned back, but made no more advances. That's what the manuals all said was supposed to happen, but she'd never had to deal with it before. She felt a small burst of surprise that the manuals were right.

A few days later, their presentation gained the highest rating in the class. Afterwards Vericour suggested a celebratory drink in Q-town, the little cluster of commercial establishments just outside the gates. 'You're certainly good luck,' he said. 'I hope we're on the same team for E and E. They say no one ever makes it all the way through the field exercise without getting captured, but you might be able to pull it off.'

'I doubt it,' Esmay said. 'The instructors know the terrain backwards and forwards. Just like natives.'

'Well – it would be more fun with you, anyway. So – will you come?'

'No – remember I'm taking extra classes, and I have a final in Admin Procedures tomorrow.'

'My sympathies.' Vericour bowed elaborately, and Esmay laughed. So he was no Barin – he was still fun to be around. She went back to her quarters and tore into the Admin Procedures material until long past her usual bedtime.

The next morning, she was surprised to see Brun Meager lining up for PT with the others. During the run, she moved up beside Esmay.

'Hi – I hardly ever see you.' She didn't sound out of breath at all.

'I've got a heavy schedule,' Esmay said. Unlike many, she actually enjoyed the run, but one of the things she enjoyed about it was sinking into a meditative state.

'So I noticed. This was the only thing I could take right now where we'd overlap, but I'm going to be in your Escape and Evasion course.'

'You?' Esmay glanced at her. Brun was taller; she loped along as if she could run forever, like one of the endurance horses.

'Well – if people are out to get me, I need to learn to get away.'

'I suppose.' She could also learn to let her security personnel guard her the way they were supposed to, and quit putting herself into dangerous situations. But that was for someone else to say.

'And I wanted to ask you – if we get a choice – I'd like to be on your team.'

Great. Just what she needed, a spoiled rich girl on her team. Esmay glanced at her again, and scolded herself. Brun might be spoiled but she was willing to work and learn – not every rich girl would pile out of bed at that hour to do PT with a lot of grumpy soldiers. Admiral Serrano had sponsored her; that had to be worth something. Rumor had it she didn't ask any favors in her classes, either.

'I don't know if we get a choice,' Esmay said. 'But if it's possible, it's all right with me.'

'If you ever wanted, we could go into Q-town together,' Brun said, an almost wistful note in her voice.

'No time,' Esmay said. Q-town held no attraction for her; if she wouldn't go with Vericour, she certainly wasn't going with a civilian.

'You don't ever go?'

Esmay shrugged. 'No – they have good steaks in the mess.'

'Um. And good steaks constitute your definition of entertainment?' That had a slight edge to it.

'No – but I wouldn't expect you to find much entertainment there either.'

'Well . . . I like a drink with friends now and then,' Brun said. 'Or a meal outside, just because it is outside.' They ran on a ways, and then she said. 'That redheaded lieutenant – Vericour. He's a friend of yours?'

'We were classmates,' Esmay said. 'And we've been assigned some problems together.'

'But you like him?'

'He's nice,' Esmay said. She couldn't figure out what Brun was driving at. Did she want an introduction? 'He goes to Q-town fairly often.'

'I know,' Brun said. 'I've seen him there with friends – I wondered why you didn't go.'

'Schedule.' It was harder to talk when she was used to solitude in the mornings. 'I've got a final this morning,' she said, hoping Brun would take the hint.

'What in?' Brun asked. As if she were really interested, which seemed unlikely.

'Administrative Procedures,' Esmay said.

'Sounds dull,' Brun said. 'But I guess I should let you review it in your head.'

That would have been nice, but they were almost back to the starting point. Esmay was glad she'd spent the extra hours the night before.

'There's going to be an ensign in our class,' Vericour said, as they headed toward the first of the Escape and Evasion classes.

'An ensign?' Esmay hoped her face didn't reveal anything. Barin had left a message saying he was down, but she hadn't seen him yet; she had back-to-back classes. 'So?'

'Well . . . this is a bit upper-level for an ensign, don't you think? But I hear he's a Serrano; that probably explains it.'

'Says he was on *Koskiusko*,' Vericour said. Esmay finally realized

401

he was fishing, and what he was fishing for. She wanted to strangle him.

'Let me see,' she said, and stopped at the next dataport to suck the class list. 'Oh . . . yes. Barin Serrano. I know him.' She hoped that was sufficiently casual. Her eye ran on down the list and got snagged on Brunhilde Meager. She had hoped someone would talk the girl out of this; the class was known to be dangerous, but there she was.

'And . . . ?'

She gave Vericour a glance that moved him back a half step. Good. 'And he's a fine junior officer – what more do you want?'

'Was he on your crew on the Bloodhorde ship?'

'No.' And she was not going to tell Barin's secrets, either; Vericour could find out for himself.

In the classroom, she saw Brun first; the tall blonde was leaning on a desk, surrounded by male officers, while her bodyguards stood by the wall, looking as blank as robots. She had, Esmay had to admit, an infectious laugh and a smile that lit up the room. Esmay moved to a seat midway up on the left side, and then spotted Barin, front row right, already seated and looking compact and composed.

Should she go up there? But she was already in her seat, and Vericour was in the next . . . it would be obvious if she moved. Barin turned, as if her glance were a warm hand on his neck, and spotted her. He smiled, nodded; she nodded in return. Enough for now; they could talk later. Although . . . certain paragraphs in the professional ethics lectures came back to her. They would have to be careful. They were not presently in the same chain of command, but she was senior enough that the relationship would be called 'not recommended.'

At the chime, the instructor came in; he looked as if he'd been slow-dried over a fire . . . the color of jerky and not any more extra fat. Lieutenant Commander Uhlis, his name was.

'Escape and evasion,' he said, without preamble. 'If you're lucky, you'll never need this course, but if you need it and haven't mastered it . . . you'll be dead. Or worse.' He glanced around the room, then his gaze rested on Barin.

'I understand that Ensign Serrano already has experience as a

402

captive,' Lieutenant Commander Uhlis said. 'But none at all in escape.' Esmay gave him a sharp look. His tone was ambiguous, edged in some way she could not yet determine.

Barin said nothing; the others had turned to look at him.

'It is the duty of a captured officer to attempt to escape, is it not, Serrano?' The edge was sharper, sarcasm at the least.

'Yes, sir.'

'Yet . . . you did not.'

'I did not escape, sir.'

'Did you even *try*?' Contempt now. Esmay could feel the tension in the room.

'Not effectively,' Barin said. 'Sir.'

'I would have thought a *Serrano* the equal of a few Bloodhorde thugs,' Uhlis said. 'Would you care to explain to the class your mistakes?' Put that way, it was not a request.

'Sir, I was careless. I thought the person I saw in the inventory bay, wearing a Fleet uniform with Fleet patches, was Fleet personnel.'

'Ah. You expected the Bloodhorde to be fur-clad barbarians carrying swords—'

'No, sir. But I didn't expect them to be laying an ambush in the inventory bay. As I said, sir, my carelessness.'

'And precisely how did they capture you, Ensign?'

Esmay could tell from the quality of Barin's voice that he was both angry and shamed. 'I was climbing an inventory rack – the Deep Space Repair has automated inventory racks some twenty meters tall, but the machinery had been shut off. Ship regulations required using safety harness and line, so I was clipped into the ladder I was climbing. The parts trays were far enough apart that someone could lie flat in them; when I climbed up that far, I found a gun to my head.'

'And did you struggle?'

'Yes, sir. But between the harness and the ones who grabbed my legs, and getting knocked unconscious, not effectively.'

'I see.' Uhlis eyed the rest of the class. 'The lesson here is that a moment's inattention – a brief lapse of caution – can and someday will result in your capture. The ensign thought that he was safe, aboard a Fleet vessel, even though he knew intruders had penetrated the ordinary defenses. He saw nothing, heard nothing, smelled nothing, felt nothing – and no doubt convinced himself that anything out of the ordinary was the result of the overall emergency situation. Someone else would take care of it. He is lucky to be alive, presumably only because his captors thought he might be useful that way.'

Uhlis paused, long enough that a discreet rustle indicated uncertainty among the other students. 'But the ensign did something right. Two things, in fact. He stayed alive, when it might have been easier to die. And he worked through his post-capture trauma properly, as his reactions just now proved.'

A hand shot up on the far side of the room. 'Sir – I don't understand.'

'Lieutenant Marden, I presume?'

'Yes, sir.'

'Kindly identify yourself next time. And haste, in this course, can get you killed. When you don't understand, *wait*. Be still. Listen. You might learn something that will save your life.'

Everyone was very still; Esmay found it hard to breathe. Even Brun had gone immobile, she noticed.

'But since I was going to explain anyway, I will now. Ensign Serrano could, no doubt, have changed his captors' decision to keep him alive, by being too much trouble, while not able to escape. From my understanding, having reviewed his debrief, he had no real opportunity to escape. Therefore, his duty was to stay alive, if possible, by not driving his captors to kill him. This he did, enduring physical abuse without losing control, making no threats, being as passive as possible. Second, he cooperated fully with remedial therapy. Some rescued captives cannot face what they consider the shame of such therapy; although they cannot evade a minimum requirement, they do not cooperate, and do not receive the benefit of it. Ensign Serrano, by all reports – and of course most of this is confidential, so I have only the output summary – cooperated completely, and his therapists were convinced that he had no residual psychological deficits.' Another pause, which no one interrupted.

'Some of you, no doubt, thought I was being rough on Ensign Serrano – sarcastic, critical. I was. I was testing for myself the validity of the therapists' report, before putting him through the trauma of this course, where any unresolved issues might make him a danger to himself and others. He passed *my* test. The rest of you . . . we'll just have to see about.' Uhlis turned to Barin. 'Ensign Serrano.'

'Sir.' The back of Barin's neck was no longer flushed.

'Congratulations.'

'Sir.' Barin's neck reddened again.

'I presume you've all read the introductory material for this class,' Uhlis said. His gaze scanned the classroom. Esmay had, as usual, read beyond the introductory assignment, but she judged from the uneasy shifting of some classmates that they had not. Uhlis glanced down at his display. 'Lieutenant Taras, please explain the legal difference between military capture and hostile seizure.'

Taras had been one of the wigglers, seated two down from Esmay. She rose to her feet. 'Sir, military capture is when a unit surrenders, and hostile seizure is when they're caught off-guard.'

'And the legal situation?'

'Well . . . one is surrender and one is – being caught.'

'Inadequate. I assume you did not read the assignment, is that correct?'

'Yes, sir.' Taras looked deservedly wretched.

Uhlis looked along the row. 'Lieutenant Vericour?'

Vericour stood. 'Sir, I read it, but I am not sure I understand – I mean, it's clear when someone is kidnapped from a space station while they're on leave or something, as compared with the surrender of personnel from a damaged ship.'

'Suppose you were sure that you were facing a situation of hostile seizure: what would be your legal position?'

'Sir, the Code says that I am to attempt escape by any means possible, assisting others to escape—'

'Yes . . . and what obligation do your captors have toward you?'

'If they're signatories to the Otopki Conference, which the Benignity of the Compassionate Hand and the Guernese Republic are, but the Bloodhorde are not, they are obliged to provide adequate life support and medical care . . .'

'Well enough. Lieutenant Suiza—' Vericour sat down, and

Esmay rose. 'Please define Ensign Serrano's situation in terms of the legal issue I've raised.'

'Sir, although Ensign Serrano was captured on board a Fleet vessel, his situation is more like a hostile seizure than military surrender. Since the Bloodhorde are not signatories to the Otopki Conference, they acknowledge no obligation to captives under any circumstances, but Familias law still holds them responsible.'

'Very well.' Uhlis nodded; Esmay sat down, and he turned his attention to someone else. In a few minutes, he had determined exactly who had read the assignment, and who had not – and who was inclined to be hasty or foolish. Brun was one of the latter, not to Esmay's surprise. Uhlis had just called on her, and found that she had not read the assignment either, and had told her it was even more important for her than for the others.

'I don't see why,' Brun said. Uhlis looked at her, a long considering look.

'Even a civilian, Ms. Meager, is expected to abide by the basic courtesies of the class. Please request permission to speak, and identify yourself, before blurting out your ignorance. Better still, listen a little longer and see if you can learn on your own.'

Brun's neck reddened, and Esmay could see the tension in her shoulders. But she said nothing more, and Uhlis turned to someone else. Esmay could not relax no matter whose behavior was under his harrow; she almost regretted choosing this class, except that Barin was in it.

Esmay's next class was just down the hall. Barin was there when she came out of the door. 'Lieutenant – good to see you again.' His eyes said more. Esmay felt a warm glow, as if she'd stepped into a spotlight.

'Morning, Ensign,' she said, being just as formal. She could feel Vericour's interested gaze on her back. 'Glad to be off old *Kos*?'

Barin grinned. 'They tell me they'll put me on a line ship after this – assuming I pass all the courses.' In his tone was the confidence of someone who always passed his courses.

'You passed the hardest, back on *Kos*,' Esmay said seriously. 'And Uhlis knows it.'

'I would have preferred things in the opposite order,' Barin said.

'Training before performance – though you did the same trick with command, only better.'

Brun appeared suddenly at Esmay's side. 'Hi there – introduce me, Lieutenant Suiza, to this most attractive young ensign. Unless, that is, you're keeping him for yourself.'

Barin flushed, and Esmay could feel her own ears heating up. With an effort, she forced a smile onto her face and said, 'This is Ensign Serrano . . . Ensign, this is Brun Meager.' She didn't have to give a pedigree; everyone knew it.

'You must be Admiral Serrano's grandson,' Brun said, practically shoving in front of Esmay. 'I heard a lot about you – do you have a few minutes?'

Esmay didn't – it was time for her next class. She ignored the desperate look Barin gave her and abandoned him to his fate. If he couldn't handle one dizzy blonde . . .

But she had trouble concentrating on tactics, for the first time in her life. Brun was beautiful, in a way she had never been beautiful, and she had that ability to attract almost anyone. Even Esmay had liked her, in spite of disapproving; it was impossible, it seemed, to stay distant from her. Naturally she would like Barin – charming, handsome, talented – and naturally Barin . . . she yanked her mind back to the lecture, and realized that Vericour had noticed her distraction, which made it even worse.

She made it through class after class, dragging her attention back again and again from the thought of Barin and Brun. If this was what love did, she told herself grimly, no wonder they cautioned officers against it. Back on *Kos* it had seemed simple: her feeling for Barin made her stronger, more confident, happier – and her performance had soared. But that was the first burst of feeling . . . this was something else, not helpful at all. Was he having the same problem? Would loving her destroy his chances to be the officer he could be? She tried to think what her therapist would have said, but none of the phrases she remembered helped at all.

At the evening meal, she was hunched morosely over her tray when a chair scraped at her side.

'Lieutenant?' It was Barin. She felt something clench and release in her chest.

'Ensign,' she said. She felt like crying; she choked that feeling back. 'Barin – how was your first day?'

'Interesting,' Barin said. He was grinning at her in obvious delight. 'You're looking good. When Uhlis started in on me, I wasn't sure what to do – but then I figured out what he was driving at.'

'I could have clobbered him,' Esmay said, startling herself with the fierceness of that. Hunger returned, and she took a bite of bread as if it were Uhlis's flesh.

'No—' Barin paused for a spoonful of soup. 'He was right, and I did make an interesting demonstration for the class. I would bet they don't have someone like me in every class – unless they import them especially.' He looked thoughtful a moment. 'I wonder if that's why I got this course. It's just devious enough—' He shook his head. 'But you – I hear you've been taking one course on top of another. Are you getting any sleep at all?'

She felt her ears going hot, even though she knew it was an innocent inquiry into her health. 'I'm doing fine, as long as I don't do much but study.'

'Oh, I wasn't going to interrupt you,' Barin said. 'I know this is important to you. I just hoped—'

'I know,' Esmay said, into her roast beef. 'I'm just – you know it's been awhile.'

'Ah.' Barin ate some peas, then something orange that had probably started life in the squash family. 'I saw you yesterday, when I came in. Going to some class – seems like you're getting along well with the other officers.'

'Trying to,' Esmay said. 'All that you told me about the difference in cultures – it helps. Though I still catch myself about to apologize or explain far too often.'

'Glad to be of service,' Barin said. 'I was going to ask—'

'Well,' said a voice from overhead. 'I hoped to find my favorite ensign for a dinner companion, but he's already engaged—'

Esmay nearly choked; Barin turned. 'Hello, Sera Meager . . .'

'Brun. Nobody calls me Sera Meager or Ms. Meager but people who want to keep me from doing things. You don't mind if I join you, do you? I promise my watchdogs will keep a respectful distance.'

408

'Of course,' Barin said; he stood while Brun found a seat across from Esmay, exactly where Esmay did not want those clear blue eyes.

'How did the exam go?' Brun asked Esmay, with apparently genuine interest. 'Administrative Procedures, wasn't it? Sounds deadly boring to me. Forms-filling, isn't it?'

'A bit more than that,' Esmay heard herself say, with unmistakeable coolness in her voice. She cleared her throat and tried again. 'Forms-filling is part of it, but then you have the decisions of which form, and to what office it should be sent. Filling it out correctly doesn't help if you've sent the wrong level of form, or sent the right form to the wrong office.'

'Deadly boring. My sympathies. I hope my heckling you that morning didn't hurt your performance.'

'No,' Esmay said. 'I did all right.'

'All right being number one in the class. Don't hide your light, Lieutenant,' Barin said.

'Good for you,' Brun said. 'Though I can't see you as a forms-filler, I suppose into every life a few forms must fall.'

Esmay could not stay annoyed, not with that combination of interest and goodwill beaming at her from across the table. 'I thought it was boring,' she said. 'But – it was a requirement.'

'So you topped out. What I'd expect. Are you sure you won't come into Q-town, the both of you, and celebrate?'

'I can't,' Esmay said. 'The Tactics final is in two days, and our workgroup is studying tonight and tomorrow night.'

'Well, then, Ensign – do you have a final coming up?'

'No, but—'

'Then you can come, surely? If you're not in Lieutenant Suiza's Tactics class, then she's not going to be spending time with you – not that she'd cradle-rob anyway.'

'I'm hardly an infant, Brun,' Barin said, before Esmay could say anything. 'But yes, I'll be your escort . . . since your watchdogs will be along to ensure my good behavior.'

Esmay watched them go with feelings not so much mixed as churned. She did have a Tactics study group meeting, but she had hoped for a few more minutes with Barin, in which she could ask him about his interpretation of the rules governing personal relationships between officers not of the same rank, or in the same chain of command. He had grown up in Fleet; he was used to the rules. If he thought there was nothing wrong, there probably wasn't anything wrong.

Barin eyed the Speaker's daughter as they walked through to the base gates. Dangerous waters, he told himself. Professional officers did not mix with Families; the shadowy aura of Undue Influence brooded over any such liaison. Still, common courtesy to a guest of the Fleet demanded that he accompany her . . . and her security detail.

He would much rather have talked to Esmay. They had things to discuss . . . and anyway, she looked tired, strained, and he wanted to help her, ease that strain. She had been trying so hard for so long; she was on the right track now, but . . . his fingers twitched, imagining the softness of her hair, the way he could soothe the tension from her neck.

'So . . . you knew Lieutenant Suiza on the *Koskiusko*?' Brun asked.

'Yes,' Barin said, brought back abruptly from his reverie.

'Is she always so . . . stiff?'

'Stiff? She's hardworking, professional—'.

'Dull,' Brun said. But her mouth quirked.

'You can't mean that,' Barin said.

She grinned at him. 'No, I don't mean that. But I wanted to meet her, talk to her, and she's always so . . . so upright and formal. Not to mention that she never seems to stop studying. She's at the top in just about every class – what more does she want?'

'What any of us wants,' Barin said. 'To be the best.' He was aware of his spine growing slightly more rigid, and wondered why.

'It's so different,' Brun said, in a thoughtful tone. 'I've been around Royal Space Service officers for years, and they're not like all of you.'

Because they weren't really military, but that was not something to say when Brun was being trailed by six of the Royal Security's finest.

'I don't know why all this is necessary,' Brun went on. 'Professional competence I can understand, but the rules are ridiculous.'

410

Barin managed not to snort. 'What rules are these?' he asked instead.

'Oh, you know. All this formality in class – standing when the instructor enters, and saluting all the time, and everything divided by rank.'

'There are reasons,' Barin said vaguely; he didn't feel like explaining millennia of military tradition to a privileged civilian who was in a mood to dislike it anyway. 'But if you don't like it, why did you come?'

'Admiral Serrano recommended it. Over my father's objections, in fact. She said I would benefit from the chance to develop my special talents in a controlled environment.'

'That sounds like a quote,' Barin said.

'You know Admiral – oh, that's right, you are a Serrano. So you also know Heris, I'd imagine?'

'Admiral Serrano is my grandmother; Commander Serrano is one of my cousins.' No need to go into that.

'Well, then, we'll be friends,' Brun said, taking his arm in a way that made him distinctly uncomfortable. 'Now let's go have some fun.'

Barin thought longingly of Esmay, hard at work no doubt in her quarters.

3

Brun had developed a habit of stopping by Esmay's quarters every day or so, for what she termed 'a friendly chat.' Esmay did her best to be polite, though she resented the time it cost her, and even more the fact that Brun seemed to consider herself qualified to comment on everything in Esmay's life.

'Your hair,' she said, on one of her first visits. 'Have you ever considered having it rerooted?'

Her hair had been an issue since childhood; before she could stop herself, she had run a hand over it trying to smooth it down. 'No,' Esmay said.

'Well, it would probably help,' Brun said, cocking her own gold head to one side. 'You've got quite nice bones . . .'

'I have quite a nice lot of work to do, too,' Esmay said. 'If you don't mind.' And was not sure which was worse, the insults or the casual way Brun slouched out, apparently not the least offended.

One evening, she arrived with Barin, who made some excuse and left, casting a lingering glance that Esmay wished she knew how to interpret.

'He's nice,' Brun said, settling herself on Esmay's bunk as if she owned it.

'More than nice,' Esmay said, trying unsuccessfully not to resent Brun's proprietary tone. Just what had Barin and Brun been doing?

'Handsome, courteous, clever,' Brun went on. 'Too bad he's only an ensign – if he were your rank, he'd be perfect for you. You could fall for him—'

'I don't want to "fall for" anyone in that sense,' Esmay said. She was uneasily aware that her ears felt warm. 'We're colleagues—'

Brun cocked an eyebrow. 'Is Altiplano one of those places where no one can talk about sex?'

Her ears felt more than warm; her whole face burned. 'One can,' she said between clenched teeth. 'Polite people, however, do not.'

'Sorry,' Brun said. She didn't look, or sound, very sorry. 'But it must make it hard to talk about people, and to people. How do you indicate . . . preference?'

'I had none,' Esmay said. That sounded bad, even to her. 'I left my home world quite young,' she added. That wasn't much better, but she couldn't think of anything that would help.

'Mmm. So when you met attractive young men – or women – you had only instinct to help you.' Brun buffed her fingernails on her vest, and examined them critically. 'And they say the men are the inarticulate ones.'

412

'You – that's – rude.'

'Is it?' Brun didn't sound concerned; she sounded arrogant. 'If it seemed so to you, I'm sorry. I didn't intend it that way. We don't have the same rules, you see.'

'You must have some,' Esmay said. Whatever they were, they didn't match Fleet's – or Altiplano's.

'Well . . . it would be rude to discuss the grittier bits with someone who was not a friend – or while eating.'

Despite herself, Esmay wondered what Brun might mean by 'grittier bits.'

'And,' Brun went on, 'it would be rude to comment on someone's genetic makeup as revealed in their – I'm not sure what term wouldn't offend you. Body parts? Equipment?'

'Genetic makeup!' This was not what she had expected; curiosity overcame outrage.

'Whether they're a Registered Embryo or not, and what the code is.'

'You mean that's . . . visible?'

'Of course,' Brun said, still in the superior tone that was raking Esmay's patience. 'There's the registration mark, and the code number. How else are you going to be sure–? Oh. You don't do that.'

'Well, I certainly don't have any registration marks or numbers on me,' Esmay said. The thought made her skin twitch, but curiosity was a worse torment. 'Where—?'

'Lower left abdomen,' Brun said promptly. 'Want to see?'

'No!' Esmay said, with more force than she intended.

'I didn't mean that,' Brun said, not specifying. 'But surely you *have* – I mean, you're older than I am.'

'What I do is none of your business,' Esmay said. 'And I plan to keep it that way.'

Brun opened her mouth and shut it again, then gave a little shrug that irritated Esmay as much as anything she might have said. She fished in one of her pockets and brought up a tangle of wire with a few plastic beads on it. 'Here – know what this is?'

'Haven't a clue,' Esmay said, glad to be off the topic of Barin.

'According to Ty, it's a good-luck charm. I thought it was a chunk of obsolete electronics.'

413

'Mmm.' Esmay gave the little object a better look, then grinned.
'What?' Brun asked.
'Well . . . it's a good-luck charm only under certain circumstances. That is – this is the sort of thing they gave us when we started the senior scan course. You were supposed to hang it up – did Ty mention that?'
'Yes – above my desk, from the lamp bracket.'
'Uh huh. What it is, underneath the distractions of bent wire and pretty beads, is a scan device. Along about week six, if you were doing your work, you would suddenly realize that it had been transmitting everything you did and said . . . and you'd look up – everyone did – and that picture of your sudden revelation went into the class scrapbook. The earlier, the better luck . . . they'd calculated the mean, and if you beat the mean, you got extra points, depending on how early you were.'
'You mean it's . . . spying on me?'
'Well, you knew you were under surveillance.'
'I hate it!' Brun flung herself down, in a gesture that reminded Esmay of a child's petulant flounce. Esmay was not moved.
'So? You agreed—'
'I agreed to have the stupid bodyguards around, not to have them putting illicit scan devices in my room. Damn them!'
Esmay felt much older than this spoiled girl. 'They're doing their job . . . and you're not making it easier.'
'Why should I?'
'Grow up!' It wasn't what she'd meant to say, but she had been thinking it, and she couldn't hold it back any longer. To her surprise, Brun whitened as if Esmay had hit her.
'I'm very sorry to have bothered you.' She was up and out the door before Esmay could say anything. Esmay stared at the shut door a long moment. Should she apologize? Altiplano manners demanding apology for almost everything quarrelled with Serrano advice not to apologize too much; she wished she could talk to Barin about it, but she had to finish the calculations for a project in support planning. She forced herself to concentrate on the work, with the consoling thought that perhaps Brun would no longer want to be on her team.

* * *

414

But that hope disappeared when the study team assignments came out. Brun had managed, by whatever means the daughter of the Speaker of the Grand Council could use, to get herself assigned to Esmay's team in the Escape and Evasion course. Esmay told herself that was unfair; it might not have taken any deviousness at all. Perhaps she'd just asked, and they'd given. Brun's demeanor gave no clue; she gave her usual impression of complete unconcern.

'Your problem today is to assess the security problem associated with moving a high-risk individual from this room' – Uhlis pointed at it on the diagram – 'to the shuttle port, which is here.' A map graphic came up on the screen. 'You have available the materials in the box on your table; you are briefing the head of the security detail in forty-five minutes. Go.'

The first thing to do, the class rules declared, was to open the envelope in the box and find out who was commanding this exercise. To Esmay's relief, it was neither Brun nor herself. Lieutenant Marden – who had, though hastily, at least read the first assignment – seemed to have a basic grasp of the topic so far, as he handed out the materials to Esmay, Brun, and Vericour. They all set to work, and their presentation won a passing grade, though not a high one. Brun's failure to recognize a potential threat dropped their score, and Uhlis was unforgiving.

'The point of working as a team is for all of you to combine skills and knowledge, not to hide in your own narrow area of responsibility. Any of the rest of you could have noticed that Sera Meager had ignored the possibility of an aerial attack on the motor route – and should have.'

Esmay felt the sting of that. She *had* wondered why Brun didn't mention it – and she had said nothing, since she was trying to arrange the resources she supposedly had, none of which included anything she knew could take out aircars. But Uhlis's greatest scorn fell on Lieutenant Marden, as their commander. By the time he was through, Esmay was afraid Marden would be in shreds on the floor . . . as it was, he disappeared rapidly after the lab, and showed up again only at dinner. Esmay took her tray to his table.

'I should've said something,' she said. 'I did wonder about air, but since I didn't have any resources to deal with an air attack—'

415

'That was in my packet,' Marden said. 'If and only if someone mentioned it, I could call for reinforcements. I thought that meant I couldn't mention it myself, but – as you heard – that's not what it meant at all.' He stared at his plate. 'I'm not really hungry. Sorry to lower your ratings average, though.'

'Don't worry about that,' Esmay said. 'I think we were all too worried about stepping on each other's territory. Wonder if all the other groups had the same problem.'

'Well, from what I hear, no one got a satisfactory, let alone a commended. But I feel really stupid.'

'I don't think—' began Esmay. But Vericour appeared at the table.

'Do you think we'll have the same teams for the field exercise?' He sat down before either of them answered. 'I hope not – getting the Speaker's daughter through it safely is going to make it harder on us.' He turned to Esmay. 'Harder on you, in particular.'

Esmay felt moved to defend Brun. 'I don't know – she has no military background, but she is smart and willing.'

'And just about demonstrates rashness, from what I hear.' Vericour reached for the condiment tray, and sprinkled galis sauce generously over his entire plate. Esmay sneezed as the sharp fumes went up her nose. 'Sorry – I forget what this can do to sensitive noses. Mine went years ago.'

'She is the Speaker's daughter,' Marden said, in a lower voice than Vericour had used.

'Well, yes. She's also a celebrity in her own right, so she can't expect not to be talked about. She's always on some newsflash or other. You know they have a team here covering her training.'

'She can't help that,' Esmay said. 'They're always after prominent people, and she is good-looking—'

'She's spectacular,' Vericour said. 'But I can't see her sneaking across anything unobserved, can you?'

'She got from Rotterdam back to Rockhouse Major—' Marden said.

'Yes, back when no one imagined a girl like that would work her passage on an ag ship. Now they know – and you can bet she won't do that again.' He turned back to Esmay. 'Do you follow the newsflashes, Esmay?'

'No,' Esmay said. She had never paid much attention to the gossipy newsflashes, with their emphasis on fashion and celebrity.

'Well . . . if you had, you'd have seen Brun Meager in everything from formal gowns to skinsuits, posing elegantly on a horse or lounging by a picturesque beach. Flatpics of her are probably in more lockers than anyone but actual storycube stars.'

Great. Someone else who thought she was astoundingly beautiful. Esmay could picture every flaw in that face and body – not that there were many.

'But except for the daring rescue of the most noble Lady Cecelia' – that sounded like a quote from someone's purple prose – 'nothing I've read suggests she had any real sense. So now we're stuck with her . . .'

'If the teams are the same,' Marden said. 'Maybe they aren't.'

'Maybe they aren't, but I'll bet Esmay ends up on the same team. They'll want to put another woman on her team, and who else would they put? Taras? Don't make me laugh. Taras wouldn't have a chance with Brun Meager. No, they'll put the best they have, and that's you, m'dear.' Vericour bowed, grinning. Esmay felt embarrassed. How could she deal with this? It did not help that Brun chose that moment to appear at their table.

'Won't do you any good to flirt with Suiza,' she said to Vericour, apparently apropos of the bow. 'But you could always flirt with me.'

Vericour spread his hands, rolled his eyes, and then mimed a swoon; everyone laughed but Esmay. It was funny, but she was too conscious of the vivid intensity next to her to enjoy it.

'Could I talk to you a bit?' Brun said, turning to her with a more serious expression than usual. Under the eyes of the others, Esmay had to say yes.

'I know I did something wrong, but not what . . . how could I arrange air cover when we didn't have any resources? And why should I have worried about it, when the information we were given didn't mention any such threat?'

A technical problem she could answer; Esmay quickly outlined the logic behind their low score. Brun nodded, apparently paying attention, and Esmay warmed to her again.

'So . . . even if there's no evidence to indicate a certain kind of threat, you still have to counter it?'

'You have to assume your intelligence is incomplete,' Marden put in. 'It always is.'

'But if you're too cautious, you can't get anything done,' Brun said. 'You have to act, even before you know everything—'

'Yes, but with an awareness of what you don't know, and its implications,' Esmay said.

'And it's not so much what you don't know, as what you think you do know – that's wrong – that will get you killed,' Vericour said. 'It's the assumptions – that no mention of an aerial threat means no aerial threat, or no mention of piracy in a sector means there are no pirates.'

'I see,' Brun said. 'I'll try to do better next time, but I have to say I'm better at reacting quickly than seeing invisible possibilities.'

When Esmay got up to leave, Brun trailed along instead of heading for the ball courts with the others, and Esmay sighed internally. She was tired already, and had at least four hours of studying to do; if Brun insisted on talking to her, she would be up late again, and her energy was running out.

'I know you're busy,' Brun said, as they got to Esmay's quarters. 'But this shouldn't take long, and I really don't know where else to go.'

This appeal cut through Esmay's worry about her classes. 'Come on in,' she said. 'What's wrong?'

'There's something wrong with Master Chief Vecchi,' Brun said.

'Wrong? What kind of wrong?' Esmay, her mind on their previous conversation, had been expecting a question about Fleet manners.

'Well . . . right in the middle of the lecture today, he suddenly didn't make sense. He was telling us how to secure a line on a derelict in zero gravity, and he got it backwards.'

'How would *you* know?'

Brun had the grace to blush. 'I read the book,' she said. 'His book, actually. *Safety Techniques in Space Rescue.*'

'It slipped his mind,' Esmay said. 'Everyone makes mistakes sometimes.'

'But he didn't know it. I mean, he went right on, explaining things wrong. When one of the jigs asked if he was sure, Vecchi blew up . . . then got very red, walked out, and when he came back, he said he had a headache.'

'Maybe—'

'It's not the first time,' Brun said. 'A week ago, he actually inserted a Briggs pin upside down.'

'Testing you?'

'No – it was his own line, and he was about to move on it when one of the junior instructors – Kim something. Tough little woman, about half my size but can haul me up one-handed. She did. Anyway, she noticed Vecchi's mistake and fixed it.'

'Um.' Esmay couldn't think why this was her problem, except that anything that bothered Brun was her problem.

'It bothered her, I could tell. She watched everything else he did, checked it all. Not the usual cross-checks, but as if he were a student.'

'How old is Vecchi?'

'What, are you thinking he's just gotten old? He's rejuved, I know that. One of the first enlisted rejuvs.'

'When?'

Brun looked disgusted. 'I don't have his medical records – how would I know?'

'I just wondered . . . maybe it's wearing off.'

'It doesn't work that way,' Brun said. Esmay raised her eyebrows and waited. 'My father,' Brun went on. 'He's rejuved, so is Mother. Their friends . . . so I naturally know how it works.'

'And?' Esmay prompted.

'Well, the usual reason for repeating a rejuv is physical. The people I know who've had more than one certainly didn't have any mental problems. Their personalities don't change, and they're just as alert.'

'But wasn't that earlier kind of rejuvenation associated with mental degeneration?'

'Only if you tried to repeat it.' Brun made a face. 'Mother's second cousin or something did that, and it was horrible. Mother tried to keep me away from her, but you know little kids . . . I thought there must be something special in that suite if they wanted me out of it, so I sneaked in.'

'So . . . is Vecchi anything like your mother's cousin?'

'Not . . . exactly. Not as severe, anyway. You don't suppose they made a mistake and gave him the wrong kind of rejuv procedure, do you?'

'I don't know. It would help if we knew more about rejuvenation, and also about the procedure used on Vecchi.'

'I thought you could do something, since you're in Fleet.'

Esmay snorted. 'Not dig into his personnel and medical records – I have no reason to see them, and it's against regulations to snoop.'

'Not even . . . unofficially?'

'No.' She would stop this right here. 'I'm not going to ruin my career to satisfy your curiosity. If Vecchi is impaired, someone in his chain of command will notice. If I observe something myself, I can report it. But I cannot – and will not – attempt to snoop in his records. You can report it, to – oh – whoever's commanding over there. Who's the senior instructor?'

'A Commander Priallo, but she's on leave somewhere.'

'Well, find someone else – whoever is her junior—'

'I'd think you'd care,' Brun said.

'I care—' If anything at all was wrong, but this was only Brun's word. 'But I have no right to intervene; this needs to go to his commander. I suppose you could tell the Commandant.'

'Maybe I will,' Brun said, and after a moment sighed and went out. Esmay put Brun's worries out of her mind and tackled her assignments.

When the field exercise team assignments came out the next day, she found Vericour was right. Brun was on her team, and she had the smallest team of all – because her security would have to come along. How would that work? Would they really let her be roughed up? Or would they interfere in the exercise. And what would that do to the scoring?

Meanwhile, Brun maintained an indecent level of energy and enthusiasm. She learned content as fast as anyone Esmay had ever known – Esmay wondered if her intellectual capacity had ever been pushed near its limit. She did not, however, seem able to learn the attitudes that were by now second nature to those young officers for whom they were not first nature. Reprimands slid off her impenetrable confidence; suggestion and example alike had no effect.

'She's a dilettante,' Vericour said, in another of those mealtime discussions. 'Though what else could we expect from someone of her background? But she takes nothing seriously, least of all Fleet culture.'

Anton Livadhi, a cousin of the Livadhi with whom Esmay had served on *Despite*, shook his head. 'She takes us seriously enough . . . but she's not one of us, and she knows it. She wants us to be serious, while she has fun.' He had his own team for the field exercise, and they were well up the chart on the evaluations for the preliminary exercises. Esmay's team performance was only middling; Brun fluctuated between brilliant and maddening, and her security could not commit emotionally as team members were supposed to do, and still be guards. They had taken almost twice as long as the fastest team in several exercises.

Esmay began to dread the field exercise itself, four days of intense and dangerous work in the badlands west of the base. She was reasonably sure that Brun's guards wouldn't let her be killed, but that left her and Jig Medars to do the work of an entire team. Two days before the exercise, she left a lecture on ship systems maintenance and found a message on her personal comunit: Lieutenant Commander Uhlis wanted to see her at her earliest convenience. Since she had an hour between classes, that meant right now.

She could hear the angry voices from ten meters down the corridor; Uhlis's door was ajar.

'You have to see that it's impossible.' Uhlis sounded annoyed.

'Why?' Brun sounded more than annoyed; Esmay paused, wishing the door had shut firmly.

'Because you're already the target of assassins. The field exercise is by nature dangerous, and it's also impossible to secure. All it would take is one person – just one, with the right skills – to pick you off.'

'You mean to tell me that on a base covered with Fleet personnel, you can't even let me do a simple field exercise?' Scorn in that, as if Brun expected to shame Uhlis into changing his mind. That wouldn't work.

'I mean we will not approve it. Nor will your father; I have already forwarded our decision, and our reasons for it, to him. He agreed.'

'That's – that's – the stupidest thing I ever heard!' Brun's voice had gone up another notch. 'If I'm a target for terrorists, then it's perfectly clear that escape and evasion is exactly what I need to know. What am I supposed to do if I get kidnapped and need to escape?'

'The escape segment will be available – at least the urban end . . .'

'Fine. So I've broken out of some provincial jail somewhere and have to cover a hundred kilometers to a safe haven, and I have no training?'

'According to your father, you have had ample training in the basics of survival and navigation in the field, both on Sirialis and on Castle Rock. Your field skills are, in his opinion and those of our instructors who reviewed the recordings, equivalent to those of most graduates. So the escape segments should fill out your skills very well.'

Silence for a moment. Esmay wondered if she could just walk past the door now, but even as she moved, Brun stormed out, silent but obviously in a rage. She broke stride when she saw Esmay.

'You will not believe ——!' she began.

'Excuse me,' Esmay said, not wanting to hear it all again. 'I overheard a little, and I have an appointment.' Brun's eyes widened, but she moved aside. Esmay edged past Brun and into the office, where a grim-faced Commander Uhlis looked ready to melt bulkheads with his glare. 'Sir, Lieutenant Suiza reporting—'

'Close the door,' he said.

'Yes, sir.' Esmay shut the door firmly, aware of Brun hovering outside.

Uhlis took a deep breath, then another, and then looked at her with less intensity. 'I wanted to talk to you about your team assignment,' he said. 'If you overheard much of that' – he nodded at the door – 'then you know we have concerns about security. Up until last night, we still had orders to accommodate Meager and include her in all the courses, including the field exercise. However, since we now have permission from the highest levels to exclude her and her bodyguards, we need to rearrange team assignments. We're going to split the exercise, and you'll be assigned to a new team, acting commander.' He gave her a dangerous smile. 'I understand you do very well at motivating strangers, Lieutenant.'

So the camaraderie she'd built up with her team over the past week would be no use to her – and the team she went to might well resent losing its familiar commander. But at least she wouldn't have Brun to worry about.

'Thank you, sir,' she said.

'Thank me afterwards,' he said. 'If you can. Remember, your score depends on not only your own successful evasion, but how many of your team make it.'

Her new team waited for her in the afternoon skills exercise. They had a bored, wary look . . . they were, she realized, the team that Anton Livadhi had led. And Anton had remarked, just too audibly, that he had his doubts about the source of Suiza's success. 'Serrano pet' was a phrase she'd been meant to overhear; she had ignored it, but these people hadn't. Two other women, four men; she ran the names over quickly in her mind. All but one had been in her class in the Academy, but she hadn't seen any of them for years, and she hadn't been close to them even then.

That afternoon's exercise was deceptively simple. From a scatter of raw materials, improvise a way to cross a series of 'natural' barriers. Each obstacle required not only teamwork but also innovative thinking . . . none of the poles were long enough, none of the ropes strong enough, none of the assorted other objects were obviously meant for the tasks at hand. Esmay tried being forthright and cheerful, as recommended in the leadership manual, but only some of her new team responded. Lieutenant Taras was inclined to be pettish if her ideas were not accepted the first time; Lieutenant Paradh and Jig Bearlin could always think of ways for things not to work. By the time the period was over, they had completed only four of the five obstacles. Esmay was aware of the frowning instructor, ticking off points on his chart.

This team had been ranked first or second in every exercise; now they wouldn't be.

It was possible to request overtime, though it was rarely done because it imposed a twenty percent penalty on the entire score. Esmay raised her hand; Taras made a sound that might have been a groan. Esmay rounded on her. 'We are going to finish this, Lieutenant, if we have to stay here all night—'

'We can't *win*,' Bearlin said. 'We might as well take the eighty percent we've got—'

'And when you need that other twenty percent of experience, where are you planning to get it?' Esmay asked. 'We're completing this exercise, and we're doing it now.'

She expected more resistance, but despite some sidelong grumpy looks, they tackled the final obstacle with more energy than they had any of the others. Five minutes later, they had solved the problem – and although Esmay halfway expected them to dump her in the mud, they got her over the pit with the same care they expended on each other.

'Good choice,' the instructor told them afterwards. 'You wouldn't have got eighty percent before – you were about as effective as a jug of eelworms – but you've got it now.'

By the time they got back to the mess hall, Esmay felt she had a chance with this group – a slim chance, but a real one. If only she'd had a few more days before the field exercise.

The next day's prelims went better; her new team seemed willing to work together again, and they were back up to third in the daily ratings. Esmay went to her quarters to pack her gear for the field exercise, and try to snatch a few hours of sleep before time to leave.

She had everything laid out on her bunk when her doorchime rang. Stifling a curse, she went to open it. Barin might have stopped by, though she'd hardly seen him for days, except with Brun. She hoped it was Barin. But instead it was Brun, and a very angry Brun at that.

'I suppose you're proud of yourself!' Brun said first.

'Excuse me?' What was the girl talking about?

'You never did want me on your team; you haven't liked me from the beginning.'

'I—'

'And now you've made sure I can't do the field exercise, so you can take over a top team . . .'

'I did not,' Esmay said, beginning a slow burn. 'They just assigned me—'

'Oh, don't be stupid,' Brun said, flopping onto the bunk and making a mess of Esmay's careful arrangement. 'You're the heroic Lieutenant Suiza – they want you to shine, and they've arranged it. Never mind what it does to other peoples' plans . . .'

'Like yours?' Esmay said. She could feel her pulse speeding up.

'Like mine. Like Anton's. Like Barin's.'

'Barin's!'

'You know, he's really quite fond of you,' Brun said, idly prodding a stack of concentrate bars until they collapsed. Two slid off onto the floor. Esmay gritted her teeth and picked them up without comment. She did not want this. 'I was trying to find out why you're such a cold fish, and I thought he might know – and I'll bet you didn't even know the poor boy's half in love with you.'

Didn't she . . . ? Esmay contemplated for a moment the probable result of pulling out Brun's tousled gold curls by the roots.

'Of course, such an upright professional as yourself would never stoop to dally with mere ensigns,' Brun went on, in a tone that could have removed several layers of paint from a bulkhead. 'He, like the rest of us, is far beneath your notice – unless someone gets in your way.' This time she picked up a water bottle and opened and shut the spout.

'That is not fair,' Esmay said. 'I didn't have anything to do with your being taken out of the field exercise—'

'I suppose you want me to believe you support me?'

'No, but that's not the same thing. It wasn't my decision to make.'

'But if it had been—' Brun gave her a challenging glare.

'It wasn't. What might have been doesn't matter.'

'So true. You *might have been* a friend; you *might have been* Barin's lover; instead—'

'What do you mean "might have been" someone's lover?' Even

425

as angry as she was, she could not say Barin's name in that context. Not to this woman.

'You don't expect him to hang around worshipping your footsteps forever, do you? Just in case you might come down from your pinnacle and notice him? Even a bad case of hero worship yields at last to time.'

This was her worst fear, right here and now. Had it been only hero worship? Was it . . . over?

'And you, of course, were right there to help him over this unwarranted fixation . . . ?'

'I did my part,' Brun said, flipping out the gold curls with a gesture that left no doubt what she meant. Esmay had an instant vision of them strewn about the room, little gold tufts of hair like fleece on the shed floor after shearing. 'He's intelligent, witty, fun, not to mention incredibly handsome – I'd have thought you'd notice—'

A light of unnatural clarity seemed to illuminate the room; Esmay felt weightless with pure rage. This . . . *this* to be pursuing Barin. *This* to displace her, to ruin her relationship with Barin. A young woman who boasted openly of her sexual conquests, who refused to abide by any rules, who claimed to be unafraid of rape because 'it's just mechanics; and aside from that, no one can make me pregnant.' She was like Casea Ferradi, without Ferradi's excuse of a colonial background.

Hardly conscious of what she was doing, she reached out and lifted Brun off the bunk, and set her against the wall, as easily as she could have picked up a small child.

'You . . . ' She could not say the words she was really thinking; she struggled to find something hurtful enough. 'You playgirl,' she said finally. 'You come bouncing in here, all full of your genetically engineered brains and beauty, showing it all off, playing with us – *playing* with the people who are risking their lives to keep you and your wonderful family alive and safe.'

Brun opened her mouth, but Esmay gave her no chance; the words she had longed to say came pouring out.

'You wanted to be friends, you said – what did you ever do but get in my way, take up my time, and go lusting after anyone who caught your fancy? It never occurred to you that some of us have a job to do here – that peoples' lives, not just ours, will depend on how we do it. No. You want to go play in Q-town, someone should go with you . . . it doesn't matter to you if that means learning less. After all, what does it matter if you pass a course or flunk it? It's not your life on the line. You don't care whether you ruin Barin's career or not—' Not the way she herself cared; not the way she agonized over it. 'You think your money and your family make it right for you to have anyone you want.'

Brun was white to the lips. Esmay didn't care. Her anxiety about the next day, her exhaustion from weeks of extra work – all had vanished, in righteous rage. 'You have the morality of a mare in heat; you have no more spiritual depth than a water drop on a window. And someday you will need that, and I promise you – I promise you, Miss Rich and Famous – you will wish you had it, and you will know I'm right. Now get out, and stay out. I have work to do.'

With that, Esmay yanked the door open; she was ready to shove Brun out, but Brun stalked past her, under the eyes of her waiting security, who carefully looked at neither of them. The doors were not made to slam, or Esmay would have slammed hers. As it was, she restacked her gear with shaking hands, packed it, set it aside, then lay unsleeping on her bunk to wait for the alarm.

4

Brun stalked along the streets of Q-town trying to push her anger back down her throat. That sanctimonious little prig . . . that prissy backcountry *chit* . . . her family probably slopped hogs in their bare feet. Just because she herself had grown up rich, just because she could talk about sex without squinching her face up—!

427

In one corner of her mind, she knew this was unfair. Esmay was not an ignorant girl, but an accomplished older woman. Not much older, but an Academy graduate, a Fleet officer, a combat veteran – Brun would have been glad to have Esmay's experience. She wanted Esmay's respect.

But not enough to turn into a frumpy, tight-buttoned, sexless, joyless . . .

Esmay wasn't joyless, though.

Brun didn't want to be fair. She wanted to be angry, righteously angry. Esmay had had no right to ream her out like that, no right to say she had no moral sense. Of course she had moral sense. She had rescued Lady Cecelia, for one thing. Even Esmay granted that. Aside from the requisite helling around that all the people in her set went through in adolescence, no one had ever accused her of being immoral.

She hunted through her past, finding one instance after another in which she had acted in ways she was sure Esmay would approve . . . not that it was any of her business. She had protected that little Ponsibar girl at school, the one who had arrived so scared and so easy to bully. She had told the truth about the incident in the biology lab, even though it had cost her a month's detention and the friendship of Ottala Morreline. She had been polite to Great-Aunt Trema even when that formidable old lady had regaled guests at the Hunt Ball with tales of 'little Bubbles' cavorting naked in the fountain as a toddler. She'd had to fight off entirely too many of her schoolmates' brothers after that one, but she hadn't turned against Aunt Trema. She and Raffa on the island . . . they had saved each others' lives.

She could not, however, find something to plaster over all the accusations. Well . . . so what? Her standards were different; that didn't mean she had none. Just as her inner voices began to talk about that, she decided she was thirsty, and turned into one of the bars that lined the street.

DIAMOND SIMS, the sign read. Brun assumed it referred to fake diamonds, with an implication of world-weariness. Inside, the tables and booths were full of men and women who might as well all have been in uniform as in the mostly-drab shipsuits now the favorite casual wear for the military. The way they sat, their gestures . . . all revealed their profession. A few – less than a third – were in uniform. She didn't see any of the students from the courses here – not that she'd know any but those in her own section, anyway. But she hadn't wanted to see anyone she knew, anyone who would wonder where her bodyguards were. She wanted new faces, and a new start, and new proof that she was who she thought she was.

With that in mind, she edged past crowded tables to the one double seat empty toward the back. She sat down, and touched the order pad on the table – Stenner ale, one of her favorites – and put her credit cube in the debit slot. She glanced around. On the wall to her right were framed pictures of ships and people, and a display of little metal bits arranged in rows. A faded red banner hung up in the far corner; she could not make out the lettering from where she sat.

A waitress deposited her frosted mug and the bottle of ale, and gave her a saucy grin. 'What ship, hon?'

Brun shook her head. 'I'm on a course.' The waitress looked slightly surprised, but nodded and went on her way to deliver the rest of the tray to another table. Brun poured her ale. Behind her, she heard the dim confused sound of voices, and realized that there was another room – apparently private – adjoining the main room. And on her left, the long bar, the same matte black as the stuff covering ships' hulls . . . could it possibly be a section of the same material? Above it, suspended from the high ceiling, were ship models. Brun recognized the odd angular shape of a mine-sweeper among the more ordinary ovoids of the warships. And behind the bar, the expected mirrors were framed with . . . her eyes widened. She knew enough about ordnance now to recognize that every frame had once been part of a functioning weapon. In a quick glance around the room, she saw more and more . . . it was as if the inside of the bar were made of the salvaged pieces of wrecks.

She felt the hair rising on the back of her neck, on her arms. It wasn't real – it could not be real – no one would really . . . but her eye snagged on a display at the near end of the bar. *Paradox*. That name – she could not forget that name. And here was a plate – an ordinary dinner plate, its broad rim carrying the same dark-blue

429

chain design she'd seen on all the dinnerware aboard Admiral Serrano's ship, with the four lozenges that had surrounded the name *Harrier*. Here, the design inside the lozenges was slightly different . . . and the plate, sitting on a stand she was suddenly sure had been made of other debris, was brightly lit by a tiny spot that also illuminated the label, for those who were too far away to see the lozenges. Beside it was a stack of crockery.

Brun looked at the mug holding her ale, suddenly feeling almost sick. Had she been drinking from . . . ? No, it wasn't *Paradox*. But now that its frosting had melted, she could see it was etched with some design. She squinted slightly. R.S.S. *Balrog*.

She had been drinking from dead men's cups. She was sitting on . . . a seat made from salvaged bits . . . and what bits? Her elbows rested on a table made of . . . she wasn't sure what, but she was now sure it was something that had been part of a living ship, and had been salvaged from a wreck. She looked for clues – and there, in a dull-finished plaque set into the tabletop next to the menu screen, she found it. R.S.S. *Forge*, enlisted bunk 351. A tiny button to one side caught her eye; she pressed it.

The menu screen blanked, replaced by a historical note: R.S.S. *Forge* had been lost thirty-two years before, in combat with a Benignity strike force; all hands had died. This fragment had been salved twenty-eight years ago, and identified by the stamped part number (still on the underside of the table); at the time of the ship's death, enlisted bunk 351 had been assigned to Pivot Lester Green.

The table's pedestal, the note went on, was formed of a piece of shielded conduit from the same ship; the two chairs were both from *Forge*, but one was from the enlisted mess and the other had been that of the senior weapons tech serving the aft starboard missile battery. The five people who had taken that position during *Forge*'s final battle were all listed: Cpl. Dancy Alcorn, Sgt. Tarik Senit, Cpl. Lurs Ptin, Cpl. Barstow Bohannon, Sgt. Gareth Meharry.

Brun's breath caught. Bad enough that all the names were listed, real people who had lived real lives and died a real death. But Meharry . . . she had known Methlin Meharry . . . was this a relative? A . . . parent? Aunt? Uncle?

Each name was linked, she realized, to some other information. She didn't want it; she didn't want those names to be any more real than they already were. But Meharry – she had to know. She activated the link.

Gareth Meharry had been twenty-six when he died; his family tree, spread across the screen, with Fleet members in blue, was more blue than gray. His parents (both now deceased, one in combat) had been Fleet; of his four sibs, two were active-duty Fleet, and two were married to Fleet members. Methlin Meharry was his sister . . . hard to think of that tough veteran as anyone's sister. One of his nieces – her niece too – was named after her. So there would be another Methlin Meharry someday, and with both parents, and aunts and uncles, in Fleet, there was every chance that she would go into Fleet.

Sudden curiosity – and an escape from the weight of tragedy that was making it hard to concentrate – sent Brun back to the main menu. Sure enough, below the lists of drinks and food, she found data access choices. From this table, she could check on the publicly accessible records of anyone in Fleet.

Esmay – she wondered if there were other Suizas in Fleet. She entered the name and waited. Up on the screen came only one name, and Fleet's choice of data for public consumption. Name . . . she had not known that Esmay's full name was Esmay Annaluisa Susannah Suiza. Planet of origin: Altiplano. Family background . . . Brun caught her breath. In a few crisp sentences, she was informed that the Suiza family was one of the three most prominent on Altiplano . . . that Esmay's father was one of the four senior military commanders . . . that her uncles were two of the others, and that the fourth was considered to be a Suiza choice. That the military influence on Altiplano's government was 'profound.'

Brun tried to tell herself that a senior military commander on a backwater planet was nothing special – her father's militia, back on Sirialis, was just a jumped-up police force. Its commander, though given the title 'General,' had never impressed her as the regulars of Fleet did. But Altiplano . . . she read on . . . had no Seat in Council. It had no Family connections at all. Which meant – she wasn't sure what, but she suspected that a General Suiza had a lot more power than old General Ashworth.

431

Of Esmay herself, there was little: a list of her decorations, with the citations that went with them. Conspicuous gallantry. Outstanding leadership. Outstanding initiative. A list of the ships she'd served on. Her present assign-ment, to Training Command's Junior Officer Leadership Course.

Well. Brun sat back, aware of tension in her neck and shoulders, the feeling that she'd got herself in well over her head in more than one way. She returned the screen to its default, and thought of ordering a snack. But it would come on a plate from some wrecked ship. She didn't think she could face that. As it was, she already had tears in her eyes.

'Something wrong?' asked a deep voice behind her. She turned.

He was stocky, heavy shoulders thick with muscle; his bald head, like Oblo's, deeply scarred. His eyes were scarcely higher than hers; he was in a hoverchair. Brun kept her eyes from dropping to see why with an effort – but that gave him a clear look at her face.

Out of the scarred face, brown eyes observed her with more insight than she liked. His wide mouth quirked.

'Lady, you're not Fleet, and you don't know what you've gotten yourself into, do you?'

The 'lady' threw her off-stride for a moment. In that pause, he jerked his head toward the farthest angle of the back.

'Come on over here, and let's get you sorted out,' he said. She was moving before she realized it, compelled by something in his voice. His hoverchair turned, and slid between the tables; Brun followed.

Two tables away, someone called, 'Hey! Sam!' He turned his head slightly – he could not, Brun realized, turn it all the way – and raised a hand but did not answer. Brun followed him and found a half-booth: enclosing bench and table, with space on the other side for his hoverchair.

'Sit,' he said. Then, over his shoulder to a waitress, 'Get us a pair of Stenners, and some chips.' His gaze returned to Brun, as disturbing as ever.

'I'm not really—' Brun began.

'That much I know already,' he said, humor in his tone. 'But let's see what you are.' He ticked off points with a stubby finger

432

that looked as if it had been badly moulded of plastic. 'You're Thornbuckle's daughter, according to your credit chip, and according to the class list over there—' He jerked his head in the direction of the Schools. 'You're Brun Meager, choosing to use your mother's family name. Target of assassination attempts—' Brun noted the plural and wondered how he knew. 'By your instructors' reports, physically agile and strong, bright as a new pin, quick learner, gifted with luck in emergencies. Also emotionally labile, argumentative, arrogant, stubborn, willful, difficult. Not officer material, at least not without a lot of remedial work.'

Brun knew her face showed her reaction to that. 'And why not?' she asked, trying for a tone of mild academic interest.

He ignored the question and went on. 'You're not Fleet; no one in your bloodline's been Fleet for over two hundred forty years. You come from a class where social skills are expected in a normal person your age. Yet you come into a Fleet bar—'

'There's nothing *but* Fleet bars in Q-town,' Brun muttered.

'And not only a Fleet bar,' he went on, 'a bar with special connotations, even for Fleet personnel. Not all of them will come here; not all of them are welcome here. I've seen kids with what you would call no social background at all come through the door and recognize, in one breath, that they don't belong here. Which makes me wonder, Charlotte Brunhilde Meager, about someone like you *not* noticing.'

Brun glared at him. He gazed back, a look neither inviting nor hostile. Just . . . looking . . . as if she were an interesting piece of machinery. That look didn't deserve an answer, even if she'd had one, which she didn't. She didn't know why she'd ducked into this doorway instead of another. It was handy; she'd wanted a drink; when the thought of a drink and a doorway offering drinks overlapped, she went in. Put that way it didn't sound as if she were thinking straight, but she didn't want to think about that. Not here; not now.

'You know, we've got security vid outside,' the man said, leaning back a little. 'When your cube ID popped up on my screen, I ran back the loop. You were stalking along the street like someone with a serious grievance. Then you hitched a step, and turned in here, with just a glance at the sign. Anyone tell you about this place?'

'No.' Even to Brun's present mood, that sounded sulky, and she expanded. 'I was given a list of places that catered to various specialties, mostly sexual. They have a code of light patterns in the windows, the briefing cube said. Anything else was general entertainment.'

'So, just as it seemed on the vid, you were in a rage, thought of getting a drink, and turned into the first bar you saw.' His mouth quirked. 'Really high-quality thinking for someone of your tested intelligence.'

'Even smart people can get mad,' Brun said.

'Even smart people can get stupid,' he replied. 'You're supposed to have a security escort at all times, right? And where are they?'

Brun felt herself flushing again. 'They're—' She wanted to say *a royal pain*, but knew that this man would think that childish. Everyone seemed to think it was childish not to want half a dozen people lurking about all the time, looming over private conversations, listening, watching, just . . . being where she didn't want them to be. 'Back at the Schools, I suppose,' she said.

'You sneaked out,' the man said, with no question at all in his voice.

'Yes. I wanted a bit of—'

'Time to yourself. Yes. And so you risk not only your own life, which is your right as an adult, but you risk their safety and their professional future, because you wanted a little time off.' Now the scorn she had sensed was obvious in his expression and his tone. Those brown eyes made no excuses, for himself or anyone else. 'Do you think your assassin is taking time off, time to have a little relaxation?'

Brun had not thought about her assassin any more than she could help; she had certainly not thought about whether an assassin kept the same hours as a target. 'I don't know,' she muttered.

'Or what will happen to your guards if you get killed while they're not with you?'

'I got away from them,' Brun said. 'It wouldn't be their fault.'

'Morally, no. Professionally, yes. It is their job to guard you,

434

whether you cooperate or not. If you elude them and are killed, they will be blamed.' He paused. Brun could think of nothing to say, and was silent. 'So . . . you got mad and barged in here. Ordered. Started looking around. Noticed the decor—'

'Yes. Pieces of ships. It's . . . morbid.'

'Now that, young lady, is where you're wrong.'

Faced with opposition, Brun felt an urge to argue. 'It is. What's the point of keeping bits of dead ships, and – and putting peoples' names on them, if not morbid fascination with death?'

'Look at me,' the man said. Startled, Brun complied. 'Really look,' the man said. He moved the hoverchair back a little, and pointed to his legs . . . which ended at what would have been mid-thigh. Brun looked, unwillingly but carefully, and saw more and more signs of old and serious injury.

'No regen tanks on an escort,' the man said. 'It's too small. A buddy stuffed me in an escape pod, and when old *Cutlass* was blown, I was safely away. By the time I was picked up, there was no way to regrow the legs. Or the arm, though I chose a good prosthesis there. They'd have given me leg prostheses too, but I had enough spinal damage that I couldn't manage them. Now the head injuries—' He dipped his head, showing Brun the scars that laced his head. 'Those were from another battle, back on *Pelion*, when part of a casing spalled off and sliced me up.'

He grinned at her, and she saw the distortion of one side of his mouth. 'Now you, young lady, you don't have a clue what using part of *Cutlass*'s hull as my bar means to me. Or to any of the men and women who come here. What it means to have crockery from *Paradox* and *Emerald City* and *Wildcat*, to have cutlery from *Defence* and *Granicus* and *Lancaster*, to have everything in this place made of the remnants of ships we served on, fought on, and survived.'

'I still think it's morbid,' Brun said, through stiff lips.

'You ever killed anyone?' he asked.

'Yes. As a matter of fact, I have.'

'Tell me about it.'

She could not believe this conversation. Tell him about the island, about Lepescu? But his eyes waited, and his scars, and his

435

assumptions about her ignorance. Which of these finally drove her to speak, she could not have said.

'We – some friends and I – had taken an aircar to an island on Sirialis. It's a planet my father owns.' She didn't like the sound of that, now; she wasn't boasting, but it sounded like it. He didn't react. 'We didn't know that there were . . . intruders. A man – he was a Fleet officer—'

'Who?'

She felt a reluctance to answer, but could think of no way to avoid it. 'Admiral Lepescu.' Was there a reaction? She couldn't tell. 'He and some friends – at least, I was told they were friends – had transported criminals . . . well, not really criminals, but that's what they said . . .' He shifted, with impatience she could almost feel. 'Anyway,' she said, hurrying now, 'he and his friends transported these people to the island, to hunt. To hunt them, the supposed criminals. Lepescu and his friend stayed on a nearby island, which had a fishing lodge on it, and flew over every day to hunt. The hunted had cobbled together some kind of weapon, and shot down our aircar, thinking we were Lepescu. They captured us. When they realized their mistake, we realized that we would all be hunted; Lepescu would try to cover up his crimes.'

'And no one knew he was on this planet?' The man's voice conveyed his disbelief.

'Dad found out later that one of his station commanders had been bribed. There was so much traffic in the system – it was the height of hunting season, with lots of guests coming and going – that the others had not noticed an extra ship at one station.'

'Umph.' Disbelief still in that, but a sharp nod made Brun go on with her story.

'So Raffa and I went off to an old hideout I remembered from childhood,' Brun said. She felt herself tense, felt the fine sweat springing out on her skin. She didn't like thinking about that night or the next days. She rattled through the story as fast as possible: how she and Raffa had each killed one of the intruders and acquired their weapons, the discovery that the intruders had poisoned the water, their flight to the cave, and the final confrontation in the cave when Lepescu had been killed by Heris Serrano.

The man's expression changed at the mention of Serrano, but he said only, 'So you yourself actually killed someone who was trying to kill you . . .'

'Yes.'

'And did you enjoy it?'

'No!' That came out with more force than she intended.

'You were scared?'

'Of course, I was scared. I'm not a . . . a . . .' *Military freak* hovered on her tongue, but she was able to choke it back.

'Militarist crazy?' he asked. Brun stared. Mind-reading was impossible, wasn't it? Then he sighed. 'I do wish that somewhere in history people would quit diminishing courage in military personnel by assuming they aren't subject to normal emotions.'

'Lepescu didn't seem to have any,' Brun said.

'Lepescu was a serious problem,' the man said. 'He damn near ruined the Serrano family, through Heris; he was probably responsible for more deaths than the enemy in any engagement he had to do with. But he was hardly typical. Even in his own family, there are good officers, not that any of 'em will have a career now.'

He took a long swallow of his ale, then put the mug down and gave her another straight look.

'So . . . back to you. What put you in a rage?'

'An argument.'

'With whom?'

'Esmay Suiza,' Brun said. Anger burst out again. 'She was like you – she thinks I'm just a spoiled rich girl helling around the universe having fun. She had the nerve – the gall – to tell me I had no moral structure to my life.'

'Do you?'

'Of course I do!'

'What, then, do you conceive as the purpose of your life? What is it that you do, to justify your existence? What are you here for?'

Put that way, in his easy voice that carried neither praise nor blame, Brun found the answers that floated into her mind clearly inadequate. She was her father's daughter; she existed to . . . to be her father's daughter. No. She didn't want to be just her father's daughter, but she had found nothing else.

'I've helped people,' she said lamely.

'That's nice,' he said. She wasn't sure if sarcasm edged his tone or not. 'Most people have, at one time or another. You saved your friend's life on that island. That's a point for you. Is that your mission, saving peoples' lives by killing those who want to kill them? If so, I must say you're woefully undertrained for that and overtrained for other things.'

'I . . . don't know.' Brun took another sip of her ale.

'Mmm. You're in your mid-twenties now, right? By your age, most young people without your . . . advantages . . . are showing more sense of direction. Consider the officer you quarrelled with. By your age, she had chosen a profession, left home against some resistance to pursue it, and performed capably in her choice. She was not flitting around having adventures.'

'Just because I'm rich—'

'Don't try that,' he said; this time contempt laced his voice. 'It has nothing to do with wealth; your father, for instance, shows every sign of being an honorable, hard-working man whose service to the Familias – and his own family – are his mission. Your sister Clemmie, even before she married, had chosen to work in an area of medicine where her skills and ability actually served someone else. You, on the other hand, while willing to help out friends, have no consistent direction in your life.'

'Yes, but—'

'So I would say Lieutenant Suiza has the right of it. You are a fine lady, Brun Meager, but you aren't anything else. And some-day, if you haven't developed the spiritual muscle, you're going to find yourself in a situation you can't handle – and with no tools at all to deal with it.'

Brun glared at him, unable to think of anything to say.

'All of us here have been in those situations,' he said, after a pause. 'Brains aren't enough. Physical strength isn't enough. Life will throw things at you that brains and strength can't deal with. Smart people and strong people can both go crazy – or worse, go bad like Lepescu, convinced that whatever they want must be acceptable, or should be acceptable. There must be spiritual strength.'

'And you think I don't have any?'

He shrugged. 'That's not for me to say. I would have to say you haven't *shown* any yet. You haven't shown any ability to see yourself as you really are, for instance – and self-examination is one good clue to an individual's spiritual state. You have the capacity, certainly – anyone does – but you haven't developed it.'

'I think you don't know what you're talking about,' Brun said. She drained the rest of that mug of Stenner. 'You haven't any idea what my life has been like, or what I've done, nor does your wonderful Lieutenant Suiza. You think being rich had nothing to do with it? Let me tell you something . . . the rich learn early on that you can't trust anyone – *anyone* – but the other rich. And you Fleet people are just the same. You don't trust anyone who's not born to Fleet. Nothing I did would make any difference. You all decided I was just a spoiled rich girl, from day one, and there was no hope of changing your minds. What passes for your minds.'

She pushed herself away from the table and made her way outside, carefully not meeting anyone's eyes. She had had it; there was no way to do what she wanted to do as long as no one would give her a fair chance. She would leave Copper Mountain; she would figure out for herself what she needed.

By the time she got back to base, she had cooled down enough to be icily polite to her security escort. They were icily polite in return. It was long after midnight; she could hear the snarling of the transports picking up teams for the field exercise. The exercise she should have been on.

She checked the outbound shuttle and transport schedules. No doubt there would be formalities, but she should be able to get away before Esmay came back. She put her name on the list for an appointment with the Commandant of Schools in the morning, and went back to her quarters to take what rest she could.

When she went in, it was clear that the Commandant already knew something. She could see it in his face, and before she even sat down, he started to apologize.

'Sera Meager, I understand a junior officer acted very inappropriately—'

'You had scan on Lieutenant Suiza?'

He coughed. 'On . . . you, Sera Meager. I'm sorry, but for your own safety—'

It was intolerable. She could not even have a quarrel without someone listening in. 'Well, I suppose you got an earful.'

'Lieutenant Suiza was totally unprofessional; you have my – Fleet's – apology . . .'

'Never mind that. She was rude, yes, but she made it clear I will never be accepted on my own merits. And I'm placing an undue burden on your staff, trying to keep me safe. I'm resigning my place, or whatever you call it.'

'Does your father know?'

She could have slugged him, but his question was another proof that she was right. 'I am informing him by ansible transmission this morning, sir, as soon as public hours open. I plan to take Fleet transport to the nearest civilian transport nexus—' She could not think of the name. 'I will probably lease a vessel from there.'

'You need not hurry . . .'

'I would rather be gone before the field exercise is over,' Brun said. She was determined not to see Esmay Suiza again. Or Barin Serrano, for that matter – she could just imagine what his grandmother would say.

'I see.' His lips compressed. 'Again, while I think your decision is probably best under the circumstances, you have my assurance that Lieutenant Suiza's behavior will not go without official rebuke.'

Exhaustion rolled over her suddenly like a heavy blanket. She didn't care about Lieutenant Suiza; she just wanted to be away from these people with their punctilious rules, their unbending righteousness.

'I will cooperate with all necessary procedures,' Brun said, pushing herself up. What she really wanted was a week's sleep; she could get that once she left this miserable place. She put on her public persona to get through the remaining hours; she smiled at the right time, shook the right hands, murmured the right pleasantries, assured everyone that she had taken no offense, harbored no grievances, had simply come to the conclusion that this was not right for her.

By nightfall, her father had replied to her request that he send his personal militia to replace the Royal Space Service security when she reached civilian space. He had agreed – with what enthusiasm she could not judge – to her plan of spending a few months visiting relatives and business contacts before returning to Sirialis for the opening of the hunting season. At local midnight, she boarded the shuttle offplanet . . . and hoped that Esmay Suiza was having a miserable time, wherever she was.

Thirty hours into the field exercise, Esmay wondered why she had ever thought this was a good idea for an elective. She had led her team safely through the first third of the course; they had spotted and evaded a number of traps. But they were hungry, thirsty and tired now, and she was fresh out of ideas. Ahead lay grassland – just grassland – to the line of fence that represented safety. They hadn't been spotted in the broken ground, but out there they couldn't hide – and it was too great a distance to cross in a rush. If they stayed where they were, they'd probably be found, and anyway they wouldn't get the extra points for getting to the safehold.

'A tunnel would be handy,' Taras said.

She was right, of course, but why were her good ideas so impractical?

'I don't suppose we could find an animal burrow?'

'I doubt it.' Briefing had said the native animals were all under five kilos. Of course, briefing had left a lot out. Esmay held them all where they were until dusk, then they began a slow, careful crawl through the grass toward the fenceline.

The hood cut off sight instantly; she struck out uselessly, knowing it was useless. Her blows fell on air, but the blows aimed at her landed . . . knocked her sideways, back, sideways again, until she finally fell, her head slamming into a hummock she had not been able to see. She tasted blood; she'd bitten her tongue in that fall. Before she could react, the assailants grabbed arms and legs, and in seconds she was immobilized like a calf for branding.

Had it been like this for Barin? No, for him it had been real . . . but the harsh voice that promised pain was real now, too. A fist grabbed her hair through the hood, and yanked her head back.

Think of something else, Barin had said. It does help, though you don't believe it at the time. That was in the manual, too, so others had found it useful. As she felt rough hands on the fastening of her clothes, and the cold edge of a blade, and then the tug as her clothes were cut away, her mind slid back toward that other time, in childhood.

No. She would not go there. She would think of something that made her feel strong.

What came into her head was the argument with Brun. In her head, in this pain-filled dark, she could think of much more to say than she had said. As the hours passed – hours she could not count – she elaborated on the argument and its causes, all the way back to that first meeting with Brun, and imagined herself and Brun and Barin. What each said, what each was thinking, what each thought the other was thinking. The verbal assaults of her captors became the things Brun had said, or would have said if she'd thought of them. The blows they dealt were the blows Brun would have dealt if she had dared fight openly.

But in the story she was telling herself, she gave as good as she got – better, in fact. For Brun's attacks, she now had the right counterattacks. For Brun's invincible arrogance, she now had a response that brought Brun to her knees, that forced her to acknowledge Esmay's position, skills, knowedge . . . In her mind, at least, she could triumph.

She was vaguely conscious that her captors were considerably annoyed with her for some reason, but nothing mattered as much as Brun's appropriation of Barin, and her own determination to defend – not territory, exactly, but her chance at—

As suddenly as it began, it ended. She didn't notice at first, though as she came back to real space and time, she was aware that her mind had noticed, and had begun pulling her back from the story she'd been writing in her mind. She felt the cool blunt snout of a hypospray against her arm, then a wave of returning clarity. When she opened her eyes, a medic smiled at her, and gave the code phrase that meant the exercise was over. And Lieutenant Commander Uhlis, looking no grimmer than usual, reached out a hand to help her up.

'Suiza, you're tougher than I thought. Whatever you were doing inside your head worked – keep it in mind in case you need it.'

She felt shaky when she stood, and only then noticed that her hands were bandaged. He nodded at them. 'You'll need an hour or so in the regen tank. The team kept thinking they could get to you in just another little bit. But it's all within regs.' Now she could feel the pain, working its way past the restorative drug. Uhlis put out his arm again. 'Better take hold – we'll get you into the transport. You're the last here—'

'The team?' she asked.

'You all passed,' he said. 'Even Taras. I don't know how you got her through it, but you did.'

'She did,' Esmay said. She felt distinctly odd, with the combination of stimulant and residual imagination, but managed not to throw up or fall down. Once in the transport, she tried to let herself relax, but she couldn't quite. It could still be a trick . . . it could still be . . .

She woke briefly back at the base, when the medics were easing her into the regen tank; one glimpse of her hands was enough. She didn't fight the sedative they gave her, but slid into unconsciousness.

By the time she got back to her quarters, she was more than ready for solitude and sleep. The pain was gone, and there were no visible bruises, but her body insisted that something traumatic had happened. The medics said she'd feel much better in the morning, that tank healing often left people feeling slightly disoriented and peculiar.

She had just decided not to bother with undressing, when her comunit chimed.

'The Commandant wishes to see you at your earliest convenience,' the voice in her ear said. 'He will expect you within ten minutes.'

She tried to shake herself awake, staggered into the shower, and into a clean uniform. What could the Commandant possibly want? Some administrative matter, no doubt, but why the hurry?

5

The Commandant did not look as if this were just an administrative matter. Esmay came to attention and waited. Finally he spoke.

'I understand you had an . . . er . . . disagreement with the Speaker's daughter, Brun Meager.'

As if she didn't know who it was; as if she did not know with whom she had quarrelled. And could this be what it was about? A simple quarrel?

'Yes, sir.'

'The . . . er . . . surveillance recordings indicate that you criticized Sera Meager on grounds of her moral failings . . .'

'Sir.' Certain phrases came back to her memory for the first time in days, as if highlighted in flame.

'Do you really think that was appropriate professional demeanor, Lieutenant?'

'If you have the tapes, you know why I said what I said,' Esmay said. She wished she'd been more tactful, but it was petty of Brun to have reported their argument.

'Let me put it another way, Lieutenant.' The voice was a shade cooler; Esmay felt it on her skin, like a cold breeze stiffening the hairs of her arms. 'Whatever the provocation, do you think it is appropriate for a Fleet officer to lecture a civilian – a prominent civilian – as if they were rival fishwives?' Before Esmay could think of anything to say, he want on. 'Because, Lieutenant, I can tell you that I do *not* consider it appropriate. I consider it an embarrassment, and I am quite seriously disappointed in your performance. Allowances have been made for your background—'

Esmay stirred, but he held up a warning hand and went on.

'Your background, as I said, would be some excuse, if you were not from a prominent family on Altiplano, and if you had not previously commented on the greater formality of manners there. I hardly think you would have spoken to a civilian guest of your father's in such terms as you used to Sera Meager.'

'No, sir.' She wouldn't, because no young woman of family would have behaved like Brun Meager. She tried to think of an equivalent crime, and couldn't. But no use explaining . . . that never did any good.

'And then to make comments where someone in the media could hear you—!'

'Sir?' She had no idea what that was about.

'Don't tell me you don't know about that!' He glared at her.

'Sir, after the argument with Brun, I finished packing and then left on the field exercise. I didn't talk to anyone else about anything at all; I didn't talk to anyone about her during the exercise, and I just got back from medical . . . I'm sorry, sir, but I *don't* know what you're talking about.'

He looked slightly taken aback, someone in a righteous rage who had stumbled over an inconvenient contrary fact.

'You spoke to no one?'

'No one, sir.'

'Well, you must've been loud enough for someone to overhear, because it certainly made the news.'

There would have been no media on a military installation on Altiplano. It wasn't fair to blame her because they'd let media follow Brun around and poke into every cranny.

'You of all people should know that Fleet is under great suspicion at this time – between the mutinies and the Lepescu affair – and the last thing we need is some wild-eyed young officer accusing the Speaker's daughter of immorality. That does us no good with the Grand Council, or for that matter with the populace at large. Do you understand?'

'Yes, sir.'

'I wonder. You are an intelligent officer, and supposedly talented in tactics, but . . . in all my years, I don't think I've ever seen as egregious an example of bad judgement. You've

445

embarrassed me, and you've embarrassed the Regular Space Service. If you didn't have such a good record previously, I would seriously consider having you up for conduct unbecoming an officer.'

All she had done was tell a rich spoiled brat the plain truth . . . but clearly some unpleasant truths were not to be told. Brun was the one who had done wrong, and now *she* was in trouble. Her head was pounding again.

'Let me tell you what you're going to do, Lieutenant. You are going to avoid any interviews on any topic whatsoever. You are going to make no comments whatever about Sera Meager, to anyone. If asked, you will say you lost your temper – which clearly is the case – and you have no more to say. I would have you apologize to Sera Meager, except that she chose to leave this facility – and no wonder – and I doubt she wants to hear from you anyway. Is all that clear?'

'Yes, sir.'

'Dismissed.'

Esmay saluted and withdrew, angry with both herself and Brun. She shouldn't have said what she said – all right, she could admit she'd been too angry to think straight. But Brun had taken advantage of her, time and again – and to go complain to authority was . . . was another proof of her childishness.

She was supposed to meet Barin – he'd left word on her comunit – but she really wanted to crawl into her bunk and sleep another twelve hours. At least, she thought, he wouldn't waste their time talking about Brun.

Brun was the first topic he brought up. 'You were pretty hard on her,' Barin said, after mentioning that he'd seen the newsflash along with everyone else in the class. 'She's not as bad as all that . . .'

'She is,' Esmay said. It was too much; she was not going to let Brun get away with ruining this, too. She saw his face change his expression harden against her. Sorrow cut through her, but her anger pushed her on, forcing her against the blade of his disapproval. 'She had no right to come after you; if she had one scrap of morality—'

446

'That's not fair,' Barin said. 'She does. It's just that – that someone like that—'

'The richest girl in the Familias Regnant? The rules are different for the rich, is that what you're saying?'

'No – yes, but not the way you mean it.' The slight emphasis he put on 'you' stung; he had meant it to, Esmay was sure.

'The way I mean it is that people who have her advantages ought to have used them for something more than personal pleasure.'

'Well, had you told her that we were . . . anything to each other?'

'No, I did not.' Esmay could feel her own face getting stiff. 'It was none of her business. It has nothing to do with me and you; it has to do with her assumption that anyone she wants should climb in bed with her . . .'

'Anyone!' Barin looked startled, then amused, then alarmed. 'She didn't try to get you—?'

'No!' Esmay shook her head, which was beginning to throb in the old way. 'She didn't, of course she didn't. It's just that she went after you, and you're an officer of Fleet, and younger than she is—' Too late she remembered that she herself could not be simultaneously older than Brun and co-equal with Barin. Her voice wavered; she gulped and went on. 'It was – was – unseemly. Chasing junior officers.'

'Esmay, please.' Barin reached out but drew back his hand before touching her. 'It was perfectly natural. And all she did was ask. When I said no, she didn't bother me. Perfectly polite, perfectly within the bounds of courtesy.'

'You said no?' Esmay managed to get out around a dry lump in her throat.

'Of course I said no. What do you think?' His heavy Serrano brows drew together. 'You thought I *slept* with her? How could you think that?' Now he was angry, black eyes flashing and a flush coming up in his face.

Esmay felt panic rising in her. He hadn't slept with Brun? Had Livadhi lied? Misunderstood? Not known? She could say nothing. Barin, glaring at her, nodded sharply as if her silence confirmed some dire suspicion.

447

'You thought I did. You thought just because I shared a few meals with her while you were busy, just because we talked, just because she's a rich girl, that I'd leap into her bed like a tame puppy. Well, I'm no one's pet, Esmay. Not hers, and not yours. If you really cared for me, you'd know that. I'm sorry you understand so little, but if you want to succeed in Fleet, you'd better get off your moral high horse and start dealing with reality.'

He was gone before she could say anything, and long before anyone could have suspected what she had once worried they might suspect. She made it to her quarters at last, and spent another night not sleeping, staring at the ceiling over her bunk.

When they met in class the next day, Esmay could do nothing but stare miserably at the back of Barin's head. He did not turn to look at her. When called on, he gave his answers in his familiar crisp voice; she found that she could do the same, though she wasn't at all sure how her brain could keep working when her heart was lying in a sodden heap somewhere below her navel.

She had never been in love before. She had heard others describe similar symptoms, but had thought they exaggerated. They did not exaggerate, she decided; in fact, they had not begun to describe the misery she felt. They had all lived through it; she supposed she would too, but she wasn't sure she wanted to.

To her surprise, she received a high score on her field exercise. It did not make her feel better, though her subdued acceptance of the certificate seemed to please Lieutenant Commander Uhlis. She could feel the subtle withdrawal of her classmates, even those like Vericour who had been friendly all along.

Anonymity had been a lot easier than disgrace.

On the day Barin was due to leave, she made her way to the exit area; she felt she had to make some contact with him, or she might as well jump off a tower. Her hands were icy; she could feel her heart pounding as she spotted him across the room.

'Barin—'

'Lieutenant.' He was coolly polite. She didn't want coolly polite.

'Barin, I'm sorry. I didn't mean to insult you.' That came out in a rush, almost all one word.

448

'No apologies necessary,' he said, almost formally. She thought she saw a bit of warmth in his eye, but nothing more. He wasn't going to reach out for her, not here in public, and he showed no signs of wanting a more private conversation.

'I just – don't want us to be enemies,' Esmay said.

'Never!' He took a breath. 'Never enemies, Lieutenant, even if we can't agree.' A long pause, during which Esmay heard what he did not say aloud – or what she imagined he was saying. She didn't know which. 'Goodbye, Lieutenant, and good luck on your first assignment in command track. You'll do fine.'

'Thank you,' Esmay said. 'And good luck to you.' Her throat closed on the rest of what she wanted to say: We could stay in touch. We could plan . . . No. She had ruined what they had, and that was it.

They shook hands, formally, and then saluted, formally, and then he moved over to the line forming for his shuttle. Esmay did not wait to see if he would turn around and wave. She was sure he wouldn't.

She had not been outside the gates of the facility before, but now she found herself wandering out to Q-town in the kind of numb misery she thought she'd never feel again. She didn't want to see anyone from her class in the mess hall, but she had to eat before leaving, or she'd throw up. Someone had said – who was it? She couldn't recall, someone on *Koskiusko* – that while she was on Copper Mountain, she'd have to visit Diamond Sims. She spotted the sign down the street, and made for it.

'Lieutenant Suiza!' The man in the hoverchair called to her almost as soon as she cleared the door. 'I'm glad you came. I'm Sam – I run this place.'

Someone was glad to see her? She glanced around, recognizing with a strange shock what this bar was about, and made her way toward the back.

'We're honored you came by,' the man said. 'Major Pitak said you might, if you had time.'

'Sorry it took me so long,' Esmay said. 'I was doubling courses—'

'Yeah – we keep track of people at the school, so I knew you were busy. Didn't expect you before now, and didn't know if you'd have time. When's your shuttle?'

'About five hours.' Esmay took the seat he indicated.

'You in trouble about that Meager woman?' he asked.

Brun again. Esmay managed a nod, and hoped that would indicate she didn't want to talk about it.

'It's partly my fault,' the man said. 'She came in here hopping mad that night, and shot off her mouth in front of the whole room. We think what happened is that one of the newsies on her tail got it with a spike-mike from out on the street. Least, nobody that was here will admit to telling it.'

'It's – not worth worrying about,' Esmay said. 'It happened; I can't change it now.'

'You sound like someone who needs a steak,' the man said. He raised his hand, and a waitress appeared. He glanced at Esmay. 'Steak all right? Onions?'

'No onions, thanks.' Not with a shuttle liftoff. But she nodded to the rest of his suggestions, and soon the sizzling platter appeared.

When she had started eating, the man went on chatting. 'She's a pretty thing, but stubborn as a stump. A good argument against letting civilians train at our facilities, no matter whose children they are. It does no good to mix with the Families. They employ us; they cannot *be* us.'

For some reason – perhaps the energy imparted by the steak – Esmay was moved to argue. 'She had a lot of talents we could use—'

'Oh, certainly, if she had any discipline at all . . .'

'She did pull off some good stuff I heard about,' Esmay said. 'Helping that old lady – she worked hard on that.'

His eyes twinkled. 'You'd make a silk purse out of any sow's ear, would you, Lieutenant? A good attitude for a young officer, but you'll find some of 'em smell of pig no matter what you do. So where are you going now?'

'I'm not sure,' Esmay said. 'They're supposed to have my assignment ready by the time I get to sector HQ. They may bury me in paperwork—'

450

'No, I don't think so,' the man said. 'Even if you're in trouble now, it will pass, and they're not going to waste a young officer with real combat ability.'

'I hope not,' Esmay said.

Junior Officer Assignment Section, Regular Space Service HQ

'We're going to have to find something else,' the admiral said. 'I know what we thought we were going to do with Lieutenant Suiza, but we certainly cannot reward her performance with a plum assignment.'

'We needed her the way she was—' the commander said.

'The way we thought she was. Thank any deity you like that we brought her in for training before assigning her permanently to command track. Imagine the mess she could've caused as a cruiser captain, if all this had slid by.'

'I still find it hard to understand. There was nothing – *nothing* – in her record to indicate that kind of character flaw, rather the opposite.'

'There was nothing in her record to indicate her ability in combat until Xavier,' the admiral said. 'If she could hide that kind of talent, and she did, then this is no more difficult. And after all, she'd never been in contact with any of the Families before – Altiplano has no Seat in Council.'

'There is that.' The commander looked thoughtful. 'I wish we knew whether there was anything more to it.'

'More? Verbal assault on the Speaker's daughter isn't enough?'

'Well . . . is it just personal, or is it political? Is she the spearpoint for something?'

'I don't know, and at the moment I don't care. We've wasted entirely too much money and time on this young woman, and we're going to have to figure out a way to get repaid without risking the welfare of the Fleet.' The admiral looked around the table. 'Someone had better have an idea how.'

Down at the far end, a lieutenant commander raised her hand. 'Sir, she's elected to take both the basic level Search and Rescue as well as Escape and Evasion, right?'

'Yes . . .'

'SAR is chronically short of junior officers for both ship XOs and SAR team leaders, and those are command track billets. There are at least three openings for lieutenants in Sector VII alone.'

The admiral thought a moment. 'Relatively small ships, elite crew, operating independently for the most part – yes. She'd be under really close supervision; if she messes up, or tries to foment some kind of action, her captain would know for sure. Good. What have you got?'

'*Shrike*, I thought. Podaly Solis is commanding it, and his exec just applied for family leave.'

'Mmm. I don't know about having her second in command . . .'

'My thought was, it puts her more directly under the captain's supervision than she would be as a team leader. And we have no doubts about Solis; he helped us clean out that mess at Sector HQ, as I'm sure the admiral recalls.'

'Yes, that's true. Probably the best we can do. Blast the girl; why couldn't she have been as good as she seemed?'

Sector VII HQ, Aragon Station

Esmay arrived at *Shrike*'s dock area to find it in perfect order; the guard saluted crisply and checked her orders.

'I'll just let the captain know – we didn't expect you until early next shift.'

'*Gossamer* came in early,' Esmay said.

She wondered what her father would think now, both about her promotion and the trouble she was in. She was sure he'd followed her career as best he could from Altiplano; her promotions and awards were matters of public record, and the news media had covered the *Koskiusko* affair. Her thoughts drifted to her great-grandmother – so fragile, so embedded in her culture's past. What would she think? For an instant, she wished she could sit beside that low chair, and pour out the whole story. Surely her great-grandmother would understand about Barin; surely she would feel the same way about Brun.

* * *

Captain Solis greeted her with reserve; she did not know whether it was his habitual mood, or whether he had been informed of the trouble she was in.

'You're quite inexperienced to be taking over as number two,' he said. 'I understand you have a distinguished combat record, especially considering that you were not in command track at the time. But the executive officer of an SAR – that's asking rather a lot of you.'

'I'll do my best, sir,' Esmay said.

'I'm sure you will. Your experience on a DSR will be some use, and I see you stood well in your classes in both search and rescue and escape and evasion. Still, it will be a stretch, and you might as well be prepared.' He gave her a long look. 'Now, about this other problem – your quarrel with the Speaker's daughter.' He shook his head. 'If I'd been your CO, I'd have had you up for conduct unbecoming. He didn't, and so far you have no record here, but I warn you – I will not tolerate disrespect for the civil government of the Familias Regnant. Officers do not play politics. We serve; we do not interfere.'

Esmay wanted to say that Brun was not her father, and had no official position of her own, but she knew she must not. Why did they keep thinking that her opinion of Brun's behavior had anything to do with her loyalty to the Fleet? 'Yes, sir,' she said.

'You will find no support for any Family games on my ship,' he went on. 'And no room for grandstanding, either. You do your job, and do it well, and you'll get the appropriate credit in your fitness reports. Nothing more, nothing less.'

'Yes, sir.'

'I'll expect you back here in two hours for a briefing. Dismissed.'

It was cold comfort that her duffel was all in her compartment when she got there. At least her new position ensured a compartment, even on so small a ship. She glanced around. Bunk, storage lockers, desk, cube reader, and – to her surprise – a row of display screens above the desk. Esmay inserted her datawand into the slot, and these screens flashed to life. One displayed the orders of the day; another gave the status of the two SAR teams and their vehicles; yet another listed stores, crosslinked to consumption rates.

Esmay stowed her gear in the lockers – she had nothing to put in two of them – and changed into a clean uniform. She did not look forward to the next meeting with her captain.

He was, however, slightly more affable. 'I hate losing Colin,' he said. 'But his wife was killed in a traffic accident while she was downside arranging for their children to change fosterage. It's going to take him quite a while to sort everything out . . . the kids have outgrown the grandparents, and the retired uncle who was going to take them was killed in the same accident.' He shook his head, then smiled at Esmay. 'You'll find we have good teams, Lieutenant. And a tour on an SAR is always interesting. We deal with problems that the big boys ignore – everything from private yachts stranded by jump-drive blowouts, to collisions. You will learn a lot. And since we didn't expect you until tomorrow, you're not on the watch list yet, which gives you time to poke around and start learning your job.'

'All I've had was the basic SAR course, sir,' Esmay said. 'They assigned me before I had time for the advanced . . .'

'Better than nothing,' he said. 'And if you know you don't know, you'll ask questions instead of blundering around causing trouble. Now – the duties of exec on this ship are different than on line ships. That's because our mission is different. There's the basic stuff, of course – but I'd like you to look at this—' He handed over a data cube. 'And of course you'll want to meet everyone – we'd planned a get-together this evening, at 1900—'

'That's fine, sir,' Esmay said. 'I can get unpacked, have a chance to look this over . . . unless you have something now.'

'No, that's fine. We're not kicking out of here until day after tomorrow anyway. There's a meeting tomorrow, which you'll have to attend as my representative – you haven't been with the ship quite long enough to take over full prep.'

Alone in her cabin – her name was already on the door, she noticed, with the permanent engraving EXECUTIVE OFFICER underneath – Esmay inserted the cube the captain had given her into the reader. She knew what an exec did – or thought she did. Run the ship, basically, under the captain's command. But on

454

a Search and Rescue ship, the exec also had the responsibility of supervising all rescue efforts, while the captain concentrated on ship security – of both this ship and the rescued one. She blinked at the listing for the security detachments – she had not realized that an SAR ship would carry marines, though it made sense. Most of the time when ships needed rescue, it was the result of some deliberate act, and the troublemakers might still be in the area.

And she'd had only the basic course . . . so it was definitely going to be a case of 'sergeant, put up that flagpole' if they had a rescue call before she had learned the rest of the stuff she needed. Which meant she had better make friends with the sergeant equivalents.

She scrolled quickly through the headings of her job description to the ship's table of organization, and began to figure out who would do the actual work, while she 'supervised.' These were the key people she must have on her side. The words in the leadership manuals were fresh in her mind. The five rules of this; the seven principles of that. She reminded herself where the cube of those manuals was. She would review it as soon as she'd finished the captain's cube. She knew she could lead, when she let herself remember it.

Shrike mounted two complete rescue teams, cross-trained in both gravity-field and zero-gravity work. Like most of the smaller SARs, the gravity-field training specialized in low-pressure and vacuum work. Most of their calls would be to space stations or ships in deep space. A forensic team and a lab full of analytical gear suggested that SAR might include something more than accident assistance. And the medical support team was substantially larger than a ship this size normally carried, including both major trauma regen tanks and two surgical theaters, with all that implied. Again, it reminded her of a miniature of *Koskiusko*.

Rescue One was commanded by a lieutenant she remembered from the Academy as a clown of sorts, Tika Briados; he didn't seem clownish now, as he led her around the ready room with its racked suits and equipment. It all seemed a jumble to Esmay, though an orderly one – she recognized only about half the equipment and wondered how long it would take to learn the

455

rest. Rescue Two's commander was a jig she'd never met before, Kim Arek; she was eager and energetic, busily explaining things that Esmay hoped she could remember. She kept nodding, and found herself liking Jig Arek for her single-minded enthusiasm.

Going through both rescue team areas had taken hours, she found when she finally got away from Arek, and she needed to get ready for the meeting with the other officers. She did hope they weren't all going to mention Brun Meager.

The wardroom was crowded when she got there.

'Lieutenant Suiza – glad to meet you.' The blocky major who thrust out his hand reminded her of Major Pitak. 'I'm Gordon Bannon, pathology.'

'Officers—' That was Captain Solis, who stood; the others quieted. 'This is Lieutenant Esmay Suiza, our new executive officer. Some of you have heard of her—' There were murmurs that Esmay hoped referred to her earlier exploits. 'She's fresh out of Copper Mountain, with the basic course in SAR, so I'm sure you'll all cooperate in educating her into the real world.' He sounded friendly enough; this was clearly an old joke, for their chuckle had no edge to it.

After that, the others came up one by one to introduce themselves, Esmay began to relax as she chatted with them; they were clearly more interested in how she might perform here than in anything which had happened in her past.

In the next few days, she threw herself into her work, loading her scheduler with everything she could think of, or that anyone suggested. When *Shrike* left the base, she was just beginning to think she had a handle on her assignments. *Shrike* would patrol alone through the sector, ready to assist in any emergency that fell within its mission statement. According to those who had been aboard longest, days might go by with nothing happening, or disasters might overlap . . . there was no way to predict.

'The ship's a part-container, part-bulk hauler that lost power on insertion . . . the insystem drive's functioning at maybe twenty percent. They say it's fluctuating, and they can't make orbit. We've advised them that there's a registered salvage company in this system; the captain sounds unhappy with that. Says he's had trouble before with salvage companies.'

The first emergency since she'd come aboard. Esmay listened to the précis of the problem, and tried to remember which protocol this fell under.

'He wants Fleet assistance.' Captain Solis looked at Esmay. 'We have a responsibility in such cases, but we must also consider our responsibility to the whole area. So I want an estimate on the time it will take us to skip-jump over there, rig grapples, and put him in tow, then sling him back toward the orbit he wants. He's not an emergency.'

'Sir.' Esmay ran the numbers quickly. 'Sixty hours, allowing a safety margin for rigging the grapples; he should have standard tug connections, but just in case.'

'Well, then . . . let's go catch us a freighter.'

Esmay watched the approach plots carefully on the bridge displays. External vid showed a bulbous, almost spherical ship with rings of colored light indicating tug grapple connections.

'Ugly, isn't it?' asked Lieutenant Briados. The Rescue One commander was on the bridge to watch the approach. 'You'd think they could design big freighters with some character, but they all look pretty much alike.'

'It would hold a lot of soldiers,' Esmay said, the first thing that came into her mind.

Briados laughed. 'I can tell you're off a warship. Yeah, it could, but it hasn't got insystem maneuverability worth spit. Even with the insystem drive working.'

'How do they even know where to mount the drives? What's the drive axis?'

'Well, they want low-speed maneuverability near stations, so they mount two, usually, out near the hull and separated by sixty degrees; the drive axis is the chord perpendicular to the chord between the drives, in the same plane.' It took Esmay a moment to work that one out, but she nodded finally.

Captain Solis turned to her. 'All right, Suiza – let's see how you handle this. Just pretend you've been doing it for years.'

Her stomach churned. She nodded to the com watch, and

picked up the headset to talk to the freighter captain, explaining that a team would be boarding.

'We just wanted a tow,' the captain said. 'I don't see why you want to board.'

'It's R.S.S. policy to board all vessels seeking assistance,' Esmay said, repeating what Captain Solis had told her. 'Just a routine, sir.'

'Damned nuisance,' the captain said.

'Think of it as practice,' Esmay said. 'If we didn't practice close-hauling and boarding, we might not be quick enough for someone with a serious emergency. After all, it might be your ship . . .'

'Oh, all right,' he said. 'Just as long as you're not planning to practice cutting holes in my hull.'

Shrike deployed standard tug grapples, backed up by its military-grade tractor. In this instance, the grapples homed neatly on the freighter's signal, and locked on as *Shrike* maintained matching course and velocity. The tractor snugged the SAR ship closer still. Esmay gave the orders that sent Jig Arek and her team across a few hundred meters of vacuum to the other ship.

Rescue Two made its way in and out of all the holds, while *Shrike* boosted the freighter gently on its way, then returned before Solis ordered the grapples retracted.

'Captain – what were they looking for?' Esmay asked.

'Just practicing,' Solis said.

She looked at him; finally he grinned at her.

'All right. You might as well know. Sector's concerned about possible shortages in the munitions inventory. We think some stuff's being diverted from Fleet to civilian use. So the admiral says to check every ship that asks us for a boost. It is good practice, including the use of the warhead detection equipment.'

'What's missing?' asked Esmay.

Solis spread his hands. 'I've been told I don't need to know, but since they specified the equipment we were to use looking for it, I'd say someone's misplaced some of the more effective nukes.'

'Ouch.'

'Exactly. If our stuff's being transshipped on civilian freighters, it could be going anywhere. To anyone. Probably not the Benignity – they have their own munitions industry, and plenty in stock. But any of the lesser hostile powers, or domestic malcontents . . .'

'Or simply pirates,' Esmay said.

'Yes. Anyone who wants a big bang.'

6

Elias Madero, owned by the Boros Consortium, followed a five-angled route that had proved lucrative for decades. Olives and wine from Bezaire, jewels mined on Oddlink, livestock embryos from Gullam, commercial-grade organics from Podj, entertainment cubes from Corian, which had FTL traffic from deeper insystem, and the largest population in the area. She was a container hauler, picking up at each port the hold-shaped containers that had been filling since her last visit there. Her crew, most of them permanent, often had no idea what was in the containers. The captain did, presumably, and also the Boros agents at each port. But the containers had no accessible hatches – one advantage of container ships was supposed to be the impossibility of petty pilfering by crews – so they had no idea that the container in Hold 5 which was supposed to be filled with 5832 cube players was actually full of arms stolen from a Fleet stockpile. The other containers in Hold 5, which should have had entertainment cubes to be played in the cube players, contained more illicit weaponry, including thirty-four Whitsoc 43b11 warheads, their controlling electronics, and the arming keys.

Boros' agent at Bezaire would not have been happy to find the contents of that container, since she had a contract to supply the cube players and the entertainment cubes supposedly filling the rest of Hold 5.

Elias Madero came out of FTL flight, retranslating to normal space, to traverse the real-space distance between two jump points in the same system, colloquially known as Twobits. This shortcut had been marked 'questionable' on standard charts for years, because the presence of two jump points in the same system was believed, on theoretical grounds, to lead to spatial instability of the jump points. If the insertion point shifted, an inbound ship might find itself emerging too close to a large mass, with no time to maneuver clear. But the nearest greenlined route meant three more jump point calculations, and added eleven days to the Corian-Bezaire passage. Since jump point temporal coordinates were fuzzy anyway, many commercial haulers used shortcuts to ensure that they met contractual delivery dates . . . while filing flight plans that were all greenlined.

This crew had made the traverse before, many times, without incident. The jump points had not shifted in the past fifty years, while the possibility that they might kept the system uncrowded.

On this trip, system insertion went as smoothly as usual, and the *Elias* transferred to insystem drive without a hitch.

'That's done, then,' Captain Lund said to his navigator, clapping a hand on the man's shoulder. 'Four days, and we'll be out of here again. I'm going to bed.' Custom and regulation both required that a captain be on the bridge during jump point insertions; Lund had been up three shifts running because of a minor engineering problem.

His navigation officer, a transfer from *Sorias Madero*, a sister ship, nodded. 'I have the course laid, sir. By my calculations, ninety-seven point two hours.'

'Very good.'

Captain Lund, balding and stocky, waited until he was in his cabin to take off his jacket and kick off his shoes. He hung the jacket up neatly, set his shoes side by side, laid his trousers, neatly folded, over the back of his chair, with his shirt over them. This was his last cycle . . . when he reached Corian again, he would retire at last. Helen . . . his grandchildren . . . the neat little house set high on a slope above the valley . . . he drifted into sleep, a smile on his face.

The sharp yelp of the emergency alarm woke him. He touched the comunit above his bunk.

'Captain here – what is it?'

'Raiders, sir.'

He sat up, ducking automatically from the overhanging cabinets. 'I'm on my way.'

Raiders? What kind of raiders would hang around a route where almost no ships went? No ships, really – he'd never found any indication that others used this two-jump transit.

Had they been tailed through FTL? He'd heard rumors that Fleet was developing some kind of scan that worked in FTL. The Benignity? Certainly not Aethar's World, and they were across Familias space anyway.

From the bridge, the situation was clear. Two of them, their weapons systems lighting up the scan board with red threats. On the com screen, a hard-faced man in a uniform he didn't recognize was speaking in accented Standard – an accent he hadn't heard before, with the words pulled out twice as long.

'You surrender your ship, and we'll let the crew off in your lifeboats—'

Captain Lund almost choked. What good would lifeboats be, in a lifeless system that no one visited because of the paired jump points?

'Wheah's yoah captain? I wanna talk to him.'

Lund stepped up to the comunit, and nodded to his exec, who stepped back.

'This is Captain Lund. Who are you and what do you think you're doing?'

'Takin' yoah ship, sir.' The man favored him with a tight grin that did not look at all friendly. 'In the name of sacred liberty, and the Nutex Militia. We apologize for any . . . ah . . . inconvenience.'

'You're pirates!' Lund said. 'You have no right—'

'Them's harsh words, sir. We don't like disrespect for our beliefs, sir. Let me put it this way – we have the weapons to blow

461

your ship away, and we're offerin' you a chance to save your crews' lives. Some of 'em, anyway. If you surrender your ship, and allow us to board without resistance, we will swear not to kill any of your legal crew.'

Lund felt that he had waked into a nightmare, and his mind refused to work at its normal speed. 'Legal crew?'

'Waal . . . yes. We're aware, you see, that you work for a corporation with obscene and unnatural views about moral issues. In our books, there's things that just ain't natural and normal, let alone *right*, and if you have people like that on board, then they'll have to face justice.'

Lund glanced around; the faces on the bridge were tense and pale. He thumbed the com control to prevent his words going out in transmission. 'Do any of you have the slightest idea who these crazies are? Or what they mean about natural and un-natural?'

The junior scan tech, Innis Seqalin, nodded. 'I've heard a little about the Nutex Militia . . . for one thing, they think it's wrong for women to be spacers, and for another, they don't tolerate anything but what they call normal sex.'

Lund felt his stomach churn. If they didn't allow women in space, what kind of sex did they think was normal? And why not allow women in space? 'Is it . . . something religious?'

'Yes, sir. At least, they say it is.'

Lund felt even sicker. Religious nuts . . . he had gone to space to get away from them back on his home world. If these were the same sort . . . he had too many crew at risk.

'I'm warnin' ya,' the pirate officer said. 'Answer, or we'll blow your holds . . .'

'All right,' Lund said, as much to gain time as anything. 'I'll send my people to the lifeboats—'

'We'll see a crew list,' the man said, smiling unpleasantly. 'Right now, afore you can doctor it up. If a life-boat separates before we've approved the list, we'll blow it.'

Lund's mind raced into high gear. The crew list did not mention gender – and certainly not sexual preferences – so if he could just keep the medical records out of their hands . . .

'And the medical records,' the man said, 'in case you got some

462

of them so-called modern women that don't have good women's names.'

He could refuse, but then what? According to scan, he was facing weapons easily capable of blowing his ship. But they wouldn't want to blow his ship . . . they would want the cargo, and perhaps the ship itself, intact.

'Personnel and medical records aren't networked,' he said, thanking whatever gods were around, including those he didn't believe in, for the fact that this was standard, and known to be standard.

'Ten minutes,' the pirate said, and clicked off.

Ten minutes. What doctoring could he do in ten minutes? And why hadn't he denied the presence of women right away, so that he might have had a chance to pass them off as men? But the ship's tiny medical staff had been listening, and Hansen gave him a call.

'I'm changing the genders, and stripping out all reference to gender-specific medications . . . six minutes for that. What else do you think?'

'Sequalin says they have some weird beliefs about sexual practice – but I don't know which.'

'Umm. If they go to space in single-gender ships, maybe they have obligatory homosexuality in space? I could code everyone as male/male preference.'

'Yeah, but if we're wrong . . . I don't know.'

'And what about the children?'

Elias Madero, like most commercial ships, carried some of its crew's children aboard. Children had been found well worth the extra work and worry, in terms of keeping a crew entertained and cooperative. Right now there were six, four under school age and two taking a work-study tour as junior apprentices.

'We put the kids in the core, where the scans are least likely to find them. Sedate the littles. If they just rob the ship and go on . . . the older ones can come back out and send a message. Got to clear out the nursery, though . . .'

'Do it,' Lund said. 'But don't code gender preference. Just leave it.' How was he going to hide the women? And what would happen to them if they were found?

* * *

463

Hazel Takeris, age sixteen, had found her first working trip to be as dull as her father had warned – but she wouldn't have missed it for anything, certainly not another five terms at the Space Dependents Middle School on Oddlink Main Station. So she had willingly performed the routine chores allotted to the apprentices, reminding herself – when enthusiasm for washing dishes or scrubbing the deck flagged – that she could have been listening to Professor Hallas discourse on the history of a planet that lay – to Hazel's mind – in the dim past of human history. A long way away, and very far back, and who really cared which millennium had produced which oddly named king or scientist.

When the alarm came, she was doing inventory of the galley stores, as ordered by the cook. She heard nothing of the ensuing discussion, because Cookie had told her to get back to work, and be sure her count was right. Thirty-eight three-kilo sacks of wheat flour. Six half-kilo boxes of sodium chloride salt, and four of a 50/50 mix of potassium and sodium chlorides. Eight –

'Haze – drop that and listen up.' Cookie's face was an odd shade, the rich tan paled and splotchy. 'Get four emergency ration kits, and go to Core 32. Hop it!'

'What – ?' But apprentices didn't ask questions, not when a crew member looked like that. Hazel grabbed four emergency kits, and as she went past Cookie dumped two more on top of them. She scurried as fast as she could through the corridors, turned into the drop to the Core, and met her dad, who was even paler than Cookie.

'Haze – gimme two of those – now go to 32. We're going to lock you in. I put your suit in there already. Put it on, and wait. Be sure you wait long enough.'

She had grown up a spacer's child; she could figure it out. 'Raiders,' she said, trying to keep her voice steady.

'Yeah. Go on, now. You and Stinky will be awake; we've sedated the littles, and they'll be in Core 57 and 62. Oh – and remember, it's the Nutex Militia.'

Hazel fell down the drop, landing easily, feet first, on the pad. Thirty-two was clockwise four; she had known the geography of this ship from early childhood. Thirty-two's hatch was open; she slid in, dumped her rations, pulled the hatch shut, and locked it from inside. Her suit stood slumped in one corner, along with a stack of extra oxygen tanks. She got herself into it, her fingers shaking, fumbling at the catches and seals.

She started to report herself secure, on suit com, and then didn't – what if the raiders were already aboard? No one had told her when to expect boarding; no one had told her when to come out. Wait long enough? How long was that? How was she supposed to know?

In her suit, she could not quite lie down in the compartment, but she propped herself corner-to-corner, so that if she fell asleep, she would not fall and make a noise. She had the helmet open to ambient air – no sense in wasting suit air yet, and the helmet would snap shut automatically at any drop in pressure. She looked at her suit chrono, and marked the time. Wait long enough. She wished she knew how long.

She wished she and Stinky had been in the same compartment so they could talk. As the two apprentices, they had formed a natural alliance. Besides that, they liked each other's parents, and had spent the voyage trying to maneuver her father and his mother into some kind of arrangement. So far the adults had been resistant, but she and Stinky hadn't given up hope. Surely everyone felt the same urge to partner that she and Stinky felt . . . that's how adults came together to have children, after all.

Locked in the empty compartment, it finally occurred to Hazel that the straightforward solution would have been for her and Stinky to partner, and leave the parents alone . . . but she wasn't ready to partner anyone. Not yet. Later . . . she allowed herself a few delicious minutes of imagining what it would be like if Stinky were in the same compartment, without the pressure suits or the adult supervision. She had thoughts like that, even though she had chosen to take the treatment to delay puberty; she might look only ten or eleven, but she was sixteen for true.

She pulled her mind away from that to the littles, locked away in other compartments. Sedated, her dad had said. How long would the sedation last? Brandalyn was always first up in the morning, bouncing around . . . would she come out of sedation first? Had they put her in the same compartment as her sister? Surely they'd thought of that. Stassi was quieter, and very attached to her big sister. The other two littles, Paolo and Dris, were cousins.

She looked at the chrono. Only fifteen minutes had passed. That couldn't be long enough. The raiders might not have boarded yet. She might have to wait hours.

Her suit transmitted nonspecific vibrations that she could not identify – except that they were different from those she knew so well after all these months aboard. One hour, two, three. How long did raiders stay aboard a ship to plunder it? Docked at a regular cargo station, the automated handlers could unload a hold in seven hours and twelve minutes – if nothing went wrong. Would the raiders try to unload an entire hold? All the holds? Would they have the right equipment? How long would it take them?

It would be easier to steal the whole ship; she felt cold as she thought of it. If they did, if they took the entire ship . . . then what would happen to her? To Stinky? To the littles?

She heard noises – nearby noises. It must be the raiders, because no one had unlocked her compartment yet. Shuffling, thumping – then a shriek that stiffened her. Brandy, that would be; they had all joked that she had a scream that would slice steel plates. The child screamed again. Hazel clambered up, clumsy in the suit, and tried to unlock the hatch. She had to stop them – she had to protect the child. She had the lock undone when the hatch was yanked out of her grip, and two big men grabbed her, one for each arm, and pulled her out of the compartment. She could see Brandy kicking and screaming in the grip of another, who was trying to gag her with a length of cloth. Stassi was crying, more quietly, in the grip of another; the two little boys clung to Stinky, who looked as scared as she felt.

'A girl,' one of the men said. 'The perverts.' Brandy's scream choked off; the man holding her had managed to tie the gag. 'You take her,' he said, shoving Brandy into Hazel's arms. 'And bring her along.'

She held Brandy to her, trying to comfort the child, who was sobbing into the gag. Stassi clung to one leg and Paolo to the other. Stinky carried Dris. The raiders pushed her along, back up toward the bridge.

The first thing she saw, coming into the bridge, was her dad's body in a pool of blood. She almost dropped Brandy, but the child clung to her, legs and arms fastened tight. There were other bodies, all people she knew – Baris the navigator, and Sig the cargo chief, and – and Stinky's mother, gagged and bound, but glaring furiously. All the women of the crew, she noted, were lying there in a row, bound and gagged. Captain Lund faced the bridge access, bound to his command seat. And all the armed men wearing the same uniform as the ones who had captured her.

The leader turned to Captain Lund. 'You lied to us, captain. That wasn't very smart.' He drawled the words out, an accent that Hazel had never heard before.

'I . . . wanted to save the children.'

'God saves the children, by giving them to those who will bring them up in righteousness.' The leader smiled, a smile that made Hazel feel cold inside.

Captain Lund looked at Hazel, then at Stinky. 'I'm sorry,' he said. The leader slammed his weapon into Captain Lund's head.

'You don't talk, old man. Nobody talks to our children but our family. And you're going to be really sorry that you lied . . .' He turned to his men. 'Get goin' now . . . let's check these heathen sluts out, see if any of 'em's worth botherin' with.'

Hazel lay in the compartment that had been the spare passenger cabin, trying to hug all the littles at once. Dris was still dozing, and she didn't know if that was the sedative or the lump on his head. Paolo whimpered softly; Stassi had her whole hand in her mouth, sucking furiously. Brandy was out cold, snoring through the gag. Hazel wanted to take it out, but she was afraid of the man with the weapon who stood by the hatch. She was afraid of everything. She had to pretend not to be, because the littles needed her; she was the one person they knew, the one person who could make them feel safe, if anything could after what they'd been through. How could you make someone feel safe if you didn't feel safe yourself?

She still could not believe it was all real. The soreness in her own body was real, and the hunger, and the fear, but – had she really seen all she remembered? The women who had been her aunts, her mentors, since her own mother died, all . . . she didn't even know the words for what had been done to them, except the killing at the end. And poor Captain Lund . . . she had known him since she could remember, a gentle man, a kind man . . . and they had stuffed his mouth with the tongues of the women, and then . . . and then shot him, at the last.

Paolo whimpered a bit louder; the man by the hatch growled. Hazel stroked the child's back. 'Easy,' she murmured. 'Sshh.' She wouldn't think about it any more; she would think only of the littles, who needed her.

'These are the rules,' the raider said. Hazel sat on the deck, with Brandy in her lap and the others nestled against her. 'Look at me,' the raider said. Hazel had been looking at the littles, because she'd been slapped already for looking – staring, the man had said – at one of the raiders. Now she looked up, her shoulders hunching. 'That's right,' the man said. 'You look when I tell you to, where I tell you to. Now listen. These are the rules. You don't look at our faces unless you're told to. You don't talk. You – girlie – you can whisper to the babies if you have to, but only if none of us's talkin'. You keep the babies clean and fed; you keep the compartment and all the rest clean; you do whatever you're told. No talkin', no arguin', nothin'. If you want to keep your tongue in your head.'

The grown women hadn't believed that, at least not at first. And they had died. She had to keep her tongue, to comfort the littles.

'Now what do you say?' the man said, leaning close. She was too scared to answer; he'd just told her not to talk. He grabbed her hair and yanked her head back. Her eyes watered. 'I'll tell you what you say, girlie. Nothing. You bow your head, when you're told what to do, and you say nothing. Women are not to speak before men. Women are to be obedient in silence. You understand?'

Trapped, terrified, she tried to nod against the pull of his hand on her hair. He let go suddenly, and her head bobbed forward.

'That's right,' he said. 'Bow your head in respect, in obedience.' He straightened up and took a step backward; Hazel watched his boots. 'Now you get busy, girlie, and get these brats cleaned up.'

She needed clothes for them; she needed cleaning supplies. She wanted to ask . . . and she wasn't supposed to talk.

'One of us'll bring you what you need,' he said. 'Food and water, as long as you're obedient. Decent clothes for the babies. There's nothin' on this heathen ship fit for you to wear; you'll have to make somethin'. We'll show you pictures. You've got the sink and toilet in there; you'll wash their clothes in that.'

She wondered why, when the crew laundry would return the dirtiest clothes clean, dry, and unwrinkled, in only a few minutes. She didn't ask.

The supplies came a short time afterwards. Packets of food, powdered milk to mix with the water in the bathroom, sheets and towels and a sack of children's clothes, soap and shampoo, combs and brushes. Even a few toys: two dolls, blocks, a toy groundcar. Hazel was grateful. She handed each of the littles a sweetbar, and rummaged through the sack of clothes . . . there was Paolo's tan jumpsuit, Brandy's striped shirt, Stassi's flowered one, Dris's gray jumpsuit. But none of the girls' jumpsuits, nor the shorts they wore with shirts.

The littles were so dirty – she couldn't tell which were smudges and which were bruises. As they finished their sweetbars, she herded them into the bathroom, and used the towels and soap to clean them up. Then she got them all dressed, as much as possible, and folded the rest of the clothes. Four more shirts, four more jumpsuits . . . three sets for each child, if only they'd been complete. And for herself . . . nothing but a long-sleeved pullover that was really Stinky's; it had been in her compartment because she'd traded shirts with him, this last segment. She didn't put it on because she had nothing to wear with it . . . the thought of wearing that on her top, and nothing below, was worse than nothing at all.

She stacked the clothes neatly in one corner, and put the food in another. She let the children sort through the toys. Brandy chose blocks, as always; Stassi hugged her doll to her chest, fiercely. Paolo began handing blocks to Brandy, while Dris put the other doll in the groundcar and rolled it along the floor.

The hatch slammed open, startling her; she almost looked up but remembered in time. The littles did look up, but quickly glanced away, toward her.

'Why aren't you dressed, girlie?'

She must not speak. She didn't know how to answer without speaking. She shook her head, spread her hands.

The boots moved closer, the big hands tossed aside the neat stack she'd made of the clothes, and came up with Stinky's pullover. The man threw it at her. 'Put this on, girlie. Now.'

She fumbled her way into it. 'You wrap yourself in one of them sheets.' She hadn't thought of that; she scrambled across the deck, grabbed a sheet, and wrapped it clumsily around her body. How could she make it stay? Something thumped on the deck in front of her – a small canvas bag. 'That's a sewing kit – if you can't sew, better learn. Make yourself something decent from the sheets. Cover your arms, everything to the ankles. Don't make the skirt too full. Only decent married women wear full skirts. Make them girl babies skirts too; sew 'em to their shirts.' He walked around, stood over the littles.

'What's this?' She didn't look up; didn't answer. 'Now girlie, you got to teach these babies right. Girls play with girls; boys play with boys. Girls got dolls; boys got boys' toys. You keep 'em separate, you hear?'

But Brandy and Paolo were friends; they'd played together since infancy. And Brandy always played with blocks and building toys. Hazel crouched, scared and furious both, as the man knocked down Brandy's block tower, and moved her near her sister. 'You – take this doll.' Brandy took it, but Hazel could see the anger in her eyes, almost enough to overcome the fear. Paolo, left with the scattered blocks, had already picked one up and was reaching toward Brandy. 'No!' the man said. 'No blocks for girls. Blocks for boys.' Paolo looked puzzled, but Brandy let out a furious screech. Casually, the man slapped her against the bulkhead. 'Shut up – you better learn now, sissie.'

The next days were, if possible, a worse nightmare. The littles could not understand any of the restrictions; Hazel struggled to keep them separated as the raiders demanded, to keep them engaged with 'appropriate' toys, to keep the compartment clean enough, herself 'decent,' and still figure out how to make the garments the raiders demanded she furnish for herself and the girls. She had never sewn anything in her life; she had seen Donya using the sewing machine to create artworks they sold when they stopped at Corian, but clothes came from shops, or – in emergencies – the fabricator. You put in the measurements, dialled the style, and out came clothes. She had no idea how to turn flat cloth into the tubelike garment in the picture the raiders showed her.

It wasn't a practical garment anyway. Snug tubes for the arms, a long one covering her from armpits to ankles . . . no one could sit comfortably, walk comfortably, climb and play and do things in a shape like that. But she didn't argue. She struggled to figure out the odd implements in the sewing kit: dangerous thin sharp bits of metal that had no place around small children, reels of fine thread, scissors, a long tape marked off in sections that corresponded to no measuring system she knew, a short metal strip – also marked in sections – with a sliding part.

Sewing by hand was much harder than it looked, though when she figured out that the tiny cup-shaped thing would fit over her finger and protect it from pricks of the long sharp thing that the thread fit through, she got along better. The fabric seemed to have a mind of its own; it shifted around as she tried to poke through it. But finally she had a long straight skirt attached to the bottom of her pullover, and skirts on the girls' shirts. They hated them, and pulled them up around their waists to play . . . but that, it turned out, was something else forbidden to girls.

'You were reared among heathen,' the man said. 'We know that, and we make allowances for it. But you're among decent folk now, and you must learn to act like decent folk. It is forbidden for any female to show herself off to men; these girl babies must be decently covered at all times.'

Then why, Hazel wanted to scream, won't you let us have underwear? Long pants? And how can you call a toddler playing on the floor a female showing herself off to men? She said nothing, but bobbed her head. She had to protect the littles, and she could do that only by being there – being able to sing them to sleep, to comfort them in a murmur that grew softer day by day.

She had no idea how much time had passed when the daily

471

visitor first took the boys out of the compartment. By then, of course the raiders knew all the children's names. At first, Paolo and Dris hung back . . . but the man simply gathered them up and carried them out. Hazel was terrified – what would they do to the boys? But in the time it took to feed the girls their lunch, the boys were back, grinning from ear to ear. Each held a new toy – Paolo had a toy spaceship, and Dris had a set of brightly colored beads.

'We had fun,' Dris said. Hazel shushed him, but Paolo spoke up.

'We can talk. They said so. Boys can talk all they want. It's only girls have to be quiet.'

Brandy scowled. 'Gimme!'

'No,' Paolo said. 'This is mine. Girls can't play with boys' toys.' Brandy burst into tears.

After that, day by day, the boys were weaned away from the girls. Daily visits outside the compartment – they returned with glowing reports: they could run up and down the corridors; they could use the swings in the gym; they could use the computer in the schoolroom. The men fed them special foods, treats. The men were teaching them. The men read to them from books, new books, stories about animals and boys and exciting stuff. They were gone hours a day now, returning to the compartment only for baths and bed. Hazel was left with the girls, the two dolls, and the endless sewing.

'You teach those girl babies to sew,' Hazel was told. 'They're old enough for that.'

They didn't want to learn, but that made no difference. Hazel realized that. But . . . no books at all? No vid, no computers, no chance to run and play? She didn't ask. She didn't dare. She didn't even dare tell them stories, the stories they knew, because the compartment was rigged for scan. She had been warned to talk no more than necessary . . . telling them stories would, she knew without asking, be breaking the rules.

The days dragged by. Stassi, though younger, was better with needle and thread than Brandy. Her stitches were ragged and uneven, but she could get them lined up into a sort of row. Brandy, more active by nature, fretted and fumed; her thread kept getting into knots. Hazel tried to find ways to let the child work

472

off her wild energy, but in that small space, and hampered by a long skirt, the child was constantly being frustrated. She cried often, and had screaming tantrums at least once a day.

Hazel would like to have had a screaming tantrum of her own, and only the littles' need for her kept her quiet.

7

Brun Meager exchanged the squad of Royal Security guards for ten of her father's personal militia from Sirialis with considerable relief. She had known some of these people for years, and although she would rather have travelled alone, this was the next best situation. With them, she visited the Allsystems Leasing office and chose a roomy private yacht for the next stage of her journey. If she was not going to have Fleet's respect anyway, there was no reason to endure discomfort. She chose the highest-priced food and entertainment package, and paid extra for an accelerated load-and-clearance that would get her on her way quickly. Allsystems checked her licenses, and those of the militia who would act as crew, and – in less than 24 hours – she had undocked and headed for her first destination. From now until the Opening Day of the hunt on Sirialis, she was free of schedules and demands, except those she chose for herself.

Since it was handy – relatively – she decided to check out her holdings within the Boros Consortium. It was something her father would approve of, the kind of grownup, mature behavior he claimed she didn't show often enough. And it was a long, long way from Castle Rock.

She spent two days with the accountants at Podj, feeling virtuous and hard-working as she waded through stacks of

473

numbers, and then decided to skip Corian – where there would be more news media, since it was a shipping hub – and go straight to Bezaire. She plotted the course, calculated the times . . . and scowled at the figures. If she went to Bezaire by any of the standard green-lined routes, she wouldn't have time to visit Rotterdam before the start of the hunting season on Sirialis. But she was determined to visit Lady Cecelia and discuss with that other adventurous lady those things which she could not say to her parents. She could skip Bezaire – but she didn't want to skip Bezaire.

She looked at the navigation catalogs again. A caution route would save her five days, but that really wasn't enough. Maybe the Boros pilots that ran the circuit all the time knew of a shortcut . . . she called up their time-on-route stats. Supposedly they all took greenlined routes . . . but the on-time figures were improbably high for the Corian-Bezaire leg of the journey. They had a shortcut; she was sure of it. Now who might be willing to let her in on the secret?

For the rich and beautiful daughter of Lord Thornbuckle, a stockholder, the secret wasn't that hard to find. A double-jump-point system where the two jump points had been stable for over fifty years. Fleet had warnings about systems harboring two jump points, but Fleet had warnings about everything. Brun grinned to herself as she plotted a jump direct from Podj to the first of the double jumps. A nice slow-vee insertion in such a small-mass vessel, and she would be safe as safe – and have plenty of time to visit Lady Cecelia.

Jester slid through the first jump point, and scan cleared. Brun checked the references, and grinned. The second jump point was right where it was supposed to be . . . an easy transit. She was tempted to make a flat run for it – nothing else should be insystem – but checked for beacons anyway.

Four popped up on the screen. Four? She punched the readout, up came *Elias Madero*, which should have cleared the system three days before, and three ships with non-Familias registry.

'Jump us out now!' Barrican said. Brun glanced at him; he was staring at the scan monitor.

'They won't notice us for another few minutes,' Brun said. 'Whatever's going on, we can find out and—'

'We're scan-delayed too,' he said. 'They aren't where you see them, whoever they are. And it's trouble—'

'I can see it's trouble,' Brun said. 'But if we're going to get them help, we need to know what kind – who it is, what's going on.'

'It won't help anyone if we're blown away,' Calvaro said. He had come up behind her. 'This thing can't fight, and we don't know what those are – they might outrun us.'

'We're little,' Brun said. 'They'll never even notice. Flea on the elephant.'

'Milady—'

That did it. Her father's men, protecting her father's daughter; they probably thought she would faint at the sight of blood. When would her father realize that she was grown, that she was capable . . .

'We're going to sneak in closer,' she said. 'And look. Just look. Then we can jump out and tell Fleet what's happened.'

'That's foolish, milady,' Calvaro said. 'What if they—'

'If they're pirates, they'll think we're too small to bother with.' She pushed back memories of that lecture on recent incursions from outlying powers. These were not the Benignity – she had seen Benignity ships on scan. Nor the Bloodhorde, which was all the way across Familias space and probably still licking its wounds after the *Koskiusko* mess. These were common criminals, and common criminals were after the big, easy profit . . . not chasing a small yacht with a few insignificant passengers.

'If you would jump out now, we could be back in range of the Corian ansible in just a few hours—'

'And have nothing much to say. No, we need to record some data, at least the beacon IDs of those other ships—' She grinned at them, and saw the grin have its usual effects. Her father's employees had been putty in her hands since she had convinced the head cook to give her all the chocolate eclairs she could cram into her mouth. Nor had she been sick, which only proved that the stuffier grownups were entirely too cautious.

Sneaking nearer with the insystem drive just nudging them along was dead easy. Brun napped briefly, slightly worried that one of them might figure out the lockout code she'd put on the nav computer so that they couldn't go into jump while she was asleep. But they hadn't. They'd tried – she could see that in their expressions, a mix of guilty and disgruntled – but she'd used a trick she'd learned at Copper Mountain and it held.

Scan delay was down to one minute by then. One of the mystery ships was snugged up to the merchanter, and one was positioned a quarter second away. The third . . . her breath caught. The third had moved . . . on an intercept course.

It couldn't have seen *Jester*. The yacht was too small; they could have spotted the bobble near the jump point, but after that – after that she had laid in a straight course and they could have extrapolated.

She should have jinked about. In the back of her mind, a nagging voice told her that she should have done what Barrican said, and jumped out right away. The pirates could not possibly have caught her then. Now – if they had military-grade scans – she flicked off the lockout. She could jump from here; there were no large masses to worry about. She had no idea where they might come out, jumping this far from the mapped points, but it had to be better.

She set up the commands, and pushed the button. A red warning light came on, and a saccharine voice from the console said 'There are no mapped jump points within critical; jump insertion refused. There are no mapped jump points . . .'

Brun felt the blood rush to her face as she slapped the jump master control the other way. A rented yacht, with standard nagivation software . . . she had not thought about that, about the failsafes it would have built in, which she would not have time to bypass. Of course Allsystems Leasing would protect their invest-ment by limiting the mistakes lessees could make.

She looked at the insystem drive controls. The yacht's insystem drive, standard for this model, should be able to outrun anything but Fleet's fastest – but only if she could redline it. She noticed that the control panel stopped well below what she knew was its redline acceleration. Still, it was all she had.

'Milady—' Barrican said softly as she reached out.

'Yes—'

476

'They might not have seen us, even so. If you don't do anything, they might miss us still.'

'And if they don't, we're easy meat,' Brun said. 'They've got the course; a preschooler could extrapolate our position.'

'But if we seem to be unaware of them, they might still consider us unimportant. If you do anything, they'll have to assume you have noticed trouble.'

What she had noticed was how stupid she'd been. Someday you'll get into something you can't handle by being bright and pretty and lucky, Sam had told her. She'd assumed someday was a long way away, and here it was.

'We have essentially no weapons,' she said softly, though there was no need for quietness. 'So our only hope of escape is to get within effective radius of that jump point – unless they do ignore us, and somehow I don't think they will.'

On scan, the other ship's projected course curved to parallel theirs. Another of the smaller ships now moved – and moved in the blink-stop way of a warship that could microjump within a system.

'We can't outrun *that*,' Brun said, under her breath. 'Two of them . . .'

'Just go along as if we had no scans out at all,' Barrican advised.

It was good advice. She knew it was good advice. But doing nothing wore on her in a way that action never did. Second by second, *Jester* slid along much more slowly than it had to; second by second the unknown ships closed in. What kind of scan did they have? Koutsoudas had been able to detect activity aboard other ships – could these? Would they believe that a little ship on a simple slow course from jump point to jump point would notice nothing?

Seconds became minutes, became an hour. She had shut down active scan long since; passive scan showed *Elias Madero* and the third unknown in the same relative location, with the other two flanking *Jester*. They were approaching the closest point to the merchanter on their projected course to the second jump point. If they got by, if they weren't stopped, would that mean they were in the clear?

*　　*　　*

477

There was no logical alternative. One could always choose certain death . . . but it was amazingly hard to do. So this was what Barin had faced . . . this was what the instructor had been talking about . . . Brun dragged her mind back to the present. The yacht had a self-destruct capability; she could blow it, and herself and her father's loyal men. Or she could force the raiders to blow their way in, and not wear a pressure suit – that would do it. But . . . she made herself look at the faces of the men who surrounded her, who were about to die for her, or with her.

'I was wrong,' she said. 'No comfort now, but – you were right, and I was wrong. I should have jumped right back out.'

'No matter, milady,' said Calvaro. 'We'll do what we can.'

Which was nothing. They could die defending her . . . or be killed without fighting; she did not believe the raiders' would spare them.

'I think we should surrender,' she said. 'Perhaps—'

'Not an option, milady,' Calvaro said. 'That's not a choice you can make; we're sworn to your father to protect you. Go to your cabin, milady.'

She didn't want to. She knew what was coming, and it was not death she feared, but having forced these men into a position where they had to die – would die – in a futile effort to protect her. *I'm not worth it*, she wanted to say . . . to admit . . . and she knew she must not say that. She must not take their honor from them. They thought her father was worth it, or – again Esmay's words rang in her head – they thought *they* were worth it. She said their names, to each of them: Giles Barrican, Hubert Calvaro, Savoy Ardenil, Basil and Seren Verenci, Kaspar and Klara Pronoth, Pirs Slavus, Netenya Biagrin, Charan Devois. She could find no words for them beyond naming them, recognizing their lives. She gave them all she had, a last smile, then went meekly to her cabin as they wished. It wouldn't work; she would die at the end, but . . . they would not have to see her dead or captive. They could die remembering that smile, for all the good it did . . . and she did not even know if they believed in an afterlife where such a memory might be comforting. She wrote their names, over and over, on many scraps of paper and tucked them in places she hoped the

478

raiders would not find. They deserved more, but that was all she could do.

When the cabin hatch gave at last, she faced the intruders with her personal weapons, and the first one to try the opening fell twitching. But the small sphere they tossed in burst in a spray of needles . . . and she felt the fine stinging all up her body. Her hand relaxed, her sidearm fell, she felt her knees sagging, and the deck came up to meet her.

She woke with a feeling of choking, tried to cough loose the obstruction, and then realized it was a wad of cloth tied in her mouth. A gag, like something out of an ancient story. Ridiculous. She blinked, and glared up at the men standing over her. They were in p-suits, helmets dangling in back. Her body still felt heavy and limp, but she could just move her legs when she tried. Then they spoke to each other in an accent so heavy that she could hardly understand it, and reached for her. She tried to struggle, but the drug made it impossible. They dragged her upright, then out through the twisted hatch into the main passage of the yacht . . . over the bodies of her guardsmen . . . through the tube they'd rigged between the yacht and their ship, whatever it was.

They pushed her into a seat and strapped her in, then walked off. Brun wiggled as much as she could. Her arms, then her legs, began to itch, and then tingle. So . . . the drug was wearing off, but she didn't see how she could get away. Yet. *Your first duty is to stay alive.*

Several more men came through the tube . . . was that all? Or had some stayed aboard the yacht, and if so, why? She felt her ears throb as they shut the exterior lock, then the interior lock. They must have cast off the yacht . . . someone would find it. Someday. If another Boros ship came this way, if another Boros ship even noticed a minor bit of space debris . . .

The ship she was on shuddered uneasily – jump? – then steadied again. Three of the men were still back by the airlock. Now they went to work . . . Brun craned her head, trying to see. Her ears popped again. Something clanked; the ship made a noise like a tuning fork dragged on concrete, then stopped. The men moved on into the airlock, and – judging by the sounds –

undogged the outer hatch. Colder air gushed in, chilling her ankles. She heard loud voices from the other – ship, it must be – and those men leaving.

The ones who'd originally brought her aboard reappeared, now in some sort of tan uniform instead of p-suits, unstrapped her, and hauled her upright. If she could break loose, while they thought she was still weakened – but three more appeared at the airlock. Too many, her mind decided, even as her body tried to twist. Too much drug, she realized, as her muscles refused to give her the speed she was used to. Well, if she couldn't fight, she could at least observe. Tan uniforms, snug-fitted shirts over slightly looser slacks, over boots. Brown leather boots, she noticed when she looked down. On the collar, insignia of a five-pointed star in a circle.

Once she was through the airlock, she saw the Boros Consortium logo on the bulkhead . . . so she must be on the *Elias Madero*. The men hustled her down the passage – wide enough for a small robot loader – past hatches with symbols and labels she felt she should recognize. Past a galley with its programmable food processor humming, past a gymnasium . . . to the bridge, which reminded her instantly of the bridge where she'd stood when she'd broken the second mate's nose . . .

But the man who stood in the center of the bridge was no merchant captain.

He had to be the commander. He wore the same uniform as the others, but the star-in-circle insignia on his collar was larger, and gold instead of silver. She met his gaze with all the defiance she could muster. He looked past her to her escort.

'Got the papers?' He had the same accent as the others.

'Yep.' One of the other men came forward with her ID packet. 'She's the one, all right. We checked the retinal scans and everything.'

'You done good, boys.' The commander glanced at her papers, then at her. 'Not a single shred of decency, but what can you expect of that sort?' The other men chuckled. Brun struggled to spit out the gag; she knew exactly what she wanted to say to this . . . this person. The commander came closer. 'You're that so-called Speaker's daughter. You're used to having your own way, just like your daddy. Well, all things come to an end.' He waited a moment, then went on. 'You probably think your daddy will get you out of this, like he's gotten you out of all your other scrapes. You may think he's going to send that *Regular Space Service*' – he made a mockery of Fleet with that tone – 'to rescue you. But it ain't gonna happen that way. We don't want your daddy's money. We aren't scared of your daddy's power. They won't find you. No one's gonna find you. You're ours, now.'

He grinned past her, and the other men chuckled.

'Your daddy and that Council of Families, they think they got a right to make the laws for everybody, but they don't. They think they got a right to set fees and taxes on everybody comes through their so-called territory, but they don't. Free men don't have to pay any mind to what perverts and women say. That's not the way God made the universe. We're free men, we are, and our laws come from the word of God as set forth by the prophets.'

Brun wanted to scream at him: *They will destroy you*, but she could not make a sound. She thought it at him anyway: *You can't do this; you won't get away with it; they will come after me and blow you to bits*.

He reached out to her face, and when she turned away he grabbed her ears with both hands and forced her to face him. 'Now your daddy may try – or maybe, because he'll know we've got you, he'll have the good sense to let us alone if he doesn't want to see his little girl in pieces. But he's not gonna get you back. No one is. Your life just changed forever. You're gonna obey, like the prophets said women should, and the sooner you start the easier it will be on you.'

Never. She threw that at him with her eyes, with every fiber of her body. Maybe she couldn't do anything now, but now was not forever. She would get free, because she always did come out on top. She was lucky; she had abilities they didn't know about.

But the fear edged closer. Someday, Sam had said, Esmay had said, your luck will run out. Someday you'll be helpless. Someday you'll be stuck. And what will you do then?

The words she had thrown at them sounded thin now, faced with these men. But she had meant them. She would not give up; she would not give in. She was Charlotte Brunhilde . . . named for queens and warriors.

He moved his hands down the sides of her head to her neck. 'You don't believe me yet. That's fine . . . doesn't matter.' He slid his hands out her shoulders, then curled his fingers into the neck of her jumpsuit. Brun would have curled her lip if she could. Here it came, the predictable move of a storycube male captor. He was going to rip her clothes off. He would be surprised when he tried; she hadn't spent all that money for custom-tailored protective shipsuits for nothing. But he didn't try to rip the suit, just ran his fingers inside the neck, feeling the cloth. 'We'll need the slicer, boys.' Well, hackneyed, but smarter than dirt, maybe.

The knife the other man handed him was large enough to gut an elephant, Brun thought. He wanted her to be impressed with it – some men always thought bigger was better – but she had seen knives that big before.

'Now the first thing,' the man said, sliding the tip of the long blade into the neck of her suit. 'Women don't wear men's clothes.' *Men's* clothes! How could anyone mistake a custom outfit designed for her body as a man's outfit? With those darts, it wouldn't have fitted any male she'd ever seen. But the man was still talking.

'Women who wear men's clothes are usurping men's authority. We don't put up with that.' He made a single rapid slice downward, and the shipsuit opened from neck to crotch. He could just as well have pulled the tab, but he had to make a dramatic thing out of it, ruining an expensive shipsuit.

'Women are not allowed to wear trousers,' he said. Brun blinked. What did pants have to do with it? Everyone wore pants if they were doing the kind of work in which pants were more comfortable. But this was probably just an excuse to cut her clothes off. He inserted the tip of the knife into the lower end of the opening, and sliced open the leg of the shipsuit . . . then the other leg. Brun stared ahead. They would want her to react; she wouldn't react. 'Women are not allowed to wear men's shoes.' At a nod from the commander, two men grabbed her legs and pulled off her boots. Stupid, stupid, stupid. Custom-made boots, *her* boots, and she was a woman, and therefore those were her bare feet thudded on the cold deck.

Next the commander gestured and someone behind her pulled the ripped sides of her shipsuit behind her. This she'd expected.

Her chin lifted. *Take a good look. You'll pay for every leer.* But the commander's frown was not a leer. He was staring at her abdomen, at the Registered Embryo logo with its imprinted genetic data.

'Abomination . . .' breathed one of the other men. 'A construct—' He pulled out his own big knife, but the commander's gesture stopped him, just as Brun was sure she would be gutted right there.

'It's true that none of the Faithful can tamper with God's plan for their children, but this woman is the result of tampering. What was done to her was not her responsibility.' Brun relaxed muscles she didn't realize she'd tensed. The man leaned over, peering at the mark, then rubbed his finger over it. Brun thought of kneeing him in the face, but there were still too many of them . . . she would have to wait.

'I don't like it,' one of the others said. 'What perversions have they bred into her . . .'

'None that will survive our training,' the commander said. 'And she is strong, well-grown. By all reports, she carries genes for intelligence and good health. It would be a waste not to make use of them.'

'But—'

'She will be no threat to us.' He looked Brun full in the face. 'You – you are thinking still that you will be rescued, that you can go back to your abominations and perversions. You do not yet believe that your old life is over. But you will soon. You have already spoken the last words you will ever speak.'

What did that mean? Were they going to kill her after all? Brun stared back, defiant.

'You will be used as you deserve . . . and as a mute breeder, you will be no threat, no matter what.'

Brun felt a shock as her mind caught up with that. Mute? What was he . . . were they going to cut out her tongue? Only barbarians did things like that . . .

He laughed then, at a change in expression she did not know she'd made. 'I see you understand – that much, at least. You're not used to that – not being able to plead and beg and wheedle your way around your weakling father. Or the other men you've whored with. But that's over. The voice of the heathen will be heard no more; yea, the tongues of those who know not God will be silenced. And, as the holy words also say, Women shall keep silence before men, in respect and submission. You were born in sin and abomination, but you will live in the service of God Almighty. When it is time, when *we* choose, you will sleep, and when you awake, you'll have no voice.'

Her body jerked, in spite of herself . . . she struggled, as she had not struggled before, knowing it was useless. The men laughed, loud confident laughter. Brun fought herself to stillness, hating the tears that stung her eyes, that ran down her face.

'We'll put you away now, to think about that. I want you to know ahead of time, to understand . . . for this is part of the training you will receive, to learn that you have no power, and no man will listen to you. You are silenced, slut, as women should be silent.'

It could not be happening. Not to her, not to the daughter of the Speaker of the Grand Council. Not to a young woman who could rappel down cliffs, who had earned badges in marksmanship, who could ride to hounds, who had never done anything she didn't want to do, with anyone she wanted to do it with. Things like this happened, if they happened, in dull history books, in times long past, or places far away. Not to her. All this, she knew to her shame, was in her eyes, was in the tears, in the shaking of her body, and the men laughed to see it.

'Take her back – be sure you've cuffed her. Start an IV, too. Just saline, for now.'

For now. For however long. She believed, suddenly. It was real, it was happening . . . no, it couldn't be! The men holding her moved her firmly along, her bare feet stumbling on all the rough places where her boots had protected her. She was cold, frozen with a fear she had never understood when she saw the storycubes or read the old books in her father's library.

In the compartment, four of them laid her on the bunk, ignoring her struggles, and cuffed her hands to the sides, her feet together. She tried to plead with her eyes: loosen the gag, just for a minute, please, *please*. They chuckled, confident and amused. Another one came, with a little kit, and turned her arm . . .

inserting the IV needle deftly. She stared up at the bag of saline hanging from a hook overhead.

'When we're ready,' one of them said, 'we'll put you to sleep.' He grinned. 'Welcome to the real world.'

She hated them; she writhed with fury. But it was too late for that.

She would go to sleep . . . it would be a dream, when she woke. A bad dream, a scary dream, and she would go tell Esmay about it and apologize for having laughed at Esmay. She would . . .

She woke to a sense of pain, and fought her way to consciousness. No gag in her mouth; she could breathe through it. Had they – ? But she could feel her tongue, too large it seemed, scrubbing around in her mouth. So they hadn't. At least not yet. She swallowed. Her throat felt raw and scratchy. She looked around, cautiously. No one . . . she was still cuffed to the bunk, with the IV running in her arm, but no one was there. She took a breath of pure relief . . . ahhh.

And froze in horror. No sound. She tried again. And again. No sound but the rush of air in her throat, which hurt a lot now. She tried to whisper, at least, and realized that she could shape words, she could make hisses and clicks (though moving her tongue made the pain in her throat worse) but she could get no real volume out, hardly enough sound to carry across a small room.

Almost at once, the door slid aside, and the one who had inserted the IV came in.

'You need to drink,' the man said. He held a straw to her mouth. 'Swallow this.'

It was cold, minty. She could swallow . . . but she could not say anything. Her throat hurt as the liquid went down, then eased.

'You've realized what we've done,' he said. 'Cut your vocal cords, some muscles. Left your tongue – you can eat normally, and swallow, and all the rest of it. But no speech. And no, it won't grow back. Not the way we do it.'

It had to be a dream, but she had never felt a dream this real. The cold air on her skin, the ache from being bound in one position too long, the pain in her throat, and . . . and the silence

485

when she tried to speak. She tried to whisper, to mouth words, but at that he put a hand on her mouth.

'Stop that. You don't talk to men, ever. Make faces at us, and you'll be punished.'

It wasn't making faces, it was communication. How could he not know that?

'Nothing you have to say is important to us. Later, if you're obedient, you can lipspeak to other women, in the women's quarters. But not now, and never to men. Now – I'm going to examine you. Do as I say.'

His examination was clinical and complete, but not brutal; he handled her body with the same smooth competence she had received from doctors in her father's clinics. He spoke the results aloud, for a recorder. Brun learned that she was now catalogued as Captive Female 4, slut, gene-altered, fertile. Her instant satisfaction at the error in that disappeared when he held up her fertility implant, and she realized they had removed it. Through the haze of drugs, she now felt the pain in her left leg, from the incision. She was fertile, then – or soon could be, if they also knew about fertility drugs. She thought they probably would.

When he was through, the man called others; they carried her from that compartment to another, somewhat larger, but empty of anything she could use as a weapon against them or herself. She was still cuffed, this time one arm to the corner of the bunk. Beside her the men left a soft tube of nutrient gel and a carisack of water. She had just dozed off when the commander appeared with the man who had waked her.

'How long?'

'Well, she'll be strong enough in another two or three days, but she won't ovulate for another twelve to fourteen. I gave her the shots, but it takes that long to cycle.'

'We'll move her in with Girlie and the babies when she's strong enough. She can start sewing, though I doubt she knows any more about it than Girlie did.' He stepped up to the bunk. 'Now you know we spoke truth; living among liars as you did, you might have doubted us. Now your next lesson. You aren't who you were. No one will ever call you by that heathen name you used. Where you're going, no one will even know it. Right now you have no name at all. You're a slut, because you aren't a virgin or a wife. Sluts are any man's pleasure. When you've borne your third child, if anyone wants you and if you've been obedient, you'll be available for junior wife.'

He left, taking the other man with him, before she even thought to curse him in whispers. Brun wanted to cry, but tears would not come. Instead, despair settled over her like a dark blanket, tucking itself around her mind until she could see nothing else. She struggled against it briefly, but it held her as firmly as the cuff on her arm, and she was so tired.

She slept again, and woke. Her throat hurt; she sucked at the nutrient tube, and the chill gel eased it again. The move to the other compartment had to be better, Brun thought. If she lay there alone she would go crazy. Another human – even women belonging to these men – had to be better.

Hazel looked up from the littles only as far as the men's waists . . . she saw the woman's bare legs and almost forgot to keep her gaze down. They had told her about this woman, and Hazel's heart had ached for her . . . but it frightened her, because they had shown Hazel pictures of what they'd done to her, and threatened to do the same to Hazel and the littles if Hazel disobeyed. Now they pushed the woman down onto the pallet along the wall. Hazel pulled the littles back into the corner. The woman was pale, almost as white as milk, and dark bruises stood out on her skin. She had a rough red scar on her leg, and her face . . . Hazel didn't want to look at her face, but the burning blue eyes seemed to reach for hers and demand a response.

'Girlie, you take care of her. Feed her. Make sure she eats and drinks and goes to toilet. Keep her clean. But don't talk to her. Understand?'

Hazel bobbed her head. They'd told her and told her – if she talked to the woman they were bringing in, they'd do the same to her. And to both the littles. She couldn't let that happen.

'You teach her to sew, if she doesn't know how. Make her a decent dress. We'll bring more cloth.'

Hazel bobbed her head again. The men left, leaving the strange woman alone. Hazel hitched herself across the deck, being careful not to uncover her legs, and retrieved the food sack. She held out a tube of paste concentrate. The woman put her hand in front of her mouth and turned away. Hazel went back to the littles, who were staring at the woman with wide eyes.

'Who she?' asked Brandy, barely breathing the words.

'Shhh,' Hazel said.

'No clothes,' breathed Stassi.

'Shh.' She handed the littles their dolls, and started them on the dancing game she'd devised.

Every word Brun had said to Esmay seemed etched on her skin in acid. Simply a matter of practice, she'd said. Just think of pistons and cylinders, she'd said. Easy . . .

In the silence, in her mind, she apologized again and again, screaming the words she could not say. How could she have been so wrong? So stupid? So arrogant? How could she have thought the universe was set up for her convenience?

Her body ached, raw and sore from waking to sleeping again. They had all used her, over and over, for days . . . how many days she didn't know. Through one cycle, at least, for she had bled heavily. They didn't touch her then, and would not even enter the compartment. Not until she was 'clean' again . . . and then it started all over.

When her breasts swelled up, sore to the touch, she winced away from one of them. He stopped. 'Slut . . .' he said warningly. Then he prodded her breasts, and moved away. She lay slack, uncaring. If it wasn't hurting right now, that was enough. Another one came . . . the one, she now recognized, who was some kind of medic. He felt her breasts, took her temperature, and sampled her blood. A few minutes later, he grinned.

'You're breeding. Good.'

Good? That she was carrying the child of one of these disgusting monsters? He seemed to read her feelings in her face.

'You won't be able to do anything unnatural. If you try, we'll confine you alone. Understand?'

She glared at him, and he slapped her. 'You're just pregnant, not injured. You will answer appropriately when I ask you a question. Understand?' Against her will, she nodded. 'Get dressed now.'

Under his gaze, she fumbled back into the ugly tubelike dress the girl had made for her and tied the tapes that held it closed. She threw the square of cloth that covered her arms around her shoulders. They hadn't figured out yet how to put sleeves in the dress.

'Come along,' he said to her, and led her back to the compartment where the girl and the little ones waited. The girl looked at her, then looked away. Brun wasn't sure how old the girl was; she looked very young, perhaps eleven or twelve, but if she'd had an implant to retard puberty, she might be as old as eighteen. If only they could talk – even write notes back and forth . . . But there were no writing materials in the cabin, and the girl refused to talk, looking away when Brun tried to mouth words at her.

Day followed day, unbearable in their sameness. Brun watched the young girl try to quiet and entertain the two little ones, feed them, keep the compartment clean. She was always gentle with the younger girls, always busy in her care for them. The girl accepted Brun's help, but seemed afraid of her. When the girl held out food she had been ordered to give Brun, she looked down or away.

Brun had no way of telling time, except by her body's growth. When she felt the first vague movement that could not be ignored, she burst into tears. After a while, she felt someone patting her head gently, and looked through tear-stuck lashes to see one of the babies – the one the girl called Stassi. The child put her head near Brun's.

'Don' cry,' she said very softly. 'Don' cry.'

'Stassi, no!' That was the older girl, pulling the child away. Brun felt as if she'd been stabbed in a new way. Did the girl think she would hurt the child? Was she to have no one to comfort her? She struggled to hold back the sobs, but couldn't.

To get her mind off herself, she tried to pay more attention to the others, especially the older girl. The girl could not be one of them – not originally. She sewed clumsily, with no real knowledge of how to fit cloth to human shapes. When the men dropped off garments to be mended, Brun could see that they had been made

489

originally with great skill . . . with hand sewing, like the most expensive 'folk' imports, the stitches subtly imperfect. Surely a girl of their people would know, by that age, how to do it right. She glanced at the girl, whose brown hair hung down like a curtain to either side of her face. She didn't even know the girl's name . . . the men always called her Girlie, and the little ones Baby.

If the girl weren't one of theirs, where had she come from? No clues now . . . the pullover that formed the top of her dress might have come from anywhere, one of the millions sold in a midprice shop at any spaceport. Spaceport? Had she been snatched off a space station? Or a ship? By the color of her skin and hair – by her features – she could have come from any of a hundred planets, off any of a thousand ships. And yet – she was herself, an individual, just as Brun was. She had a past; she had hoped for a future. Ordinary . . . but very real. Brun found herself imagining a family for the girl, a home . . . wondering if the little ones were her sisters or just other captured children. How did the girl stand it?

Tears choked her again; she clenched her hands to her swelling belly. The girl flashed her a quick look, wary. Then, for the first time, she reached out a hand, and patted Brun's. That did it. Brun cried harder, rocking back and forth.

8

Some days after boosting the trader on its way, *Shrike* nosed into the spindown military docking collar at Overhold, the larger of the two orbital stations serving Bezaire, as gently as a spider landing on a tree. Esmay carried out the docking sequence under Solis's watchful eye; it was her first docking. Everything went smoothly; Solis nodded as the status lights flicked to green, and then spoke to the Stationmaster. 'R.S.S. *Shrike* docked; permission to unseal?'

'Permission to unseal. All personnel leaving ship must be ID'd at the security desk opposite the docking bay.'

'Understood, Stationmaster. We anticipate a brief visit, and no station liberty. My quartermaster will be coming out to arrange for some supplies.'

'Right, *Shrike*. You do have a hardcopy packet in the tank.'

'Thank you, sir.' Solis grimaced as he flicked off the screen. 'Idiot civilians . . . says that right out on the station com, where anyone with a halfway decent datasuck could get it.' He turned to Esmay. 'Lieutenant, you'll take the bridge while I'm on station picking up our mail. I anticipate being gone less than an hour. If I'm delayed, I'll call you.'

'Sir.' Esmay toggled the internal com. 'Security escort to the access for the captain, on the double.'

'And . . . I think we'll do a practice scan, as well. Nobody's checked Overhold since Hearne was by, and there's no reason to trust her data. You can set that up while I'm gone.'

Nothing showed up on the scan by the time Solis returned, and he sent Esmay off to other routine duties. Half a shift later, Chief Arbuthnot came back from the station in a state of annoyance and reported to the cook while Esmay was in the galley inspecting the sink traps.

'They don't have any Arpetan marmalade in, and we need it for the captain's birthday dinner. I always get it here; it's better quality than out of stores at HQ. They say they don't expect any until the Boros circuit ship comes in. You know how fond he is of Arpetan marmalade, especially the green gingered.'

'Odd. Wasn't that ship supposed to be in already?' The cook glanced up at a schedule on the bulkhead. 'We usually get here a week or so after her.'

'Yes, but she's not. They don't sound very worried, though.'

Esmay reported that conversation, minus the specifics of a treat for the captain's birthday, to Captain Solis.

'They don't seem concerned . . . interesting. I think perhaps we'll have a word with the Boros shipping agent here.'

The Boros agent, a flat-faced woman of middle age, shrugged off Captain Solis's concern.

'You know yourself, Captain, that ships are not always on time. Captain Lund is getting on a bit – this was to be his last circuit – but we are confident in his honesty.'

'It's not his honesty I'm questioning, but his luck. What was his percentage of late arrivals?'

'Lund? He's better than ninety-three percent on time, and in the last five years one hundred percent on time.'

'Which you define as . . .'

'Within twenty-four hours, dock to dock.'

'On all segments?'

'Well . . . let me check.' The woman called up a file and peered at it. 'Yes, sir. In fact, on the segment ending here, he's often twelve to twenty-four hours early.'

'When would you have reported an overdue ship, if we hadn't asked?'

'Company policy is to wait three days . . . seventy-two hours . . . for any run, and add another day for each scheduled ten days. For *Elias Madero*, on this segment, that would come to ten days altogether. And from day before yesterday, when she was due, that's . . . seven days from now.'

Captain Solis said nothing on the way back to the ship, but called Esmay into his office as soon as they arrived.

'You see the problem . . . scheduled transit time is seventy-two days, from Corian to Bezaire, dock to dock . . . most of that time spent on insystem drive. If you consider beacon-to-beacon time, she should have been off-scan only sixteen days.'

'What's the scan data from Corian?'

'Normal exit from system. The approved course was like this—' Solis pointed it out on the charts. 'That makes the scheduled transit fairly tight . . . if the company really schedules things that tight, then it makes sense to allow some overage. But I'd expect someone on this route to be over the alloted time at least thirty percent of the time. And the *Elias Madero* wasn't. Does that tell you anything?'

'They've been using a shortcut,' Esmay said promptly. 'They'd have to.'

'Right. Now we have to figure out where.'

'Someone at Boros should know,' Esmay said.

'Yes – but if it's an illegal transit, unmapped or something, they may not want to tell us. Tell me, Lieutenant, who would you recommend for a little quiet questioning?'

The crew list ran through Esmay's mind, unmarked by any helpful notes on deviousness; she hadn't been with them long enough to find out. She fell back on tradition. 'I would ask Chief Arbuthnot, sir.'

'Good answer. Tell him we need someone who would be confused with a shady character, someone who can get answers out of a rock by persuasion.'

Chief Arbuthnot knew exactly what Esmay wanted and promised to send 'young Darin' out at once. The answer that finally came back several days later was expected, but not overly helpful.

'A double-jump system,' Solis said, when he had taken the data and dismissed the pasty-faced Darin. 'Hmm. Let's see if we can get confirmation out of someone at Boros. They probably ran into a shifting jump point.'

'Why would someone retiring risk that?' Esmay wondered aloud.

'He probably thought it was stable. Some of those systems are stable for decades, but that doesn't mean they're safe.'

Something tickled Esmay's mind. 'If . . . they were carrying contraband . . . then the time gained in a shortcut would give them time to offload it. Or if someone knew they had contraband, it'd make a fine spot for an ambush.'

'Well . . .' Solis raked a hand through his hair. 'We'd better go take a look and see . . . I have to hope it's not a shifting jump point . . .'

By this time, the local Boros agent was quite willing to list the *Elias Madero* as missing. Even so, it took Solis another two days to locate someone higher in the Boros administration who could confirm not only the existence, but the location of the shortcut.

'There's an off odor about this whole thing,' he said to Esmay. 'Normally I'd expect reluctance to admit to using a dangerous route, but there's something more. Or less . . . I'm not sure. Now – how would you plot a course to this place?'

It was not, Esmay discovered, a simple matter. The shortest route would have been to reverse what the trader's course would have been, but Fleet charts did not list any insertion data for the outbound jump point.

'Besides,' Solis said, 'if we go in that way, we'll cross any trail they made. We need to come in the way they did.'

'But that'll take much longer.'

Solis shrugged, a gesture which did nothing to mitigate the tension of his expression. 'Whatever happened has already happened. My guess is that it happened days before we got to Bezaire. So what matters now is to find out what happened, in as much detail as possible. That means approaching the system with all due caution.'

All due caution meant spending twenty-three days jumping from Bezaire to Podj to Corian, and from there to the shortcut jump points. Esmay set up each course segment, and each time Solis approved.

Shrike eased its way into the system with what Esmay hoped would be low relative velocity. So it proved . . . and as scan steadied, she could see that the system held no present traffic.

'But over here, Lieutenant, there's some kind of mess – I can't tell if it's distortion from interaction of the two jump points or leftover stuff from ships. If it's ships, it's more than one.' The senior scan tech pointed to the display.

'Huh.' Esmay looked at the scan herself; ripples and blurs obscured what should have been a steady starfield. 'What's the range?'

'Impossible to say right now, Lieutenant. We don't know how large it is, so we can't get a range . . . but to me, the texture looks closer to this than the other jump point.' The scan tech glanced at the captain.

'We'll continue on course for two hours, then see what parallax gives us,' Solis said.

In two hours, the area of distorted scan was hardly larger.

'Well, Lieutenant,' Solis said, 'we can risk a micro-jump, run in a few light-seconds, and see what happens . . . or we can sneak up on it. What's your analysis of the relative risk?'

Esmay pointed to the scan display. 'Sir . . . this knot in the grav readings ought to be the second jump point, and if it is, it hasn't shifted. Nor has this one. Which suggests that we're definitely looking at transit residue . . . and therefore, unless it's an entire Benignity battle fleet, it's not that big. So . . . it's close, but not within a light minute – we could jump in fifteen-second incre-ments, and have a safe margin.'

'If it's only transit residue, you're right. If it's also debris – it's been expanding from its source – and we don't know the location of its source – at some velocity we also don't know, for at least – I'd say thirty days. Worst-case: *Elias Madero* was carrying the missing weapons, and for some reason they all detonated . . . how much debris, in how big a volume, are we talking about?'

'I don't know, sir,' Esmay said, feeding numbers into the calc subunit as fast as she could.

'Nor do I, and that's why we'll jump in *one*-second bursts, with the main shields on full.'

Solis brought *Shrike* toward the anomaly in repeated small jumps. At twenty-one light-seconds in, the scan was markedly different. Now they could see clearly that more than one ship had been involved.

'Let's just sit here and look at this,' Solis said. On insystem drive, *Shrike* was hardly sitting still, but it would still take her hours to reach the distortion. 'Do we have any indication at all of an original track?'

'Very attenuated, sir, but this might be the merchanter's original trace—' Scan switched filters and enhancement to pick out, in pale green, a faint, widened trail. 'If we take the centerline of that, we get appearance at the incoming jump point, and progress consistent with an insystem drive of its class up to this point—' He pointed to the confusion of stronger traces. 'But there's a more recent trace, much smaller.'

'So . . . assume for the moment that we have found the merchanter's incoming trace, and it's a perfectly straightforward course toward the second jump point, just as they'd done before. There's no bobble indicating slowdown until the mess?'

'None, Captain, but the traces are so old I can't be sure.'

'Right. But I'm assuming that for now. She comes in, she heads for her outbound jump, and . . . runs into a bunch of other ships. Trouble, no doubt. Do we have *any* older traces?'

'No, and from this angle it'd be hard to see 'em.'

'Fine, we'll go up and take a look there.' Solis put his finger on the chart. 'A thirty-two-second jump to these coordinates. I want to be well outside the zone of distortion.'

Scan blurred and steadied again. 'Now,' Solis said, 'I want to find out where those other ships came from, and in what order.'

Esmay found this tedious, but knew better than to say so. Surely the fastest way to find out what had happened to the *Elias Madero* would be to go in and look. The system was empty – what could be wrong with that?

The scan tech raised his hand. 'Captain, the merchanter – or the ship that made the incoming trace – left by the second jump point.'

'What!'

'Yes, sir. Look here. There's five outbound traces: three maybe patrol-size craft, one very small – my guess is it's whatever little ship overlay the merchanter's trace on the way in – and the big one, the merchanter itself.'

'Then why hasn't it shown up?' Solis muttered.

'They . . . raiders don't steal entire ships, do they?' Esmay asked.

'Not . . . often. But . . . if she was carrying weapons . . . they might. Let's think this through. We have one large ship – we're assuming for now it was the Boros ship – coming in, running into something, and then leaving by the second jump point. One little ship, sometime later, following it in and out—'

'Excuse me, Captain, but the little ship's departure trace is the same age as the others. Within a few minutes, anyway.'

'So . . . they had arranged a cleanup? Someone to follow behind and make sure the merchanter went through?' Solis shook his head. 'But then we still don't know who the other three ships were. Which way they came in. Any other traces?'

More color shifts on the scan monitor, as the tech cycled through all the enhancement possibilities. Suddenly three pale blue tracks showed up, angling from the second jump point to make a wide circuit and end up positioned along the merchanter's track.

'There they are, sir. Came in by number two . . . and set up an ambush, looks like.'

'So I see. Good job, Quin. Well, that seems clear enough. Someone knew the merchanter was coming, and wanted it; someone came in and set up either an ambush or a rendezvous.' He grinned at Esmay. 'Now, Lieutenant, we'll go in and see what evidence we can pick up.'

The first evidence was a scatter of what was clearly debris.

'So the ship blew?' Esmay asked. 'Or was blown?'

'No – not enough debris.' The scan tech pointed out figures along the side of the screen. 'I've been keeping track of the estimated total mass of all fragments, and it's less than would fit into one of the five cargo holds of the freighter we're hunting. Moreover, if it was from an explosion, it would be much more scattered by now. This was dumped from something with very low relative vee, perhaps given just a little push in addition. My guess is that someone captured it and took it.' She reset one of the fine-grain scans. 'Let's see if we can find any bodies.'

Hour after hour, then day after day, the painstaking work went on. The SAR ship located and identified one piece of debris after another, all the while plotting location and vector on a 3-D display. Hundreds, thousands, of items . . . and then, the bodies they had known must be there, that they had both hoped and feared to find. They gathered the bodies into one of the vacuum bays, tagging them with numbers, the order in which they were retrieved. Men, women . . . the men in shipsuits, with their names stenciled on back and chest, as expected; the women . . .

'Their tongues have been cut out,' the medic said. 'And they're naked.' Esmay could hear the strain in his voice. 'I can't tell, out here, if it was done before or after death.'

'I never heard of the Bloodhorde making it into this sector,' someone said.

'This isn't Bloodhorde work . . . they mutilate males as well, and this isn't their typical mutilation anyway.'

Lieutenant Venoya Haral, Major Bannon's assistant, piled the items on the table. Bannon himself was in the morgue, working on the recovered bodies. 'All these things were all marked and recorded in place,' she said to Esmay. 'Now we need to know what they tell us about the crew and the raiders.'

'Didn't Boros give us a crew list?'

'Yes, but crew lists aren't always dead accurate. Someone gets sick or drunk and lays off for a circuit, or someone's kid comes along for the ride.'

'Children?'

'Usually. Commercial haulers often have children aboard, especially those on stable runs like this. We haven't found any juvenile bodies yet – which doesn't mean anything either way. They're smaller, and less likely to be picked up. We're still missing five adult bodies, including the captain. Let's see.' Haral started sorting items into classes. 'ID cases . . . put those down at that end. Grooming items. Recording devices . . . *aha.*' She started to pick it up and shook her head. 'No . . . do things in order. But I can hope that this recorded something useful.'

'Here's a child's toy,' Esmay said. It was a stuffed animal, in blue and orange, well chewed by some child. She didn't want to think about the fate of those children on the merchanter. She had to hope they were dead.

'Good. Stick it over there, and anything else that looks like it belongs with children. Where was it found?'

Esmay referred to her list. 'In the back pocket of a man whose shipsuit read "Jules Armintage." '

'Probably picked it up off the deck where some youngster dropped it. How was he killed?'

Esmay looked back at the list. 'Shot in the head. Record doesn't say with what.'

'The major will figure that out. Oh, here's something—' Haral held up a handcomp. 'We might get some useful data off that, if they used it for anything but figuring the odds on a horse race. Didn't you have background in scan?'

When they had catalogued the items, Haral began examining them. 'You don't know how to do this yet,' Haral said. 'So I'll give you the easy stuff. See if any of those cubes have data on them. They're pretty tough, but the radiation may have fried 'em.'

The first cube seemed to be a record of stores' usage by the crew over the past eight voyage segments; it listed purchases and inventory levels, all with dates. The second, also dated, was from environmental, a complete record of the environmental log covering thirty days six months before.

'One of a set,' Haral said. 'But it gives us some baseline to go on, if you find the one that should've been running when the ship was taken. It suggests they blew the ship, but there's not enough debris.'

'It was found in . . . caught in the crevice of a lifeboat seat, the record says.'

'Um. Someone tried to take the environmental log aboard a lifeboat, and the lifeboat was blown. That makes sense. They may have put all the logs aboard it.'

'What would that be, on a merchanter?'

'Environmental log, automatic. Stores inventory. Captain's log – how the voyage was going, and so on, and might include the cargo data. Accounting, which would definitely include the cargo data, pay information. Crew list, medical – pretty sparse, on a vessel like this with a stable crew. Communications log, but some merchanters put that in the captain's log.'

Esmay slotted the next cube into the reader. 'This looks like communications. And the date's recent . . . fits with the ship's last stop. *Elias Madero* to Corian Highside Stationmaster . . . to Traffic Control . . . undock and traffic transmissions and receptions.'

'Good. Let me see.' Haral came over and peered at the screen. 'This is really good . . . we can match this against the records at Corian, and see if anyone tampered with the log. Wish they'd put it in full-record mode, but that does eat up cube capacity. Let's just see how far it goes . . .'

'*Elias Madero* – you get your captain to the com. You surrender your ship, and we'll let the crew off in your lifeboats.' The voice coming out of the cube reader's speakers startled them both.

'What is *that*—' Haral leaned forward. 'My God – someone had the sense to turn on full-record mode when the raiders challenged them. No vid yet, but—'

The screen flickered, changing from text to vid. A blurry image formed, of a stern man in tan – Esmay thought it might be a uniform, but she couldn't tell. Then it sharpened suddenly.

'Got the incoming patched directly to the cube recorder, instead of vidding the screen,' Haral said. They had missed a few words; now another voice spoke.

'This is Captain Lund. Who are you and what do you think you're doing?' A shift in the picture, to show a stocky balding man who was recognizable from the crew list Boros had supplied. It was definitely Lund. The recording continued, including Lund's off-transmission commands to his crew.

Haral paused the playback, and sat back. 'Well, now we know what happened to this ship . . . and we know they had kids, and hid them. Question is, did the raiders find them? Take them?'

'Must have,' Esmay said, feeling sick at the thought. Four preschoolers, the age she had been when – she pushed that away but was aware of a deep rage stirring to action. The person who had had the sense to put this cube in the lifeboat – who had thought to switch to full-mode recording – had also quickly shot vid from the children's records. So they knew the children's names, and had faces to go with them. Two girls, sisters. Two boys, cousins.

'The vid quality is good enough that we should be able to read the insignia on those uniforms, see if intel has anything on them. Faces – we may have them in the file somewhere. And that's the most audio we've ever had from raiders. Interesting accent.'

But all Esmay could think about was the children, the helpless children. She turned the orange and blue toy over and over in her hands.

One by one, the rescue crews located and retrieved the bodies.

'We've got too many bodies,' the team chief said. 'How many were on the merchanter's crew?'

'So some raiders died,' Solis said. 'I'm not grieving.'

'These men have been stripped – not like the others. Would the raiders have stripped and dumped their own dead?'

'Unlikely. Stripped, you say? Why these men?'

'Dunno, but there's no ID on them at all. We can take tissue samples, but you know what that's like—'

'No fingerprints, retinals?'

'Nope. All burned. After death, the medic says; they died of combat wounds.'

Solis turned to Esmay. 'Ideas, Lieutenant?'

'Unless we've stumbled into some local fighting ground . . . no, sir.'

'The merchanters look like ordinary spacers,' the medic said. 'Light-boned, small body mass . . . merchanters nearly always run with low grav because it feels good. Varying ages – the cook was two years older than the captain, all the way down to the kid.' The scrawny teenager who'd been in a fight before he was shot. 'But these others . . . they could be Fleet, except that they don't have Fleet IDs. Look at the muscular development – and their bone mass indicates regular hard exercise in a substantial field, at least standard G. Even though the raiders burned off the fingerprints, we can see enough callus structure on the hands that's consistent with weapons use . . .'

'Assuming it was the raiders, why wouldn't the raiders want them identified? If their primary target was the merchanter – which seems obvious – and they left the crew identifiable, what was it about these?'

'Don't know. Military, not Fleet . . . a Benignity spyship, maybe? A probe from the Guernesi? But – why would the raiders care if we knew that? Unless they're from the same source – but that would imply that these are *their* people, and we've already said they probably aren't. About all we can be sure of is that they weren't merchanter crew.'

'We can't do a genetic scan?'

'Well, we could – if we had one of the big sequencers. The forensic pathology lab at Sector would have one, but that still doesn't tell you much. Maybe a rough guess at which dozen planets the person came from, but the amount of travel going on these days, it's less and less accurate. I'm running the simpler tissue scales here . . . but I don't expect anything to come up. If someone reports missing persons, and has their genome on file, that would do it.'

*   *   *

'We're finding less each sweep,' Solis said. 'Time to move on. This jump point has how many mapped outlets?'

'Five, sir.'

'All right. We'll hop to Bezaire, where the merchanter was headed, and report to Boros on what we found. I don't expect to find any trace there – we'd have noticed it when we were there before – so we'll have to let HQ decide if they want us to check each of the other known outlets or send someone else. Prepare a draft report for Sector HQ, and we'll pop that onto the Bezaire ansible when we get there. Include a recommendation to interdict this route, and a request for surveillance of all the outlets . . . not that it will do any good.'

Shrike popped out in Bezaire's system, and Esmay oversaw the signal drop to Fleet Sector HQ. Scan reported no traces matching that of the *Elias Madero* . . . no other ship of that mass had been through in over a hundred days, according to the Stationmaster.

'I told you that before.'

'Yes, but we have to check.'

'The Boros Consortium local agent wants to talk to you.'

'No doubt.' Solis looked grim. 'I want to talk to Boros, as well. We'll need a real-time link.'

Bezaire Station, Boros Consortium Offices

'Not . . . *all* of them?' The Boros agent paled.

'I'm sorry,' Solis said. 'Apparently the ship was captured – there is evidence under imminent threat of heavy weapons – and although the crew had been promised safe exit in a lifeboat, they were instead killed.'

'The . . . children?'

'We don't know. We found no children's bodies, and we know the crew had concealed them in one or more core compartments.'

'But – but who—?'

'We don't know yet. We've sent the data we have back to headquarters; someone will figure it out, I'm sure. Now, about the deceased—'

502

The agent drew herself up. 'You will of course release the remains to Boros Consortium, for transmittal to the families—'

'I'm afraid we can't at this time. We have positively identified all adult crew personnel and one apprentice, but it's possible the bodies bear additional evidence of the perpetrators. We must continue to examine them.'

'But – but that's outrageous.'

'Ma'am, what was done to these people was outrageous. We must find out who did it, so that we don't have more of this—'

'What was done . . . what *was* done?'

'There was . . . mutilation, ma'am. And that's all I care to say until forensics is through with the remains. I can assure you that all due care will be taken to return remains to family members as soon as possible.'

When the crew remains and the other debris had been transferred to the courier that would take it to sector HQ, *Shrike* went back out on patrol.

'We don't try to pursue?'

'No. Not our job. We can't tangle with three armed ships, and we have no idea where, besides Bezaire, that jump point leads. Someone's going to have to explore it blind. The trail's cold, and growing colder. We did what we could – we have hull signatures on the raiders, or close to, we know what happened to the crew—'

'But not if there were weapons aboard—'

'No. But I'd say it was a fair bet that there were. We'll just have to keep eyes and ears open.' He looked at her with what might almost be approval. 'You're asking good questions, though, Lieutenant Suiza.'

9

Barin returned the sentry's salute as he came to the access area for the *Gyrfalcon*. At last, he was going aboard a real warship, to a proper assignment. Not that he would have missed the time on *Koskuisko*, and meeting Esmay. He quickly turned his mind from that painful thought – meeting her was one thing, but their relationship now was something he could have missed quite happily. But this – since he'd been out of the Academy, this was his first regular assignment, and he was more than happy to get it.

As he expected, when he reported aboard he was called to the captain's cabin. Captain Escovar . . . he had looked Simon Escovar up in the Captains' Lists. Escovar was a commander, with combat experience at Patchcock, Dortmuth, and Alvara; he had, besides an impressive array of combat decorations, the discreet jewels that denoted top rank in academic courses ranging from his cadet days at the Academy to the Senior Command and Staff Course.

'Ensign Serrano,' he said, in response to Barin's formal greeting. 'Always glad to have a Serrano aboard.' The twinkle in his gray eyes suggested that he meant it. 'I served under your . . . uncle or great-uncle, I suppose. There are too many of you Serranos to keep straight.' Barin had heard that before. And the Escovars, though an old Fleet family, had never had as many on active service at one time as the Serranos. 'You've had an unusual set of assignments so far, I see. I hope you won't find us too mundane.'

'By no means, sir,' Barin said. 'I'm delighted to be here.'

504

'Good. We have only three other command-track ensigns at the moment, all with a half-standard year on this ship.' Which meant they already knew things he would have to scramble to learn. 'My exec is Lieutenant Commander Dockery. He has all your initial assignments.'

Lieutenant Commander Dockery spent five minutes dissecting Barin's past career and preparation, pointed out that he was a half year behind his peers, and then sent him on to Master Chief Zuckerman to get his shiptags, data cubes, and other necessities. Barin came out of Dockery's office wondering if Zuckerman was another step on the 'cut the ensigns down to size' production line.

Master Chief Zuckerman nodded when Barin introduced himself. 'I served with Admiral Vida Serrano on the *Delphine*. And you're her grandson, I understand?' Zuckerman was a big man, heavily built, who looked about forty. Rejuv, of course; no one made master chief by forty.

'That's right, Chief.'

'Well. How may I help you, sir?' A lifetime's experience with the breed told Barin that the twinkle in Zuckerman's eye was genuine . . . for whatever mysterious reasons senior enlisted sometimes decided to like young officers, Zuckerman had decided to like him.

'Commander Dockery told me to acquaint myself with the starboard watch orders—'

'Yes, sir. Right here.' Zuckerman fumbled a cube out of a file. 'This has your schematics, your billeting list, your duty stations. Now you can either view it here, or check it out; if you check it out, it's a level-two security incident, and I'll require your signature on the paperwork.'

'I'd better check it out,' Barin said. 'I'm on duty four shifts from now, and I'm supposed to know it by then.'

'You'll do fine, sir,' Zuckerman said. He rummaged a bit in a drawer and came up with an array of papers. 'Captain likes hardcopy on all checkouts of secured documents, so it really is paperwork.'

Barin signed on the designated line, initialled in the spaces. 'When do I have to have it back?'

'Fourteen hundred tomorrow, sir.'

Barin smiled at him. 'Thanks, Chief.'

'Good to have you aboard, sir.'

There were worse ways to start ship duty than by having a master chief for a friend; Barin went off to put his duffel in his quarters considerably cheered. He knew Zuckerman would be as critical – perhaps more critical – than another man; he knew he would have to live up to Zuckerman's standards. But if a master chief took a youngster under his wing, then only a fool would ignore the chance to learn and prosper. It was probably due to his Serrano inheritance – but that worked both ways, and it was pleasant to have it working his way for once.

Young officers in command track were expected to know every-thing moderately well; ensigns rotated through various systems and sections of the cruiser, learning by doing – or, as often, by making mistakes less critical at their level than later on. The other three ensigns aboard had all started at the bottom – environmental – and completed their two-month rotation there, so Barin expected his first assignment: unaffectionately known as the 'shit scrubber special.'

'Your nose is unreliable,' he was told by the environmental tech officer he reported to. 'You think it stinks – and it does stink – but your nose gets used to it. Use your badges and readouts, and any time you're actually opening units, suit up. This stuff is deadly.'

Barin wanted to ask why they weren't all dead then, but he knew better than to joke with someone like Jig Arendy. It was clear from her expression that she took sewage treatment very seriously, and – he suspected – spent every spare moment reading up on new technology.

She led him through the system he would help maintain, explaining every color-coded pipe, every label, every gauge and dial. Then she turned him over to Scrubber Team 3, and told him to do a practice inspection of the system from intake 14 to outputs 12 to 15. 'And you can't use that old saw about flagpoles,' she warned him. 'This is my test team, and they'll do exactly what – and only what – you tell them.'

Barin heaved an internal sigh, but started in. He remembered almost everything – he forgot to have them turn off the check-valve between primary feed and the intermediate scrubbers – and Arendy gave him a grudging thumbs-up. Then she spent ten minutes with the flow diagrams explaining exactly why that check-valve should be closed during routine inspections.

In a few days, Barin felt he was fitting in well. All four command-track ensigns bunked together; they were pleasant enough, and genuinely glad that someone else had the scrubber duty for the next two months. Meals in the junior wardroom enabled him to meet the other juniors – jigs and lieutenants – who were his immediate superiors. Jig Arendy, he discovered, could talk about something other than sewage; she turned out to be an avid follower of celebrity newsflashes. She and a handful of others discussed celebrities as if they were family members, endlessly poring over their clothes, their love affairs, their amusements. When she found he'd been at Copper Mountain with Brun Meager, she wanted to know all about it. Was she really as beautiful as her pictures? What kind of clothes did she wear? Had there been many newsflash shooters around?

Barin answered what he could, but luckily it did not occur to Arendy that he himself might have been a target of Brun's attention. When the wardroom discussions of Brun became uncomfortable, he took himself off. He would much rather listen to Zuckerman's tales of the old days in *Delphine*, with his grandmother. She'd never told him about the time a missile hung in the tube with a live warhead.

He mentioned that to Petty-light Harcourt, while they were replacing a section of feeder pipe.

'Zuckerman is . . . well, he's Zuckerman,' the petty-light said.

Barin was surprised at the tone. P-lights knew more than he did, and he'd never met one who didn't admire a master chief. But Harcourt sounded unsure. He thought of asking more, but decided against it. Whatever it was, a mere ensign shouldn't be getting involved. If Harcourt had a serious problem, he also had the seniority to feel comfortable taking it to his own commander.

He had come to that decision when Harcourt sighed, an expressive sigh, and went on.

'It's like this, sir . . . Zuckerman's got a fine record, and I'm not saying anything against him. But he's . . . changed, in this last tour. He's not the man he was. We all know it, and we make allowances.'

But allowance shouldn't have to be made, not for a master chief. Harcourt was still looking at him, and Barin realized he was expecting a comment.

'Family?' he murmured. It must've been the right thing to say, because Harcourt relaxed.

'I wouldn't bring this up with a junior officer, begging your pardon sir, but you *are* a Serrano, and . . . well . . . the chief's always talking about the time he served with a Serrano on *Delphine*. It's not anything we – I – can understand. It's not all the time. Just sometimes he's . . . it's like he forgets things. The kind of thing you just don't forget, not with his years. We – I – have to have someone check his pressure-suit settings, for instance. One emergency drill, he didn't even have his suit sealed.'

He shouldn't be hearing this. Someone considerably senior should be hearing this. Because anything which could make a man like Chief Zuckerman forget to seal his suit was too much for an ensign to handle.

'I did say something to Major Surtsey,' Harcourt went on. 'He arranged to have the chief called in for a random health survey, but . . . that was one of his good days. And on his good days, he's sharper than I am. And then the major was reassigned, and I . . . I was just . . . I don't quite know how far to take this.'

So the sticky problem had just been handed off to a very junior ensign. With the Serrano reputation. No good to tell Harcourt that he didn't feel comfortable with it either . . . the job description for ensigns did not include comfort.

'And you'd like me to take this on upstairs?' Barin asked.

'It's up to you, sir,' Harcourt said. 'Although . . . if I could make a suggestion . . .'

'Sure,' said Barin. Having hooked the ensign, of course the petty light could play him.

'Commander Dockery is . . . prefers to have . . . all the ducks in a row, sir, if you know what I mean.'

'In other words, I should investigate this myself, and have some documentation?'

'Well . . . yes, sir.'

He would have to have something, that was certain, something more than the word of a petty-light who might have some grievance Barin didn't know about. 'I'll have a look,' he said to Harcourt, who looked satisfied with that. He himself had no idea how to go about finding out if a senior NCO was going bonkers for some reason.

He remembered what Brun had said about that man at the Schools . . . what was his name? She'd claimed he was making too many mistakes, but that was right before she and Esmay had the big fight. Barin had no idea what had happened after that, if anyone else had confirmed Brun's suspicions. She was, after all, only a civilian, and she might not have told anyone else.

Still, he paid close attention to Zuckerman every time his own duties took him that way. The man seemed much like every other master chief he'd met, decades of experience providing him with a depth of knowledge and competence far beyond the ability of an ensign to assess. Zuckerman could be missing whole chunks, and he'd never know it. He liked Zuckerman, and Zuckerman seemed to like him; he felt that Zuckerman would have liked almost any Serrano. He hoped he wouldn't find anything to worry about; he worried that he might miss something important.

But most of the time he was too busy to worry, too busy to find time to visit Zuckerman. He had his own work, in an area remote from Zuckerman; he had watches to stand, inspections to take, duties that kept him busy. He had peers, the other ensigns in both command and technical tracks, whose personalities and relationships became ever more important as time went on. Jared and Leah were already engaged; Banet recorded a cube every other day for someone on *Greylag*. Micah had quarreled with Jared over plans for the ship's Commissioning Day festivities, and Leah had blown up at Micah in the junior wardroom in a way that reminded Barin painfully of Esmay.

He tried not to think of Esmay. As time wore on, he could not stay angry, but he remained confused. They had liked each other a lot, back on *Koskiusko*; they had shared secrets neither had told anyone else. He had expected her to welcome his presence at Copper Mountain – and granting that she had been extremely busy and tired, there was still something else different about her, a new reserve, a tension. And then there'd been Brun, always around when he wanted to talk to Esmay, always with time on her hands. Exuberant when Esmay was reserved. Jolly when Esmay was serious. Fun when Esmay was . . . he would not say dull, because to him she was never dull, but . . . busy, tired, not really present when she was sitting right beside him.

Perhaps she never had loved him. Perhaps it had worn off, and she was too kind to say so. That didn't make sense, though, if she was angry because she thought Brun had tolled him into her bed. He thought of sending mail . . . but after all, their quarrel wasn't *his* fault.

As he came to know the other junior officers better, he noticed that he kept running into one in particular: Casea Ferradi. He'd heard of Casea Ferradi back at the Academy, but she'd graduated before he started. He knew how rumors grow with time, and assumed that the stories of her beauty and her behavior were both inflated.

Barin first noticed Lieutenant Ferradi because of her hair – that uncommon golden blonde, like Brun's, but different. Brun's hair had a life of its own; it curled vigorously even when just groomed, and when she was upset or excited, and raked her fingers through the curls, it looked like an uncombed poodle. Lieutenant Ferradi's hair lay in a sleek wave beside her perfect cheekbones. Blondes were rare in Fleet. Perhaps that accounted for Lieutenant Ferradi's nickname, Goldie, which he heard in the junior wardroom the first night.

He noticed her next because she kept showing up where he was, and speaking to him. She was a jig on the watch rotation, so of course she would be where he was part of the time. But he began to realize that he saw her more than any other jig, even when she wasn't on shift watch.

He hadn't thought about her being in Esmay's class at the Academy until she brought it up.

'You know Lieutenant Suiza, don't you, Ensign?' That, while initialling the midwatch report.

'Yes, sir.'

'I wonder if she's changed much,' Ferradi said. 'We were classmates, you know.'

'No, sir, I didn't know that.' He wondered if she might have some insight into Esmay's recent behavior, but felt reluctant to ask her.

'I mean,' Ferradi went on, as she fiddled with the datawand, 'she was such a stiff, formal person. Not really friendly. But from what everyone says, she's such a born leader – so I was wondering . . .'

Tiny alarm bells rang in his backbrain, but his forebrain was ahead of them. 'She's fairly formal, yes . . . but I believe it has something to do with her background.'

'Oh yes.' Ferradi rolled her eyes. 'Both of us were the colonial outcasts, you know. I'm Crescent Worlds – I think they expected me to insist on wearing one of those trailing silk things.' Her hands fluttered and waved. Barin had no idea what she meant, and his expression must have showed it because she laughed.

'Oh – I guess you haven't seen the bad storycubes about us. I think they got the costumes from back on Old Earth, because of course no one actually wears them. Long flowing garments that cover young women from head to toe, but flutter fetchingly in the breeze.'

Barin had no time to pick out what detail had set off the alarms again, because she'd gone on, her pleasant, slightly husky voice soft and amused.

'But Esmay – Lieutenant Suiza – she told me once her whole family was military. Very formal, very correct. Which is why I can understand her having a quarrel with the Speaker's daughter, but not how she could lead anyone anywhere.'

Barin had his mouth open before caution stopped him; he had to say something. 'I – didn't know the quarrel was common knowledge.'

Ferradi laughed again. 'I don't see how anyone could keep it quiet. It was on the newsflashes, after all. Screamed like a harpy, is what I heard, and told the Speaker's daughter she had no more morals than a tavern whore.'

'It wasn't like that!' Barin said. He couldn't have said how it wasn't, since Esmay had been loud and insulting, but his instinct was to protect Esmay.

Ferradi looked at him with an indulgent smile that made him feel like a small child. 'That's all right, Ensign; I'm not asking you to turn your back on a Fleet hero.'

She made him feel uncomfortable. She was always looking at him . . . he would glance up and discover those clear violet eyes, and an amused quirk to her mouth. She seemed to impinge on his space in a way that Esmay never did. Brun, though she had been overtly interested in his body, had backed off without rancor when refused. But this . . .

He went into the gym convinced that whatever was going on was his fault. He had done something – what, he couldn't figure out – that aroused her interest. He climbed onto the exercise machine he'd reserved, and set the controls. Past the warmup phase, into the sweaty part of the workout, his mind drifted to Esmay. She was exec of a specialty ship now; he could imagine her in a rescue situation . . . she might do something spectacular, and get back in everyone's good graces.

'Hello, Ensign.' The husky voice broke his concentration. There beside him, on the next machine, was Ferradi. Barin blinked, confused. She hadn't been signed up for that machine; he'd made sure of that. But now she was warming up, her body as sleek as her golden hair in a shiny exercise suit that outlined every curve. Barin, panting slightly, nodded a greeting.

'You're a hard worker,' she said, starting her own machine. 'I guess that goes with being a Serrano, eh?'

He had to say something; she was still looking at him and it would be rude to ignore her – possibly even insubordinate.

'It's . . . expected . . . sir,' he said.

'No need for formality in the gym,' she said. 'I approve . . . of the attitude, and the results, Barin.' Her look ranged over him, with particular attention he couldn't mistake.

Well, he would have to say something . . . but before he could, Major Oslon climbed onto the machine on Ferradi's other side.

'Hey, Casea . . . let Serrano finish his workout. He's too young for you anyway. I, on the other hand . . .'

She gave Barin a last lingering look before turning to Oslon. 'Why, Major . . . you're incorrigible. Whatever makes you think I'm after Ensign Serrano?'

'Glad to know you're not. I must have been misled by the fit of that exercise suit.'

'This old thing?' Barin had seen less obvious flirting from professionals at the trade, but Oslon didn't seem to mind. He and Casea bantered awhile, and when he invited her to a game of parpaun, she agreed – with a last lingering look at Barin that bothered him all over again.

A few days later, Barin was on his way through Troop Deck on a routine inspection of the traps in the heads – hairballs in the traps were a constant problem. A peculiar *crunch* caught his attention. He hesitated. Another, and then another. Which compartment was it in? He looked around, trying to locate the sound . . . slightly behind him, and to the right. A slither-and-bump, followed by the sounds of something heavy being dragged, came next, and pinpointed the source: D-82.

Barin looked in, to see Master Chief Zuckerman, face almost purple with rage and exertion, dragging someone by the heels.

'Chief – what's going on?'

'Outa my way!' Zuckerman said, breathing heavily. The Chief did not seem to recognize him; his eyes were dilated.

'Chief—' Barin could not see clearly past him, but the limpness of the legs Zuckerman held bothered him. He lifted his gaze a little . . . down the row of racks to one with a depression where someone had been sitting . . . a needler case on the pillow . . .

'Chief, put that down.' Barin had no idea what had happened, but it was trouble all the same. He reached back for the alarm beside the hatch.

'Oh, no you don't, you *puppy*!' Zuckerman dropped the man's feet and charged. Barin ducked aside, and Zuckerman kept going, bouncing off the opposite bulkhead. By then Barin had slapped the alarm, cutting in local scan.

'Security, ASAP!' Barin said. 'Man down, possible assault!'

513

Zuckerman turned, more slowly than he'd charged. 'Not *possible* – the bastard attacked me. Me, a master chief with . . . with . . . twenty . . . twenty . . .' He shook his head. 'He shouldn't have done that. Not right.'

'Chief,' Barin said, cautiously. 'What happened?'

'None of your lip, boy,' Zuckerman said. His eyes narrowed. 'What the devil are you doing wearing officers' insignia? That's illegal. You want to get tossed out? You take those pings off your uniform this minute, Pivot.'

'Master Chief Zuckerman,' Barin said. 'I asked you a question.' For the first time in his life, he heard the Serrano bite in his own voice – the family pride that knew, bone-deep, what it was.

Zuckerman stared at him, his face blanking a moment. Then he looked confused. 'Uh . . . Ensign . . . Serrano? What's . . . what's that you were asking me, sir?'

'Chief,' Barin tried again, but cautiously. Where was Security? How long would it be? 'I'm watch officer today. I heard something funny, and came to look. You were in 82, dragging someone, and there's a needler case on a rack.' He paused. Zuckerman stepped forward, but Barin put up his hand. 'No. Don't go in there. Security's on the way; I want nothing disturbed. Can you tell me what happened?'

'I – he – he was going to kill me.' Zuckerman was sweating now, his face shiny with it. His hands opened and closed rhythmically. 'He pulled a needler; he said he'd never be caught.' He shook his head, then looked at Barin again. 'Son of a bitch actually tried it – if I didn't have good reflexes, I'd be dead in there. So I – so I grabbed his hand, got the needler, and – and hit—' He turned pale and sagged against the bulkhead. 'I hit him,' he whispered. 'I hit him . . . and then I hit him . . . and—'

'Chief. Stay where you are. Can you do that?'

Zuckerman nodded. 'Yes, sir. But I – but I don't know—'

'Just *stay* there. I need to check the guy. What's his name?'

'Moredon. Corporal Moredon.'

'All right. I'm going in; I want you to stay exactly where you are.' Again, the Serrano tone – he could hear it himself; he could see its steadying effect on Zuckerman.

Moredon lay where Zuckerman had dropped him, unmoving.

514

Barin stepped closer. Now he could see the bruises and blood on the man's head, and a long streak of blood on the deck where he'd been dragged. Was he breathing? Barin couldn't tell; he knelt beside the limp body. Yes. Through the open mouth he could just hear a low snore, and feel the moist breath against the back of his hand.

He stood up, and went back to the corridor. Zuckerman stood where he'd been told, and down the corridor came a Security team, with medical assist.

'Sir?' said the sergeant in charge of the Security team. His gaze flicked quickly from Barin to Zuckerman, down to Zuckerman's hands, back to his face, and Barin could see the puzzlement in his eyes.

'There's a man down in 82,' Barin said crisply. 'Head injuries, but he's breathing. You'll need to secure the area for forensic examination, and look for a loose needler.'

'Yes, sir,' the sergeant said. He waved the medical team forward, and gave the necessary orders to his team. Then he glanced at Barin again. 'Did . . . uh . . . the man in there attack Chief Zuckerman, sir? Or you?'

'If you please, Sergeant, just see to it that the area is secured, and that the injured man is treated appropriately.' Before the sergeant could comment, Barin turned to Zuckerman. 'Chief, I need you to come with me to make a report. Can you do that?'

'Of course, sir.' Zuckerman straightened up. 'What's the problem?'

Barin wished he had an answer for that. 'We'll let the Exec sort it out,' he said. It occurred to him, as he led the way back up to command deck, that perhaps he should have brought along an escort. What if Zuckerman got violent again? Surely he wouldn't, but all the way up to command deck, his neck prickled at the thought of Zuckerman behind him.

He met Lieutenant Commander Dockery coming down the ladder from command deck, and came to attention.

'What is it, Ensign?'

'Sir, we have a real problem. Permission?'

'Go ahead . . . wait, who's that with you?'

'Chief Zuckerman, sir. There's been an incident—'

'I know you called for Security. At ease, both of you. Spit it out, then, Ensign.'

Barin spit it out, aware all the time of Zuckerman – his age, his seniority, his record – standing there looking entirely too confused still.

Dockery glanced at Zuckerman. 'Well, Chief?'

Zuckerman's voice trembled. 'Commander, I . . . I don't quite know what happened . . .'

'Did this individual attack you?'

'I – I think so. Yes, sir, he did. It's – I can almost see it—'

Dockery gave Barin a look he could not interpret. 'Did you . . . do anything with the Chief, Ensign?'

'No, sir.'

'Was he sedated by security?'

'No, sir.'

'You came up here with someone you're accusing of assault, without sedating him or putting him under guard?'

'Sir, he'd calmed down. He wasn't—'

Dockery touched one of the com panels on the bulkhead. 'XO to med, stat response team to my location.' He turned back to Barin. 'Ensign, the Chief is clearly not himself. He needs medical evaluation prior to anything else.'

'I feel fine, Commander,' Zuckerman said. Indeed, he looked like the model of a master chief. 'I'm sorry to have upset the ensign; I'm not sure why . . .'

'Just routine, Chief,' Dockery said. 'Just a checkup, make sure you aren't coming down with something.'

A team of medics arrived, carrying crash kits. 'Commander?'

'Chief Zuckerman's had a little spell of confusion this morning. Why don't you take him down to sickbay and check him out. He might need a little something to calm him.'

'There's nothing wrong with me,' Zuckerman protested. Barin noticed his neck flushing again. 'I'm . . . sorry, Admiral!' He stared at Barin and saluted stiffly. Barin felt a coldness settle into his belly; he returned the salute, just to get Zuckerman to relax. 'Whatever you say, Admiral,' Zuckerman said, though no one had said anything in the surprise of seeing a master chief confuse a grass-green ensign with an admiral.

'Just a checkup,' Barin said, afraid to let his gaze wander to see how Commander Dockery was taking this. Zuckerman was staring at him with an expression halfway between fear and awe. 'It'll be fine, Chief,' he said, putting what he could of the Serrano voice in it. Zuckerman relaxed again.

'By your leave, sir.'

'Go along, then,' Barin said. The medics led Zuckerman off, with the obvious care of professionals ready to leap to action.

'Well, Ensign,' Commander Dockery said. 'You've made a right mess of things, haven't you?'

Barin knew better than to protest that it wasn't his fault. 'I know I did something wrong, Commander, but I'm not sure what I should have done.'

'Come along, and I'll tell you as we go. Down on Troop Deck, wasn't it?' Dockery strode off, leaving Barin to follow. Over his shoulder, he asked, 'And just how much of Zuckerman's problem did you know about?'

'Me, sir? Not much . . . another NCO had said something, but he said it had been checked by another officer and nothing was found.'

'Did you look for anything? Or did you just ignore it?'

'I looked, sir, but I didn't know what to look for. The times I talked to him, Chief Zuckerman seemed fine to me. Well, there was once . . . but it didn't seem that important.'

'And you didn't see fit to pass on what this other NCO told you?'

Barin began to see the shape of his sin looming ahead. 'Sir, I wanted to have something definite before bothering you.'

Dockery grunted. 'I'm just as unhappy to be bothered with trifles as anyone else, Ensign, but I'm even more unhappy to be bothered with a large problem that someone let get big because he didn't know what to do about it.'

'I should have told you right away, sir.'

'Yes. And if I'd chewed on you for bringing me vague un-substantiated reports, well – that's what ensigns are for. To provide jaw exercise for grumpy executive officers. If you'd told me, or this other mysterious NCO had told me – and who was that, by the way?'

'Petty-light Harcourt, sir.'

'I thought Harcourt had better sense. Who'd he tell before?'

'Uh . . . a Major Surtsey, who was transferred out. He said they'd done a med check, and found nothing.'

'I remember . . . Pete told me about that before he left, but said he hadn't found anything definite. I said I'd keep an eye out . . . thinking my officers would have the good sense to pass on anything they heard . . .'

'Sorry, sir,' Barin said.

'Well. All you youngsters make mistakes, but mistakes have consequences. In this case, if I'm not mistaken, the ruin of a good man's career.'

They were on Troop Deck now, and Dockery led the way to the right passage and compartment as if he never needed to stop and think. Barin supposed he didn't.

The security team had cordoned off the passage, and as Dockery arrived so did a forensics team.

'Commander . . . all right to go on and start collecting evidence?'

'If it's been scanned. Come on, Ensign, I want to show you how to do this.'

If Barin had not been so aware of his failings, it would have been a fascinating hour. But it was followed quickly by a less pleasant time in Dockery's office.

'Remember – the chewing out you get for bothering me with a nonproblem problem will never be as big as the one you get for not bothering me with a real problem.'

'Yes, sir.'

'Unless Zuckerman turns out to have an unsuspected medical problem – and anything big enough to excuse this would probably get him a medical out – he's in big trouble.'

Something tickled a corner of Barin's mind. Medical problem? He cleared his throat. 'Sir – ?'

'Yes?'

'I – something I just remembered, sir, about another senior NCO back at Copper Mountain.'

'Relevant to this?'

'It might be, sir. But it's not something I observed myself, it's just that when you said medical problem . . .'

'Go on, Ensign.'

Barin related the story of the master chief whose crew was covering up for some strange memory lapses as succinctly as possible. 'And, sir, back on *Koskiusko*, I remember being told that the master chief in inventory had had a breakdown after the battle . . . everyone was surprised, because he'd been in combat before, and he wasn't directly involved anyway.'

'And . . . you're wondering what affected three master chiefs? Do you have any idea how many master chiefs there are in the whole Regular Space Service?'

'No, sir,' Barin said miserably. So this one had been a stupid idea, too.

'Of course, by the time they're master chiefs, most of the problem cases have been eliminated,' Dockery said. 'But it is odd. I'll tell the medics and see if anyone has any ideas.'

But his sins had earned him yet another chewing out, this time at the captain's hands.

'Ensign, Commander Dockery has had his chance at your backside – now it's my turn. But first, let's see if you understand what you did wrong – or rather, didn't do right.'

'Yes, sir. I knew about a problem, and did not keep Commander Dockery or you advised.'

'Because—?'

'Because I thought I should gather more data, keep a record of incidents, before bother – before telling anyone else.'

'I see. Serrano, there are several possible motives for that action, and I want a straight answer out of you. Were you trying to protect Chief Zuckerman's reputation, or get yourself a bit of glory by bringing me a nice juicy bone?'

Barin hesitated before replying. 'Sir, I think . . . I was confused at first. I was surprised when the other NCO told me about Zuckerman; my first thought was that he had something personal against Zuckerman. But when he said he'd reported it before and that a major had taken it seriously . . . I thought it might be a real problem. Except that medical hadn't found anything. I didn't know why the NCO had confided in me, in particular – it made me uncomfortable. So I thought I'd keep an eye out, and document anything I noticed—'

519

'And did you notice anything?'

'Not anything I could put a finger on, sir. There was less respect for Chief Zuckerman than I would expect to find among enlisted, but not enough to be insubordination. I noticed that he was not intervening in some situations where I'd have expected his influence. But he'd made only two actual errors that I'd documented – and even master chiefs are human. I didn't want to go around asking questions – he deserved better than that—'

'Wait there. You are telling me you made the judgement – that you felt qualified to make the judgement – that Zuckerman "deserved better" than your asking questions about him? Zuckerman liked you, that much is clear. Were you swayed by his favoritism to your family, or were you just out of your depth completely?'

'Sir, I know now that I was out of my depth, but I didn't recognize that at the time.'

'I see. And you thought you'd keep a quiet eye on him, document any problems, and bring your report to – exactly whom did you expect to bring this report to, assuming you came up with something?'

Under that cool gray gaze, Barin's mind kept trying to blank out. But a lifetime's experience gave him the right answer even in his panic. 'To Chief Zuckerman's commander in the chain, sir. Which would be Lieutenant Commander Orstein.'

'That much is correct. And what did you expect to happen when you presented such a report?'

'Sir, I thought Commander Orstein would review it, perhaps make his own investigation, and then take whatever action he felt necessary.'

'And it would be out of your hands?'

'Yes, sir.'

'And what did you think Orstein would do with you, the pup who dragged in this unsavory prize?'

'I . . . hadn't thought about that, sir.'

'I find that hard to believe.'

'Sir, no one could be happy to find a master chief losing his . . . losing effectiveness, sir. Master chiefs are . . . special.' That wasn't the right word, but it was the only one he could think of.

520

'Yes, they are. So, if I read between the lines correctly, you figured Lieutenant Commander Orstein would chew you out and then – maybe – undertake his own investigation.'

'Yes, sir.'

'Tell me, Serrano, if you had found additional problems, are you certain you'd have risked that chewing out to report on Zuckerman?'

'Yes, sir!' Barin couldn't keep the surprise out of his voice.

'Well, that's something. Let me reiterate what I'm sure Dockery told you: it is annoying for a junior to show no initiative and bother a senior with minor problems, but it is dangerous and – in the long run – disloyal for a junior to conceal a serious problem from a senior. If you had reported this sooner, Chief Zuckerman's problems – whatever they are – could have been dealt with properly, in the chain of command, and I would not have been caught flat-footed and embarrassed. I presume you understand this, and I presume you won't do it again. If you do, the trouble you're in now will be as a spark compared to a nuclear explosion. Is that clear?'

'Yes, sir.'

'Then get out of here and do better.'

10

R.S.S. Gyrfalcon

Lieutenant Casea Ferradi knew she looked like a recruiting poster. She intended to. Every hair on her head lay exactly where it should, and under perfectly arched brows her violet eyes sparkled with intelligence. Her features – strong cheekbones and clean-cut jawline, short straight nose and firm but generous lips – fit anyone's image of professional beauty.

It had been worth the risk of early biosculpt. All she had ever wanted was to be a Fleet officer – no, to be honest, a Fleet commander. She had first imagined herself in command of a starship when only a child, her parents had told her. Casea Ferradi was born to be a hero, born to prove that a Crescent Worlds woman could do anything.

Being a girl on the Crescent Worlds had been the first handicap, and the second had been her face and body – typical of her colony, but not like anything she'd seen in a Fleet uniform on the newsfeed vid. Delicate features, narrowing to a pointed chin, sloping wine-bottle shoulders, and generous hips – all prized in her culture – did not fit her dream.

Her parents had been shocked when she told them what she wanted – but at ten, even girls could speak to the sept as a whole, not just parents, about important decisions like marriage negotiations. She had taken her argument to the Aunts' Gossip, where her desire to go offworld was quickly approved – she was too intelligent by far to fare well in the local marriage market. Biosculpting, though – it wasn't until her father's mother approved that she knew she had a chance.

'They will not know she is from here, if she looks so different, so her unwomanly behavior will not disgrace us.'

Three years of surgery – of the pain that strengthening her redesigned body caused her – and then she took the Fleet entrance exams, passed them, and left home forever.

Once at the Academy, Casea discovered that her new shape was not considered sexless and unfeminine by her peers. Her honey-blonde hair, falling sleekly to a razor-cut angle, was unique in her class. She had all the interest she could handle, and discovered that the behaviors she'd observed in her older sisters and cousins had quite an effect on the young men in her class.

Protected by the standard implant provided all Academy cadets, she moved from interest to experimentation, and from experimentation to enthusiastic activity. Lectures on the ethics of personal relationships rolled off her confidence without making any impact. If Fleet had been serious about it, she reasoned, the young men of renowned Fleet families wouldn't have been so eager to take her to bed, and the young women would not have received implants. And after all, the young men and women of the Chairholding Families made no secret of their sexual activity – Casea watched enough newsflash shorts to know that.

She was angered, rather than alarmed, to discover that some of her classmates were making snide remarks about her behavior.

'Casea – if it's alive, she'll take it to bed,' one of the women drawled in the shower room one morning. That wasn't fair; she had no interest in the ugly or dull.

'She'll get herself in trouble someday,' another one said, sounding worried.

'No – not the way she's going. Which of those guys is going to accuse her of seducing *him*?'

Others simply radiated quiet disapproval. Esmay Suiza, whom she had expected to be a natural ally – they were each the only cadet from their original worlds – turned out to be either a sanctimonious prig or a sexless lump. Casea wasn't sure which, but didn't care. After the first year, she gave up on Esmay: she hadn't the right qualities to be the plain friend of a popular beauty, and Casea could not tolerate the chilly, stiff earnestness of the girl.

But after graduation, she slowed down – sex itself was no longer as exciting – and began to consider her targets with more care. Her cultural background had taught her to look for more from a liaison than physical pleasure alone. Carefully, with an eye out for trouble, she explored the limits of Fleet's policy on what was delicately termed 'personal relationships.'

In her first assignment, she discovered that if she stayed away from men already considered 'taken' by other women, she could hunt at will without arousing comment. So that had been it! She felt a happy glow of contempt for the idiot girls who hadn't simply told her which boys they fancied themselves. Testing this understanding, she turned her violet eyes on a lonely jig, who was quite happy to console himself with a lovely ensign.

But he wasn't enough. She wanted someone in command track. All the command track jigs aboard were paired already – she wrinkled her nose at the two who were wasted on each other, as she thought – and she was not attracted to the single male lieutenant. A major? Could she? She did not doubt her ability to get his interest, but – regulations were supposed to prevent him from dallying with junior officers in his chain of command.

Regulations, as everyone knew, could be bent into pretzels by those with the wit to do so. Still it might be better to look elsewhere . . . which led her to a major in another branch of technical track. It never hurt to have a friend in communications. On her next assignment, he was followed by a lieutenant in command track, and then – with some difficulty in detaching from the lieutenant – by another major. She learned something from each about the extent of her talent, and what advantages could come from such close associations.

Now, though, she was through with casual liaisons. She had found the right man. Against all expectations – she was sure that her grandmothers and aunts would be amazed – she had found a respectable, intelligent, charming young man whom even her father would consider eligible. That he was an ensign, and she a lieutenant, two ranks higher, meant nothing to her. He was mature for his age, and best of all . . . he was a Serrano. Family is everything, she had heard all her life. The one-eyed son of a chief is better than a robber's by-blow. And better family than Serrano – grandson of an admiral, with other admirals in the family tree – she could not hope to find.

The only snag was that rumor said he was, or had been, interested in Esmay Suiza. Casea discounted that. Esmay had been a nonentity, even aside from being a prig. Not pretty, with a haphazard set of features topped with fluffy, flyaway hair of nondescript brown. The boy had hero worship, that's all it was. Suiza had turned out to be a hero of sorts, but nothing could make her beautiful or charming. And now, if rumor were true, she was in trouble for being untactful – Casea could believe *that*, no question. If she ever had a lover, which didn't seem likely, it would be someone as unspectacular as herself, another nonentity, probably just as tactless and doomed to as inglorious a career.

Still, Esmay's present disgrace would make it easier for Casea to pursue Barin Serrano unhindered. And surely that Serrano grandmother wouldn't want him connected to someone like the bad Lieutenant Suiza. It would take very little, Casea thought, to make absolutely sure that no one ever admired Lieutenant Suiza again.

Elias Madero

It was getting harder to get up off the floor to use the toilet; Brun realized that in addition to the pregnancy she was getting weaker because she didn't exercise much. How could she? The compartment would have been small for one person; with an adult woman, a girl, and two small children, it was impossibly crowded. And at any time, one of the men might look in; she could imagine how they would react if they caught her doing real exercises. She tried to make herself pace back and forth, but she quickly ran out of breath, and leaned on the bulkhead panting. The girl watched her with a worried frown, but looked away when Brun tried to smile at her. As Brun had shared more of the work, the girl had accepted that help, but always with reserve.

That night when the lights dimmed, signalling a sleep period, the girl slept at her back, curled around her. Brun woke to a breath of air in her ear. She started to lift her head, and felt a gentle push downward. The girl?

'*Elias Madero*,' came the words. 'Merchanter.'

Brun squirmed as if trying to find a comfortable position. Merchanter . . . the merchanter ship. This girl must be off that ship. Excitement coursed through her . . . she knew *something* now.

' 'M Hazel,' the girl breathed. Then she too squirmed, as if moving in her sleep, and rolled away.

The rush of joy from those five words burst through her. This must have been how Lady Cecelia felt, when she first made contact with the world again.

A wave of shame followed. Lady Cecelia had been locked in paralysis and apparent coma for months . . . and months more of painful rehab . . . and she had been old. Brun was young, healthy . . . *I am not defeated. I am only . . . detained on the way to victory.* So she might bear children for these animals . . . so she might be a prisoner for months, for years . . . but in the end, she was who she was, and that would not change.

She rolled over with difficulty, and looked through narrowed lids at the girl . . . at Hazel. She had been impressed before at the girl's patience, her consistent gentleness with the little girls, her endless invention of quiet little games and activities to amuse them. But she had given up hoping for any real contact, after the first long stretch of days . . . the girl was too scared. Now she appreciated the courage of this thin, overworked, terrified girl . . . still a child herself . . . who cared for two younger children and Brun. Who dared, in the face of threats, to say a few words of comfort. She had lost everything too – parents, most likely. Were these children even her sisters? Maybe not, but no one could have done more for them.

She pushed herself up to use the toilet; on the way back she noticed that Hazel had rolled over again, as if offering Brun a niche convenient to her ear. Brun lay down, grunting, and pretended to sleep. Her arm slid sideways, touched Hazel's. She twisted – she was uncomfortable – and traced the letters of her name on Hazel's arm before moving her arm away.

Hazel turned, burying her face under her hair, and a soft murmur came to Brun's ear. 'Brun?'

Brun nodded. A wave of excitement ran through her; the baby kicked vigorously as if aware of it. Someone besides the men knew who she was . . . an ally. She had made contact . . . it wasn't much, but it gave her hope, the first real hope she'd had.

The next day, she watched Hazel covertly. The girl seemed the same as always – busy, careful, quiet, patient, warm with the children and remote with Brun. When Brandy's restlessness grew toward a tantrum, Hazel intervened, steadied her . . . and Brun was reminded of an expert trainer with a fractious young horse. When she thought of it that way, she began to grasp how Hazel was using the children's need to steady herself. She could be calm, she could follow the senseless rules, because she had someone for whom she was responsible.

And who was Brun's responsibility? The words she had heard from Lieutenant Commander Uhlis came back to her. If she had been a Regular Space Service officer, her duty would have been clear – to escape, or if that was not possible, to live, gathering information, until she could escape. But she wasn't. And even if she had been – even if she pretended to be – was that duty enough to sustain a lifetime such as she faced? What if she never had a chance to escape?

The baby inside her moved, as if it were doing a tumbling act. Surely one baby couldn't make that much disturbance. Some people would say that it was her responsibility, but she did not feel that – it had been forced onto her, into her, and it was not hers at all. It was an abomination, as the men claimed she was.

Was she then her own responsibility? Her mouth soured. Not enough to make a lifetime as these men's slave tolerable, or even bearable. She had spent too many hours already planning how she could escape life, if not them, once they lowered their guard. Eventually they would.

But . . . what if there were a chance, however slim, to keep Hazel and the little girls from her own fate? Somewhere, she was sure, her father was searching. Fleet was searching. It might be years; it might be too many years . . . but it might not. Hazel was compliant not entirely from fear, but also from hope, the hope that some help might come – if she had not had some hope, she would never have dared share her name, and her ship's name, with Brun. So she, Charlotte Brunhilde Meager, could fix her mind on Hazel and the little girls – on saving them.

She did not let herself think again about how unlikely success was. Instead, she began thinking what information she needed, and how to get it. And she quit trying to catch Hazel's eye, quit trying to entice her into communication. The last thing she wanted now was trouble for Hazel.

Only a few days later, the men came for both of them, and the little ones. Brun almost panicked – had they realized Hazel had talked to her? That she had written her own name on Hazel's arm? But they were led along the corridors, farther than Brun had ever gone. Her bare feet were sore; her pregnancy made her awkward at the hatches. To her surprise, the men were patient, waiting while she lifted one leg then the other. They helped her down a slanting surface . . . to a space that opened out around her. She looked, her eyes unaccustomed to the distances after those months in the compartment. The docking bay of a space station, it looked like. All around were men, only men . . . she and Hazel and the two little girls were the only females. The men guided her, gently enough, to a hoverchair. With Hazel walking beside her, the men pushed her chair a long distance. Chair and all, she was moved through another docking bay into a shuttle. Only five men now. At their command, Hazel strapped the children into seats, and herself into another. The men locked the hoverchair down.

When the shuttle hatch opened, Brun smelled what could only be a planet. Fresh air . . . growing things . . . animals . . . hope rose in her again. Planets were big; if she could once get loose, she could find a way to hide, and then to escape. But right now she could barely stand in this gravity, and the heat almost took her breath away.

The men moved her hoverchair from the shuttle, through a low-ceilinged boxlike building, and then into a wheeled vehicle, also large and boxlike, where they locked the chair down again. It had no windows in back, but up front she could see out . . . until a partition rose to cut off her vision. Panic choked her – she was alone in that back compartment; Hazel – the only person she knew – hadn't come with her. Hazel wouldn't know where she was, no one would know, she was going to be lost forever.

Hazel watched under lowered lids as they took the pregnant woman away in a groundcar. She still wasn't sure of the woman's name, even though the woman had traced it into her palm. Could 'Brun' be right? What kind of name was that? A nickname for something, most likely, but they had not dared talk enough to make sure. Her yellow hair shone in the sun of this planet, much longer than it had been when Hazel had first seen her.

'I'm taking the children,' one of the men with her said. The others nodded, and moved away.

'Come along, Girlie,' he said. Hazel followed him, a little breathless with the unaccustomed exercise and the oppressive heat, Brandy holding one hand and Stassi the other. She wondered where the boys were – she hadn't seen them for a long time. She wondered even more about Stinky, and pushed that thought aside too.

The man led them through a gate and across a wide paved space

528

so hot her feet burned. The little girls began to whimper. The man turned. 'Here,' he said. 'I'll carry them.' He scooped them up; they stiffened, turning their faces to Hazel's, but they didn't cry out. 'Only a little farther,' he said. Hazel stepped as lightly as she could. He stopped at last, beside a row of groundcars. A strip of something soft lay there. 'Stand on that,' he told her. Hazel stepped onto it – and it was cool beneath her feet. She let her breath out in a sigh. He put the little girls down and they each grabbed a hand.

He punched something on a control panel set on a post, and one of the groundcars popped its doors. The man got in, fiddled with the controls, then put his head back out. 'All of you, into the back,' he said. Hazel pushed the little girls into the back of the groundcar – it was soft inside, with cool air coming out of vents. After she climbed in, the door closed without her touching it. She noticed that there were no door handles on the inside, either.

'I'm taking you home, for now,' the man said. The car moved off. Hazel looked out the windows . . . but they were frosted, so she couldn't see. Between the back seat and the front, a dark panel had risen so that she couldn't see out the front, either. The car moved smoothly, though, with no sudden jerks. After some time, the car stopped, and the man opened the door from the outside.

'Come along now,' he said. 'And be good.'

They were on a wide paved street between stone buildings perhaps two stories tall, with a park of some kind just down the block. Hazel caught a glimpse of bright flowers arranged in some sort of pattern, but dared not take a real look. Instead, she followed the man across a stone-flagged walk to the entrance of the nearest building, a heavy carved door opened by a shorter man wearing white trousers and overshirt.

Her escort led them into the house, down a hall, into a large room with big windows opening on a garden. 'Wait here,' he told Hazel, pointing to a place near the door. She stood, holding the little girls to her. He walked across the room, and sat in a chair that faced the door. A girl about Hazel's age, wearing a plain brown dress, scurried into the room, carrying a tray with a pitcher of some liquid and a tall mug. Hazel noticed that she kept her eyes lowered, moving with quick short steps that didn't stretch her ankle-length skirt. Hazel did not dare to watch her all the way to the man's chair, but she heard the gurgle of liquid, the tinkle of a spoon in a glass, stirring. The girl left, her busy feet slipping hurriedly past Hazel. Did she look at Hazel? The littles were looking at her; Hazel squeezed their shoulders in warning.

Across the silent room, she could hear the man swallow. Then more footsteps, from outside the room, hurrying. Short light steps, short heavier ones, and someone running . . . as those legs flashed past her, bare to the knee, in sandals, Hazel realized it must be a boy.

'Daddy!' The boy's voice was still a shrill piping, but full of joy. 'Youah home!'

'Pard!' The man's voice, for the first time that Hazel had heard it, expressed something softer than command. 'Were you good? Did you take care of your mothah?'

'Yes, *sir*.'

'That's my boy.'

The others were passing her now. She saw the small bare feet of three girls, the slim skirts that hobbled their ankles, and – so astonishing she almost forgot and lifted her eyes – a woman's feet angled up on high pointed heels, beneath full skirts that rustled when she walked.

The girls rushed forward; the woman strode, her heels clicking on the floor. Hazel peeked through lowered lids . . . to see a child hardly bigger than Brandy throw herself at her father's lap, giggling. 'Daddy!' she said . . . but softly. A larger girl, head down, moved up to nestle against his side. One still larger moved to his other side.

The man kissed each girl, murmuring something in a voice that made Hazel want to cry. Her father had made that soft voice for her, when she sat leaning against him, her head resting on his shoulder. A sob rose in her throat; she choked it back, and stared at the floor again. She could feel the littles trembling; they wanted a cuddle too; they would break away any moment now. She clutched at them harder.

'I brought you something,' the man said. 'Looky there.' Hazel could feel, as if it were sunlight, their gazes on her and the littles. 'Found them on a merchanter we captured. The girlie's a bit old,

530

but biddable. Been no trouble. The two little uns . . . well, one of 'em's too talkative. We'll just have to see.' He swallowed again. 'You take 'em on back and get 'em settled. Girlie's virgin all right. Doc checked.'

The woman's shoes clicked, closer and closer. Hazel saw the wide skirt . . . a wife's skirt? . . . and then a firm hand on her shoulder, pushing. She obeyed, walking ahead of the woman, bringing the littles with her. She had no idea what was coming, but . . .

'You kin look at me,' the woman said. 'In here.' Hazel looked up. The woman had a broad, peaceful-looking face, with a crown of gray-brown hair in a braid above it. She had big broad hands, and a big broad body. 'Let's see you, honey . . . that's the ugliest dress I ever did see.'

Hazel said nothing. She wasn't about to get into trouble if she could help it.

'Didn't your folks teach you anything about sewing?' the woman asked.

Hazel shook her head.

'You kin talk, too,' the woman said. 'As long as you keep it low. No hollerin'.'

'I . . . don't know how to sew,' Hazel said softly. Her voice felt stiff, it had been so long since she said a whole sentence.

'Well, you'll just have to learn. You can't go around lookin' like that. Not in this family.'

Hazel bobbed her head. Brandy tugged on her hand.

'Hungry,' she said.

The woman looked down at the littles, her face creased with something Hazel could not read. 'These littl'uns yours?' she asked. 'Sisters?'

'No,' Hazel said.

'No, *ma'am*,' the woman said sharply. 'Didn't your folks teach you any manners?'

'No . . . ma'am,' Hazel said.

'Well, I sure will,' the woman said. 'Now let me think. You littl'uns will fit into Marylou and Sallyann's things, but you, Girlie . . . and we have to find a name for you, too.'

'My name's Hazel,' Hazel said.

531

'Not anymore,' the woman said. 'Your old life is gone, and your old name with it. You put off the works of the devil and the devil's name. You will put on a godly name. When we find the right one.'

In the next weeks, Hazel settled into a life as unlike that she'd known as the raider's ship had been. She slept in a room with ten other girls, all near or just past puberty but unmarried: the virgins' bower. Their room opened onto a tiny courtyard separated from the main garden by a stone screen and walled off from anything but their room. The room's other entrance was to a long corridor that led back to the main house without passing any other door.

'So we're safe,' one of the other girls had explained the first evening. She had helped Hazel unroll her bedding onto a wooden bunk, helped her straighten the cover properly. These were all, she discovered, daughters of the man who had brought her here . . . daughters of four wives, who had produced all the other children in the house. Only the children of his first wife were permitted in the great room . . . and only when he summoned them. The others, when he wanted to see them, went to the second parlor.

'Y'all are the first outlanders in our household,' one of the other girls said.

'Can't no one have outlanders unless they've got enough children to dilute the influence of y'all's heathen ways,' another girl said.

'So we can teach you right from wrong,' yet another said.

In short order, Hazel was clad in the same snug long skirt and long-sleeved top as the others. She learned to shuffle in quick steps . . . she learned how to navigate the corridors and rooms of the big house, that seemed to sprawl on forever. She learned to stand aside respectfully when the boys ran down the hall, to duck her chin so that even the little boys, looking up, did not meet her gaze.

Once a day, she was allowed to sit with Brandy and Stassi, if all her work was done. At first they ran to her and clung, silent, crying into her shoulder. But as the days passed, they adjusted to whatever their life was like. She had asked, but they found it hard to tell her . . . and no wonder. They had been hardly able to talk clearly when the ship was taken, and too many things had happened. They had eaten honeycakes, or they had new dresses, was all they could say. At least they were being fed and cared for, and they had a little time each day to play in the garden. She saw them with the other small girls, tossing back and forth weighted streamers of bright colors.

Her work was hard – the other girls her age were accomplished seamstresses, able to produce long, smooth straight seams. They all knew how to cut cloth and shape garments . . . now they were learning embroidery, cutwork, lacework, and other fine needlework. Hazel had to master plain knitting, crochet, and spend hours hemming bedsheets and bath towels. Besides sewing, she was taught cooking – to the wives' horror, she did not even know how to peel potatoes or chop carrots.

'Imagine!' said Secunda, the master's second wife. 'Letting a poor girl grow up knowing so little. What did they expect you to do, child? Marry a man so rich and dissolute he would expect your servants to do everything?'

'We had machines,' Hazel said.

'Oh, *machines*,' Prima said. She shook a finger at Hazel. 'Best forget about machines, girl. The devil's ways, making idle hands and giving women ideas. No machines here, just honest women doing women's work the way it should be done.'

'Prima, would you taste this sauce?' Tertia bowed as she offered it.

'Ah. A touch more potherb, m'dear, but otherwise quite satisfactory.'

Hazel sniffed. She had to admit that the kitchen smelled better than any ship's galley she'd ever been in. Every day, fresh bread from the big brick ovens; every day, fresh food prepared from the produce of the garden. And she liked chopping carrots – even onions – better than those long, straight seams. The women even laughed – here, by themselves, and softly – but they laughed. Never at the men, though. None of the jokes she'd heard all her life, bantering between the men and women of the crew. She wanted to ask why; she had a thousand questions, a million. But she'd already noticed that girls didn't ask questions except about their work – how to do this, when to do that – and even then were often told to pay better attention.

She did her best, struggling to earn her daily visit with Brandy and Stassi. The women were quick to correct her mistakes, but she sensed that they were not hostile. They liked her as well as they could have liked any stranger thrust into their closed society, and they were as kind as custom allowed.

The closed car had gone an unknowable distance – far enough for Brun to feel mildly nauseated – when it stopped finally. Someone outside opened the door; a tall woman – the first woman she had seen on this world – reached in and grabbed her arm.

'Come on, you,' she said. After so long in the ship, the accent was understandable, if still strange. 'Get out of that.'

Brun struggled up and out of the car with difficulty, not helped by the woman's hard grip. She looked around. The groundcar looked like an illustration out of one of her father's oldest books, high and boxy. The street on which it had driven was wide, brick-paved, and edged with low stone and brick buildings, none more than three stories tall. The woman yanked at her arm, and Brun nearly staggered.

'No time for lollygagging,' the woman said. 'You don't need to be sightseeing; get yourself inside the house like the decent woman you aren't.' Brun could not move fast enough to satisfy the woman, even with one of the men helping – she was too big, too awkward, and the stones of the front walk hurt her feet. She glanced up at the building they were urging her towards and nearly fell up a stone step. But she had seen it – made of heavy stone blocks, it had no windows on this side, and beside the heavy door was a tall stout man who had the body language of every door guard Brun had ever seen. A prison?

It might as well have been, she found when she was inside and the matron was listing the rules in a harsh voice. Here she would stay until her baby was born, and a few weeks after, with the other sluts – unmarried pregnant women. She would cook, clean, and sew. She would be silent, like all the others; she was there to listen, not to talk. If the matron caught her whispering or lipspeaking with the other women, she'd be locked in her room for a day. With that, the matron pushed her into a narrow room with a bed and a small cabinet beside it, and shut the door on her.

Brun sagged onto the bed.

534

'And no sitting on the bed during work hours!' the matron said, flinging open the door with a bang. 'We don't put up with laziness here. Get your sewing basket; you have plenty to do.' She pointed at the cabinet. Brun heaved herself up and opened the door; inside was a round basket and a pile of folded cloth. 'Decent clothes for yourself, first of all,' the woman grumbled. 'Now come along to the sewing room.'

She led the way along a stone-floored corridor to a room that opened on an interior court; five pregnant women sat busy at their handwork. None of them looked up; Brun could not see their faces until she was sitting down herself. One had a wry face, pulled to the right by some damage; Brun could see no scar, and wondered what had caused it. But the warden tapped her head with a hard finger. 'Get busy, you. Less lookin', more sewin'.'

'You did *what*?' Pete Robertson's voice rose sharply.

The Ranger Captain looked even more like a sick turkey gobbler, Mitch thought.

'We captured the trader without any trouble; the crew and captain lied, and the females was all using abominations, so we killed 'em. There were five children aboard, though: three girls and two boys, and those we brought home. They're in my household now. We were still in the system, learning the big ship's control systems before taking it through jump, when this little yacht came in—'

'And you couldn't let it go—'

'Not after it slowed down and was sneakin' up on us, no. It would've got all our IDs. They might've traced back to where we got the ships from. So we grabbed it, and found a mighty important passenger, so she thought herself.' Mitch grinned at the memory of that arrogant face.

'Abomination!' Sam Dubois hissed.

'She's a female, like any other,' Mitch said. 'I had her gagged, and muted her without letting her speak – she can't have contaminated any of us. Our medico said she was pure in blood, and after he took out her implants and made her a natural woman again—'

'She's one of them Registered Embryos,' Sam said. 'And you call *that* pure in blood?'

'Mixing genes from more'n one person – she might as well be a bastard—' Pete added. 'You know what the parsons say about them.'

'She's a strong, healthy young female who's now pregnant with twins,' Mitch said firmly. 'And she's mute, and she's safely in a muted maternity home. She's not going to cause any trouble. You better believe I was firm with her – she's quiet and obedient now.'

'But why did you send the yacht back?' asked Pete.

If they were asking questions and not yelling at him, he was over the hump.

'Because it's about time we got a little respect, that's why. The talk on the docks is that we're just a bunch of pirates like any others. Common criminals. That's what the Guernesi are sayin' in their own papers; they're not tellin' the truth about us. So we make it clear we aren't goin' to put up with it – they can't just ignore us. God's plan isn't goin' to be held back by such as them. Besides that, once they started lookin' for that female – and they would look, considerin' who her father is – they could've found things we don't want them to know.'

'And you bring the whole Familias down on us,' Sam hissed. 'Biggest power in this part of the galaxy and you have to make them mad—'

'I'm not afraid of anything but God Almighty,' Mitch said. 'That's what we all swear to, 'fore we're sworn in as Rangers. Fear God but fear no man – that's what we say. You goin' back on that, Sam?' He felt strong, exultant. New children in the home, shaping well. That yellow-haired slut carrying twins – God was on his side for sure.

'There's still no sense leadin' trouble home,' Pete said.

'I didn't,' Mitch said. 'Sure, I claimed what we did for the whole Militia – but I didn't leave one scrap of evidence which *branch* it was. By the time they figure it out – if they figure it out, which I doubt – we'll be raisin' enough hell right there in Familias space that they won't have time to bother us. If they make one move against us, we blow a station or two – they'll back off. I told 'em that. Nobody goes to war for one female.'

* * *

536

Brun fretted in the confines of the maternity home. She was allowed to go into the walled courtyard, hobbling around the brick paths on her swollen, sore feet. In fact, she was required to walk five circuits each day. She was allowed to go from her dormitory to the kitchen, to the dining hall, to the bathing room or toilet, to the sewing room. But the only door out was locked – and more than locked, guarded by a stout man a head taller than she was. The other occupants, all five of them, were as mute as she. The woman in charge – Brun could not think of any word that fit her position – was not mute, but all too verbal. She ordered the pregnant women around as if she were the warden in a prison. Perhaps she was; it felt like a prison to Brun. She had to spend so much time a day sewing: clothes for herself, clothes for the baby to come, clothes for herself after the birth. She had to help in the kitchen. She had to clean, struggling to push a heavy wet mop across the floor, to scrub out the toilets and sinks and shower stalls.

What kept her going was the thought of Hazel, somewhere with those two small girls. What was happening to Hazel? Nothing good. She promised Hazel – she promised herself – that she would somehow get Hazel out of this.

She was examined every day . . . and as her time came nearer, she found a whole new source of fear. One of the other women, cutting carrots beside her in the kitchen, suddenly bent and pressed a hand to her side. Her mouth opened in a silent yell. Brun could see the hardening under her maternity shift.

'Come along, you,' the warden said. She glared at Brun. 'You help her, you.' Brun took the woman's other arm, and helped her stumble down the corridor, into rooms Brun had not yet seen. Tiled floor . . . narrow bed, too short to lie on . . . as the woman in labor heaved herself onto it, she realized that this – this utterly inadequate ramshackle arrangement – was where women gave birth. Where she would give birth. The woman writhed, and a gush of fluid wet the bed and splashed onto the floor.

'Get basins, you!' the warden said to Brun, pointing. Brun brought them. When was the warden going to call the doctor? The nurses?

There were no doctors, no nurses. The warden was the only

attendant, along with whatever women were in the house. The others edged in – some of them had done this before, clearly. Brun, forbidden to leave, stood against the wall, alternately faint and nauseated. When she sagged, one of the others slapped her face with a wet rag until she stood straight again.

She had known the facts of human reproduction since childhood. In books. In instructional cubes. And she knew – or she had known – that no one who had access to modern methods still gave birth in the old way. And certainly no one, no one in the whole civilized universe, gave birth like this, without medical care, without life support, without anything but a grim old woman and other pregnant women, in a room with unscreened windows, with the blood and fluids splashing onto the bare floor, splashing onto the women's bare feet. Her father's horses had better care; the hounds had cleaner kennels for whelping.

She tried not to look, but they grabbed her, forced her to look, to see the baby's head pushing, pushing . . . her body ached already in sympathy.

The baby's first cry expressed her own rage and fear exactly.

She could not do it. She would die.

She could not die; she had to live . . . for Hazel. To keep Hazel from this horror, she would live.

11

Castle Rock

Lord Thornbuckle, Speaker of the Table of Ministers and the Grand Council of the Familias Regnant, successor to the abdicated king, had spent the morning working on the new Regular

Space Service budget proposal with his friend – now the Grand Council's legal advisor – Kevil Starbridge Mahoney. All morning a succession of ministers and accountants had bombarded them with inconvenient facts that cluttered what should have been – Lord Thornbuckle thought – a fairly simply matter of financing replacements for the ships lost at Xavier. They had decided to lunch privately, in the small green dining room with its view of the circular pond in which long-finned fish swam lazily, in the hope that the peaceful spring garden would restore their equanimity. A spicy soup and slices of lemon-and-garlic roasted chicken had helped, and now they toyed with salad of mixed spring greens, putting off the inevitable return to columns of numbers.

'Heard from Brun lately?' Kevil asked, after reporting on his son George, now in law school.

'Not for several weeks,' Thornbuckle said. 'I expect she's in jumpspace somewhere; she wanted to visit Cecelia's stud before coming home for the hunt opening day.'

'You don't worry?'

'Of course I worry. But what can I do about it? If she doesn't show up soon, I'll put someone on her tail – the problem is that as soon as I do, the newsflash shooters will know where to look, and the real sharks follow the bait.'

Kevil nodded. They had both been targets of political and private violence, as well as intrusive newsflash stories. 'You could always use Fleet resources,' he suggested, not for the first time.

'I could – except that after Copper Mountain I'm not at all sure it's safe to do so. First she's nearly killed right on the base – they still haven't figured out who was shooting at her – and then the heroic Lieutenant Suiza takes it upon herself to question Brun's morality.'

Kevil held his silence but one eyebrow went up. Thornbuckle glared at him.

'I know – you think she's—'

'I didn't say a word,' Kevil said. 'But there are two sides or more to any quarrel.'

'It was unprofessional—'

'Yes. No doubt about that. But if Brun were not your daughter, I think you would find it more understandable.'

Thornbuckle sighed. 'Perhaps. She can be . . . provocative. But still—'

'But still you're annoyed because Lieutenant Suiza wasn't more tactful. I sympathize. In the meantime—'

The knock on the door interrupted him; he turned to look. Normally, no one disturbed a private meal here, and that knock had a tempo that alerted them both.

Poisson, the most senior of the private secretaries attached to Lord Thornbuckle's official position, followed on that knock without waiting. Unusual – and more unusual was his face, pale and set as if carved from stone.

'What is it?' asked Thornbuckle. His gaze fixed on the package Poisson carried, the yellow and green stripes familiar from the largest of the commercial express-mail companies, Hymail.

'Milord – milord—' Poisson was never at a loss for words; even when Kemtre abdicated, he had been suavely capable from the first moments. But now, the package he held out quivered from the tremor in his hands.

Thornbuckle felt an all-too-familiar chill as the food he had just eaten turned to a cold lump in his belly. In the months of his Speakership, he had faced crisis after crisis, but none of them had arrived in a Hymail Express package. Still, if Poisson was reacting like this, it must be serious. He reached out for the package, but had to almost pry it from Poisson's grip.

'You opened it,' he said.

'With the others that came in, yes, milord. I had no idea—'

Thornbuckle reached into the package and pulled out a sheaf of flatpics; a data cube rolled out when he shook the package upside down. He glanced at the first of the flatpics and time stopped.

In a distant way, he was aware of the way the other flatpics slid out of his grasp, and fell slowly – so slowly – turning and wavering in the air on their way from his hand to the floor. He was aware of Poisson with his hand still extended, of Kevil across the table, of the beat of his own pulse, that had stumbled and then begun to race.

But all he could see, really see, was Brun's face staring into his with an expression of such terror and misery that he could not draw breath.

'Bunny . . . ?' That was Kevil.

Thornbuckle shook his head, clamping his jaw shut on the cry he wanted to give. He closed his eyes, trying to replace the pictured face with one of Brun happy, laughing, but – in his mind's eye, her haunted frightened gaze met his.

He didn't have to look at the rest. He knew what had happened, without going on.

He had to look. He had to know, and then act. Without a word, he passed the first flatpic to Kevil, and leaned over to pick up the rest. They had landed in a scattered heap, and before his hands – steady, he noted with surprise – could gather them together a half-dozen images had seared his eyes: Brun naked, bound to a bunk, a raw wound on her leg where her contraceptive implant had been. Brun in her custom protective suit, with a gag in her mouth, being held by gloved hands. Brun's face again, unconscious and slack, with some kind of instrument in her mouth. Brun . . . he put the stack down, and looked across at Kevil.

'My God, Bunny!' Kevil's face was as white as his own must be.

'Get us a cube reader,' Thornbuckle said to Poisson, surprised that he could speak at all past the rapidly enlarging lump in his throat.

'Yes, milord. I'm—'

'Just do it,' Thornbuckle said, cutting off whatever Poisson had been planning to say. 'And get this cleared away.' The very smell of the food on the table nauseated him. As Poisson left, he retrieved the flatpic Kevil had, and turned the whole stack carefully upside down. Two of the serving staff came and cleared the table, eyeing them worriedly but saying nothing. They had just gone out when Poisson returned with a cube reader and screen.

'Here it is, milord.'

'Stay.' Poisson paused on his way back out.

'Are you sure?' Kevil asked.

'The damage is done,' Thornbuckle said. 'We'll need at least one of the secretaries to handle communications. But first, we need to see what we're up against.' He did not offer Kevil the other flatpics.

The image on the cube reader's screen wavered, as if it were a copy of a badly recorded original, but it was clear enough to see Brun, and the heavily accented voice on the audio – a man's voice – was just understandable. Thornbuckle tried to fix his mind on the words, but time and again he lost track of the man's speech, falling into his daughter's anguish.

When it was done, no one spoke. Thornbuckle struggled with tears; he could hear the other men breathing harshly as well. Finally – he could not have said how long after – he looked up to meet their gaze. For the first time in his experience, Kevil had nothing to say; he shook his head mutely. Poisson was the first to speak.

'Milord – will want to contact the Admiralty.'

'Yes.' A rough croak, all he could make. Brun, Brun . . . that golden loveliness, that quick intelligence, that laughter . . . reduced to the shambling, mute misery of that recording. It could not be . . . yet, though recordings could be faked, he knew in his heart that this one had not been. 'The Admiralty, by all means. We must find her. I'll go – get transport.' He knew as he said it how impossible that could be. In Familias space alone, there were hundreds of worlds, thousands perhaps – he had never actually counted – where someone might be lost forever. Poisson bowed and went out. He had not told the man to be discreet – but Poisson had been born discreet.

'We will find her,' Kevil said, the rich trained voice loaded with the overtones that had moved courtrooms. 'We must—'

'And if we don't?' Thornbuckle felt his control wavering, and pushed himself up out of the chair. If he stood, if he walked, if he acted, perhaps he would not collapse in an agony that could not help Brun. 'What am I going to tell Miranda?'

'For now, nothing,' Kevil said. 'It might still be a fake—'

'You don't believe that.'

'No. But I want someone expert with image enhancement to work on it before you tell her.'

'Look at those,' Thornbuckle said, gesturing at the pile of flatpics on the table. He stared out into the green and gold garden, the water dimpling as a breeze swept across it. Behind him, he heard Kevil's breath catch, and catch again. Then the chair moved, and he felt more than heard Kevil come up behind him.

'We will get her back,' Kevil said, this time with no courtroom overtones. It was as if the rock itself had spoken. Not for the first time, Thornbuckle was aware of the depth of character that lay behind Kevil's easy, practiced manner. 'Do you want me to concentrate on the search, or the administration?'

'I have to go,' Thornbuckle said.

'Then I'll work with – whom do you want to act as Speaker while you're gone?'

'Could you?'

'I doubt it, not without starting a row. Your best bet would be a Cavendish, a de Marktos, or a Barraclough. I can certainly stay as legal advisor, and hold the carnage to a minimum. But you're the only one everyone trusts right now. Almost everyone.'

'Your transportation is here, sir.' Poisson again.

'I'll come with you this far,' Kevil said. It was not a question.

'Thank you.' Thornbuckle did not entirely trust his voice. 'I'll . . . just wash up, I think.' He gathered up the flatpics and the data cube, stuffing them back into the striped package. Kevil nodded and went on toward the side entrance.

Thornbuckle looked at his face in the mirror after splashing cold water on it. He looked . . . surprisingly normal. Pale, tired, angry . . . well, that he was. After the shock, the pain, came the anger . . . deep, and burning hotter every moment. Without his quite realizing how, it spread from the thugs who had perpetrated this most recent abomination to everyone who had contributed to it . . . the blaze spreading back down the trail Brun had taken, outlining in flame every person who had influenced her on that path.

When he left the dining room he was still in shock . . . by the time he arrived at the Admiralty, he was already beginning to think whom else to blame. Kevil, sitting beside him in the groundcar, said nothing to interfere with the inexorable progress of his rage.

At the Admiralty's planetside headquarters, a commander awaited him . . . someone he remembered from the briefings of the past week, when the replacement of ships from the Xavier action had been under discussion. He realized with a shock that Poisson had not told them what this was about – and then that Poisson had been right.

He nodded to the commander, and as soon as they were inside said, 'This is not about the budget; I need to speak to the highest ranking officer present.'

'Yes, sir; Admiral Glaslin is waiting. Secretary Poisson said it was confidential and urgent. But since I had met you before, he thought I should be your escort.'

Admiral Glaslin – tall and angular, with a heronlike droop of neck – met him in the anteroom and led them into inner office. 'Lord Thornbuckle – how may we help you?'

Thornbuckle threw the package on the desk. 'You can find these . . . persons . . . and my daughter.'

'Sir?'

'Look inside,' Kevil said quietly. 'Lord Thornbuckle's daughter has been abducted and mutilated—'

The admiral's mouth opened, then he shut it firmly and emptied the contents of the package onto his desk. At the sight of the flatpics, his face paled from its normal bronze to an unattractive mud color. 'When did you get this?'

'Just now,' Thornbuckle said.

'It was delivered sixty-four minutes ago, at the palace, as part of the normal Hymail Express daily delivery; Secretary Poisson opened it because it was labelled *Personal*, and when he realized its nature, brought it immediately to Lord Thornbuckle.' Kevil paused in his recitation until the admiral nodded. 'We were eating lunch, at the time. We have also viewed the data cube.'

'Same as the flatpics?'

'The data cube contains both a video record of the capture and an apparent surgical procedure, and audio threats against the government of the Familias Regnant.'

'Lord Thornbuckle?' The admiral looked at him.

'I – didn't hear most of the words. Kevil will be correct, however. I want a copy, when you've made one—'

The admiral looked at Kevil. 'Do you think that's wise – ?'

'Dammit, man! I'm the Speaker; I know what I need!'

'Certainly. But I must tell you – this will have to go to the Grand Admiral—'

'Of course. The sooner the better. You have to find her—' Thornbuckle forced himself to stand, to shake the admiral's hand, to turn and walk out of the office, down the polished corridors, to the entrance where his car waited.

Twelve hours later, Thornbuckle woke from a fitful doze at the approach of the Grand Admiral's aide.

'They're here now, milord.'

The conference room, as secure as any room could be, was crammed with officers. Thornbuckle reminded himself that the blue shoulder-flashes were Intelligence, and the green were Technical. At one end of the long black table, Grand Admiral Savanche leaned forward, and at the other was the only empty seat in the room, waiting for the government's senior civilian representative: himself.

He edged past the others to his place, and stood there facing Savanche.

'You've seen the recording,' Lord Thornbuckle said. 'What I want to know is, what kind of force are you committing to getting her back?'

'There's not a damn thing we can do,' Grand Admiral Savanche said. After a brief pause, he appended, 'Sir.'

'There has to be.' Thornbuckle's voice was flat, even, and unyielding.

'We can search,' Savanche said. 'Which we're doing. We have experts going through the intel database, trying to figure out who these people are, and thus where they might be.'

'You have to—'

'My Lord Thornbuckle. Your daughter has not made any official checkpoint since Podj, sixty-two days ago. We have already begun running the traffic records and sightings from all stations – but there are thousands, tens of thousands, of stations, just in Familias space alone. You have three orbiting your own Sirialis. With the staff we can release for this, that's going to take weeks to months, just to sift the existing data.'

'That's not good enough,' Thornbuckle said.

'With all due respect, my lord, given the recent incursions by the Compassionate Hand and the Bloodhorde, we dare not divert resources from our borders. They can certainly add surveillance for your daughter or her ship to their other duties; those orders have gone out. But it would be suicidal to put all Fleet on this single mission.'

'Tell me what else you have done,' Thornbuckle said.

'We know that she leased the yacht *Jester* from Allsystems; ten personnel identified as your personal militia boarded with her. Allsystems has provided us full identification profiles for that ship; if it shows up in Familias space, within range of any of our ships, we will know it. We know that she took it from Correlia to Podj without incident. Do you know where she was going next?'

'No.' He hated admitting that. 'She – she said she wanted to visit several friends, and check into some of her investments, before coming to Sirialis. She had no itinerary; she said if she made one, the newsflash shooters would find her. She said she'd be at Sirialis for the opening day of the hunt.'

'So – you expected her to be out of contact.'

'Yes. She had mentioned visiting Lady Cecelia de Marktos on Rotterdam, and perhaps even Xavier's system.'

'I see. So when would you have considered her overdue?'

'I was beginning to worry – I expected her to call in more often—'

'You see, milord, it's a very large universe, and she is only one person. Our technicians are still working on the data cube and the flatpics, but so far nothing definite has shown up. The cube itself is one of the cheap brands sold in bulk through discount suppliers; the image has been through some sort of editing process which removed considerable data. The flatpics were taken with old technology, but the prints you have are simply copies of prints, not prints from negatives. That again reduced the data available for analysis.' Savanche cleared his throat. 'Right now, there is nothing whatever to give us any idea what we're dealing with, let alone where she is.'

'But they said they were the Nutaxis something or other—'

'New Texas Godfearing Militia, yes. Something we never heard of before; it sounds utterly ridiculous to me. We are making discreet inquiries, but until something comes along – some confirmatory evidence – this might as well be the act of lunatics.'

'And how long will that take?' Thornbuckle asked. 'Don't you realize what's happening to her?'

Savanche sighed, the creases in his face deepening. 'It will take as long as it takes . . . and yes, I understand your concern, and I can imagine – though I don't want to – what may be happening to her.'

R.S.S. *Gyrfalcon*

'Ensign Serrano, report to the Captain's office. Ensign Serrano, report to the Captain's office.' What had he done wrong this time? Lieutenant Garrick turned to look at him, and then jerked her thumb toward the hatch. Barin flicked the message-received button, and headed up to Command Deck.

When he knocked, Captain Escovar called him in at once. He was sitting behind his desk, holding what looked like a decoded hardcopy.

'Ensign, you knew the Speaker's daughter, didn't you?'

For an instant Barin could not think who this might be – what chairman, what daughter. Then he said, 'Brun Meager, sir? Yes, sir, I did. I met her at Copper Mountain Schools, and we were in the escape and evasion course together.'

'Bad news,' Escovar said. 'She was on her way back to her family home when her ship was attacked by raiders.'

Brun dead . . . Barin could not believe that vivid laughing girl was dead . . .

'She was *alone*?'

'Not quite. She'd chartered a small yacht, about like one of our couriers, and she had a small security detachment, her father's private militia.' Escovar paused, as if to make sure that he was not interrupted again. Barin clamped his jaw. 'The ship has not been found, but a message packet was sent to her father, via commercial postal service.' Another pause. 'The Speaker's daughter . . . was not killed. She was captured.'

Barin felt his jaw dropping and bit down hard on everything he felt.

'The raiders . . . wanted her family to know that they had taken her, and what they had done.' Escovar made a noise deep in his throat. 'Barbarians, is what they are. Information has been forwarded to me; it should arrive shortly.' He looked at Barin, over the top of the hardcopy. 'I called you in because we have no adequate professional assessment of this young woman's temperament and abilities. I know she was referred to Copper Mountain by Admiral Vida Serrano, apparently on the advice of Commander Serrano. But her Schools files were wiped, when she left, as a security measure. If anything is to be done for her, we need to know what she herself is capable of, and what she is likely to do.'

Barin's first impulse was to say that Brun would always come out on top – it was her nature to be lucky – but he had to base this on facts. He wasn't going to make rash assumptions this time about what he knew and what he merely surmised.

'She's very bright,' he began. 'Learns in a flash. Quick in everything . . . impulsive, but her impulses are often right.'

'Often has a number attached?'

'No, sir . . . not without really thinking it over. In field problems, I'd say eighty percent right, but I don't know how much of that was impulse. They didn't let her do the big field exercise, for security reasons. She did have a problem . . .' How could he put this so that it wouldn't hurt her reputation? 'She was used to getting what she wanted,' he said finally. 'With people – with relationships. She assumed it.'

'Um. What did she try with you? And I'm sorry if this is a sore subject, but we need to know.'

'Well . . . she found me attractive. Cute, I think was her word.' Like a puppy, he had thought at the time; it had annoyed him slightly even as he was attracted to her energy and intelligence. 'She wanted more. I . . . didn't.'

'Aware of the social problems?'

'No, sir. Not exactly.' How could he explain when he didn't understand it himself? 'Mostly . . . I'm . . . I was . . . close to Lieutenant Suiza.'

'Ah. I can see why. Exceptional officer by all accounts.'

Then he hadn't heard. Barin felt a chill. He didn't want to be the one to tell the captain about Esmay's stupid explosion, or the quarrel they'd had.

'Brun is . . . like Esmay – Lieutenant Suiza – with the brakes off. They're both smart, both brave, both strong, but Brun . . . when the danger's over, she's put it completely aside. Lieutenant

Suiza will still be thinking it over. And Brun would take chances, just for the thrill of it. She was lucky, but she *expected* to be lucky.'

'Well, I know who I'd want on *my* ship,' Escovar said. Then he touched a button on his desk. 'Ensign, what I'm going to tell you now is highly sensitive. We have some information on the young woman's condition after capture, but that information must not – *must* not – spread. It will, I think, be obvious to you why, when I tell you about it. I am doing this because, in my judgement, you may be able to help us concoct a way to help her, if you have enough information. But I warn you – if I find out that you've slipped on this, I will personally remove your hide in strips, right before the court-martial. Is that clear?'

'Yes, sir.' Barin swallowed.

'All right. The raiders left behind a vid they made of her after the capture. It's one of the ugliest things I've ever watched, and I've been in combat and seen good friends blown to bits. It is clear from this vid that the raiders intend to take her to one of their home planets and keep her there as breeding stock—'

'What!' That got out past his guard; he clamped his teeth together again. He'd thought of rape; he'd thought of ransom; he'd thought of political pressure, but certainly not that.

'Yes. And they've mutilated her: they've done surgery and destroyed her vocal cords.' He paused; Brain said nothing, trying not to think of voluble Brun silent, unable to speak. Rage rose in him. 'We do not at this time know where she is; we do not know if she is still alive or not – though we suspect she is. We do not know her physical condition at any time subsequent to the vid left by the raiders. It may be impossible to find her.'

Barin wanted to argue, to insist that they must – but he knew better. One person – even Brun, even the Speaker's daughter – was not enough reason to start a war.

'I see no reason for you to view the vid,' Escovar said. 'It makes voyeurs of us, who would least want to participate in something like that. But this may be a requirement later, and you need to know that for calculated cruelty without much actual injury, this is the worst I've seen. The important thing is that what you know about her might make rescue possible. We don't want to shoot her by accident because we failed to understand her way of thinking.'

'Yes, sir.'

'I would like you to record every detail you can remember about her – anything, from the color of her underwear to every preference she ever expressed. We're trying to get more information from other people she knew, but you and Lieutenant Suiza have the advantage of understanding the military perspective, and having known her in a dangerous situation.'

'Yes, sir.'

'I put no deadline on this, but I do consider it urgent. The longer she is in their hands, the more likely that permanent damage will result, not to mention political chaos.' Barin digested that in silence. He dared not ask how her father was taking it – the little bit that he knew.

'Is her voice – permanently gone?'

'No way to tell until she's retrieved. The surgeon who viewed this tape says it depends on the exact type of surgery they performed. But she could always be fitted with a vocal prosthesis. If the only damage is to the vocal cords, she can whisper – and a fairly simple prosthesis will amplify that. However, they may have done more damage that we don't know about, and since their intent is to silence her, they may punish any attempt to whisper.'

'But how are we going to find her?'

'I don't know, Ensign. If you come up with any ideas, be sure to share them. We have been assigned to the task force charged with finding and rescuing her.'

Only a day later, Escovar called him into the office again. 'They found the yacht. It was dead in space, tethered to an unmanned navigation station; local traffic hadn't noticed it. It was found by the maintenance crew that went out to service the station. Empty, and so far no idea where it came from. Forensics will be all over it . . . there is evidence of a struggle inside.'

Barin's heart sank, if possible, even lower. A vid of Brun was one thing, but her yacht, empty and bearing signs of a fight, was not something likely to have been faked.

'Did she say anything to you – anything at all – that might give us a clue to where she could have been when she was attacked?'

'No, sir. I brought the notes I've made—' Barin handed them

over. 'Mostly we talked about the courses, about the other students and instructors. Quite a lot about Lieutenant Suiza, because Brun – Sera Meager – asked about her.'

Escovar flipped through the pages, reading rapidly. 'Here – she mentioned owning a lot of stock – did she ever say in which companies?'

'Not that I remember,' Barin said. 'She may have, but that didn't really interest me. She talked about hunting – on horseback, that is – and bloodstock, and something about pharmaceuticals, but I don't know anything about that, so—'

R.S.S. *Shrike*

They had been in jump for eight standard days, and Esmay had spent much of the last two shifts in the SAR ready rooms, briefing the specialist teams on the wonders of EVA during FTL traverses. Solis had asked her to work up a training syllabus. She would have expected this to take only an hour or so, but the teams had ever more questions – good questions. If it had been possible, they would have gone EVA on *Shrike*; Esmay was glad to find that the fail-safe of the airlocks worked here as well as on *Koskiusko*, and no one could get out.

'We really should practice it, though,' Kim Arek said. She had the single-minded intensity that Esmay recognized as her own past attitude. 'Who knows when we might need it?'

'Someone should develop suit telemetry that works outside the jump-space shielding,' someone else said. 'The temporal distortion could kill you if you didn't know when your air was running out.'

'What techniques do you use when your air is running out?' Esmay asked. 'I know what the manuals say, but the only time I saw my gauge hitting the red zone, I found "stay calm and breathe slowly" wasn't that easy.'

'No kidding.' Arais Demoy, one of the neuro-enhanced marines, grinned at her. 'Imagine what it's like when you're not even on a ship, but knocked loose somehow. That happened to me one time, during a ship-to-ship. That's why we have suit beacons in the space armor. Try to go limp, if you can – muscle contraction uses up oxygen – and think peaceful thoughts.'

551

The ship shuddered slightly, and everyone swallowed – the natural response to a downjump insertion; the insystem drive had been on standby for the past half hour, and now its steady hum went up a half tone.

'Prayer doesn't hurt,' added Sirin. 'If you're any sort of believer.'

Esmay was about to inquire politely which sort she was, when the emergency bells rang.

'XO to the bridge; XO to the bridge—' She was moving before the repeat.

'Captain?'

Solis was glaring at her as if she had done something terrible, and she couldn't think of anything. She had been in his good graces; he seemed to have put aside his earlier animosity.

'We have received a flash alert, Lieutenant.'

War? Esmay's stomach clenched.

'Lord Thornbuckle's daughter has been taken captive by an unknown force which threatens reprisals against Familias should any action be taken to rescue her. She has been mutilated—'

'Not . . . Brun!?' Esmay could feel the blood draining from her head; she put out a hand to the hatch coaming.

'Yes. There is, apparently, incontrovertible evidence of this capture. All ships are to report any trace of an Allsystems lease yacht *Jester* . . .' Solis shook his head, as if to clear it, and gave Esmay another long challenging look. 'You don't seem pleased that your prophecy that Sera Meager would come to grief has been fulfilled—'

For a moment she could not believe what he said. 'Of course not!' she said, then. 'It has nothing to do with – I never wanted anything bad to happen—'

'You had best hope, then, that she is recovered quickly and in good health,' Solis said. 'Because otherwise, what everyone will remember – as I'm sure her father remembers – is that you bawled her out and she stormed away from Copper Mountain in a temper. You might as well realize, Lieutenant Suiza, that your future in the Regular Space Service depends on her future – which right this moment looks damned bleak.'

She could not think about that; it was too dire a threat to think about. Instead, her mind leaped for any useful connection. 'That trader,' she said. Solis looked blank. 'The little ship,' Esmay said. 'The one that trailed it in, the five bodies that weren't crew, but had been mutilated. That could have been Brun's ship.'

Solis stared at her, then blinked. 'You . . . may be right. It could be – could have been. And we sent the tissue for typing—'

'Sector HQ forensics – but they'll be coded as related to the *Elias Madero*. And we don't have any beacon data on the little ship.'

'No . . . but we have a mass estimate. All right, Suiza – and now, one more time, and I want the truth: is there even the slightest glimmer of satisfaction?'

'No, sir.' She could say that with no hesitation. 'I was wrong to lose my temper at the time – I know that, and I would've apologized if she'd still been there when we got back from the field exercise. And I would not wish captivity on anyone, any time, least of all someone like her . . .'

'Like her?'

'So . . . free. So happy.'

'Umph. Well, I'm mostly convinced but I doubt anyone else will be. Better see you don't make any mistakes, Suiza. With the data we have aboard, we're sure to be called back to confer with the task force. You will be questioned about her, and one wrong word will ruin you.'

Esmay put that out of her mind, and instead thought of Brun the laughing, Brun the golden. She had not thought of herself as religious – in her great-grandmother's sense – for years, but she found herself praying nonetheless.

Aragon Station, Sector VII HQ, Task Force Briefing

Barin found himself in the very uncomfortable position of being the youngest person at a very ticklish conference. He knew why he was there: he had trained with Brun on Copper Mountain; he and Esmay had saved her skin. he had known about her disappearance almost from its discovery for precisely that reason. But nothing in his training had prepared him to sit at a table with a Grand Admiral, his admiral grandmother, two other three-star admirals, a sprinkling of commanders – his cousin

Heris among them – and the Speaker of the Council of Families of the Familias Regnant.

Nothing except growing up Serrano, which at the moment he felt was a distinctly overrated qualification.

Brun Meager's father, Lord Thornbuckle, was far beyond distraught . . . balanced on the thinnest knife-edge of stability Barin had ever seen in a previously functioning adult. In the harsh light that shone onto the polished table, Barin could see the fine tremor of the man's hands, the glitter of silver in his close-cropped blond hair as his head shifted in tense jerks from side to side, when someone spoke.

You've got to tell them everything. That's what his captain had said. Everything. But how could you tell a roomful of brass, in front of the woman's father, about her less admirable behavior? He sat very still and hoped against hope that something would interrupt this before he had to hurt a man already hurting so much. .

'Grand Admiral Savanche, we have a flash-priority message—'

Savanche pushed himself back. 'This had best be worth it.' Barin knew that despite this almost-regulation growl, he was secretly glad to have something break the tension of the briefing. Savanche took the message cube, and put it in the player.

'It's from Captain Solis, aboard the search-and-rescue ship *Shrike* . . . they were pursuing leads in the disappearance of a Boros Consortium merchanter, and have been out of contact for weeks. He just heard about the yacht's disappearance, and – you'd better see this for yourself.' He transferred output to the room's main screen.

Onto the screen came a section of star chart, with a corner window of Captain Solis.

'—trace of a very small craft in the system as well,' he was saying. 'We presumed at first that it was the raider's tail on the *Elias Madero*. When we located debris and bodies from the merchanter, amounting to the entire adult crew and one juvenile apprentice – but not the other apprentice, nor four small children – we also located five bodies which were not crew, and which we could not identify. My forensics team believes them to have been military, but they weren't Fleet, and the usual identification sites had been mutilated.'

'There were ten . . .' breathed Lord Thornbuckle.

'We sent off a report on this to Sector, top priority, when we got back to Bezaire, but we had to use a commercial ansible. At that time we had not received word that the Speaker's daughter was missing. However, when we came out of jump at Sil Peak, we received that news and specifications of her ship. My Exec, Lieutenant Suiza, immediately thought of the other bodies we'd found. The ship trace we found is consistent with a yacht of the stated mass. We have the recovered bodies in storage; please advise next move.'

'We own stock in Boros,' Lord Thornbuckle said. 'She was out there – she'd said she wanted to look into the olive orchards on . . . whichever one it is, I can't think. It has to be her . . . her yacht. Her guards . . .'

'Do you know anything about them, Lord Thornbuckle?'

'They're from my militia. Brun had . . . not gotten along with the Royal Space Service security personnel who had gone with her to Copper Mountain. There had been an incident—'

'And you say there were more than five—'

'Yes . . . there should have been ten.' Lord Thornbuckle stared at the table between his hands. 'She thought that was too many.'

'Well, it's imperative that we get what evidence Solis has gathered as soon as possible.' Savanche's eye swept the room and lighted on Barin. 'Ensign – go find my signals chief and tell her I want a secure link to *Shrike*.'

'Sir.' Barin found the Grand Admiral's staff signals specialist hovering outside the room – someone had anticipated the need – and sent her in. He was glad to be out of there, and hoped he wouldn't be called back. *Shrike* . . . Esmay was on *Shrike*. He wondered how she was taking the news.

12

Shrike came into the system like an avenging angel, a high-vee insertion through a lane cleared for that purpose, and then shifted insystem in a series of microjumps . . . reducing a normal eight-day down transit to a mere eleven hours. Three tugs went out to meet her, and dragged her toward the station at a relative velocity that seemed reckless. Barin, aboard *Gyrfalcon*, lurked in scan and watched along with everyone else.

'Ensign—' He glanced back to find his captain beckoning, and followed him to his office.

'We've been getting realtime downloads from *Shrike* for the past hour,' the captain said. 'I want you to hand-carry this to the Grand Admiral's office – it's for his eyes only, and I want you to put it in his hands personally.'

'Sir.' Barin took the rack of four data cubes – a *lot* of data – and headed for the Grand Admiral's temporary suite of offices. He'd been couriering one thing and another since they'd arrived, so the Admiral's staff listened when he said. '—in his hands personally.'

'You'll have to wait, though. The Admiral's receiving a delegation from the Guernesi Republic.'

'Fine.' Barin found a spot out of the way of the traffic through the outer office, and let his mind wander to *Shrike*'s arrival . . . and her executive officer. Would he have a chance to see Esmay? Not likely; *Shrike*'s captain would certainly be the one coming to any briefings. Perhaps this new information would divert attention from his supposed expertise on Brun, which seemed more tawdry every time he thought of it. So she had wanted to bed him – so what? So she had been, in his mind, a difficult and headstrong individual . . . but whatever she had been, she didn't deserve what had happened to her. Once again he saw the video clip of the surgery and felt his own throat close; he swallowed with an effort.

'Hello, Ensign Serrano—'

His eyes snapped to the left, where Lieutenant Esmay Suiza stood with a challenging look . . . and a lockbag of data, no doubt.

'Lieutenant!'

'Wool-gathering?' she asked, in almost the tone of the old Esmay, the Esmay of the *Koskiusko*.

'Sir, my mind had wandered—'

'Just another minute, he said,' the clerk at the desk interrupted. 'If the lieutenant wouldn't mind going in with Ensign Serrano—'

'Not at all,' said Esmay.

Barin tried not to stare, but – she looked so good. Nothing like Casea Ferradi; if she was priggish in some ways, she was at least clean.

The Admiral's door opened, and a harried-looking commander waved them both in. 'Come on Serrano, Suiza – he's waiting for both of you.'

From within someone said 'No!' very loudly. Barin paused. 'I won't have her – I don't want to see her.' The commander holding the door closed it again. '—all her fault!' leaked out just before it snicked shut.

Thornbuckle. Still angry, still unreasonable . . . Barin gave Esmay a sidelong glance; she was staring straight ahead, almost expressionless. He wanted to say something – but what? – but the door opened again, this time to Grand Admiral Savanche.

'Lieutenant, I believe you have a hand-to-hand for me?'

'Yes, sir.' Esmay's voice expressed no more than her face as she handed him the databag.

'Very well. Dismissed.' He turned to Barin. 'Come along in, Ensign.' Barin tried to catch Esmay's eye, but she looked past him. He followed Savanche into the conference, his heart sinking rapidly past the deck toward the gravitational center of the universe.

'The tissue typing confirms that the unidentified bodies found at the site of the *Elias Madero* hijacking were those of five members

557

of the ten from Lord Thornbuckle's personal militia: Savoy Ardenil, Basil Verenci, Klara Pronoth, Seren Verenci, and Kaspar Pronoth. This very strongly suggests that Sera Meager's ship was there at the time, and may have attempted to intervene.'

Which meant that they knew, at last, where Brun's yacht had been when she was attacked. At last they could narrow the search to something other than all space everywhere. *Shrike*'s subsequent search for traces of the *Elias Madero* narrowed it further. Barin tried to fix his mind on the evidence and its logical consequences, but Esmay's set face kept intruding. She had been wrong, yes – but Lord Thornbuckle's outburst, his refusal to see her, was profoundly unjust. Brun's situation was not Esmay's fault.

'The Guernesi are working on data cubes recovered from the *Elias Madero*; they have already identified the organization – apparently it really is the New Texas Godfearing Militia, and they are attempting to find out which branch captured Sera Meager.' The briefing officer, a commander Barin did not know, paused for questions. One only came, from Lord Thornbuckle.

'How long . . . ?'

When the conference was dismissed, Barin fully intended to go looking for Esmay. He wanted her to know that he, at least, was no longer angry with her. But the ubiquitous Lieutenant Ferradi caught him first. By the time he'd finished running the errands she assigned, he was due back aboard *Gyrfalcon* for his watch.

Captain Solis met Esmay at the docking hatch for *Shrike*. 'We need to talk,' he said. He looked more tired than angry. 'So far no one aboard knows about this – and I would prefer to keep it as quiet as possible.'

'Sir.' She hadn't done anything at all, but follow orders and take the data where she'd been told.

He sighed. 'Near as I can tell – and I should be able to tell, or what am I doing with my rank? – your outburst back at Copper Mountain was just that, an outburst. You've done a good job for me; you're an effective leader. You fit your history, is what I'm saying. But acts have consequences, including mistakes, however rare.'

Esmay thought about saying something, but decided there was no point.

'Lord Thornbuckle needs a villain,' Solis said. 'And since he can't get his hands on the real villains, he's picked you. He refuses to have you involved in planning the rescue; he doesn't even want you on the base. There's a very limited amount that we can do, given his position and his state of mind. However, I consider your knowledge of Sera Meager – and the investigation of the *Elias Madero* hijacking site – to be important resources. I've gone on record as saying so, and had my tail chewed by Admiral Hornan.'

'Yes, sir,' Esmay said, since the long pause suggested the need for some comment.

'You're going to have to stay out of everyone's way – I won't say I'm restricting you to *Shrike*, because that would be unfair, but until I can get you some kind of assignment that uses your talents, I strongly recommend that you consider spending most of your time there – and make sure you don't run afoul of Lord Thornbuckle or Admiral Hornan. The latter won't be easy – he's taking his position as Sector Commandant very seriously, and he would like to lead the task force when it acts. Since the Serranos are in Thornbuckle's bad graces, he may well get that assignment.'

'Yes, sir.' Why were the Serranos in trouble? That made no sense to Esmay, but clearly she should stay away from Barin until she got that figured out. The last thing she wanted was to get a Serrano in worse trouble.

'And if you do mingle, watch what you say – because someone else will be.'

'Yes, sir.'

'I'll do my best to keep you informed of the progress of the investigation and planning – now, get in there and keep my ship the way it should be.'

'Yes, sir.' Esmay saluted and went aboard, very little cheered by the knowledge that her captain no longer thought of her as a monster. Clearly, enough other people did.

In the next few days, Barin did his best to search the station, but he did not see Esmay in any of the places where off-duty officers congregated. Her name was never down for a machine or swim lane at the gym; he could find no logon records at the library; she had no assigned quarters. Could she still be living aboard *Shrike*?

He called up the ship's entry and found her listed as the XO – at least that was right – but no personal comcode number. He didn't want to call the ship's general number and have her paged; in the present climate, that might get them both in more trouble.

The next briefing began with a presentation by one of the Guernesi.

'Thanks to the data cubes recovered by *Shrike*, and skillfully enhanced by your technicians, we're able to identify the raiders as members of a religious-military organization which controls some six Earth-type planets in this area—' He pointed to a chart on display. 'You'll notice that these are in the angle, as it were, between Guernesi and Familias space.

'Let me give you a little necessary background on the group that calls itself the New Texas Godfearing Militia, or the Nutex Militia, for short. Our historians have done extensive research on the fringe religions that formed colonies in the early days of expansion from Old Earth, because we've had unpleasant contact with many of them. This one claims to descend from founders in Texas – one of the United States, which was in North America, for those of you with an interest in Old Earth geography.'

'I don't see the relevance,' Lord Thornbuckle said. 'We can learn the history later—'

'I believe you will, sir. Their present beliefs are relevant to your daughter's situation, and to any hope of intervention on her behalf. Their present beliefs grow out of their mythologized view of Texas history.' He took a breath and went on. 'Now, this state had at one time been – very briefly – an independent nation. As with other nations swallowed up by larger political units, a portion of its population clung to that memory and caused trouble. In the late twentieth, their reckoning, one of many militias and terrorist religious groups active in the United States was something called the Republic of Texas. At that time, it was not affiliated with a particular religious position, and did not have as rigid a view of gender roles as some others. But it existed in the same soup, as it were, and the flavors melded.'

'Was it involved in terrorist acts at that time?' asked Admiral Serrano.

'We think originally not, except in collecting arms, evading taxes, and causing the local government as much administrative trouble as possible. However, in one recorded standoff with the authorities, its members did take hostages, and did announce an intent to form a separate government and bring down the existing one. It failed. But that failure led to an affiliation with the survivors of a failed religious fringe group. They explained the Republic of Texas failure as resulting from lack of faith, and explained their own as resulting from lack of military experience. That group bore the rather cumbersome name of the Republic of Godfearing Texans Against World Government. It quickly splintered, as such groups often do, into several, each of which had similar, but doctrinally distinct, beliefs. One of these called itself the New Texas Godfearing Militia. This particular branch believed that the decay of society which led to acceptance of tyranny was due to the influence of women, and that women had been allowed beyond the bounds set by God in Holy Scripture. Many other such groups existed at the time – universal education for women in North America was then fairly recent, and their entry into employment was blamed for male unemployment and discontent. Historians have found many texts advocating the return of women to 'traditional' roles, defined very narrowly.

'It is this branch of the original which made it to space, under a colonization contract which they promptly disavowed. They organized their own colonial government, based on a military unit found in the original state. Apparently, a mythology had arisen surrounding the Texas Rangers, so they denoted their elected officials "rangers," and appended the names of historical figures from the brief period of Texas nationality. That's important, because we have learned to track splits in the original group by their choice of names for their rangers. For instance, there's a branch that denominates their leaders Rangers McCullough, Davis, King, Austin, and Crockett. Another uses Crockett, Bowie, Houston, Travis, and Lamar. However, they all have in common a council of five rangers, headed by a captain. We've included a listing for each of the six known branches.

'Because this group formed by splintering, and considers individual liberty of utmost importance – individual liberty of males, that is – they are constantly breaking up and reforming alliances among themselves.'

'Do they exchange prisoners?' asked another admiral.

'Almost never. We've retrieved a few men from them, by hefty threats. But never women. There's a double problem with their attitude towards women. They believe that allowing women in space, for instance, is a form of neglect – that men are bound by faith to protect women. So if they capture women, they consider that they are actually saving them from a worse fate.'

'But they mutilated and killed those women—'

'That's the other problem. Their religious beliefs are, as with most such groups, extremely rigid on anything having to do with sex or reproduction. They believe women were created by God to serve men and bear children . . . and that they must be guided, if children, or forced, if adults, into the role divinely intended for them. They also believe that only male-female sexual activity is permissable; anything else is what they call abomination. So also is contraception and genetic engineering. So if they capture women who have contraceptive implants, evidence of genetic engineering, or who are, by virtue of their rank or behavior, "usurping the authority of men," they usually kill them.'

'Brun's a Registered Embryo,' Lord Thornbuckle said. 'She's got the mark – what would they think of that?

'Abomination, certainly. Interfering with God's plan for humans . . . and I assume like most unmarried young women, she also had a contraceptive implant?'

'Of course,' Lord Thornbuckle said. 'And beyond that, REs require a positive fertility induction. Brun wanted the implant mostly so she'd be like her friends, some of whom weren't Registered Embryos.'

'It's surprising they didn't kill her,' the Guernesi went on. 'They must have considered her political importance worth taking the chance that God would punish them for allowing her to live. That's undoubtedly why they did such a thorough job with muting her, and proceeded immediately to induce fertility. In their own minds, they were reclaiming her for God's purposes, and sending a message to you and the rest of the Familias—'

'Then they're free-birthers—'

'Rabidly so; each adult male is entitled to as many wives as he can support, and free access to what they call "whores of Satan." All live-born children, however, are considered equally legitimate property of the acknowledged father – and if no father boasts of it, there are always people ready to adopt. If any of their own women rebel – and it does happen – they are muted and handed over to these breeding houses.'

'How do you know so much?' Thornbuckle asked.

'Well, we share a border with two of the five systems they control, and they've come after our people repeatedly. Their beliefs name us as one of the abominations. If anyone is interested, we can provide copies of what they consider to be divinely inspired prophecy and law. They also trade with us, in very limited ways – in spite of our being, in their view, perverts and abominations, they have need of our skills sometimes. In order to protect our people, we've had to find out more about them. In fact, I'm afraid we may be indirectly responsible for this incursion into Familias space.'

'What!'

'They had attacked one of our passenger ships, the third time in only a few months. It got away, but we felt they were becoming too bold. So, we smacked them, hard – went in and blew some of their fixed defense platforms, and told 'em God was punishing 'em for their errors. They know most of our people are what they call "spiritual" – though of course, not the same faith. Anyway, my guess is that they reacted to this by looking for some way to regain their prestige. Stayed away from us – and the Emerald States, on their other side, had whacked 'em before they bounced off us – so they went after you. I should warn you – they probably have agents somewhere in your commercial networks, because every time *we've* caught them trying to hijack a big cargo ship, it's had illegal arms shipments on it.'

'There was nothing like that on the *Elias Madero* manifest . . .'

'No. There wouldn't be. The way they operated in our space was they'd get something on a shipping agent, get the access to a hold – sometimes only one, sometimes several – then they'd have it stuffed with anything they could buy on the gray market.' He tipped his head. 'Lot of it came from the Familias, you know. You folks have a thriving arms industry.'

'We're not alone in that,' Lord Thornbuckle muttered.

'No. But of the stuff we've confiscated when we've caught them, around seventy-three percent comes from Familias sources, eleven percent from ours, and the rest from the Emerald Worlds.' He paused; no one said anything. 'I'd recommend a very thorough look at the Boros Consortium shipping agents, especially the one upstream of where the attack occurred. They don't usually wait long to grab after they've coerced someone into loading. Patience is not their strong point. You might also want to check your official military inventories; in both the Emerald Worlds and the Guerni Republic, they've attempted to gain converts within the military. Their emphasis on male supremacy and personal honor does find welcome in some cultures, and you're a multicultural entity.'

A chill fell on the room; Barin recognized both fear and denial in the silence. As if they did not already have concerns about loyalty, after Lepescu and Garrivay. But before any of the military spoke, Thornbuckle did.

'So now you've narrowed it to – what – five planets? Six? But she could be anywhere.'

'In theory, yes. But here's what else we've got . . .' A still shot of enhanced vid went up. 'Thanks to *Shrike's* extensive scavenging of the hijacking site, and the quick thinking of someone in the *Elias Madero* crew, we have video data of the hijackers themselves. 'You can see that enhancement gives us the engraving on the leader's insignia . . . here . . . you can just make out BOWIE. So we know that this raid was led by a Ranger Bowie, and we know from other sources that only two of the settlements, Our Texas and Texas True, now title one of their rangers "Bowie." Knowing that, we'll need to get visual confirmation of *which* Bowie we're dealing with – and that may take some time.'

'She doesn't *have* time,' Thornbuckle said. 'We have to find her . . .'

Barin saw the sidelong glances; he had heard the rumors, too. They had worse problems than a missing woman and threats against the government. Something would have to be done.

'We have field agents working on it,' Grand Admiral Savanche said. 'Since the Guernesi told us to expect terrorist attacks from these people, we've put out specific warnings to law enforcement on all orbital stations, shipyards, and in the larger cities.'

Zenebra, Main Station

Goonar Terakian had come into the Rusty Rocket for a quiet conversation with his cousin Basil Terakian-Junos, out of the hearing of their other relatives and shipmates. They had business no one else needed to hear. Midweek, mid-second shift, they might have been lucky enough to find the bar empty except for Sandor the bartender and possibly Genevieve. Genevieve, Sandor said, was off somewhere shopping. But the bar wasn't empty. Propped against the bar was a young man whose shipsuit bore an unfamiliar patch, but his condition was all too familiar.

'You don't have a clue what's coming to you,' the young man said. He was very young, and very drunk. Terakian ignored him, and ordered for himself and Basil. Perhaps the young fool would go back to talking to himself.

But he didn't. When Terakian moved to the far end of the bar with Basil, the young man followed.

'The blow is about to fall,' the young man said. He had an accent you could slice for baklava. 'And yet you walk in darkness, unaware.'

'Go away,' Basil said.

'You will not give the orders then,' the young man said. 'It will be too late for you, then.'

Terakian looked past him at Sandor, who rolled his eyes but said nothing. Drunks are drunks, an occupational hazard. But the Terakians were old customers, so he approached the young man. 'Are you drinking or talking?' he asked.

'Gimme another,' the young man said. He swayed slightly but he wasn't out yet, and Terakian figured he wouldn't remember anything anyway.

'About the Vortenya contract,' he said to Basil, turning his back on the drunk. 'What I heard from Gabe on the *Serenity Gradient* is that they're planning—'

The drunk tapped his shoulder, and Terakian turned angrily.

The drunk shook a finger in his face. 'You don't know what's coming to you,' he said again.

'What are you talking about?' Terakian said, more than a little annoyed. 'All I know that's coming to me is a half share in the ship when my uncle dies.' He grinned at his cousin, who grinned back.

'Issa secret,' the young man said. 'But you'll know. You'll *all* know.'

'Sounds like a threat,' Basil said. 'Oooh . . . I'm so scared . . .'

'You better be,' the young man said. His bleary gaze focussed again. 'All you . . . abominations.'

'Egglayer!' Terakian's cousin said. He had a temper, and the scars to prove it.

But the young drunk didn't rise to that insult. He smiled an ugly smile. 'You'll be sorry. When the stations blow, and the wrath of God smites—'

'Here now,' Sandor said. 'No god-talk in this bar. If you want to fight over religion, do it somewhere else.'

The young man pushed himself back from the bar, took a few unlevel steps, then folded over and vomited copiously.

'I hate righteous drinkers,' Sandor said, reaching for the vacuum nozzle racked behind the bar. 'They can't hold their liquor.' He looked at Terakian and his cousin. 'You ever seen him before?'

'No,' Terakian said. 'But there's been a few of those patches around the last day or so, over in D-dock.'

'Well, stick your head out and see if you spot any station security while I clean up. Don't want any trouble with the law for having served to a minor or something.' Sandor yanked on the vacuum hose, and hauled it around the end of the bar toward the mess.

Terakian, who came through this station every two months, regular as clockwork, knew most of the station employees. He glanced down toward Friendly Mac's Exchange & Financing, and saw Jilly Merovic on her beat. He waved; Jilly waved back, and crossed the corridor, moving at her usual quick walk.

'Jilly's coming,' he told the bartender.

'Good.' Sandor had already sucked up most of the vomit, but the young man was sprawled unconscious. 'Help me turn him over, will you?'

566

'Leave 'em face down, our ship medic says,' Basil said.

'Well, then, pick up his head so I can suck up the rest of the puddle.' Basil grimaced, but pulled the young man's head up by the hair as Sandor passed the vacuum intake under his face.

'What's going on?' Jilly asked from the doorway.

'New customer – he drank too much, threw up, and passed out on me.'

'Um. You get his ID?'

'It *said* he was twenty-seven.'

'All right, Sandor, I'm not accusing you of selling to minors. I just wanted to know if he had any medicals.'

'Nothing stamped.'

Jilly squatted beside the sprawled figure, then glanced up at Terakian and his cousin. 'Either of you know him? Did he seem distressed?'

'No, we didn't know him, and he seemed drunk,' Basil said. Terakian gave him a warning look; Basil was the kind to resent the interference of fate. They could always do their business later, if he didn't cause enough trouble to get them noticed.

'He was making threats,' Terakian said. 'Called us abominations, and said we'd get what was coming to us.'

Jilly had opened the man's ID packet but she looked up at that. 'Abominations? Are you sure that's what he said?'

'Yeah. And something about stations blowing up. Typical mean drunk, is what I thought. Probably his captain told him off, or his station molly took up with someone else.'

'Ever hear of a ship called the *Mockingbird Hill*?' Jilly asked.

Terakian shook his head. 'No . . . what is it?'

'An unaffiliated trader. This is Spacer First Class Todd Grew.' She scanned the ship patch on the man's arm, then looked at the readout on her handcomp. '*Mockingbird Hill* all right, and she's berthed in D-dock. Paid up a thirty-day docking fee, and her cargo is listed as light manufactory.'

'Aren't you going to call his ship for transport back?'

Jilly gave Basil a look that chilled Terakian to the bone, though he got only the edge of it. 'No. Ser Grew deserves only the best medical treatment. You two keep watch on the door – if you see anyone looking for Mr. Grew, go cause trouble. Whatever you do, don't let them in here.' Then, to the bartender. 'I'll need your comjack.'

'But you have your—'

'Now,' Jilly said, with sufficient force that the bartender stepped back. Terakian was glad to see another man react the way he felt. He nodded at Basil and they went to the door as Jilly had ordered. He couldn't hear what she said . . . but a long life in Familias spaceways left him no doubt as to the identity of the men in unremarkable clothes who came through the bar's back door and bundled Todd Grew into a gurney before he woke up. Even as they were taking him out the back, one of them approached Terakian.

'May I see your ID please?' It was not really a request. Terakian pulled out his folder; the man glanced at it, and without looking up said, 'Officer Merovic says she knows you – has for years.'

'That's right,' Terakian said. Cold sweat trickled down his back, and he hadn't even done anything wrong. That he knew of. 'Off the *Terakian Blessing*, Terakian and Sons, Limited.'

'And you?' the man said, looking at Basil.

'Basil Terakian-Junos. Off the *Terakian Bounty*.'

'Cousins,' the man said. 'You're the brawler, aren't you?'

'I can fight,' Basil said.

'Basil—'

'It doesn't bother me,' the man said. 'Just wanted to be sure I had the right Terakian cousins. Now let me give you some advice.' Orders, he meant. 'This never happened, right?'

'What?' asked Basil.

Terakian elbowed Basil. 'We just came in here for a little family chat—'

'Right. And you saw Officer Merovic and bought her a drink.'

'Yessir. And nobody saw anything?'

'That's it. I know how you people are with your families, but I'm telling you, this is not a story to tell, and there's no profit to be made off it.'

Terakian doubted that – anything Fleet security cared about this much usually involved plenty of profit – but he was willing to concede that he couldn't make anything off it.

'And how long should our family conference continue?' he asked.

'Another fifteen minutes should about do it,' the man said pleasantly.

Fifteen minutes. They still had time to deal with the Vortenya contract negotiations, if Jilly didn't insist on sitting with them for her drink.

Aragon Station, Sector VII HQ

'Thanks to an alert security force on Zenebra, we now have both proof of planned terrorist attacks, and some more specific information about Sera Meager's most probable location.'

'And that is?'

'An unaffiliated trader, *Mockingbird Hill*, bought used from Allsystems Salvage four years ago . . . showed up at Zenebra Main Station, and paid thirty days' docking fee upfront. That in itself was a bit surprising, but the stationmaster just listed it in the log, and didn't specifically alert Fleet; we hadn't given out a list of warning signs, because we didn't want to cause widespread panic. One of the crew, however, got drunk in a spacer bar, spewed his guts out, and had said something to the locals which alerted security. They called Fleet, and when we interrogated him, we found he was one of that cult, and the trader was stuffed with explosive, designed to blow any station they chose. They hadn't intended to blow Zenebra, particularly, but they were sited there in case called on to act somewhere in that sector.'

'And Sera Meager?'

'According to one of the others, the Ranger Bowie on the vid from *Elias Madero* is from the branch known as Our Texas; this group was from Native Texas, who are apparently allied with them at present.'

'And the Guernesi have agents in place on . . . let's see here. Home Texas, Texas True, and . . . what do you know? Our Texas.'

'Yes . . . and that agent should be able to confirm whether they still have a Ranger Bowie, and whether we've got the right man – and planet.'

Caradin University, Department of Antique Studies

Waltraude Meyerson, peering through the eyepiece of the low-power microscope at an exceedingly rare photograph which might – if she was lucky – finally answer the question of whether a certain Old Earth politician was male or female, ignored the comunit's chime until it racked up into an angry buzz. She reached out blindly, and felt around on her desk until she found the button and pushed it.

'Yes!'

'It's Dean Marondin . . . we have an urgent request for a specialty consult in your field.'

'Nothing in my field is urgent,' Waltraude said. 'It's all been dead for centuries.' Nonetheless she sat back and flicked off the microscope's light.

'It's a request from the highest authorities . . .'

'About ancient history? Is it another antiquities scam?'

'No . . . I'm not even sure why, but they want to know about Old Earth politics, North American . . . so of course I thought of you.'

Of course. She was the only North Americanist on the faculty, but chances were that some idiot bureaucrat wanted to know the exchange rate of Quebeçois francs to Mexican pesos in a decade she knew nothing about . . .

'So what's the question?'

'They want to talk to you.'

Interruptions, always interruptions. She had taken the term off, no classes, so she could finally put together the book she had been working on for the past eight years, and now she had to answer silly questions. 'Fine,' she said. 'I'll give them fifteen minutes.'

'I think they need longer,' the dean said. 'They're on their way.'

Great. Waltraude stood up and stretched, working out the kinks that hours over the microscope had put in her back, and looked vaguely around her office. 'They' implied more than one – they would want to sit down, and both chairs were piled with papers. Some people thought it was old-fashioned to have so much paper around, but she was – as she insisted – old-fashioned herself. That's why she'd gone into antique studies in the first place. She had just picked up one stack, and was looking for a place to put it, when the knock came at her door. 'Come in,' she said, and turned to find herself facing two men and two women who scared her into immobility. They looked as if they should all be in uniform, though they weren't.

'I'm sorry if we startled you,' said one of the women. 'But – do you know anything about Texas?'

Three hours later she was still talking, and they were still recording it and asking more questions. She was no longer scared, but still confused about why they'd come.

'But you really should ask Professor Lemon about that,' she said finally. 'He's the one who's done the most work on North American gender relations in that period.'

'Professor Lemon died last week in a traffic accident,' the woman said. 'You're the next best.'

'Oh. Well—' Waltraude fixed the other woman with a gaze that usually got the truth from undergraduates. 'When are you planning to tell me what's going on?'

'When we get you to Sector VII Headquarters,' the woman said with a smile that was not at all reassuring. 'You're now our best expert on Texas history, and we want to keep you alive.'

'My sources—' Waltraude said, waving at the chaos of her office. 'My book—'

'We'll bring everything,' the woman promised. 'And you'll have access to Professor Lemon's as well.'

Lemon had refused for years to share his copy of a Molly Ivins book Waltraude had never been able to track down through Library Services. He had even reneged on a promise to do so, in exchange for her data cube of thirty years of a rural county newspaper from Oklahoma. Access to Lemon's material?

'When do we leave?' asked Waltraude.

13

Sector VII HQ

'The admiral wants you,' the jig said. Esmay looked up from her lists. What now? She hadn't done anything bad again, surely.

'On my way,' she said, forcing cheerfulness into her voice. Whatever it was would be made no better by a long face.

In Admiral Hornan's outer office, the clerk nodded at her soberly, and touched a button on the desk. 'Go right in, Lieutenant Suiza.'

So it was serious, and she still had no idea what was going on. They had chewed all the flavor out of her sins so far; what else was there to attack?

'Lieutenant Suiza reporting, sir.' She met Admiral Hornan's eyes squarely.

'At ease, Lieutenant. I'm sorry to say I have sad news for you. We have received a request relayed by ansible from your father for you to take emergency leave . . . your great-grandmother has died.'

Esmay felt her knees give a little. The old lady's blessing – had she known? Tears stung her eyes.

'Sit down, Lieutenant.' She sat where she was bidden, her mind whirling. 'Would you like tea? Coffee?'

'No . . . thank you, sir. It's – I'll be fine in a moment.' She was already fine; a translucent shield protected her from the universe.

'Your father indicates that you and your great-grandmother were close—'

'Yes, sir.'

'And says that your presence is urgently needed for both legal and family matters, if you can possibly be spared.' The admiral's head tilted. 'Under the circumstances, I think you can well be spared. Your presence here is hardly essential.' He might as well have said it was grossly unwelcome; Esmay registered that but felt none of the pain she would have felt before. Great-grandmother dead? She had been a constant, even in self-exile, all Esmay's life, all her father's life.

'I – thank you, sir.' Her hand crept up to touch the amulet through her uniform.

'I'm curious to know, if you would not mind telling me, what legalities might require a great-grandchild's presence at such a time.'

Esmay dragged her mind back to the present conversation; she felt she was wading through glue. 'I'm not entirely sure, sir,' she began. 'Unless I am my great-grandmother's nearest female relative in the female line . . . and I'd have thought it was my aunt Sanibel.'

'I don't follow.'

Esmay tried to remember birth years – surely it had to be Sanni, and not herself. But Sanni was younger than her father. 'It's the land, sir. The estancia. Land passes in the female line.'

'Land . . . how much land?'

How much land? Esmay waved her hands vaguely. 'Sir, I'm sorry but I don't know. A lot.'

'Ten hectares? A hundred?'

'Oh no – much more than that. The headquarters buildings occupy twenty hectares, and the polo fields are—' She tried to think without counting on her fingers. 'Probably a hundred hectares there. Most of the small paddocks up by the house are fifty hectares . . .'

The admiral stared; Esmay did not understand the intensity of that stare. 'A small paddock – just part of this land – is fifty hectares?'

'Yes . . . and the large pastures, for the cattle, are anywhere from one to three thousand hectares.'

He shook his head. 'All right. A lot of land. Lieutenant – does anyone in Fleet know you are that rich?'

'Rich?' She wasn't rich. She had never been rich. Her father,

573

Papa Stefan, her great-grandmother . . . the family as a whole, but not her attenuated twig on the end of the branch.

'You don't consider thousands of hectares a sign of wealth?'

Esmay paused. 'I never really thought of it, sir. It's not mine – I mean, it never was, and I'm reasonably sure it's not now. It's the family's.'

'My retirement estate,' the admiral said, 'Is ten hectares.'

Esmay could think of nothing to say but 'Sorry,' and she knew that was wrong. .

'So might I conclude,' the admiral went on, in a tone of voice that set Esmay's teeth on edge, 'that if you were to . . . choose to pursue family responsibilities, rather than a career in Fleet, you would not be starving in the street somewhere?'

'Sir.'

'Not that I'm advising you to do so; I merely find it . . . interesting . . . that the young officer who was capable of telling the Speaker's daughter she was a spoiled rich girl is herself . . . a rich . . . girl. A very rich girl. Perhaps – for all the reasons you elucidated for Sera Meager's benefit – rich girls are not suited to military careers.'

It was as close to an instruction to resign as anyone could come, without saying the words. Esmay met his eyes, bleak misery in her heart. What chance did she have, if senior officers felt this way about her? She wanted to argue, to point out that she had proven her loyalty, her honor – not once, but again and again. But she knew it would do no good.

The admiral looked down at his desk. 'Your leave and travel orders have been cut, Lieutenant Suiza. Be sure to take all the time you need.'

'Thank you, sir.' She would be polite, no matter what. Rudeness had gotten her nowhere, honesty had come to grief, and so she would be polite to the end.

'Dismissed,' he said, without looking up.

The clerk looked up as she came out.

'Bad news, sir?'

'My . . . great-grandmother died. Head of our family.' Her throat closed on more, but the clerk's sympathetic expression looked genuine.

574

'I'm sorry, sir. I have the leave and travel orders the admiral told me to prepare . . .' The clerk paused, but Esmay offered no explanation. 'You've got a level two priority, and I took the liberty of putting your name on a berth for the fastest transit I could find.'

'Thank you,' Esmay said. 'That's very kind—'

'You're quite welcome, sir; just sorry it's for a sad occasion. I notice your end-of-leave is given as indeterminate – I'm assuming you'll notify the nearest sector HQ when you know how long you'll need?'

'That's right,' Esmay said. The familiar routine, the familiar phrases eased the numbing chill of the admiral's attitude.

'That would be Sector Nine, and I'll just add the recognition codes you'll need – and here you are, sir.'

'Thank you again,' Esmay said, managing a genuine smile for the clerk. He, at least, treated her as if she were a normal person worth respect.

Her transport would undock in six hours; she hurried back to her quarters to pack.

Marta Katerina Saenz, Chairholder in her own right, and voter of two other Chairs in the Family sept, had been expecting the summons for weeks before it came. Bunny's wild daughter had at last fallen into more trouble than youth and dash could get her out of, though the news media had been fairly vague about what it was, having had her listed first as 'missing' and then as 'presumed captured by pirates.' She suspected it might be worse than that; pirates normally killed any captives or ransomed them quickly. Bunny, who had succeeded Kemtre as the chief executive of the Familias Grand Council, had actually done quite well in the various crises that had followed the king's abdication – the Morellines and the Consellines had not in fact pulled out; the Crescent Worlds hadn't caused trouble; the Benignity's attempt at invasion in the Xavier system had been quickly scotched. But rumor had it that his daughter's disappearance had sent him into a state close to unreason. Rumor was usually wrong in details, Marta had found, but right in essence.

She herself was the logical person to call in for advice and help. Family connections and cross-connections, for one thing, and –

paradoxically – her reputation for avoiding the hurly-burly of political life. Her axes had all been ground long since, and stored in the closet for future need. Several of the Families had already contacted her, asking her to make discreet inquiries. Moreover, she had helped Bunny in the Patchcock affair, and she knew the redoubtable Admiral Serrano. In addition, whatever trouble Brun had gotten herself into involved this side of Familias space – that was clear from the number of increased Fleet patrols, and the way her own carriers were being stopped for inspection. So it was natural that someone would think of asking her to – what was the phrase? – 'assist in the investigations.'

She did not resent the call as much as she might have a decade or so earlier. That affair on Patchcock had been much more fun than she'd expected, and the aftermath – when she'd tackled Raffaele's difficult mother about the girl's marriage – even more so. Perhaps she'd had enough, for a while of secluded mountain estates and laboratory research. Perhaps it was time for another fling.

Though by all accounts this would be no fling. When she boarded the R.S.S. *Gazehound*, which had been sent to fetch her, she was given a data cube which made that clear. Marta had met Brun more than once, in her wildest stages, and the vid of Brun helpless and mute was worse than shocking. She put it out of her mind, and concentrated instead on testing her powers with the crew of the R.S.S. *Gazehound*.

Captain Bonnirs had welcomed her aboard with the grave deference due her age and rank; Marta had managed not to chuckle aloud at that point, but it wasn't easy. He seemed so young, and his crew were mere children . . . but of course they weren't. Still, they responded to her as her many nieces and nephews had, treating her as an honorary grandmother. For the price of listening to the same old stories of love, betrayal, and reconciliation, she could acquire vast amounts of information the youngsters never knew they were giving.

Pivot-major Gleason, for instance, while apparently unaware of any conflict between his loyalty to the Regular Space Service and that to his family, was carrying undeclared packages from his brother to his sister-in-law's family: packages that, under the scrutiny now given such mail, would have been opened and inspected by postal authorities. He didn't see anything wrong with this; Marta hoped very much he was merely hauling stolen jewels or something equally innocuous and not explosives.

Ensign Currany, in the midst of asking advice on handling unwanted advances from a senior officer, revealed that she had a startling misconception of the nature of Registered Embryos which suggested a political orientation quite different from that she overtly claimed. Normally this wouldn't have mattered, but now Marta had to wonder just why Currany had joined Fleet – and when.

She discovered that an environmental tech had a hopeless crush on the senior navigator, who was happily married, and that the curious smell in the enlisted crew quarters emanated from an illicit pet citra, kept in a secret compartment in the bulkhead behind a bunk. It was brought out to show her, and she enchanted its owners by letting it run up her arm and curl its furry tail around her neck. She overheard part of a furious argument between two pivot-majors about Esmay Suiza – one, having served aboard *Despite*, insisted she was loyal and talented; the other, who had never met her, insisted she was a secret traitor who had wanted Brun to be captured and had probably told the pirates where to find her. She would like to have heard more of that, but the argument ended the moment they realized she was lurking in the corridor, and neither would talk more about it.

By the end of the twenty-one-day voyage, she was remembering exactly why she normally lived in isolation: people told her things, they always had, and after just a few weeks of it, she felt stuffed with the innumerable details of their lives and feelings. Therapist had never been her favorite self-definition.

Marta prepared herself for her first meeting with Bunny; she knew, from the tension all around her, that whether she liked it or not, she was everyone's favorite candidate for therapist where Bunny was concerned. She swept into the room with her usual flair, hoping it would have its usual effect on him.

This time it did not. Lord Thornbuckle looked up at her with the expression of a man very near the edge of sanity. Desperate, exhausted . . . not the expression one wanted to see on the chief executive of the Familias Regnant, someone on whose judgement the security of the entire empire depended.

Marta moderated her instinctive verve, and instead walked quietly across the room to take the hand he held out to her.

'Bunny, I'm so sorry.'

He stared at her silently.

'But I know Brun, and if she's alive, we can and will help her.'

'You don't know' – he swallowed – 'what they did to her. To my *daughter*—'

She did know, but clearly he needed to tell her. 'Tell me,' she said, and held his hand through the recitation of all the horrors he knew Brun had endured, and the ones that might have followed. She interrupted this latter list.

'You can't know that – you can't know, and until we know for certain, you must not waste your strength worrying about it.'

'Easy for you to say—'

'It was my niece you sent off to rescue Ronnie and George,' Marta said crisply. 'It is not easy to say, or to do, but people of our rank have responsibilities. Yours is heavy, but not beyond your strength, if you will quit adding to the load by imagining even more horrors.'

'But Brun—'

'What you are doing by tearing yourself up does not help her.'

'I don't know what to do . . .'

'Where's Miranda?' Bunny's exquisitely beautiful wife was, under her beauty, a woman of spun-steel endurance, capable of enforcing sense on her husband – one of the few who could.

'She's . . . back on Castle Rock. I didn't want her out here.'

'Then, in her place, I will tell you what to do. Eat a hot meal. Sleep at least nine hours. Eat another hot meal. Don't talk to anyone about anything important until you have done so. You will be even more miserable if your bad judgement, born of hunger and exhaustion, harms Brun's chances.'

'But I can't just sleep—'

'Then get medication.' Marta paused a moment for that to take effect, and went on. 'Bunny, I'm terribly, terribly sorry that this has happened . . . but you simply must not go into this as you are.'

578

'Who called you here?' he asked, at last reacting to her immediate presence.

'It doesn't matter. I'm here; I belong here, because those people are only a jump point away from my home; and I'm taking charge of you, at this moment, because I'm older, meaner, and you daren't hit me.'

With that, she punched in a call to the infirmary and the kitchen, and stood over Bunny until he had downed a bowl of soup and a plate of chicken and rice. Then she insisted that he take the medication provided, and nodded to his valet. 'Don't let him up until morning, or he's slept ten hours, whichever comes latest. Then make him eat again.'

From the startled, but relieved, expressions of those around her, Marta judged that no one else had been able to make the Speaker see reason. He was, after all, the Speaker of the Grand Council. She felt her lip curling. That was exactly why she let someone else vote her Seat most of the time, all this ridiculous social etiquette getting in the way of common sense.

Her next stop was a brief call on Admiral Serrano, who was said to be in line to command the task force. On her way through the interminable layers of military bureaucracy between the outer and inner office, she heard a sleek blonde female officer murmur to another woman, 'Well, it was Suiza, after all.' Both shook their heads.

Marta decided she didn't like the sleek blonde, on no more evidence than the unlikely perfection of her bone structure and perfect grooming. She said nothing, but filed the comment away.

Vida Serrano looked almost as harried and exhausted as Thornbuckle had. Marta blinked; she had not expected this.

'What happened to you?'

'Lord Thornbuckle,' Vida said. 'He's furious with the Serrano family in general, and me in particular.'

'Why?'

'Because he thinks it was his daughter's attachment to my niece Heris which led her into what he calls "dangerous interests." Of course, there was that regrettable incident at Xavier, but it certainly wasn't Heris's fault. Then I recommended that she go to the Fleet training facility at Copper Mountain to get some practical knowledge – and I had hoped, some discipline as well – but that blew up in our faces when she was shot at, then quarrelled with Lieutenant Suiza and stormed off on her own. Still, it was my recommendation, so it's my fault.' She heaved a sigh and managed a weary smile. 'I really had thought she was ready for something like Copper Mountain. Lord Thornbuckle himself introduced his daughter to Lieutenant Suiza, but apparently that young woman is not at all what she seemed.'

'I'm confused,' Marta said, sitting down firmly. 'I thought young Brun had managed to get herself captured by pirates and hauled off somewhere. I saw the vid of her mutilation, that's all. But I've heard nasty comments about Lieutenant Suiza from more than one person, and this is the first I've heard of Brun taking any military training. And "shot at" – was that part of a course, or something else?'

'One thing at a time,' Vida said, suddenly looking more like the admiral she was. 'Brun was accepted as a civilian trainee – she signed up for courses in search and rescue, and similar adventurous things. I was hoping, frankly, that she'd realize how well her talents suited us and join Fleet formally.'

'Brun?' Marta snorted. 'You could no more make that girl into an officer than a mountain cat into a sheepdog.'

'So it seems. Perhaps she was on her best behavior with me. At any rate, while she was there, she was the target of at least two assassination attempts – one nearly fatal, in part because she insisted on doing what everyone else did, and eluding her assigned security detail. Her father wanted her to leave, and she refused. He recognized Lieutenant Suiza from all the publicity, and tried to enlist her help in making his daughter cooperate with her security detail. Apparently his daughter did agree, and things went along fairly well for a few weeks. Witnesses say that she kept trying to make friends with Suiza, who wasn't willing.'

'Why?' Marta asked.

Vida shrugged. 'Who can know? She was taking extra courses herself, doubling up, but all we know for sure is that she and Brun quarrelled the night before the field exercise in escape and evasion. Lieutenant Suiza was extremely rude and abusive – I've heard the tapes myself – and according to some sources, she had been previously heard to make disparaging remarks about the senior Families and the Grand Council. Highly unprofessional.'

'Why didn't this come out at the time of the courts-martial?' Marta asked. 'Surely if she'd had a bad reputation, it would have been a matter of some interest during the investigation of the mutiny.'

Vida threw out her hands. 'I don't know. I wasn't involved in that investigation, except in the most preliminary stages; all the background work was done at headquarters. Frankly, I had trouble believing that of her – I'd met her several times, you know – but the scan record is undeniable. Moreover, she admits she said those things to Sera Meager.'

'Odd,' Marta said. She filed that away in the same mental cubbyhole as the sleek blonde's remark. 'So – what happened to Brun, then?'

Vida related what was known. 'We're keeping it as quiet as we can, which isn't very. The newsfeeds have agreed, for now, but who knows when they'll change their mind? Clearly these people want it known: they keep leaking vid and other material – everything except location – to the newsfeeds. Worse, we still do not know where she was taken – and until we know that, we can hardly formulate a plan to get her out. The Guernesi are cooperating in every way, but so far we are still sifting through a very large sandpile looking for one very small diamond.'

'Well.' Marta gazed past Vida at the wall screen – a pattern of slowly shifting bands of color – for a long moment. 'I'll tell you what I've accomplished. I put Bunny to bed with his stomach full of decent food, and I think I've terrorized the medical staff into keeping him down for at least ten hours.'

'I am impressed.'

'You should be. I presume you wanted me for my knowledge of the region?'

'Your ships travel it regularly – we wondered if there was anything in any of the logs that might reveal a trace of the ship or ships that Brun was on.'

'What are we looking for?'

'A Boros Consortium container ship – a heavy – called the *Elias*

Madero, perhaps traveling in association with one or more ships of about patrol-class.'

'I presume you want this information extracted without informing my entire staff?'

'If possible, yes.'

'I'll do the datasuck myself.' Marta stood up. 'Now you, m'dear, need to take my advice to Bunny. A hot meal, a long sleep. For a woman your age, you look like hell.'

Vida laughed. 'Yes, Marta. Are we convening the aunts' coven again?'

'No . . . Cecelia would be no help on this, and her feelings for Brun would be almost as obstructive as Bunny's. You and I should be able to handle it.'

'If your esteemed friend will quit putting obstacles in my path,' Vida said, shaking her head. 'He's so convinced there's a conspiracy of Serranos, I'm lucky to be still on the task force.'

'Um. I'll see what I can do, when he's had some sleep. I should at least be able to insist on his eating and sleeping on a sane schedule. Now, what can you give me for doing the suck on my own database?'

'Well . . . we've gathered the best we've got. Take your pick – here's my private list.' Vida handed over a data cube. 'You might want to work through Heris; she's got the really good techs with her at the moment.'

'Fine. Now what's our conference schedule?'

Between meetings and a long and abortive attempt to extract data about the Boros ship from her own databases (no one had reported anything like it), Marta pottered about, as she thought of it, listening and learning how Fleet fit together. Much like any large organization, including her own pharmaceutical firms, but subtly different. Yet it was made up of people, and people were people the universe over.

Take this matter of Esmay Suiza. She had heard of Suiza – everyone with a newsfeed had heard of Suiza, first for the Battle of Xavier, and then for the *Koskiusko* affair. A rising young hero, a tactical genius, a charismatic leader. And she was here, executive officer of a ship in the task force . . . but she was *not* here . . . nowhere in the lists of officers tasked with this or that planning, was Esmay Suiza listed. Her captain sat in on some meetings . . . she never had, it seemed.

It seemed stupid. Suiza was the obvious source of recent, detailed knowledge of Brun's performance and attitudes. Surely Bunny's irrational dislike wasn't affecting everyone's judgement. Was she on some secret assignment? When she turned out to be on leave, that seemed the most likely explanation. But according to gossip, she was in disgrace, and had been sent away.

A cover story, of course. Marta wondered what kind of cover story they'd concocted. She knew what she would have done. She managed to be in one of the rec rooms one evening, looking by design as close to a potty old woman as she could manage, and kept her ears open.

Of course, they all knew who she was, in a way. Ordinary old civilian women weren't hanging out in the junior officers' recreation room. But they all had grandmothers, and she had perfected an earthy chuckle in the years of having nieces and nephews and cousins visiting. Soon she had a circle around her, bringing her drinks and snacks, and chatting happily.

She didn't even have to drop the topic herself. A female ensign nudged another. 'Look – there's Barin now.'

They both looked, and Marta looked too. A darkly handsome, compact young man with a worried expression made his way across the room to the drinks dispenser; that same sleek blonde followed him.

'With Casea on his heels,' the other ensign said.

'Lieutenant Ferradi to you, Merce – she is senior.' That was a male jig, whom Marta had already pegged as stuffy and overly precise.

'She is what she is,' the ensign said. Her eyes slid to Marta, encountered the unexpected, and she blushed.

That confirmed what Marta had already expected. These young people – so transparent.

'It's too bad,' the first ensign said. 'I'd like to get to know him, but I can't—'

'Well,' said the jig, 'she may be . . . whatever . . . but she's better than Suiza, and that's who he was supposed to like before.'

Marta gave him a smile for doing her work for her, and cocked her head. 'Suiza? That girl who's the hero?'

Nervous glances, eyes shifting from side to side. No one spoke for a moment, then the first ensign said quietly, 'She's – not such a hero right now, Sera.'

'Why?' asked Marta, ignoring the signals that this was a ticklish subject. Directness often worked, and besides, it was more fun. But this produced more sidelong looks, more shifting about. Finally, the same ensign answered.

'She – said bad things about the Speaker's daughter. Said she didn't deserve to be rescued.'

Marta blinked. That was not the kind of cover story she would have invented, and it wasn't something Admiral Serrano had told her. She had mentioned a row at Copper Mountain, but nothing since. That kind of rumor could hang around and damage someone's career years later. 'Are you sure?' she asked.

Nods, some reluctant. 'It started before, is what I heard,' the jig said.

'It's all rot!' another jig said. 'I don't believe it – someone made it up—'

'No, it's true. They have a tape. I heard Major Crissan talking to Commander Dodd, and he said he heard it himself. She quarrelled with Sera Meager at Training Command, something about a course they were both in, and they nearly asked for her commission.'

'I don't see what you could say bad enough for that.'

'Well . . . it had something to do with her loyalty, or something.'

Something something something. A clear sign of uncontrolled rumor, Marta thought. She prodded a bit.

'Well, but – she is a hero, isn't she? I mean, she brought her ship back and saved Xavier . . .'

'Yes, but why? That's what they're asking now. People I know who knew her in the Academy say she wasn't that talented then. She wasn't even command track. How could she get that good without anyone knowing, unless she had help? And not wanting to rescue Sera Meager—'

'I'm sure she does,' said Suiza's defender, getting red in the face. 'But nobody listens—'

584

'Just because you have a bad case of hero worship, you can't ignore the facts. Sera Meager is a Chairholder; we exist to protect Chairholders, and—'

'What class was she in?' Marta said, before that turned ugly.

That led to an explanation she did not want about the way the Academy named its classes, on a rotation having nothing to do with the standard calendar. 'So anyway,' that informant finished up, when Marta felt her eyes about to glaze over, 'she's in Vaillant class, six years ago.' Marta converted that quickly to standard dates, but reminded herself that she'd probably have to ask for classmates by the Fleet's peculiar reckoning. But her informant went on, clearly in earnest to be complete. 'Her classmates will be jigs – that's lieutenant, junior grade, sera – and lieutenants. Everyone who doesn't mess up badly is promoted from ensign to jig at the same time, but there's a selection board for lieutenant, with a 12-month range. Lieutenant Suiza was promoted in the first selection; some of her classmates will be promoted in the next few days.'

So, to find Esmay's classmates, she could confine herself to lieutenants, for the most part. And some of them promoted behind her might have reason to wish her ill. Casually, without apparent intent, Marta began trolling through the assortment of lieutenants. Most were, she found, either classmates or within one year of Esmay Suiza's class. Some had hardly noticed her at the Academy; others claimed to have known her well. And a few had more immediate information to share.

'I just can't believe it,' said the redhaired lieutenant with the mustache. Vericour, his name was. 'I mean – Esmay! Yes, she got angry, and yes, she said things she shouldn't have – but she'd been working twice as hard as anyone else. They should have cut her some slack. You'd have thought she murdered the girl.'

'You're a friend of hers?'

'Yes . . . at least, we were together at Training Command; we studied together sometimes. Brilliant tactician – and a nice person, too. I don't think she ever said half of what people say—'

'Perhaps not,' Marta said.

'But Admiral Hornan says I should stay away from her – she's poison. And Casea Ferradi claims she was saying all sorts of things in the Academy . . . but why they listen to Casea, I can't figure out.'

'Casea?'

'Classmate of ours. She's from a colonial world too – one of the Crescent Worlds group, can't remember which. Tell you the truth, before I met her, I had heard the women there are . . . well . . . shy. Casea was an education in that respect.'

'Oh?' Marta gave him a grandmotherly smile, and he blushed.

'Well . . . junior year . . . I mean I'd heard about her, and she . . . she said she liked me. I suppose she did, as long as it lasted.'

'She likes men . . .' Marta said, trailing it out.

'She likes sex,' Vericour said. 'Sorry, sera, but it's the truth. She went through our class like – like—'

'Fire through wheat?' suggested Marta. 'And now she's always with that Ensign Serrano, isn't she?'

'Poor kid won't know what hit him,' Vericour said, nodding. 'I'd heard she was after bigger game, working her way up – but maybe she thinks the Serrano name's better than rank alone. And right now, when they're under a cloud, what with Lord Thornbuckle being so angry with them, she probably thinks she has a better chance.'

'She is attractive,' Marta said. 'And I suppose she's efficient in her work?'

'I suppose,' Vericour said, without any enthusiasm. 'I was never on the same ship.'

'I wonder if Ensign Serrano is actually taken with her.'

'It wouldn't matter,' Vericour said gloomily. 'She has her ways, has Casea.'

A few days downside, working through the civilian databases and ansible, gave her even more insight into the Suiza controversy. She had identified five classmates, including the sleek blonde Ferradi, who were actively spreading, if not inventing, wicked-Suiza stories. All five were at least one promotion group behind Suiza. If that wasn't the green-eyed monster, she didn't know what was. Suiza's former co-workers and commanding officers, on the other hand, seemed incredulous that anyone would believe such stories. One and all, they insisted that if she had had an argument with Brun Meager, and if she had been insulting, then Brun must have deserved it.

Marta wasn't sure about that – couldn't be, until she met Esmay Suiza in person – but she was willing to swear that whatever the nature of the original offense, malice and envy and spite had blown it out of all proportion.

The nature of the original offense still eluded her. Unless Suiza had snapped under the pressure of work – which didn't seem likely given her history – Brun had precipitated the fight. How? Given Brun's past history, the most likely cause was that she'd come between Suiza and a lover, but gossip didn't credit Suiza with any lovers. Indeed, gossip went the other direction. Block of ice, cold fish, frozen clod. Barin Serrano was supposed to have liked her, when he was on *Koskiusko*, but that could be mere hero worship, and Vericour had said Suiza was cool to him at Copper Mountain.

What could Brun have done? Marta was careful not to ask this question of the youngsters. Most of them, it was clear, thought that being the victim of piracy turned Brun into a shining martyr figure, untainted by any human error other than getting caught. Marta knew better. Brun was, by observation and Raffaele's report, intelligent, quick-witted, brave, and full of mischief as a basket of kittens. If she had wanted some reaction from Suiza she did not get, she might well have put all her inventive genius to work making trouble. That still led back to interference with a man Suiza wanted – but the problem was that Suiza supposedly had no preferences. Unless it was Barin, but for that she had no evidence.

14

The pains started at night. Brun woke up, to find herself knotted around her hardened belly. It eased, but she knew at once it was not a cramp from supper. It was . . . what she most feared. She lay back, stretching a little. She was just dozing off when another pain curled her forward again.

She had no watch, no clock. She had no way to tell how the pains quickened. She had to use the toilet suddenly. Levering herself out of bed, she went into the corridor. Down the length of it, she saw the glint from the door-guard's eyes watching her. Damn him. She struggled toward the toilets, but another pain caught her, doubling her up against the wall. Through a haze of pain, she saw the guard stand up, move toward her. The pain eased; she leaned on the wall but went on. Into the toilet room . . . at least they had toilets, she thought muzzily. She was hardly a meter from it when fluid gushed down her legs, hot and shocking.

'You!' It was the warden; the guard must have wakened her. 'Come on!' The woman grabbed her arm, pulled. Yelled at the others to wake up. Brun doubled up again; the woman tugged at her arm. But it hurt too much; she was too weak. She sagged to her knees, gasping. It was unfair that she couldn't scream, unfair that this pain could not be met as it should be, with the protest it deserved.

Now the other women were around her, tugging and pushing, but she huddled there on her knees, unwilling to rise. Why should she? Suddenly the warden stuck something under her nose, an acrid smell that made her throw her head up to escape it. With a grin of triumph, the woman yanked on her arms again. With the others' help, she got Brun up, and together they half-dragged, half-carried her down the corridor and into the birthing room. By then the pain had eased, and Brun clambered onto the birthbed herself. She might as well.

To her surprise, the rest of the birthing went faster than the one she had watched. Weren't first births supposed to be slower? She couldn't remember; she couldn't think. One pain after another flowed down her body, pushing, pushing . . . the other women wiped her face with damp cloths, stroked her arms. The warden alone scolded her, telling her to breathe or push, waiting with a folded towel for the baby that was – surely – just about to come.

And then it did – with a last wrenching pain, she felt the pressure ease suddenly; a thin cry rose from nowhere. The women all gasped together; the warden scowled.

'Too little. You have puny babies.'

But then another pain struck, and Brun curled into it.

'Ah—' The warden handed off the first baby to one of the other women. 'Two babies! Good!'

The second was born crying lustily. The warden put them on Brun's chest. 'Give suck,' she said. Brun had no idea how, until the warden turned the babies and pressed Brun's nipples into the little mouths. 'Help her,' she ordered one of the other women. She herself washed Brun, while the others cleaned the room.

By afternoon, Brun was back in her own room, lying exhausted on her bed, with a baby on either side. She felt nothing for them. They were no more her babies than . . . than any stranger's baby. Less. They had been forced on her; strangers had made use of her body to produce them.

Two babies. Brun slid into darkness on that thought.

'No breeding for half a year,' the warden told her the next day. 'You feed your babies; you help with work here one month, then you go to the nursery. Nursery for five months – maybe with twins, six months. Then to breeding house.'

Half a year . . . she had half a year to get strong, to escape, to find a way to contact someone who would let her father know where she was.

But in the days after the birth, Brun began to despair again.

How could she help Hazel if she couldn't find her? How could she find her when she couldn't ask questions? She lay motionless unless the warden prodded her to get up . . . she fed the babies only when ordered, ate only when ordered. Feeding the babies hurt; she had not imagined that babies would suck harder than her lovers had. But she was too weak, too miserable, to do more than hiss in pain each time someone put them to her breasts. She didn't notice when someone took the babies away, bringing them to her only for nursing. Someone had to put them to her breasts; someone had to clean them – and her – when they soiled her.

Then one day a cooler wind blew through the doors and windows, carrying with it a scent of harvest fields. And something – something familiar. Brun shifted in her chair; the babies shifted. One of them lost its hold on her nipple, and whimpered. Without noticing, she moved it back. Something – what was it? She dozed again, but woke at the next cool gust. Oak leaves, stubble fields. Hunting, if she were home. All at once the full memory hit her: Opening Day, with all three hunts gathered before the big house, the clop of the horses' feet, the panting and whining of hounds, the clink of glasses, the voices . . . but even in imagination, she saw herself silent, unable to reply to the greetings. She saw the faces of friends staring at her, shocked, disapproving . . . and she was standing barefoot on the sharp gravel, all the others on tall horses, hard-hooved horses stamping near her bare feet . . .

She would never be home. Her thoughts slid down the same spiral of depression . . . but this time stopped short of darkness. No. She was young, she had a long life to live. Lady Cecelia had survived without a voice, and she had been blind and paralyzed as well. Help had finally come; she, Brun, had been part of that help. Somewhere, people were trying to plan help for her. She had to trust that, believe that her family and friends would not leave her here forever, alone. She had survived so far; she had borne twins with no medical care worth mentioning, and lived . . . she would live to hunt again. She would ride; she would speak, and those who had silenced her would listen. Her head came up.

'This is good,' the warden said, coming out to pat her on the shoulder. 'Many mothers feel sad after babies, especially twins. But now you're better. Now you will be all right.'

She was not all right, but she could be . . . perhaps. Brun fought the darkness back, made herself begin to live again. The next day, she reached out for the babies as they were brought to her. She didn't even know what they were . . . not only whose, who was the father, but whether they were boys or girls. She looked. Boys. Both boys . . . one with pale orange hair, one with darker, thinner hair. She could see nothing of herself in either one, and she knew that one of the men had had red hair and a shaggy red beard.

She still felt nothing for them, not even the mild flicker of interest she used to feel for other women's babies. She had thought babies amusing at times, when they were older than this and had learned to smile. She had felt the odd pang of tenderness . . . but not now. These were just . . . little animals who had lived in her flesh, and now fed at her expense. At least the nursing was less painful – even a relief, when her breasts were swollen with milk.

She watched the other women with their babies. Muted though they were, they clearly loved the babies, cuddling them, stroking them, laughing soundlessly when one of the infants did something amusing. They spoke to them in hissing whispers and little clicks whenever the warden was far enough away. They peered at each other's babies, smiling and nodding over them – and the same with her twins. She could not reciprocate.

Now that she could force herself to her feet again, she was expected to help with the work. But she had never cared for an infant, let alone in these primitive circumstances. The wrapping of diapers baffled her completely.

'It's as if she never did anything until now – can you believe a grown woman not knowing how to peel vegetables? To put a child to breast?' The warden complained to the other women, who nodded and hissed in response.

Brun seethed. She could have told them why she didn't have their backwards, primitive skills. She had not been trained to make beds and clean toilets and chop vegetables and wipe the bottoms of dirty little brats. She held pilots' licenses on half a dozen worlds; she could ride to hounds with the Greens; she could take down and reassemble the scan systems of a medium cruiser as fast as any technicians . . .

591

And here her skills were worth nothing. They thought she was stupid or crazy, because she couldn't do what they did so easily.

'She's an abomination. Of course the heathen don't teach their daughters properly.' That was the warden's explanation for everything she did wrong.

She was not a heathen, nor an abomination, but surrounded by those who thought she was, she found it harder and harder to remember her real self. It was easier to scrub the floor the way the warden insisted on, even if it would have been more efficient the other way. Easier to change the babies the way she was told, to cut vegetables the way she was told.

If only she had been really stupid . . . but her intelligence, recovering from the birth, awoke again. Recipes were boring, perhaps, but she remembered them just the same, automatically assigning them to categories. Sewing was even more boring than recipes, poking a needle in and out of cloth over and over. Why did they have to do everything the hard way? Not everything, she reminded herself . . . just the work assigned to women. Electricity for light, running water . . . but only men had access to computers and all that computers stood for.

Scraps of history she had hardly listened to in class floated up from a retentive memory. There had been other societies which resisted making life easier for women, because then they might turn away from the traditional role of wife and mother. Way back on Old Earth, cultures which didn't let women drive groundcars or fly or learn to use weapons – others which forbade women to teach in mixed classes, to become doctors. But that was long ago and very far away . . . and this was here and now.

In the quick glimpse she caught of the street when she and the babies were transferred to the nursery, she could not distinguish any landmarks. It was a chill, raw day; she shivered in the wind that whipped down the street. She was put in the back of the same kind of closed groundcar, where she could see nothing of her route, and driven some incalculable distance with four definite turns.

The front of the nursery looked slightly more welcoming, with shuttered windows instead of blank stone overlooking the street.

A distant roar – Brun looked up to see the obvious plume of a shuttle launch in the distance.

'Eyes down!' said the driver, slapping at her head. But she exulted . . . she knew now where the spaceport was, or at least what direction.

Inside, the matron greeted her less harshly than the warden at the maternity house, and she could hear women's voices in the distance. Women's voices? The matron led her to a room large enough for a bed, two cribs, and a low wide chair with a leg rest that was obviously intended for nursing. She had a small closet, a chest, and the inevitable sewing basket was on a bedside table.

The matron helped her settle the babies in their cribs, helped her make the bed, and then led Brun off to show her the house. In the upstairs rooms, the more privileged women could look out through slatted shutters to the streets below – but Brun had only a glimpse before the matron pulled her away. An upstairs sewing room had rear-facing windows that looked out on a long, walled garden full of fruit trees; a few apples hung from some of them. Beyond the wall – Brun tried not to stare, told herself she would have time to look later – beyond the wall she could see a street, and the buildings across it . . . and beyond more buildings, open land, rough fields and distant hills.

The women in the nursery had slightly more freedom. They were supposedly regaining their strength for another pregnancy; they were encouraged to walk out in the orchard, as well as do the housework and cooking. Not all the women were muted, either. They had come, Brun learned, from other maternity homes or from private homes . . . servant women whose children would be reared elsewhere when they returned to their duties. The women who supervised them inspected the babies and mothers daily for cleanliness and any sign of illness, and supervised the preparation of household chores and cooking, but otherwise treated their charges with pleasant firmness. The muted women had perhaps less pleasantness and more firmness, but no active unkindness.

They continued to teach Brun the skills they thought all women should have. Brun had not known that such things were possible, but she watched the other women produce socks and gloves and mittens from several wooden sticks and balls of fuzzy yarn. She was handed a pair of sticks, and shown – over and over – how to cast on, how to knit a plain stitch. It was the most boring thing she'd ever done, the same little movement of the hand over and over and over, even worse than sewing seams. Then they handed her another stick, and taught her to knit a tube. Something clicked in her mind – this sort of thing, done with finer yarn and on a machine, made some of the things she'd worn. Sweaters, for instance: three tubes sewn together. Stockings . . . leggings . . . tubular knits. It was interesting in an intellectual way, one of the few things that was.

It got colder, and Brun shivered. The other women, warm in their knitted shawls and sweaters, shook their heads at her.

'You must work faster,' one of them told her. 'You will be cold if you have no winter clothes.' In winter, they explained, they wore long knitted stockings under their skirts, held up with a peculiar arrangement of straps and buttons. The stockinged feet did not break the rules against shoes, because they were not hard-bottomed. In households, some women even wore backless clogs in wet or snowy weather, if they needed to go to market, but here they would not.

Here also Brun was formally introduced to the beliefs of her captors. They assumed that outlanders had no morals, and no beliefs worth mentioning. So they began with the basics, as Brun assumed children were taught. God, a supernatural being who had created the universe. Man, the glory of creation. Woman, created to be Man's comfort and help. Evil powers, rebellious against God, who tempted Woman to usurp Man's position.

For once muteness had its utility; Brun could not be made to recite the Rules and Rituals, as the other women did. And since women did not 'discourse' – a word which they interpreted to mean speaking or writing about Godly matters – she was not asked to write answers to the questions asked ritually of others. Women were not encouraged to read or write anyway – although recipes and compendia of other household knowledge were permissable. But they clearly feared contamination by anything a heathen abomination such as a Registered Embryo might commit to paper, or do to a book she read from. She was not allowed to read or write anything at all. They could not test her memory, or her understanding.

But she had an excellent memory. She could not hear the same words over and over without storing them away. The words of the prophets . . . the word of God Almighty. The rules and their corollaries . . . quite reasonable, if you accepted the premises, which Brun did not. If in fact you believed that women had been created as men's servants and comfort, then . . . anything women did which was not serving men would clearly be wrong. And this was not something women could determine. Only God could make the rules, and only men could interpret them.

It all made sense, except that it was ridiculous, like the ridiculous logic of paranoia. The notion that she was not as much a person as, say, her brothers . . . or, to go one step away, that Esmay Suiza was less a person than Barin Serrano . . . was absurd. She knew that. She knew how to demonstrate that, if only she could have explained; she was sure that every woman in the nursery would understand, if only . . .

But she was mute, all her knowledge and intelligence locked away. In her world, in the world she knew, the individual's voice was honored; parents and teachers and therapists like those who had worked with Lady Cecelia tried to ensure that each person had every opportunity to communicate. She remembered Cecelia's struggles, and the many who had helped her. Here, no one thought an abomination had anything useful to say. As long as she could understand and obey, that was enough.

She ached, burned, to free this world's women . . . to show them that they were as human as men. In her mind, in the dark hours, she made all the speeches, wrote all the lectures, proved over and over and over again to an audience of shadows what she could never say.

In the daytime, Brun forced herself to walk on the gritty paths, toughening her feet as well as her legs, whenever exercise was permitted. She walked in all weathers, even when frost and snow numbed her to the knees before she was halfway to the first trees. The twins weighed her down – but she thought of them like the heavy packs in training. Additional strength would come from lugging them around . . . she would be stronger sooner, and more able to escape. Twice a day she walked the length of the orchard and back . . . soon she'd be able to walk farther, in the lengthening days that must mean a warmer season was coming. She even welcomed the hard work of mopping and cleaning, as she felt herself growing stronger. In the evenings, in her room, she attempted the exercises that had once come so easily. At first she worried that they would notice, and forbid them, but no one commented. Other women too, she discovered, did exercises to tighten their slack bellies, to recover flexibility.

In the darkest times, she practiced the swift movements of unarmed combat . . . only two or three strokes each time, in case of observation, but a little every day. She matched hands and feet against each other, the quietest way she could think to achieve the hardening she needed for a killing stroke.

The showings, where proven breeders were displayed for men who might choose them next time, were less humiliation than she'd expected, and more worrying. In the showings, she did her best to look exhausted, weak, helpless, broken. It wasn't hard to look tired . . . she pushed herself to shaky exhaustion every day. But she could feel the muscle building on her legs again, in her arms, in her abdomen. Would they believe that came from carrying the babies? From walking in the orchard? From the simple exercises the others did?

But they could not expect what she intended to do with the muscles she built with such effort. Eyes squeezed shut, she reminded herself which basic moves would build the strength and speed she needed for killing.

The other women did not so much avoid her as ignore her. When the babies were wriggling happily on quilts on the floor, they exclaimed over the strength and vigor of her boys as they did over the qualities of their own. The staff gave her directions – which chores to do – in much the same tone as anyone else. The speaking women naturally talked most to each other; the muted women had a private language of gesture, and a public one of broader gestures and elaborate lipspeaking and hisses. The speaking women would include the mutes if one of the muted women made the effort to get their attention. Some even befriended one –

for cooperative baby care made friendships useful for both. But Brun could not enter into the lipspeaking of the other muted women. Occasionally, if she were alone with another woman, and faced her directly, she could make herself understood with a combination of gesture and mouthing – if the topic was something obvious. *Where is the sewing basket*? or *What is that*? They were willing to show her where things were, or how to do a chore. But she had no topics in common with them, except babies, and she did not care that much about the babies, any of them. They were all – hers and the others' – proof of what she hated. And she knew they saw her as a dangerous person . . . tamed by muting, but potentially a source of soul-killing deviancy. Her lack of interest in the babies was another proof, to them, of her unnatural, immoral upbringing.

The babies were moving from creeping to rocking on their hands and knees when a new mother arrived at the nursery. She was very young, and had a slightly dazed expression. The other women spoke to her in short, simple sentences, a little louder than usual. Brun wondered if she'd been drugged, though she had seen no evidence that women were given drugs. On the third day, she approached Brun. 'You're the yellow-hair from the stars?' She had the usual soft voice, but a little hesitancy in it.

Brun nodded. Up close, she decided that it wasn't drugs, but some innate problem, that gave the girl that odd expression and halting speech . . . and the social unawareness that let her approach the unapproachable.

'You traveled with another girl – more my size – and two brats?'

Brun nodded again.

'She said you was nice. She liked you. She said.'

Brun looked hard at the girl. She had to be talking about Hazel. Where had she seen Hazel?

'She's doin' fine. I just thought you'd like to know.' The girl smiled past Brun's shoulder, and wandered off, leaving Brun tethered to the twins.

Hazel was all right. A surge of relief swept through her. When had that girl had left wherever Hazel was, to go to maternity – or was Hazel in maternity? Brun shook her head; she could not keep track of time. It was hot, or it was cold, daylight or dark; that was all she knew. But Hazel was all right, less time ago than Brun knew for sure. If only she knew *where*.

Several days passed before the girl sat down beside her again to nurse her baby.

'They call her Patience now,' the girl said. 'It's a good name for her 'cause she never makes trouble. She's real quiet and works hard. Prima says they'll be able to marry her as a third wife for sure, maybe even a second, even though she can't sew good. They been trainin' her for market girl, and she goes there by herself now.' A wistful note in that soft voice – had this girl wanted to go to market? By now Brun was sure the girl was retarded; no one would let her go out alone for other reasons than the restrictions on women. 'But she doesn't have your yellow hair,' the girl said, staring at it with frank admiration. 'And she won't talk about the stars, 'cause Prima said not to.'

Brun could have strangled her, for having a voice and not saying what Brun really needed to know. She picked up a twin and removed from his mouth the pebble he'd put there. She could not feel any affection for them, but she wasn't about to let a child – any child – choke to death.

'She don't look big enough to have babies, though,' the girl said, petting her own child. 'And her blood's not regular yet. The master says—'

'Hush, you!' One of the women in charge came by and tapped the girl on the head. 'You're not here to gossip about what your master says. You want your tongue pulled?'

The girl's mouth snapped shut, and she clambered out of the chair, holding her baby to her.

The women shook her head at Brun. 'She's simple, she is. Can't remember from day to day what the rules are, poor thing. We have to keep an eye on her, so's she doesn't get herself in trouble. If she gets in the habit of talking about her master here, even to you, she might do it back at her house and then they'd have to punish her. Best nip it in the bud.' She patted Brun's head, almost affectionately. 'That is pretty hair, though. Might win you a chance at wifing, when you've borne your three. Just you give me a nod, if the girl starts talking about men's doings again, like a good girl, eh?' Brun nodded. As long as they'd let the girl talk to her.

598

The girl avoided Brun for days. But late one evening, she slipped into Brun's room.

'She don't scare me,' she said, clearly untruthfully. 'I'm from Ranger Bowie's house; he's the only one can mute me. They can't. And he wouldn't, long as I don't argue or nothing. Telling you about Patience isn't arguing. It's explaining. Explaining is fine as long as it's not men.'

Brun smiled, a smile that seemed to crack her face. How long had it been since she last smiled?

'I wish they hadn't muted you,' the girl said. 'I'd sure like to know what it's like out there . . . Patience, she won't tell me about it.' She stopped, listening, then crept closer. 'I wisht I had your hair,' she said, and put out a hand to stroke it. Then she turned and vanished into the dark corridor.

Brun traced what she'd heard on the wall, fixing it in her mind, as she once would have repeated it aloud. Ranger Bowie. What an odd name. She didn't remember the men using any name like that on the ship . . . had they even called each other by name?

The nondescript man in the checked shirt bellied up to the bar and ordered. Beside him, two men were talking about the Captain's choice of policy.

'Well, we're free men but I don't see any call to stomp in an ant bed. It's my right, but I'm not stupid enough—'

'You're calling the Captain stupid?'

'I'm saying that taking outlander women for our own needs is one thing, but taking that one – and then bragging about it – is just asking for trouble.'

'It proves we're strong.' That speaker turned to the man in the checked shirt. 'And what's your opinion, brother?'

He smiled. 'I heard she had yellow hair.'

The first speaker snorted. 'Everybody knows that. They're hoping she'll put her hair on her babes.'

Someone down the bar leaned forward. 'You talkin' about that gal from space? The yellow-haired slut? She had twins, did you hear? One redhead, one dark. Odds on, they're double-fathered.'

'No!' The man in the checked shirt widened his eyes, the perfect picture of a country bumpkin in for one of the festivals.

'I'd bet on it. She won't be out for another two months, though. They say the twins need her milk longer, being smaller.'

'Ah. I'd hoped.'

The other men looked at each other, sly grins twitching their mouths. This one probably had only one wife, and her homely as a tree.

'Well, who wouldn't? Don't get that many blondes, do we? Put your name on the list, is all I can say. They're showing her now, if you want to see if it's worth the tax.'

'Before I put down on the list, believe I will.'

'Crockett Street Nursery, then.'

He was not the only one who wanted to see the out-worlder blonde mute, who had birthed twins. They'd been confirmed fraternal and double-fathered, which meant she might throw twins again. A woman who could drop two eggs at a time was even more desirable. He took his number, and when it was called pushed into the room with the others in that group.

At first he wasn't sure. He had been shown pictures – moving and still – of Brun in childhood, adolescence, and adulthood. Closeups, distance shots, everything. He had thought nothing could disguise her. But the yellow-haired woman before him was not the same Brun – if it was Brun at all. Her slender strength was reshaped now – her body blurred and broadened with the children she'd carried, her breasts heavy with milk. She stood heavily, arms hanging by her sides. Her yellow hair was long, lank, nothing like the lively tousled curls in the pictures. Her blue eyes were duller, almost gray. But his practiced eye noted what was not concealed . . . the bone structure of her face, her shoulders, the exact shape of her fingers and toes. This had to be the woman he sought. He looked for the RE tattoo, but the short wrap such women were allowed during a showing covered the area where it might have been.

Two guards stood with her, their staves held to prevent the men from touching her.

'Devil's own,' one of the men near him muttered.

'Satan's snare,' said another. 'Good thing they muted her.'

'Yup. But the babies look strong.' The babies were on display as well, naked cherubs in a playpen. They grinned toothlessly at the watching men.

'Not worth it to me,' said a black-haired man, and spat on the floor. 'I'm not risking my soul for that.' He pushed past the others and walked out.

Another laughed. 'There speaks a man without the tax. She was just as wicked afore he looked at her.'

'And it's our duty to convert the heathen,' said another. 'I reckon another couple of birthings'll convert her.'

'What – you'll bid for her wifing?'

'Might do. Might do worse.'

'Might do better . . .' They chatted on. Brun stared past them. Why didn't she lower her gaze, he wondered, the way the other women did. Then he knew why . . . she was neither virgin nor wife, and the worst had happened already. What could they do to her now? He shivered, and the man next to him glanced over.

'What is it, brother?'

'Nothing.'

Hazel's duties as a servant required her to go into the street each day with the garbage. When she had demonstrated that she would perform this task exactly as directed, looking neither to right nor left, even when unaccompanied, Prima decided to try her out as a market girl. She was still clumsy in her sewing; she would be more marketable for other skills. As near as she could tell, from what she dared let the girl tell her about the abominable behavior of those outworld heathens, the girl had been among merchants and traders all her life.

So, first in the company of Mellowtongue, Hazel went to the market to carry home those items which the garden did not produce. She was required to look at the ground two paces before her, and carry the basket at waist height, and speak to no one, not even if spoken to. Mellowtongue answered those inquiries which must be answered. Hazel performed exactly as ordered, on that and all the trips that followed.

The first time she was sent out alone, for just one item, she was watched, from a distance, by one of the other servant women, one too senior to be a market girl, but reliable in her gossip. She went directly to the correct stall, waited with head down until the stallkeeper called her house name, and held out the basket and payment without looking up. She was sent again, and then again, and then – in company with the head cook – learned to haggle respectfully with the stallkeepers.

She took nothing on herself; she pilfered no treats; she was submissive even to the unfair scolding of the cook on the matter of some wilted greens.

So, in a few months, she was sent regularly to market on market days. And there, by keeping her ears stretched to the fullest, she heard gossip about the yellow-haired outlander, the heathen woman who was in the maternity house . . . and then had birthed twins . . . and then nearly died of the birth sadness . . . and then moved to the nursery. Days later she heard which nursery. Days after that, one detail after another trickled into street talk. She said nothing; she asked no questions, and told no tales. When market girls from other houses tried to make friends, with quick murmurs, she ignored them.

She kept her eye on Brandy – now Prudence – and Stassi – now Serenity. Day by day, the little girls seemed to forget their former life. Quick, bouncy, darting Brandy was still more active – but she had transferred her passion for blocks and construction toys to sewing and weaving. Already she had made a stuffed doll for Stassi, and then a dress to put on it. She seemed to grasp easily the way that cloth could be shaped to fit bodies. She was fascinated by the movement of the great looms in the weaving shed, and had explained to Hazel (who could not figure out how they worked) how the rise and fall of rows of little rings would produce different patterns in the cloth. Both girls had friends their own age, and seemed far more attached to the women who cared for them than to Hazel.

Reluctantly, Hazel gave up the idea of including the littles in an escape. They were too small; they could not run and climb and fight. They would be obvious – no way to conceal the fact that they were children, and they had had no training in the boys' world, so they could not pass as boys. Most of all – she could see that they were happy and secure, and that the women of the household liked them. Even Prima, inclined to be stiff with the

602

other women's children, had smiled at Brandy-Prudence, and stroked her dark curls. If she could get away – if she could get Brun away – the littles would not suffer for it. No one here blamed children for things like that. They would be cared for better than she could care for them – better, she suspected, than the Distressed Spacers' Home would care for them if she did get them back to Familias space safely. And . . . they were happy. They had lost one family, one world – she could not tear them away from another.

So she waited her chance. She could live here the rest of her life . . . she had the knack of fitting in, she always had . . . but she didn't want to. She had to admit she liked the food, the beautiful garden, the sense of security, the luxury of what seemed infinite space in which to move – she had never realized just how *much* space a person on a planet might have available, how big 'outdoors' actually was. But she remembered too well the comfort of her old clothes, the freedom of movement, the friendships not bound by gender or race or beliefs. Here she would always be an outsider; she wanted to feel part of a family again. She missed the technology, the sense she'd had, in *Elias Madero*, of being part of a greater civilization spread across the universe.

Besides, there was the blonde lady. They had exchanged names. On the whole world, only she knew who Hazel really was, where she was from – and on the whole world, only she knew that the blonde lady's name was Brun. She, Hazel, could survive here, but that lady had no chance.

Brun. She rehearsed the name, keeping it alive. Even at the time, even frightened as she had been, and determined to protect the littles, she had felt a stubborn flare of rage at what the men had done to the other woman. Muting Brun had been wrong, even more wrong than muting a woman brought up in their world. Nothing anyone did – nothing, not ever – deserved that punishment. And Brun had done nothing, any more than Hazel had. They had been wrong; they had stolen her, and then they had stolen her voice.

Hazel knew Brun would want to escape. Any woman would, who had lived in freedom. And Brun . . . even at the worst, Hazel sensed a burning determination to do more than survive. But voiceless, locked up as she was, with twin babies, she could not possibly do it alone. Hazel would have to figure out a way. It wasn't going to be easy, not with babies . . .

To herself, in the night, she rehearsed – but only in her head, never aloud – the things she knew to be really true. She was Hazel Takeris; her father had been Rodrick Takeris, on the engineering staff of the *Elias Madero*, commanded by Captain Lund. She had passed her G-levels and qualified for junior apprentice in a competitive exam; her pay scale had been upgraded once on the voyage.

Brandy and Stassi had been Ghirian and Vorda's daughters, but Ghirian and Vorda were dead. The blonde woman was Brun, and her father was named something like 'rabbit.' Out there among the stars was a universe where girls could wear whatever they chose, look men in the eye, choose their own careers and partners. Someday . . . someday she would find it again.

15

All the way to Sector IX HQ, where she switched to civilian transport, Esmay felt she had a fiery brand on her forehead and back, defining what most Fleet personnel thought of her. She kept to herself as much as possible, trying to think how to explain to her father her precarious state in Fleet. Perhaps the funeral and its aftermath would distract him. For it seemed she was in fact her great-grandmother's heir.

Her previous visit to Altiplano had begun with pomp and ceremony; this time she had the ceremony, but no pomp, and no newshounds. Her father met her in the inbound reception lounge; she almost did not recognize him in the formal mourning garments of black, with elaborate curlicues of black braid on breast and sleeves of the tight short jacket with its black-beaded collar, the full black pants tucked into low black boots with turned-up toes, and the flat black cap with the shoulder-length tassel hanging past his left ear. Left ear, heart ear, direct line of descent . . . that came back to her at once.

He had brought one of the estancia maids to help her into the clothes she must wear. In the ladies' retiring room, she changed from Fleet uniform to the layers of white: long pantaloons under a petticoat, a short white chemise. The outer layers were all black, like her father's. Wide-sleeved black blouse finely tucked down the front, full black skirt, black brocade short vest heavily over-beaded in jet, a wide black waistcloth in a diamond-patterned weave, black-on-black. Women's boots, with the top rolled down to reveal the black silk lining. On her head, a stiff black cap sitting squarely across her brow, with a rolled knob at either side. Esmay had seen this at other Landbride ceremonies; she had never expected to wear it, and she had never witnessed the whole ceremony – outsiders never did.

The weight of the clothes burdened her almost as much as the secrets she carried.

Slowly, in a cadence old as the mountains, they walked from the reception area to the shuttle bay. She was used to being a half step behind him, if not more; but now, slow as she walked, he would walk slower.

It was real. She was the Landbride. For no one else would her father slow his steps.

On the shuttle down, he spoke briefly of the arrangements, then left her with a sheaf of old-fashioned paper . . . the family copy of the old rites in which her great-grandmother had lived her long life. Esmay read carefully. She could have a coach – she *would* have a coach – but the more she could do by herself, the better. She had never witnessed the ceremony of Land-bride's Gifting, though she had heard others talk of it. At the shuttlefield, it was just past sunset, with a fiery glow behind the mountains. By the time they were out of the city, night closed around them; Esmay switched on the light in the passenger compartment and kept reading. Then her father touched her arm, and pointed ahead. Esmay switched the light off and peered into the darkness.

On either side of the road, flickering lights resolved into rows of black-clothed figures holding candles . . . the car slowed and stopped. Her father handed her out. Esmay this time was first in lighting the candles at the shrine . . . remembered without prompting the words, the gestures, the entire ritual. Behind her, she heard the respectful murmurs.

They walked from there, slowly, up to the great entrance and up the long drive, and the others closed in behind them. The house loomed, darker than the darkness around it. Then candlelight appeared from inside – the family, each carrying a candle. Esmay entered a chill dark space where normally light and warmth held sway. No fires would be kindled until after the ceremony; luckily the new rules had allowed fire and light during her travels, until she arrived onplanet.

She walked through the house, and lit one of the tiny candles in each room – a promise of the Landbride's coming. Then through, and out to the Landbride's Gift, the heart of the holding, and the place where the first Landbride in her heartline had made claim long, long ago.

There the priest waited for her, with the basket that held the braided coil of her great-grandmother's hair. Esmay shivered suddenly, her imagination caught on the possibility – no, the certainly – that someday her own unruly hair would be coiled in such a basket, its strands, however short or meagre, braided formally and tied off with silk cord.

Her great-grandmother's body had long been buried, of course, and the new pale gravestone set above it. But her hair awaited this final ceremonial dance. No musicians played. In the dark night, by flickering candlelight, Esmay led the women of the estancia in slow procession around each Landbride's gravestone, starting with the oldest, and ending with the latest. The men, standing around the margin of the space, stamped a slow rhythm, but did not follow.

When the dance was done, Esmay took the silvery braid from its basket and held it high, turning to show it to everyone.

'The Landbride . . .' came the hushed whisper from many throats. 'The Landbride has died . . .'

606

'She who was Landbride is no more,' Esmay said.

'She has gone into darkness,' the people said.

'She has returned to the land,' the priest said. 'And her spirit to the heavens.'

'Her power is released,' Esmay said. She untied the silk cord, and untwisted the strands of the braid. The night wind sighed down off the mountains, cold around her legs even through the layers of clothes. Candle flames streamed sideways; a few went out.

'Into the heavens . . .' the people said.

Esmay untied the second cord, at the top of the braid, and held the loosened braid high in her open hands. A gust of wind picked up one strand, then another. She heard the next gust coming, shaking the trees around the glade. When she felt it, she leaped up, tossing the hair free . . . and landed in darkness, all the candles blown out.

'Now is the death; now is the sorrow born!' In darkness and windy cold, the people cried out, and burst into the formal wails of mourning. One voice, quavering, old, sang the story of her great-grandmother's life, a counterpoint to the mourning cries. It had been a long life; it was a long dirge, and it ended only when the darkness crept back under the trees with approaching dawn. Light strengthened moment by moment; one by one the mourners fell silent, until at last there was no sound nor movement. Far off, it seemed, a rooster crowed, and another answered.

The priest with his tall black hat had turned his back, to face the sunrise. The women helped Esmay back through the crowd, into the curtained tent she had not seen for the darkness. Quickly they stripped off the black vest, waistcloth, skirt, blouse, boots. Over the pure white underclothes, they helped her into the Landbride's traditional outfit: white blouse, with wide pleated sleeves ending in a hand's width of frothy lace; white skirt pinstriped in green; white doeskin vest embroidered and beaded in brilliant color with flowers and vines and fruit . . . and to top it all, the hat with its two blunt points, from each of which a gold tassel fell past her ear to her shoulder. Around her waist, the scarlet and purple striped waistcloth, folded and tied precisely. In its folds, a narrow belt to which was hung on her right hip a sickle's curved blade, its metal varicolored with age, but its edge still gleaming. On her left side, slung from a shoulder strap, she had a pouch of seed. Soft green boots, lined in yellow silk, would come later – for the first, she would go barefoot.

Back outside, the risen sun streamed through the trees in long red-gold shafts, but the dew beneath her feet felt icy cold. Someone behind her struck a bell, and at its lingering mellow tone, the priest turned to face her. He raised on outstretched hands a long sharpened stick. The men moved to stand behind him.

'From night comes day,' the priest said. 'By the grace of God. And from the death of one comes the life of another, as the seed in the ground dies to live as the grain that blows in the sun.'

Esmay lifted her arms in the ritual gestures.

'Does any here challenge the Landbride's lineage?' the priest asked. 'Or is there cause she should not be wed?'

Silence from the people, and the nervous chattering of a treehopper, who cared nothing for ceremony. The priest waited out a full count of a hundred – Esmay counted it out in her own mind – then nodded.

'So it shall be . . . this bride to this land, to the end of her life, or her willing gift to her heir.' He held out the digging stick.

The next part had seemed ridiculous and more theatrical than archaic when Esmay read it, but wearing the old costume in the early morning light, with the digging stick in her hand (far heavier than she expected), and the sickle and seeds . . . it felt right in a way she had not imagined.

She strode out into the little circle of grainland kept for this purpose, and planted carefully each year. Though the season was wrong, and what she planted would not grow, it still felt connected to some larger ritual which would work, which would bind the land to her, and her to the land. She was not sure she wanted that, but she was sure what she had to do.

With the digging stick, she pried up the three holes at the corners of an equilateral triangle, pushing through the earth until they were big enough. Old stains on the tip of the digging stick made clear how deep was the right depth. Her helpers picked up the loosened clods and put them in a copper bowl. Then, taking the old sickle blade which would have no handle until this was over, she laid the edge of the blade to the palm of her left hand. It hardly hurt at first, and the blood ran redder than her sash into the bowl, into the clods of earth, darkening them. When it was enough, the women nodded, and she held out her hand for someone to bind in the kerchief that would henceforth be laid under the kitchen hearthstone.

Her hand was beginning to throb. Esmay ignored it, and hung the sickle back on her belt. Then she spat into the bowl, onto each clod. The women nodded again, and she stepped back. They poured a few drops of water from a jug of springwater and, using paddles carved of wood from orchard trees, kneaded the earth and blood and water into a ball.

Esmay took five seeds from the sack and dropped them carefully into the first hole – and the women laid a small lump of the mixture in the bowl on top of it. Again . . . and again. Then the women set the bowl on the ground in the triangle, and divided the remaining lump into five smaller ones, each carefully shaped into a loaf, and laid a tripod of sticks over them, with a tuft of dry bristlegrass atop. The priest approached, and took from around his neck the crystal that formed the center of his scapular, the symbol of the star. But so early in the morning, it could not focus enough sunlight . . . no. For one of his assistants brought forward a pot, in which was a coal from the fire on the hearth, kept live since that fire had been quenched.

The fire, fed carefully, baked the earthen loaves hard and dry. While it baked, the musicians began to play, wild heartrending dances. When it was baked, the Five Riders came forward. Esmay broke the lump apart, and each took a section, mounted, and rode away. They would place the loaves in the boundary shrines, where the earth from her planting, her blood, and her spit, would declare the land hers. It would be days before the last one, far to the south, was set in its little stone house.

By now, the smells of food had wafted across from the kitchens; with the Landbride's dawn, fires could be lit, and cookstoves heated. Fresh hot bread, roast meat . . . Esmay sat on a throne piled with late flowers as the feast was carried out to her guests.

609

When the crowd around her thinned, her cousin Luci came up. 'I have your accounting,' she said. 'The herd has done well.'

'Good,' Esmay said. She sipped from the mug someone had handed her, and felt dizzy from the fumes alone. 'Could you get me some water? This is too strong.'

Luci laughed. 'They want to follow the old ways into the bedding of the Landbride, do they? I'll bring you water.' She darted off, and was back soon, this time with a handsome young man at her heels.

'Thanks,' Esmay said, taking the jug of cool water.

When the long ceremony was over, Esmay's stepmother led her to the suite her great-grandmother had occupied. 'I hope you will stay awhile,' she said. 'This is your home . . . we can redecorate the rooms—'

'But my room's upstairs,' Esmay said.

'Not unless you wish it. Of course, if you insist . . . but this has always been . . . it's the oldest part of the house . . .'

She was trying to be tactful, and helpful; Esmay knew that, just as she knew that she was too tired, after all this, to discuss anything calmly. What did it matter, after all, where she slept?

'I think I'll lie down awhile,' she said instead.

'Of course,' her stepmother said. 'Let me help you with these things.'

Her stepmother had hardly touched her, as near as she could remember – it felt strange indeed to have help from her. Would she have helped, years ago, if Esmay had let her? A disturbing question, which she might reconsider after a long nap. She was in fact a deft maid, quick with the fastenings, and she knew exactly when to turn away, the outer garments folded carefully in her arms, and leave Esmay alone.

Esmay woke in late afternoon to the chill light of an overcast sky – clouds had moved in. Nothing looked right . . . and then she remembered. She was not upstairs, not in her own bed, but in great-grandmother's. Except it was her own now, in a way that the bed upstairs had not been . . . hers not by custom, or assignment, but by tradition and law. Everything was hers now . . . this bed, the embroidered panel on the wall with THE EYES OF GOD ARE ALWAYS OPEN on it (her great-grandmother had done the needle-work herself, as a young girl), the chairs . . . and the walls around them, and the fields around the walls, from the distant marshy seacoast to the mountain forests. Fruit trees, olive trees, nut trees, gardens and ploughland, every flower in the field, every wild creature in the woods. Only the livestock might belong to others – but it was she who would grant grazing rights, or refuse them, which land could be put to plough, and what would be pasture.

She pushed the covers aside, and sat up. Her stepmother – or someone – had laid out more normal clothes. Not anything she'd brought, but new – soft black wool trousers, and a multicolored pullover top. Esmay found the adjoining bath unit, and took a shower, then dressed in the new clothes.

In the hall, Luci was talking quietly to Sanni and Berthold. Sanni looked at her, a long considering look. 'You slept well?' she asked. Esmay had the feeling that the question meant more than it said.

'Yes,' she said. 'And now I'm hungry again.'

'A few minutes only,' Sanni said, and turned toward the kitchen.

'Welcome home,' Berthold said. He looked slightly wary.

'Thank you,' Esmay said. She was trying to remember if her new status changed anything but the land titles . . . was she supposed to change the terms of address for Berthold and Sanni, for instance?

Her father came out of the library wing. 'Ah – Esmay. I hope you're rested now. I don't know how long you can stay, but there's a great deal to be done.'

'Not until after eating,' Sanni said, reappearing. 'We're ready now.' Esmay realized they had been waiting for her.

The meal made clearer than any explanations how her status had changed. She sat at the head of the table, where her great-grand-mother had sat on the rare occasions she joined the family at table . . . which deposed Papa Stefan from his position as her repre-sentative. She had not imagined he could look so small, hunched over his plate halfway down the table. She ate slowly, watching and listening, trying to feel out the hidden currents of emotion.

Her stepmother and her aunt Sanni, for instance, were eyeing each other like two cats over a plate of fish. In what way were they rivals? Her father and Berthold, though studiously polite, seemed both particularly tense. Of the youngsters, only Luci was at the table – the young ones, she supposed, had been fed informally earlier.

'Have you decided whom to name as your heir?' her stepmother asked. Sanni shot her a look that should have had gray goose-feather fletching, it was so sharp.

'Not now,' her father said.

'No,' Esmay said. 'I haven't – it's all too new. I will need to consider carefully.' She would need to look at the family tree; she had no idea who might be eligible. It might even be Luci. That wouldn't be so bad.

'The paperwork starts tomorrow,' her father said. 'All the judicial red tape.'

'How long does that last?' Esmay asked.

He shrugged. 'Who knows? It's not something we've done for a long time, and since then some of the laws have changed. It's no longer enough for the family to swear agreement to the whole change; it has to be done piece by piece.'

It sounded far worse than Administrative Procedures. If the whole family had to pledge peaceful acquiescence to the change in ownership of each field, each woodland patch . . .

'At least, much of it can be done by proxy, now. My guess is that it will take hours, if not days – and all to do over again when you abdicate.' He sounded more tired than resentful; Esmay considered that he had probably taken on most of the family responsibility on her behalf since her great-grandmother died.

'If she abdicates,' Papa Stefan put in. 'She should stay, marry well, and be the Landbride we need. She's been a hero to the world – she has proved herself – but they cannot need one young hero as badly as we need her here. She could retire now.'

Her father gave her a look, and a tiny lift of the shoulders. He knew what her career meant to her, as he knew what his meant to him – but there was much he didn't know, as well, and at the moment, Esmay could almost see the wisdom of leaving Fleet before they forced her out.

'It may not be me that you need, Papa Stefan, but someone who has lived here all along, who knows more—'

'You can learn,' he said, his spirits rising as he had someone to argue with. 'You were never stupid, just stubborn. And why should you serve the Familias Regnant? We have not even a Seat in their Grand Council. They do not respect us. They will use you up, and discard you at the end, whenever you displease them, or they tire of you.'

That was too near the mark; Esmay wondered if some word of her disgrace had leaked through the newsnets. But Berthold jumped in.

'Nonsense, Papa. Young officers of her quality are rarer than diamonds at the seashore. They won't let her go easily. Look what she's already done.'

'Finished eating, is what she's done,' her stepmother said. 'Dessert, anyone?'

Esmay was glad enough to have the subject turned, and accepted a bowl of spiced custard gratefully.

Next morning, the legal formalities began. Her father had brought an entire court to the house: judge, advocates, recording clerks and all. First, although Esmay had openly accepted her heritage in the ceremony, she must now swear that she had done so and sign the Roll, her signature beneath her great-grandmother's, where anyone could compare its slightly awkward simplicity to the lovely old-fashioned elegance of her great-grandmother's writing. But three lines above, someone had signed in awkward childish letters that looked even worse.

Once she was sworn in as heir, the true Landbride, the real work began. Every Landsteward, including Papa Stefan and her father, had to submit an accounting of the management of each division of the Landbride's Gift. Esmay learned things about the family estancia she had never known, because in her great-grandmother's long tenure as Landbride, changes had been made before Esmay was born which had now to be explained. From the trivial (the decision to move the chicken yard from one place to another, to accommodate a covered passage to the laundry) to the major (the sale of almost a third of the cattle lands to finance artillery

613

and ammunition for her father's brigade in the Uprising, and its eventual repurchase), the last 70 years of history were laid out in detail.

Esmay would have stipulated that the accounts were correct, if she could, but the judge would have none of it. 'You were away, Sera. You cannot know, and although these are your family, and you are naturally reluctant to consider them capable of the least infidelity or dishonesty, it is my duty to protect both you and the Landbride Gift itself. These accounts must be scrutinized carefully; that is why we brought along the accountants from the Registry.'

And how long would that take? She did not want to spend days sitting here watching accountants pore over old records.

'Meanwhile, Sera, as long as a representative of your family is here to answer any questions, we need not detain you.'

That was a relief. Esmay escaped, only to be captured by Luci, who had in mind a lengthy discussion of the herd she managed for Esmay. From one accountant to another – but Luci was so eager to explain what she'd been doing, that Esmay did not resist as she was led through the kitchens, out the back of the house, and into the stable offices.

'You hadn't said what direction you wanted to take,' Luci said. 'So I decided to sell the bottom ten percent at the regional sales, not under your name. Your reproductive rates are above the family average, but not much—'

'I didn't know they could be improved at all . . .'

'Oh yes.' Luci looked smug. 'I started reading offworld equine reproductive journals – couldn't afford a lot of what they talked about, but I made some changes in management, and everyone smirked at me until the first foal crop. Then they said it was normal statistical variation – but your second foal crop hit the ground this year, and it was a point ahead of last year's.'

Esmay had never had any interest in equine reproduction, but she knew natural enthusiasm when she saw it. She had definitely picked the right manager for her herd . . . and maybe more than that.

'What did they say about selling off the bottom end without the family name? They were branded, weren't they?'

'No . . . I decided to defer branding until after the cull period. Papa Stefan was angry with me, but it was your herd, so he couldn't stop me.'

'Mmm. And what criteria are you using for culling?'

'Several things.' Luci ticked them off on her fingers. 'Gestational length – early or late is one cull point. That could be the mare, but there's evidence it may be the foal, too. Time to stand and suck, and vigor of suckling; if they're outside a standard deviation on time to standing, or if they don't have a strong suck, that's another cull point. You already have good performance mares in that herd – but you'll benefit by having additional survival vigor.'

Esmay was impressed. 'I assume you'll cull mares later?'

'With your permission, yes. And while they're young enough to sell on . . . according to the articles I read, after three foals you should know if length of gestation, foaling problems, foal vigor, and milk production are due to the mare. I can show you the references—'

'No, that's all right. You've done very well. Tell me what you think we should do with this herd.'

'Produce exportable genestock,' Luci said promptly. 'We have the perfect outcross genome for at least five other major horse-breeding worlds. All our horses have been performing – we've culled for soundness, speed, and endurance. I entered a query in one database, to see if anyone knew of, or would be interested in, what we've got, and the response was promising. Here on Altiplano, with the reputation our family has, we can sell live animals, but the export costs are far too high to export anything but genestock . . . so I would concentrate on the most salable genestock.'

'Sounds good to me,' Esmay said. 'When do you think we might see a profit on it?'

Luci looked thoughtful. 'Not immediately. Since we usually do live breeding, and have never exported genestock, we'd need an investment in equipment. I put the income from the cull sales into a fund for that, pending your approval.'

'Would genestock from the rest of the family holdings, or from Altiplano in general, be salable?'

'I would think so. Possibly even other livestock, like our cattle . . .'

'Then I'll see if it's possible to make an investment from family funds, and then you could rent the facilities.'

'Would you really?'

'If it's possible, yes. Why not? It would benefit not only our family, but all Altiplano.'

Luci nodded, looking satisfied. She made a notation in one of her books, then gave Esmay a challenging stare. 'You look worse than you did when you left,' Luci said.

'You have less tact,' Esmay said, nettled.

'Was it the fighting?' Luci asked. 'They say the Bloodhorde is terrible.'

'No.' Esmay turned over a leaf in the studbook. 'I don't really want to talk about it.'

Luci cocked her head. 'You weren't this grumpy before, either. You looked horrible for a day or so, then better – and you were helpful to me. Something's wrong.'

The girl was persistent as a horsefly, with the same ability to go straight to the blood of it. It crossed Esmay's mind that tactical ability could be shown in more than one way.

'I have had some problems. There's nothing you could do.'

'Well, I can wish the best for you.' Luci moved restlessly from door to window and back. 'If you were my age—' A long pause, which grew uncomfortable.

'What?' Esmay said finally.

'I'd say you were lovesick,' Luci said. 'You have all the signs.'

'Lovesick!'

'That's just the way Elise said it, when she thought no one knew. But they did. Is it lovesickness, or something else?'

'Luci.' There was no way to explain. She tried another approach. 'There are things I can't tell you about. Fleet things. Sometimes bad things happen.'

'Esmay, for pity's sake – I grew up in a military household. I can tell worry about a war from a personal worry, and you needn't try to pretend that's what's going on.'

'Well, it is, Persistence. Great-grandmother died; I've had to take on the whole estate; there's a lot to worry about.'

Luci turned the conversation back to the horses, and for an hour they spoke only of this line or that, this outcross line or another. They walked up to the house together, still deep in the intricacies of fourth-generation distribution of recessives. At the door Luci said, with the most spurious wide-eyed innocence Esmay had seen, 'Are you going to marry and settle down here, cousin, the way Papa Stefan wants?'

In the hearing of half the kitchen staff and Berthold, who had wandered into the kitchen before the meal as usual. Silence fell, until one helper dropped her knife.

'I'm a Fleet officer,' Esmay said. 'You know I told everyone I would have to appoint a trustee, and an heir.'

'Yes,' Luci said. 'I know that. But you hadn't spent even a week on Altiplano yet. You could change your mind, especially if things aren't going well in your Fleet.'

Berthold snorted. Esmay could have done without that; Berthold's humor was uncomfortable at best.

'You see what she's like,' he said, around a couple of olives he'd filched.

'I'm ready for lunch,' Esmay said. 'And those had better not be the export-quality olives . . .' Her warning glance took in the cooks and Berthold. He wagged a finger at her.

'You sound exactly like Grandmother. She could squeeze oil out of the very smell of olive.'

'Lunch,' Esmay said, leading the way. 'A morning spent with lawyers and accountants, then Luci, has starved my brain.'

Darien Prime Station

Pradish Lorany turned the pamphlet over and over in his hands. He wasn't sure about this. Yes, it was totally unfair that Mirlin had taken the children and moved away – that Sophia Antera had been promoted over his head – that over half the seats on the station citizens' council were held by women. He loathed the very thought of artificial births and manipulation of the human genome – if that wasn't interfering with God's plan, he couldn't think of anything that was. But while he agreed in principle that society was corrupt and degraded, and that it all began with the

617

failure to understand the roles God had ordained for men and women, he could not quite convince himself that therefore it naturally followed that blowing up people was a Godly act. Especially since Mirlin and the children would die, too. He wanted respect from women, and leadership by men, and an end to tampering with human reproduction, but . . . was this the way to do it?

He thought not. He made up his mind. He would continue to support the Gender Defense League; he would continue to argue with his former wife that she was misunderstanding his reasons for disciplining the children by traditional methods . . . but he would not attend the next meeting with the representative of the Godfearing Militia who had attempted to recruit him to help place explosive charges.

In a spasm of disgust, he threw the pamphlet toward the orifice of the station's recycling system, but he turned away before it slid into the chute . . . and did not see it miss, to land right in front of the PLEASE ENSURE TRASH ENTERS HOPPER sign.

Nor did he see the prune-faced old woman who glared at his retreating back as she stooped to pick up the crumpled pages and put them in carefully – but who stopped, her attention arrested by the glaring grammatical error in the first sentence. Sera Alicia Spielmann, as ardent a grammarian as she was a supporter of public neatness, took the pamphlet home to use as a bad example in her next complaint to the local school trustees . . . but when she read it, she called her friend whose grandson was a member of station security, instead.

She did not connect the 'lazy litter-bum' or her own actions with the discovery, two days later, of the corpse of one Pradish Lorany who had been brutally attacked in his own apartment. Others made that connection.

16

Altiplano, Estancia Suiza

After lunch, Luci followed Esmay into the Landbride's quarters with obvious intent. Esmay, who'd been hoping for a time alone to think things over, decided she would have more peace if she let Luci talk herself out. 'So what is it now?' she asked, half laughing. 'Do you have five other schemes for the estancia, or are you planning to take over the government?'

Luci, it seemed, loved a boy – young man, actually – in a neighboring household. 'Your father is set against it – I don't know why,' she said. 'It's a good family—'

'Who is it?' asked Esmay, who had a suspicion. At the name, she nodded. 'I know why, but I think he's wrong.'

'Is this another of those things you can't tell me about?' Luci asked with a pettish note in her voice. 'Because if it is, I think it's mean to let me know you know . . .'

'Come all the way in, and sit down,' Esmay said, shutting the door carefully. No one would disturb them now. She gestured to one of the comfortable chintz-covered chairs, and sat in another one herself. 'I'll tell you, but it's not a pleasant tale. You know I was miserable the last time I was here, and I suppose no one told you why . . .'

'No one knew,' Luci said. 'Except that you had some kind of fight with your father.'

'Yes. Well . . . there are too many secrets going around, and now that I'm Landbride, I'm going to do things differently. Back before you were born, when I was a small child, and my mother had died, I ran away.'

'You!'

'Yes. I wanted to find my father, who was off at war. I didn't understand about war . . . it had been safe, here. Anyway, I ended up in a very dangerous—' Her throat closed, and she cleared it. 'A village right in the middle of the war. Soldiers came.'

'Oh – Esmay—'

'I was . . . assaulted. Raped. Then one of my father's troops found me – but I was very sick . . .'

'Esmay, I never heard of this—'

'No, you wouldn't have. They hushed it up. Because the soldier that did it was in my father's brigade.'

'No – !' Luci's face was white to the lips.

'Yes. He was killed – old Seb Coron killed him, in fact. But they told me it was all a bad dream – that I'd caught my mother's fever, which I may have, and anything else was a fever dream. All those nightmares I had – they made me think I was crazy.'

'And you found out, finally—?'

'Seb Coron told me, because he thought I knew already – that Fleet's psych exams would have found it and cured me.' She took a deep breath and let it out slowly. 'So . . . I confronted Father, and when I identified the face in the regimental rolls, he admitted it. That it had happened, that I remembered correctly.'

From white, Luci went rage-red. 'That's – hideous! Lying to you like that! I would've—'

'And the thing is,' Esmay went on, remotely cheered by Luci's response. 'The thing is, the person who did it was of that family. The man you love is his nephew, his older brother's son—'

Luci's face whitened again. 'Arlen? You can't mean Arlen. But he was killed in action – they have a shrine to him in the front hall.'

'I know. He *was* killed in action – by Seb Coron for assaulting a child – me.'

'Oh . . . my.' Luci sat back. 'And his father was com-manding something – so your father didn't tell him—? Or did he?'

'I don't know if his family knows anything at all, but even if they do it was all kept quiet. He got his medals; he got his shrine in the front hall.' She could not quite keep the bitterness out of her voice.

'And your father doesn't want anything to do with their family . . . I understand . . .'

'No . . . they stayed friends, or at least close professionally. I think my father considered it an aberration, nothing to do with his family. I danced with his younger brother when I was fourteen, and he said nothing. He'd have been delighted if I'd married Carl. But he's worried now, because he knows I know, and he isn't sure what I'll do.'

'I'll – I'll break it off, Esmay.' Luci's eyes glittered with unshed tears.

'Don't be ridiculous!' Esmay leaned forward. 'If you love him, there's no reason to break it off on my account.'

'You wouldn't mind?'

'I . . . don't know how I'd react, if he looks much like Arlen did. But that shouldn't matter, to you or the family, if he's suitable otherwise. Is he a good man?'

'I think so,' Luci said, 'but girls in love are supposed to be bad judges of character.' That with a hint of mischief.

'Seriously . . .'

'Seriously . . . he makes my knees weak, my heart pound, and I've seen him at work – he wants to be a doctor, and he helps out in the estancia clinic. He's gentle.'

'Well, then,' Esmay said, 'for what good it will do, I'm on your side.'

'What good it will do? Don't be silly – you're the Landbride. If you approve a match, no one's going to argue with you.'

That had not occurred to her, having never contemplated a match herself. 'Are you sure?'

'Of course I am!' Luci grinned. 'Didn't you realize? What happened when you—' She sobered suddenly. 'Oh. Did it – what happened – make you not want to marry?'

'It may have,' Esmay said, ever more uncomfortable with where this was heading, onto turf that Luci clearly knew well. 'I didn't think of it at the time – I just wanted off-planet. Away from it all.'

'But surely you've met someone, sometime, who made your knees weak?'

Before she could say anything, she felt the telltale heat rushing to her face. Luci nodded.

'You did . . . and you don't want anyone to know . . . Is it something . . . outworldly?'

'Outworldly?' Barin was an outworlder, but she wasn't sure that's what Luci had meant.

Now it was Luci blushing. 'You know – those things people do that – we don't do here. Or at least, not officially.'

Esmay laughed, surprising both of them. 'No, it's nothing like that. I've met people like that, of course – they don't think anything of it, and they're quite ordinary.'

Luci had turned brick red by now. 'I always wondered,' she muttered. 'How . . .'

'We had that in the Academy prep school,' Esmay said, grinning as she remembered her own paralyzing embarrassment. 'It was part of the classes on health maintenance and I nearly crawled under the desk.'

'Don't tell me; you can show me the data cube,' Luci said, looking away. Then she looked back. 'But I do want to know about him – whoever it was – is?'

'Was,' Esmay said firmly, though pain stabbed her. 'Another Fleet officer. Good family.'

'Did he not love you?' Luci asked. She went on without waiting for an answer. 'That happened to me – the second time I fell in love, he didn't care a fig about me. Told me so quite frankly. I thought I'd die . . . I used to ride out in the woods and cry.'

'No, he – he liked me.' Esmay swallowed and went on. 'I think – I think he liked me a lot, actually, and I—'

'Well, what happened, then,' Luci said.

'We . . . quarrelled.'

Luci rolled her eyes. 'Quarrel! What's a quarrel? Surely you didn't let one quarrel end it!'

'He's . . . angry,' Esmay said.

Luci looked puzzled. 'Is he violent when he's angry? You still love him – that's obvious. So why—?'

'It's – mixed up with Fleet business,' Esmay said. 'That's why I can't explain—'

'You can't stop now,' Luci said. 'And I'll bet most of it's about you and him anyway, and nothing to do with any universe-shattering secrets. You trust me with your horses

622

and your money; you ought to trust me to keep a few stupid secrets about Fleet.'

The logic made no sense, but Esmay was past caring; she'd held it in as long as she could; she had to talk to somebody. As simply as she could – which turned out to be not very simply at all – she explained about Barin, about her transfer to command track, and her arrival at Copper Mountain. And Brun. When she first mentioned Brun, Luci stopped her.

'So – *that's* the rat in the grain bin.'

'She's not a rat . . . she's a talented, bright, attractive—'

'Rat. She went after your man, didn't she? I can see it from here. Used to getting what she wants, probably started falling in love at twelve—'

Esmay had to smile at Luci's tone. 'It's not that simple, though. I mean, that's what I thought – that's what other people said, with all the time she spent with Barin—'

'And why weren't you spending time with him?'

'I was taking double courses, that's why. They both had more time off – everyone had more time off than I had. And then she talked to me . . . she said she wanted to be friends, but she was always telling me how to dress, how to do my hair—'

Luci pursed her lips. 'You could use some advice there—'

'It's *my* hair!' Esmay heard her own voice rise, and brought it down with an effort. 'Sorry. She wanted to talk about Altiplano, and about our customs, and it sounded so . . . so condescending, and one day she was talking about Barin, and I just . . . blew up.'

'Told her to keep her sticky fingers off your man, did you?'

'Well . . . not exactly. I told her—' She didn't want to repeat those angry phrases, which echoed in her head sounding far worse than they had at the time. 'I called her names, Luci, and told her she had no morals worth mentioning, and should go away and quit corrupting people.'

'Oof. I can see I don't ever want you mad at me.'

'And then I had to leave for the field exercise in Escape and Evasion – no, I'll tell you about that later – and when I came back she'd left Copper Mountain, and my commander was furious with me for what I'd said to her. She was under surveillance, being the Speaker's daughter, so they had it all recorded, and somehow the news vids had got hold of it. Barin – I thought he'd slept with her, and then he was mad at me for thinking he would. And as if that weren't bad enough, she was later captured by pirates, and they tortured her and took her away – and everyone's blaming me.'

Luci gave her a long, cool look and shook her head slowly. 'Landbride you may be, and Fleet officer, and decorated hero, but you've been acting like a schoolgirl with her first crush. Your brains have all gone to mush.'

'What!?' After the previous conversation, she had expected some form of sympathy, not this.

'Yes,' Luci said, nodding. 'I guess I can see why – no background at all. But still – what a wet ninny you've been! Let me tell you something, cousin, if you don't get yourself back to wherever Barin is and tell him all about it – why you blew up at Brun, and that you love him – you will be confirmed as a total complete idiot.'

Esmay could say nothing for the shock; she was aware that Luci was thoroughly enjoying what must be her first chance to lecture an elder.

'All right, this was your first love affair. But you've made every mistake there is.'

'Like what?' Esmay said.

'Like not telling him. Not telling this Brun person. She may be the sort who snatches other peoples' lovers for the fun of it, but if you didn't even *tell* her—'

'How could I? We hadn't – and anyway there are the regulations—' Quickly she outlined the relevant portions of the code of conduct.

'Poppycock,' Luci said confidently. On a roll, ready to lecture, apparently for hours – Esmay wondered if she had been like this with Brun. No wonder Brun had flounced away; if she'd known how to flounce, she'd have done it herself. 'You weren't exploiting Barin; emotionally you're younger than I am. You could be reasonably careful and professional without turning into an icicle.'

'I don't know . . .'

'I do. You are a fool if you sit here playing about at being Landbride, when you don't really care about this land at all—'

'I do so care about the land!'

624

'In the abstract, yes. And you'd like it to be here, unchanged, when you visit. But you can't convince me that you feel really passionate about whether coastal pastures are crossfenced to allow HILF grazing or left open and grazed in alternate years.'

'Er . . . no.' Esmay scrabbled at her memory, trying to think what 'HILF grazing' was.

'Or whether we quit buying cattelope breeding stock from Garranos and develop our own breed, and if so, on what criteria.'

'Not really . . .' She hadn't known they had been buying cattelope from the Garranos.

'Or whether to bring in new rootstock for the nut trees, or top-graft with the latest varieties onto the old.'

'I suppose not.' Rootstock? Top-graft? She had not suspected her great-grandmother of knowing anything about any of this.

'Well, then. You have always wanted a wider world, and you made your way into it. You found love there – that *proves* it was the right choice for you.' That was a line of reasoning Esmay had never heard, let alone thought of, before. 'Don't let anyone take it away from you,' Luci finished, triumphantly.

'They can,' Esmay said bleakly. 'They can ask me to resign my commission—'

'Have they?'

'No, not yet. But Admiral Hornan hinted at it.'

'There's more than one admiral, surely. Esmaya – you are older than I am, and you are the head of my family now, but you cannot be a good Landbride if your heart is somewhere else. You want a career in Fleet, you want this man Barin – *go get them*. No one in our family has ever been shy about going after what he or she wanted. Don't break with tradition.' Luci sat back, arms crossed, and gave Esmay a challenging stare.

The tumult inside subsided gradually. It seemed so simple to Luci, and it wasn't simple . . . and yet it was. If she had a goal – and she did – then why wasn't she pursuing it? Why had she been sidetracked? And, more importantly, what could she do about it?

'They're organizing an attempt to free Brun,' Esmay said. She could talk calmly now. 'The ship I was on is part of it. I should be part of it, but Lord Thornbuckle is blaming me for the whole thing – he insists that he doesn't want me to have anything to do with it. And someone I knew in the Academy is sticking to Barin like dried egg to a plate—'

'He's the sort of man other women want,' Luci said, with no heat. 'You said that—'

'Yes . . . but she's a bad one, really.'

'So what would it take to get you back in Barin's good graces, so you can find out if he still loves you, and back in your admiral's good graces?'

'I don't know . . .' She paused. 'I don't know if Barin will ever forgive me . . .'

'He might not,' Luci said frankly, 'But you won't know that until you see him again. And the admiral?'

'I suppose – if I could convince them somehow that I don't hate Brun, and I didn't ever say that she deserved what she got—'

'They think you said that?'

'Casea – the woman who's after Barin – says I did. Says she knew me at the Academy and I was always saying things about the senior Families. Of course I didn't . . .'

'Muerto de Dios,' Luci said. 'I would have a knife for that one if I saw her. But if she's having to lie about you to keep Barin away from you, then he's not that eager for her. Go back, Esmay. Go back and make them know how good you are.'

'And you, cousin?'

'And I will breed horses, and – with your consent and support – marry the man I love and have babies.'

'And be Landbride someday?' Esmay asked, after a decent interval.

'That is entirely up to you,' Luci said. 'I don't want that job too soon, I can tell you. At least let me prove my abilities with your herd before I take on another.'

Esmay sat alone as the light dimmed, thinking over what Luci had said. She knew what she wanted – she was supposed to be a tactical genius – so it should be possible to figure out what she could do to get herself out of the mess she was in. If she could retrieve her intelligence from the mush her emotions had made . . .

And yet, what she wanted had more to do with emotions then

brains: what she wanted was love, and respect, and honor, and the sense that she was serving something worth serving.

She could do nothing about it here. With every passing minute, she realized that no matter how hard she worked, or how pleasant a life she could contrive here, as one of the wealthiest women on the planet, she would never satisfy her own desires, her own needs, by being a Landbride, even the best Landbride she could be. She would always know she had run away from trouble. She would always know she had failed. In her mind's eye, she could see herself – her civilian self – meeting an older Barin far in the future. They would be polite. He would admire, politely, her empire. And then he would go away, and she . . . she blinked back tears, and pushed herself up from the chair.

The judge and the advocates and auditors were annoyed when she walked in on them, and insisted that she must soon return to Fleet.

'We understood you had indefinite leave.'

'My pardons, sirs, but there are events afoot which I cannot discuss, but which make it very desirable that I return as soon as I can. I must know how long this will take.'

'We could, if we hurried, have the transfers ready within five days . . .'

Esmay had already looked up the commercial passenger schedules. 'Sirs, the next ship leaves in five days, but the one after is another twenty days. I'm sure you can have all ready in four days, with all the cooperation and resources of this house.'

'It will hardly be possible,' said one of the advocates, but the judge waved him to silence.

'You have honored Altiplano already by your deeds, Sera; for you, this is possible. Not easy, but possible.'

'My thanks are eternal, and I will place the household at your service.'

On the last of the four days, having signed the last paper, Esmay asked her father to come to the library, scene of that earlier confrontation. This time, however, she put that aside, and asked his advice. With the same precision and organization that she might have briefed someone on a military problem, she told him what she faced. 'So you see, far from being a credit to our house, I

627

am in disgrace,' she said. 'But I cannot change that here – and if I stay here—'

'I see,' he said. He nodded, sharply. 'You are a credit to this house, Esmaya, and to Altiplano; you will never be a disgrace in my sight. But I agree: for your own sake, you must clear your name. If you cannot, you are always welcome to return, and you must not give up your Landbride Gift until this is over. Stand or fall, it will be as the Landbride Suiza.'

She had been more than half afraid he would demand that she give it up; her eyes filled.

'As for the matter of the Speaker's daughter – you were wrong, there, and you know it. Her rudeness does not excuse yours. But your reasons for not claiming the man's affection make sense to me, though perhaps not to those with different ways. Still – they will not hold it against you, if you can prove that you wish her no harm, and can convince her, when and if she is rescued. As for the man – even I have heard of Serranos. A remarkable family, and well suited to this house. You must have made friends, Esmaya, and this is the time to call on them.'

'Approach them?'

'Yes. When under attack, seek allies – you cannot fight all Fleet alone, and when people are lying about you, you need those who will not. If you say nothing, if you avoid them, they can more easily believe the lies are true.' His voice grew husky. 'Thank you, daughter, for your great courtesy in confiding this to me . . . I always did care for you.'

'I know.' She did know, and she also knew it had not been enough – but it was all he had to give. Bitterness rolled over her one last time, and then washed away.

With her family's advice in her ears, and more resources than she had ever had at her disposal, Esmay chose to take the fastest transport she could find. Civilian fast-transit passenger ships were almost as fast as Fleet, and more reliable in schedule – she would not risk being told there was no more room when she held first-class tickets. She had never traveled this way before. In her stateroom, with access to the first-class exercise and entertainment facilities, she thought of Brun, who had grown up thinking this was normal.

628

If captivity and brutality were bad for an ordinary person, how must they be for a girl who had experienced luxury, with very whim indulged? How could she withstand the shock? She had taken the E&E course, yes, but Esmay doubted she had taken the lectures about nonresistance, passive resistance, seriously. Brun had no habit of passive survival. She had no experience of being silenced, of having no one listen to her. She would fret, rebel, bring on herself more punishment and abuse. Only if she had a possibility on which to focus her mind and effort – only if she could imagine herself into a different future – would Brun be able to concentrate her resistance into that hope, and not waste herself on futility.

So far as Esmay knew, from the little she'd been allowed to know after being banished in disgrace, the planning had concentrated on a covert operation to extract Brun, with no consideration of her own need for activity. They were clinging to the hope that she had survived, but they didn't consider finding a way to include her help in her own rescue. They were thinking of her as a passive object, something to be snatched from a thief – just as her captors had thought of her as a passive object, some valuable to be stolen and appropriated for their own use.

Just as she herself had been only an object to the man who raped her in childhood – and had himself been only a disgusting object to the sergeant who killed him – and she again had been only an object when her family ignored her memory of the rape and made her into the outcast with nightmares who lived at the far end of the house. She wondered suddenly if Brun's family had ever seen her as a person, not a decorative object . . . if all her wild behavior had been as much a cry for recognition as Esmay's dreams.

And she, too, had treated Brun as a silly piece of decorative statuary – she had not seen the person behind the pretty face, the lovely hair, the exuberance. Familiar guilt rolled over her, and she pushed it away. Guilt would not help. Remorse would not help. Brun the person was in trouble, and Esmay the person would have to figure out how to help her – and not by ignoring the person she was.

She put her mind back on the problem, as she spent an hour in the ship's countercurrent swim salon.

Brun was, or had been, pregnant. Would pregnancy give her a reason to stay alive, or not? Would babies? She had told Esmay, the day of the disastrous argument, that she didn't want children . . . but that didn't mean she hated them.

That stuffed toy. Esmay stopped swimming, and the pool's current pushed her back to the edge. That stuffed toy from the *Elias Madero* . . . there had been children aboard, and no children's bodies had been found. If – perhaps – the Militia had kept the children, if Brun had been with them, would that give her a focus? Something to live for? Some reason to be patient, in a way that nothing in her past had made her be patient?

It might. Esmay climbed out of the pool, dried off, and went back to her stateroom hardly noticing those who spoke to her. She spent the last days of the transit putting together everything she remembered about the debris from the trader, and Brun, and trying out one scenario after another. If she had fixed on the children as a means of staying sane, she would want to bring them out too. How could that be done? Esmay didn't let herself think it might be impossible.

Sector VII HQ

Casea Ferradi was having more luck with blackening Esmay Suiza's name than with capturing Barin Serrano. She had managed to get herself assigned to Admiral Hornan's personal staff with only the slightest, insignificant pressure on the major – now lieutenant commander – she'd known so well on her first ship. Everyone knew she'd been Suiza's classmate, so her opinion had been asked more than once – she hadn't had to create opportunities to talk about Esmay. With Suiza off on leave to her home planet, Casea didn't even have to worry about contradiction.

'And she really said she thought the Great Families were a ridiculous institution?'

Casea didn't answer directly; she stared thoughtfully into the distance in a way that suggested noble reticence. 'I think it's because Altiplano has no Chair in Council,' she said, after a long pause. Neither did the Crescent Worlds, but that didn't matter. 'There's no tradition of respect, you see.'

'I'm surprised they didn't notice anything when she was in the Academy,' Master Chief Pell said. He was, though enlisted, senior enough to have access to files in which Casea had particular interest.

'She kept a low profile,' Casea said. 'Actually, so did I – we were both outsiders in a way, you know. That's why we were together so much, and why I didn't realize that what she said was important.' She shook her head, regretting her own innocence. 'Then I got absorbed into things, you see, and just . . . didn't notice.'

'It's not *your* fault,' Pell said, just as she had meant him to say.

'Perhaps not,' Casea said. 'But I still feel bad about it. If I'd only known, maybe all this could've been prevented.'

Pell looked confused. 'I don't see how—'

She should have picked a brighter one. 'I mean,' Casea said, edging nearer to her intended message, 'if I'd realized how bitter she was toward the Families, perhaps she would never have had any influence on Sera Meager.'

Pell blinked. 'You can't mean – she actually had something to do with the capture itself? I thought that was accidental; she just happened to enter the same system where they were plundering that merchanter . . .'

'A very handy coincidence, don't you think? And Sera Meager had traveled widely . . . I find myself wondering why she happened to take that particular shortcut at that particular time.'

'And you think Lieutenant Suiza told her about that? Or told them—'

'I don't suppose we'll ever know,' Casea said. The chances of this rescue succeeding were, in her unspoken opinion, so close to zero as made no difference.

'But – but does the admiral know about this? That would be treason . . .'

'I'm sure someone else has thought of it,' Casea said. 'I'm only a lieutenant, and it occurred to me . . .'

631

'But you knew her before,' he said. 'Those more senior might not know what she said at the Academy.'

'Well . . .' Casea feigned reluctance, though it was getting harder. She had trailed this particular theory across several potential helpers, and so far had no takers. Even Sesenta Veron, who had been telling his own wicked-Suiza stories, thought it was impossible.

'I think you ought to tell the admiral,' Pell said. Then, with returning caution, 'It would help if you had any documentation.'

'I'm afraid not,' Casea said. 'The only files which might contain useful references are all well out of my clearance.'

The following silence lasted so long she almost gave up, but at last Pell's sluggish processors put two and two together. 'Oh! You need access. Er . . . what files did you have in mind?'

'I did just wonder if anything had come up during the investigation of that mutiny.'

'But surely you don't think – I mean, she was *decorated* for that action—'

'I think they might have been asking questions they didn't ask before,' Casea said. 'Even if they didn't look too carefully at the answers.'

Pell shook his head. 'It won't be easy, Lieutenant, but I'll see what I can do. I'll have to see who I can talk to over in legal . . . but I'll let you know.'

'Thanks,' Casea said, giving him the full benefit of her violet gaze and her smile. 'I just want to help.'

Barin Serrano was used to Fleet politics; he had grown up in that dangerous sea. He navigated the tricky currents of influence at the task force headquarters with care, noticing which competing Fleet families were taking advantage of Lord Thornbuckle's present annoyance with the Serrano name. The Livadhis were split, as usual: some were proclaiming their friendship and loyalty to various Serrano seniors like his grandmother, while others were passing snide remarks in the junior officers' recreation areas. Barin ignored the insults, but kept track. Someone in the family would need to know this, when he had enough data.

In another compartment of his busy brain, he began looking for signs of trouble in other master chief petty officers. Once is accident, twice is coincidence . . . he was willing to admit that Zuckerman could be an accident, and the others he'd heard of only as rumors, but if they were true . . . something was going on. His captain would've reported it, but in the present crisis, would anyone listen?

His duties consisted mostly of hand-carrying data cubes back and forth; he spent plenty of time kicking his heels in someone's front office, and thus had plenty of time to chat with people with lots of time-in-grade.

'. . . Like you take Chief Pell,' an impossibly perky female pivot-major was saying. 'I don't know if it's the strain of all this, or what, but he's not the man he was last Fleet Birthday.'

'Really?' Barin's mental ears rose.

'No. Why, the other day I had to look up access codes for legal investigations for him – I'm not even supposed to know the lockout sequences, but he started asking me to keep track of that six months ago – and he couldn't remember *any* of them.'

'My, my,' Barin said, his mind flickering over the reasons why Admiral Hornan's chief administrative NCO would be poking into legal investigations now, when supposedly the admiral was after Barin's grandmother's job as task force commander. Was he trying to get something on Heris Serrano, who had been through a sticky legal process? 'I don't suppose you'd know whose files he was sucking . . . ?'

'That awful Esmay Suiza,' the pivot-major said, with a toss of her head. 'The one that practically *sold* poor Lord Thornbuckle's daughter to the pirates.'

Barin managed not to leap over the desk and snap the girl's neck, but it was an effort.

'Whatever gave you that idea?' he murmured.

'Well, everybody knows she hated her. And I heard Lieutenant Ferradi say that if everyone had known what *she* knew about Lieutenant Suiza, she'd never have been allowed *near* Sera Meager.'

Barin mentally moved a marker in his head to change Casea Ferradi's label from 'nuisance' to 'enemy.'

'She's so beautiful, isn't she?' cooed the pivot-major.

'Mmm?'

'Lieutenant Ferradi. You're lucky she likes you; she could have any man on the base.'

'She probably has,' Barin said without thinking; he looked up to find her outraged, glaring at him. '—Them all thinking about her,' he amended quickly. She held the glare long enough to let him know she wasn't convinced, then relaxed

'She's a fine officer, and Chief Pell thinks so too. So does the admiral.'

Did he . . . did he indeed. Barin went out thinking hard in several directions, and nearly ran over the fine, beautiful Lieutenant Ferradi.

'Oh – Ensign—'

'Yes, sir?' He managed to smile at her.

'Have you heard anything from Lieutenant Suiza?'

'No, sir. I believe the lieutenant is on leave, isn't she?'

'Yes, but – actually I wanted to talk to you about her.'

Now it was coming. He gripped his temper firmly by the collar, and waited.

'I know you . . . used to be friends.'

'We served together on *Koskiusko*,' Barin said.

'I know. And I heard you were friends. And I'm sorry, but – I think you should know that continuing that friendship would not be in your best professional interest.'

As if Ferradi cared about his professional standing, other than to take advantage of his family name.

'I have not had any contact with Lieutenant Suiza since Copper Mountain,' Barin said.

'Very wise,' she said, approving.

Barin headed back to *Gyrfalcon*'s berth, hoping that Captain Escovar was aboard. This time he knew when to call for help.

17

Escovar was not aboard; he was at another meeting.

'Is there something I could answer?' asked Lieutenant Commander Dockery. Barin hesitated only a moment.

'Yes, sir, quite possibly, but it would be better somewhere else.'

'Trouble?'

'Perhaps.'

'Sten, you have the bridge,' Dockery said. And to Barin, 'Come on, then – we'll use the captain's office.'

Barin had just time to realize that he might be scuttling several careers, not just his own, when Dockery turned to him.

'Out with it, then. Found another problem with master chiefs?'

Barin's jaw almost dropped. 'As a matter of fact, sir, possibly yes. But that's not my main concern.'

'Which is?'

Best get it out quickly, before he was tempted to soften it. 'Sir, an officer from this ship has accessed records which she has no legitimate interest in, and may have given false information about someone else.'

'Hmm . . . that's a serious charge about an indefinite – I presume you have a name for each of these?'

'Yes, sir.' Barin took a deep breath. 'Lieutenant Ferradi talked a master chief named Pell – who incidentally is known to his juniors to be forgetting things this past year – into accessing Lieutenant Suiza's legal records from the court-martial.'

'It didn't occur to you that she might have had orders to do so? She is on Admiral Hornan's staff for the present . . .'

'No, sir. If she'd had orders, she'd have gone through channels, not Chief Pell.'

'And you also accuse her of giving false information about Lieutenant Suiza? What kind of false information?'

'She's said a lot of things about what Es – what Lieutenant Suiza was like in the Academy. Now I was too far behind to have witnessed any of this directly, but other people who were there don't have the same account at all.'

Dockery pursed his lips. 'I know that Lieutenant Ferradi's been interested in you, Ensign – it's been fairly obvious. Scuttlebutt had it that you were . . . "falling under her spell," I believe, is the term I heard used most. Are you sure this isn't just a lovers' quarrel you're trying to make official business? Because if so, you're about to be in more trouble than you were in over Zuckerman.'

'No, sir, it is not a lover's quarrel. I have no interest in Lieutenant Ferradi and never did.'

'Mm. The other rumor was that you had been in love with Esmay Suiza—' Barin felt his face getting hot; the exec nodded. 'And so the other possibility I see is that you're accusing Lieutenant Ferradi of unprofessional behavior toward another officer because you're still besotted with Suiza and can't stand to hear her criticized.'

'Sir, I became . . . very fond of Lieutenant Suiza when we were both on *Koskiusko*. I think she's a fine officer. We quarrelled at Copper Mountain, over what she'd said to Brun Meager' – and to him, though he wasn't going to mention that at the moment – 'and I haven't seen her since. Whether I have a bad case of hero worship, which is what Lieutenant Ferradi's told me, or a friendship, or – or something else, doesn't really matter. What does, is whether the stories Ferradi's spreading about her are true.'

'If they were true, what would you think?'

Barin felt a pain in his chest squeezing out hope. 'Then, sir – I would have to change my opinion.'

'Barin, I'm going to tell you something, in confidence, because right now you need to know it. Casea Ferradi has been trouble for every commander she's had – it's why she's at the back of her class's promotion list – but she's never quite managed to get herself thrown out. If Lieutenant Suiza hadn't had that quarrel

636

with Sera Meager, if Lord Thornbuckle hadn't fastened on her as the scapegoat in this mess, no one would be paying the slightest attention to Ferradi's accusations. Now they are – and if she's so far overreached herself as to break regulations concerning legal paperwork, we've got her at last. Tell me, do you know if Koutsoudas is still running scan on your cousin's ship?'

'I think so, sir.' Where was this leading?

'Good. We're going to need really good scan to catch her in the act, because she's no dummy. And by the way, good job on finding Pell. We've found two others here . . . though we haven't figured out what the problem is yet.'

A half hour later, Barin was on his way to the berth of the *Navarino*, his cousin Heris's ship. Heris was at home to family members – he had the distinct feeling that if he'd been an ensign named, perhaps, Livadhi or Hornan, he might have cooled his heels for an hour before getting in to see her.

'You want my scan techs sucking for you? What's wrong with yours? Escovar's always been able to pick good people.'

Dockery had left it to him how much to tell, but this was family. Barin made it as short as he could, emphasizing that he had thought at first it was Heris's record Ferradi was after, in order to help Hornan wrest command of the task force from Admiral Serrano.

'Are you *involved*?' The emphasis clearly meant culpable as well.

'No, and yes,' Barin said. 'Lieutenant Ferradi also happens to see me as her ticket to the Serrano dynasty.'

'Does she now?' Heris looked suddenly very dangerous indeed, as if a sleeping falcon had waked, and aimed its deadly gaze at a target. 'And what do you think she's done, that you need Koutsoudas to discover?'

'Gone hunting in supposedly secure legal files, and possibly altered data, sir.' That last was his own guess; Dockery hadn't been impressed by it, but he was sure that if Ferradi would lie verbally, she would not be above fudging the records. Why else risk tinkering with those files at all?

'Ah. Well . . . tell you what. You can have a couple of hours of Koutsoudas' time – but I get the whole story afterwards.'

637

'Yes, sir.'

'And your captain owes me dinner.'

Now how was he going to explain *that* one? He returned thoughtfully to *Gyrfalcon*'s berth, and reported his success to Dockery. 'Koutsoudas will be along after lunch, sir,' he said at last.

'Good. In the meantime, I want you to go destroy property and get yourself chewed out.'

'Sir?'

'Go find Lieutenant Ferradi – which shouldn't be hard, as you say she's been adherent – and figure out some way to damage her datawand. I want her to have to initialize another. I don't care how you do it, as long as you don't damage the lieutenant – but I will mention that just dropping one in an alcoholic beverage is not sufficient. On the other hand, the application of sufficient point pressure is.'

Barin set out on this mission with the uneasy feeling that Dockery's past might be more interesting than he had thought. When – and why – had Dockery discovered that dropping a datawand in alcohol wouldn't damage it?

Ferradi found him just as he was turning into the junior officers' mess and recreation area. 'Lunch, Ensign?' she asked brightly.

'Oh – yes. Excuse me, Lieutenant—' He made a show of patting his pockets. 'Drat!'

'What?'

'I was supposed to check on something for Commander Dockery, and then Major Carmody asked me something else, and – I forgot my datawand. It's back aboard. I'll have to go back – unless I could borrow yours, sir?'

'You should carry it with you all the time,' Ferradi said, pulling out hers. 'What did Dockery want?'

'Spares delivery schedule,' Barin said promptly. 'He says they've shorted on pre-dets the last four times. You probably know all about it.'

'Oh – yeah. Everyone's complaining.' She handed over the wand, and Barin looked around. The nearest high-speed dataport was out in the corridor.

'I'll just be moment,' he said. 'I heard they have Lassaferan snailfish chowder today—' Sure enough, she went on to the serving tables. Snailfish chowder was a rare treat.

Barin found the high-speed port and jammed the datawand in. Nothing happened; it lit up normally. He pulled it back out, looked around, and shoved it in as hard as he could. Its telltales came up normal again. He pulled it out and looked at the tip. Someone had designed it to withstand normal carelessness . . . and he realized that a high-speed dataport probably had internal cushions to protect the port side of the contact as well. Fine. Now what? She'd be looking for him any moment.

A thought occurred. He went back into the lounge, waved to Lieutenant Ferradi, who had found a seat at a small table facing the entrance, and pointed at the head, then strode quickly in that direction, as if in urgent need.

Heads were full of hard surfaces; Barin tried one after another, between flushes, until he'd produced a crumple at the datawand's tip by catching it between the door and its jamb, and then squashing it with the door as a lever. He'd had no idea datawands were that tough.

'Sorry, sir,' he said to Lieutenant Ferradi, as he seated himself and handed her the wand. 'Some kind of bug, I expect.'

She had tucked it away without looking at it. 'So – you're not having chowder?'

'No, sir. In fact, I think I'll just sit here, if that's all right.'

'Of course.' She gave him one of her looks from under long eyelashes. Despite his opinion of her, he felt a stir . . . and she knew it. He could have strangled her for that alone. He hoped very much he'd done enough damage to that datawand.

Esmay changed into her uniform aboard the ship that had brought her, and took the tram over to the Fleet side.

'Lieutenant Suiza,' she said to the security posted at the entrance to the Fleet side of the station.

'Welcome home, Lieutenant.' The greeting was merely ritual, but she felt welcomed nonetheless. Beyond the checkpoint, the corridors were busy. No one seemed to notice her – and no reason why they should.

She paused to check the status boards. The task force was still here; her ship was still docked at the station. She entered her name and codes, and found that she was still on the crewlist, though coded for 'leave status: away.' All other leaves had been cancelled.

'Well, if it isn't Lieutenant Suiza,' came a voice from behind her. She turned, to find herself face to face with Admiral Hornan. He was looking at her with considerably less than pleasure. 'I thought you had indefinite leave.'

'I did, sir,' she said. 'But we got everything taken care of back home, and I came back at once.'

'Couldn't leave it alone, could you? Think you'll have a chance to gloat over the Speaker's daughter, if we get her out?'

'No, sir.' Esmay managed to keep her voice level. 'Gloating was never my intention.'

'You did *not* think she richly deserved what she got? That's not what I heard.'

'Sir, I neither said, nor thought, that Brun deserved being kidnapped and raped.'

'I see. You did, however, say that she wasn't worth going to war over.'

'Sir, I said that no one makes war over one person, not that she wasn't worth it. That is what others have said, as well.'

The admiral made a noise somewhere between a grunt and a growl. 'That may be, Lieutenant, but the fact remains that what is on the record is your statement that she wasn't worth a war.'

Before she could answer – if she could have thought of an answer – the admiral turned away. So much for making allies. She couldn't think of anything she might have said to change his mind.

Esmay had never really thought about the people who might be annoyed, or envious, because of her success. That first triumph had felt so fragile: she had not planned to be the senior survivor of a mutiny, and her struggle to bring her ship back to Xavier, and help Commander Serrano, had been a desperate struggle, one she did not expect – even at the last moment – to win. How could anyone resent it when it was clearly more luck than skill? As for the *Koskiusko* affair . . . again, it was pure luck that she had been there, that she had not been snatched, like Barin, by the Blood-horde intruders.

But now, thinking about it, she realized that her peers were used to thinking of her as a nonentity, no threat to their own career plans. They had kept a closer eye on more credible rivals. The very suddenness of her success must have made her seem even more dangerous – to those inclined to think that way – than she really was. They would doubt her real ability, or fear it.

So she had . . . enemies, perhaps . . . in Fleet. Competitors, anyway. Some would want to frustrate her goals; others would want to ride her coattails to their own.

Once she'd thought of it, she felt stupid for not thinking of it before. Just as people had interacted with her without knowing what her internal thoughts and feelings were – seeing only the Lieutenant Suiza who was quiet, formal, unambitious – so she had interacted with the others without knowing, or caring much, what their internal motivations and goals were. She had been concerned what those senior to her thought of her performance, of course . . . she paused to consider that 'of course,' then set that aside for later. The problem was, until recently she had been just existing alongside others, unaware of them except where interaction was required. So she had no idea which of them thought of her as a rival, and which as a potential friend. Except for Barin.

She arrived at her assigned quarters still thinking this over. She had unpacked her duffel and was looking up references on the cube reader when the doorchime sounded. When she opened the door, she was facing an elderly woman she had never seen before in her life, a civilian woman who carried herself with the confidence of an admiral – or a very rich and powerful person.

'You don't look like a desperate schemer,' the old woman said. Her night-black hair was streaked with silver, bushing out into a stormy mass, and with her brilliantly colored flowing clothes, she looked like a figure out of legend. Granna Owl, or the Moonborn Mage or something like that. 'I'm Marta Katerina Saenz, by the way. My niece Raffaele went to school with Brun Meager. May I come in?'

'Of course.' Esmay backed up a step, and the woman came in.

641

'You are, I presume, Lieutenant Esmay Suiza, just returned from leave on Altiplano?'

'Yes . . . Sera.'

Marta Saenz looked her up and down, very much as her own great-grandmother had done. 'You also don't look like a fool.'

Esmay said nothing as the old woman stalked about the room, her full sleeves fluttering slightly. She came to rest with her back to the door, and cocked her head at Esmay.

'No answer? Indirect questions don't work? Then I'll ask outright – *are* you a heartless schemer, glad to make profit out of another woman's shame and misery?'

'No,' Esmay said, with as little heat as she could manage. Then, belatedly, 'No, Sera.'

'You aren't glad the Speaker's daughter was captured?'

'Of course not,' Esmay said. 'I know that's what people think, but it's not true—'

The old woman had dark eyes, wise eyes. 'When you have called someone – what was it? oh, yes – a "stupid, selfish, sex-crazed hedonist with no more morals than a mare in heat," people are going to get the idea you don't like her.'

'I didn't *like* her,' Esmay said. 'But I didn't want this to happen to her.' She wanted to say *What kind of person do you think I am?* but people had been thinking she was bad for so long she didn't dare.

'Ah. And did you think she was morally lacking?'

'Yes . . . though that still doesn't mean—'

'I honor your clear vision, young woman, which can so easily find where others are lacking. I wonder, have you ever turned that clear vision on yourself?'

Esmay took a deep breath. 'I am stubborn, priggish, rigid, and about as tactful as a rock to the head.'

'Um. So you're not casting yourself as the faultless saint in this drama?'

'Saint? No! Of course not!'

'Ah. So when you decided she was lacking in moral fiber, you were comparing her to an objective standard – ?'

'Yes,' Esmay said, more slowly. She wasn't even sure why she was answering this person. She had been over this so often, without convincing anyone.

The old woman nodded, as if to some unheard comment. 'If I were simply going by Brun's past behavior, I'd say there's a man at the bottom of this.'

Esmay felt her face heating. Was she really that transparent? The old woman nodded again.

'I thought as much. And who, pray tell, is the young man on whom Brun set her sights, and whom you think you love?'

'I do love—' got out before Esmay could stop it. She felt her face getting hotter. 'Barin Serrano,' she said, aware of being outmaneuvered, outgunned, and in all ways outclassed.

'Oh, my.' That was all the old lady said, though she blinked and pursed her lips. Then she smiled. 'I have known Brun since she was a cute spoiled toddler they called Bubbles—'

'Bubbles?' Esmay could not put that name with what she knew of Brun. 'Her?'

'Stupid nickname – gave the girl a lot of trouble, because she thought she had to live up to it. But anyway, I've known her that long, and you are right that she was as badly spoiled as it's possible for a person of her abilities to be. My niece Raffaele was one of her close friends – and Raffa, like you, was one for getting other people out of scrapes. She got Brun out of a lot of them.'

Where was this leading? Esmay wasn't sure she was following whatever chain of logic the old woman was forging; she was still too shaken at having admitted – to a stranger – that she loved Barin Serrano. She was hardly aware that the emotional atmosphere had changed, that the old woman wasn't as hostile as she had been.

'Tell me that Brun Meager has *no* morals, and I find myself defending her. But tell me that she cast covetous eyes on your young man, and I am not only willing to believe it, but not even mildly surprised. She's been that way since she first discovered boys.'

Was that supposed to excuse her? Esmay felt the familiar stubborn resentment. The old woman paused; Esmay said nothing.

'If you're thinking that making a habit of stealing other women's men is even worse than happening to fall in love with one of them, which is what your face looks like, that's true. She collects them like charms on a bracelet, with reprehensible lack of concern for anyone's feelings. Or she did. Raffa said she'd been more . . . er . . . discreet in the past few years. Apparently someone she took a fancy to refused to have a fling with her.'

'Barin . . . didn't,' Esmay said. Then, realizing how many ways that could be taken wrong, she tried to explain. 'I mean, he wasn't the one, but he also didn't. He said . . .' Her voice failed her. After a miserable pause, during which she wished she could evaporate, the old lady continued.

'But what you should know is that while Brun's moral qualities are certainly immature, the girl had the right instincts about many things. She's been wild, heedless, rebellious – but she's not wittingly cruel.'

'She said things to me, too.' That sounded almost childish, and again Esmay wished she could just not be there.

'In the heat of an argument, yes. She would. Both of you sound rather like fishwives in the tape.' The old lady picked up and put down a datawand and a memo pad. 'Suppose you tell me how you met her, and what happened then?'

Esmay could see no reason for doing so, but she felt too exhausted to protest. Dully, she recounted the story of her first sight of Brun arguing with her father, and what followed, up to the point where Barin arrived.

'Let me see if I have this right. Brun admired you, wanted to be your friend, but you found her pushy and uncomfortable.'

'Sort of. I'd seen her throw that tantrum with her father—'

'That sounds like her – and like her father, for that matter. Stubborn as granite, all that family. Back when her father was a boy, he had almost that same argument with *his* father. But since he was only ten years old, it was easier to deal with. So, from the first, Brun impressed you as spoiled and difficult, and you wanted no part of her.'

'Not exactly,' Esmay said. 'If I hadn't been so busy, taking double courses, I might've had time to talk to her. She kept wanting to go off somewhere and have a party, when I had to study. But that doesn't mean I wanted her to get hurt.'

'And knowing Brun, she would've counted on her charm – she probably couldn't figure out why you weren't being friendlier. A natural ally, she would have thought – ran away from a repressive home and made a career for herself, and *her* family isn't interfering.'

'I suppose . . .' Esmay said. Had that been what Brun was thinking? It had not occurred to her that Brun could ever think of them as having much in common.

'And then, on top of that, she made a play for your man. I wonder if she was serious about that, or if she just thought he could help her get to you?'

'She asked him to sleep with her,' Esmay said, angry again.

'Ah. Unwise of her, at best. And you suddenly thought of her as a rival, a sneak, and a slut, did you?'

'Mmm . . . yes.' Put like that, it made her seem even more naive than she was. If that were possible.

'And you got mad and reamed her out for it. But, my dear, had you ever bothered to tell her you were in love with the man?'

'Of course not! We hadn't made any promises . . . I mean . . .'

'Have you told *anyone*?'

'Well . . . only when I went home for Great-grandmother's funeral, I told my cousin Luci.'

'Who is how old? And what did she say?'

'She's eighteen . . . and she said I was an idiot.' Esmay blinked back sudden tears. 'But she – she's had those years at home, and her mother – and no one ever told me—'

The old lady snorted. 'No, I don't suppose how to conduct a love affair is one of the courses taught at the Academy or the prep school.'

'What they said was not to become involved with people above or below in the same chain of command, and avoid all situations of undue influence.'

'That sounds like a recipe for confusion,' Marta commented.

'In the professional ethics segment at Copper Mountain,' Esmay said, 'there was more about that – and I started worrying about what I might do to Barin—'

'Professionally, you mean?'

'Yes – I'm two ranks senior, he's just an ensign. It seemed natural at first – and we weren't in the same chain of command – but maybe I shouldn't, anyway. I told myself that,' Esmay said, aware of the misery in her voice. 'I tried to think how to talk to him about it, but – but *she* was always there, and I didn't have time—'

'Oh . . . my. Yes, I see. She had the experience, and you didn't. She had the time, and you didn't. And you would not see her being concerned about her effect on his career, either, I daresay.'

'No. It was always "Barin, since Esmay's being no fun, let's go into Q-town for a drink or something." '

'I've met the young Serrano,' Marta said. Her finger traced a line on the built-in desk. 'Handsome boy – seems very bright. His grandmother thinks rather well of him, and tries not to show it.'

'How is he?' asked Esmay, her whole heart waiting for the answer.

'Thriving, I would say, except for the woman he's got on his trail. One Lieutenant Ferradi, as slickly designed a piece of seduction as I've ever seen. I wonder who did her biosculpt. He's at that age, Lieutenant Suiza, where young men of quality are full of animal magnetism and some women behave like iron filings. Tell me, if you will, who noticed whom first between the two of you?'

'He – came to me,' Esmay said, feeling the heat in her face.

'Ah. No iron filing tendencies in you, then. Typical – the magnets prefer to join other magnets: like to like.'

'But I'm not—'

'A magnet? I think you misjudge yourself; people often do. The most distressing bores are most sure they fascinate; the least perceptive will tell you at great length how they understand your feelings; every hero I ever knew was at least half-convinced of his or her own cowardice. If you were not a magnet, so many people could not be so angry with you.'

Esmay had never looked at character that way, and wasn't sure she agreed. But Marta went on.

'You're a born leader; that's clear from your record. That, too, is a magnet quality. You repel or you attract . . . you are not, as it were, inert. Brun's the same – and when magnets aren't attracted, they're often repellent to one another. You got, as it were, your like poles too close together.'

'I suppose . . .'

'Tell me, if you hadn't been working so hard, and if Barin hadn't been there, do you think you'd have found anything to like in Brun?'

'Yes,' Esmay said after a moment. 'She could be fun – the few times we had a few minutes together, I enjoyed it . . . I could see why people liked her so much. She lights up a room, she's bright – we were on the same team for the E&E class exercises, you know. She learned fast; she had good ideas.'

'Good enough to get herself out of her present predicament?'

'I . . . don't know. They wouldn't let her take the field exercise – that's one thing she blamed me for, and I had nothing to do with it. But against a whole planet – I don't think that would've helped. What worries me is that they aren't paying attention to her character in the planning—'

'I thought you said she had none—'

Esmay waved that away. If this woman, even this one woman, would listen to what she'd worked out, maybe it would help Brun. 'I don't mean sexual morality. I mean her personality, her way of doing things. They're talking – they were talking – as if she were just a game piece. Unless she's dead, she's planning and doing *something* – and if we don't know what, we're going to find our plans crossing hers.'

'But the Guernesi said there's no way to communicate with her – that pregnant and nursing women are sequestered, and besides, she can't talk.' Still, Marta's eyes challenged Esmay to keep going.

'She needs to know she's not forgotten,' Esmay said. 'She needs to know someone thinks she's competent—'

'You sound as if you thought you understood her,' Marta said.

'They silenced her,' Esmay said, ignoring that invitation. 'That doesn't mean she can't think and act. And – did they tell you about the children on that merchant ship?'

Marta frowned. 'I . . . don't know. I don't think so. What does that have to do with Brun?'

Quickly Esmay outlined her new theory. 'If they didn't kill those children, if they were taking them, they'd have put Brun in with them. That might be enough to keep her alive – if she

647

thought she had a responsibility to the children. And she'd be planning some rescue for them, I would bet on it.'

'I suppose it's possible . . .'

'And besides, for her to come out of this in the end, even if she is rescued, she needs to feel that she had some effect. It's one of the things they taught us, and Barin knows from experience . . . a captive who is just rescued like a . . . a piece of jewelry or something . . . has a much harder time regaining a normal life. She was not just captured; she was muted, and then raped – made pregnant. All her options closed. They should be thinking beyond getting her out, to getting her out with some self-respect left.'

Marta looked at her with a completely changed expression. 'You're serious . . . you couldn't have come up with that if you didn't really care. That's good thinking, Lieutenant – excellent thinking. And I can tell you that you're right – the planning group is not considering any of those things.'

'Can you get it across to them?'

'Me? It's your idea.'

'But I don't know how to get anyone to listen to me. They're so convinced I wanted something bad to happen to her, none of them will let me near the planning sessions, let alone speak. If you tell them, maybe they'll consider it.'

'You're not asking for credit—'

Esmay shook her head. 'No. Brun's the one in critical danger. Of course, I'd like to be the one to come up with the best solution . . . but it's better that someone comes up with it, than have it ignored.'

'I'll . . . see what I can do,' Marta said. 'In that and other situations.'

Admiral Serrano frowned as the door opened, but her expression eased as Marta Saenz swept through. 'Marta! I heard you were back from downside. We missed you the past few sessions. Lord Thornbuckle was actually making sense when you left, but he's foaming at the mouth again.'

'I was prowling amongst the troops, as you'd put it. And I just had a little conversation with your Lieutenant Suiza,' Marta said.

'Her.' The admiral frowned again. 'A very disappointing decision, encouraging her switch to command track. She's not working out at all.'

'You've got the bull by the wrong leg,' Marta said. 'Did you know the girl was besotted with your grandson?'

'I know they formed an attachment on *Koskiusko*, which I'm glad to see is no longer important.'

'Oh, but it is,' Marta said. 'The silly child fell madly in love for the first time in her life, and nothing in her background told her what to do when a rich, beautiful, charismatic blonde moved in on her love life.'

'But she's – what? – almost thirty.'

'She's also Altiplanan, lost her mother when she was five, and apparently no one told her about anything to do with love. So when she finally fell, she fell like the side of a mountain. Something she heard in a class on professional ethics started her worrying about whether she should have – as if rules ever affected gravity or love – and while she was fumbling around trying to put her emotional affairs in order, Brun started playing come-hither with your grandson. Who resisted, by the way, but Esmay didn't know that when she blew up.'

'I can hardly believe—'

'Oh, it's true. And your grandson is equally besotted with her, though he's tried to fight it. He was angry and hurt that Esmay didn't trust him, and – since he wasn't the one feeling unsure and jealous – he was appalled at her attack on Brun.'

'Where did you get all this . . . inside knowledge of my grandson's head?'

'His heart, not his head. By poking around being a nosy old woman and then a more . . . er . . . traditional grandmother than you are. He could hardly confide his guilty passion to you, now could he? Not when his lady love was in your black book and he knew your position was shaky, with dear Admiral Hornan doing his best to grab your command.'

Admiral Serrano looked thoughtful. 'They both still think they're in love, do they?'

Marta chuckled. 'All the symptoms. They blush, they tremble, they look shy – it's rather sweet, actually, as well as unmistakeable. I admit my fondness for young love, messy though it often is. It's

649

why I helped Raffa and Ronnie get free of their appallingly stiff-necked parents. So you can quit looking for hidden political motives in Lieutenant Suiza's behavior – this is the oldest story in the book.'

'That may be, but it doesn't excuse—'

'What she said? No. But if her commander had known from day one that this was a squabble over a man, would he have handled it the way he did?'

Admiral Serrano pursed her lips. 'Well . . . probably not. We do get late bloomers from time to time, and they do usually make a mess of things at least once.' The admiral sounded thoughtful, less harsh.

'Making a mess of love is part of growing up,' Marta said, nodding. 'Making a mess of someone's career, however, requires the connivance of others.'

'I don't follow you.' But the dark eyes were alert, watchful.

'Well . . . as the resident sweet old lady in this facility—' The admiral snorted, and Marta flashed a quick grin but went on. 'The youngsters tell me things. They always have. It's why I was Raffa's favorite aunt. I'd already begun to wonder how so shining a young hero could become everyone's favorite wicked woman quite so fast. I suspected that someone else's interest lay in making Lieutenant Suiza look as bad as possible, and I found that the tainted effluent, as it were, led to a few sources quite remote from Copper Mountain. That's why I went planetside, so I could do a little discreet database poking from a civilian facility.'

'And you found – ?'

Marta held up her hand and ticked off points on her fingers. 'I found Academy classmates of Esmay's who were jealous of her success – who resented her honors – who would be quite happy to see her back in tech track, or out of Fleet, because she can fight rings around them. Much that's been attributed to her has come from these sources, and they've put the worst possible interpretation on what she *did* say. The people who've actually served with her are confused and upset right now, but find it hard to believe she could be the way she's now being painted. I found others who want to get influence with your grandson because he's a Serrano

. . . who are very glad to put a barrier between him and Lieutenant Suiza.'

'All very interesting – but are you sure you're hearing the truth?'

'Vida – remember Patchcock? My nose for this kind of nastiness—'

'Yes . . . all right . . . but that doesn't get Lieutenant Suiza off the hook for what she actually said and did. And there's a witness to her saying that Brun wasn't worth starting a war over.'

'So did I, m'dear. So did you. So did the Guernesi ambassador, more than once. We wrapped it in platitudes, but you know and I know that no one – not even the Speaker, and certainly not his daughter – is worth starting a war for. Taken in context, what she actually said cannot be construed to mean that she thought all those things attributed to her.'

The admiral spread her hands. 'So – what do you propose to do about this? Since you came here, I presume you have a plan in mind.'

'Well . . . having played fairy godmother to at least three other romances recently – you know about Raffa and Ronnie, but you don't know about the others – I feel I'm on a roll where love is concerned. If Esmay and Barin can work out their problems—'

'You mean you aren't planning to do it for them?' That with a challenging grin.

'Of course not.' Marta made a prim face. 'Children learn by doing. But if they can work it out – and since they're both still smitten, I expect they can – that will take the teeth out of some of the other criticisms. After all, if a Serrano is her lover—'

'Ah – so *that's* why you tackled me first. So I wouldn't tell young Barin to avoid her?'

'Got it in one. Incidentally, if you thought Suiza was bad, you ought to see what's working on him now. One of Esmay's classmates, and a very sleek piece of work she is, too. Knows everything Esmay doesn't know about men, and since she's also a colonial, from one of the Crescent Worlds, you have to wonder where she got that kind of skill. Rumor has it, from seducing her senior officers.'

'Pull in your claws, Marta – I won't do anything to warn Barin off. And I already know about Lieutenant Ferradi – she may have done even worse than you know, according to Heris. If so, her doom is about to be upon her: Heris lent Koutsoudas to the cause.'

'You're going to tell me, I trust? No? Wicked woman – but then you are an admiral.' Marta's chuckle ended. 'There's another thing, though. Lieutenant Suiza, when I talked to her, had what I think are some very good insights into Brun's situation and some concerns about the planning. She is convinced that no one will listen to her, and asked me to pass these ideas on, as my own. I'd much rather get her involved in the planning herself—'

'Can't be done,' Admiral Serrano said crisply. 'Lord Thornbuckle's adamant. Apparently he had liked her when he met her at Copper Mountain, and feels that this proves she is . . . treacherous, was his word. He will not have her involved at all. And I doubt you can change his mind. Not in the time we have left.'

She glanced at the wall calendar and Marta followed that glance. A red rectangle covered the most probable dates for the end of Brun's pregnancy; a green one covered the time the Militia were known to allow before rebreeding a captive. That was their target; somewhere in that period they had to extract her – or face even more difficult problems.

'All right. One war at a time. I'll present Esmay's ideas; they certainly make sense in terms of my knowledge of Brun's character.'

18

Marta found Esmay at work in a cubicle, paging through a report, looking thoughtful.

'I've just talked to Admiral Serrano,' Marta said. Esmay flushed a little, the reaction Marta had hoped for. 'I told her I thought the reports of your hardheartedness and political ambitions were exaggerated . . . and why.' The flush deepened, but Esmay said nothing. 'You will find that she creates no barrier to your relationship with Barin . . .'

'If I ever have one,' Esmay said. She looked up, tears standing in her eyes. 'What if he won't speak to me?'

'Well, then, you have to see that he does.'

'But Casea's always around—'

Marta sat very straight. 'You are not going to make that mistake again! Think, child! What do you know about that young woman? Does she have a good reputation?'

'No . . .' Esmay's voice trembled slightly.

'Do you really think Barin is the kind of man who prefers that kind of woman?'

'No . . .' Her voice failed completely.

'Then quit being a wet lump, and give him some help in getting free of her. Be someone he can prefer, with some reason.' Marta cocked her head. 'Personally, I'd recommend a good haircut, to start with. And a really well-cut exercise suit.'

Esmay flushed again. 'I – I couldn't.'

'What – you can't show what you've got, because she's displaying herself like a fruit basket? What kind of nonsense is that? Come along—' Marta stood up, and watched Esmay rise slowly. 'I know perfectly well you're just moving things around in here trying to look busy. Your commander's angry with you, nobody has any real work for you – so I'm demanding your services as an escort.'

'But you—'

'My dear, before you embarrass yourself again, I'm not just Raffaele's aunt . . . I hold my own Seat in Council, though I usually let Ansel vote it for me, and if I wanted to grab any officer up to and including Admiral Serrano for an escort, no one, least of all Vida, would stand in my way. Bunny himself is putty in my hands when I'm in this mood. And you are, after all, the Landbride Suiza. Now come along and quit making difficulties.'

Marta was glad to see the salutary lift of spine which that produced, and thoroughly enjoyed her sweep through the corridors of the HQ complex, with Esmay Suiza a silent shadow at her side. She could almost see the shock, and imagined it trickling icewater-like down certain spines. The particular blonde spine she most wanted to discomfit didn't appear – well, that would come later.

Esmay hung back as Marta led her toward the doors of the most fashionable salon in the city. She had heard of Afino's – including from Brun, who had recommended it heartily.

'No one's ever been able to do anything with my hair,' she said miserably, as she had more than once on the way downside. 'It's too fine, and thin, and it frizzes—'

'And probably all you do is wash it, brush it, and cut it off when it gets too long,' Marta said. 'Listen – you are not your hair. You have choices. You want Barin, and you want to regain your professional reputation. This will help.'

It still seemed more than a little immoral. Her hair had always been her downfall, in the style sense, and she could think of nothing that would improve it but yanking it out and starting over from the genome. The serious noises the head of the salon made when he looked at her scalp made her want to sink through the floor.

'You have the fine hair,' he said. 'Perhaps your parents also, or perhaps you have had a high fever when you were young?'

'Yes, I did,' Esmay said.

'That may be it. But it is very healthy; you have not been doing anything stupid, as some women do. And you are a Fleet officer – you want something practical, easy to keep, but looking more . . . more . . .'

'More like it's intended to be something,' Marta put in. 'Less like dryer fluff.'

'Ah. A more permanent solution would be the genetic one, but you said the matter was urgent.'

'Yes. Although in the long run, Esmay, he's right – it's expensive, but you can have your hair genetically reprogrammed.'

So – even a salon like this thought that replacing it from the roots out was the best approach. But she hadn't actually thought it was possible.

'It would change your genetic ID slightly,' the man said. 'You would have to report it to your commander, and they would have to approve, and then change your records. But it has been done. On the other hand, there's nothing wrong with your hair as it is, once we determine the best way of cutting it.'

With scissors, Esmay thought but did not say.

Three hours later, she stared at her reflected image with astonishment. It was the same hair, but somehow it had consented to take a shape that suggested both competence and charm. Smooth there, a bit of curl here. Fluff was perhaps the wrong word . . . but she couldn't think of another. She looked like herself, but . . . more so. And under the tutelage of the salon's staff, she had learned to do it herself, from sopping wet to final combing.

After that, Marta dragged her off to the neighboring dress shop. 'You need off-duty clothes. I've seen you in those exercise suits.'

'I sweat,' Esmay said, but with less strength in the protest.

'Yes, but you don't have to sweat while eating dinner.' Marta prowled, sending Esmay into the changing room again and again until she was happy with the result – by which time Esmay was finally beginning to understand what the fuss was about. The blue and silver exercise suit was as comfortable as the ones she usually wore, but looked – she had to admit – stunning. And the others . . .

'The people you think were born looking good were born looking red and wrinkly just like everyone else,' Marta said. 'Yes, there are faces more beautiful than others, bodies more easily draped than others. But at least half the people you admire aren't, on form alone, beautiful. They make the effect they have. Now some people don't care about effect, and don't need effect, and nobody needs it all the time. At home, when I'm out in the garden, I look like any plump old woman in dirty garden clothes. I don't care, and neither does anyone else. But when I'm being Marta Katerina Saenz, with a Chair in Council, I dress for effect. Right now you need all the effect you can manage: it will do no good, and much harm, for you to skulk around headquarters looking ashamed of yourself. It helps people think you're guilty.'

Hair, clothes, even a session in a day spa, from which she emerged feeling utterly relaxed. Two days after they'd left, when her new clothes were stowed in her compartment, Marta led her back to the lieutenant commander in charge of Esmay's section.

'Here she is – you can have her back for a while, but I may need her again. Thank you, Lieutenant Suiza; you've been most helpful.'

Lieutenant Commander Moslin looked from one to the other. 'You're . . . satisfied, Sera Saenz?'

'With Lieutenant Suiza? Of course. Best personal assistant I ever had. Excuse me; I mustn't be late to meet Admiral Serrano.' With a wave, Marta departed, leaving Esmay under the lieutenant commander's mistrustful gaze.

'Well . . . I thought she was Lord Thornbuckle's friend, and here she's sticking up for you . . .'

'I think,' Esmay said, following Marta's briefing, 'I remind her of a niece or something. But of course I did my best.'

'Yes. Well. I suppose you can get back to that report you were working on . . .'

Esmay could feel his gaze on her as she walked off. She knew he had sensed some difference, but couldn't pinpoint it. She could . . . and was amazed that she had never bothered to learn such simple things before. She saw Casea Ferradi coming toward her, and assumed the expression Marta had recommended. Sure enough, Casea almost stumbled.

'Lieutenant Suiza—'

'Hello, Casea,' Esmay said, inwardly amazed and delighted.

'You're – I thought you were on leave.'

'I'm back,' Esmay said. 'But busy – see you later.' It could be fun. It could actually be fun. Buoyed up by that thought, she smiled serenely at Admiral Hornan around the next corner.

Barin came to attention. 'Ensign Serrano reporting, sir.'

His grandmother looked up. 'At ease, Ensign. Have a seat. We have family business to discuss.'

Family business did not put him at ease, but he sat and waited. His grandmother sighed.

'Marta Saenz tells me that you and Lieutenant Suiza had a row over Brun Meager.'

656

Barin almost let his jaw drop, but tightened it in time. 'That's . . . not exactly how it happened, sir.'

'Mmm. Well, however it happened, and whatever the current status of your feeling for Lieutenant Suiza may be, I wanted you to know that from my perspective, as your grandmother, I have no advice to give. About her, at least. About someone else you've been seen with, I have the advice you can probably guess. As an admiral, I would like to see Lieutenant Suiza perform at her best – she has a strikingly good best – and would like whatever circumstances might contribute to that end, to happen. So if you feel you can do her some good, go ahead.'

'She's – not speaking to me.'

'Are you sure? Perhaps she thinks you're not speaking to her. Especially since there are others who might have an interest in keeping you two apart.'

'Lieutenant Ferradi—' Barin said, through clenched teeth.

His grandmother looked at him as if he were a toddler; he knew that look. 'Among others. Barin, you're old enough to know how our family name attracts envy as well as admiration. Lieutenant Suiza's rapid rise to fame and promotion has had a similar effect. It has come to my attention that there are people who feel it in their interests to have you and Lieutenant Suiza at cross purposes. If you did not care for her, it would be one thing, but since you do, it seems to me that it is a matter of family honor not to let them succeed. Subject, of course, to your own feelings.'

'Ah . . . yes, sir – Grandmother.'

She gave him a frank grin. 'Sir Grandmother must be an unusual title, but I'll take it. Seriously, Barin – do you love this woman?'

'I thought I did, but—'

'Well, think again. Think, but also feel. It is not for me to play Cupid; if you two are meant for each other, you shouldn't need a Cupid. But take nothing for granted. Clear?'

'Yes . . . Grandmother.'

'Good. If there's fallout, I'll deal with it. I trust your judgement, Barin – just be sure you have enough data to base it on.' She paused, but he said nothing. What was there to say? With a crisp nod, she reverted from grandmother to admiral. 'Now – how's that investigation of Lieutenant Ferradi coming?'

'I don't know,' Barin said. 'Both my captain and my exec told me to keep my nose somewhere else, so I have.'

'Amazing,' his grandmother murmured, in a tone that made his ears heat up. 'Well, we're closing in on our active dates – it would be a help to me to know what's going on. I'd like you to go mention that to Heris, and let her murmur it to your captain's ear – or whatever it takes. Klaus still wants my job, and since he hasn't commanded anything but a desk for the past nineteen years, I'm unwilling to let him make a hash of it. Your ostensible message to Heris is that we're having a family celebration since the Fleet Birthday festivities will be very restrained this year. This is what you can – and should – tell anyone. But carry this—' she handed over a data strip. 'For her hand only, and use the family hand-shake.'

'Yes, sir.'

'Dismissed.'

'She's a natural-born weasel,' Koutsoudas said, pointing out the graphic he had made of Lieutenant Ferradi's illicit activities in the legal database. 'If we hadn't had that primed datawand, she might've got away with it, even with me on scan.'

'Well, what has she done?' asked Captain Escovar.

'She used Pell's access codes into the first level, and then someone else's – would you believe Admiral Hornan's?'

'How'd she get those?'

'I have no idea, sir.' Koutsoudas was watching the vid screen now, on which Lieutenant Ferradi's neat blonde head was bent studiously over a console. 'Possibly from Pell . . . and while it's none of my business, you should probably know there's rumors that Pell's been called in for an off-cycle physical.'

'So he has,' Escovar said.

'And three other master chiefs here as well . . . it's making some of us nervous, tell you the truth.'

'In what way?'

'Beyond my area of expertise, sir.' Koutsoudas had the expression of a man not in the mood to trust anyone.

'Mm. Concerns have been expressed at higher levels than mine, as well.'

'Just as well, sir. Ah – there she goes.' Onscreen, Ferradi inserted her datawand into a port in the console. 'Bet she inputs a file this time – look at her left hand. Yeah – there it is.' On Koutsoudas' graphic, an orange line snaked along a tangle of other lines, and made its way into a blue box, where it flashed steadily. 'Altering data, sir: that's one hundred percent clear.'

'Do we know what the data were prior to alteration?'

'I don't, no sir. But I do know there was a secure backup made last night, blind copy to a storage unit she'll never find. And the trace on her wand will prove she altered something, and where in the file it is.'

'These are very serious charges, Commander Escovar,' Admiral Hornan said. 'I've found Lieutenant Ferradi to be a most efficient officer . . .' His glance at Barin mixed suspicion and resentment in equal portions. Barin reminded himself that this man was his grandmother's rival.

'The admiral is right – these are serious charges. That is why I brought them to you rather than calling Lieutenant Ferradi in myself. Under the circumstances – political as well as military – it seemed preferable to have you in on this from the beginning—'

'Not the beginning, if you've already done the investigation—'

'Only enough to be sure the original allegation was founded on fact, Admiral. There's more to do—'

'Well, let's just hear her side of it—' Hornan touched his comunit. 'Lieutenant Ferradi, would you come in, please?'

'Right away, Admiral.' The slightest pause, then, 'Should I bring the latest information from that database search the admiral asked about?'

'Uh – not right now, Lieutenant.' A flush crept up Hornan's neck. Barin dared a sidelong glance at Escovar and saw that he had not missed it. So . . . just how deep into this was Hornan?

In only a few moments, Casea Ferradi came into the admiral's office, wide-eyed and smiling, a smile that widened into a quick grin meant to be complicit when she saw Barin, and sobered when no one smiled back.

'Admiral?'

'Casea – Lieutenant – these officers have made some serious charges against you. I want to know what you have to say.'

'Against me?' For just an instant, in profile, Barin saw a flicker that might have been panic, but her calm returned. 'Why – what am I supposed to have done?' She looked at Barin. 'Did I bother poor Ensign Serrano? I didn't mean to . . .'

Hornan cleared his throat. 'No . . . Lieutenant, I must ask: have you accessed any Fleet records which you are not cleared to access?'

'Of course not,' Ferradi said. 'Not without specific orders to do so.'

'Which would give you authorization, yes. Are you sure of that?'

'Yes, Admiral,' Ferradi said. Barin watched the pulse in her neck beat a little faster.

'Have you altered any data in any records whatsoever?'

'You mean like – watch records or something? No, sir.'

'Or in a database? Have you ever intruded into a database and altered records?'

'Not without specific orders to do so, no, Admiral.' But that telltale pulse was faster now.

'Then if I told you that you were alleged to have intruded into the records of the investigations surrounding the mutiny on *Despite*, and alleged to have changed certain files containing interview data on Lieutenant Esmay Suiza, you would deny it.'

'I would, Admiral.' Ferradi flushed suddenly. 'I deny it absolutely, and moreover I would consider the source.' She rounded on Barin. 'Ensign Serrano, Admiral, has a grudge against me . . . he thought his family position gave him a right to . . . to take liberties beyond his rank. I had to be quite firm with him and he knows I could have reported him for harrassment. He probably made up this nonsense just to get back at me—'

Barin felt the blood rushing to his head, but a stern look from Escovar kept him silent. Admiral Hornan gave a short nod in Barin's direction, and cocked his head at Escovar.

'Well, Commander? I find the foolish behavior of a hot-blooded young man of a high-status family more likely than illegal acts by someone like Lieutenant Ferradi . . .'

'Admiral, with all due respect, that won't do. Lieutenant Ferradi was pursuing Ensign Serrano, not the other way around. I knew it, and so did everyone else on the ship. You will find references to Lieutenant Ferradi's behavior in her previous fitness reports; her present position in the last promotion cohort of her class reflects that behavior.'

'That's not true!' Ferradi said. Her high color was patchy now, flushing and fading on those perfect cheekbones.

'And while her sexual proclivities would not, in themselves, be cause for disciplinary action as long as she did not interfere with anyone's fitness for duty, her intrusion into secured databases, her altering of the data, and her lies about other officers – including Ensign Serrano – would be.'

'And you think you have proof of this?' Hornan asked. Barin watched Ferradi pale, as the change in his tone and expression got through to her. He could almost feel sympathy, because in that moment Hornan was changing sides, preparing to divest himself of an embarrassment.

'Yes. We have the records of such intrusion, from a datawand initialized for Lieutenant Ferradi, along with vid records of her using it that are contemporaneous with the intrusion and alteration.'

'I didn't . . .' Ferradi breathed. But the admiral did not look at her now.

'How detailed are these records?'

'Extremely, Admiral. They include all the authorization codes she used to complete her intrusion, and to fake – I presume – the orders for the alterations.'

Now the admiral did look at Ferradi, and Barin hoped very much no such look would ever be turned on him. 'I would have to see such proof,' he said slowly, with almost no expression. 'But if you have it—'

'We do, Admiral.'

'Then Lieutenant Ferradi is, as you say, facing serious charges. Lieutenant, your datawand, if you please.'

Ferradi pulled it out slowly, and laid it on the admiral's desk.

'And that report you were working on is – where, Lieutenant?'

'On my desk, Admiral. But the admiral knows who—'

'You will consider yourself confined to quarters, Lieutenant. You will speak to no one except the investigating officer, when such has been appointed.'

'But Admiral – it's a plot – it's—'

'Dismissed, Lieutenant.'

Barin shivered as she turned and passed him. He had disliked her; he had come to despise her; for what she had almost done to Esmay, he could have hated her. But he would have wished on no one the devastation he saw deep in those violet eyes.

When the door had closed, Escovar said, 'Admiral – she used your access codes. I'm afraid there's no way to keep that out of the records.'

'Well – she would, wouldn't she, if she wanted to alter data? She'd have to have someone with enough authority.'

'Did you give her those codes?'

Hornan pulled himself up. 'Commander, I may have been an idiot, but you are not the person who will handle the investigation of this matter. It goes to internal security, as you very well know. And I will answer their questions, to the best of my ability, but not yours.' He paused, then went on. 'I supposed you're going to tell me I now have to revise my opinion of Lieutenant Suiza?'

'No, Admiral, I'm not. What the admiral thinks of Lieutenant Suiza is the admiral's business; she's not my officer. But if the data are tainted—'

'Oh yes, oh yes.' Hornan waved a hand. 'First things first. We have to inform internal security, and then Grand Admiral Savanche. He's going to be so pleased about this! Just what he needs, something else to worry about—' He hit the comunit control so hard it double-buzzed. 'Get me internal security—'

'Admiral Serrano's going to have a clear run with the task force,' Escovar commented on the way back to *Gyrfalcon*.

'Why, sir?'

'Because Hornan's not going to risk what you might say if he tries for it. Don't play stupid, Ensign – you know as well as I do that he must have been involved at some level. For one thing Ferradi isn't smart enough to get his codes without his help. And Pell couldn't help her – he couldn't remember his own codes, let alone the admiral's. Now if that civilian – Lady Marta whatshername – can put a collar on Lord Thornbuckle, we might finally get this rescue attempt off the ground.'

'Sir.'

'It's been a mess,' Escovar went on, lengthening his stride. 'It wouldn't have been easy anyway, but Thornbuckle's been more hindrance than help, and Hornan has kept putting obstacles in the way – and I would never have suspected that nailing Ferradi would get rid of the other problems, too.'

Such as what to do about Esmay Suiza. Barin waited for his captain's dismissal, then made his way to the first public com booth he could find, and looked up Esmay's comcode. She had one now, he was glad to see.

Her voice answered, crisp and professional.

'Lieutenant – it's Ensign Serrano. I—' How was he going to say this? 'I'd like – I need – to talk to you.'

A long pause, during which he felt himself turning hot, then cold, then hot again.

'In the office, or – I mean—' Her voice had softened, and sounded almost as tentative as his.

'Anywhere. There's something you need to know, and be-sides—' *Besides, I love you madly* was not something he could say over a public line.

'How about the base library. Ten minutes? Fifteen?'

'Fifteen; I'm just outside *Gyrfalcon*.'

He made it in ten, nonetheless, not realizing until he almost overran a pair of commanders strolling ahead of him just how fast he was going. Patience. Calmness. He paused in the library entrance, and didn't see her coming in either direction. Ducked inside, and – there she was.

'Lieutenant . . .'

'Ensign.' But her eyes glowed; her whole being glowed. And there were people who had thought he might be attracted to Casea Ferradi!

'I'm so sorry—' he said, and found that his words had tangled with hers. The same words. Silently, he looked at her, and she looked back.

*   *   *

663

Waltraude Meyerson had been watching the young female officer's lame attempt to pretend an interest in the online catalog. She was waiting for someone; it was not the first time Waltraude had seen a student hanging around waiting for another; she could not mistake it. Sure enough, a few minutes later a young male officer arrived. They spoke; they paused; they blushed and stammered. It was all very normal, but also very distracting when she was trying to correlate Professor Lemon's data with her own for the impeccably organized report she would present in a few hours.

The librarian was, of course, nowhere to be seen; he never was at this time of day. That didn't bother Waltraude ordinarily, since she didn't need his help to navigate her own and Professor Lemon's databases, but he was responsible for keeping order. Without his direction, and left to their own devices, these two would murmur sweet nothings for hours . . . she knew their type. Waltraude rose to her full height and cleared her throat. The two looked at her with the guilty expression typical of young love.

'This is a library, not a trysting place,' Waltraude said firmly. 'Kindly go pursue your passion elsewhere.' Shock blanked their expressions for a moment, then they turned and left quickly. Better. Perhaps now she could find a way to convince these military people that the key to extracting people from a hostile society would come from better thinking, not more guns.

'I love you madly,' Barin said, the moment they got out the door.

'Me, too,' said Esmay, and blinked back tears. Then she giggled. 'Wasn't she *awful*?'

'Yes – oh, Esmay, let's not ever *ever* fight again.'

'My cousin Luci says people in love can fight and get over it.'

'And her background is—?'

'More experience than I've got. She said I was an idiot.'

'Maybe,' Barin said, daring to close in, after a quick look up and down the corridor, and smell her hair. 'But you're *my* idiot.' He looked her up and down. 'Dear idiot. Lieutenant, sir.' He felt like dancing down the corridor, or walking on his hands, or something equally ridiculous. 'Oh, and by the way – Lieutenant Ferradi is confined to quarters and will be facing charges.'

'What!?'

'I can't tell you all of it – I mean, I'd better not, at least not out here, but that's why I had to avoid you after you got back – I was supposed to pretend to go along with her.'

'I think she lied about me,' Esmay said.

'She did more than that – she was trying to insert incriminating stuff in your old personnel and legal files. But we really shouldn't discuss that right now.'

'Fine. Let's discuss—'

'Us,' Barin said. 'Maybe with something to eat?'

'So – now that your agent has confirmed that she's there, and knows where she is – we get to the specifics.' The speaker, a commander with the shoulder flashes of headquarters staff, put up a chart. 'It's not unheard of for men to sneak over the back wall of the nursery compound for a quick poke at some woman they particularly want. He can grab her, bundle her into his groundcar, and be out of the city in twenty minutes.'

It sounded like a ridiculous plan to Marta, but she had given up trying to convince them that they had to cooperate with Brun, not treat her like lost luggage. She glanced across the room at Professor Meyerson, who had come with her usual stack of books, papers, and data cubes. Meyerson had footnotes and bibliography to back up her views – which were similar to Marta's – but that hadn't worked either.

'What if she resists?' asked a female commander across the room. 'How will she know this man is our agent?'

'He can tell her,' the first commander said.

And she's supposed to believe that, Marta thought, after almost two years of captivity? It might work, or Brun – being Brun – might clobber the fellow and take the car herself. And then where would they be? She would have no idea where to go, and they would have no idea what had happened.

'He tells us that for enough money he can get her passage offworld in a small atmospheric shuttle. He will take her out of the city, provide a disguise, and then send her to this other person. Our present plan is to insert an SAR – which can approach quite close in microjumps – to pick her up, with the rest of the task force standing by at a distance in case of trouble.'

Someone else asked the question Marta wanted to ask, about system defenses, and she listened to the answer with half her mind, the other half wondering what Brun was doing. Not sitting still waiting to be rescued, that much she was sure of.

Brun picked up the paring knife, and slid it into her sleeve. The matron was supposed to count the knives each day, but she didn't. She liked to doze in her own room, after swigging from an earthenware jar, and a good half the time left the kitchen unlocked. Brun had checked that repeatedly, making sure that her theft had a reasonable chance of going unnoticed.

The knife's pressure against her arm, under the bands she'd tied to hold it, gave her courage again. She had waited as long as she could; she dared not wait longer for rescue. Neither she nor her babies had to live in this place . . . but when she laid the blade to the moist soft neck of the sleeping redhead (she was sure which *his* father was), she knew she could not do it. She didn't love the babies, not as mothers were reputed to do, the way the other mothers here seemed to love theirs, but she didn't hate them, either. It was not their fault; they had not engendered themselves on her unwilling body.

She could not take them with her when she escaped, though. She was going to have to disguise herself as a man, somehow . . . and men did not carry babies around the streets, even if two squirming and all-too-vocal babies would not have slowed her down too much. If she left them behind, they would be squalling for their next meal in just an hour or so . . . yet she could not face killing them, just to give herself a longer start.

Another idea occurred to her. Though the nursery had no drugs that she knew – and she knew nothing about which, if any, of the herbs in the pantry might put the babies to sleep, there was a simple soporific available to anyone with access to fruit and water and a little time.

In late afternoon she walked as usual in the orchard, carrying one baby on her back and the other in front. Her feet had toughened; the gravel paths no longer hurt her. Beneath the long skirt, her legs had developed ropes of hard muscle from the exercises she'd sweated on. Without the babies, she would be able to move fast and far; she would be able to fight, if she was not taken off-guard. She did not intend to be off-guard again. If only she knew *where* . . . where to find Hazel and the little girls, where to find open country in which – she was sure – she could hide.

Out of sight of the house, she slid the knife into her hand, and then laid it in the crotch of an apple tree. She checked to be sure that the blade would not glint in the light and catch someone's eye. She stuffed some of last year's fallen leaves around it, and strolled on, coming back to the house with a spray of wildflowers in her hand.

Two days later, she pilfered a jug from the kitchen. She carried it into the orchard, concealed in the sling she now used to carry the babies. It was the wrong season for ripe fruit, but she had dried fruit, always available to the women, honey, and water.

The mix fermented in only a few days of warm sunshine. It smelled odd, but definitely alcoholic. She tasted it cautiously. It had a kick . . . enough, she hoped, to put the babies heavily to sleep.

Sector VII HQ

As the task force planning crept onward, Marta kept a weather eye on Bunny. He had not softened his opposition to Esmay Suiza, even when it became obvious that much of the evidence against her had been lies and more lies. Why not? She had known him most of his life; he was neither stupid nor vicious. His reputation for staying calm in a crisis, and being fair to all parties, had made him the one person the Grand Council would trust after Kemtre's abdication. So why was he, at this late date, trying to make sure Suiza didn't go with the task force?

She was tempted to contact Miranda, conspicuously absent, but refrained. Never get between man and wife, her grandmother had taught her, and in her life she'd seen nothing but grief come of it when someone tried. So, five days before the task force was due to depart, she tackled him privately.

'Don't start,' Bunny said, before she even opened her mouth. 'You're going to tell me Suiza isn't that bad, that she's earned her slot as exec on *Shrike*, that it's not fair to pull her off—'

'No,' Marta said. 'I'm going to ask you why you blame Suiza for Brun's behavior.'

'She drove her into a frenzy—' Bunny began. Marta interrupted. 'Bunny – who chose Brun's genome pattern?'

'We did, of course—'

'Including her personality profile?'

'Well . . . . yes, but—'

'You told me before, you deliberately chose a risk-taking profile. You chose outgoing, quick-reacting, risk-taking, a girl who would always find the glass half-full, and think a roomful of manure meant a cute pony around the corner.'

'Yes . . .'

'And you got a charming, lovable scapegrace, full of mischief as a basket of kittens, and you enjoyed it for years, didn't you?'

'Yes, but—'

'You spoiled her, Bunny.' He stared at her, his ears reddening. 'You chose for her a personality profile, a physical type, and a level of intelligence which would *predictably* make her likely to get into certain kinds of trouble . . . and what did you do, in her young days, to provide the counterbalance she needed, of judgement and self-control?'

'We'd had other children, Marta. We were experienced parents—'

'Yes, for the bright conformists you designed first. And they turned out well – you had given them what they needed.' Marta calculated the pause, then went on. 'Did you give Brun what she needed?'

'We gave her everything—' But his gaze wavered.

'Bunny, I know this sounds like condemnation, but it's not. Brun is a very unusual young woman, and she would have needed a very unusual childhood to bring her to her present age able to handle her talents safely. It's no wonder you and Miranda, enchanted just like everyone else with that explosion of joy, didn't provide the kind of background that would do her good.' She paused again; Bunny almost nodded – she could see the softening of the muscles in his neck. 'But it's my opinion that your real objection to Esmay Suiza – perhaps unknown to you – is that she's like Brun with a throttle, with controls. And her father, whatever he's like, did a better job for his daughter than you did for yours.'

Bunny reddened again. 'She's not anything—'

'Oh yes, she is. Have you read the combat reports on her? I have. Intelligent, very. Charismatic – yes, especially in a crisis. Risktaker – she came back to Xavier and saved the planet – and incidentally, Brun. Brun thought they had a lot in common; that's why she was dogging Suiza like a little girl tagging a big sister.'

'I . . . can't believe that.'

'I can't believe you're still not seeing your own part in this. That's why you didn't want Miranda out here, isn't it? She'd admit it, and she'd argue with you.'

'I . . . I . . . can't . . .'

'Bunny, it's still not your fault. I think you made mistakes, but so does every parent – your father certainly did with you. But it's also not Lieutenant Suiza's fault. She didn't drive Brun into a mindless frenzy that lasted thirty-odd days. She had a quarrel which would've been over with the next day if they'd had a chance to make up – and in your heart you know that. Channel your rage where it should go, to those thugs who took her, and quit trying to lay your guilt on Suiza.'

He was looking away from her; she waited until the muscle in his jaw quit twitching.

'We need everyone's best, to get her out,' Marta said, more gently. 'Lieutenant Suiza's best is very good – and it could save Brun's life.'

'All right.' He had not moved, but the tension had gone out of him. 'As far as I'm concerned, she can go. But . . . but if she does *anything* to harm Brun's chances—'

'I will personally take her hide off in strips,' Marta said. 'Nice narrow ones, very slowly. With Miranda on the other side, and Vida Serrano in the middle. And you can have her kidneys on toast, for all I care.'

That got a laugh, though a choked one. 'It's so small a chance,' Bunny said, after a pause. Marta could hear the tears close to the surface. 'So small . . .'

'You just increased it,' Marta said. 'Now – shall I tell the admiral, or will you?'

19

The man in the checked shirt, true to his persona as country bumpkin in the city, had wandered up and down the various streets, visiting the breeding houses once or twice, and coming again to look at the showing of the yellow-haired infidel from space. He had told several men at the bar he frequented that he was afraid she wouldn't be released for breeding before he had to go back 'up the hills.' Finally one of the men made the suggestion he'd been waiting for . . . go around to the back of the orchard, and wait for her. No harm done if she was bred a few weeks early, and likely no one would ever know. Watch a day or so, see when she went out, and who went with her.

He was watching when she went to the last-but-one apple tree and put something in its crotch. Well. That was interesting. She looked a lot more like what he'd expected out here, in the orchard, than during the showings. But would she cooperate, when the time came? If she wouldn't, he'd have to drug her – and she would be difficult to lug over the wall, big as she was. And it looked like she might have plans of her own . . . he hoped they wouldn't trip him up. He walked on, and made his arrangements. He needed a groundcar; he walked across the city to rent it for cash from the spaceport vendor.

Simplicity – an apt name, Brun thought – had told her about all sorts of things the other women mentioned only in passing. She realized that they could not imagine not knowing, while Simplicity was fascinated anew with every detail of her life. Unlike Brun, she kept track of time, and in her artless chatter had revealed the clues that let Brun begin tracking market days even while confined to the nursery. She had not previously paid attention to what the staff carried in their hands when they went out . . . but now noticed the size and shape of the baskets and bags, and their contents when they returned. From that, she thought she had a schedule figured out. Someone went out every day to get small amounts of fresh greens. Three times a week, several of the staff women went out and returned with a wide variety of supplies, not merely food but also needles, pins, thread, yarn, scrub brushes, hairbrushes, soap . . . whatever was needed for daily work which the women could not supply for themselves.

Starting with their holy day, they had market day, then skip two, then market day, then skip one, then market day, then holy day. The week's rhythm revolved around the holy day, rising in tension toward it . . . so Brun decided that the first market day would be the best for her purposes. Several of the staff women would be gone, and everyone would be more relaxed after the rigors of the holy day . . . ready to do the least in daily chores, to relax with the babies in the garden enclosures in the soft spring air. None of them walked as much in the orchard as she did, unless the staff directed, which they did only around harvest time.

The hard thing would be to find the house where Hazel stayed, since she could not ask questions – and to conceal her muteness. She did not know if men were ever muted – probably not, since their beliefs required them to recite from the sacred texts daily – or whether some men might be mute from birth or accident, but she suspected that a mute man might be subject to investigation. Still, she knew it was a large household near a market.

Simplicity had described the house at length: its gardens, its weaving shed, its woolhouse, its several kitchens, the quarters for children, for wives, for the master – she had once been allowed to sweep there, but she had knocked over a little table. They had not punished her, but she had been banished to parts of the house with fewer breakables . . . which had been a relief, Simplicity had said, smiling, because she didn't have to worry so much. What she could not describe – what it never occurred to her to describe – was its location. Brun realized the girl had hardly ever been out of

671

it, and thus had no way to describe where it was in relation to anything else.

On the midweek market day before she planned to go, Brun decided to test her plans. She would nurse the babes to fullness, mingling a little of the home brew into her milk . . . they were greedy feeders, and she had discovered that if she dripped sugared fruit juice down her breast, they'd take it along with her milk. Then she'd see how long they slept . . . which would give her some idea how long she had to find Hazel.

She finished her chores, and noticed that all but two of the staff had left to go to market. She picked up the babies, and caught the attention of one of the remaining staff women. She nodded toward the orchard.

'Go ahead, then. A good day for a walk,' the woman said. Brun mimed eating. 'Oh – you want to take your lunch out there? Fine. I'll ring the bell for you to come back, in case you fall asleep.'

Brun took a small loaf of bread, fresh-baked that morning, and sliced off a hunk of cheese, laying the knife neatly back in its place. The woman had poured her a jug of fruit juice and water – and on this day, Brun noticed that this was an unnecessary courtesy. She smiled; she could not help it. The woman smiled back, clearly pleased.

She could not afford this . . . offer of friendship, if that's what it was. She took the jug and her lunch, tucked them into the sling where the redhead lay content, shifted the back sling until the other baby was balanced better, and moved out onto the paved terrace between the nursery buildings and the orchard.

She strolled, in her usual way, along the right-hand path, pausing now and then to look up into the trees at the hard green fruit that would be ripe in a few months. This was not the day; this was merely practice. Why, then, was her heart beating so wildly that she felt it must be drumming loud enough to hear? Why was her breath coming short? She tried to relax, reaching out to stroke a branch heavy with fruit. But the babies caught her tension and began to squirm and whimper. The one in back flailed at her head with his arms.

That, oddly enough, steadied her. She moved on, more quickly now – though today there was no hurry – to her favorite spot near the far end of the orchard. When she'd first made it this far, up the little rise, she'd been able to see the building through bare branches, but now the orchard trees were in full leaf, and she knew they could no more see her, than she could see them.

She laid the babies down on the little quilts folded into the slings, and put her lunch down as well. The babies rolled and played, cooing, making wide-handed swipes at each other. She bit off a hunk of bread as she watched, thinking over her plan again, trying to improve it. But it was such a tissue of improbables . . . if she made it twice as good, she would still have less than one chance in a hundred of success.

The darker one found a leaf to explore, and managed, with great effort, to pick it up. The redhead noticed his brother was no longer paying attention, and put his own foot in his mouth instead. Brun finished eating, and by then they were getting fussy, looking at her. In her mind, she heard a voice somewhere between her own and Esmay's: *All right then. Let's do it.*

Nursing both at once was harder now that they were bigger, but she was used to it. She leaned back against the tree, and let her mind drift . . . one way or another, in less than seven days, she would be somewhere else. Maybe dead . . . she wasn't going to be taken alive, not again. But maybe . . . somewhere . . . she couldn't picture it, quite. Her mind threw up pictures from her past life – hills, valleys, forests, fields, island beaches, rocky ledges. The shuttlefield on Rotterdam, then the shuttle, rumbling down the runway, taking off, the sky darkening, darkening, the stars . . .

She shook her head abruptly. The twins had taken most of her milk; it was time to try out her brew. She added a little honey, to make it sweeter, and dribbled it into their mouths as they sucked. Redhead made a face, and snorted before going on, but the dark-haired one didn't pause in his rhythm.

She had no idea how much to use. Not as much today; she didn't want anyone to notice, and worry about them. Did babies go to sleep with a spoonful or a cup? She had no idea. Their sucking slowed, finally, and their mouths fell away . . . they gained a kilo whenever they fell asleep, she thought. Carefully, she laid them on the little quilts. Asleep like this . . . she could almost . . . but no. Not now. She told herself firmly what she already knew: they would be loved, cherished, given every opportunity this world held, because they were boys. That their mother had been an outlander heathen abomination would not affect the care given them.

They would look this way – this vulnerable, this beautiful – when she left them on the market day after the holy day. She stared at them, eyes narrowed. She could leave them – she *had* to leave them – and she would leave them.

She levered herself up and stood, fastening her dress and then stretching. She found the knife she had hidden, and turned it in her hands. She could go now . . . no. Better stick to her plan, such as it was. But one thing she could do, with a knife in hand. She might die – it was likely. Her family might not know where she was. But she could leave a record that would not be found until fall, if they noticed it then.

With the sharp tip of the paring knife she marked the tree under which the babies lay, thin scorings that would scar into visible marks later. Maybe. Her name, every syllable of it.

She wanted to write more. She wanted to scribble with that knife blade on every tree, saying what had been smothered all this time . . . but she stopped herself. No more indulgence. She had to try the wall today, to measure her strength against its height. She tied a length of yarn around the knife and hung it around her neck, then took the cloth strips she'd made and bound them tight around her breasts. When it was time to go, really time, she would bind her breasts before she fastened her dress . . . but this was only practice.

With a last glance at the sleeping babies, she turned and walked over to the wall. A last glance back, to make sure she could not been seen through the thick leaves . . . no. She turned to the wall again, steeling herself. It was the quiet time of day, after lunch. Chances were there was no one on the other side right now. If there were . . . if they saw her . . . she hesitated. Today was not *the* day. She didn't have to jump the wall today, and it would be disasterous if she were caught unprepared.

She looked back at the babies. Still sleeping. When she turned again to the wall, a man was looking over it. Brun stood frozen, immobilized with shock.

The man stared at her. 'Brun?' he said softly.

Her heart lurched, then pounded. Someone who knew her name – who *used* her name. It must be a rescue. She nodded, giddy with relief.

'Can you climb over?'

She nodded again, and a wad of brown cloth flew toward her. She dropped back, furious. But his voice came over the wall, urgent and barely loud enough to hear. 'Put that on. Cover your dress, and your hair. Not many have such light hair. Then wait for me to call – I'm watching for groundcars. Don't bring the babies; they'll be cared for.'

The babies. She had given them only a few drops each – would they sleep long enough? She yanked her long skirt up around her waist and ran to them, fumbled at the jug, and poured more of the honeyed brew onto her hand. Would they suck? Could they swallow? Their mouths caught at her finger, sucking, and she dribbled more brew into each mouth. Then she dragged the garment on – a hooded cloaklike thing, too warm for the day – and ran back to the wall. Even in those few moments, she was aware how *good* it felt to have her legs free, not bound by the narrow skirt. While she waited, she thought how to make him understand that they had to find Hazel and the little girls. She could not go without them; if she could not save her babies from this world's horrors, she must save them.

'Now,' he said. She stood up; the wall was not as tall as she was, and she made it easily. It was wide enough to lie on; she rolled the cloak around her and then dropped off, to be steadied by his waiting arm. 'Are the babies inside?' he asked. 'When will they cry?'

How did he think she could answer that? She mimed drinking, then sleeping, and he nodded.

'Come along,' he said. 'We have to get to the car.' He took her arm. 'Look down,' he reminded her. Fuming, Brun looked down at the rough pavement and went where he directed. She didn't want to argue with him in the street, where anyone might see, but she had to convince him about Hazel.

He stopped beside a groundcar parked in a row. He opened the driver's door, and then the back doors popped open. 'Get in,' he

675

said. She looked him full in the face, and mouthed *Hazel*. He paled. 'Look *down!* Get *in*,' he said. 'Before someone notices.'

She slipped into the back seat, and leaned forward, waiting for him. As soon as he closed his own door, she tapped his shoulder. He glanced back.

Hazel.

'I can't understand you. What's wrong?'

Damn the idiot fool. How had Lady Cecelia kept from bursting? There on the seat beside him were a map and notebook, with a pen. She reached over and snatched at it, wrote GET HAZEL in large letters, and then RANGER BOWIE HOUSE. He read, then paled even more.

'We can't do that! No one can get in there! Dammit, woman, you want off this planet or not?'

She tapped GET HAZEL again, glaring into his face, trying to give him a mind-to-mind transfusion of her determination.

'Who the hell is Hazel, anyway?'

She wrote again: GIRL ON SHIP. GET HER AWAY TOO.

'Can't do it,' he said, starting the groundcar. 'Now you sit back, and I'll take you where it's arranged—' The barrier between them started to rise; Brun lunged forward, putting her weight on it, and the barrier stopped, its mechanism whining loudly. 'Get *back*, you fool.' The mechanism that moved the barrier gave a grinding noise and died; the barrier slid back the small distance it had risen. She paid no attention, wriggling over the barrier into the front passenger seat. Up here the windows weren't frosted. The man jerked the groundcar out of its parking space and accelerated. 'Gods, woman, if they see you up here—'

She held the paper out: GET HAZEL.

'I can't, I tell you! The five Rangers are the most powerful men in town. Ever since Mitch Pardue got elected Ranger Bowie, he's been angling for the Captaincy. I can't barge in there and get some fool girl. I got you; that's what I contracted to do.'

Brun glanced at the groundcar controls, at his movements as he turned, slowed, sped up again, made another turn. Simple enough. After the next turn, she grabbed the wheel and yanked it hard. He yanked back, and stared at her long enough to almost hit another groundcar. 'Dammit! Woman! It's no wonder they muted you – Heaven knows what you'd say if you could talk!'

She scribbled rapidly on the notebook. GET HAZEL. IT'S MARKET DAY – SHE GOES OUT. MARKET NEAR RANGER BOWIE HOUSE. She pushed that in front of his face; the groundcar swerved again; she lowered it slightly, so he could read and see over it.

'Can't do it. Too dangerous. I have it all planned out—'

She poked a finger into his ear, hard, and laid the pruning knife on his thigh, pointed where he could not ignore it. The groundcar swerved wildly, then he got it back on his side of the street. 'You're crazy, you are. All right, we'll drive past Ranger Bowie house. And the damn market. But you've got to get in the back. If anyone sees—' He glanced at her, and she bared her teeth. 'All right, I said. I'll do it; we'll go past. But you're going to get us killed—'

With some care, Brun reversed herself into the back seat, making sure that she had enough weight on the barrier to prevent its coming back up, if the controls weren't actually broken. She laid the knife at the back of his neck . . . it would do no good there, unless it was strong enough to slide between the vertebrae, but she judged it too obvious to hold it to his throat.

'They told me you were wild, but they didn't tell me you were crazy,' the man grumbled. Brun grinned. They hadn't known what had been done to her, or they'd have known how crazy she was.

'That's Ranger Bowie's house,' the man said finally. Brun stared, uncertain. It was one of five huge houses arranged around the sides of a plaza . . . in the center was a huge five-pointed star outlined in flowers and grass. Pretty, really, if you weren't trying to escape the place. 'Ranger Houston, Ranger Crockett, Ranger Travis, and Ranger Lamar. Ranger Travis is Captain right now. The nearest market to Ranger Bowie's house is down this street . . . the women's service door is right down there, see?'

Brun saw a shadowed gap in the long stucco wall. As they drove past, she could see the door set back from the sidewalk, and the little alcove for the gate guard. They went past one cross street, then another. Ahead, down this street, a rope blocked off traffic beyond the next cross street.

'That's the market – groundcars can't go there. Nor you. Now you've seen there's nothing we can do, we can—'

Brun pressed the tip of the knife just below his ear. With her other hand she scrabbled for the pen and notebooks, and printed, GO AROUND, KEEP LOOKING.

On the third circuit, Brun spotted a woman walking toward Ranger Bowie House, baskets in each hand, still some blocks from it. Something about the quick, short shuffle caught her eye. She tapped the driver's shoulder.

'That her?' He eased the car closer.

It was hard to tell . . . the dark head bent forward, the slim body gliding along with those short, quick steps enforced by her dress. But as the car slid past, Brun caught a glimpse of the serious face, that tucked-in lower lip. She tapped the man's arm again, hard.

'I'm gonna regret this, I know I am.' But he pulled the car to the curb and got out.

'You. Girlie.' Hazel stopped, eyes on the ground. 'You from Ranger Bowie House?' She nodded. 'I got business there. Get in back.' He popped the rear doors. Brun could *feel* Hazel's confusion, her uncertainty, her near-panic. 'Hurry up now,' he said. 'I don't want to have to tell Mitch you're lazy.' She ducked into the car, then, eyes still down. Then she saw Brun, and her eyes widened. Brun grinned. The driver got back in, grumbling, and tried to raise the shield, but the mechanism made only a faint noise and the barrier didn't go up. 'Sit low,' the driver said, and drove off quickly.

'Brun . . . what . . . where . . . ?' Hazel's voice was soft as mothwings.

Brun mouthed *escape*, but Hazel shook her head. So Brun made a rocket of one hand, and jerked it upward. Hazel stared, then grinned.

'Really?' Hazel almost bounced on the seat with excitement, but her voice was soft. 'I was trying to figure a way – I'd found out where you were, an' all, an' I told Simplicity as much as I could without getting in trouble, hoping she'd see you—'

Brun nodded. She mimed the groundcar taking them to the rocket. She didn't know if that was the plan – she still didn't know

678

what the plan was – but surely that was the gist of it. Then she showed Hazel the notebook and wrote LITTLE GIRLS.

'We can't take them,' Hazel said.

YES.

'No – we can't – I already decided that, months ago. They're happy, they're safe, and they wouldn't make it anyway.'

Brun stared at Hazel. This . . . *child* had decided? But Hazel's expression didn't waver. She was not just a child.

'We have to,' Hazel said. 'Leastways—' Brun winced at the local expression. 'At least,' Hazel corrected, 'we have to try. You, for sure. And your babies?'

Brun shrugged, and wrote: CAN'T TAKE THEM. TOO RISKY. TOO LITTLE.

'See? Same with Brandy and Stassi. We can't do it.'

The driver spoke up. 'Glad one of you's got sense. All right now . . . we got us a little problem. I'd planned to pass Brun off as a man – brought along men's clothes for her; they're under the seat there – but I don't know what to do about . . . Hazel.'

Brun mimed a purchase to Hazel, and nodded to the driver. *Tell him.* Hazel looked scared, her mouth pinched tight. Then, in a high thin voice she said, 'Brun says buy some.'

'Buy some! Buy some, she says. And just how am I supposed to stop and buy some?'

But he pulled over a few streets further on, and made his way to a sidewalk vendor. Brun, peeking over the barrier, saw him choose blue pants, a brown shirt, and high-topped boots like most of the men wore, and a hat. He was back in just a few minutes, and when he started the car again, he threw the clothes over the barrier.

'You change now, both of you. Put your dresses under the seat. I'll get rid of 'em later. You'll have to cut your hair, but not here – mustn't leave hair in the car. I've got knives for both of you.'

As the car sped on, over the streets and then into the country-side on a roughly paved road, Brun and Hazel struggled with the confined space in the back seat, each other, and the clothes they had to get off and put on. Brun, having more to take off, went first; Hazel helped her bind her breasts as flat as she could. Then Hazel, and Brun tore a strip off the bottom of her dress to flatten Hazel as well. Getting into the long pants while trying to stay low, out of sight of passing groundcars, meant lying across the seat – and each other. Hardest to put on were the boots – stiff leather on feet that had been bare for more than a year. It would all have been funny if they hadn't been so afraid of being caught, and they actually did giggle when they finally stuffed the hated dresses under the seat. Brun felt it had been worth it already – she had not laughed, really laughed, since her capture, and even though she could make no sound, the laughter eased her. Hazel tucked her hair up, and jammed the hat on her head; Brun pushed her hat down on top of her head.

Hazel, Brun thought, looked like a real person again. She sat leaning forward now, eyes sparkling with excitement, her face no longer obscured by hair. Her clothes fit a little loose and the sleeves of her shirt were up the wrist a little, as if she had almost grown out of them. Hazel looked at her, smiling, and then lifted Brun's hat to push her hair more firmly under it. Brun felt that her own pants were bulky and too loose – but anything was better than that clinging skirt.

Their driver glanced back. 'Not likely to be seen, out here,' he said. 'You do look different, I'll say that. You aren't embarrassed to wear men's clothes?'

Brun shook her head.

'Well, that's good, because they're gonna be looking for two women in dresses, not two men. Remember now, you have to walk like men – big steps – and look other men straight in the eye. We – they – don't like shifty folk. Now I'm gonna let you off up here in about a mile—' Whatever distance that was . . . Brun still hadn't figured out feet and inches and ells. 'And then you'll have to hike over them hills—' He pointed at a line of hills ahead. 'Soon's you're out of sight, you got to cut your hair *real* short, like no woman would. So you can take your hat off without bein' spotted as women. You take your hat off to womenfolk, even though they aren't supposed to look at you – it's polite. And men'll see you.'

The map he gave them, along with a canteen and a packet of food, was supposed to guide them on the next stage. Brun looked at it and grinned in relief. Someone had marked it in standard measurements, not this planet's idiot miles. Someone had also printed, in a hand she thought she knew, *Brun – we're here*.

From the pulloff, a trail led up into the hills. A sign-post had a string of names on it; Brun ignored them. After a few wavery strides, her legs remembered how to stretch, and she found her balance in the ridiculous boots. Hazel staggered once, grimaced, but moved up beside her.

They were out of sight of the road in less than a hundred meters, and into thick scrub. Brun made scissor movements next to her head, and Hazel nodded. They slipped off the trail and into the head-high bushes, to do some barbering.

Brun made it clear, with gestures, that they must catch the hairs they cut off. She had no idea what to do with them, but they weren't going to leave them around as obvious trail markers. As her hair came off, as the wind reached her scalp, she felt her brain cooling, felt the lessons she'd been taught in the Fleet Escape and Evasion course coming back to her. She twisted the cut hanks of her own hair into a roll of the appropriate size, put it in one of the spare socks, and stuffed it down the front of her pants. Hazel goggled, then choked back a laugh that was half shock. Brun shrugged, and swaggered a few steps. *We're men; we need men things.* Hazel had less hair for hers, but she was younger anyway. And it did make her look more like a boy.

She struggled up the trail in those ridiculous boots . . . she'd have been more comfortable barefoot but men didn't go barefoot. Stupid people, she thought. Only really stupid people would assign footgear on the basis of gender rather than use, and choose these blistering boots for walking somewhere.

Hazel would have talked, but Brun waved her to silence. Voices carried, in the open, and Hazel's soft voice wasn't very boylike. Brun didn't know if she could do a boy's voice, and didn't want to find out she couldn't.

So when they heard the men talking, she had a few seconds warning. She caught Hazel's eye, jerked her chin up, and walked on. Around the next curve in the path came a pair of men, dressed much as she and Hazel were, though one of them had a bundle on his back. Brun stared straight at the first man, then the second, and tightened her lips. They gave her a short nod, and strode by in silence. Brun felt herself start to shake and lengthened her stride. Hazel grabbed her arm and squeezed, hard. Brun nodded. Neither looked behind as they struggled on up the hill.

They had made it over the first ridge, and halfway up the second, when Brun's breasts began to throb. She glanced at the sky. Drat. The twins would be waking now, beginning to whimper, even if no one had found them before.

'What?' asked Hazel softly. Brun put her hands to her breasts and winced. Hazel said 'Swelling?' Brun nodded. Minute by minute, they throbbed more, until she felt she could not stand it . . . but her feet hurt almost as much.

Take your pick, she thought. At least you're out here. And she took as deep a breath as she could of the fresh hill air. She would walk her feet to bloody stubs, and let her breasts explode before she would go back to that miserable nursery.

'You miss your babies?' Hazel asked.

Brun shook her head violently. Hazel looked shocked; Brun regretted her vehemence, but . . . she felt what she felt. If they had been someone else's babies, she might have felt a pang of softness for them, she had liked babies, when someone else took care of them – but not these. She set her face resolutely to the trail and struggled on.

Near sundown they came to the clearing marked on Brun's map. Here they were supposed to be met . . . or she was; whoever it was wouldn't expect Hazel.

The man who stepped out of the shadow of the trees not only didn't expect Hazel, he didn't want her. 'I didn't get paid for two,' he said roughly. 'What are you trying to pull, missy?' Brun glared at him. Then she took the notebook from Hazel and wrote SHE GOES TOO.

'I wasn't paid . . .' the man began. Brun made the universal signal for money – and saw it recognized, proving once again that humans had a common origin, something she'd been willing to doubt this past year and more. She pointed to the sky, then rubbed her fingers again. Money there, if you get us there. The man spat.

'All right. But I don't want to hear any complaints when it's crowded in the shuttle.'

Brun stared around. Shuttle here? This was no shuttlefield. But the man was walking quickly along the shadowed edge of the clearing, and she followed.

'We got us a ways to go, and I guess it's lucky I brung a extra. Hope you can ride.' With that, he ducked into the trees and Brun smelled . . . horses.

This was not how she'd planned to ride again. She had imagined herself on one of her father's hunters, galloping over the fields of home. Instead, Brun had to stretch her sore legs on the wide barrel of a brown horse with all the character of a sofa, because Hazel, who had never been on a horse before, had to have a saddle. The man swore he couldn't ride bareback – and if he was used to that armchair for a saddle, no wonder. At least her body had not forgotten that balance.

'By God, you *can* ride,' the man said, as she moved up beside him. Brun smiled, thinking nonsmiling thoughts, and he looked over at Hazel. 'That's it,' he said. Brun glanced over; Hazel looked terrified. She was clutching the knob that stuck up from the front of the saddle as if it could anchor her, and trying to strangle the horse with her legs. Brun caught her eye, and gestured down her own body: *Sit straight, head up, relax your legs.* Hazel straightened.

They rode through the night, meeting no one at all on the trail. Brun shifted as one spot after another wore raw. She had wanted to wear pants again; she had wanted to ride again, but this – she thought of the old saw about being careful what you asked for. The man spoke occasionally: 'That way's Lem's cabin.' 'Over there's the pass to Smoky's place.'

When first light began to give shape to the treetops on the slopes above them, their guide slowed. 'It's only a tad more,' he said. 'Just down this slope.' At the foot of the slope, they came out of trees and brush to find a long grassy field ending in a steep hill. Brun could not see anything resembling a shuttle. Was this a trap after all? But the man led the way along the edge of the field, and she realized it might be a grass runway. It was longer than it looked; when she glanced back along it, the far end was hidden in ground fog. The hill, as they neared it, revealed a hangar door set into it. That was promising. Set back under the trees was a log cabin with a peaked roof; beyond it was a larger log building, a barn, and in between was an enclosure of peeled poles where two more horses and a cow munched hay.

The man led them up to a gate set into the enclosure, and swung off his horse as if he'd only ridden an hour or so, not all night. Neither Brun nor Hazel could dismount alone. The man had to help them, pushing and tugging. He swore at them. Brun wished for the ability to swear back. She had not been on a horse in years, and in between she'd borne twins – what did he expect after riding all night bareback? She was sure she'd worn all the skin off her thighs and buttocks. As for Hazel, she'd never ridden before; she'd be lucky if she could walk at all in a few hours.

In the cabin, a stocky woman prepared breakfast for all of them. She never looked at them, never spoke, but set plates in front of them and kept them full. Brun raged inwardly, but they could not take all the women on this planet. I will come back, she vowed silently. Somehow . . .

After breakfast, Brun managed to stand up; she gave Hazel a hand. Outside, the man was opening the hangar door, and at last Brun could see what was waiting for them. Her grin broadened. It was a little mixed-purpose shuttle, the same kind she'd been in when Cecelia had sent her back to Rockhouse. She could fly it herself if she had to. She thought briefly of knocking the man on the head and doing just that, but she had no idea how he planned to evade Traffic Control – if this place even had Traffic Control. It did have warplanes, though, and she had no desire to meet them.

With considerable difficulty, Brun helped Hazel up the narrow ladder into the shuttle. The man was already busy at the controls; he glowered when Brun made her way forward and settled herself in the other control seat. 'Don't touch anything!' he said sharply. Brun watched. Everything looked much the same as on Corey's ship. Although the names of the measures were strange, she could identify most of the instruments. The man ran down the same sort of checklist.

The little craft bumped its way down the field, engines screaming, gaining speed with every meter. But could it possibly be enough? The trees at the far end approached too rapidly – Brun could remember going much faster than this at Rotterdam. Suddenly, the shuttle rose into the air as if hoisted on a crane . . .'

'Short field ability,' the man said, grinning. 'Surprised you, didn't I? She needs a third less runway, and she can clear a hundred feet when she goes up.'

Sun streamed in the cockpit windows; Brun stared avidly at the control panel. Her mind had been so hungry, all this time, for something real, something to do. She glanced back at Hazel; the girl grinned, pointing to the gauges. Yes – a spacer girl, she would have had the same hunger. But now Hazel was looking out and down, at the shadowy folds of hills and valleys receding as they rose. Was this, perhaps, her first planet? Brun had never thought of that. Higher . . . there was a river, winding between hills, with a roll of ground fog like wool resting on the hill to windward. The craft climbed steeply, and the view widened every minute. Over there should be the city they came from, with its spaceport . . . yes. Small – smaller than she expected, though the spaceport had landing space enough for a dozen shuttles.

The radio crackled; their pilot spoke into his headset, but it was so noisy Brun couldn't hear what he said. Higher . . . higher . . . the morning sky that had been a soft bright blue darkened again. The gauge that must be an altimeter had reeled off thousands and ten thousands, but Brun didn't know what the unit of measure was. It neared sixty thousand somethings, and passed it. Then the pilot pulled the nose up even higher, and pushed a button on the left side of the cockpit. Acceleration slammed her back in her seat as a penetrating roar came from behind. The sky darkened quickly to black; stars appeared.

She noticed a streak of sunlit vapor climbing below them; their pilot yelled something into his headset. The vapor trail turned away. The pilot pointed through the front window. Brun peered back and forth, not seeing what he meant, until Hazel tapped her arm. 'Ten o'clock, negative thirty . . . their space station.' Then she could see it, as its shape passed over a sparkling expanse of white cloud on the bulging planet below. She had been there, on the inside, unable to see . . . and now she was here. Free. Or almost free.

The man handed Brun a headset; she put it on. Now she could hear him. 'Changing from lift engines to insystem – we're supposed to rendezvous with something out here. Dunno if it's military or civilian or what. They gave me code words to use.'

The craft lurched as he switched from one drive to another, then the artificial gravity kicked in, and she might as well have been sitting in a model shuttle on some planet's surface. Quiet, too, just as it should have been, with only the faint crisp rustle of the ventilation system. She glanced back at Hazel, who was grinning ear to ear. It felt right to her as well, then. She peered out at the stars, burning steadily . . . but she could not recognize any of the geometry. What system was this?

'Might's well take a nap, now she's on auto,' the man said. He switched off the banks of instruments useless with this drive, yawned, and hung his headset on a hook. 'I'm going to.' He closed his eyes and slumped in his seat.

Brun slid her headset down around her neck, but did not follow his example. Too much was at stake.

'I'm really tired,' Hazel whispered. 'And my legs . . .'

Brun mimed *sleep* at her, and watched as Hazel dozed off. The man was snoring now, snores of such complexity that she was sure he couldn't have faked them. She put out her hand to the controls, and he didn't stir.

So here she was, on her way . . . she touched her knives, reminding herself that she was not going to be recaptured, if anything went wrong. And out there somewhere, Fleet waited. She was sure it would be Fleet; her father would not have risked anything less in taking on a whole planet. She hoped it wasn't far out, and she hoped very much that whatever ships were there did not include one Lieutenant Esmay Suiza. She was not ready to face that, on top of everything else.

An hour passed, and another, and another. Despite herself, she yawned. She would have taken a stimulant if she'd had one; she scolded herself for eating such a big breakfast. Another yawn . . . Her eyes sagged shut, and she struggled to open them, only to yawn again. She looked at her shipmates. The man was snoring in a different pattern now, but just as loudly. Hazel slept neatly as a cat, curled into herself on the bench seat. Brun tried pinching herself, changing position, taking deep breaths . . . but in that steady, warm stillness, she slept in spite of herself.

20

Brun woke abruptly with the feeling that something was very wrong. They were in free fall . . . but they had been on insystem drive, with the artificial gravity on. The pilot was awake, and changing switch positions on the main board. Brun looked at Hazel, who was also awake, hanging upside down above the bench where she'd slept. She reached back, tapped her arm, and nodded toward the pilot.

'What are we doing?' Hazel asked. Her voice was high with tension.

'End of the line, girlies. I been talking to them over there—' He gestured, and Brun looked out to see a dark shape against the starfield. What it really was, or how far away, she couldn't tell, but she could see the ovoid shape of a warship. Fleet? 'I get more from them, for turning you in, than from you, for taking you on. An abomination was one thing – I didn't bargain on a runaway from Ranger Bowie's house.'

Not Fleet. Brun's stomach tightened. The pilot smirked at them, and opened his mouth to speak into the headset. Brun uncoiled from her seat, twisting in midair, and slammed both booted feet into the side of his head. Hazel squeaked – no other word for that short alarmed sound, but then pushed off the overhead to get her forearm around the man's neck and hold it against the tall seatback while Brun untangled herself from the cords and wires her attack had landed her in.

'What do I do if he—' Hazel began, when the man jerked against her arm, and then grabbed at her arm and tried to free himself. But he was strapped in, and Brun already had her knife out, and a firm hold on the back of his seat for leverage; she jammed the knife under his ribs and up, just as she had been told. He twisted, struggling, for a moment longer, then slumped . . . that long elephant-skinning knife had the length to reach his heart. Brun stared at Hazel, who was white with shock.

But they had no time for shock. Catching her feet under the copilot's seat, she unhooked the pilot's harness, and started pulling his body out of the seat, pushing it to the back. Drops of blood followed it, floating, dispersing.

'Can you . . . pilot?' Hazel asked. Brun grinned at her and nodded, then clambered into the seat. Hazel climbed over the pilot, still snorting a little but beyond help, and made it into the copilot's seat, strapping herself in quickly.

Insystem drive . . . where was insystem drive again? And she didn't want to run them right into that warship . . . she gestured to Hazel: rotate us, point us that way. Parallel to the warship's axis, toward what she hoped was its stern. Hazel touched the controls, and the stars wheeled crazily. Brun ignored that, and her ears, and found the inset black square that should be the insystem drive startup. She pushed it. Nothing happened. What else . . . oh. Yes. Safety release . . . she tried again, in sequence. Release, startup, drive on . . . and the sudden apparent lurch of the dust in the cockpit told her they were under drive again. Now for the AG . . . down there. One tenth . . . and the dust settled, leaving the cockpit clearer. Behind her, the pilot's body thumped to the deck. A little red globule slid past her gaze and attached itself to her shirt . . . blood. The pilot's blood.

And she'd never thought about what would happen if she'd cut his throat in zero-G. They could be drowning in the stuff, unable to see any of the controls . . .

Maybe her luck was back. But she wouldn't count on it. She notched up the insystem drive. If she had the pilot figured right, he was a smuggler or something and his personal shuttle would be overpowered, up to and maybe beyond the structural limits of the craft. She found the accelerometer, and the V-scale, but the blasted thing was in mph, whatever that was, rather than meters per second. Still – it was fast, and going faster.

Hazel touched her arm. She had found the scan controls. Two

screens came up: systemwide and local. Local was the problem, Brun thought. The warship behind them was lighted up like a Christmas tree with active weapons scans. But according to Esmay, anything as small as a shuttle was hard to hit . . . if it was far enough away. Well, the answer to that was to get far enough away – and that meant speed. She notched the drive up again. The little craft still felt stable as rock. Corey's had gone faster – she notched it up again, and again.

Hazel tapped her arm. On the system scan, several ships were flagged with weapons markers. And behind, the warship had swapped ends and was in pursuit.

It had always been a small chance. She'd known that. Better to die out here, than back there. She hoped Hazel felt that way – she cocked her head at the girl.

'It'll be close,' Hazel said. 'But I like it.'

Well . . . close or not, that was the right attitude. Brun pointed at the drive controls, and mimed shoving it to the line. Hazel looked at the scan, and nodded. What the hell, Brun thought. It can't be worse. She rammed the control all the way to the end of the slot. The drive rose from a deep whine to a high one, and the shuttle vibrated down its length.

And behind them, on the scan, an explosion marred the pattern. If she had not accelerated –

'We could jump, couldn't we?' Hazel asked. 'These shuttles are jump-capable.'

They could jump, but where? Supposedly, there was a Fleet ship insystem, waiting to pick them up. If only she could find that –

Another explosion; the little ship shivered as fragments impacted its minimal shields.

'Another one!' Hazel said, pointing. Brun glanced at the scan – and saw another weapons-lighted warship. They weren't going to make it through this – she might as well jump, and sort it out later, if she could. She found the jump controls, and started the checklist . . . never leave out the checks, Oblo had told her, because you can get killed just as dead by a malfunction as by an enemy.

Navigation computer on; target jump point selected; insertion velocity – not good, but she dared not slow. Her hands raced over the controls, but she left nothing out. When she was ready, she tapped Hazel on the shoulder, and pointed to the jump-initiation control. Hazel nodded, and Brun pushed it.

Nothing happened. Brun pushed it again – some of these controls stiffened if not used regularly.

'It's asking for a validation code,' Hazel said, nudging Brun and pointing. On a side panel, a small display had lit, with the words VOICE RECOGNITION VALIDATION REQUIRED PRIOR TO JUMP INSERTION.

Brun hissed. The one thing they couldn't do was produce an approximation of the pilot's voice, and whatever code words he'd used. She slammed her fist once more against the useless button, and turned her attention to what they *could* do.

This system was woefully short of useful pieces of rock, at least near the planet. No moons to land on – she would have given a lot for a moonlet with caves to hide in. So – make use of the terrain you've got, her instructors had said. No terrain in space, though. If she could get back to the planet, they could hide out in the wilderness . . . or they could be recaptured as they tried to land. That was worse than death; she'd dive this thing into the ground before she let that happen. She glanced at Hazel. The girl was pale-faced, but calm, waiting for Brun to do something.

Terrain. It all came back to escape and evasion, and in space that meant outrun or hide out. They couldn't outrun the warships, and there wasn't any place to hide. Except – what if they went straight for the *Elias Madero*, docked at the space station? Could they get in it from outside? Hide in it? It would take a long time to find them, time in which Fleet might be coming. Or might not.

She looked around the cockpit. Somewhere, the pilot must have had local space charts – they had not run into any of the things which must be up here, the various satellites and stations. She didn't spot charts, but she did spot a noteboard. She scribbled *Local charts* on it and handed it to Hazel. Hazel said, 'We're not going back, are we?'

Not exactly, Brun thought, and mouthed. *Hide.* Hazel seemed to understand the mouthed words, and nodded.

Backed off from its maximum velocity, the little ship could

maneuver surprisingly well. Brun kept an eye on the scans as she jinked back and forth, counting to herself in a random sequence she'd once memorized for the pleasure of it. Her other eye was on the fuel gauge – rapid maneuvering ate up fuel at an alarming rate.

'Local nav charts up on the screen,' Hazel said. Brun spared a glance. Little satellites, big satellites, space stations – she hadn't realized this place had more than one station – and a large number of uncategorized items. Most were drifting in a more-or-less equatorial orbit, though a few were in polar orbits. In size, these ranged from bits as small as pencils to stations a kilometer across. She needed something big enough – an orbital station would be perfect, but of course there wouldn't be one.

Hazel leaned past her and tapped something. Brun glanced again. Something long and skinny, much bigger than the shuttle, and marked on the chart with a large red X. The shuttle shivered, as a near miss tore at its shields. Whatever it was would have to do. She nodded at Hazel and pointed to the nav computer. She couldn't figure a course to it in her head, not and dodge hostile fire. In a moment or two, the course came up on the nav screen, along with an estimate of fuel consumption. Very close . . . they'd have to spend fuel to dump vee, and spiral around the planet on a much longer approach than Brun really wanted, with ships shooting at her.

And if she was really lucky, maybe the two enemy ships would run into each other, and remove that problem.

Minute by minute, as the shuttle curved back toward the planet, Brun expected the bright flash that would be the last thing she ever saw. Behind – to either side – but none of them as close as they had been. The boost out had taken hours . . . how long would it take to get back using all the power she dared? How much of the outbound trip had been unpowered? How long had she slept before waking to zero G? She didn't know; she didn't have time to think about it, only time to watch the scans, and the nav screen, and do what she could to conserve their fuel.

'One's out,' Hazel said suddenly. Brun nodded. One of their pursuers had miscalculated a boost, and was now out of sight behind the planet. The other, farther away, was probably out of missile range – at least, nothing had blown up anywhere near them for some time. The other red-marked icons she could see now were farther away, and didn't appear to be chasing her. Yet. She could have used Koutsoudas' enhanced scan; she didn't even know what size those things were. Even ordinary Fleet scan would have told her that, and located any Fleet ships insystem as well.

They might actually make it. She glanced at the fuel gauge again. Enough to decelerate to match their target . . . and that small margin over which would give her a chance to try a last wild gamble. She linked the autopilot to the nav computer for the approach, trusting the universe enough to take this moment to stretch before trying to dock to an uninhabited derelict.

The little shuttle lay snugged to the station, hidden from several directons by the sheltering wing of the station. Brun hoped its thermal signature would be hidden as well, but she didn't trust it. They might be detected from the ground as well as space. She looked around. The dead pilot nuzzled the stained plastic of the bulkhead, held there by one of the ventilation drafts.

They needed pressure suits. While she wasn't actually naked, she felt the hungry vacuum outside . . . her clothes were no protection. They needed to get off the shuttle, and onto something bigger, with more air.

They needed a miracle.

Make your own miracles, Oblo had said. The Escape and Evasion instructors had said the same thing.

Brun spotted what might be a p-suit locker, and aimed Hazel at it. Sure enough, inside was a smudged yellow p-suit easily large enough for either of them. One p-suit, not two. Hazel clearly knew how to check out a suit; she was running the little nozzle of the tester down each seam. Brun waited until Hazel had checked it all, including the air tanks.

'It's fine,' Hazel said. 'Both tanks full – that's six hours, if I understand their notation.'

Six hours for one person. Could Fleet get from where it was to here in six hours? Not likely. The shuttle's air supply was much bigger – they would have air for four or five days – but if the warships found the shuttle, they would be dead before then.

Priority one: find another p-suit.

Priority two: find air.

'Weapons would be nice,' Hazel said, surprising Brun again. The girl seemed so docile, so sweet . . . was she really thinking . . . ? From her face, she was.

With the helmet on, Hazel tested her com circuit. She would use it, they'd decided, only to tell Brun she was on the way back . . . no need to let everyone on the planet know where they were, if they hadn't been spotted.

With Hazel gone, Brun took the opportunity to search the dead pilot. Like all the men, he had packed a small arsenal: a knife at his belt, another in his boot, and a third up his sleeve, as well as a slug-thrower capable of putting a hole in the hull – what did he want with that aboard a ship? – a needler in the other boot, and two small beamers, one up the other sleeve, and one tucked into the back of his belt.

Hazel's voice over the com: 'Bringing suits.' Suits? Why suits plural? Brun hissed the two-syllable signal they'd devised for acknowledgement. 'Problems . . .' Damn the girl, why couldn't she say more . . . or nothing?

Soon enough – sooner than Brun expected – she heard the warning bleat of the airlock's release sequence, and then muffled bumps and bangs as Hazel cycled through. An empty p-suit came out first, scattering glittering dust from its turquoise skin. Turquoise? Brun rolled it over, and there on the back was a label – BlueSky Biodesigns – and a code number whose meaning she could not guess. Hazel next, in the pilot's dirty yellow p-suit, towing another turquoise model. Then two spare breathing tanks, lashed to the second p-suit. When they cleared the hatch, Brun reached behind her to dog the inner lock seal, as Hazel popped her helmet seal.

'Brun – it's really strange in there. I found a suit locker right away, but the tank locker beside it was empty. So I had to hunt around. And I've never seen a station like it—'

Brun tapped her shoulder, and Hazel stopped. Brun wrote LABORATORY. GENETIC ENGINEERING.

'Oh. That might explain the broken stuff, then. But listen, Brun, the oddest thing . . . remember how this p-suit's fitted for males? All the suits in the station lockers – the ones I looked in, anyway – are fitted for females. That's why I brought two. It's a lot more comfortable . . . and near's I can tell these suits have all the functions we need. And I found women's clothes scattered around, soft shipsuits. Better'n these rough things, if your legs are as sore as mine.'

Brun hated it when haste blurred Hazel's accent into conformity with that of the locals. But she was right. Already Hazel was unsuiting, packing the pilot's p-suit away with practiced skill as she came out of it, hardly swaying as she steadied herself with first one hand then another. Brun opened the first turquoise suit and found the clothes. Soft fleecy pants and tops, in colors she hadn't seen for far too long: bright, clear, artificial colors. Hazel had brought an assortment, bless her, different sizes and colors.

'You're so much taller,' Hazel said, 'I hope what I got is big enough . . .'

Brun nodded. She watched Hazel try to wriggle out of her clothes, wincing, and struggle into the softer ones. She chose dark green; the top had an embroidered design of flowers and swirls. Brun had found a pair of black pants that seemed longer than the rest, and a cream-colored shirt that was bigger around – even bound, her milk-swollen breasts had added to her size.

'Should we use the shuttle's wastecan before we suit up?' Hazel asked.

Brun shook her head. They would need every recycled bit of air and water. She started trying to shuck her own pants and realized that she was simply too stiff; it hurt too much. Hazel moved to help her; Brun held one of the grabons, and gritted her teeth as Hazel started to pull the stiff pants down.

'Is this the pilot's blood, or yours?' Hazel asked.

Brun shook her head, shrugged, and then nodded. It made no difference – the pants had to come off. Hazel worked them free, muttering.

'You're raw . . . from the riding, I hope. I didn't know it was so much worse without a saddle, or I'd have switched off with you—' She couldn't have done it, but Brun appreciated the offer, even as the breath hissed between her teeth.

'We have to put something on this,' Hazel said finally. The chill air bit into the raw places and Brun shuddered at the thought of anything touching her. 'I'll look.' Moments of silence; Brun kept her eyes shut and tried to steady her breathing. It wasn't as bad as being raped; it wasn't as bad as being pregnant; it wasn't nearly as bad as childbirth. She had survived all that; this was just . . . an inconvenience. She opened her eyes and smiled at Hazel, who was watching her with a worried look. 'I found a medkit, and put it in the other p-suit,' Hazel said. 'One of those emergency kits they always put near suit lockers.' Brun nodded, and freed a hand to wave a go-ahead signal.

The bite of the painkilling spray would have gotten a yelp from her if she'd had the voice to yelp with, but the almost-instant cessation of pain was amazing. She'd forgotten how fast good meds worked. Hazel followed that with a spray of antibiotic and skin sealant. Brun unpeeled her hands from the grabon, and was able to snag the soft black pants she'd chosen and put them on herself.

Then into the p-suits, where the plumbing fixtures connected as they ought, and all the gauges and readouts worked. Brun sniffed the air coming from the nose filters – nothing she could smell, and the ship's suit-check said it was safe. They filled the suits' water tanks from the shuttle tanks. Brun folded an extra set of shipsuits into padding for the back of her p-suit, and Hazel followed her example. They packed up all the food they could find in the shuttle, and stuffed the p-suits' external storage.

All this had taken longer than Brun hoped, but according to the shuttle's scans, no active scan had pinged them yet. Now, she finished setting up the autopilot for what she hoped would be an effective screening action. Ideally, they would have been able to tie into the shuttle's scans from within the space station, and send it off under remote control. But Brun had long since given up waiting for ideal conditions. She would send it off on a time delay, giving them time to get well into the station. Hazel had left the outer lock open, with an air tank lashed in the gap just in case some officious bit of old programming was still operating and tried to shut it . . . so they didn't have to worry about entrance.

With the little fuel left aboard, she couldn't set up a very complicated course, and she had to assume that ground-based radars had plotted their whereabouts anyway. Probably one of the warships was even now maneuvering in for an attempt to re-capture them. For maximum acceleration, Brun decided to run the takeoff and insystem drives together . . . something no experienced pilot would do, but it was the only way to get the ship well away in a hurry.

When she was done, she nodded at Hazel, and they both sealed up. They had made their plans; they had said all they had to say, until they were in the station. They crammed into the tiny airlock, and cycled out.

Outside was a confusion of highlight and black shadow; Brun followed Hazel along the length of the shuttle's hull to the station's wing. From here, she could see that there was a shuttle docking bay – if she'd known that, they could have been safe inside hours ago, because it looked as if it had passenger tubes still deployed. No time for that now. Hazel led her from one grabon to another toward the emergency lock portal.

They were almost to the portal when the grabon she held bounced in her hand, then vibrated strongly. Brun looked back. The shuttle's dual drive had come alive, and the little ship slid away from the station, its takeoff reaction engine exhaust glowing against the dark. It moved faster – faster – out into the sunlight, where it glittered like a bright needle.

Would their pursuers believe it? The course she'd plotted would have been hazardous for an experienced pilot, requiring extreme maneuvers to reverse-burn and survive atmospheric reentry, but it was the most direct way to the ground – if you didn't mind burning up along the way. They had no women pilots; even with what they knew of her background, they might think – she hoped they would think – that she was a panicky female who didn't understand orbital mechanics, who was running directly for cover.

She hadn't grown up hunting foxes for nothing.

She looked around again, trying to spot any of the warships. There, possibly – a dark shape blotting out part of the starfield. And there, below them, the more pointed shape of another shuttle, against the cloudfield on the planet below.

She felt her lips stretching in a grin that had no humor in it. Coming to catch her, were they? They'd get a surprise . . .

R.S.S. *Shrike*

Sneaking a task force into a system with a single mapped jump point had taken considerable tricky navigation, especially since they knew few details of the defensive layout. Esmay, as *Shrike*'s executive officer, had checked and double-checked every one of the short FTL hops that had brought them into the system via the jump point in another, nearby – nearby in stellar terms. But it had been a difficult period; some of the jumps had required flux levels well above those recommended. Once in the system, microjumps with low relative-vee insertion had hopped them in, apparently without detection, until they were positioned to observe the escape.

For days now they had hung unnoticed, well above the ecliptic, monitoring all transmissions from the planet. Far out, the rest of the task force waited in case of need, trading hours of scan lag for obscurity. *Shrike* had acquired several specialist crew who – according to Admiral Serrano – would enhance their chances if anything went wrong. This included Koutsoudas at scan, and Warrant Officers Oblo Vissisuan and Methlin Meharry, all three of whom had worked with Brun before. Esmay, watching Koutsoudas' enhanced scan at work, helped map everything it picked up.

At present, the enemy warships insystem included four lightweights in classic tetragonal array around the planet about half a light-second out, and another lightweight docked at the orbital station. Of the lightweights, three were escort-size, and two patrol-size. Three light-minutes out, something that massed like a half-sized cruiser seemed to represent the enemy's idea of a forward defensive force. All these had their weapons systems live, a careless convenience that made it easy for Koutsoudas to analyze them.

Word on the extrication had been mixed. The Guernesi agent in place had sent off a signal at the agreed frequency, but with 'cows' instead of 'cow' and mention of a price increase. The plan had not included bringing the babies . . . what could the plural mean? Had there been another woman with Brun? That could be disastrous; pursuit might follow more quickly or the other woman might resist. Esmay wondered if the second person could be the older girl from the merchanter.

Koutsoudas, listening in on transmissions, picked up something about 'Ranger Bowie's patience' having disappeared, and more about a search under way for 'the abomination.'

'They know she's gone – I hope she got clean away.'

'That's probably why Ranger Bowie's patience is gone – he captured her.'

'Maybe.'

When Koutsoudas acquired the shuttle's signal hours later, the tension increased again. Esmay felt she could hardly breathe. Now on the scan screens, the bright dot moved out, and out, coming ever nearer. If the plan worked perfectly, in a day or so they would rendezvous with the little craft, take Brun aboard, and jump outsystem before the enemy realized they had been there. Then – with Brun safe – the rest of the task force would have time to blockade the planet and start negotiating the return of the other prisoners. If the plan didn't work . . . a cascade of contingency plans devolved from any point of discovery.

'Go get some food, people,' Captain Solis said. 'It's going to be a long wait. Suiza, that means you, too – go eat, then sleep; be back in four hours.'

Esmay tore herself away from the screens, and found she could actually down a full meal – she had skipped a couple without even noticing. She knew she should sleep, but she lay on her bunk not sleeping, thinking of Barin over on *Gyrfalcon*, of Lord Thornbuckle back at Sector, of the remarkable Professor Meyerson . . . the alarm woke her, and she rolled off her bunk, smoothed her hair – much easier, these days – and headed for the bridge.

There she found a grim mood unlike that earlier.

'That sonuvabitch has sold them out,' Koutsoudas said. He bent over the scan. 'He's cut out the insystem drive, put 'em on a zero-G ballistic for that Militia ship—' The enemy ships were still holding their tetragonal formation.

'What're our options?'

'We can microjump between them and the warship, but the backwash might get 'em. Stuff I'm getting is a minute old; we aren't sure where they are.'

'It's worth a try.'

'Wait!' Koutsoudas held up a hand. 'Hot *damn* . . . she wasn't fooled—'

'What's – ?'

'There – I can't get focus on the cabin good enough, but there's something going on . . . what – there's *three* people in there, not two!'

'Rotation!' called another scan tech. Koutsoudas glanced at his screen.

'You're right, Atten. Let's see . . .' But they all saw that the shuttle's icon had come alight with the cone that meant acceleration. The cone lengthened, then lengthened again. Vectoring away from the planet, past the warship . . .

'Gotta be Brun,' Koutsoudas said. 'She's remembered to run past him. Come on, girl, knock it to the wall.'

Moment by moment the cone lengthened, an arrow angled away from the planet, toward the distant freedom of deep space. But the little ship was deep in the gravity well, and the warship had the high ground.

'Weapons discharge!' yelled the other scan tech. They groaned; the shuttle was still in easy missile range of the warship. But just before the plotted course intersected, the cone lengthened again.

'That girl's born to win,' Koutsoudas said. 'She sucked that out of 'em like a pro. 'Course, their systems are optimized to hit big slow things – notice it didn't blow where it should have. They didn't change the arming options. Hope she figures that out. They'd have to be lucky—'

'Another enemy ship on the chase!' said the other tech. 'Intersecting – more weapons discharges.' The second ship, one of the patrol class, had left its station on the tetragonal array, and boosted to intercept.

Koutsoudas grunted. 'Come on, girl – do something—' The cone shifted shape, its tip changing direction, the colors fragmenting and reforming. 'Dammit, not that!'

'She's trying to dodge – she can't make it that way. It gives 'em time to get in position.'

'It might work – if they don't think to reset their targeting options – if they don't get a lucky hit. But she'd do better to run this way. If she knew we were here . . .'

Esmay watched the displays, her heart pounding. She could imagine herself in Brun's place – every move Brun made was one she would have made, again and again.

'She's heading back—' the scan tech said. 'Is she going to try to land on the planet?'

'No,' Esmay heard herself saying. 'She's heading for the orbital stuff.'

'You think so?' Koutsoudas asked, without looking up. 'And what makes you think that, Lieutenant?'

'It's her style. She'd have tried to jump, and something prevented her – that ship should have jump engines, but maybe they're not working. Failing that, a straight run would make her an easy target . . . so she dodged about, but that uses fuel. So she's looking for cover.'

'That's a lot of thinking for someone just hauled out of prison,' someone said.

'She wouldn't panic,' Esmay said. 'She's smart, brave, and a risk-taker.'

'That's the truth.' Koutsoudas flashed a quick grin. Then he sobered. 'But she's in real trouble here – unless she's planning to toss herself out the door in a p-suit and hope they shoot the shuttle down. And – there's still two live ones in the shuttle. She brought someone with her.'

'If they have multiple p-suits,' Esmay said, 'she'll probably try that. But given what we know about these people, I doubt there were p-suits for all of them aboard. We should microjump in closer.'

'And tell their system we're here? Before the rest of the task force comes in? I thought you were the one who said one woman wasn't worth a war.'

Would they always misinterpret that? Anger put an edge to her voice that even she could hear. 'When there was a chance to get her out without one, no. In present circumstances, when a covert extrication has gone sour, it's the only way to get close enough to do her any good.'

Captain Solis gave her a long look. 'You would risk the entire operation—?

'Microjump to within fifteen seconds scan delay, yes, sir, I would. Give 'em something else to think about. They know she was intended to meet something; they don't know what.'

'They don't know for sure it was in this system—'

'If the pilot turned, he'd have told them everything up to the recognition codes. They know someone's waiting for her. We might as well show something – any delay can help her, and we can maneuver sufficiently for the integrity of this ship.'

'Suiza, that sounds a lot more like the hero of Xavier.' He turned to the communications officer. 'Give me a tightbeam, and load a compressed summary of scan; we'll also drop a beacon. Thirty seconds to jump, people.'

Shrike popped out of its microjump at low relative system velocity, and the scans cleared.

'Total blackout two minutes forty-five seconds,' Koutsoudas said. Scan lit with the shuttle's beacon and the others – three escort-size warships, two patrol-size, something that massed like a half-size cruiser, and a clutter of small craft. All blazed with live-weapons warning icons. 'They'll acquire us in a second or so – and we should be picking up active scan signals shortly – there . . .' The warships icons all showed acceleration cones; those already under boost had the skewed cones of ships changing direction. 'Looks like we're sucking 'em off the shuttles.' The skewed cones lengthened as those ships pulled away from their pursuit, to redirect their attention to the newcomer.

The shuttle's position had moved; it was clear now that it was running back toward the planet, with rapid changes of acceleration to make it a difficult target. The screens blinked as the SAR kinked in a tiny microjump, then cleared again. The enemy icons responded more slowly this time. Good. Anything to confuse them, distract them. Another jink, to within a half-second, and then another. A distant explosion, where one of the enemy had released a missile at more than maximum range, to detonate uselessly. It was low enough now to be in the orbital trash. It disappeared around the far side of the planet from them. Long minutes passed, while they waited, jinking in random sequence microjumps to keep the enemy guessing. If Brun had slowed enough, it would be another hour and a half before the icon reappeared.

Too soon, they saw it again, now moving rapidly in a suicidal dive for the surface.

'They'll burn up on the first pass, going like that,' Koutsoudas said. 'What the hell is that girl thinking of? Did she lose control of the ship?'

'Maybe she doesn't have enough fuel for a proper descent,' someone else said. 'Maybe she'd rather burn—'

'She's not in the ship,' Esmay said. She could feel her heart pounding; she knew without question what Brun had done.

'What, you think it's flying itself? You're the one said they probably didn't have p-suits; they couldn't have spaced themselves.'

'Unless they found something with p-suits, or an air supply,' Esmay said. 'If they did . . . I can see Brun sending the shuttle off as a decoy.'

'The only active station – the only thing up there with air and p-suits – is the main station, where *Elias Madero* is docked,' Koutsoudas said. 'I can guarantee they didn't dock there – leaving aside the fact that if they did, they'd have been captured, because it's occupied.'

'Uh-oh.'

They turned. The Militia ships had not waited to see if the shuttle would burn. From safely outside the danger zone, they'd sent missiles in pursuit, and a dying flare of the screen showed that they'd hit it.

'Well,' Captain Solis said. 'That's that. Barring Lieutenant Suiza's unlikely suggestion that there are two p-suits now floating somewhere in orbit, they're dead. No one survives a direct hit on a shuttle.'

Esmay had been flipping through Koutsoudas's scan catalog of the orbiting trash. 'Here's something – and it's consistent with the origin of that burn.'

'It's derelict,' Koutsoudas said after a quick glance. 'There's an old reactor at the core, but the rest of it's at ambient temp.'

'It's big enough,' Esmay said. 'The shuttle course tracks back—'

Koutsoudas sighed, and pulled up an enlarged version of the thumbnail in the catalog. 'Look – it's big, but it's a wreck. Even from here you can see that whole sections are open to vacuum . . .'

Esmay blinked. Open to vacuum they were, but – she remembered the Special Materials Fabrication Unit, open just like this. 'Could it have been a vacuum processing or manufacturing facility?'

'They don't have anything like that,' Captain Solis said. 'They buy or steal their space-made products.'

'They do now,' Esmay said. 'Didn't the Guernesi ambassador mention a facility that used to be here – from before the Militia took over this planet?'

'The operative word is derelict, Lieutenant. Even if Brun and her companion made it there, it won't do them any good. No air, no food, no effective shields, no weapons.'

'It might've had p-suits, sir. Even if it was ransacked by the Militia, they might not have taken everything. I think she's there, and I think we should go get her.'

'I think you're trying to redeem your career, Lieutenant, at the cost of other peoples' lives.' Solis glared at her.

Silence descended on the bridge; Esmay could hear every breath anyone took. Then she heard her own.

'Sir, the captain has a right to whatever opinion of me the captain holds. But that woman – those women – have one chance only for survival, and that's someone on our side getting to them with air and protection before either their air runs out or the bad guys figure out that the shuttle was a decoy. If the captain thinks I'm a conniving glory-hound, there are others on this ship who can do the rescue. But it needs to be done.'

Solis gave her a long look, which she met squarely. 'You would volunteer for such a mission?'

Of course leaped into her mouth, and she bit it back. 'Yes, sir.'

'Mmm. Who should go, do you think?'

'A full SAR team, sir. Even though we know of only two personnel who may have medical problems, we should anticipate that the Militia may send a boarding party . . . having figured Brun's thinking just as I have. We may be fighting; we will, at the very least, be doing a rescue under hostile conditions.'

Solis looked around the bridge, and his gaze came to rest on Koutsoudas. 'You've worked with Brun Meager—'

'Yes, sir.'

'What do you think?'

'Sir, I think Lieutenant Suiza's right about how Brun thinks – she's very quick, very ingenious, and willing to take risks. If she did dock to any of the junk we've found orbiting this planet, that derelict station is the obvious place. If she's not dead, then that's where she'll be. Suiza's also right that if she did dock there, it would've been detected by any decent ground-based sensing system. We can't assume they don't have one. If I were the Militia, I'd have shuttles on the way – and in fact, we've spotted shuttle takeoffs, three altogether.'

Solis looked past Esmay. 'Meharry – you're also specially assigned to this mission – what's your assessment?'

'The lieutenant's on target, Captain. And the longer we sit around here jawing about it, the worse off Brun's going to be.'

'Would you trust Lieutenant Suiza on a mission like this? Or is she grandstanding?'

Esmay was aware of Meharry's unquiet presence behind her. Rumor had spread many stories of Meharry, most of them unpleasantly concentrating on her lethal talents. 'With me along, sure, Captain. Personally, I think she's straight, but if I'm there she won't have a chance to screw up.'

'Lord Thornbuckle has insisted all along that Sera Meager would not want to see Lieutenant Suiza,' Solis said, his tone still cool.

'I think Brun would be glad to see anyone on our side,' Meharry said. 'And from what I saw at Xavier, and heard from people on *Kos*, the lieutenant is ideally suited to this sort of thing.' That could be taken more than one way, but Esmay wasn't feeling picky.

'Very well. Lieutenant, you'll take Team One, and Warrant Officers Meharry and Vissisuan.' Esmay did not need to be told that they would be watching her, as much as helping Brun.

Freed at last to do what she knew she was best at, Esmay felt her spirits rising. Their mission was beyond difficult – but so had others been. Brun might not be on the derelict, or if she was, she might already have died from any of a thousand things. If they found her, they might find a corpse, or they might all be blown up by a Militia missile, aimed or stray.

None of that mattered now. Clear in her mind was the plan, as if someone had drawn it in scarlet ink on white paper . . . she heard herself explaining it in crisp phrases to the others. And they responded to her confidence, her enthusiasm.

By the time she was in the pinnace, her p-suit on but not sealed, and the gloves flipped back, the first flurry of action had settled to a purposeful, organized bustle.

The captain's voice in her ear caught her attention. 'Lieutenant – you were right about two things. Koutsoudas says he's picked up a single signal from the derelict, something he believes only Sera Meager would send. Fleet frequencies, Fleet codes, and a message that the fox has gone to ground. And there's at least one shuttle headed for the derelict. We can't get you there before it arrives; our jump limit will leave you at least five minutes behind them.'

'Yes, sir.'

'The rest of the wave's insystem, and I've been in contact with the admiral. I'm sending both SAR teams, and the other pinnace will have all the supplies we can stuff into it. You have discretion to use whatever force is necessary to protect Sera Meager and her companion. We will be sending reinforcements when we've dealt with the other ships, but that may be some hours. Is that clear?'

'Yes, sir.' Hours . . . it might be days before they were re-inforced. And they would have no heavy weapons. The sonic riot-control generators used in aired-up stations wouldn't work on a derelict open to vacuum . . . what could she use? 'Meharry—'

'Yes, sir.' Meharry's eyes had a feral glitter reflecting Esmay's own enthusiasm.

'Captain tells me we're going to be docking five minutes behind a hostile shuttle. The station's supposedly not aired up – at least, some of it isn't aired up. We'll need more than small arms.'

'On it.' Meharry ducked out, leaving Esmay staring at blank air. Well, she'd been with Heris Serrano for years . . . and this was how it was supposed to work . . . tell the good ones what to accomplish and then get out of their way. But she hadn't expected to feel quite this . . .

'Lieutenant—' It was a squad of the neuro-enhanced troops, heavily laden with weapons segments; their sergeant handed her a screenful of official numbers and letters for her signature – if they came back without all eight CFK-201.33-rs, it would be her job to explain where they had gone . . . and she hadn't a clue what they *were*, or any of the long list of components below them. She ran her command wand aross the bottom of the list, and handed it back.

'We'll be first out as usual . . .' the sergeant said, with not quite a question mark.

'Right,' Esmay said, dragging her mind back from Meharry's disappearance and the mysteries of Fleet inventory control to the immediate tactical problem. 'And with hostiles ahead of us, and no idea whether our rescue targets have pressure suits.'

'Piece of cake,' the sergeant said. 'None of the hostiles are going to be female, from what I hear, and our targets are. So we just shoot the bad boys, and leave the girls alone.'

21

What now?' asked Hazel. Brun shrugged. She needed to think. She was hungry, thirsty – she sipped at the helmet tube – and very, very sleepy. And her legs hurt; the anesthetic spray was wearing off.

What could they do, with the few weapons they had? She could almost hear Commander Uhlis's voice yelling at her in the class: your best weapon is between your ears. Yes, and she'd like to keep it there, preferably in one piece.

'If we could get the artificial gravity on,' Hazel said, 'then we could turn it off.'

Brun supposed she meant in order to confuse their enemies – but it would gain them only minutes, if that. It would certainly reveal their presence – the gravity generator wouldn't be on if no one was here. A vague plan began to form in her brain, shapeless as rising mist.

Exploring the controls while in a p-suit was a lot safer than playing around with them otherwise; Brun grinned as she remembered Oblo's cautionary tales. She prodded one after another, seeing what worked.

'Lights!' Hazel said. That was obvious. But was it lights in this room or overall? Brun waved a wide-armed gesture; Hazel nodded and pushed off to explore. Brun peered at the panel. If she could figure out how to bring up station scan, there should be an idiot display somewhere on the main board that would tell her what she needed to know, in several languages and nonverbal symbols. Since the controls worked at all, she ought to be able to bring up station scan.

The rocker switch, when she found it, was located underneath a foldout panel. Brun pushed it with a silent prayer for luck . . . and the displays came up, flickering badly at first but steadying. How long had they been off? And what was powering them now? She looked for the idiot display.

There. As she'd expected, one of the languages on the display was her own . . . another was Guerni. She couldn't read the third at all, but that didn't matter now. She flicked through the opening menu: station layout, environmental system controls, life support, emergency procedures (which included a section on biohazard containment), power system, communications.

Station layout made clear what the place had been – a biological laboratory of some kind; probably – Brun thought – one of those fairly common at colony startup, which tailored biologicals for the specific conditions found downside. Many colonies had them . . . but why, then, was this one derelict?

The station had been clearly divided into living space for the workers, and eight labs separated by locks and seals – three on one arm, and five on the other. The big open gap was, Brun saw, out near the end of one arm; they had docked under a solar-collecting panel halfway down the other.

Deep in the station's core, the system's expert slept, as it had slept for decades of local time. All peripherals were offline; all sensors

707

shut down. Its last instruction set lay uppermost, ready to execute if anyone turned on the power, but hard vacuum and random radiation had changed a few bits here and there. Normally that would have been no problem; its self-repair mechanisms were necessarily robust, designed for industrial use in space. But they were not designed for decades on a derelict that had been vandalized in a hurry, its expert laid to rest in half the time required.

When the lights came on, a trickle of power ran through its connections, shunted there by the designers who intended the expert to be functioning whenever the station was occupied. Slowly – slowly for its design – the expert woke, layer by layer. Power in the lines meant someone had returned; that gave permission for it to draw power on its own and engage the self-check and self-repair routines. The topmost instruction set began executing, inhibiting return of some active functions. Those who inhabited the station now might be either legitimate employees or intruders . . . if they were intruders, the expert was not to reveal itself by independent action, but instead isolate them and transmit a call for help.

Passive scan devices collected information. Two humans, female by all parameters, wearing female-design employee p-suits whose code numbers were in the directory: emergency evacuation suits from Laboratory Two. The expert engaged suit telemetry cautiously; the suits' inhabitants didn't notice. Neither human fit a known profile, but a quick check of the decay data from the reactor indicated that it had been decades since the expert was put to sleep. Therefore it was unlikely that these employees would be known to it.

One, in the control room, was following a rational restart procedure on station control functions. The expert did not interfere, but observed. She seemed to know what she was doing. The other was exploring the corridor leading to the second arm. The expert turned its attention to the outside world.

Hazel came back to the control room. 'Lights are on all down that corridor. I couldn't see into all the compartments, though. The ones I could, some were dark and some weren't. You must've hit a main switch.'

Brun nodded, and pointed to the panel that controlled lighting. It indicated power to the lights throughout, with a summary of lights switched off, and lights not functioning even though switched on. She pointed at other panels; Hazel leaned closer. She had found the power reports for both the internal reactor – now nearly depleted, and producing less than 40 percent of its former power – and the solar panels, also below nominal. With the damage they'd seen on the outside, she could believe that. Still, the station had been designed to support research and manufacturing; the power still available would easily restore life support throughout, if they could find the air for it.

The air for the central core she had already found – the heat generated by the reactor had nurtured the base beds of the environmental system all these years, and the slowly accumulating air had been stored under pressure. But should they air up? External air would free them from the need to carry tanks around, and extend the effective life of the ones they had. Yet airing up the station would prove someone was aboard – it would be easily detectable from the outside. Moreover, if intruders blew the station, and they didn't have their suits on, they'd die.

Brun was still mulling this over when Hazel brought her a handcomp with voice output . . . Brun grinned, and grabbed it. It had the standard plug connections, so Brun jacked it into the suit intercom connection on the outside, and tapped some of the preset message keys. She had a choice of three languages, and twenty preset messages. 'All correct,' said a tinny male voice with a strong accent. She looked at Hazel and cocked her head.

'I didn't hear it,' Hazel said. 'Maybe you have to hit the transmit key inside the helmet to transmit to other suits.'

A nuisance. Brun fumbled with the comp and bumped the helmet transmit button with her chin as she keyed the preset message. 'All correct.'

'Got it!' Hazel said. 'Now maybe we can find one with more capability.'

'All correct,' Brun tapped again. Then she hit each key once, to be sure what the messages were, and again to practice how to say 'Help!' and 'Danger!' and 'Shift report.' One of the keys transmitted no voice signal, but an electronic bleep that was probably,

Brun thought, some kind of ID code for a central computer. She hit that one only once.

Besides the preset messages, the handcomp had key input for other data. Brun tried tapping out 'Does this work?' but Hazel shook her head.

The expert system awaited whatever instruction would follow the authorization signal. 'Does this work?' fit no protocol, but its natural-language processing was up to the task of interpreting it. It must mean 'Did the expert system receive that authorization and can it receive keyboard input?'

'At your service,' it transmitted through the correct frequencies. Both humans stopped in the way that humans did when presented with novel or unexpected data.

'What was that?' asked the one who had not transmitted the authorization code. The expert waited for the other to reassure her, meanwhile retrieving a complete suit readout indicating fatigue toxins and mild hypothermia and analyzing the vocal patterns to conclude that this individual was a pubertal human female, a native speaker of Gaesh with the accent common to the nearby merchanters of the Familias Regnant rather than that of the Guerni Republic. It instructed the suit to warm up a bit, and increase oxygen flow.

Meanwhile, the other, without speaking, was tapping rapidly on the keyboard of her handcomp. The expert was able to interpret, despite errors in input, that she knew she was communicating with an expert system.

'The system will take over vocal communication,' the expert said to the other one.

'All correct,' Brun transmitted, hoping Hazel would understand that the expert was going to relay from her own keyed input.

'There are vocal synthesizers of more power and suitability in laboratory 1–21,' the expert said. 'Although major equipment was destroyed, my optical sensors report that some of the small synthesizers seem to be unbroken.'

'Can you guide us there?' Brun asked, aware that the expert was echoing her input as a voice to Hazel.

'Easily, but I have instead empowered a mobile unit to fetch them. Spacecraft approach; my analysis suggests that they are upcoming from the surface.'

'Plan?' Brun asked.

'Data,' the expert replied. 'Non-enemy spacecraft in system . . . too far away.'

Non-enemy . . . Fleet?

'Can you contact them?'

'Tranmitters nonfunctional. Estimated time to restore transmission capability . . . 243 standard seconds. What are the parameters?'

Hazel, who had said nothing for several exchanges, said, 'How could we know Fleet frequencies and codes?'

Brun smiled to herself. She knew. One after another, she entered the figures, carefully defining each: frequencies, frequency changes with intervals, identification codes, including the one she had been given once as her personal ID. Then, with great care, she entered the message she wanted to send. Her eyes kept blurring, but she blinked the tears back fiercely. Time enough to cry if she got Hazel to safety.

And the little children. But she could not think of that now. One thing at a time.

'These frequencies and codes are not those in my library for the Regular Space Service of the Familias Regnant,' the expert said. It was capable of expression, and it sounded fussy.

'Check date,' Brun keyed in. 'Codes change.'

A long pause ensued. 'It has been a very long time,' the expert said finally. 'I assumed the date was an error resulting from damage done when the station was overrun . . .'

'Time to intruder arrival?' keyed Brun. Some expert systems were complex enough to lose themselves in endless recursive self-examination. 'And transmitter function?'

'Ninety-seven seconds until transmitters functional; I will send your message as soon as confirmed. There is a high probability that nontarget vessels may be able to intercept the message; you have provided no cipher.'

'They already suspect we're here,' Hazel said, voicing Brun's thought. 'And if the Militia know we're here, it's better that Fleet knows it too. I suppose, Brun, it's because of your father—'

'All correct,' Brun keyed. She really did want a better voice synthesizer; her fingers were already tired, and she had a lot more to say.

'ETA of intruder shuttles from the planet now ranges from one hour ten minutes, to three hours one minute,' the expert said. 'Unless they change course, which they have the capacity to do . . . now, three shuttles apparently approaching from the planet.'

Three shuttles . . . why did they think they needed four shuttles to capture two women? Or were they coming out to fight Fleet with shuttles? Surely they weren't that stupid.

'Weapons discharge,' the expert system said. 'Nearby ship, identifying itself as Militia cruiser *Yellow Rose*, launched missiles at Fleet vessel of unknown type.'

The enemy shuttle had been run right into the gaping hole in one arm of the station. No doubt the Militia knew what was open and what wasn't – assuming they were the ones who'd made it a derelict. If they'd been in a regular warship, Esmay would have lobbed a missile into that bay, and blown the shuttle first off. But an SAR shuttle did not normally venture into hostile territory; it mounted no external weapons, and they had had no time to improvise. With that in mind, Esmay kept the length of the station between her shuttle and the enemy's, and snugged in under one of the power panels at the far end. Again, mission constraints changed the usual procedures. They dared not blow a hole in the derelict's hull, lest Brun and her companion be hiding behind just that piece of hull. They shouldn't be, but no one knew what conditions were like inside. Moreover, it would take at least four hours to rig one of the portable airlocks and carefully incise a new hole in the station hull. So the teams would have to insert through a known entrance, which all concerned knew was the best way to make a target of themselves.

The best they could hope for was that the Militia intruders weren't already in place. The neuro-enhanced squad didn't seem too worried. Esmay, waiting near the tail of the line, saw the bulky figures pause at the emergency lock, and then move in, far faster than she had expected. Perhaps this meant the station had no air pressure.

'Lieutenant, the artificial gravity's on.'

That shouldn't be . . . the station was a derelict. But she could feel through her own body the tug of a gravity generator. Which meant a sizeable power source, more than could be accounted for by the tattered, misaligned power panels. Would there be air? Had Brun turned things on? Esmay shook those questions off. What mattered now was getting in. If there was gravity, then the fighting would not favor the zero-G trained.

Inside, they were met with the chaotic remnant of systematic vandalism, all visible under ordinary ceiling panel lights. P-suits cluttered the corridor, all turquoise with a BlueSky logo and code number on the back. Someone had drawn five pointed stars and other curious symbols on the corridor bulkhead in brown pigment – or blood. The tank locker beside the suit locker was empty of breathing tanks. Air pressure was as near vacuum as made no difference . . . but why was there any pressure at all? Why were the lights on?

Esmay tried a cautious hail on the frequency Koutsoudas had given as that of Brun's transmission . . . no reply.

Nothing damaged a man's reputation more than unruly women. Mitch Pardue knew even before he launched that he could kiss the Captain's position goodbye for at least ten years. He might even be voted out as Ranger Bowie. Even if he got them back, those fool women had cost him something he'd worked for twenty years and more.

The abomination he could understand. She was crazy, even without a voice. But the girl's defection hurt. Prima had been so fond of her, and the other wives as well. She'd worked hard, and they'd treated her like one of the family. Maybe that was the problem. Maybe they'd been too lenient. Well, he wouldn't make that mistake with the little girls. That bossy one, already showing off in the weaving shed – he'd see that she didn't stay bossy. As for Patience . . . he'd already half-promised her as a third wife to a friend of his, but now that wouldn't do.

Why couldn't the girl have realized how much better off she was in his household? Why were women so perverse, anyway?

He almost let himself think God had erred in creating women

713

at all, but pulled back from that heresy. That's what happened if you started thinking about women – they led the mind astray.

If they were on the derelict station – and he was certainly sure they were – he would capture them and make an example of them. The yellow-haired abomination they would have to execute; he hated killing women, but if she escaped once, she might again. The girl . . . he would decide that later, after he learned exactly what had happened. When they'd finally found a witness, it seemed that a man had told her to get in the car. If so, she might not be guilty of anything but stupidly following a man's orders, which was all you could expect of a woman. He hoped that was it.

'Ranger Bowie!' That was his pilot. He leaned into the cockpit. 'What, Jase?'

'There's a weird ship out there, scan says.'

Weird ship. It must be a ship the women had planned to meet. 'What's our defense say?'

'Says it's weird, Ranger. Not anything they know, a lot smaller than a cruiser. But it can do those little short jumps like the Familias fleet—'

'It's looking for them,' he said. 'It's not a warship, or it'd have shot up our ships first thing, same as we would. A little transport of some kind.' The worst of it was that it meant the Familias now knew where they were – and more ships might follow. Sufficient unto the day is the evil thereof, he told himself. First things first. Get these women under control, or all hell would break loose.

Though if he'd known, he might've asked for a shuttle of space-armored troops from the *Yellow Rose*. Their p-suits were hardened, but not against the kind of weaponry a Fleet vessel would have. Still, they'd probably hold their fire if they thought the Speaker's daughter was in the midst of it.

His uncle had been one of those who trashed this godless excrescence in the first place; he'd grown up on the stories. They'd talked about blowing it up time and again, but always decided it might be useful someday. Useful! Just showed what happened when you compromised on a moral duty. He watched as the pilot brought them in to the old shuttle bay. When he felt the solid

714

clunk of the shuttle's grapples on the decking, he stood and pushed his way back to the hatch.

'Now y'all listen here,' he said. 'We're goin' in to look for those women. Not to play around gapin' at stuff, or even takin' the time to trash it. There's warships insystem; we need to get this done and get back where we can do some good. Understand?'

They nodded, but he had his doubts.

'All the weapons they can have is what that guy had in his shuttle. Maybe a couple of knives, a .45 or two. And they're women, and not used to zero-G or vacuum. They'll have p-suits on, probably ones that don't fit good. So we don't have anything to worry about if we use sense. Just don't go wanderin' off where one of 'em can blow you away too easy. And be sure your personnel scans are set on high power.'

He pulled his helmet shield down, locked it, and checked the suit seals of the man in front of him; the man checked his. Terry Vanderson – good man, reliable. Then he turned and led the way out of the shuttle's airlock.

The regular airlock from the shuttle dock to the station corridor operated normally, but there was no air inside. He'd expected that. The women would've taken a tank or so from the shuttle when they left it, and they'd be low on air by now.

Inside the airlock, they stood in a short corridor that ended in a T-intersection. He'd looked at his uncle's old notes, and knew that each arm of the station was a warren of laboratories and storage rooms – they would have to clear each of these. He looked at his scanner. Nobody near – but they would check, then close and secure each compartment.

'Don't forget the overheads,' he reminded his men. Not that they needed it; they'd been on more than one hostile boarding.

Lewis and Terry peeled off to check the outer end of the arm. It seemed to take forever, but it probably wasn't more than five minutes before they were back. Now they moved along the corridor toward the station hub.

'I can't believe this,' Oblo muttered. 'They're just walking along like they're on a picnic.' On scan, the twenty suited figures moved in a clump, checking compartments and doors, but without any real caution. Nobody on point, nobody watching their backs. 'And they're not in space armor, just p-suits. Brun could just about take them herself, if she had any kind of weapon.'

'They think they're up against two unarmed women,' Esmay said. 'Once someone calls to tell them we're here—'

'Someone should have, by now,' Oblo said. 'Unless they're not listening.'

That led to questions Esmay had no time to answer. Was there someone else in the Militia eager to have this mission fail? And why?

The assault troops moved forward, secure in the knowledge that their armor would foil scan not specifically designed to penetrate it. Esmay felt the familiar surge of excitement; she wanted to be up with them, but more important was finding Brun and the girl. Scan showed a pair of p-suited life signals on this side of the core, in a compartment off a side corridor. The problem would be letting them know she and the others were friendly – the armor, designed for combat effectiveness, did not have insignia in the visible spectrum.

All the compartments in that wing had been checked and secured, and Mitch Pardue felt pretty good as he led his men into the central core. Careful scanning had shown nothing there – the women, if they were alive, would be huddling somewhere in the far wing, close to the hotspot where they'd had the shuttle. He felt a pleasant tension as he thought of them – of the fear they would be feeling, the helplessness . . .

'Let's go, boys,' he said, and stepped out into the wider space of the core corridor.

They passed what had been a lounge area, the chairs now in a random tumble on the deck, and came to the control area. Here, Ranger Bowie paused. It had been a little surprising to find the artificial gravity still on – he clearly remembered his uncle talking about how they had pushed the bodies down the corridors in zero-G – and he wondered if perhaps the women had knocked the controls about by accident.

'Wait a minute,' he said to the others. 'I wanta check on somethin'.' They drifted across the space with him, as interested

716

in the old station as he was. He leaned over the control panel, trying to read the labels . . . not in decent Tex, but in scripts he recognized as those used in the Familias Regnant, the Guerni Republic, and the Baltic Confederation. Heathens, all of them. Sure enough, the dust had been messed around; he could see what might be the marks of suit gloves here and there. He saw the gravity control panel, and was reaching for it when his vision blanked and he was pulled violently backwards.

'Lambs to the slaughter,' Esmay heard through her comunit. 'We should space 'em now, or you want prisoners?'

'Can you get any ID?'

'Well, one of 'em's got that star thing on his p-suit, and he looks like the leader of the bunch that took the *Elias Madero*.'

'Yes, we want prisoners,' Esmay said firmly. 'Especially that one.' She wanted to hear how it went, but finding Brun was still a priority, and the scan traces kept moving – as if Brun were deliberately evading them. Perhaps she was.

'Team Blue!' That was from outside, from the other team's scan specialist.

'Lieutenant Suiza here.'

'Two shuttles approaching, with unshielded transmissions. They're planning to go in and kill everyone they find.'

That made no sense – and then it did. If these people were as given to factionalism as reported, then this would be an excellent chance for one faction to rid itself of the leaders of another.

'They know we're here, right?'

'Yeah – but they think they can take us. I estimate twenty per shuttle – total of forty, say again four-zero armed personnel. No heavy weaponry.'

That was lucky. If they'd had heavy weapons, or ship weapons, they might have decided to blow the station.

'Have they indicated where they're going to land?'

'One of them coming into the same shuttle bay as the first. They want to get in behind the others – the one's going to come in on the end of this wing.'

'Ah . . . the old pincers movement.'

'Yes, sir.'

'Mr. Vissisuan,' Esmay said. 'Expect forty intruders, in two shuttle loads, small arms only. According to backscan, they know we're here, but think we'll be easy to subdue. They've divided their force, and expect to catch us between them.'

'Sir. Plan?'

'Until we have Brun and the girl safely away, that has to be our first priority. Right now it looks like Brun is between us and the incoming shuttle. So we'd better move fast. Beyond that, secure the prisoners we have, and take prisoners if possible.' If they could pick off some high-ranking Militia, perhaps they could avoid a battle and get the children out safely.

Brun hoped the expert system knew what it was doing. It kept shifting them from one compartment to another, supposedly far from the Militia's personnel scans. It said it was still trying to retrieve a better vocal synthethizer, too, and had dispatched another two mobile units. She wanted to ask if it had received any answer from Fleet – surely they'd be doing *something* – but she simply could not get her fingers to work on the keyboard, and Hazel could not understand her gestures. She was so tired . . . she hoped it was only exhaustion and not hypoxia.

'Brun – wake up!' That was Hazel's voice; she sounded on the edge of panic. 'I feel things in the decking – vibrations—'

It must remind her of her own capture. Hiding in these vandalized rooms, waiting for someone to come, not knowing who – it must bring back all her nightmares. Brun tapped her arm, and grinned. Hazel grinned back, but there was no mirth in it.

She could feel the knocks and vibrations herself. Someone closer, and more than one. She tried again with the compad keyboard, and keyed 'Fleet assistance'?

'I'm not sure,' the expert system said in her ear. 'There have been two landings, another two are imminent. Multiple intruders aboard, hostile to one another.' Then some of them must be friendly, Brun thought. But she wasn't sure. 'Not all the same shapes of shuttles, but no recognizable ID codes from the ones that appeared nearby.'

Appeared? Launched from a larger ship that had microjumped nearby?

'Try Fleet codes on com channels,' Brun keyed.

'I cannot access any transmissions from one set of intruders,' the expert said. 'I don't know what frequencies to use.'

Shielded suit communications. That sounded more and more like Fleet, but how could she contact them? Someone should be listening in for unshielded transmissions – 'All bands,' Brun said. 'Use the codes I gave you.'

The deck bucked, and Brun and Hazel lost contact in the low gravity, bouncing into one of the bulkheads. Brun's compad flew another way, its jack yanked from her suit connection. Hazel scrambled after it, as another series of vibrations and blows shook them. Something must have rammed the station, something with a lot more mass than a single person. Brun could see into the next compartment, where the bulkhead had torn loose at the corner, leaving a triangular hole. The station could be coming apart around them; they might be flung loose into space, tiny seeds from a puffball head.

Brun fought down the panic. Right now, right this instant, they still had air, they still had intact p-suits, and they weren't freezing or full of holes. Hazel edged back to her and held out the compad and connector.

The scan tech watching the incoming Militia shuttles reported that one was likely to impact rather than dock. 'He's coming in with way too much relative vee; gonna knock this station sideways – counting down . . . seven, six, five, four, three, two, one—' The deck bucked; in the minimal artificial gravity, a cloud of dust rose and hung like a tattered curtain. 'They've made a mess out of the end of that arm, but don't seem to have damaged themselves much, worse luck.'

'Keep us informed,' Esmay said. She had Meharry and five others with her as she tried to follow Brun's scan signal through the maze of passages.

'Lieutenant!' That was the backdoor scan again. 'I've got transmissions in Fleet code from the station itself – identifies itself as the station expert system.'

'What's it want?'

'Says two employees told it to contact us and gave it the

codes. Says it's trying to protect them, and can we prove we're friendly?'

'The only person here who might know any Fleet access codes was Brun – but she was supposedly unable to talk.'

'But it can't contact this individual now – says a communications device failed.'

Great. 'Can it direct us to her?'

'It says yes, but it won't until we can prove that we have a legal right to be here, and that she knows us.'

Worse and worse. Expert systems had a reputation for rigid interpretation of rules.

'Tell it to confirm to her that we respond to Fleet codes, and ask her to sign a yes or no acceptance of our ID.'

'Yes, sir.' A pause followed, then, 'It's trying, sir.' After another pause, 'It says she wants to know who it is. A name.'

Esmay thought a moment. According to her father, Esmay was the last person Brun would want to see, or should see. But that was a name she'd know.

'She knows us, Lieutenant,' Meharry said. 'Methlin and Oblo – she'll recognize that.'

'Go ahead,' Esmay said. 'Tell it that.'

Another brief pause, and then, 'It's agreed. It's going to mark the way, and tell Sera Meager someone's coming.'

'Tell it to give her a description of our suits, so she'll know us from the others,' Esmay said.

Now her helmet display lit with the icons of the intruders: twenty red dots displayed on a graphic of the station wing. Esmay followed the expert system's directions with her team; the others moved down the main corridor to intercept those landing.

Here in the secondary corridor, occasional turquoise p-suits lay like dead bodies. Every one gave Esmay a chill, but the expert urged them on, via the relay through the scan tech. At last, a compartment door slid open ahead of them. Cautiously, Esmay edged forward . . . and there they were. Brun, recognizable through the facemask of the p-suit, and a scared-looking young girl. Meharry moved past Esmay and cleared her helmet face-shield so Brun could see her. Brun staggered forward, moving as if she had serious damage, and fell into Meharry's grip.

'Medical team,' Esmay said. They came at the double, and unfolded the vacuum gurneys that allowed life-support access to a p-suited patient outside pressure. Only then did she think of asking scan for the frequency that the expert and Brun's suit must be using. She glanced around the compartment, to see an obvious gap where bulkhead sections had warped apart. Was that from the recent impact of the Militia shuttle, or old damage? She couldn't tell; it didn't matter.

Brun struggled to free herself from Meharry's grip, and gestured at the girl. The medics unfolded another of the gurneys, and unzipped it. They rolled each woman into her own, then zipped and sealed, and popped the tanks. The transparent tents inflated, leaving sleeved access ports for treatment.

The girl started talking right away. 'Please – she can't talk – she needs a way to communicate—'

'Sure, hon . . . what's your name, now?'

'Hazel – Hazel Takeris. And she's Brun – she was using a compad with voice output, but the plug broke.'

Esmay found the compad, and slid it into the transfer portal of Brun's gurney. She could see Brun cycle it through, then hold it without using it. Plug broken? It must mean that she had needed to plug it into her p-suit. Brun made the universal sign for *Air up?* and Esmay responded. Brun popped an arm seal on her suit, just as their safety instructor had taught them: never trust anyone's word on air pressure. Then she peeled back one glove, and tapped one of the compad's keys.

'All correct,' announced the audio pickup from inside the gurney.

'Sera Meager?'

'All correct.'

'Can you describe your current status?'

'No.' That, as Esmay could see, was another button. The thing must have had preprogrammed messages. What was the keyboard for, then?

'Can you type complete answers?'

'No.'

Esmay turned away to consider their overall position. The Militia that had crunched into this wing were about halfway to their part of the wing, though coming down the main corridor.

'Trouble . . .' scan said. 'Big trouble.'

'Bad guys on the other end are carrying explosives. Can't see if the ones on this end are, but they could be.'

The mobile units available to the expert system were secondary models which had survived the initial vandalization by looking like simple boxes. It had taken longer than the expert expected to recharge one of them, get its tracks moving, and send it off to Laboratory 1–21 to look for voice synthesizers. But now it was on its way. The expert kept an area of higher artificial gravity moving along with it, to keep its tracks in firm contact with the deck plating. The expert prided itself on carrying out all orders, no matter how complex, simultaneously. It dispatched another, and then another, in case the first should be disabled somehow. Clearly it was important to get a communications device to the taller human.

The first unit reached the lab, and extended a pincer-arm to pick up one of the synthesizers, just as an impact rocked the station. The unit flipped off the deck, and out of the area of higher gravity; it flew across the lab, into the corridor, and impacted the opposite bulkhead just behind the group of neuro-enhanced marines that had stalked past. The rear marine slagged it before it had time to fall to the floor, yelling 'Hostile!'

'What is it?' Kim Arek asked. She was surprised and delighted to find that her voice didn't crack.

'This thing just flew out the hatch at me—'

'Something bounced loose by the hit?'

'Looked like one of those robot bomb-crawlers, what I saw of it.'

'Well . . . keep an eye out for others.'

Pete Robertson, Ranger Travis and Captain of Rangers, had plenty of time to think on the way up from the surface. It was all Mitch's fault, and God's judgement on Mitch's hasty ways and unhealthy attachment to outlander technology was about to land on all of them. He made up his mind, and called the others – they would make sure no one used that heathen station for anything ever again, and that Mitch paid the price for his unbelief.

722

He had no real hope that they'd get out of this in good shape – not with the appearance of enemy ships in the system – but at least they'd take care of their own dirty laundry first. And Mitch would never be Ranger Captain: he would see to that himself.

The two enemy shuttles that had docked to the derelict would present no problem if they simply blew the derelict up – and he'd toyed with the idea of having *Yellow Rose* and *Heart of Texas* do that before they went out to fight the invaders, but he'd rather do it himself. It felt right.

So, huffing a little in his hardened p-suit, he shuffled carefully off the shuttle with the rest of the Travis crew, and led the way down the corridor that lay open before him. Sam Dubois, Ranger Austin, had landed at the far end of the long structure – both groups would set explosive charges as they converged on the enemy, and then retreat – and blow the station. The odd thing was, his personnel scanners detected only a small cluster of life forms way up ahead, in the central core, and two off to the right somewhere. Hadn't Mitch caught the women yet? He smiled to himself, forgetting for the moment the missing enemy from the shuttles.

When the little tracked crawler trundled out of a side corridor, he spun and with practiced ease drew and fired. Bullets ricocheted off the thing's hard shell and holed the bulkhead in a scattered pattern. The machine came on, a jointed arm holding some device . . . behind it was another one, just coming into view around a corner.

'Git those!' he said, and drew again. Behind him, the Travis crew clumped up, and someone's shot shattered the device the thing was holding. But the crawlers came on, more slowly. 'They can't catch us,' he said. 'Come on—' and turned back to move on the way they'd been going.

Which was now blocked by huge figures in black armor, holding weapons he'd never seen.

'Get'm boys!' he yelled, and fired.

Then the strange weapons belched streams of something gray that shoved him back into his men, and glued them all into one immobile mass. When the next explosion came, from the far end, he had a sudden stark fear that it would ignite the charges his crew

723

had left behind, and blow them all. He was not, he discovered, nearly as ready to meet his Maker as he'd always claimed.

'Dumber than dirt,' Jig Arek said, with some satisfaction. 'You'd think they never heard of riot control.'

'We still have one bunch loose,' Oblo said.

'Belay that,' Meharry said, in what for Meharry was a tense voice. 'We've got worse problems. Brun and Suiza fell off the station.'

22

One moment, Esmay had been checking where everyone was; the next, with no warning, the gurney tent ruptured; air puffed out. Live fire, it had to be. Esmay threw herself on the gurney, covering Brun's body, and slammed Brun's faceshield shut. Even through her armor, she could feel Brun breathing; she could see Brun's face, rigid with fury or terror – she couldn't tell which – but the mask was clear, which meant that air and filters were both working. She pushed herself up a little and locked the elbow position so her armor wouldn't crush Brun if something hit her hard. Something thumped into her armor once, and again; someone fell over her; excited voices yelled in her suit com. She ignored them; she and her armor were between Brun and whatever was going on, and someone else could handle that.

Then the deck bucked hard, buckled, and the damaged bulkhead peeled away. She caught a glimpse of other suited figures tumbling – someone grabbing for the other gurney – and some blow thrust her toward the opening, out into the brilliant sunlight.

By the time she realized she was tumbling outside the station, she knew she was still clinging to Brun, the armor's power-assisted gloves clamped to the frame of the gurney. The view beyond shifted crazily: light/dark, starfield/planet/station. She tried to focus on the helmet readouts, and finally found the ones that gave an estimated relative vee to her 'ship' – the station – a mere 2.43 meters per second.

Brun, when she looked, was staring back at her with no recognition. Of course not – Esmay had never changed her faceshield to allow it. Impossible now. She had no idea what to do, but she knew one thing *not* to do – let go of the gurney frame. Her suit had the beacon.

'Lieutenant!' That loud shout in her helmet com got her attention; she hoped it was the first call.

'Suiza here,' she said, surprised that her voice sounded as calm as it did.

'Lieutenant, have you got the gurney?'

'Yup,' Esmay said. 'She's alive; air's flowing.'

'What about you? Somebody thought they saw a plume.'

Another look at her helmet readouts was not so reassuring. Her own air was down, and the gauge was sagging visibly. *I've been here before*, she thought, remembering her first terrifying EVA from *Koskiusko. And I didn't like it then.*

'Low,' she said. 'And going down.'

'The blast may've pulled your airfeed loose – can you check it?'

'Not without letting go of the gurney,' Esmay said. 'And I'm not going to. What's the situation?'

'They're dead; we've got two dead, and four tumblers, counting you and the gurney as one. Max has you all on scan. We'll have a sled to you in less than ten minutes.'

She didn't have ten minutes.

'What is your air?' That was Meharry.

'Three minutes,' Esmay said. 'If it doesn't leak any faster.'

'Is Brun conscious?'

'Yes. She's looking at me, but she can't see me – my helmet shield's still mirrored.'

'I'm going to transmit to her, tell her to see if she can stop your leak.'

725

'No – it's too dangerous.'

'It'll be more dangerous if you pass out and can't help guide the sled in.'

She could see the change in Brun's expression, though Meharry hadn't patched the transmission to her. Then Brun wriggled around, wrapping one arm in the straps waving from the gurney, and reaching around behind Esmay. Her arm wasn't long enough; she tapped Esmay's shoulder.

If Esmay let go with one hand, and turned, Brun might be able to reach whatever it was. But she might lose her grip on the gurney – they might not find her. Brun's tap the next time was a solid slug. Esmay grinned to herself. Whatever the damage, Brun hadn't changed in some essentials. Carefully, slowly, Esmay loosened her grip on the gurney frame on that side, and transferred her grip to one of the grab straps on Brun's p-suit. Brun wriggled more. The air gauge quit dropping . . . stabilized . . . at eight minutes.

'Eight minutes,' Esmay reported to Meharry.

'She's got the luck, that one,' Meharry said. She did not say whether eight minutes would be enough. Esmay told herself that one minute of oxygen deprivation was within anyone's capacity. Brun bumped against her, flinging out an arm and leg. What was the idiot doing – oh. Slowing rotation. Esmay extended her legs on the other side. The confusing whirl of backgrounds slowed, as they lay almost crosswise of each other, forming, with the gurney frame, a six-spoked wheel rolling slowly along.

Then Brun reached up with her webbing-wrapped arm, and pushed up Esmay's mirrorshield before Esmay could bring an arm in to stop her. Her eyes widened. Then she grinned, as mischievous and merry a grin as Esmay had ever seen on her face. She used the same arm to work free the thermal-packed bag of IV fluids sticktaped to the gurney, and very deliberately used her glove's screwblade attachment to poke a hole in it. Then she winked at Esmay, looked past her – moved the bag around – and squeezed.

A stream of saline jetted out, instantly converted to a spray of ice crystals that glittered in the sun. Esmay wondered if Brun had just gone completely insane. Then she realized what it was. For all the good it would do, Brun was trying to use an IV as reaction mass to get them back to the station faster.

Esmay did her best to hold still, even as her air ran out, and the hunger for oxygen overtook her, urging her to run, struggle, fight her way out of the dark choking tunnel that was squeezing the life out of her.

She heard voices before she could see; the steady quiet voices of the medics, and somewhere beyond, quite a bit of cursing and yelling.

'What's her pO_2 doing?'

'Coming up. Caught it in time . . .'

'We're going to need another can of spray over here—'

'My God, what'd they do to them?'

'It was the horse, I think—' That in a tentative, soft voice.

Esmay opened her eyes to see unhelmeted faces bent over her. She wanted to ask the logical question, but she would not ask that one. One of the medics anticipated her.

'We're in the shuttle again. Our targets are alive, no wounds taken in the shootout. We lost two dead, eight with minor injuries. The station's pretty much gone and there's a fight going on upstairs somewhere. And now you're with us, we don't have to worry about you any more.' The medic winked. 'But I do have to do a mental status exam.'

Esmay took a deep breath, and only then realized that she still had something up her nose feeding her oxygen. 'I'm fine,' she said. 'What else is going on?' She tried to sit up, but the medic pushed her back.

'Not until we're sure of your blood gases. Your suit telemetry said you were out of air for about two and a half minutes before we got you reconnected, and that's on the edge of the bad zone.'

'I'm fine,' Esmay said.

'You're not,' the medic said, 'but you will be when we're done with you.' She inserted a syringe into the IV line Esmay had not noticed until then, and a soft gauzy curtain closed between Esmay and the rest of the universe.

Barin had the uncomfortable honor of observing the whole collapse of the 'simple, straightforward extrication' from the bridge of *Gyrfalcon*. Most of the carnage had already happened by the time *Shrike's* signal reached them, and his grandmother ordered the rest of the task force to jump in. They popped out less than thirty light seconds from the planet, only ten from the nearest enemy ship. *Gyrfalcon's* first salvo took it out; the cruiser's massive energy weapons burned through its shields in less than a second.

'Not used to facing real firepower,' Escovar said calmly.

'Captain – *Shrike* has recovered one shuttle – casualties . . .'

Please, please, let it not be Esmay . . . Barin clenched his hand on the ring he had bought for her.

'Firing solution on second enemy ship – RED for *Shrike*—'

'Hold!'

'Got it!' That from *Navarino*, whose clear shot at the second enemy ship had blown it as cleanly as their own had the first.

'Third target running – headed for jump point—'

That would be the job of *Applejack*, the cleanup light cruiser . . . Barin watched scan intently as the enemy ship headed toward the minefield *Applejack* had spent the past six hours sowing around the jump corridor.

Hazel had seen the bulkhead peeling back, and felt a moment of complete panic – not now, not after all they'd been through – but someone's gloved hand caught the bar at the end of her gurney, and wrapped a quick line to it, then secured the line to a stickpatch. But – when she looked – she could see a tumbling, receding shape that had to be Brun and someone holding her.

She said nothing – there was enough noise on the comunits anyway – until someone asked if she was all right.

'Yes, but – what about Brun?'

'We'll get them back,' a reassuring voice said. 'Don't you worry. And we'll get you into a shuttle.'

'Yeah, before this place breaks up completely . . .'

She was passed from one set of hands to another – each carefully attaching her to another set of secured lines before releasing the first – and then finally through the cargo hatch of a shuttle. People moved past her, all busy, all doing something she hoped would rescue Brun. She had heard of Fleet SAR all her life, but she'd never seen it in action. She'd had no idea that SAR teams wore black p-suits that looked like space armor from storycubes. She'd expected them to wear bright colors with flashers or something to make them easier to see.

'Hey there – can you tell us your name again?' That was a blonde woman with sleepy green eyes.

'Hazel Takeris,' Hazel said. 'Of the *Elias Madero*.' Her throat closed on all the things she had meant to say, that she'd rehearsed in her head so many times.

'We're going after Brun now,' the woman said. 'There's a beacon on the officer with her – we can't lose her.'

Hazel felt better, but she could sense more tension in the people around her. Something was still wrong.

'What is it?'

'Nothing to worry about,' the woman said. 'Only this was supposed to be a quick, simple extrication . . . and we didn't know about you—'

'I'm sorry,' Hazel said automatically. The woman looked startled.

'Don't *you* be sorry. It's those idiots who planned it who need to be sorry.'

The woman looked aside suddenly, and Hazel turned her head to see what it was. The cargo hatch gaped again, and three more black-suited figures swam in, pushing another, attached to Brun's gurney.

'Hatch closed,' she heard through her com.

'Air up! Air up!'

'Patch it into the suit, dammit!'

Hazel could just see Brun's turquoise suit . . . surely she had air, from the suit tanks. The others cut off her view.

'Air pressure's nom,' someone said.

Then they moved, coming past her with the black-suited figure. Two of them stripped off suit gloves, and opened the other's black suit with some tool – and it flipped back like a beetle's carapace. Hazel stared – it *was* space armor. Inside, a limp figure . . . she could see a pale face, slack-mouthed. Busy arms, hands – and then someone tapped her shoulder.

'You don't want to watch,' the green-eyed woman said. 'It gets

729

messy. And since they're working on her, they asked me to do an initial assessment on you. Any trouble breathing?'

'No,' Hazel said, 'but—'

'Fine, then. You want to open your helmet? We can talk off the coms that way, save interference.'

Hazel realized she could reach up and open her faceplate. The woman had opened hers, as well, and was folding back her gloves.

'You got any broken bones you know of?'

'No . . . is Brun all right?'

'She's fine – she's got her own team working on her.'

'But who was that—'

'Lieutenant Suiza – just a little hypoxia, don't fret.'

She wished people would quit telling her not to worry. She glared at the green-eyed woman.

'I'm not a child, you know.'

'You sure look like one.'

'Well, I'm . . .' She wasn't even sure how old she was. How long had she been a captive? At least a year, because Brun had those babies. 'I'm seventeen,' she said.

'Mm. Well, I'm thirty-eight, and my name is Methlin Meharry. Want to tell me how you got away?'

'I was coming back from market—' Hazel began, and she'd gotten as far as cutting off their hair with the long knives when she heard someone working on the officer – on Lieutenant Suiza – let out a happy *Yes!*

'She coming around?' Meharry asked.

'Any minute now.' One of the others came over to Hazel.

'All right – let us professionals at her.' And to Hazel, 'Let's get you out of that p-suit and see what shape you're in.'

'You be gentle now,' Meharry said.

'You should talk,' the medic said, without rancor. 'Considering your rep.'

'I could get out of this myself—' Hazel started to say, as the medic reached through the sleeves to unfasten her p-suit.

'Yes, but we want you in the tent in case the shuttle has pressure problems . . . unlikely but it's a zoo out there.' The medic peeled back her pressure suit section by section; Hazel heard exclamations from those working on Brun and craned her head, trying to see, just as her attendant peeled the leg sections of the suit and the clothes underneath. 'My God – what did they do to them!'

'I think it was the horses,' Hazel said. 'We rode horses all night.'

'Horses! We send a task force halfway across the cluster, and they're getting you out on *horses*?'

'It makes you really sore,' Hazel said. 'And the clothes were stiff.'

'Barbarians,' someone muttered. 'Should have spaced the lot of 'em.'

Shrike scooped up the shuttle, and medics moved Hazel and Brun into the spacious sickbay. 'Regen for you,' said the green-coated medic when he'd peeled away the gurney's tent and draped a gown over her. 'You'll feel a lot better after an hour – maybe two – in the tank.' Hazel wasn't about to argue; she saw that Brun was being led to the other tank. She settled into the warm, soothing liquid, and dozed off.

Brun was furious. They were talking over her head again, as if she weren't there, and no one had thought to get her a voice synthesizer. Three hours aboard, and they continued to treat her like an idiot child.

'She'll need another five hours of regen for those abrasions,' one medic said. 'And I still think we should order a parasite scan.'

Brun reached out, caught hold of his uniform, and yanked hard. He staggered, then turned.

'Are you all right? All right?' He spoke a little too slowly, a little too loudly, as if she might be a deaf child.

Brun shook her head and mimed writing a message.

'Oh – you want to say something?'

Yes, she wanted to say something, something very firm. Instead, she smiled and nodded, and mimed writing again. Finally, someone handed her a pad.

HOW'S ESMAY? she wrote.

'Lieutenant Suiza is fine,' the medic said. 'Don't worry – you won't have to see her again. It was strictly against orders—'

What were they talking about? Brun grabbed the pad back. I WANT TO SEE HER.

'That's not a good idea,' the medic said. 'You weren't supposed to see her at all. We understand how traumatic it was—'

Brun underlined the words I WANT TO SEE HER and shoved the pad back at him.

'But it was all a mistake . . .'

SAVING MY LIFE WAS A MISTAKE? That came out in a scrawl he had to struggle to read.

'No – her being involved. Your father said, under no circumstances should you have to see her, after what she said about you.'

Her father. Rage boiled up. Carefully calm, she printed her message. I DON'T CARE WHAT MY FATHER SAID. ESMAY SAVED MY LIFE. I WANT TO SEE HER. NOW.

'But you can't – you need more time in regen – and besides, what will the captain say?'

She could care what the captain said. Or her father. She had not come back to the real world to be told she couldn't talk to anyone she pleased, even if she couldn't talk.

'She's getting agitated,' someone else said. 'Heart rate up, respirations – maybe we should sedate—'

Brun erupted from the bed, ignoring the remaining twinges, and slapping aside the tentative grab of the first medic. The other one picked up the injector of sedative spray. With a kick she had practice in secret for months, she smashed it from his hand; it dribbled down the bulkhead. She pointed a minatory finger at the medics, picked up the pad, and tapped the word NOW.

'Good to see you up,' came a lazy voice from the entrance. Brun poised to attack, then realized it was Methlin Meharry, whose expression didn't vary as she took in the two medics, the smashed injector, and Brun with the short hospital gown flapping about her thighs. 'Giving you trouble, were they? All right boys – out.' The medics looked at each other, and Meharry, and wisely chose withdrawal.

Brun held out the pad.

'You want to see Suiza? Why, girl? I thought she trashed you at Copper Mountain, upset you so you ran away home.'

Brun shrugged – it doesn't matter – and tapped the pad again.

'Yeah, well, she did save your life, and you saved hers I guess. Or helped. Your father thought seeing her would be a terrible

732

trauma. If it's not – well, it's your decision.' Meharry's mouth quirked. 'You might want to put on some clothes, though . . . unless you want her to come down here.'

Brun didn't. She was more than ready to get out of sickbay. Resourceful as ever, Meharry quickly found Brun a shipsuit that almost fit. It wasn't quite as soft as the shipsuits Hazel had found on the station, but it fitted her better.

'Now – it's customary to make a courtesy call on the captain. Since the captain told the lieutenant not to let you know she was there, and she did – this could be a bit tricky. Just so you know.'

Meharry led her through a maze of corridors to a door that had Lt. E. Suiza, Executive Officer on it. Meharry knocked.

'Come in,' Esmay said. When Meharry opened the door, she was half-sitting on her bunk; she looked pale and tired.

Brun wants to see you,' Meharry said. 'She kind of insisted, when the medics wanted to sedate her . . .'

Brun moved past Meharry, and held out the pad on which she'd already scribbled THANK YOU.

Esmay stared at it, then at Brun, brow furrowed. 'They don't have a speaker device for you! What are they thinking of!' Esmay looked almost as angry as Brun felt.

THEY'RE WORRIED ABOUT MY STABILITY.

'They ought to be worried about your voice, dammit! This is ridiculous. That should be the first thing—'

THANK YOU, Brun wrote again. MY FATHER GAVE YOU TROUBLE?

Esmay flushed. 'They got the tape of what I said to you that night – and I'm sorry, it really was insulting—'

YOU WERE RIGHT.

'No – I was angry, that's what. I thought you were stealing Barin – as if he were my property, which is disgusting of me, but that's how I felt.'

YOU LOVE BARIN? That was something that hadn't occurred to her, even in the months of captivity. Esmay, the cool professional, in love?

'Yes. And you had so much more time, and when I was working I knew you were spending time with him . . .'

TALKING ABOUT YOU.

733

'I didn't know that. Anyway – I said I'm sorry. But they think – they thought – I had something against you and your family. Your father didn't want me involved in the planning, or with the mission. But that's not the important thing – the important thing is getting you a voice.' Esmay thought for a moment. Meharry. Meharry knew everyone and everything, as near as Esmay could tell. If that device on the station had survived, Meharry would know where it was, and if it hadn't, she'd know what would work.

'A speech synthesizer? Sure – I can get you one. Just don't ask where.'

Ten minutes later, a young pivot, so new he squeaked, delivered a briefcase-sized box that flipped open to reveal a keyboard of preprogrammed speech tags as well as direct input.

'Here,' Esmay said. 'Try this.'

Brun peered at it, and began tapping the buttons. 'It looks like the one Lady Cecelia used on Rotterdam,' said a deep bass voice.

Esmay jumped, then started laughing.

'Let's see what this one sounds like,' the box said, this time in a soprano.

'I didn't like that one, let's try this . . .' came out in a mezzo; Brun shrugged. 'I'll keep this one.'

'I wonder why they didn't do this first,' Esmay said. 'If they had a speech synthesizer aboard, why not give it to you right away.'

'Arrogance,' Brun keyed in. 'They knew what I needed; why ask me?'

'Brun, I'm so sorry—'

'Don't waste time. Thank you. You saved my life.'

Esmay was trying to think how to answer that one when Brun's next message came out.

'And by the way, who's doing your hair? It looks good even after being squashed in a suit.'

'Sera Saenz – Marta Saenz – took me to this place, Afino's.'

'Raffaele's Aunt Marta? You must have impressed her if she took you there. Good for you.'

Esmay could not believe how fast Brun was keying in the words, as if she'd used one of these for years. 'You're good with that thing,' she said.

'Practice,' Brun keyed. 'With Cecelia. And you cannot know how good it feels. Now – what's going on with Fleet and the planet? Hazel wants to get the other kids out.'

'And your babies,' Esmay said. 'Your father's adamant about that: he's not leaving his grandchildren there.'

'He can have them.' Brun's expression dared Esmay to question that, and she didn't.

'I don't know what the whole situation is,' Esmay said. 'Because, since I'm in disgrace for letting you know I was here, they won't tell me. You're on a search-and-rescue ship; there's a task force with us, but what we're doing is microjumping around keeping out of the way of the Militia warships.'

'Who can I talk to?' Brun keyed. 'Who's giving the orders?'

'On this ship, Captain Solis. For the task force, Admiral Serrano.'

'Good. I need to talk to her.'

'Admiral Serrano?' Esmay remembered in time that Brun already knew the admiral . . . she might in fact listen. 'I can get you as far as Captain Solis, but there's a blackout on communications with the task force.'

'Captain Solis first,' Brun keyed in. Esmay nodded and led the way without another word. Brun glanced at Esmay. Besides the more effective haircut, there was something else different. She realized, as Esmay led her through the ship and she saw others defer to her, that Esmay might indeed be in disgrace but she was far more than Brun had imagined. This was what she'd been like at Xavier, or on *Koskiusko*? Her own idiocy struck her again, the way she had condescended to this woman, the way she had assumed that Esmay was no more than any other student, no more than, for instance, herself. That man in the combat veterans' bar had been right – she had not understood at all.

They paused at a cross-corridor while what looked to Brun like huge people in armor moved past.

'Feeling better, Lieutenant?' one of them asked.

'Fine, thanks,' Esmay said. She turned to Brun. 'They were on the team that got you out.'

'Thank you,' Brun keyed quickly. She hit the controls to save that phrase; she was going to need it a lot.

* * *

Captain Solis stood as Brun came in and reached to shake her hand. 'We are so glad to have you back!'

'I'm glad to be back.' Brun had anticipated the need for that phrase, and had it loaded.

'Your father did not want you bothered by Lieutenant Suiza, but I understand that you wanted to see her—?'

'Yes.' This had to be done word by word, carefully, and Brun took her time. 'I wanted to apologize to her for my behavior on Copper Mountain. It was made clear to me during my captivity just how badly I had misjudged her. And I wanted to express my profound gratitude for her efforts on my behalf.'

'You don't know most of it,' Captain Solis said. 'She is the one who insisted that you were probably still alive after your escape shuttle blew up – that you could have engineered that as a decoy – and said we had to go find you.' He spared Esmay a glance that Brun could tell was more approving than usual. 'I could almost change my mind.'

'I changed mine,' Brun keyed in.

'Well, now that we've got you and the other – Hazel Takeris, is that her name? – we can jump safely back to the task force and get out of here with no more disruption.'

'No.' Brun keyed, and switched to the masculine voice output for emphasis.

Captain Solis jumped; she bit back a grin. It would not do to laugh at the man. 'But— what—?'

'We must get the other children,' Brun keyed. 'From the ship Hazel was on.'

'I don't see how,' Captain Solis began.

'We must,' Brun said.

'But Hazel said they were safe – that they had adjusted to their new family—'

'We cannot leave little girls, Familias citizens by birth, to be brought up in a society where they can be muted like me for saying the wrong thing.'

Solis looked at her. 'You're naturally overwrought,' he began. Brun stabbed at the keyboard with such emphasis that his voice trailed away, and he waited. 'I am tired, sore, hungry, and extremely tired of having no voice, but I am not overwrought.

736

Could you define the right amount of "wrought" for someone in my position? Those children were stolen from their families – their parents were murdered horribly – and they're in the control of people who were willing to kidnap, rape, and abuse me. How dare you suggest that they are safe enough where they are?'

'Sera – it's not my decision. It will be the admiral's, if she can make it without authorization from the Grand Council, which I doubt.'

'Then I will see the admiral,' Brun said.

'It will be some time before we can rendezvous safely,' Solis said. He gave Esmay a long look. 'And for the time being, Lieutenant, could you find quarters for our guest? I know we're crowded with extra crew, not to mention prisoners—'

'Yes, sir,' Esmay said.

'Prisoners.' That came out in a flat baritone, after they'd left the bridge.

'Two groups,' Esmay said. 'Three different shuttle loads came up to the station after you; one blew itself up, but we caught two.'

She wanted to see them. She wanted to let them see her, free and healthy and – no. She would get her voice back first, and then she would see them.

'Something to eat?' she keyed.

'Right away,' Esmay said, and led her to the wardroom. Brun sat revelling in food which someone else had cooked – flavors she was used to, condiments she liked, anything she chose to drink, while watching Esmay covertly. What *had* Afino's done to her hair? And for that matter, what could she do about her own hair, which she'd hacked off so blindly with a knife?

Several days later, with her hair once more a riot of tousled curls, thanks to the crew's barber, she was ready to tackle Admiral Serrano.

'You are coming with me,' Brun said. 'I need you; I trust you.'

'You could take Meharry—'

'Methlin is a dear person . . . ' Esmay blinked, imagining what the redoubtable Meharry would think to hear herself so described. 'But she is not you. I need you.'

'I'm the executive officer; I can't just leave the ship.'

'Well, then, the admiral can come here. Which do you think she'd like least?'

Put like that, there was no question. Esmay tracked down Captain Solis and received permission to accompany Brun to the flagship.

'And it has not escaped my notice,' Solis said, 'that almost two years without a voice has not begun to stop that young woman giving orders. We had better get her commissioned, so at least it's legal.'

Our Texas, Ranger Bowie's Household

Prima had known, from the beginning, that this was big trouble coming. She could hardly believe Patience had run off – and in fact it seemed she had been abducted. That happened sometimes, girls stolen away, but usually no one would bother a Ranger's household. And the man had said, loud enough to be heard, that he had business with Mitch.

She hadn't wanted to tell Mitch until she knew for sure what had happened. Mitch was at a meeting, an important meeting. But his younger brother Jed had stopped by, as he often did, and when Tertia came in to report that Patience had still not come home, he took it upon himself to find Mitch. He liked to give orders, Jed did, and Prima knew that his ambitions went beyond being a Ranger's brother. He wanted that star for himself, and Mitch couldn't see any danger in it.

And then Mitch had come home, in a rage with her for not supervising the girl better; it seemed the woman who'd been captured at the same time as Patience had disappeared from the Crockett Street Nursery. He'd called the older boys and they'd all gone out to search, and he'd sent for the parson to come and preach at her and the women all afternoon.

It was more than a nuisance; it was baking day, and they had to leave the dough rising to sit in silent rows and listen to Parson Wells lecture them on their laziness and sinfulness. Prima kept her eyes down, respectfully, but she did think it was a shame and a nuisance, to stop hard-working women in their work and make them listen to a scolding about their laziness. And he would go on and on about their sins tainting their children. Prima had trouble with that bit of doctrine: if, hard as she tried, her faults had made poor Sammie a cripple, and Simplicity stupid, then how could the outland women – who had arrived after lives of sin and blasphemy – bear such beautiful, healthy children?

Mitch had come home late that night, having found not sight nor word of Patience . . . or, presumably, the other woman, the yellow-haired one. Prima wanted to ask about the yellow-hair's babies, but she knew better. He was in no mood to tolerate any forwardness, even from her. She set the house in order, and waited by the women's door, but he never came to her. Early the next morning, she heard him leave the house; when she peeked, Jed was with him. She had hardly slept. She heard the roar of a departing shuttle from the spaceport, and sometime later, another, and another.

A few hours later, a tumult from the boys' section drew her to its entrance. She could hear their tutor hollering at them, trying to quiet them . . . and then Randy, Tertia's youngest boy, shot out the door with a clatter of sandaled feet.

'Daddy's dead!' he was screaming, at the top of his lungs. Prima caught him. 'Lemme go! Lemme go!' He flailed at her.

The tutor followed close behind. 'Prima – put him down.'

The tutor, though a man, was not Mitch, and she dared look at his face, pale as whey. 'What is it?' she asked.

'That abomination,' he said, through clenched teeth. 'She stole a shuttle, and tried to escape. Ranger Bowie and others went after her; there's been—' Light stabbed through the windows, a quick shocking flash of blue-white. Prima whirled, suddenly aware of her heart knocking at her ribs.

The tutor had opened the window and peered out and up. Prima followed him. Outside, cars had stopped cantways, and men were looking up. Prima dared a look into the sky, and saw only patches of blue between white clouds. Ordinary. Unthreatening.

'I want to see the newsvid,' she said to the tutor, and walked into the boys' part of the house without waiting for his permission.

23

The newsvid had two excited men yelling into the vid pickup. Prima could hardly make out what they were saying. Escape, pursuit, invasion . . . invasion? Who could be invading them? And why? Mobilization, one of the men said.

'What is it?' she asked again. The older boys were already moving toward their gunboxes.

'It's the end of the world,' one of them said. Daniel, she thought. Secunda's third.

'Don't be silly,' another said. 'It's the heathen, come to try to enforce their dirty ways on us.'

'Why?' Prima asked. In all her years, no one had ever bothered Our Texas, and she saw no reason why anyone would.

'Don't worry,' Daniel said, patting her shoulder. 'We'll protect you. Now you get on back to the women's side, and keep order.'

Prima turned to go, still unsure what had happened, and what it could mean. In the kitchen, Secunda and Tertia were quarrelling over the meaning of the bright light, and both turned to her for an answer. 'I don't know,' she said. Who could know? Temptation tickled her . . . no, she dared not risk her soul asking an outlander such questions, but . . . she made up her mind, and went out to the weaving shed.

'Miriam!' The outlander woman turned from her loom. Her face was tight with tension; she must have seen the light too. 'Do you know what that light was?'

Miriam nodded.

'Was it from space? From ships?' Another nod, this time with a big grin, a triumphant grin. Miriam mimed a rocket taking off, shooting another rocket.

Invaders. There *were* invaders. 'Who?' Prima asked the air. 'Who would do this? Why?' She jumped when Miriam touched her arm. 'What?' Miriam mimed writing. Writing . . . Mitch, she recalled, had threatened to take Miriam's right hand if she didn't quit writing; she'd hoped it wouldn't be necessary because the woman was a gifted weaver. Now she led Miriam to the kitchen and gave her the pad of paper and marker they used for keeping accounts.

Light is weapon Miriam wrote. Prima squinted, trying to read as fast as Miriam wrote. Weapon, that was clear. *Ionizing atmospheric gases.* That made no sense; she didn't know any of the words. Miriam, glancing up, seemed to guess that. *Made air glow* she wrote. Well, but how could air glow? Air was just air, clear unless there was smoke in it.

'Who?' Prima asked again. 'Who would attack us?'

Miriam scribbled rapidly. *Guerni Republic, Emerald Worlds, Baltic Confederation, Familias Regnant* . . . Prima had no idea what those were, besides godless outlanders. *Battle in space, not attacking here. Someone you stole from.*

'We don't steal!' Prima said, narrowly stopping herself from slapping Miriam. 'We are not thieves.'

Stole me, Miriam wrote. *Stole children, women, killed men.*

'That's not true. You're lying. The children had no families, and you women were rescued from a life of degradation . . .' But her voice wavered. Miriam had been here for more than ten years; if she still believed she had been stolen, if she had not understood . . .

I can prove it. Miriam wrote. *Get to a transmitter – call – find out who that is, and ask them.*

'I can't do that! You know it's forbidden. Women do not use men's technology.' But . . . if she could find out. If it was possible . . .

I know how. Miriam wrote. *It's easy.*

Forbidden knowledge. Prima glanced around, realized that the others in the kitchen were staring, trying to understand this conversation. 'I – I don't know where such machines are,' she said finally.

I know how to find them.

'How?'

Tall thin things sticking out the top of buildings.

'It's still forbidden.' Thinking of looking up at tall thin things made her dizzy in her mind. Thinking of touching men's machines was worse.

We can look at the newsfeed. She must mean the machine kept for the women to watch religious broadcasts.

'How? I don't know how to set it up.'

I do.

Miriam went to the closet where it was kept, and pulled it out. More than a little afraid, Prima helped her pull it, on its cart, into the back kitchen where there were extra electrical outlets. Miriam uncoiled the nest of wires that Mitch had left, and plugged this one and that one into the back and sides of the machine. Prima had no idea which went where, and kept expecting the machine to burst into flame. Instead, it made a faint frying noise and then a picture appeared, the same background as the one she'd seen on the boys' side. This time only one man looked back at her. Miriam kept tinkering with the machine, and suddenly it had a different picture, crisp and colorful . . . men in strange uniforms, very odd-looking.

Prima felt faint suddenly. Some of those odd-looking men in uniform were women. The view narrowed, concentrating on one of them, a woman with dark skin and eyes, and silver hair. Miriam touched one of the machine's front controls, and a voice spoke.

'—Return of children captured with the piracy of the ship *Elias Madero*. Return of infant children born to Sera Meager during captivity—' Prima felt behind her for the table and leaned against it. That yellow-hair . . . this must be about that yellow-hair. '—Ships are destroyed; your orbital station is destroyed. To avoid more damage and loss of life, you are urged to cooperate with us. This message is being transmitted on loop until we receive a reply.'

Ships destroyed. Mitch's ship? Was he dead? Prima felt the weight of that loss. If Mitch was dead, someone else would be Ranger Bowie, and she – she and the rest of Mitch's wives and children – would belong to Mitch's brother Jed, if he lived. Jeffry, if Jed had died.

The sound of gunfire in the street brought her upright. 'Turn that off,' she said to Miriam. 'Before we get in trouble. Put a – a tablecloth over it.' She knew she should put it away, but if Mitch was not dead there might be more news of him, and she could not bring herself to lose that connection. 'It's past lunchtime, and we haven't served,' she scolded, brushing past the questions the other women wanted to ask. 'Feed the children, come on now. Feed them, put the babies down for naps. What would Ranger Bowie think, if he saw us like this!'

They were washing up when Jed arrived, white-faced and barely coherent. 'Prima – it's terrible news. Mitch is dead or captive; all the Rangers are. Get me food, woman! I have to – somebody has to take over—' Prima scurried out, driving the maids away; she would serve him herself. Safer. When she had piled his plate with roast and potatoes and young beans, she summoned Miriam.

'Turn it on, but keep it low. Be ready to hide it again.'

The next time she came through the kitchen, all the grown women were clustered around it. This time the face on the screen was a woman in a decent dress – or at least a dress. Dark hair streaked silver – an older woman.

'She says the yellow-hair was a big man's daughter.'

Oh, Mitch . . . ambition diggeth pits for the unwary . . .

'She says our men murdered people and stole things . . .'

'That's a lie,' Prima said automatically. Then she gasped as the screen showed Mitch – sitting miserably at a table, not eating, with men she knew around him. Terry . . . John . . . and there was the Captain, Ranger Travis.

'—Rangers are either captive, or dead.' That was the voice from the machine, with its curious clipped way of speaking. The way Patience had spoken at first.

'Prima! Get out here!' That was Jed, bellowing as usual. Prima scurried away, resenting once again that part of Scripture which would give her to this man just because he was Mitch's brother.

*   *   *

743

Mitch Pardue came to in the belly of the whale, a vast shadowy cold cavern as it seemed. He blinked, and the threatening curves around him resolved into something he recognized instantly as part of a spaceship. Not the shuttle, though, and not the space station he'd been on. He looked around cautiously. There on the deck nearby were a score of his fellows, most still slackly unconscious, one or two staring at him with expressions of fright.

Where were they? He pushed himself up, and only then gathered his wits sufficiently to realize that he was dressed in a skimpy shipsuit with no boots, with plastic shackles on his ankles. He felt his heart pounding before he identified the fright that shook him. He cleared his throat . . . and stiffened in outrage and terror. No. It could not be. He tried again, forming a soft word with his mouth, and no sound emerged.

He looked around frantically – on one side of him the bodies of his own crew, men he knew well, now more of them awake, and mouthing silent protests. On the other, another clump of men he knew – Pete Robertson's bunch, he was sure – beginning to stir, to attempt speech, to show in their faces the panic and rage he felt in his own.

The troops that entered sometime later did not surprise him; he braced himself for torture or death. But after checking his shackles, they simply stood by the bulkhead, alert and dangerous, waiting for whatever would come.

He should rally his men and jump them. He knew that, as he knew every word of Scripture he'd been told to memorize. But lying there, mute and hobbled, he couldn't figure out how. He turned his head again, and saw Terry watching him. *Get ready* he tried to mouth. Terry just stared at him blankly. He nodded, sharply; Terry shook his head.

The women had been able to lipspeak to each other; some of them had a hand language too. Men should be able – he tried again, this time looking past Terry to Bob. Bob mouthed something he couldn't figure out in return, and looked scared. Mitch was plumb disgusted. Giving up this way, what were they? He rolled over to attempt something with Pete, but one of the guards had moved, and was making very clear gestures with his weapon. Mitch looked closer. *Her* weapon.

'Stop it,' she said. 'No whispering, no mouthing.' She had a clear light voice that didn't sound dangerous, but the weapon in her hands was rock-steady. And he didn't doubt the others would get him if he tried anything with her. Down the row someone made a kiss sound, a long-drawn smooch. Mitch looked up into dark eyes like chips of obsidian and didn't make a sound. Another of the soldiers walked up to the smoocher and deliberately kicked him in the balls. He could not scream, but the rasping agonized breath was loud enough.

Another group of soldiers arrived; Mitch found himself suspended between two in space armor, propelled down a corridor to a large head. 'Use it,' said a voice from inside the helmet. Man's or woman's, he couldn't tell, but he had urgent need. So did the others, alongside him. From there, they were taken to a compartment with a long table set with mealpacks.

He shouldn't eat. He should starve himself, rather than eat with these infidels. He tried to signal his team, figure out a way to stop them, but four of them were already tearing open the mealpacks. He sat rigid, jaws clamped on his hunger, while the others ate. After a short time, two of them dragged him away to a small cubicle where he faced someone in a fancier uniform.

'You won't eat?'

He shook his head.

'We'll feed you, then.' And in the humiliating struggle that followed, strong arms held him down while he was force-fed some thick liquid.

'You do not have the option of suicide, or resistance,' the officer said coolly, when they dragged him back to the same cubicle. 'You will cooperate with us, because you can do nothing else.' After that, they took him back to a different compartment, a small solitary cell.

Mitch had, once or twice in his young days, travelled under a fake identity on Familias-registry ships; he had seen a few of the big commercial orbital stations. But nothing he had seen was like the interior of an elite warship. He wanted to despise it; he wanted to sneer at the exaggerated courtesy, the grave ritual, the polish and precision . . . but without a voice he could do nothing but experience it, and in that experience realize how foolishly he had misjudged his opponents. He had called down God's wrath on his people, and here was the instrument of that doom: sleek, shining, perfectly disciplined, and utterly deadly.

He wanted to defy them. He wanted to hate and defy and condemn and resist to his last breath, but he kept thinking of Prima and Secunda . . . of the smell of bread from the ovens, the bright flowers in the gardens, of the sound of children's voices echoing through the halls, the slap of the boys' sandals when they ran; the clump of the bigger boys learning to walk in boots, the soft patter of girls' feet . . . the feel of their soft little arms around his neck, the smell of their hair. His wives. His children. Who would be someone else's, who might be forced out to work in someone's fields, who might be crying, unprotected, afraid, because of him — he woke sweating, his own eyes burning.

In the empty hours, staring at the blank walls, he saw deeper into himself than he ever had, or wanted to. God was punishing him for his ambitions. That was only right, if he had done wrong. But his family — why should they be punished? His appetite disappeared, this time from no rebellion but sadness . . . and his captors did not force him to eat, this time.

Someone knocked, then entered. A man — he was grateful for that, at least — but in a uniform he had not seen before.

'I'm a chaplain,' the man said. 'My own beliefs are not yours, but I am assigned to help members of Fleet with matters of belief and conscience.' He paused, paged through a small booklet. 'I think your nearest word for me would be *pastor* or *preacher*. You are being returned to Familias space for trial, and our laws require that anyone facing charges of such gravity must be granted spiritual consolation.'

What spiritual consolation could an unbeliever, a heathen, give him? Mitch turned his face to the bulkhead.

'We have only the smallest chance to get those children out alive,' Waltraude said. 'I know you want nothing to do with this Ranger Bowie — but unless he tells his wife to give them up, she won't. And he is the only one who can influence his brother, who has now inherited responsibility for his wives and children.'

'But it's ridiculous! Why can't we talk to her?' Admiral Serrano said.

'I see no reason to negotiate with him – he's our prisoner; he's going to get a good, quick, legal trial and the death sentence—'

'Do you want those children? Their families do. Their families will want to know why all these lives were expended for the Speaker's daughter . . . and children of their own family left in slavery.'

'Oh – all right.'

Mitch had not been to the bridge of a warship of this size; he was almost drawn out of his misery by the size, the complexity, the implications of power.

His guards led him before a woman – a woman in night-dark uniform, with insignia that he recognized as an admiral's rank, and bright-colored ribbons on her chest. And he stood before her, barefoot and voiceless, and wanted to see in her the very image of Satan . . . but could not.

'You have a choice, Ranger Bowie,' she said, in the quick speech of these people. 'Your former prisoner, Hazel Takeris, insists that you truly love your wives and children.'

He nodded.

'We are going to retrieve the other children you stole from the *Elias Madero* when you murdered their parents. However, your – the other men, on the surface – show no signs of cooperating with us. We are concerned that harm might come to your wives and your children, if they attempt to interfere with us . . . and we wish no harm to them. We want no child hurt, not so much as scratched. Do you understand?'

He nodded again, though he wasn't sure he believed it.

'We do not make war on children . . . though you did. But we will have those children returned to their families, whatever it takes, and that might endanger other innocents. So – here is your choice. We can restore your voice, for you to transmit a command to your family, to release those children. Or, if you refuse, you can remain mute until your trial – however long that might be.'

He might talk again? He might have a man's voice again? He could hardly believe it – but all around, he saw men and women listening as if they believed it.

'Our landing craft are ready to launch,' the admiral said. 'If they are fired on, they will return fire. If they are obstructed, they will fight through . . . and your people, sir, have nothing capable of resisting them. So it rests with you, how this will be.' She paused, then went on. 'Will you give these orders, or not?'

It was cooperating with the devil, to take a woman's orders – a woman soldier, an abomination of abominations. For a moment he thought of the weapons hidden in the city, the chance that the other men might be able to launch them. Yet – he could almost feel against his cheek the soft cheeks of his daughters, could almost hear his children's laughter. Kill them? Put them at risk? He had never killed a child in his life – he could not – but these people could, or said they could . . .

He nodded.

'You will. Good. Take him to sickbay, and have the treatment reversed, then bring him back to the bridge.'

He was a traitor, a backslider . . . all the way to sickbay, he trembled with the conflict inside. His guards said nothing to him, guiding him along with impersonal efficiency.

'We have to put you to sleep briefly,' the medic explained. 'Just long enough to relax the throat muscles—'

He woke as from a moment of inattention, and felt a lump in his throat. When he cleared it – he could hear it. 'I – can – talk . . .'

'Not to me, you can't,' said one of his guards. 'You can say what the admiral says you can say. Now come along.'

He sat where they told him to sit, and faced the little blinking light that was a video pickup, and though his voice trembled at first, it steadied as he went along.

'Jed, you listen to me. This is Mitch, and yes, I'm a prisoner, but that doesn't matter. I want you to let the people that are landing take those outlander children with them. Prima knows which four. And send to Crockett Street Nursery for those twins, the yellow-haired sl – woman's twins. I want all six of 'em released to the people that are comin' for 'em. Prima, you get those children dressed, now . . .'

'Signal coming up, Admiral—'

'Let's see it—'

It was a vid, from his home: Jed, looking angry, with Prima, well behind him, hands clasped respectfully in front of her. They were in the small living room, the one where he'd met the others so often, with the fireplace at one end and the conference table at the other.

'Mitch, I don't believe it's you, or they've drugged you, or somethin'. It's some kind of trick. An' I'm head of the family now, and I'm not about to let any children of this house into the hands of those – those godless scum!'

Mitch felt the sweat spring out on his face, his hands. 'Jed, you have to. They're comin' anyway – if you cause 'em trouble, they'll be more people dead. Children dead, most likely—'

'Then they'll go to the Lord. I'm not—'

Behind Jed, Prima had moved. Without looking up to face the vid pickup, she had stretched out her hand and touched the fireplace poker in its stand. Mitch's breath caught in his throat.

'—Not going to let the honor of our name be smirched because you got yourself caught like a weakling—'

Prima held the poker . . . she held it easily, in a grip strengthened by kneading bread dough, wringing out wet wash, lifting babies. He knew the strength of those massive shoulders, those arms.

'Jed, please . . . don't risk the other children for those few – it's not worth it – please, Jed, let 'em go.' Before worse happened, before Prima did something he would have to notice. He struggled to keep his gaze on Jed.

'If they want a fight, they can have it!' Jed looked at much triumphant as angry. 'The preachers have already told us to gather and fight—'

'The preachers—!' Mitch could hardly keep talking, as he watched Prima walk softly, softly on her bare feet, coming up behind Jed, raising the poker. Horror and hope warred in him – that any woman would strike a man, let alone strike without warning – that maybe, without Jed, the children would be safe . . .

'You could stop them,' Mitch went on, struggling to make Jed understand, Jed who had never understood anything he didn't want to. He should warn Jed; he should admonish Prima. But the children— 'You could convince them, if you'd try—' And on the screen Prima looked up at last, straight into the vid pickup, and smiled. 'Do it!' Mitch said, not entirely sure who he was talking to, and as Jed opened his mouth, the poker slammed into his head with all the strength of Prima's shoulders and arms . . . and blood spurted up, and she hit him again, and again, on the way down . . .

'Prima!' he yelled, and his throat cramped, closing on more. She looked up at the vid again, her face settling into its usual calm from an emotion he had never seen before. 'Don't let them hurt the children,' he said; his voice creaked like that of a young rooster learning to crow. 'Don't let them hurt—' His voice failed again; tears stung his eyes.

Prima's voice on the link was far steadier than his had been. 'I want to see . . . what kind of people they are, you would trust with our children.'

'Be careful,' he managed to whisper. 'Please . . .' He was pleading with a woman . . . pleading . . . and that was wrong, but his throat hurt, and his heart, and he wanted no more pain, for him or the children. The screen in front of him blanked, and then he curled around his misery like a child around a favorite toy.

'I want to go,' said Hazel. 'I should – the children know me; they won't be as scared. Brun would go if she could.' Brun was sedated, in regen after an attempt at the delicate surgery that might restore her voice. She wouldn't be out for another three days, at the soonest.

'Not a bad idea,' Waltraude Meyerson said. 'And I, of course.'

'You! You're not only a civilian, but you have no role in this . . .'

'I'm the resident expert you brought along – I should get to see these Texas mythologists on their own turf. And I would recommend, Admiral Serrano, that you send a member of your family – perhaps that grandson who keeps hovering around looking hopeful.'

'I hardly think Barin's an appropriate choice,' the admiral said.

'These people care about families. If you send a family member, you are showing that you will risk family to save family. It is also as well that he is male – that will be more acceptable, as long as there are women along.'

'I see. And whom else would you recommend? Do you have the entire mission plan in mind?' Sarcasm, from Admiral Serrano, affected most people like being in close proximity to a large industrial saw, but Professor Meyerson didn't flinch.

'No, that is your area of expertise. Mine is antique studies.'

Hovers held position above the streets, and a mobile squad kept pace with them, helmet shields down.

'Looks kind of silly,' Hazel said, 'with the streets empty.'

'The streets wouldn't be empty if they weren't there,' Barin said. His helmet informed him of the location of hotspots in the buildings; they were clustered behind every screened window niche. He hoped none of them had weapons that could penetrate their body armor . . . he hoped even more that Ranger Bowie's transmission had convinced them not to fight. Right now the Fleet forces were on Yellow Two, which meant that even if they were fired on, they were not to return fire without authorization.

Hazel pointed out the main entrance to the house, and the side street that led to the women's entrance. 'I came through this door only once, when he brought me here.' Barin noticed that she did not say the man's name or title. 'I used that other door to take out refuse or go to the market.'

'But you think we should go in here?'

'It establishes authority,' Professor Meyerson said. She had elected to wear a skirt, though she agreed to wear body armor under it, which made her look considerably bulkier.

She led the way up to the door; it swung open just before she reached it. A stout woman wearing a blue dress with a wide flounced skirt glared at them. She had a flowered kerchief tied tightly around her head.

'That's Prima,' Hazel said softly. 'The first wife.'

'Ma'am,' Professor Meyerson said. 'We've come for the children.'

Prima yanked the door wider. 'Come in. Which one of you is the yellow-hair?'

'She couldn't come,' Hazel said. 'She's getting medical treatment for her voice.'

'She abandoned her babies – abominations like her don't deserve children,' Prima said.

'Are they here?' Hazel asked.

751

'Yes . . . but I'm not convinced they should go . . .'

Hazel stepped forward. 'Please – Prima – let the children come.'

'I'm not giving those sweet girls up to some disgusting heathen,' Prima said. She had the taut look of someone willing to die for her convictions.

'It's just me,' Hazel said softly. 'You know me; you know I'll take care of them.'

'You – you traitor!' Prima's face had gone from pale to red, and tears stood in her eyes.

'No ma'am . . . but I had my family to think of—'

'We were your family – we treated you like family—'

'Yes, ma'am, you did. As well as you could. But back home—'

'And you!' Prima turned on Professor Meyerson. 'You're what – a woman *soldier*! Unnatural, disgusting—'

'Actually, I'm a historian,' Meyerson said. Prima looked blank. 'I study Texas history.'

'You – what?'

'That's right. I came to learn about you – about what you know of Texas history.'

Prima looked thoroughly confused, then focussed on Barin. 'And you – who are you?'

'Admiral Serrano's grandson,' Barin said. Then, when Prima seemed not to understand, he said, 'The woman you may have seen in transmission – dark, like me, with silver hair? She's commanding the task force.'

'A *woman*? Commanding men? Nonsense. No men would obey her—'

'I do,' Barin said. 'Both as admiral and as my grandmother.'

'Grandmother . . .' Prima shook her head. 'Still . . . do any of you have a belief in God?'

'I do,' Barin said. 'It is not the same as yours, but in my family we have always had believers.'

'Yet you are a soldier alongside women? Commanded by women?'

'Yes, sometimes.'

'How can that be? God decreed that women bear no arms, that they enter into no conflicts.'

'That is not the doctrine I have been taught,' Barin said.

'You are a pagan who believes in many gods?'

'No, in one only.'

'I do not understand.' Prima looked closely into his face. 'Yet I see truth in your face; you are not a liar. Tell me, are you married?'

'Not yet, ma'am, but I plan to be.'

'To a . . . another of these woman soldiers?'

'Yes.' If he survived this. He wished very much Esmay were with him.

'Do you swear to me, on the holy name of God, that you are taking them to their families?'

'Yes,' Barin said. Prima deflated; her face creasing into tears. Barin moved nearer. 'Let me tell you about their families, ma'am, so that you will understand. Brandy and Stassi – Prudence and Serenity, as you call them – have aunts and uncles. Their dead mother's sisters and brother; their father's sister. Paolo's grandfather and uncle, and Dris's aunt and uncle. We have brought recordings of them, asking for the safe return of these children.'

'They are happy here,' Prima said. She looked down and away; she had the look of someone who will argue to the end but knows she cannot win. 'It will hurt them to move them now.'

'They are happy now,' Professor Meyerson said. 'They are small children, and I know – Hazel told us – that you have been kind to them. But they will grow older, and you are not, and cannot, be the same as their own family. They need to know their own flesh and blood.'

'They will cry,' Prima said, through her own tears.

'They may,' Professor Meyerson said. 'They have had a difficult few years, losing their parents and then coming to such a different place, and leaving it again. They cried when they came here, didn't they? But in the end, all children cry over something, and that is not reason enough to leave wrong as it is, and good undone.'

'I am undone,' Prima said, folding her apron. 'But I had to try—'

'You are a loving mother,' Professor Meyerson said. Barin was surprised at this; he had not thought of Meyerson as having, or caring about, families. Yet her tone of absolute approval seemed to settle Prima. 'I want you to see recordings of the children's families.'

'I don't have to – I believe you—'

'No, but it may help you understand.' She nodded to Barin, who set up the cube reader and display screen. 'We have brought our own power supply, since your electrical lines carry the wrong voltage for our equipment.'

'This is men's work,' Prima said.

'God gave eyes to men and women,' Professor Meyerson said. She put the first cube into the reader. 'This is a recording of Brandy and Stassi's parents before they were killed.'

On the screen, a woman with a long dark braid over her shoulder cradled a baby in her arms. 'That's when Stassi was born; their mother's name was Ghirian. Her parents were from Gilmore Colony. Brandy was a year old then.' A man appeared, holding an older infant in his arms. 'That's their father, Vorda. He and Ghirian had been married eight years. His family had been merchant spacers for generations.'

'They – were married?'

'Oh yes. And very much in love, though I understand from Hazel that you do not value romantic love between men and women.'

'It doesn't last,' Prima said, as if quoting. Her eyes were fixed on the screen, where the affection between mother and father, and parents and children, was obvious. 'It cannot be depended on to make a strong family.'

'Not alone, no. But along with honesty and courage, it's a good start.'

The screen flickered, and now showed a slightly older Brandy, stacking blocks with an unsteady hand.

Prima sucked her breath through her teeth. 'Boy's toys—'

'We value all the gifts God has given a child,' Professor Meyerson said. 'If God did not mean her to build, why would he have given her the ability? They sent this recording to her grandparents; her mother's father was a construction engineer in Gilmore. He was pleased that his granddaughter had inherited his gift.' The child pushed the blocks over, gave a dimpled grin into the camera, and stood up, dancing in a circle. Then her mother came into view, carrying Stassi, now a wiggly toddler herself. She reached out and caught Brandy to her, gave her a little hug. Professor Meyerson turned up the sound of the cube reader.

'—So we've decided to take them with us. Captain Lund says that'll be fine; there are two children about the same age, and a couple of older ones. The ship has a fully equipped nursery and playroom, with all the educational materials you could hope to see, so don't worry about them falling behind. It's as safe as being onplanet – safer, in some ways. No *bugs*!' The woman grimaced. 'And no weather. I know, I know – you like the changing seasons, but with these two if it's not colds in winter it's allergies in summer.'

Professor Meyerson stopped the reader. 'That was made just before they rejoined the *Elias Madero*, about a year before they died.'

'Was there sickness on the ship after all?'

'No.' Could she not know? Was it possible? She glanced at Hazel, who shook her head. 'They were killed in the capture of the ship, ma'am.'

'No . . . it must have been an accident. Mitch would never kill women—'

This was farther than they'd meant to go; they'd assumed the wives knew how outworld children were taken. Professor Meyerson said nothing, clearly at a loss to think how to put it. Prima blanched.

'*You* think – you believe our men killed the parents, orphaned those children on purpose? Killed *mothers*? That's why you attacked us?'

'They considered them perverts,' Professor Meyerson said. 'That's what was on the recordings.'

'I don't believe it! You're lying! You have no proof!' She grabbed Meyerson's arm. 'Do you? Does your . . . your *device* show anything like that?'

24

'Heads up—' That murmur in Barin's ear got his attention away from Prima. 'May be trouble on the way – some kind of gathering across town—' A tiny picture flashed on the corner of his helmet display. Someone in a bright blue bathrobe or something similar yelling at a bunch of men.

'Excuse me, ma'am,' Barin said. 'Do you know what this might be?' He transferred the image to the larger screen they'd been using for the cube reader.

Prima glared at him, but turned to look. Her face paled. 'It's Parson Wells—'

'A parson is a religious leader,' Professor Meyerson said with renewed confidence. 'Amazing – look at that garment—'

'It's a cassock,' Prima said.

'No, it's not a cassock,' Meyerson said, as if correcting a child. 'Cassocks were narrower, black, and buttoned up the front. This is the variant of academic regalia which was popular in one branch of Christianity—'

'Professor . . . I don't think that's the most important thing.'

'But look at that – those men are carrying replica Bowie knives – and that looks like a replica of an actual twenty-first century rifle—'

'Professor – we need to get the children and get out of here,' Barin said. 'We don't want a conflict – we want them safe—'

'Oh. Yes, of course.' Meyerson flushed slightly. 'Sorry. It's just – seeing things I've only read about before – it's quite exciting. I wish I had more time—'

'Not this visit,' Barin said. He turned to Prima. 'Please, ma'am – the children?

'Come with me, then.' She was still angry, but clearly the view on the screen meant more to her than to the professor. 'I want you to see where they were housed, how they were cared for, so you can tell their families—' She led the way down the corridor to the women's wing. Through windows, Barin saw a garden brilliant with flowers, centered by a fountain – then a wall, then another garden.

'The children's garden,' Hazel murmured. 'The little girls were allowed to run about some there.' It was empty now. The scent of warm, fresh-baked bread wafted along the corridor, as Prima opened another door. 'Kitchen's down there – she's taking us to the sleeping area for the youngest—'

Another courtyard, this one paved with broad stone slabs and shaded by a central tree. Prima turned, led them down a narrow exterior hall, and into a large room. Here a dozen beds were lined up along either wall. On five of the beds, children sprawled asleep.

'Here is where they slept,' Prima said. 'This is the quiet time after lunch, and these younglings are napping. Prudence and Serenity are too old for naps now; they'll be in the sewing parlor.' She led them on, to a room where two older women and a dozen young girls from Hazel's age down were sitting, heads bent, over their sewing. Only the women looked up; the younger one stood. 'It's all right, Quarta. They do have families, real families.'

Now the children looked up, shyly, staring at the intruders. Barin smiled at them; he didn't want to be a frightening memory. Two of the children stared at Hazel a long moment, then one of them said, 'Patience—?' softly.

'Yes,' Hazel said. 'I'm back. Do you remember your Uncle Stepan?' The child nodded, her face solemn.

'He wants to see you again, and so does your aunt Jas. We can go home now, Brandy.'

The girl's face lit up and she dropped her sewing – then she looked cautiously at the older women.

'You may go with Patience – Hazel – now, Prudence.'

The girl ran to Hazel and hugged her. 'I didn't forget, I promise I didn't forget!' She leaned back, looking up at Hazel's face. 'Home to the ship? Will Mama be there? Can I use the computer again? Can I have books?'

The other child, younger and shyer, had to be led from her seat . . . but when she realized she was actually leaving, she clung to Brandy's hand and smiled.

The other girls stared, faces solemn. Clearly they had no idea what was happening.

Barin glanced at Prima, hoping she would make the necessary explanation. The older woman grimaced, but complied.

'Prudence and Serenity are going back to their own families,' she said. 'We wish them God's blessings in their new life.'

'But who will protect them?' asked one of the other girls. 'Is that man their father? Their uncle? Why are those women holding weapons?'

'We will protect them,' Barin said. Shocked looks from all of them. 'In our home, women can be soldiers or work on space-ships—'

'That's wrong,' said one of the older girls firmly; she picked up her sewing. 'It's wrong for women to meddle in men's things.'

Quarta reached out and tapped the girl lightly on the head with her thimbled finger. 'It's wrong for children to instruct their elders. But I believe, Faith, that you are right and these heathens will not prosper.'

The boys were in the boys' wing; Prima despatched one of the other women to fetch them, while she herself led them to the nursery to pick up Brun's twins. They seemed healthy, happy babies, scooting about on the floor in a way that suggested they would soon be crawling.

'Simplicity . . .' Hazel breathed, nodding toward a young woman who sat rocking her baby. The girl looked up with a shy smile; her eyes widened when she saw the others. Hazel picked up one twin, and Prima carried the other; by the time they were back to the front hall, the boys were there, looking worried and uncertain.

'Paolo!' Brandy said. 'We're going home!' She reached out to hug him, but he moved aside.

'I don't think—'

'You need to hear this, Ensign—' That in his earplug. Automatically, he switched audio to the speakers of the cube reader.

'—Satan's snares!' the man in the blue robe was saying. 'God's judgement has fallen on those Rangers, and on their families, for their sins. Suffer not the wicked to prosper, nor the ungodly woman to speak—'

'He means you,' Professor Meyerson said to Prima. 'You're in danger now.'

'We must retake the Rangers' houses, and cleanse them of the filth of contamination – destroy the infidels with holy fire—'

'Not that there's anything really to worry about,' the marine major said; his voice overrode the other man's on the com. 'All they've got is old-fashioned small arms and big knives. You'll be safe enough in the ground transport—'

'No,' Hazel said. 'They have whatever was on *Elias Madero*. They said so, when they were talking after I was captured.'

'What *was* on *Elias Madero*?' Barin asked. 'Ship weapons?'

'I don't know, but something bad, something they'd stolen from Fleet.'

A cold wave ran down Barin's spine, as if someone had swiped along it with a piece of ice. The Guernesi had talked about arms traffickers and stolen weapons . . . and Esmay had mentioned that her captain was concerned about missing nuclear warheads.

'Major, it could be a lot worse than that – these guys may have our missing nukes.'

A pause, in which the ranting voice went on about sin and defilement and tyranny. Then: 'I *knew* we shouldn't have brought a Serrano along. Things always get *interesting* with a Serrano along. All right, Ensign, suppose you tell the admiral while I see what I can do to keep these guys from using whatever it is they've got.'

Barin had just presence of mind to sever the connection to the cube reader's speakers, then switched channels to contact *Navarino* in orbit.

'We're on it,' he was told first. 'Monitoring all local transmissions . . . and we have scan working on locating any fissionables. Get those kids out now, if you can.'

'I don't want to be another man's servant,' Prima said suddenly. 'I don't want my children brought up in another man's house . . .'

Barin spared her a glance, but no more; he was trying to patch into ship's scan and see if he could spot anything. Then Prima grabbed his arm.

'You – your grandmother is really the commander? And you are a man of her family – you must give me your protection.'

'I'm trying,' Barin said.

'I want to go,' Prima said. 'Me, all my children. Take me to my husband.'

Barin stared at her, startled out of his immediate concern. 'Take you—? You mean, to the ship?'

'Yes. That man—' She pointed at the now-blank screen. 'He will give me to someone else; he may tell them to mute me just because I have talked with you – and if he knew I had killed Jed last night, he would certainly do so.' Heavily, with no grace at all, she knelt in front of Barin. 'I claim you as my protector, in place of my husband.'

Barin glanced around; Professor Meyerson had her usual expression of alert interest, and the guards looked frankly amused. 'I – let me talk to my grandmother,' he said. When in doubt, ask help.

'No – it is you I claim.'

'She means it,' Meyerson said. 'And she'll probably do something drastic if you don't agree.'

And he had always wanted command track. Well, he had it now. 'Fine,' he said. 'You're under my protection. Get your household together—'

'I can't speak for the other wives,' Prima said.

'Would he give *them* away? Mute *them*?'

'Yes . . .'

'Then you jolly well *can* speak for them, and you have. Get them together; don't bring anything but warm bodies.' He chinned his comunit. 'Major, we're going to be bringing out the whole household. I don't even know how many—' He looked at Hazel, who shook her head. Even she didn't know. 'More transports,' he said, trying to think if they'd have shuttle space. If they crammed in, if nobody blew the shuttles on the way up—

People started crowding into the front hall: women, carrying babies; girls leading younger girls, boys pushing younger boys ahead of them, and one man – a narrow, angular fellow that Barin disliked on sight. They all stared at Barin and the guards, but there was less noise than he expected. The girls were all looking

760

silently at the floor; the boys were all staring silently, with obvious awe and longing, at the soldiers' weapons.

Prima made her way through the crowd and dipped her head to him, which made Barin acutely uncomfortable.

'May I speak?'

'Yes,' he said. 'Of course.'

'I have sent messengers to the other Rangers' house – by the women's doors – to their ladies.'

'What? No!' But even as he said it, he realized it must be so. 'You think—'

'You said I could speak for the other wives. As you are my protector, so you are theirs, through me; it is your people who killed their husbands, after all.'

Barin looked over the crowd that filled the hall from side to side, and was packed into the rear passages – somewhere between fifty and a hundred people, he was sure, and made the easy calculation.

'We need more shuttles,' he murmured to himself. And what of the male relatives of the other Rangers, who were surely in their houses as – what was his name? That fellow Ranger Bowie had been talking to – had been here. Wouldn't they resist? He could not possibly get that many people out of a city in riot, without casualties. A child whimpered, and someone shushed it.

'What's your situation, Ensign?'

Waiting for inspiration, he could have said. Instead, he gave his report as succinctly as possible, into the hissing void of the comunit, which hissed emptily at him for long enough to make him worry. Then his grandmother's voice in his ear.

'Am I to understand that you have undertaken the evacuation to our ships of the entire civilian population of that misbegotten excuse for a city?'

'No sir: only about five hundred of them. Rangers' households.'

'And upon whose authority?'

'It . . . had become a matter of family honor, sir. And Familias honor.'

'I see. In that case, I suppose we are bound to support your actions, if only to have you present and accounted for when the bill comes in.' His grandmother, according to rumor which he had

761

never cared to test, could remove a laggard officer's hide in a single spiraling strip, from crown of head to tip of toe, without raising her voice. He felt dangerously close to finding out whether she would use its full powers on a callow young descendant.

'Contact!' That was the marine major in charge of the landing party. 'We are being fired upon; say again: we are receiving hostile fire.'

'Engagement code: open green.' His grandmother's voice when speaking to the others was flat and edgeless. 'Say again: engagement code is open green.'

Open green . . . new objective, new rules of engagement. She had given it to him. Barin felt a simultaneous lift and sink of the heart which almost made him sick, then he steadied to it.

'In support of Ensign Serrano and an unknown number of civilians, in the hundreds, who will be embarking for evacuation – open green.'

He could hear the suck of the major's indrawn breath: the ground support more than adequate for a small party was far from adequate to protect and escort hundreds.

'Support on the way—'

He tried to calculate how long it would take, whether they would have to draw shuttles and troops from the other cruisers, from *Shrike*. Then he shook his mind away from that, which was someone else's task, to his own, which was organizing this mass into the most protectable, in the safest possible place to await what his grandmother would send.

To Prima, still waiting before him, he said, 'They will send more shuttles, but it will take time. We will keep you as safe as possible, but—' But . . . if the rioters knew where the nukes were, if they could trigger them, there was no safety. '—If you know anything of outland weapons, where they are hidden, it would help.'

'I know somethin'.' That was a boy, perhaps thirteen, now waving his arm.

'What?' he asked.

'Daddy gave Uncle Jed his key, an' told him right afore he left to go hunt down that runaway girlie.'

Key. That would be an arming key. Barin's stomach curled into a tight cold knot.

'And where's your uncle Jed, do you think?'

'On the floor in there—' Prima waved toward a door across the hall. 'I couldn't think what to do, so I left him—'

'Check it,' Barin said to the guards. One of them went in, shutting the door behind him on the smell of death that had puffed out into the hall.

'Looks like an arming key, on a chain around his neck. In the pockets – another key, different – looks like he has the primary for one system, and the secondary for another.'

But how many systems were there, and how many men held the keys, and did they know in what order to use them? He could not count on the other Rangers' wives to poleax their husbands' relatives.

'We have two arming keys,' Barin reported to the major. 'From Ranger Bowie's brother. I expect each Ranger had one or more keys and left them with a successor.'

'How many troops do you have with you?'

'Only the four, as escort.'

'Damn. We need to get those keys out of those houses, before we all form a pretty fireworks display. These guys are insane – you should see how they're acting out here.'

Barin could hear, in the distance, noises like those on a live-fire range.

Esmay Suiza, back on the bridge of *Shrike* where she belonged, discovered that everyone aboard – including Captain Solis, who had given up the last of his doubts about her intentions – was treating her with excessive care. All the special crew borrowed from *Navarino* had gone back to their ship – Meharry, she knew, would not have treated her as if she were delicate crystal, just because she'd had a spell of hypoxia. She felt quite fit for regular duty, more than willing to go back to work rather than sit by Brun's side as she dozed in regen. If she could have been on *Gyrfalcon*, with Barin, that might've been different, but soon enough they'd be back at some base, where they could finish what they'd started.

'I'm fine,' she said, to the third offer of a chance to take a break. 'It's my watch—' She caught the edge of a significant glance from Solis to Chief Barlow on communications. 'What? Am I making mistakes?'

'No, Lieutenant, you're doing fine. It's just that there have been
. . . developments.'

Something cold crawled through her chest, down toward her
toes. 'Developments?'

'Yes . . . while you were offwatch, the landing party went down
to retrieve those children . . .'

'What's wrong?'

'There've been . . . complications. And – Admiral Serrano's
grandson is down there.'

Barin was down there? 'Why?' came out in an accusatory tone
she had not meant to use to her captain. 'I mean,' she said, trying
to recover, 'I didn't think an ensign would be chosen for such a
team.'

'He wasn't, originally. But he's there now, and since you and
he – well, so I understand—'

'Yes,' Esmay said firmly. Whatever else might be secret, that
wasn't any longer.

'He's managed to get himself into a right mess, and we're
supposed to help him out, but I do not think you should be on the
team. You've already had your stint at suited combat—'

'I'm fine,' Esmay said. 'I am perfectly recovered, passed by
medical, 110 percent. It is of course the captain's choice—'

Solis snorted. 'Don't start *that* again. One time for each trick.
Besides, he had to chew his nails over your exploits on the station;
it's only fair for you to reciprocate.'

'War isn't about fair,' Esmay muttered. To her surprise, that got
a flashing smile.

'You're right there, Suiza, and if I decide your talents are
needed, be sure I'll send you. If you can assure me that being
in love with the admiral's grandson won't warp your judgement or
affect your performance.'

'I'm not in love with the admiral's grandson,' Esmay said. 'I'm
in love with Barin. Sir.'

Another look between captain and chief; she felt her ears
heating.

'Wonderful,' Solis said, in a tone that could be taken in several
ways.

*   *   *

The crackle of gunfire was nearer, as was the *crump* and crash of Fleet light-duty guns. Barin felt he should be doing *something* with his menagerie, but he couldn't figure out what. If he took them out in the street to head for the port, they could be shot; if he kept them here, they were a grand target.

'Serrano – taxi's here, room for fifteen.'

That simplified things slightly. 'Sera Takeris, Professor – take the *Elias Madero* children, the babies, and – let's see—' Room for fifteen adults . . . make that two adults, four small children, and – surely he could cram in ten babies. No, another adult and ten babies. 'Prima, bring eight more babies, if you have them, and a reliable woman to care for them.'

That turned out to be a gray-haired woman as wrinkled as dried fruit; in less than three minutes he had ten babies, the four little children, and the adults all out the door and into the first ground transport vehicle. It clanked off noisily. Barin looked up the street, to the flower-decked park at the end of it. In the middle, a great stone star-shape. The points of the star were blunted, he noted, and seemed to have bronze plaques set on them.

Suddenly as he watched a door opened across the street, and a woman scampered toward him, eyes on the ground. When she neared him she stopped short. Behind him, Prima cried out, and the woman dashed on, brushed past him, and began chattering to Prima as fast as she could.

'An' Travis's little brother, he tooken this key and he putted it into this thing, this box thing, and then Travis's Prima she whapped him with her skillet, that she was carryin' from the kitchen all full of hot grease and fried chicken, an' that box was buzzin' and buzzin' and she said come quick tell you 'cause one-a her outland mutes she wrote BAD, BAD, BAD, GET HELP QUICK in the grease.'

Prima looked over her head at Barin. 'It's a bomb,' he said, hoping she had that much knowledge. 'The keys turn it on—'

'Like a light?' she asked. 'A . . . switch?'

'Yes. If they're the bombs taken from us, it takes at least two keys to arm them . . .' But if they'd been stolen elsewhere, he didn't know. 'So no one can do it by accident,' he said. 'The keys have to be used in the right order.'

'Where are the keys?' Prima asked the woman.

'I dunno, ma'am, she only tol' me to come tell you 'cause you'd sent word we's to get out and Ranger Travis's brother he said no, and we was all whores of Satan and deserved to die anyway.'

'I'll send—' Barin said, but Prima held up her hand.

'They won't trust you; they might trust my women. You want to be sure no one uses both keys?'

'Any keys, if we're not too late.'

Prima despatched another cluster of women, who followed the first back across the street. The next armored transport arrived. One baby left, then half a dozen toddlers, and women to care for them, crammed into that one. He noticed that Prima had no hesitation about which to choose, and those waiting their turn made no attempt to crowd or protest. One more would make a shuttle load – the shuttle they'd come in on.

Two sets of keys he was sure – almost sure – hadn't been used. At least three more, and he would be lucky if that was all . . .

An explosion, up the street, and a gust of acrid smoke blew past, followed by the rattle of something hard on the house walls and the street. Before he could dare a cautious look, he heard the major in his earpiece.

'Something just blew in that pretty little park up the block from you, Ensign. Looks like it took the top off that decorative star—'

Barin looked out to see, through the cloud of dust and smoke, an ominous shape rising slowly from the bright red and yellow flowerbeds.

'I think we found the nukes,' he said, surprised at the even tone of his voice. 'They had a silo under that thing. And somebody used both keys.' For all the good it would do, he gestured to Prima to have everyone get down on the floor, and then replaced and locked his own helmet. He would like to have said goodbye to Esmay, but—

'It's not moving any more,' said the major. 'What's your visual on it, Serrano?'

Barin peered cautiously around the doorframe, wondering only then why he'd left the door open. 'It's – about thirty feet above ground, and . . . not moving.'

'Waiting an ignition signal?' asked another voice in his ear.

'Don't know. Our birds would be out and flying by now,' said the major. 'Is this just a way to blow up the city?'

Pleasant thought. He had not thought of that, and hoped very much that hypothesis was wrong.

The first armored transport, back for another load, ground its way around the corner, as if nothing else mattered, and paused by the door. Brain shrugged: if that thing blew where it was, it wouldn't matter whether people were in the house or the transport – they'd be safely dead. He nodded at Prima, who pointed at heads until the transport driver insisted not one more would fit in.

'Shuttles incoming—' Of course, if it blew as the shuttles were landing, all those would die too. His decision to save more lives just might be the cause of losing more lives.

And he'd asked for command track.

One after another, the shuttles left shockwaves that rattled the windows and sounded like heavier guns than any that had spoken yet. He counted – two, four, six . . . how many were they sending in one flight? Nine, ten, eleven, twelve – they must have stripped every shuttle from *Navarino*, and most from the other ships as well. Thirteen . . . the rolling thunder went on, and he lost count. Well, if you were going to commit to something, you committed in strength.

Now a nearer roar, with an unpleasant groaning whine to it. 'Troop drop.' He peeked out again, to see the first shuttle doing a low flyby, its drop bay open and marines falling, then steadying on their gravpads, to form up with the others. A blinding-bright bar of blue light stabbed across, toward the north. A second shuttle, this one fatter and even slower, crawled past with its cargo bay open and disgorging dark blots he hoped were more weapons and some faster transport. A distant loud rumble suggested that other shuttles were landing.

'Equipment—' On grav sleds, big enough to hold twenty armored troops . . . steering carefully down to the wide streets around the central plaza. Once they'd gone to open green rules, attempts to match technology to that of the planet had gone by the boards. Well, it would be quicker . . .

Another distant *crump*, and another, and a column of black

smoke – Barin could almost feel sympathy for the men with their rifles and their long knives. A grav sled settled outside the door, and its six occupants rolled off, leaving room for the women and children.

Prima had them ready, and sent them out the door without a word. 'First shuttle's off,' Barin heard in his ear. So the original mission was accomplished, if they got those safely to a ship. The grav sled took off, with a whine and a whirl of dust; the next settled in its place, and Prima directed a file out to it.

'We're loading in all the streets,' Barin heard. He could see, from the door, the sleds landing and taking off in three of the streets around the plaza. He glanced around, and saw that one more sled load would do it for this house. 'It's your turn,' he said to Prima.

'She's not goin' ' a male voice said. 'She deserves to die, the murderin' whore.' The scrawny man, the one he had not liked but had ignored after the first glance, had his long knife out, and held to Prima's neck. Her eyes looked at him, a look that might have been warning, but was not fear.

Then the neuro-enhanced female marine who'd been checking the back rooms broke his arm like a soda straw, smashed him into the wall, and caught Prima before she fell. Her neck bled – but not the lethal spurt of a severed artery. The marine slapped a field dressing on it. Prima looked at Barin.

'You're a good protector,' she said, then quickly lowered her eyes.

'No, she is,' Barin said, nodding to the marine, who pushed up her faceplate so that Prima could see. Prima stared.

'You're . . . a woman?'

'Yup. And a mother, too. Hang in there, lady, you're gonna be fine.'

The last load went quickly; Barin swung aboard the grav sled and watched others loading and taking off as they swung above the city and headed for the spaceport. There he found, instead of the chaos he expected, a perfectly ordinary Landing Force Traffic Control section. 'Ah – Ensign Serrano's last load, fine. Bay 23, that'll finish that shuttle load—'

Bay 23 had a shuttle labelled R.S.S. *SHRIKE*. Barin helped his passengers from the grav sled to the interior with its narrow benches designed for troops in armor, not civilians in dresses. He started helping them strap in, ignoring the pounding of his heart which had speeded up at the thought of seeing Esmay again.

'Barin!'

His heart stopped completely, then raced on again. She was there, alive and well, waving from the front. He nodded, grinning but speechless with feeling, and went on with his work. He felt the shuttle lurch, then the lump-lump-lump of the wheels on the runway.

'You know her?' Prima asked him, a hand on his wrist.

'Yes. She's—' How could he say it to her? He didn't even know what words would make clear to her what his culture meant by engagement. Prima's eyes flicked to his face, then back down. She nodded.

'I will be an obedient second wife,' Prima said. 'After you execute my husband Mitchell.'

Barin could think of nothing whatever to say to that, and the rising thunder of the shuttle engines made further conversation impossible anyway.

Far below, as the last shuttle rose into the sky, the men at last made it to the Rangers' houses, the armory, the meet-ing hall. The houses were empty, but for a dead man or two in each; and the keys – the keys they needed so badly – were missing.

Mitchell Pardue had been told that his wives and children were safe, but he hadn't believed it. Not until Prima stood before him, properly barefoot but quite improperly dressed in a bright orange shipsuit with a sheet tied around it for a skirt.

'We have a new protector,' she told him. She glanced at his face, then down respectfully. 'Of the Serrano family.'

'Prima – you can't just—'

'I reckon you lied to me, husband,' Prima said. She looked at him again, this time steadily. 'You said they was all orphans. You said those outlander women was all you ever found. You never told me you *killed* parents, in front of their children, that you killed *women*, even *mothers*.'

'I—'

'As far as I'm concerned, they might as well mute you, Mitchell Pardue, because if your tongue cannot speak the truth, why speak at all?'

And after that, he found he had little need to speak, and no one to speak to. In a last act of kindness that tore his heart, his captors showed him video of his children playing in the ship's gymnasium.

They were almost to the Security station at the Fleet entrance to Rockhouse Major when they spotted the crowds on the other side of the barrier. The security detail moved on ahead to take up their positions.

'Oh Lord, the media!' Brun's new voice, still furry and softer than it had been, but strengthening steadily. Esmay glanced over at her.

'You knew it would be here.'

'I suppose so, but I could hope. And you know, I used to love being the top newsflash attraction.'

'Well, Barin can almost top you this time,' Esmay said, with a wicked smirk.

Barin flushed. 'I do not really have nineteen wives—'

'No, but do you think the media cares? It's a great story.'

'Esmay—'

'I wouldn't tease him,' Brun said. 'After all, you could be a sensation yourself—'

'Not me, I'm the plain one.'

'I don't think so. Landbride Suiza in love with a man encumbered by nineteen fanatic cultists, and having gone from villainess of my abduction to hero of the rescue force? We might as well face it – we're *all* condemned to a spot on the evening news.'

'So . . . what's your advice, O experienced target of the press?'

'Relax and enjoy it,' Brun said. 'In fact – let's give them a real show. After all, it's ours. We're heroes of the hour – let's do it right.'

'I hesitate to ask,' Barin said, with a glance at Esmay. 'Do you know what she means?'

'No,' Esmay said, 'and I don't want to, but we will.'

'Link arms and I'll show you,' Brun said.

'We can't do that; we're sober, serious professionals, Fleet officers—' But Brun had already grabbed her arm, and they came out of the gate like a trio of chorus dancers, into the lights and hubbub.

'All we have to worry about,' Brun was saying brightly, eyes sparkling, golden curls tossing, 'is pirates, thieves, traitors, smugglers, assassins, and the occasional nutcase.'

Esmay looked past Brun to Barin. 'Do you want to duck her in the fountain, or shall I?'

'Let's do it together,' Barin said, suggestively.

'Always,' Esmay said.

Elizabeth Moon joined the US Marine Corps in 1968, reaching the rank of 1st Lieutenant during active duty. She has also earned degrees in history and biology, run for public office and been a columnist on her local newspaper. She lives near Austin, Texas, with her husband and their son.

Find out more about Elizabeth Moon and other Orbit authors by registering for the free monthly newsletter at www.orbitbooks.net

THE SERRANO SUCCESSION

Omnibus Three

Elizabeth Moon

Two action-packed SF epics available in one volume

CHANGE OF COMMAND

The Speaker of the Grand Council has been assassinated, and battle lines are quickly drawn between warring political factions. Even Fleet can no longer be depended on to keep the peace. Young Fleet officers Esmay and Barin want simply to marry. But Barin is a Serrano, the most influential of Fleet families, and Esmay is Landbride of the planet Altiplano. Their irreconcilable elders see only disaster in the match. And as Esmay and Barin struggle to appease their families, their very way of life is threatened.

AGAINST THE ODDS

The worst has happened and Fleet is tearing itself apart. Some mutineers see injustice in the unequal spread of rejuvenation drugs, which offer virtual immortality to the rich. Other rebels are simply thirsty for power, or for blood. And when Esmay Suiza-Serrano is unceremoniously booted out of Fleet, the apparent victim of Family politics, she has no idea of the whirlwind of conflict that awaits . . .

TRADING IN DANGER

Book One of Vatta's War

Elizabeth Moon

Ky Vatta is a highly promising military cadet with a great future ahead of her, until an apparently insignificant act of kindness makes her the focus of the Academy's wrath. She is forced to resign, her dreams shattered.

For the child of a rich trading family, this should mean disgrace on a grand scale. And yet, to her surprise, Ky is offered the captaincy of a ship headed for scrap with its final cargo.

Her orders are absolutely clear, but Ky quickly sees potential profit in altering the parameters of the journey. Because, whatever the risks, it's in her blood to trade – even if the currency is extreme danger.

COYOTE

Allen Steele

Embark on an incredible journey of courage, ambition and discovery.

Forty-six light years from Earth, six moons orbit a gas giant three times the mass of Jupiter. Each has been designated a name from the animal demigods of Native American mythology: Dog, Hawk, Eagle, Coyote, Snake and Goat.

Only the fourth moon, Coyote, is likely to sustain life. The crew setting out on Mankind's greatest adventure know that the success of the mission will depend on how well they adapt to their new home. There will be no going back.

But Coyote is also known as the trickster.

SHADOW WARRIOR

Chris Bunch

The epic space adventure trilogy is one blistering volume from the master of military SF.

The Great War is over. The last pockets of resistance long eliminated. For many, the alien Al'ar are now little more than a memory. But there is one man who cannot forget: Joshua Wolfe. Friend, prisoner, then betrayer and executioner of the Al'ar. To humans he is a hero, a legend.

To the aliens he is the Shadow Warrior, master of the arts of killing. And his story has only just begun . . .

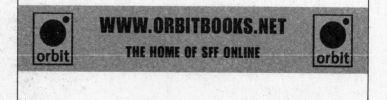